THE BEST OF THE BEST
HORROR OF THE YEAR

10 YEARS OF ESSENTIAL SHORT HORROR FICTION

Also Edited by Ellen Datlow

THE BEST OF THE BEST
HORROR OF THE YEAR

10 YEARS OF ESSENTIAL SHORT HORROR FICTION

EDITED BY ELLEN DATLOW

NIGHT SHADE BOOKS
NEW YORK

Night Shade books may be purchased in bulk at special discounts for sales promotion, corporate gifts, fund-raising, or educational purposes. Special editions can also be created to specifications. For details, contact the Special Sales Department, Night Shade Books, 307 West 36th Street, 11th Floor, New York, NY 10018 or info@skyhorsepublishing.com.

Night Shade Books™ is a trademark of Skyhorse Publishing, Inc. ®, a Delaware corporation.

Visit our website at www.nightshadebooks.com.

10 9 8 7 6 5 4 3

Library of Congress Cataloging-in-Publication Data is available on file.

Cover design by Erin Seaward-Hiatt
Cover artwork by Santiago Caruso (Volume One), Santiago Caruso (Volume Two), Allen Williams (Volume Three), Allen Williams (Volume Four), Allen Williams (Volume Five), Pierre Droal (Volume Six), Noia Hokama (Volume Seven), Blake Malcerta (Volume Eight), Kevin Peterson (Volume Nine), and Chenthooran Nambiarooran (Volume Ten)

Print ISBN: 978-1-59780-983-2
Printed in the United States of America

Thank you horror writers for giving me hours of enjoyment over these last ten years.

Thank you to my editor Jason Katzman for shepherding through the first ten volumes of the series and hoping we work together on many more.

Thank you to all you readers out there who love horror fiction as much as I do.

TABLE OF CONTENTS

INTRODUCTION

Welcome to this celebration of the last ten years of great short horror fiction.

After editing the horror half of *The Year's Best Fantasy and Horror* for twenty-one years, the series was discontinued, but Night Shade Books stepped up and agreed to have me edit a horror annual, *The Best Horror of the Year*. Now, after ten years going strong, we're presenting a Best of the Bests, including many of my favorite stories chosen from the first ten volumes of the ongoing series.

I've picked between two and four stories from each of the ten volumes. One thing I realized during my reread is how much high-quality short horror fiction is being published now, more so than even ten years ago. Established authors continue to produce top-notch work, and it's always a kick to pick a story by someone I haven't published before. I never even think about that during the selection process, but it is something I note when summing up the year.

There are zombies and vampires and serial killers and ghost stories and Lovecraftian horror herein, proving something I've consistently emphasized when on panels that are intended to bemoan the tired old tropes of horror: there's a reason these tropes/monsters don't go away. They are not tired, they are not worn out. And as long as writers take a fresh look at them and continue to create bracing takes on them, they will never be. Trust me, you'll see.

◄○►

I haven't read more than a handful of novels since I started working on my bests of the year because most of my time is taken up reading short stories. However, I thought I'd note a few of my favorites of the last ten years:

Sharp Teeth by Toby Barlow (Harper) is a werewolf novel told in verse, but don't let that scare you away. It's free verse, not rhyming, and the book is wonderfully gripping in part due to its compression of language. Go and read it, you won't be disappointed. Highly recommended.

The Shadow Year by Jeffrey Ford (William Morrow) is a satisfying expansion of Ford's novella "Botch Town," creating a sharp snapshot of growing up on Long Island, New York, in the early 1960s. Two brothers and their young sister investigate mysterious occurrences in the neighborhood, partly with the help of the sister's seemingly preternatural powers of detection. The adult narrator looking back at a dark year in his family's hometown never intrudes on the story, and the characters are so realistic that it's almost painful to read about them. Highly recommended.

Let the Right One In by John Ajvide Lindquist (Quercus) was originally published in Sweden in 2004. It made a huge impression when it was published in the United States and the United Kingdom in 2007, and the movie based on the novel was released in 2008. I saw the movie first and although I ended up enjoying the movie more than the novel, the novel is also quite good. Oskar, a bullied twelve year old, lives with his divorced mother in a housing complex, just outside Stockholm. Mysterious neighbors move next door, heralding several brutal murders in the area. Oskar meets one of the new neighbors, Eli, a 200-year-old vampire child as lonely as he is. There are some nice touches as their relationship develops. And there are also some terrific scenes indicating what happens when a vampire doesn't follow its own kind's rules, such as when it enters a dwelling uninvited. Both novel and movie do a terrific job of depicting pre-teen loneliness and the cold, bleak Swedish winter.

Darling Jim by Christian Moerk (Henry Holt) opens with the shocking discovery of the bodies of two sisters and their aunt in a suburb of Dublin and unfolds into even more horror, all radiating from a seductive traveling storyteller who enchants every woman and girl within reach of his uncanny charms. Darling Jim, as he is dubbed by those he seduces, entrances the inhabitants of the pubs he visits as he weaves his tale of two brothers, a wolf, a curse, and a princess. The mystery of the three deaths is painstakingly unraveled by a young mailman who really wants to be a graphic novelist as he doggedly searches for clues to the truth after accidentally discovering the diary of one of the sisters.

The City & The City by China Miéville (Del Rey) is a dark, metaphysical police procedural that opens with the discovery of a body. The mystery is contingent on the unusual world Miéville creates, a world as bizarre in its way as any Miéville has previously envisioned: in an alternate reality from our own, two eastern European cities—Beszel and Ul Qoma overlap—in the same space, yet their citizens are forbidden to interact or acknowledge the existence of any person/event/physical location in the other, overlapping city. Breach is invoked for those caught breaking the law, and the guilty are taken away, never to be seen again. A detective from the Beszel Extreme Crime Squad is assigned to the murder and his life is utterly changed. It's a great read.

The Little Stranger by Sarah Waters (Riverhead) is a terrific historical novel that slowly ratchets up the tension as it becomes a disturbing psychological puzzle and haunted house story. The story is told from the point of view of a middle-aged local doctor in a post World War II Britain still suffering shortages. Dr. Faraday becomes physician to the owners of Hundreds Hall, the now-dilapidated estate on which his mother worked as a maid years earlier. Are the members of the household becoming unhinged from stress, or is there something at Hundreds that is actually trying to "get" them? Despite the house's fall into ruin, it becomes the focal point of Faraday's longed for acceptance by the local gentry and his stubborn, extreme rationalization; plus, this fixation that has dominated his imagination since childhood prevents him from actually helping before it's too late.

A Dark Matter by Peter Straub (Doubleday) is an elegant, enjoyable gem of a novel by one of the best horror stylists working in the field today. The book, which reads much quicker than its 416 pages would suggest, is about the aftermath of a cataclysmic event that took place in the sixties when a group of teenagers were led by their self-styled guru into a mystical miasma for which none of them were prepared, with dire consequences for all of them. Now, years later, the one member of the group who did not fall under the spell of the guru is driven to investigate what exactly happened to his friends.

The Millennium Trilogy [*The Girl with the Dragon Tattoo* (Vintage), *The Girl Who Played With Fire* (Vintage), and *The Girl Who Kicked the Hornet's Nest* (Knopf)] by Stieg Larsson creates one of the most memorable heroes of modern fiction: Lisbeth Salander, a young woman systematically abused by the Swedish social system from childhood, who has despite this grown into a brilliant computer hacker (although she's lacking "people" skills). The three books make up a fascinating fictional study of government-wide corruption and truly live up to the first book's original title *Men Who Hate Women*. The books are dark, violent, sexy, and riveting.

Dark Matter by Michelle Paver (Orion Books) is a suspenseful ghost story about a 1937 British arctic scientific expedition to Gruhuken, an isolated Norwegian bay. There are rumors that Gruhuken is haunted. The story is told mostly in the form of a diary written by Jack Miller, a twenty-eight-year-old desperate to escape London where he feels he's a failure. Reminiscent of Dan Simmons's brilliant epic novel *The Terror* in its depiction of the cold and bleakness of the Arctic winter, *Dark Matter* is a smaller, more intimate story, told in one voice. But the increasing claustrophobia, the sense of entrapment, and the haunting itself is all extraordinarily effective.

The Silent Land by Graham Joyce (Gollancz/Doubleday) is a dark fantasy about death, but it's a contemporary, lush, joyous celebration of life, love, and trust in the face of mystery and fear. A married couple skiing in the Pyrenees are engulfed by an avalanche. Jake digs Zoe out and they make their way back to their hotel, which is deserted. From there, things take a strange turn as food left out by the missing hotel staff remains fresh over a period of days, people appear and disappear, and the couple believe that they must be dead—or in some kind of weird stasis. Just as you think you know where the plot is heading, the reader (and the characters) come across another little twist and turn. I, for one, was delighted to have followed the road.

The Devil All the Time by Donald Ray Pollock (Doubleday) is horrific at times but would be difficult to classify as horror—which shouldn't put off those who enjoy a good dark mainstream novel about rural southern Ohio and West Virginia and the people who live there. The story has the rawness and unpredictability of the movie *Winter's Bone* (I haven't yet read the Daniel Woodrell novel). Among the characters are a man who believes that only by making more and more elaborate animal sacrifices can he save his dying wife, a murderous couple who pick up and torture young men, and a pair of scam artists posing as a preacher and his acolyte. Highly recommended.

Feast Day of Fools by James Lee Burke (Simon & Schuster). Although I enjoy the Dave Robicheaux novels a lot, I—like his creator—sometimes need a break from them. So Burke's novel, featuring Sheriff Hackberry Holland, a man haunted by his experiences as a POW in the Korean War, is welcome. Holland has been central to two of Burke's previous novels, including the early *Lay Down My Sword and Shield* with Holland having recently returned from the war. *Feast Day of Fools* is not supernatural but is a dark, complex, riveting story about evil doings and good deeds taking place along the Texas-Mexico border. An alcoholic ex-boxer witnesses the torture and death of a man in the desert and reports it to the Sheriff, setting in motion events that spotlight some of the flashpoints of contemporary US society: illegal immigration, drug running, the exploitation of children, psycho killers, corrupt politicians, and religious extremists.

Raising Stony Mayhall by Daryl Gregory (Del Rey) is a wonderful novel about a newborn discovered in a snowstorm after his mother has died. He's dead. And then he opens his eyes—he's a zombie. He's named Stony by the family that takes him in and is hidden from the authorities, who would exterminate him. Against all scientific reason, Stony grows up. And that's where it gets even more interesting. This is a terrific new take on the zombie trope.

Zone One by Colson Whitehead (Doubleday) is an engrossing, realistic, horrific-with-a-touch of humor, poignant zombie novel. The zombie plague is under control and the government headquartered in Buffalo is gung ho on reconstruction, especially down in New York City. The story unfolds from the point of view of Mark Spitz, a member of one of several civilian clean-up crews stationed in lower Manhattan, assigned to mop up any surviving zombie squatters after heavy duty artillery has stormed through. As the team does its sweeps, Spitz recalls how he ended up where he is.

The Rook by Daniel O'Malley (Little, Brown) is a marvelous first novel that is dark and violent, yet laced with humor. It opens with one of the most engaging first lines I've read: "Dear You, The body you are wearing used to be mine." And so, a young woman comes to consciousness with two black eyes, dead people lying on the ground around her, and no memory of who she is or why she's in the situation in which she finds herself. The rest of the novel doesn't disappoint, with a secret agency protecting Great Britain from supernatural forces, conspiracies, and plenty of mayhem to keep the reader entertained.

The Croning by Laird Barron (Night Shade Books) was the author's first full-length novel (a short novel of about 43,000 words had been published a couple of years earlier). Barron puts his poor innocent schmo of a protagonist through torturous paces in a smashing, horrific retelling of Rumpelstilkin. Barron's an expert at depicting Lovecraftian cosmic horror, and this book—with its echoes of places and characters from his short stories and novellas—is for every reader who devours those works.

Available Dark by Elizabeth Hand (Minotaur) is the sequel to *Generation Loss*, and both are excellent, compulsively readable contemporary dark suspense novels about Cassandra Neary, a brilliant photographer who lit up the '70s punk landscape briefly but quickly, burned out with liquor and drugs. After escaping home to Manhattan after some real nastiness in Maine (*Generation Loss*), Neary is offered a great deal of money to fly all expenses paid to Helsinki and authenticate a series of five photographs purportedly taken by a famous photographer. Once there, she becomes embroiled in a Scandinavian death metal cult and sacrificial murder, ending up fighting for her life in economically destroyed Iceland. There are subtle elements of the supernatural threaded throughout this powerful novel. *Hard Light* is the third noir novel featuring Cass Neary, a former New York punk known for her transgressive photography, not to mention her very bad behavior. After fleeing Reykjavik on a stolen passport, she waits in London for her lover, and when he doesn't show up is easily enticed to attend a party hosted by a gangster, becoming involved in dirty dealings in antiques, ancient instruments of movie making, beautiful and dangerous losers and, of course, drugs and alcohol. The plot is complicated, but even if the reader might occasionally become lost in the intricacies of who did what to whom, the experience of reading this gorgeously written novel fully makes up for it.

Long Lankin by Lindsey Barraclough (The Bodley Head-UK 2011/ Candlewick) was an excellent first novel marketed as young adult. Although two of the three points of view are children's, this book should appeal to readers of any age. In the late 1940s, two young sisters from London are sent to stay with their great aunt in a small isolated village in rural England. Their aunt is strange and strict. The house is haunted, as are the grounds around it. The two child narrators overhear adult conversations and because it takes them longer to comprehend what's going on than the reader, we fear for them. There's a curse, a witch, ghosts, and a bog that can swallow a body without a trace. The unease creeps up on the reader slowly yet relentlessly, but it's the individual voices of each character that makes this novel of fear and desperation so stand out. The last fifty pages are heart-grabbing.

The Devil in Silver by Victor LaValle (Spiegel & Grau) is horrific, but the supernatural element takes backseat to the vivid, depressing, terrifying depiction of the United States' mental-health system. Pepper is big, rough, and angry, and through a moment of misplaced gallantry has ended up committed to and trapped in the New Hyde Mental Hospital, a place where the patients claim the Devil is stalking and murdering them.

American Elsewhere by Robert Jackson Bennett (Orbit) was one of my favorite novels of 2013. When a burned out, divorced, former cop inherits the house she didn't know her mother (dead many years from suicide) owned in a town no one has ever heard of called Wink, Mona Bright decides to check it out, hoping to learn more about the mother she barely remembers. As the story rolls on, it expertly blends elements of science fiction, dark fantasy, and horror, all folded into the primary mystery of this Bradburyesque town.

Night Film by Marisha Pessl (Random House) is, if possible, both a page-turner and a slow burn of a novel in one of my favorite subgenres: film horror. Scott McGrath is an investigative reporter intrigued by the mysterious, reclusive underground filmmaker Stanislas Cordova, whose movies are disturbing, horrifying, addictive, and difficult to track down. There have always been dark rumors swirling around the director's working methods and when McGrath gets too close, he's set up—leaving his reputation and career shot to Hell. But he's sucked back into the world of Cordova when the director's twenty-four-year-old daughter falls to her death in a derelict building. Fuelled by anger and bent on vengeance, McGrath sets out to prove that Cordova is responsible for his daughter's death. I particularly love the visionary weirdness reminiscent of John Fowles' great novel, *The Magus*.

The Burn Palace by Stephen Dobyns (Blue Rider Press) opens strongly with the disappearance of a newborn baby and the scalping of a middle-aged man. These incidents and other frightening occurrences are making the residents of the town of Brewster pretty jittery. There are hints of the supernatural throughout: a young boy works on developing his skills in telekinesis, local coyotes don't behave the way coyotes should, large, goat-like two-legged footprints are discovered, and a family man seemingly transforms into a rabid animal. Over the course of the novel the sense of unease created by the non-supernatural behavior of the humans in town begins to take precedence over the otherworldly, but this shift doesn't decrease the suspense. Dobyns has delved in the dark with two excellent previous novels, specifically in *The Two Deaths of Senora Puccini* and *The Church of Dead Girls*.

NOS4A2 by Joe Hill (William Morrow) is rich in characterization and a terrifically satisfying read. We follow Vic through a magical girlhood during which she discovers an impossible bridge to the past where she can find lost objects. Unfortunately, she's also noticed by an evil piece of work named Charlie Manx and his sadistic lunatic sidekick named Bing, who kidnap children and take them to a place called Christmasland, in a vintage Rolls Royce nicknamed "The Wraith." The encounter reverberates through the rest of Vic's troubled life.

The Enchanted by Rene Denfeld (HarperCollins) is a gorgeously written, exceedingly dark heartbreaker of a novel about an old, corrupt prison. A brilliant, dogged investigator takes on hopeless cases on death row, delving into childhood abuse and mistreatment for clues and mitigating circumstances to save the lives of men who have committed heinous crimes. One reclusive inmate believes that golden horses run free and wild under the prison, affecting the tides of violence that occasionally erupt behind the bars.

We Are All Completely Fine by Daryl Gregory (Tachyon Publications) is a brilliant short novel about a therapy group comprised of five men and women traumatized by violent supernatural events. As they learn to trust each other (slightly), they come to realize that their experiences might be related and that their ordeals may not be over. Clever, and filled with the kind of creeping dread at what's in the flickering shadow next to you and what might be just around the corner, that suffuses the best horror.

The Southern Reach Trilogy: Annihilation; Authority; Acceptance by Jeff VanderMeer (Farrar, Straus & Giroux) is a compulsively readable, densely rendered, magnificently weird creation consisting of three connected novels. In the first, an expedition of four is sent into Area X—a section of the US that has been infected/colonized/altered by a possible alien visitation—to explore, survey, and search for clues to what happened to earlier, missing expeditions, and to measure changes to the terrain. The second and third volumes run in counterpoint, explicating, analyzing, and breaking down the elements of the first volume. In *Authority*, the reader meets Control, a conflicted former field operative put in charge of the expeditions into Area X presumably by the influence his mother wields in the organization.

The Girl with All the Gifts by M. R. Carey (Orbit/Grand Central) is an absorbing, fresh take on zombies by the pseudonymous Mike Carey. A young girl named Melanie, along with other children around her age, are kept shackled, muzzled, and imprisoned within a mysterious compound. They are also taught by an assemblage of teachers, only one of whom seems particularly compassionate. The children are zombies but zombies varying in intelligence, unlike the "hungries" outside the compound, who only seek to consume. The compound is primarily a laboratory in which experiments are being done on the children in a desperate attempt to save the human race from extinction.

Bird Box by Josh Malerman (Ecco) was a marvelous, suspenseful horror debut about the survivors of a mass extinction of humankind resulting from madness induced by seeing . . . something. The two strands of the book follow Malorie and her two young children leaving the sanctuary they've lived in for several years and the other backtracks up to how she came to live at the house with other survivors.

A Head Full of Ghosts by Paul Tremblay (William Morrow) is a terrific novel about a teenager who manifests symptoms of schizophrenia. Doctors are no help. Her desperate father consults a Catholic priest who, feeding the father's religious mania, believes the girl is demonically possessed and pushes for an exorcism. A reality show is produced about the family and their troubles. The story is told mostly from the point of view of the eight-year-old younger sister, who adores her sister but has mental/emotional problems of her own. Because of this and her youth, she may not be the most reliable narrator. It's no coincidence that the younger of the two girls is named Meredith, shortened to Merry (pace Merricat from *We Have Always Lived in the Castle*).

Finders Keepers by Stephen King (Scribner) is terrific. I haven't been keeping up with King's novel output for a while so hadn't realized this book was a sequel to 2014's *Mr. Mercedes*, which I've not read. But that matters not. A novelist retires after writing a bestselling literary trilogy. The final book ends unsatisfactorily for at least one reader—a psychopath. There are rumors of a sequel and the unhinged reader wants to read that manuscript—at any cost, setting off a tense, terrifying series of events. This is a great novel about obsession and a writer's responsibility to his readers.

The Library at Mount Char by Scott Hawkins (Crown) was an utterly refreshing debut about gods as monsters. A young woman who, along with several other neighborhood children, was plucked from a normal life when they were all orphaned in one destructive event, is raised by a mysterious man who becomes their demanding "father." Whenever the reader is certain of what comes next, the plot veers wildly into a different, perfectly controlled direction. This is especially evident about three quarters of the way in, when the story seems to be over. It's not. A fabulous, exceedingly dark fantasy about the monstrosity of gods. By turns funny and horrifying, it hits every mark. While I don't want to oversell it, this is the finest, most satisfying dark novel I read in 2015.

Experimental Film by Gemma Files (CZP) is another great example of weird fiction about arcane secrets behind movies and movie-making. A former film teacher suffering from depression and anxiety—because of dealing with an autistic child—is pulled into a mystery that becomes more and more dangerous to her and those around her. The novel's about so much: Gods and what they require in their worship, the difference between looking and seeing, and knowing when to look away. The danger of obsession. Wonderfully creepy. Another great one from 2015.

Lovecraft Country by Matt Ruff (Harper) combines the harrowing horror of 1950s Jim Crow America with the supernatural horror of the Lovecraftian Mythos. In 1954, an African American man goes missing and his war veteran son sets out from Chicago with two companions to search for him. Each chapter tells a separate story that builds into a complete whole that exudes a sense of dread—almost more from the rampant racism than the monsters conjured up by a cult of sorcerers. But even so, this is most definitely a Lovecraftian story, with all the paranoia, conspiracies, family secrets, and cosmic horror that readers could hope for.

It's the perfect companion to Victor LaValle's novella chapbook, *The Ballad of Black Tom.* The Tor.com novella program started publishing science fiction, fantasy, and horror in 2015, but the first actual horror novella was *The Ballad of Black Tom* by Victor LaValle (acquired and edited by me). The author, who in his dedication relays his conflicted feelings about Lovecraft, reimagines "The Horror at Red Hook" with a young African American protagonist. Charles Thomas Tester is hired to deliver an occult book to an elderly woman in Queens. By doing so he becomes involves in arcane, mythos-inspired doings.

Mongrels by Stephen Graham Jones (William Morrow) is a gorgeous dark and moving coming-of-age story about a young, not-yet werewolf being brought up by his grandfather, aunt, and uncle who are all tasked with teaching him how to *be* a werewolf—what a werewolf can and can't do, what can harm or kill it. Moving gracefully back and forth over a period of several years, clues are sprinkled throughout to the history of the family.

Hex by Thomas Olde Heuvelt (Tor) is one of the most *unnerving* novels I've ever read. A small town in upstate New York is cursed by a witch from the seventeenth century, a witch with her eyes and mouth stitched up. What is especially unnerving is that the witch mysteriously appears and disappears around town at will: in the street, in shops, in homes. Everyone in town knows there are rules that must be obeyed, or harm will come to them and their loved ones. One of the rules is that outsiders must never know of the curse, so the town is basically quarantined from the rest of the world. When a new family ignorantly moves into town despite all attempts to discourage them, a string of events begin to drive the whole town batshit crazy.

Most novel-length supernatural horror doesn't work for me, as my suspension of disbelief usually falls away at some point. *Hex* manages to avoid this—perhaps because it's both supernaturally and psychologically horrific.

The Fisherman by John Langan (Word Horde) is the terrific second novel by an author who has been making his reputation in the horror field by producing consistently powerful and literate stories for the past several years. In a perfect origami of stories within stories, a fisherman relates a tale of another kind of fisherman, who is seeking more than mere fish.

The Loney by Andrew Michael Hurley (Houghton Mifflin Harcourt) was originally published by Tartarus Press in 2014 and won the prestigious Costa First Novel Award in 2015. It's a gorgeously written, powerful gothic novel about events that take place during three Catholic families' religious retreat to the wild northern coast of Lancashire, an area known as the Loney. They go there to find a cure for the disabilities of the narrator's brother, as the area is known to be ghost-ridden, full of mystery, and sometimes the provider of miracles. But there's a cost. There's always a cost. Literary horror at its best.

The Changeling by Victor LaValle (Spiegel & Grau) takes the reader for an emotionally wrenching rollercoaster ride when a horrific act destroys the seemingly idyllic life of a New York couple and their infant. Apollo Kagwa's father disappears, leaving him with strange dreams and a box of books. Apollo becomes a rare book dealer and a father himself. When his wife, Emma, starts behaving oddly, he's alarmed, but before he can do anything she does something horrible and unforgivable—and disappears. The story becomes a dark fairy tale about Apollo's odyssey into a world just beyond our ken, with magic that can empower or destroy.

The Child Finder by Rene Denfeld (HarperCollins) is by the author of the acclaimed first novel *The Enchanted*, published in 2014. Is *The Child Finder* horror? Probably not, although it is a crime novel about child abduction and abuse. A young woman, herself a former child abductee, who remembers little of her experience yet is haunted by it, has taken it upon herself to find other lost and abducted children. The book is brilliant, suspenseful, heartbreaking, and thought-provoking. One of the best novels of the year.

-◦-

Here are some of the best single-author collections I covered during the past ten years:

Mr. Gaunt and Other Uneasy Encounters by John Langan (Prime) was the first collection by the author and contains five novelettes and novellas, one novella published for the first time. Langan's work is influenced by his work in academia and his interest in the literature of both Henry James and M. R. James. I'm especially fond of the title novella, "Mr. Gaunt," but all his stories are worth reading. His fine story notes are illuminating to readers who want to know "where did you get that idea." *The Wide, Carnivorous Sky and Other Monstrous Geographies* (Hippocampus Press), published five years later, was the author's second collection of marvelously creepy short fiction. Langan especially shines at the novelette and novella length, and almost everything in the new book is those lengths. Eight were originally published between 2008 and 2010, one on the author's blog. The one original is an excellent novella. With an introduction by Jeffrey Ford and an afterword by Laird Barron.

The Autopsy and Other Tales by Michael Shea (Centipede Press) is a gorgeous, over-sized, illustrated volume of twenty-one of the late author's best stories and novellas, including some of my personal favorites: the creepy Lovecraftian, *Fat Face* and the novella *I, Said the Fly*. The book reprints all eight stories from *Polyphemus*, published by Arkham House in 1988. Laird Barron has written an introduction to Shea's work. Also included is one story published for the first time.

Northwest Passages by Barbara Roden (Prime) was an impressive debut collection of ten stories (two appearing for the first time). Four of the reprints were given honorable mentions in *The Year's Best Fantasy and Horror* series, and one was reprinted in #19. With an introduction by critic Michael Dirda.

Occultation by Laird Barron (Night Shade Books) was the second collection by a writer with a sure hand and a memorable voice. If you want literary horror with a fair share of visceral chills and the occasional shock, you'll find no better. The three originals—two novellas and a short story—are all excellent. Several of the stories have been reprinted in my Year's Best anthologies.

The Ones That Got Away by Stephen Graham Jones (Prime) is an important collection containing eleven powerful stories published between 2005 and 2010, with two new ones. Jones's work is visceral, violent, and disturbing. With an insightful introduction by Laird Barron and story notes by the author. Several of the stories were reprinted in various Year's Best anthologies, including my own.

Lesser Demons by Norman Partridge (Subterranean Press) collected ten stories published between 2000 and 2010, one new. Partridge is a writer who is equally at home in whatever genre his tale falls: hard-boiled western, contemporary noir, or monster tale. The title novelette is Lovecraftian and very effective.

Lost Places by Simon Kurt Unsworth (Ash-Tree Press) was an excellent debut collection with eighteen stories, fourteen of them never before published. The stories are varied in tone, setting, and character. Several are particularly creepy.

The Janus Tree and Other Stories (Subterranean Press) was Glen Hirshberg's third collection of short fiction and it's as good, if not better, than his first two. Included are his eleven recent stories. The title story won the Shirley Jackson Award and several others were chosen for best of the year volumes. The two originals are both chilling.

Engines of Desire: Tales of Love and Other Horrors by Livia Llewellyn (Lethe Press) was a powerful debut collection of ten stories published between 2005 and 2010, with one knockout original novelette, reprinted in the *Best Horror of the Year Volume Four*. Llewellyn is ferocious and unflinching as she creates flawed characters facing the dark in the world outside and in themselves. *Furnace* (Word Horde) was the author's second collection, featuring fourteen stories, one new. She's in the forefront of contemporary writers excelling in the horror short form. Psychosexual, provocative, sharp, complex.

Mrs Midnight and Other Stories by Reggie Oliver (Tartarus Press) was the topnotch fifth collection of horror and weird stories, with four of the thirteen stories published for the first time. Featuring spot illustrations by the author. It was one of the best collections published in 2012.

Red Gloves by Christopher Fowler (PS Publishing) was an excellent double volume of twenty-five stories celebrating the author's twenty-fifth anniversary writing horror. Fowler is both prolific and versatile, a winning combination. The first volume contains London stories, the second is made up of "world" stories. Several are original to the volume and one of them was a new Bryant and May story.

Two Worlds and In Between: The Best of Caitlín R. Kiernan (Volume One) (Subterranean Press) was, at 600 pages, a very generous helping of this excellent writer's short fiction output between 1993 and 2004. A must-have for fans of Kiernan's dark fictions. Her background in geology and vertebrate paleontology infuse her science fiction work, as well as her Lovecraftian influenced stories.

Remember Why You Fear Me was Robert Shearman's (ChiZine Publications) fourth collection of stories and the only one he categorizes as "horror" (although many of his earlier tales are dark). This volume includes twenty-one stories, ten of them new. Enjoy the feast. Before he won the World Fantasy Award in 2008 for *Tiny Deaths*, his first collection, he was best known as the *Doctor Who* writer who reintroduced the Daleks into the series. In addition to this new collection, Shearman posted a series of stories on his blog starting in 2011—some reprints, most published for the first time. The idea was, in his own words: "I wrote a book of short stories, called *Everyone's Just So So Special.* And to celebrate its release, I proposed that everyone who bought the one hundred special leatherbound editions would receive an entirely unique story of their own, featuring their name, of at least 500 words in length. And to prove that the stories really *were* unique, I'd post them all online, for all the world to see. The problem is, they're not 500 words. They're a bit longer than that. But, hey, I like a challenge." I don't believe Shearman finished his task, but what he did write is still up there, in 2018. Enjoy what comes out of this guy's brain at: justsosospecial.com

The Terrible Changes by Joel Lane (Ex Occidente Press) is an excellent collection. It contains fourteen stories, twelve previously uncollected, two published for the first time. Lane's foreword described his evolution as a writer of weird fiction and the stories range over his up till then twenty-five-year career. *Where Furnaces Burn*, also by Lane (PS Publishing), was a consistently terrific collection by a writer often named in the same breath as Conrad Williams, whose new collection I mention below. The twenty-three reprints and three original stories in the Lane volume are never less than very good, and always readable. Lane died in 2013; these two collections were published in 2009 and 2012 respectively.

Born with Teeth by Conrad Williams (PS Publishing) was another excellent volume of short fiction by this author. It has seventeen diverse horror stories originally published between 1997 and 2012 in various magazines and anthologies, including one excellent new story, which was reprinted in the *Best of the Year Volume Six*.

Windeye by Brian Evenson (Coffee House Press) presented twenty-five dark and sometimes weird stories by a writer who has been consistently praised by the mainstream, despite the fact that he mostly writes horror fiction. He's one of the few writers in the field today whose work, even in a very few pages, can pack a punch and not seem gimmicky doing so.

North American Lake Monsters by Nathan Ballingrud (Small Beer Press) was the author's first collection. Some of the nine stories are almost mainstream, I guess you could say mainstream in sensibility, but there's always a touch of the weird in them. Since publishing his first story in Scifiction in 2003, I've been astounded by his range. The one original story is a knockout, and was reprinted in the *Best Horror of the Year*.

The Beautiful Thing That Awaits Us All by Laird Barron (Night Shade) was Barron's third collection, and has eight stories originally published between 2010 and 2012, plus one new one. Barron's writing might be described as an amalgam of Lovecraftian themes and paranoia with the language and characterizations of tough men laid low (sometimes by women) of Lucius Shepard. Critics talk about Thomas Ligotti as an inheritor of Lovecraft's mantle, and that might be, but Barron at his best has pushed cosmic horror through to the twenty-first century. With an introduction by Norman Partridge. The one new story was reprinted in the *Best Horror of the Year Volume Six*. *Swift to Chase* (JournalStone) was the author's fourth collection, featuring twelve stories and novellas, one new. Barron's short fiction ranges from horror and sword and sorcery to noir and dystopic, never moving too far from the dark dark core he writes about so well.

Everything You Need by Michael Marshall Smith (Earthling Publications) was a welcome new collection of seventeen stories by one of the contemporary masters of the form. Smith's range is extraordinary, roaming equally smoothly among horror, dark fantasy, science fiction, and mainstream. There were three new stories, one of them mainstream and heartbreaking.

The Bright Day is Done by Carole Johnstone (Gray Friar Press) was a terrific debut, with seventeen stories by a British writer whose work has been published in *Black Static, Interzone*, and a host of anthologies including *The Best Horror of the Year* and *The Best British Fantasy.* Five of the stories and novelettes are new. A must read.

Night Music: Nocturnes Volume 2 by John Connolly (Atria Books/Emily Bestler Books) was an excellent second collection of thirteen supernatural tales by the Irish author of crime novels that are often imbued with the uncanny. There were five new stories and one, "Razorshins," originally published in *Black Static* several months before the collection's publication, is especially good.

Probably Monsters by Ray Cluley (ChiZine Publications) was a strong debut by a writer who has been getting increasing and well-deserved attention in Great Britain (one story won the British Fantasy Award). The twenty stories showcase his broad range, with three new stories, one of which was reprinted in the *Best Horror of the Year Volume Eight*.

Interior Darkness by Peter Straub (Doubleday) was a compilation of sixteen stories and novellas published over twenty-five years, and culled from this master stylist's three collections. Three of the stories and novellas were previously uncollected.

Ragman & Other Family Curses by Rebecca Lloyd (Egaeus Press, Keynote Edition I) was a limited edition mini-hardcover collection of four impressive new novelettes. "Ragman" and "For Two Songs" are both disconcertingly horrific. The former was reprinted in *Best Horror of the Year Volume Nine.* *Seven Strange Stories* (Tartarus Press) was the author's excellent fourth collection of eerie dark stories and novellas. Two are reprints.

Phantasms: Twelve Eerie Tales by Peter Bell (Sarob Press) was an excellent selection of seven reprints and five new stories by a formidable writer of ghostly tales.

She Said Destroy by Nadia Bulkin (Word Horde) was a smart, powerful debut collection with thirteen stories of horror and weird fiction, one of them new. Three of them were nominated for the Shirley Jackson Award.

The Night Shop: Tales for the Lonely Hours by Terry Dowling (Cemetery Dance) was the Australian, multi-award-winning author's fourth horror collection and it's a terrific sampling of his work, with eighteen disturbing stories, three of them new. It showcases Dowling at the top of his game.

The Unorthodox Dr. Draper and Other Stories by William Browning Spencer (Subterranean Press) collected ten years' worth of Spencer's most recent stories, between 2007 and 2017, which includes nine stories and one poem. His work is surreal, funny, horrific, and very well written.

⊷

Working on *The Best Horror of the Year* for so long has given me a fierce appreciation of the richness inherent in the term "horror." The stories I've chosen during the past ten years are those I've read and reread with continuing enjoyment. Because that's how I choose what goes into the anthology—I read the ones I've marked for special attention multiple times until I bring the word count of the anthology down to my annual limit. So, you can imagine just how many times I've reread the stories that made the final cut of *this* volume.

I often jokingly call myself a "pusher"—I am. A pusher of what I consider great short fiction. I want you the reader to love the stories that *I as a reader* love. I hope you'll return to these stories over and over with the same enjoyment I have. And perhaps "push" them to your friends.

LOWLAND SEA

SUZY MCKEE CHARNAS

Miriam had been to Cannes twice before. The rush and glamour of the film festival had not long held her attention (she did not care for movies and knew the real nature of the people who made them too well for that magic to work), but from the windows of their festival hotel she could look out over the sea and daydream about sailing home, one boat against the inbound tide from northern Africa.

This was a foolish dream; no one went to Africa now—no one could be paid enough to go, not while the Red Sweat raged there (the film festival itself had been postponed this year til the end of summer on account of the epidemic). She'd read that vessels wallowing in from the south laden with refugees were regularly shot apart well offshore by European military boats, and the beaches were not only still closed but were closely patrolled for lucky swimmers, who were also disposed of on the spot.

Just foolish, really, not even a dream that her imagination could support beyond its opening scene. Supposing that she could survive long enough to actually make it home (and she knew she was a champion survivor), nothing would be left of her village, just as nothing, or very close to nothing, was left to her of her childhood self. It was eight years since she had been taken.

Bad years; until Victor had bought her. Her clan tattoos had caught his attention. Later, he had had them reproduced, in make-up, for his film, *Hearts of Light* (it was about African child-soldiers rallied by a brave, warm-hearted American adventurer—played by Victor himself—against Islamic terrorists).

She understood that he had been seduced by the righteous outlawry of buying a slave in the modern world—to free her, of course; it made him feel bold and virtuous. In fact, Victor was accustomed to buying people. Just since Miriam had known him, he had paid two Russian women to carry babies for him because his fourth wife was barren. He already had children but, edging toward sixty, he wanted new evidence of his potency.

Miriam was not surprised. Her own father had no doubt used the money he had been paid for her to buy yet another young wife to warm his cooling bed; that was a man's way. He was probably dead now or living in a refugee camp somewhere, along with all the sisters and brothers and aunties from his compound: wars, the Red Sweat, and fighting over the scraps would leave little behind.

She held no grudge: she had come to realize that her father had done her a favor by selling her. She had seen a young cousin driven away for witchcraft by his own father, after a newborn baby brother had sickened and died. A desperate family could thus be quickly rid of a mouth they could not feed.

Better still, Miriam had not yet undergone the ordeal of female circumcision when she was taken away. At first she had feared that it was for this reason that the men who bought her kept selling her on to others. But she had learned that this was just luck, in all its perverse strangeness, pressing her life into some sort of shape. Not a very good shape after her departure from home, but then good luck came again in the person of Victor, whose bed she had warmed til he grew tired of her. Then he hired her to care for his new babies, Kevin and Leif.

Twins were unlucky back home: there, one or both would immediately have been put out in the bush to die. But this, like so many other things, was different for all but the poorest of whites.

They were pretty babies; Kevin was a little fussy but full of lively energy and alertness that Miriam rejoiced to see. Victor's actress wife, Cameron, had no use for the boys (they were not hers, after all, not as these people reckoned such things). She had gladly left to Miriam the job of tending to them.

Not long afterward Victor had bought Krista, an Eastern European girl, who doted extravagantly on the two little boys and quickly took over their care. Victor hated to turn people out of his household (he thought of himself as a magnanimous man), so his chief assistant, Bulgarian Bob, found a way to keep Miriam on. He gave her a neat little digital camera with which to keep a snapshot record of Victor's home life: she was to be a sort of documentarian of the domestic. It was Bulgarian Bob (as opposed to French Bob, Victor's head driver) who had noticed her interest in taking pictures during an early shoot of the twins.

B. Bob was like that: he noticed things, and he attended to them.

Miriam felt blessed. She knew herself to be plain next to the diet-sculpted, spa-pampered, surgery-perfected women in Victor's household, so she could hardly count on beauty to secure protection; nor had she any outstanding talent of the kind that these people valued. But with a camera like this Canon G9, you needed no special gift to take attractive family snapshots. It was certainly better than, say, becoming someone's lowly third wife, or being bonded for life to a wrinkled shrine-priest back home.

Krista said that B. Bob had been a gangster in Prague. This was certainly possible. Some men had a magic that could change them from any one thing into anything else: the magic was money. Victor's money had changed Miriam's status from that of an illegal slave to, of all wonderful things, that of a naturalized citizen of the U.S.A. (although whether her new papers could stand serious scrutiny she hoped never to have to find out). Thus she was cut off from her roots, floating in Victor's world.

Better not to think of that, though; better not to think painful thoughts.

Krista understood this (she understood a great deal without a lot of palaver). Yet Krista obstinately maintained a little shrine made of old photos, letters, and trinkets that she set up in a private corner wherever Victor's household went. Despite a grim period in Dutch and Belgian brothels, she retained a sweet naiveté. Miriam hoped that no bad luck would rub off on Krista from attending to the twins. Krista was an *east* European, which seemed to render a female person more than normally vulnerable to ill fortune.

Miriam had helped Krista to fit in with the others who surrounded Victor—the coaches, personal shoppers, arrangers, designers, bodyguards, publicists, therapists, drivers, cooks, secretaries, and hangers-on of all kinds. He was like a paramount chief with a great crowd of praise singers paid to flatter him, outshouting similar mobs attending everyone significant in the film world. This world was little different from the worlds of Africa and Arabia that Miriam had known, although at first it had seemed frighteningly strange—so shiny, so fast-moving and raucous! But when you came right down to it here were the same swaggering, self-indulgent older men fighting off their younger competitors, and the same pretty girls they all sniffed after; and the lesser court folk, of course, including almost-invisible functionaries like Krista and Miriam.

One day, Miriam planned to leave. Her carefully tended savings were nothing compared to the fortunes these shiny people hoarded, wasted, and squabbled over; but she had almost enough for a quiet, comfortable life in some quiet, comfortable place. She knew how to live modestly and thought she might even sell some of her photographs once she left Victor's orbit.

It wasn't as if she yearned to run to one of the handsome African men she saw selling knock-off designer handbags and watches on the sidewalks of great European cities. Sometimes, at the sound of a familiar language from home, she imagined joining them—but those were poor men, always on the run from the local law. She could not give such a man power over her and her savings.

Not that having money made the world perfect: Miriam was a realist, like any survivor. She found it funny that, even for Victor's followers with their light minds and heavy pockets, contentment was not to be bought. Success itself eluded them, since they continually redefined it as that which they had not yet achieved.

Victor, for instance: the one thing he longed for but could not attain was praise for his film—his first effort as an actor-director.

"They hate me!" he cried, crushing another bad review and flinging it across the front room of their hotel suite, "because I have the balls to tackle grim reality! All they want is sex, explosions, and the new Brad Pitt! Anything but truth, they can't stand truth!"

Of course they couldn't stand it. No one could. Truth was the desperate lives of most ordinary people, lives often too hard to be borne; mere images on a screen could not make that an attractive spectacle. Miriam had known boys back home who thought they were "Rambo". Some had become killers, some had been become the killed: doped-up boys, slung about with guns and bullet-belts like carved fetish figures draped in strings of shells. Their short lives were not in the movies or like the movies.

On this subject as many others, however, Miriam kept her opinions to herself.

Hearts of Light was scorned at Cannes. Victor's current wife, Cameron, fled in tears from his sulks and rages. She stayed away for days, drowning her unhappiness at parties and pools and receptions.

Wealth, however, did have certain indispensable uses. Some years before Miriam had joined his household, Victor had bought the one thing that turned out to be essential: a white-walled mansion called La Bastide, set high on the side of a French valley only a day's drive from Cannes. This was to be his retreat from the chaos and crushing boredom of the cinema world, a place where he could recharge his creative energies (so said B. Bob).

When news came that three Sudanese had been found dead in Calabria, their skins crusted with a cracked glaze of blood, Victor had his six rented Mercedes loaded up with petrol and provisions. They drove out of Cannes before the next dawn. It had been hot on the Mediterranean shore. Inland was worse. Stubby planes droned across the sky trailing plumes of retardant and water that they dropped on fires in the hills.

Victor stood in the sunny courtyard of La Bastide and told everyone how lucky they were to have gotten away to this refuge before the road from Cannes became clogged with people fleeing the unnerving proximity of the Red Sweat.

"There's room for all of us here," he said (Miriam snapped pictures of his confident stance and broad, chiefly gestures). "Better yet, we're prepared and we're *safe*. These walls are thick and strong. I've got a rack of guns downstairs, and we know how to use them. We have plenty of food, and all the water we could want: a spring in the bedrock underneath us feeds sweet, clean water into a well right here inside the walls. And since I didn't have to store water, we have lots more of everything else!"

Oh, the drama; already, Miriam told Krista, he was making the movie of all this in his head.

Nor was he the only one. As the others went off to the quarters B. Bob assigned them, trailing an excited hubbub through the cool, shadowed spaces of the house, those who had brought their camcorders dug them out and began filming on the spot. Victor encouraged them, saying that this adventure must be recorded, that it would be a triumph of photojournalism for the future.

Privately he told Miriam, "It's just to keep them busy. I depend on your stills to capture the reality of all this. We'll have an exhibition later, maybe even a book. You've got a good eye, Miriam; and you've had experience with crisis in your part of the world, right?"

"La Bastide" meant "the country house" but the place seemed more imposing than that, standing tall, pale, and alone on a crag above the valley. The outer walls were thick, with stout wooden doors and window-shutters as Victor had pointed out. He had had a wing added on to the back in matching stone. A small courtyard, the one containing the well, was enclosed by walls between the old and new buildings. Upstairs rooms had tall windows and sturdy iron balconies; those on the south side overlooked a French village three kilometers away down the valley.

Everyone had work to do—scripts to read, write, or revise, phone calls to make and take, deals to work out—but inevitably they drifted into the ground floor salon, the room with the biggest flat-screen TV. The TV stayed on. It showed raging wildfires. Any place could burn in summer, and it was summer most of the year now in southern Europe.

But most of the news was about the Red Sweat. Agitated people pointed and shouted, their expressions taut with urgency: "Looters came yesterday. Where are the police, the authorities?"

"We scour buildings for batteries, matches, canned goods."

"What can we do? They left us behind because we are old."

"We hear cats and dogs crying, shut in with no food or water. We let the cats out, but we are afraid of the dogs; packs already roam the streets."

Pictures showed bodies covered with crumpled sheets, curtains, bedspreads in many colors, laid out on sidewalks and in improvised morgues—the floors of school gyms, of churches, of automobile showrooms.

My God, they said, staring at the screen with wide eyes. Northern Italy now! So *close*!

Men carrying guns walked through deserted streets wearing bulky, outlandish protective clothing and face masks. Trucks loaded with relief supplies waited for roads to become passable; survivors mobbed the trucks when they arrived. Dead creatures washed up on shorelines, some human, some not. Men in robes, suits, turbans, military uniforms, talked and talked and talked into microphones, reassuring, begging, accusing, weeping.

All this had been building for months, of course, but everyone in Cannes had been too busy to pay much attention. Even now at La Bastide they seldom talked about the news. They talked about movies. It was easier.

Miriam watched TV a lot. Sometimes she took pictures of the screen images. The only thing that could make her look away was a shot of an uncovered body, dead or soon to be so, with a film of blood dulling the skin.

On Victor's orders, they all ate in the smaller salon, without a TV.

On the third night, Krista asked, "What will we eat when this is all gone?"

"I got boxes of that paté months ago." Bulgarian Bob smiled and stood back with his arms folded, like a waiter in a posh restaurant. "Don't worry, there's plenty more."

"My man," said Victor, digging into his smoked Norwegian salmon.

Next day, taking their breakfast coffee out on the terrace, they saw military vehicles grinding past on the roadway below. Relief convoys were being intercepted now, the news had said, attacked and looted.

"Don't worry, little Mi," B. Bob said, as she took snaps of the camouflage-painted trucks from the terrace. "Victor bought this place and fixed it up in the Iranian crisis. He thought we had more war coming. We're set for a year, two years."

Miriam grimaced. "Where food was stored in my country, that is where gunmen came to steal," she said.

B. Bob took her on a tour of the marvelous security at La Bastide, all controlled from a complicated computer console in the master suite: the heavy steel-mesh gates that could be slammed down, the metal window shutters, the ventilation ducts with their electrified outside grills.

"But if the electricity goes off?" she asked.

He smiled. "We have our own generators here."

After dinner that night Walter entertained them. Hired as Victor's Tae Kwan Do coach, he turned out to be a conservatory-trained baritone.

"No more opera," Victor said, waving away an aria. "Old country songs for an old country house. Give us some ballads, Walter!"

Walter sang "Parsley Sage", "Barbara Ellen", and "The Golden Vanity".

This last made Miriam's eyes smart. It told of a young cabin boy who volunteered to swim from an outgunned warship to the enemy vessel and sink it, single-handed, with an augur; but his Captain would not let him back on board afterward. Rather than hole that ship too and so drown not just the evil Captain but his own innocent shipmates, the cabin boy drowned himself: "he sank into the lowland, low and lonesome, sank into the lowland sea."

Victor applauded. "Great, Walter, thanks! You're off the hook now, that's enough gloom and doom. Tragedy tomorrow—*comedy* tonight!"

They followed him into the library, which had been fitted out with a big movie screen and computers with game consoles. They settled down to watch Marx Brothers movies and old romantic comedies from the extensive film library of La Bastide. The bodyguards stayed up late, playing computer games full of mayhem. They grinned for Miriam's camera lens.

In the hot and hazy afternoon next day, a green mini-Hummer appeared on the highway. Miriam and Krista, bored by a general discussion about which gangster movie had the most swear words, were sitting on the terrace painting each other's toenails. The Hummer turned off the roadway, came up the hill, and stopped at La Bastide's front gates. A man in jeans, sandals, and a white shirt stepped out on the driver's side.

It was Paul, a writer hired to ghost Victor's autobiography. The hot, cindery wind billowed his sleeve as he raised a hand to shade his eyes.

"Hi, girls!" he called. "We made it! We actually had to go off-road, you wouldn't believe the traffic around the larger towns! Where's Victor?"

Bulgarian Bob came up beside them and stood looking down.

"Hey, Paul," he said. "Victor's sleeping; big party last night. What can we do for you?"

"Open the gates, of course! We've been driving for hours!"

"From Cannes?"

"Of course from Cannes!" cried Paul heartily. "Some Peruvian genius won the Palme D'Or, can you believe it? But maybe you haven't heard—the jury made a special prize for *Hearts of Light*. We have the trophy with us—Cammie's been holding it all the way from Cannes."

Cameron jumped out of the car and held up something bulky wrapped in a towel. She wore party clothes: a sparkly green dress and chunky sandals that laced high on her plump calves. Miriam's own thin, straight legs shook a little with the relief of being up here, on the terrace, and not down there at the gates.

Bulgarian Bob put his big hand gently over the lens of her camera. "Not this," he murmured.

Cameron waved energetically and called B. Bob's name, and Miriam's, and even Krista's (everyone knew that she hated Krista).

Paul stood quietly, staring up. Miriam had to look away.

B. Bob called, "Victor will be very happy about the prize."

Krista whispered, "He looks for blood on their skin; it's too far to see, though, from up here." To Bob she said, "I should go tell Victor?"

B. Bob shook his head. "He won't want to know."

He turned and went back inside without another word. Miriam and Krista took their bottles of polish and their tissues and followed.

Victor (and, therefore, everyone else) turned a deaf ear to the pleas, threats, and wails from out front for the next two days. A designated "security team" made up of bodyguards and mechanics went around making sure that La Bastide was locked up tight.

Victor sat rocking on a couch, eyes puffy. "My God, I hate this; but they were too slow. *They could be carrying the disease.* We have a responsibility to protect ourselves."

Next morning the Hummer and its two occupants had gone.

Television channels went to only a few hours a day, carrying reports of the Red Sweat in Paris, Istanbul, Barcelona. Nato troops herded people into make-shift "emergency" camps: schools, government buildings, and of course that trusty standby of imprisonment and death, sports arenas.

The radio and news sites on the web said more: refugees were on the move everywhere. The initial panicky convulsion of flight was over, but smaller groups were reported rushing this way and that all over the continent. In Eastern Europe, officials were holed up in mountain monasteries and castles, trying to subsist on wild game. Urbanites huddled in the underground malls of Canadian cities. When the Red Sweat made its lurid appearance in Montreal, it set off a stampede for the countryside.

They said monkeys carried it; marmots; stray dogs; stray people. Ravens, those eager devourers of corpses, must carry the disease on their claws and beaks, or they spread it in their droppings. So people shot at birds, dogs, rodents, and other people.

Krista prayed regularly to two little wooden icons she kept with her. Miriam had been raised pagan with a Christian gloss. She did not pray. God had never seemed further away.

After a screaming fight over the disappearance of somebody's stash of E, a sweep by the security squad netted a hoard of drugs. These were locked up, to be dispensed only by Bulgarian Bob at set times.

"We have plenty of food and water," Victor explained, "but not an endless supply of drugs. We don't want to run through it all before this ends, do we?" In compensation he was generous with alcohol, with which La Bastide's cellar was plentifully stocked. When his masseuse (she was diabetic) and one of the drivers insisted on leaving to fend for themselves and their personal requirements outside, Victor did not object.

Miriam had not expected a man who had only ever had to act like a leader onscreen to exercise authority so naturally in real life.

It helped that his people were not in a rebellious mood. They stayed in their rooms playing cards, sleeping, some even reading old novels from the shelves under the window seats downstairs. A running game of trivia went on in the games room ("Which actors have played which major roles in green body make-up?"). People used their cell phones to call each other in different parts of the building, since calls to the outside tended not to connect (when they did, conversations were not encouraging).

Nothing appeared on the television now except muay thai matches from Thailand, but the radio still worked: "Fires destroyed the main hospital in Marseilles; fire brigades did not respond. Refugees from the countryside who were sheltering inside are believed dead."

"Students and teachers at the university at Bologna broke into the city offices but found none of the food and supplies rumored to be stored there."

Electricity was failing now over many areas. Victor decreed that they must only turn on the modern security system at night. During daylight hours they used the heavy old locks and bolts on the thick outer doors. B. Bob posted armed lookouts on the terrace and on the roof of the back wing. Cell phones were collected, to stop them being recharged to no good purpose.

But the diesel fuel for Victor's vastly expensive, vastly efficient German generators suddenly ran out (it appeared that the caretaker of La Bastide had sold off much of it during the previous winter). The ground floor metal shutters that had been locked in place by electronic order at nightfall could not be reopened.

Unexpectedly, Victor's crew seemed glad to be shut in more securely. They moved most activities to the upper floor of the front wing, avoiding the shuttered darkness downstairs. They went to bed earlier to conserve candles. They partied in the dark.

The electric pumps had stopped, but an old hand-pump at the basement laundry tubs was rigged to draw water from the well into the pipes in the house. They tore up part of the well yard in the process, getting dust everywhere, but in the end they even got a battered old boiler working over a wood-fire in the basement. A bath rota was eagerly subscribed to, although Alicia, the wig-girl, was forbidden to use hot water to bathe her Yorkie any more.

Victor rallied his troops that evening. He was not a tall man but he was energetic and his big, handsome face radiated confidence and determination. "Look at us—we're movie people, spinners of dreams that ordinary people pay money to share! Who needs a screening room, computers, TV? We can entertain ourselves, or we shouldn't be here!"

Sickly grins all around, but they rose at once to his challenge.

They put on skits, plays, take-offs of popular TV shows. They even had concerts, since several people could play piano or guitar well and Walter was not the only one with a good singing voice. Someone found a violin in a display case downstairs, but no one knew how to play that. Krista and the youngest of the cooks told fortunes, using tea leaves and playing cards from the game room. The fortunes were all fabulous.

Miriam did not think about the future. She occupied herself taking pictures. One of the camera men reminded her that there would be no more recharging of batteries now; if she turned off the LCD screen on the Canon G9 its picture-taking capacity would last longer. Most of the camcorders were already dead from profligate over-use.

It was always noisy after sunset now; people fought back this way against the darkness outside the walls of La Bastide. Miriam made ear plugs out of candle wax and locked her bedroom door at night. On an evening of lively revels (it was Walter's birthday party) she quietly got hold of all the keys to her room that she knew of, including one from Bulgarian Bob's set. B. Bob was busy at the time with one of the drivers, as they groped each other urgently on the second floor landing.

There was more sex now, and more tension. Fistfights erupted over a card game, an edgy joke, the misplacement of someone's plastic water bottle. Victor had Security drag one pair of scuffling men apart and hustle them into the courtyard.

"What's this about?" he demanded.

Skip Reiker panted, "He was boasting about some Rachman al Haj concert he went to! That guy is a goddamn A-rab, a crazy damn Muslim!"

"Bullshit!" Sam Landry muttered, rubbing at a red patch on his cheek. "Music is music."

"Where did the god damned Sweat start, jerk? Africa!" Skip yelled. "The ragheads passed it around among themselves for years, and then they decided to share it. How do you think it spread to Europe? They brought it here on purpose, poisoning the food and water with their contaminated spit and blood. Who could do that better than musicians 'on tour'?"

"Asshole!" hissed Sam. "That's what they said about the Jews during the Black Plague, that they'd poisoned village wells! What are you, a Nazi?"

"Fucker!" Skip screamed.

Miriam guessed it was withdrawal that had him so raw; coke supplies were running low, and many people were having a bad time of it.

Victor ordered Bulgarian Bob to open the front gates.

"Quit it, right now, both of you," Victor said, "or take it outside."

Everyone stared out at the dusty row of cars, the rough lawn, and the trees shading the weedy driveway as it corkscrewed downhill toward the paved road below. The combatants slunk off, one to his bed and the other to the kitchen to get his bruises seen to.

Jill, Cameron's hair stylist, pouted as B. Bob pushed the heavy front gates shut again. "Bummer! We could have watched from the roof, like at a joust."

B. Bob said, "They wouldn't have gone out. They know Victor won't let them back in."

"Why not?" said the girl. "Who's even alive out there to catch the Sweat from anymore?"

"You never know." B. Bob slammed the big bolts home. Then he caught Jill around her pale midriff, made mock-growling noises, and swept her back into the house. B. Bob was good at smoothing ruffled feathers. He needed to be. Tensions escalated. It occurred to Miriam that someone at La Bastide might attack her, just for being from the continent on which the disease had first appeared. Mike Bellows, a black script doctor from Chicago, had vanished the weekend before; climbed the wall and ran away, they said.

Miriam saw how Skip Reiker, a film editor with no film to edit now, stared at her when he thought she wasn't looking. She had never liked Mike Bellows, who was an arrogant and impatient man; perhaps Skip had liked him even less, and had made him disappear.

What she needed, she thought, was to find some passage for herself, some unwatched door to the outside, that she could use to slip away if things turned bad here. That was how a survivor must think. So far, the ease of life at La Bastide—the plentiful food and sunshine, the wine from the cellars, the scavenger hunts and skits, the games in the big salon, the fancy-dress parties—had bled off the worst of people's edginess. Everyone, so far, accepted Victor's rules. They knew that he was their bulwark against anarchy.

But: Victor had only as much authority as he had willing obedience. Food rationing, always a dangerous move, was inevitable. The ultimate loyalty of these bought-and-paid-for friends and attendants would be to themselves (except maybe for Bulgarian Bob, who seemed to really love Victor).

Only Jeff, one of the drivers, went outside now, tinkering for hours with the engines of the row of parked cars. One morning Miriam and Krista sat on the front steps in the sun, watching him.

"Look," Krista whispered, tugging at Miriam's sleeve with anxious, pecking fingers. Down near the roadway a dozen dogs, some with chains or leads dragging from their collars, harried a running figure across a field of withered vines in a soundless pantomime of hunting.

They both stood up, exclaiming. Jeff looked where they were looking. He grabbed up his tools and herded them both back inside with him. The front gates stayed closed after that.

Next morning Miriam saw the dogs again, from her balcony. At the foot of the driveway they snarled and scuffled, pulling and tugging at something too mangled and filthy to identify. She did not tell Krista, but perhaps someone else saw too and spread the word (there was a shortage of news in La Bastide these days, as even radio signals had become rare).

Searching for toothpaste, Miriam found Krista crying in her room. "That was Tommy Mullroy," Krista sobbed, "that boy that wanted to make computer games from movies. He was the one with those dogs."

Tommy Mullroy, a minor hanger-on and a late riser by habit, hadn't made it to the cars on the morning of Victor's hasty retreat from Cannes. Miriam was doubtful that Tommy could have found his way across the plague-stricken landscape to La Bastide on his own, and after so much time.

"How could you tell, from so far?" Miriam sat down beside her on the bed and stroked Krista's hand. "I didn't know you liked him."

"No, no, I hate that horrible monkey-boy!" Krista cried, shaking her head furiously. "Bad jokes, and pinching! But now he is dead." She buried her face in her pillow.

Miriam did not think the man chased by dogs had been Tommy Mullroy, but why argue? There was plenty to cry about in any case.

Winter had still not come; the cordwood stored to feed the building's six fireplaces was still stacked high against the courtyard walls. Since they had plenty of water everyone used a lot of it, heated in the old boiler. Every day a load of wood ash had to be dumped out of the side gate.

Miriam and Krista took their turns at this chore together.

They stood a while (in spite of the reeking garbage overflowing the alley outside, as no one came to take it away any more). The road below was empty today. Up close, Krista smelled of perspiration and liquor. Some in the house were becoming neglectful of themselves.

"My mother would use this ash for making soap," Krista said, "but you need also—what is it? Lime?"

Miriam said, "What will they do when all the soap is gone?"

Krista laughed. "Riots! Me, too. When I was kid, I thought luxury was to change the bedsheets every day for fresh." Then she turned to Miriam with wide eyes and whispered, "We must go away from here, Mimi. They have no Red Sweat in my country for sure! People are farmers, villagers, they live healthy, outside the cities! We can go there and be safe."

"More safe than in here?" Miriam shook her head. "Go in, Krista, Victor's little boys must be crying for you. I'll come with you and take some pictures."

The silence outside the walls was a heavy presence, bitter with drifting smoke that tasted harsh; some of the big new villas up the valley, built with expensive synthetic materials, smoldered slowly for days once they caught fire. Now and then thick smoke became visible much further away. Someone would say, "There's a fire to the west," and everyone would go out on the terrace to watch until the smoke died down or drifted away out of sight on the wind. They saw no planes and no troop transports now. Dead bodies appeared on the road from time to time, their presence signaled by crows calling others to the feast.

Miriam noticed that the crows did not chase others of their kind away but announced good pickings far and wide. Maybe that worked well if you were a bird.

A day came when Krista confided in a panic that one of the twins was ill.

"You must tell Victor," Miriam said, holding the back of her hand to the forehead of Kevin, who whimpered. "This child has fever."

"I can't say anything! He is so scared of the Sweat, he'll throw the child outside!"

"His own little boy?" Miriam thought of the village man who drove out his son as a witch. "That's just foolishness," she told Krista; but she knew better, having known worse.

Neither of them said anything about it to Victor. Two days later, Krista jumped from the terrace with Kevin's small body clutched to her chest. Through tears, Miriam aimed her camera down and took a picture of the slack, twisted jumble of the two of them. They were left there on the driveway gravel with its fuzz of weeds and, soon after, its busy crows.

The days grew shorter. Victor's crowd partied every night, never mind about the candles. Bulgarian Bob slept on a cot in Victor's bedroom, with a gun in his hand: another thing that everyone knew but nobody talked about.

On a damp and cloudy morning Victor found Miriam in the nursery with little Leif, who was on the floor playing with a dozen empty medicine bottles. Leif played very quietly and did not look up. Victor touched the child's head briefly and then sat down across the table from Miriam, where Krista used to sit. He was so clean shaven that his cheeks gleamed. He was sweating.

"Miriam, my dear," he said, "I need a great favor. Walter saw lights last night in the village. The army must have arrived, at long last. They'll have medicine. They'll have news. Will you go down and speak with them? I'd go myself, but everyone depends on me here to keep up some discipline, some hope. We can't have more people giving up, like Krista."

"I'm taking care of Leif now—" Miriam began faintly.

"Oh, Cammie can do that."

Miriam quickly looked away from him, her heart beating hard. Did he really believe that he had taken his current wife into La Bastide after all, in her spangly green party dress?

"This is so important," he urged, leaning closer and blinking his large, blue eyes in the way that (B. Bob always said) the camera loved. "There's a very, very large bonus in it for you, Miriam, enough to set you up very well on your own when this is all over. I can't ask anyone else, I wouldn't trust them to come back safe and sound. But you, you're so level-headed and you've had experience of bad times, not like some of these spoiled, silly people here.

Things must have gotten better outside, but how would we know, shut up in here? Everyone agrees: we need you to do this.

"The contagion must have died down by now," he coaxed. "We haven't seen movement outside in days. Everyone has gone, or holed up, like us. Soldiers wouldn't be in the village if it was still dangerous down there."

Just yesterday Miriam had seen a lone rider on a squeaky bicycle peddling down the highway. But she heard what Victor was *not* saying: that he needed to be able to convince others to go outside, convince them that it was safe, as the more crucial supplies (dope; toilet paper) dwindled; that he controlled those supplies; that he could, after all, have her put out by force.

Listening to the tink of the bottles in Leif's little hands, she realized that she could hardly wait to get away; in fact, she *had* to go. She would find amazing prizes, bring back news, and they would all be so grateful that she would be safe here forever. She would make up good news if she had to, to please them; to keep her place here, inside La Bastide.

But for now, go she must.

Bulgarian Bob found her sitting in dazed silence on the edge of her bed.

"Don't worry, Little Mi," he said. "I'm very sorry about Krista. I'll look out for your interest here."

"Thank you," she said, not looking him in the eyes. *Everyone agrees.* It was hard to think; her mind kept jumping.

"Take your camera with you," he said. "It's still working, yes? You've been sparing with it, smarter than some of these idiots. Here's a fresh card for it, just in case. We need to see how it is out there now. We can't print anything, of course, but we can look at your snaps on the LCD when you get back."

The evening's feast was dedicated to "our intrepid scout Miriam". Eyes glittering, the beautiful people of Victor's court toasted her (and, of course, their own good luck in not having been chosen to venture outside). Then they began a boisterous game: who could remember accurately the greatest number of deaths in the *Final Destination* movies, with details?

To Miriam, they looked like crazy witches, cannibals, in the candle-light. Yes, she could hardly wait to leave.

Victor himself came to see her off early in the morning. He gave her a bottle of water, a ham sandwich, and some dried apricots to put in her red ripstop knapsack. "I'll be worrying my head off until you get back!" he said.

She turned away from him and looked at the driveway, at the dust-coated cars squatting on their flattened tires, and the shrunken, darkened body of Krista.

"You know what to look for," Victor said. "Matches. Soldiers. Tools, candles; you know."

The likelihood of finding anything valuable was small (and she would go out of her way *not* to find soldiers). But when he gave her shoulder a propulsive pat, she started down the driveway like a wind-up toy.

Fat dogs dodged away when they saw her coming. She picked up some stones to throw but did not need them.

She walked past the abandoned farmhouses and vacation homes on the valley's upper reaches, and then the village buildings, some burned and some spared; the empty vehicles, dead as fossils; the remains of human beings. Being sold away, she had been spared such sights back home. She had not seen for herself the corpses in sun-faded shirts and dresses, the grass blades growing up into empty eye sockets, that others had photographed there. Now she paused to take her own carefully chosen, precious pictures.

There were only a few bodies in the streets. Most people had died indoors, hiding from death. Why had her life bothered to bring her such a long way round, only to arrive where she would have been anyway had she remained at home?

Breezes ruffled weeds and trash, lifted dusty hair and rags fluttering from grimy bones, and made the occasional loose shutter or door creak as it swung. A few cows—too skittish now to fall easily to roaming dog packs—grazed watchfully on the plantings around the village fountain, which still dribbled dispiritedly.

If there were ghosts, they did not show themselves to her.

She looked into deserted shops and houses, gathering stray bits of paper, candle stubs, tinned food, ball point pens. She took old magazines from a beauty salon, two paperback novels from a deserted coffee house. Venturing into a wine shop got her a cut on the ankle: the place had been smashed to smithereens. Others had come here before her, like that dead man curled up beside the till.

In a desk drawer she found a chocolate bar. She ate it as she headed back up the valley, walking through empty fields to skirt the village this time. The chocolate was crumbly and dry and dizzyingly delicious.

When she arrived at the gates of La Bastide, the men on watch sent word to Bulgarian Bob. He stood at the iron balustrade above her and called down questions: What had she seen, where exactly had she gone, had she entered the buildings, seen anyone alive?

"Where is Victor?" Miriam asked, her mouth suddenly very dry.

"I'll tell you what; you wait down there til morning," Bulgarian Bob said. "We must be sure you don't have the contagion, Miriam. You know."

Miriam, not Little Mi. Her heart drummed painfully. She felt injected into her own memory of Cammie and Paul standing here, pleading to come in. Only now she was looking up at the wall of La Bastide, not down from the terrace.

Sitting on the bonnet of one of one of the cars, she stirred her memory and dredged up old prayers to speak or sing softly into the dusk. Smells of food cooking and woodsmoke wafted down to her. Once, late, she heard squabbling voices at a second floor window. No doubt they were discussing who would be sent out the next time Victor wanted news of the world and one less mouth to feed.

In the morning, she held up her arms for inspection. She took off her blouse and showed them her bare back.

"I'm sorry, Miriam," Victor called down to her. His face was full of compassion. "I think I see a rash on your shoulders. It may be nothing, but you must understand—at least for now, we can't let you in. I really do want to see your pictures, though. You haven't used up all your camera's battery power, have you? We'll lower a basket for it."

"I haven't finished taking pictures," she said. She aimed the lens up at him. He quickly stepped back out of sight. Through the viewfinder she saw only the parapet of the terrace and the empty sky.

She flung the camera into the ravine, panting with rage and terror as she watched it spin on its way down, compact and clever and useless.

Then she sat down and thought.

Even if she found a way back in, if they thought she was infected they would drive her out again, maybe just shoot her. She imagined Skip Reiker throwing a carpet over her dead body, rolling her up in it, and heaving her outside the walls like rubbish. The rest of them would not approve, but anger and fear would enable their worst impulses ("See what you made us do!").

She should have thought more before, about how she was a supernumerary here, acquired but not really *needed*, not *talented* as these people reckoned such things; not important to the tribe.

"Have I have stopped being a survivor?" she asked Krista's withered back.

In the house Walter was singing. "Some Enchanted Evening!" Applause. Then, "The Golden Vanity".

Miriam sat with her back against the outside wall, burning with fear, confusion, and scalding self-reproach.

When the sun rose again she saw a rash of dark blisters on the backs of her hands. She felt more of them rising at her hairline, around her face. Her joints ached. She was stunned: Victor was right. It was the Red Sweat. But how had she caught it? Through something she had touched—a doorknob, a book, a slicing shard of glass? By merely breathing the infected air?

Maybe—the *chocolate*? The idea made her sob with laughter.

They wouldn't care one way or the other. She was already dead to them. She knew they would not even venture out to take her backpack, full of scavenged treasures, when she was dead (she threw its contents down the ravine after the camera, to make sure). She'd been foolish to have trusted Bulgarian Bob, or Victor either.

They had never intended to let the dove back into the ark.

She knelt beside Krista's corpse and made herself search the folds of reeking, sticky clothing until she found Krista's key to the rubbish gate, the key they had used to throw out the ashes. She sat on the ground beside Krista and rubbed the key bright on her own pant-leg.

Let them try to keep her out. Let them try.

Krista was my shipmate. Now I have no shipmates.

At moonrise she shrugged her aching arms through the straps of the empty pack and walked slowly around to the side alley gate. Krista's key clicked minutely in the lock. The door sprang outward, releasing more garbage that had been piled up inside. No one seemed to hear. They were roaring with song in the front wing and drumming on the furniture, to drown out the cries and pleadings they expected to hear from her.

Miriam stepped inside the well yard, swallowing bloody mucus. She felt the paving lurch a little under her.

A man was talking in the kitchen passageway, set into the ground floor of the back wing at an oblique angle across the well yard. She thought it was Edouard, a camera tech, pretending to speak on his cell as he sometimes did to keep himself company when he was on his own. Edouard, as part of Security, carried a gun.

Her head cleared suddenly. She found that she had shut the gate behind her, and had slid down against the inside wall, for she was sitting on the cool pavement. Perhaps she had passed out for a little. By the moon's light she saw the well's raised stone lip, only a short way along the wall to her left. She was thirsty, although she did not think she could force water down her swollen throat now.

The paving stones the men had pried up in their work on the plumbing had not been reset. They were still piled up out of the way, very near where she sat.

Stones; water. Her brain was again so clogged with hot heaviness that she could barely hold her head up.

"Non, non!" Edouard shouted into his phone. "Ce n'est pas vrai, ils sont menteurs, tous!"

Yes, all of them; menteurs. She sympathized, briefly.

Her mind kept tilting and spilling all its thoughts into a turgid jumble, but there were constants: *stones. Water.* The exiled dove, the brave cabin boy. Krista and little Kevin. She made herself move, trusting to the existence of an actual plan somewhere in her mind. She crawled over to the stacked pavers. Slowly and with difficulty she took off her backpack and stuffed it with some of the smaller stones, one by one. Blood beaded black around her fingernails. She had no strength to pull the loaded pack onto her back again, so she hung it from her shoulder by one broad strap, and began making her painful way toward the well itself.

Edouard was deep in his imaginary quarrel. As she crept along the wall she heard his voice echo angrily in the vaulted passageway.

The thick wooden well-cover had been replaced with a lightweight metal sheet, back when they had had to haul water by hand before the old laundry pump was reconnected. She lifted the metal sheet and set it aside. Dragging herself up, she leaned over the low parapet and peered down.

She could not make out the stone steps that descended into the water on the inside wall, left over from a time when the well had been used to hide contraband. Now… something. Her thoughts swam.

Focus.

Even without her camera there was a way to bring home to Victor all the reality he had sent her out to capture for him in pictures.

She could barely shift her legs over the edge, but at last she felt the cold roughness of the top step under her feet. She descended toward the water, using the friction of her spread hands, turning her torso flat against the curved wall like a figure in an Egyptian tomb painting. The water winked up at her, glossy with reflected moonlight. The backpack, painful with hard stone edges, dragged at her aching shoulder. She paused to raise one strap and put her head through it; she must not lose her anchor now.

The water's chill lapped at her skin, sucking away her last bit of strength. She sagged out from the wall and slipped under the surface. Her hands and feet scrabbled dreamily at the slippery wall and the steps, but down she sank anyway, pulled by the bag of stones strapped to her body.

Her chest was shot through with agony, but her mind clung with bitter pleasure to the fact that in the morning all of Victor's tribe would wash themselves and brush their teeth and swallow their pills down with the water Victor was so proud of, water pumped by willing hands from his own wonderful well.

Head craned back, she saw that dawn pallor had begun to flush the small circle of sky receding above her. Against that light, black curls of the blood that her body wept from every seam and pore feathered out in secret silence, into the cool, delicious water.

WINGLESS BEASTS

LUCY TAYLOR

The first thing I tell people headed out here is just this: Go someplace else. I mean, Death Valley got that name for a reason, right? And the Mojave, of which Death Valley's a part, is especially dangerous in ways most people don't even suspect. I know, because I've seen the results of somebody's wrong turn or ill-considered adventure. And even though I live out here and own Joe's Towing Service—which comes in handy at times—I don't patrol the off-road areas on a regular basis, just when I'm edgy or restless or when I've got reason to believe someone may be in need of assistance.

Then I lock up my double wide and head out to the back country, checking salt pans and arroyos and lake beds where those afflicted with hubris or just old-fashioned stupidity are most apt to meet with disaster.

Tragic deaths and mysterious disappearances don't deter people, though. They keep turning up, charging off into blast furnace heat, not taking along enough food or water or gas, and sometimes, inevitably, a few meet with misfortune.

Case in point: the gimp with the cane at the Bun Boy Diner this morning. Only a little after six a.m and I'm just pulling into Baker, California, a pit stop for tourists traveling on I-15 between Barstow and Vegas. The town's claim to fame is having the world's biggest thermometer (like you need that to tell you it's hotter than the devil's butthole here), which rises 134 feet over a main drag lined with two-star motels, gas stations, and shuttered convenience stores. I park my truck and amble into the Bun Boy for my usual breakfast of eggs, hash browns, and grits before I head out to Barstow to visit my girl.

Right off the bat, though, the creep at the counter gets under my skin.

Soon as I see him, a squat, toadish little man, with a shiny bald dome looks like it's been polished with Pledge and hear him yakking to Margo the waitress about his plans to go off-roading in the Mojave, I peg him for the kind of know-it-all who'll be in deep shit by sundown.

I know his type: the obnoxious braying voice of a small man trying to sound imposing, the sardonic roll of his dishwater eyes when Margo suggests that the desert is best left to the young and the able-bodied, the puffed-up way he tries to pretend the cane's not really necessary, that he only carries it "in case I encounter a rattlesnake."

"Well, no rattlers in here," I tell him and ask which of the vehicles out in the lot belongs to him.

I figure him for the owner of the Subaru Outback or the Ram1500 or even the goofy-looking Baja Beetle I saw coming in, but he slurps his coffee and says, "Mine's the red Camry. Oh, I know, go ahead and laugh, but it's got me where I need to go plenty of times."

Which amuses me, because the kind of serious off-roading he's talking about demands a lot of a vehicle—at minimum, you need a flexible suspension, high clearance, and big tires with deep open treads.

"That's the wrong ride for your purposes," I say, taking a stool next to him. "You want a vacation, forget the Mojave. Just stay on 15 north. Three hours from now you can be laying bets at a crap table in the Bellagio or getting a lap dance at Spearmint Rhino Cabaret."

He grunts, but whether it's in response to my unsought advice or to some other pain in his pancake-flat ass, I can't tell. He upends the sugar bowl into his coffee and says with disdain, "Vegas is where Satan vacations when he gets bored with hell. Myself, I prefer the purity of the desert."

Now that takes me aback, because he sure doesn't seem like a man who'd know much about purity or aspire to it or respect it, for that matter. But then, I suppose, neither do I, yet it was the austerity of the desert, the vast silence and uncompromising indifference to all human fears that lured me out here almost ten years ago, and I've never been tempted to go back to my old bad-ass life on the streets of L.A., not once.

"Joe Fitch," I say, extending a hand, which he shakes with a prissy distaste suggesting he thinks I may have recently used it for wiping my ass. I shrug off the attitude and go on. "If you're hellbent on going out there by yourself, at least know what you're getting into. You break down, you get stuck, or your GPS lies to you—and let me tell you, a GPS will lie like a ten-dollar whore—any of that happens and, in this heat, you are goddamn dead."

Maybe still worrying about our handshake, he taps a squirt of hand sanitizer from a tube on the counter into his palm, which is thick and red as a slab of raw liver. "Otis Hanks. And, no offense, but I'd prefer you not curse."

"I won't," I tell him, "except to say if you go off half-cocked in the desert without the right experience and equipment, then you are well-fucked and royally so."

Hanks scowls and I figure I'm about to get chastised for the cussing, but what he says is, "Your name's familiar. Do we know each other?"

I assure him we don't. I wonder if we might've done time together, but I'm not about to bring up the nickel I did in Lompoc for a bar fight that ended up with a manslaughter charge or the lesser run-ins I've had with the law on various occasions. My past is what I moved to the Mojave to forget.

His comment about my name rankles, but still, in the interest of fairness, I try to put some fear into Hanks, pointing out that the sun's barely up and the giant thermometer already reads over a hundred degrees, and if he has any sense at all, he'll rethink his plan for an off-road adventure in the middle of goddamn July.

But I doubt that he will, because guys like him never listen. They're like my old man, railing about sin and salvation from the pulpit of the Wrath of God Methodist Church back in California; they already got all the answers. To hear folks like that tell it, God Himself comes to them for advice.

So I tell Hanks about just a couple of the tragedies that have taken place here over the past few years; about the skeleton that was found in a desert wash by a group of kids looking for arrowheads, just west of Newberry Springs along Interstate 40 and how it turned out to be the remains of a tourist from Munich, who must've thought the Mojave was some kind of Disney World, but without the A/C, and then proceeded to stroll off into the fiery furnace with just a half gallon of water, wearing thong sandals, a tee shirt, and shorts. When they found him, his mouth and nostrils and every other orifice was stoppered with sand and the vultures had pillaged his insides like conventioneers at the Golden Nugget's buffet.

And I tell him about the woman from Huntsville, Alabama, who got the terrific idea to take her eight-year-old son camping in the Mojave a couple of summers back and how, when the road ran out and her GPS cheerfully instructed her to turn right and continue another eighteen miles into a waterless hellhole, she followed directions. A ranger found the car and the kid dead nearby a few days later. The mother's body wasn't found for months, not much more than a pile of bones, hair, and vulture scat, or so I heard.

Margo swings by with the coffeepot then and refills my mug, saying, "You setting him straight, Reverend Joe?"

This makes Hanks's squinty eyes in their nests of wrinkly, sun-cured skin flicker with curiosity. "Don't tell me you're a man of the cloth, Mr. Fitch?"

Margo grins as she pours a steaming black stream. "Old Joe here's a reverend like I'm a pole dancer, but folks here gave him that name 'cause he lives out in the nowhere by hisself like one of them—monasticians?"

"Monastics," I say, "and I'm far from that. But my father was a minister with an interest in such things. I grew up listening to him preach about the religious tradition of men who turned their backs on civilization and went out into the deserts of Egypt and the Sinai. Men like Abba Macarius and Anthony the Great who were looking to deepen their spiritual life through isolation and physical hardship. Guess I got inspired by that." I shrug. "In hindsight, it seems naive to me now, but finding God was my aim when I moved out here years back and I guess what started out as a bit of a joke at my expense..."

"...is still a joke," chuckles Margo, "but we like you now. You're one of us."

Hanks raises a brow so pale that it's almost translucent. "And did you? Find God?"

The question pokes me like a sharp stick as I fork up my eggs. "Of course not. There was nothing to find."

We sit in silence then, shoveling food into our pieholes, but I keep dwelling on his comment about my name. After a while, I get up and amble out to my truck, noting with some amusement that the Camry belonging to this guy who only requires his cane for warding off rattlesnakes is parked in a handicapped spot. I get a map from the glove compartment and come back inside.

Hanks's mouth twists in annoyance when I unfold the map, like he's worried I'm going to dip the northeast corner of Nevada into his biscuits and gravy, but I take out a pen and draw him a route through the back country to a remote, beautiful area I call the Cauldron. "It's a straight shot from the paved road. No need to even get out of your car. Other side of the salt pan, there's a Joshua tree forest and beyond that, a dune field that'll make you think you're on Mars." I pause before adding, "Probably best not to try climbing them, though."

Hanks studies the map the way a prude eyes pornography, with distaste and a thinly veiled craving, then folds it up.

"I appreciate your concern, Mr. Fitch, but as I was explaining to our waitress here while you were outside, I'm a bit of an amateur eremologist—" he sees of my puzzled expression, "—one who studies the deserts. Since my retirement, I've visited quite a few, the Gobi, the Sahara, the Atacama. I've hiked some of the world's most desolate regions and come back none the worse for it." He glances down at his right boot, which is built up higher than the left one, and yanks up a pant leg, offering a glimpse of an off-white prosthesis. "Well, except for the incident with the leg, but that was due to a sin of lust, not a hiking mishap."

Right about then Margo notices some people across the room need more water and goes hurrying over with a pitcher while I try to dispel some unpleasant images about what kind of kinky sexual shenanigans—an amputee fetish perhaps?—might result in the loss of a limb.

Hanks notes our reactions and has the grace to redden a bit. After some awkward silence, he allows as how, since he has what he calls "a flexible itinerary," he just may hang onto the map anyway. "Wouldn't mind seeing that Joshua tree forest," he says, and there's a wistful note in his voice that I haven't detected before, as though he's longing—maybe not so much to see Joshua trees—but to be somewhere, anywhere else, besides here.

When Hanks dons his safari hat and gets up to pay his tab, I throw down some bills and walk with him outside. Even with the cane, which is a striking piece of handiwork—mahogany with an intricately carved ivory handle—he creaks laboriously along, huffing like one burdened by more than just a physical disability.

My tow truck, parked a few spaces down from his Camry, catches his eye. "Joe's Towing Service. Now I recall how I know you."

I look at him quizzically.

"Two nice people I met on a trip recently said you towed their car when it stalled in the desert. Maisie and Claude from Modesto. Said if I saw you to send their regards."

I turn away and gaze up at the eyesore thermometer, which now measures a hundred and four, as ice crystals clink in my chest. "Names don't ring a bell."

Hanks sighs, as though my failure to remember the couple confirms for him some basic belief about human nature. We shake hands again and I watch him drive off, then hightail it back into the Bun Boy and make it to the can just in time to puke up a thick slop of greasy coffee, potatoes, and eggs.

What Hanks said isn't possible. No fucking way.

The last time I saw dear ol' Maisie and Claude, they were stone fucking dead and I was towing their Mazda 280z with their bodies in the back seat.

⁗

Part of me, the impulsive, hot-headed ruffian whose misdeeds inspired some of my old man's more graphic sermons wants to go after Hanks right then and there, but I choke down the urge. That was the old me. Now I know how to hang back and be patient, bide my time. That's a skill the desert has taught me.

So I climb into my truck and roar out toward Barstow, knowing I'll catch up with Hanks in due time. Right now, I need to spend time with my girl.

Opal isn't her real name, of course. I call her that, because her blue-gray eyes remind me of opals, flecked with tiny motes of cobalt and daffodil gold. She was found by a sheepherder, wandering up near Red Mountain, half naked and near death with deep, infected gashes on her shoulders and neck, like at some point she'd collapsed, and the vultures had done a little taste testing before she fought them off and got moving again. Far as anyone knows, she hasn't spoken to anyone since. The heat and the trauma of her ordeal, including whatever led to her being in that situation in the first place, has parboiled her brain. Now she occupies a room at the Rohr Convalescent Center in Barstow, a Jane Doe waiting for somebody to come forward and give her a name.

Today when I slip into her room, she's propped up in bed, a little fuller in the face than the last time I saw her, but still stiff as a scarecrow, with that tiny mummified smile on her lips that never twitches or flags, that seems to hint at a cache of secrets she's hoarding. The only part of her that moves are her half-closed, feral eyes, which scan back and forth, tock-tick-tock, as though she's mesmerizing herself by following the path of an interior metronome.

After chitchatting with one of the nurses, who stops in to say hi, I take a comb and brush from the night stand by the bed and set about braiding her hair, which has gone white over the months that I've known her. To pass the time, I talk to her like I always do, just random stuff that she's heard before, about how it was when I first moved to the desert, how that ocean of emptiness both fascinated and horrified me. Something about that burnt, hostile terrain, so purged of anything conducive to sustaining life, gave me a strange kind of solace born of pain and familiarity. I realized that my addled, punitive parents had given me something valuable after all—the ability to survive in a place so barren that few people even come here and those that do, generally don't stay very long.

And although I didn't find God in the way most people know Him, I found deities of my own understanding—hundreds of them, winged carrion-eaters reigning over a savage landscape. I recognized them from my father's sermons, these vulture-gods, and I named them after the archangels: Moloch and Charon, Metatron and Uriel and Gabriel. I recognized them at once for what they were, creatures old as the rocks and the salt pans, ancient as the bones of the finned creatures that once lived here sixty-five million years ago when the Mojave was a vast, inland sea.

I knew they must see us as we really are—wingless beasts lumbering across a destroyed landscape, while they soar on the updrafts, patient and cunning, knowing that we're here for only an eyeblink in their eternity.

The great birds appalled me at first—with their plucked, scarlet heads and seething black eyes—and their habits struck me as ghastly. After startling one outside my trailer one day, I watched it take clumsy run-ning hops, flapping furiously to get airborne, then regurgitate a gut full of stinking carrion all over the hood of my truck in an effort to lighten the load. That one, the Leaver of Offerings, was the first, and soon others came. They'd soar on the thermals for hours within sight of my home, silent and watchful, until I'd come outside and let them lead me to whatever they'd found that was dying or injured: a burrowing owl, a tortoise, a chuckwalla . . . a vagabond from Munich or a mother desperate to find help for her boy.

Opal shivers then and exhales a sound, not much more than a thin hic-cough of dread. I wonder if she's been hearing me. Doesn't much matter, she knows who I am.

Her hair looks good when I finish it, the long braids sliding over her shoulders in smooth, ghostly ropes that stand out against her dark, ruddy skin. But when I hold the mirror up so she can admire herself, her eyes ignite like a cornered bobcat's and a snarl corkscrews between her bared teeth.

I lean close, stroke a wisp of hair back off her face and whisper the same thing I always do, "Next time I come here, I'm going to kill you."

❖

Now it's Hanks's turn

On the way back toward Baker, I take a seldom-used exit and follow an unmarked dirt road until I come to the edge of the Cauldron. Here the remnant of road peters out at the edge of a cracked lake bed and I blaze across it, raising a roostertail of white sand sparkling with tiny grains of feldspar and quartz. For miles around, there's no pavement, no signs, and no help if you need it. No indication that Hanks has passed this way, either, so I head south, where the desert floor splits into a snake's nest of arroyos and the earth is so dry that sections lurch up, overlapping each other like a shelf of ceramic tiles. When my tires crunch over the baked clay, the noise is an escalation of tiny explosions and the air turns the color of cinders and chalk.

I'm following the approximate route that I mapped out for Hanks, but when I see the outline of Joshua trees in the distance, a sudden sense of unease washes over me. I've always found the trees spooky—the way the branches claw and arch in grotesque, twisted shapes, like the broken limbs of men who've been crucified. But now, when I get out of my truck to survey the terrain through binoculars, I spot the outline of a vulture amid the tree's deformed limbs. At the sight of me, the bird hisses softly. Its neck swivels around and a beak so red it might have been dipped in a wound lifts into the yellow-white glare.

It takes off, flying out toward a formation of orange sandstone that juts to the east. I follow its flight through the binoculars and zoom in on a dust-caked red fender—Hanks's Camry, left at the base of the rocks in a puddle of dwindling shade.

Towing a car so you don't damage the transmission requires care and the right implements, but not ruining Hanks's ride isn't high on my list of concerns. I hook it up to the back of my truck, tow it a half mile away and offload it behind a low rise bristling with pinon and creosote. On the passenger seat I find a modest supply of water and energy bars; a key is hidden under the floor mat. I stuff my backpack with bottles of water and granola bars, lock up the car, and pitch the key into the scrub.

What I've found is that people whose vehicles disappear in the middle of nowhere generally do one of three things: they assume they've screwed up and returned to the wrong place and commence a futile and increasingly frantic search. Or they stay calm, keep their wits about them, and try to hike out. Either dehydration and heat stroke fell them or I do the job with the crowbar I keep in my truck next to the phony maps, but either way, the birds feed. A third, smaller group, those with a naive belief in the goodness of humanity, huddle in whatever shade they can find, presumably praying for help to come, and thank God when they see me approaching—at least until they realize I'm not there on a mission of mercy.

The Modesto couple Hanks mentioned fell into that last category.

Hanks, though, does none of these things. When I hike back to the sandstone formation, there's nothing to indicate he's returned to the place where his car ought to be, no helterskelter footprints of the kind a panicked person generally leaves, no indication he's attempted to follow my tire tracks. I clamber onto the highest ridge of sandstone and do a sweep with the binoculars. I don't see him at first—his khaki clothing and tan safari hat blend in with the dun-colored sand—but the lazy swoops of vultures mark his place on the desert floor like a giant red X. He's about a mile away, heading toward the dune field, puttering along like a geezer perusing his garden. Everything catches his fancy: a thorny cactus pad, a stretch of orange dogweed, the green, tapering shafts of a cluster of desert candles.

As I watch, he looks up abruptly. Although I know at this distance, he can't possibly see me, our eyes seem to lock, and his flaccid lips smack with what an over-imaginative mind might interpret as relish. Real or not, the gaze is unsettling and I turn away. A few seconds later, when I focus the binoculars again, he's no longer there. All I see are the bristly contours of a cluster of teddy bear cholla and the slow rotation of obsidian wings against a searing hot sky.

Has he stumbled into an arroyo or collapsed in the meager shade of some creosote bushes? I press on, expecting to catch up to him quickly, but the desert seems to have licked up his life like spilled water. It's not until mid-afternoon that I spot him again, when the temperature in this part of the Cauldron must be approaching a hundred and twenty and the heat waves the vultures are riding look like curtains of shimmering gauze.

To my astonishment, the distance between us hasn't narrowed at all. If anything, Hanks has pulled farther away.

The heat's pummeling him, though, exposing his decrepitude. His head's bowed, shoulders sagging, and the hand clutching the cane by turns stiffens and then undergoes bouts of violent trembling. He no longer stops to investigate this flower or that sparkly mineral. Nor does he seem to notice the grim entourage that spirals above him like smoke rings expelled from the simmering earth. A check of my compass tells me what I already suspect, that his meandering course has begun to veer north. The straight line he undoubtedly thinks he's walking has begun to curve drastically, taking him not to the place where he left his car, but toward the Joshua tree forest.

For the next hour, I'm able to keep him in view, expecting him to drop any minute, but he soldiers on and the distance between us barely shrinks. Finally, frustrated, I break into a furious run and briefly enjoy the satisfaction all killers must feel when closing in on their prey. Yet just when I'm almost upon him, something shifts as though a key's clicked in a door of the universe, and his outline flickers and fades. What just moments ago seemed so obviously flesh and bone blurs away into shadows and sand. The vultures disperse, and a deathly stillness ensues. Suddenly I'm the only thing left alive on the earth and the single sound is the rasp of my breathing.

I check the number of full water bottles left in my pack, am shocked to discover there's only one left and that it's less than half full. I've been drinking water throughout the day, but my throat feels like I've gargled with sawdust and brine, and my lungs burn like I've inhaled the desert. Still, I'm not ready to turn back, a determination that's strengthened when I find a bright gob of blood on the rubbery pad of a prickly pear cactus. From the looks of Hanks's tracks, it appears he's faltering badly, leaning so heavily on the cane that it punches into the sand an inch or two deep.

Even as Hanks fades, so does the day. The shadows elongate and the sun blowtorches the horizon with bands of vermillion and deep mustard blue.

And the wind picks up, scouring my exposed skin and hurling huge, tangled masses of tumbleweed around like bizarre beach balls. Its bluster plays tricks with my hearing. A woman's voice—plaintive and whimpering—plays counterpoint to its keening. A second voice joins in and initiates a fevered duo—my father raging about the temptations of demons and the abyss of the damned where fallen angels feed on their prey. It's a rant as lunatic and mindless as the woman's, but more disturbing for notes of threat and contempt underlying it.

The sky suddenly looks too big to be real, a painted backdrop meant to deceive me. The gritty wind, full of sadistic trickery, is bent on erasing Hanks's tracks.

To the west, a cloud of bats rises up from a nest of creosote bushes and takes to the sky like a flurry of semaphores from the pen of a demented scribe. Instinctively I duck down and cover my head as their dark mass swarms by. The rush of their passing distracts me; the warring voices subside. My head clears, and in the distance, I see the stark outlines of the Joshua trees.

In the fading daylight, the grotesque trees appear eerie and blighted. Black, oval blooms freight their branches, giving some trees the appearance that they are ready to uproot from the earth under the weight of the vultures that roost in them. The stench of carrion wafts toward me, and a low murmur makes the hair stiffen on the back of my neck. It's the voice of a woman begging for help. Pleading for water.

Then it changes, and Hanks cries for water.

The sound, unmistakably real this time, echoes from far back in the trees. I catch a glimpse of Hanks's khaki hat as it flies off his head, of a body tumbling and falling, hitting the ground amid puffs of sand and a cascade of stones. For a second, the wind and Hanks mourn in unison. Then silence.

I run toward him, but the sunset fires scalding light into my eyes, and my strides are unsteady and blundering. A shadow coiled beneath one drooping, heavy-laden tree brings to mind a fetally curved body. I grab for it and recoil as one hand disappears into flesh so decomposed that it slides off the bone in clumps of powdery fur, while the other grasps a jawbone missing most of its teeth—the scraggly remains of a coyote or fox. Other, larger bones, flecked with threadbare scraps of cloth, suggest deaths older and feedings more savage.

"Mr. Fitch?" The words, coming from behind me, aren't so much spoken as spat, and I whirl around, arms raised but not fast enough, too late and too slow to block the knob of the cane before it staves in the flesh between my brows.

⟶⟵

"Well, finally. There you are."

I don't know how much time has passed, ten seconds or a day, but Hanks's gravelly voice is edged with impatience and thwarted intent. The cane he brandishes is slick with blood and a caterpillar-like tuft of something I recognize to be one of my eyebrows adheres to a carved notch in the ivory.

I want to seize him by his wattled neck and wring the life from him, but when he squats down and turns his vexed gaze on me, I can taste his loathing and feel the spikes imbedded in his every word, and I shut my eyes.

"You didn't hear what I was saying, did you? You were...elsewhere. No matter. I was speaking of the deserts of Norway and New England and Brazil. Can't tell you their names, because they don't exist yet. But they will. You'll see. Oh, just give it time."

I try to swallow, find my throat clogged. "I want...water."

He sneers. "Oh, don't we all!"

In the bruise-colored dusk, he hobbles back and forth, hunched and scowling like a traveler on a subway platform awaiting a long-delayed train he knows in his heart never will come.

Suddenly he spins around and wags the cane a few inches away from my face; the sudden, violent motion in front of my eyes off-kilters a slice of my brain, blurs my vision, and stymies my tongue. When I try to speak again, my parched throat produces only a feeble croak that elicits a look of disgust.

"You think you're so unique, don't you?"

He rolls up the right pant leg, reaches down and pops off the prosthesis, revealing a chewed stump of something oozing and raw, like what you'd see in some third-world butcher shop. The charnel house smell of that suppurating stump makes me gag, but what's worse is that Hanks doesn't seem unduly discomforted. Like he's been existing this way for a very long time.

He lays a paternal hand on my shoulder. "We're not so different, you and me. That woman you named Opal, the one you found near Stovepipe and chose to keep for yourself, I understand how that happened. No place lonelier than the desert, and a man has needs that a lap dance in a gentlemens' club won't satisfy. I took a woman once too for my personal use—she was a Berber girl from the Tenere whose family threw her out for being unchaste. Unlike you, though, I kept her tightly bound, so she couldn't escape into the desert where some sheepherder could find her." He exhales a snort. "A sheepherder, for God's sake! Like such occupations even exist in this day and age!"

He hops backward, stork-like on the one leg, teeters a bit, then reattaches the prosthesis. "Didn't surprise me I had to forfeit a limb. I took what didn't belong to me after all. Bitch of it was, the leg was still attached when the birds ate it."

The tears spurting through my lashes shame and shock me. They're also precious drops of moisture that I try to capture on my tongue, a futile effort that makes Hanks's eyes crinkle with contempt.

But the tears produce more tears and, after that, words that are old and dreadfully familiar. "I'm sorry, so sorry. I won't do it again. I promise I'll stop. I won't kill anyone else!"

Hanks cocks his head, perplexed and peeved-looking. Then he stands up, his creased face sad, avuncular, and kicks me in the head.

When my vision clears, Hanks is bent over me, studying my face while a black ant the size of a paperclip navigates the ruts in his forehead.

"You misunderstood me," he says, as though there's been only a slight, inconsequential interruption in our conversation. "My purpose isn't to stop you from killing. It's what you do, and you're good at it. Gifted even." He gestures toward the trees with his cane and the vultures roosting there stir, hissing softly, their naked necks stretching and curving into question marks. "Not here, though. Not anymore. From now on, yours are the deserts of the interior lands, the hellscapes of your creation. Deserts so vast you can wander for eons before finding someone to kill. Or to fuck. But don't worry. You won't be alone. After you left her this morning, someone helped Opal take a sheet into the bathroom and showed her how to hang herself from the shower curtain. She could be free now, but she'd rather be angry. She wants revenge for what you did to her. And she's still so very thirsty."

He gazes around at the skeletal trees with their dark, restless fruit and lifts up the cane. At once the vultures' hissing grows louder, unnatural, imperative.

Some of them take to the air, swooping so low that I can feel the foul breeze from their passing rustle my hair. I know there is very little time.

"The people you met in the desert," I blurt out, "Maisie and Claude, did they...?"

"Talk about you? Of course they did. But don't worry about your mama and daddy too much. They were headed to their own desert anyway. You just sent them there sooner."

Hanks's grin is inhumanly wide. His mouth creaks open like a rusty-hinged crypt and belches forth a bevy of soft, struggling things, tarry and mewling, that flee into the darkening sky and are plucked from the air by the vultures. They are the souls of the lost and the damned and I know one of them is my own.

"Safe journeys," he says, before his face is obscured beneath a barrage of obsidian wings and stabbing beaks.

◄◦►

When my screaming stops and I risk opening my eyes, the sun is still setting and constellations unknown to mortal astronomers swarm in the dome of a blazing red sky. I'm alone in a Joshua tree forest and, a few yards away, an assembly of vultures is squabbling over the remains of my foot.

Hanks is gone, but his cane lies within reach.

The birds bolt down their feast and take to the air, one by one, as a woman's voice, familiar and piteous, cries out for water. She sounds as near as my heartbeat and as far away as the other side of the moon.

After a while, I pick up the cane and start hobbling along, knowing I have all eternity to find her.

THE NIMBLE MEN

GLEN HIRSHBERG

"But the air, out there, so wild, so white…"
—Thomas St. John Bartlett, in a letter to Robert Louis Stevenson
from the Orkney Islands in the winter of 1901

Ever notice how Satie, played in the dark at just the right volume, can tilt the whole world? That night, I had *Je te Veux* on the tinny cockpit stereo, and even before the snow, the pines at the edge of the great north woods just beyond the taxiway appeared to dip and lean, and the white lines disappearing beneath the wheels of our little commuter seemed to weave around and between each other like children at a wedding dance as we made our way to the de-icing station. Then the snow started, white and winking, a drizzle of starlight, and even the air traffic control tower looked ready to lift its arms and step off its foundations and sway.

And then Alex, my junior co-pilot of four months, opened his thermal lunch box. The reek flooded the cabin and set the panel lights wavering in my watering eyes. I swear to God, the iPod gagged. Alex just sat in the steam, eyes half-closed and grinning, as if he were taking a sauna.

"God, you Gorby, tell me that isn't poutine."

"Want some, Old Dude?" said Alex, and lifted the container from the cooler.

Out the front of the plane, the world went on dancing, and the snow whirled through it. But I couldn't stop staring at the mess in Alex's container. A few limp, bloated French fries stuck out of the lava flow of industrial-colored sludge like petrified slugs. Congealed, gray lumps clung to their sides and leaked white pus.

"Is that meat?" I asked. "Cheese?"

Alex grinned wider. "It's your country. You tell me."

"Where'd you even find it? We had, what, three hours? Where does one even find poutine on a three-hour layover in Prince Willows Town, Ontario?"

"If you turn over control of the stereo, I'll put it away for a while."

We'd reached the de-icing station, and I pushed on the brakes and brought the coasting plane to a rolling stop. No matter how many times I did this, I was always surprised by the dark out here. At every other point within two miles of this tiny airport, manmade light flooded and mapped the world. But not here.

I peered through the windscreen and the wavering skeins of snow. It took a few moments, but eventually, my eyes adjusted to the point where I could just make out the de-icer truck parked a few meters off the taxiway in the flat, dead grass. Weirdly, it had its boom already hoisted, as though we were meant to make our way into the fields to get sprayed. I couldn't see either the driver of the truck or the guy on the enclosed platform at the top of the boom, because both were blanketed in shadow. But the platform looked tilted to me, almost chin-to-chest with the rotating metal stand that supported it. It reminded me of one of the dead Martians from *War of the Worlds*.

We sat and we waited. The truck didn't move.

"Peculiar," I murmured, and Alex passed his poutine container right under my nostrils. My eyes watered, and I turned on him. "What was that for?"

"You were muttering, Old Dude. Just making sure you were conscious. Now about control of that stereo. You ready to deal?"

For answer, I clicked on the intercom. "Ladies and gentlemen, this is your captain speaking. We hope all six of you have settled comfortably in your seats, that your luggage is crammed effectively between your knees and the seat in front of you—" Alex snorted at that—"and we look forward to having virtually no time to serve you during our brief skip-hop to Toronto. We will be cleared for takeoff shortly. In the meantime, sit back, relax, be happy this flight is *not* bound for Winterpeg, and please pay no attention to the gigantic, alien-shaped creature about to swoop down upon us. It comes in peace, to de-ice the wings. Also, we do apologize for the odor escaping into the cabin under the doors of our cockpit. It came with my co-pilot, and I'm afraid there's little we can do about it. If you need assistance of any kind, please don't hesitate to call on Jamie, our charismatic, experienced, and re-sourceful in-flight technician, at any time. We should be in the air shortly."

Alex laughed. "Come out with me tonight," he said. "Let's do Hogtown."

"Do it?"

"Paint it. Rock it. Suck it dry. Come on, Old Dude. You keep saying you'll let me show you *my* Toronto. I say it's time. You told me it's been three years, right? It's—*whoa*. What was that?"

He had his cap turned backward on his head, the container in his lap, and a gravy-soaked French fry halfway to his lips. For the thousandth time in the past four months—but the first tonight—I remembered how much I liked him.

"I think we just painted Prince Willows Town, Young Polyp. Milked it, licked it, whole works."

"You're babbling again, Old Dude."

"Northern lights, Alex. You've heard of them, maybe."

He shook his head. "Wrong time, right? Also too low."

As usual, he was correct on both counts. I turned back to the windscreen, peering down the tarmac toward the tops of the trees, where we'd both seen a spiraling flash of green, then aquamarine.

But there was nothing now except the snowflakes, settling in their mil-lions onto the branches of the pines as though completing some massive, unmarked winter migration. We watched that a while, and then I glanced again toward the de-icing truck. It sat silent, and the snow shrouded the high platform's window glass.

"The Nimble Men," said Alex, savoring the words.

"What?"

"Is that the coolest name you've ever heard for the aurora, or what?"

"The Nimble Men?"

"It's catchy, no?"

"How many other names do you know, Alex?"

"Well, there's *chasmata*. That's from Ancient Rome. They thought the lights were cave mouths. For sky caves. Come on, Old Dude. Trump me. What you got?"

I would have smiled if not for the de-icer, hunkered in the dead grass like a junked car on a lawn.

"Well, there's one story…" I said.

"That's the Old Dude I know. Lay it on me."

"There are several versions. Usually, it goes that sometime during the Depression, a poor woodsman went out in those woods—"

"Those woods right there?"

"Whichever Ontario woods you happen to be closest to. Didn't anyone ever tell you a ghost story?"

Alex nodded. "Carry on."

"So the woodsman was out." This time I did smile. "Rockin' the forest."

That earned me a salute with a sludgy fry.

"And while he was out, he saw the lights."

"The Nimble Men," said Alex.

I held up a finger. "But not in the sky. In the trees. The woodsman had an inkling. He raced home. When he got there, his wife said their old, sick dog had got out, and their daughter had gotten frantic and gone after him. The dog came back. But the daughter didn't. She was never seen again. The woodsman went looking with his lantern every night for the rest of his life, but he never found so much as a trace. According to some, he's still looking, and those are his lights. Hey, Alex, I don't like this."

He'd been nodding and chewing, but now lowered the cardboard fry-boat back into his lunch box and wiped his hands on his uniform pants. "You're right, Old Dude. Why are we just sitting here?"

I flicked on the radio and called the tower. "This is Northwoods Air 2-8-4."

The response was immediate, the voice so clear it might have come from inside the cabin. "Northwoods 2-8-4, go ahead."

"Bill, that you?"

"What is it, Wayne?"

"We're at the de-icer. The de-icer isn't moving."

I don't know what I expected. *We'll wake him up*, maybe. Or, *How's that?* Or, since Bill had a little of Alex's puckishness, *Moon him.*

Instead, there was a long silence. I was about to repeat myself when Bill's voice came back.

"Sit tight," he said. "Don't move."

"What—" I started, and the link closed. Went off. I tried talking into the communicator again, but it was like yelling into a fist.

"Hey, another one," Alex said, but by the time I turned, there was just the faintest blue streak, a smear on the snow-curtain.

On normal nights, the de-icer springs awake the second a plane rolls to a stop. The truck maneuvers close, and the driver makes contact over the com-link. The pilot shuts down all systems and closes the vents so no fluid gets inside the cabin. Then the platform jockey swoops in with his pod, unfolds its nozzle-arms, and engulfs the wings in a blast of bright purple antifreeze. The whole process takes less than five minutes. Sometimes less than two.

But we'd already been here quite a while. I could make out the platform jockey now, or at least his shadow. He was hunched or slumped in his pod, fifteen meters off the ground. I couldn't see his face, because he had nothing illuminated. I couldn't hear his voice, because the truck hadn't plugged into us and made contact. As far as I could tell, the truck still wasn't running its engine. This time, the glimmer in the trees flashed red, and the redness hung a moment at the very edge of the forest before winking out.

"See, I don't get it," Alex said. "It doesn't make sense."

"That's what I'm—"

"Your story. I mean, what's the deal, Old Dude? The lights came to warn him? Or they're his daughter's soul at the moment of her death? Or a presentiment of his future as the Wood-Wandering Lantern Guy? You've got to get more specific, here."

The lack of movement on the taxiway was really starting to get to me. I almost clicked on the intercom and called Jamie in to take a look. But that would only have triggered a new round of Alex-hits-on-Jamie. Not that Jamie seemed to mind.

"It's not my story. And the lights were probably all of those things, depending on the telling," I said. "You know how those stories work."

"I know that one could work better."

"What does he mean, *sit tight, don't move?*"

"Let's go see," Alex said, unhooked himself from his belts and stood.

That at least drew my gaze from the taxiway to his face. "Go where?"

"Out. Tell me you've never wanted to go out there. You ever done it? We've got a perfect excuse."

"We can't go out there."

"Why not?"

I thought about that. "Aren't there regulations? There've got to be regulations."

"And yet there you are, already unhooking your belt." His grin was an eight year-old's, and lit him all the way to his moppy curls. And there I was, unhooking my belt. "Old Dude," he said approvingly. Then he threw open the cockpit door and marched into the tiny cabin of our commuter plane, chanting, "Oh, Jamie…"

By the time I emerged, he was standing as if onstage with his arm around our blond, too-thin flight attendant, who was without doubt closer to my age than his, and facing our six passengers. All of them were apparently traveling alone, since they'd each claimed their own row—we called them rows, though they were really only sets of single seats on either side of a narrow aisle—leaving only the front empty.

"What's going on?" called an exhausted-looking grad-school type in a green McGill sweatshirt from a couple rows back.

"Who's up for hide and seek? Come on, I'll count ten," Alex said, and Jamie dropped her head and shook it and laughed.

"Excuse him, ladies and gentlemen," I said. "He's American, he's just eaten his first poutine, and it's made him punchy."

"*Avez-vous poutine?*" said a white-haired woman three rows back, perking up as though she thought we might offer her a plateful with her complimentary ice water.

"*Je l'ai fini,*" Alex said, patting his non-existent gut. I couldn't see his face, but I was sure he'd winked.

I moved to the door, unlocked it, and Jamie swung toward me in surprise. "Wayne?"

I made a waving gesture, casual as I could make it. "We're just…"

"Checking something," Alex said. "Right back, y'all."

"Checking," I said quietly to Jamie. "It's not the plane. Not to worry."

Before she could ask, and before I had time to reconsider, Alex pushed the door outward. Frigid, resin-scented air gushed into the cabin, sweeping tendrils of snow around our ankles as the folding stair lowered itself to the ground.

Jamie took an immediate step back. Because of the cold, I realized, only the cold. But Alex hesitated, too, just momentarily. In thirty-one years as a pilot, I'd never once left my plane except at a gate. Certainly not on a taxiway or runway. I stared into the blackness, the snow cocooning the world. A high, industrial whine rode the air-currents, seeming to burrow uncomfortably into my ear canals.

I glanced over my shoulder. The only passenger not watching was the chubby, middle-aged guy in the seat closest to the open door. He had his head against the window, his tie still knotted tight at this throat, his eyes closed too tightly to be sleeping. At least, that's how it seemed to me. His skin looked pale and wet as the window-glass.

"He okay?" I murmured to Jamie.

She shrugged. "He's been like that since we boarded. I don't think he's having a heart attack or anything, if that's what you're asking. Are *you* okay, Wayne? This doesn't seem…"

"You're right," I said. "Hey, Alex, why don't we just go check in with Bill again."

"Because, Old Dude," he said. "We're the Nimble Men." And with his hands artfully tucked in the pockets of his ridiculous thrift-store bomber jacket, he strolled out of the plane, down the steps to the tarmac.

Why did I go? I've wondered that ever since. Because the lifeless de-icer bothered me, sure. Because Alex's enthusiasm for everything had stirred the embers of my own, dead not so long then. But there was something else. A *need*. Sudden. Overpowering. Was it mine? I still don't know.

I went down the steps. Behind me, I heard a single, saw-edged gasp or sigh from the not-sleeping guy. I heard another sound, too, or thought I did. That high, electrical whine, though we were the only plane out here.

When I reached Alex's side, he smiled. "One small step for Nimble Men…"

To my surprise, I smiled back. "See, now you're doing it."

"Doing what?"

"Are the lights the Nimble Men? Are we?"

"You know you're the coolest pilot I'm ever going to work with in my life, right, Old Dude? You know you've ruined cockpit chatter for me forever."

"Why, thank you, Alex. Sometimes, I feel the same."

"When we get back inside, could we at least put on a *Gymnopedie*? One of the *Gnossiennes*?"

Now I stared at him. "You know Satie, too?"

"I know *Je te Veux* makes you morose."

"For a punk kid, you know a hell of a lot of things, Alex."

"That's what things are for. Right?"

"Some things," I said, and immediately wished I hadn't.

"Hey, man," Alex said.

Ignoring him, trying to ignore myself, I looked across the tarmac at the de-icer. There really didn't seem to be anybody in the truck. There was someone on the platform up there, alright, but as far as I could make out, he still hadn't even noticed us. Unless the driver had left his keys in the ignition, or we could find a good stone to throw, we were going to have a hard time getting the platform jockey's attention. The whining was louder out here, too. Or, not louder. Closer. More shrill. If it hadn't been January, I'd have thought there were gnats in my ears.

Jamie's low-heeled shoes clicked on the folding staircase, and she appeared between us. Alex put his arm around her. Lights blossomed in the closest treetops, a scatter of turquoise and Kelly green and deep pink, as though someone had scattered a handful of marbles up there. The branches rippled with the color, then swallowed it.

"Jesus," said Jamie.

Alex put an arm around her waist. "Wacky north woods beautifulness. My favorite kind."

"Is that ice, do you think? Airport lights reflecting in the branches?"

Of course, that was right. Why hadn't I thought of it? I gestured back toward the plane. "Seriously, is that guy alright?" I asked. "The passenger in 2B?"

"I think mostly he's crying," said Jamie. "I've got my eye on him."

"I know you do."

"We shouldn't be out here, Wayne." She touched my hand.

"Go inside. We'll be right back."

More lights. A royal-blue flurry this time, concentrated in the pines nearest the taxiway, maybe thirty meters away. Up in the platform pod, I could see the jockey's shadow just a little more clearly through the snow. He was turned toward the forest. I still didn't think he'd seen us.

Unease flickered through me again. It felt almost good. It filled the emptiness, or at least colored it.

As if sensing that thought, Jamie squeezed my hand. I'd worked with her a long time. I squeezed back. "Go on inside. We're coming."

"You can offer White-hair in there the rest of my poutine," Alex said. "I didn't actually finish it all. Although it's kind of cold, now."

"Bleah," said Jamie, and turned for the plane. I saw her look backward at the woods as she climbed up. Maybe she was hoping for another light show. But I had the idea she was hoping the opposite. Maybe that was just me.

The whining swelled still more. Underneath the shrillness, I could hear another sound, now. A sort of low grinding. Then that faded. I lifted my hands over my head, waved them at the de-icer platform. Next, I tried jumping up and down.

"See?" said Alex. "You're still nimble. You know she digs you, right?"

I stopped jumping. "What?"

"Jamie. She's just waiting for you to say the word. She's been waiting a long time."

"What are you talking about? She told you this?"

"She didn't have to tell me. I know. It's one of those things Alex knows."

"Let's get that guy's attention and get out of here," I said.

"I'm just telling you. She's waiting for you to say you're ready. I say it's been three years, Old Dude. And no disrespect. But I say three years is plenty. I say you're ready. *Shit.*"

It came from nowhere, wasn't anything, vanished just as quickly. A flash of green-yellow right over our heads, like lightning stabbing into the ground. Or eyes blinking.

"Did you hear that?"

"Hear it? You have ears in your eyes, Old Dude?"

"Hey," I said. Our breath plumed in front of us. "He moved."

Both of us craned our necks back, trying to see. The guy up there *had* moved. I was sure of it. But he'd stopped now. And he was still staring straight at the woods. The whining was creeping deeper into my ears again. And there was yet another sound, this one more familiar. But several blank seconds passed before I realized what it was.

"That truck *is* on," I said.

"Well," said Alex, and for the first time, I heard doubt in his voice, too. Just a flicker. But that rattled me more than anything else out here. "If it won't come to us…I guess we just go get it."

He started that way, and I followed, and the driver in the cab finally sat up. He looked astonished to see us. Then he started flinging his hands wildly in front of his face, as though he had bees in there.

"What the fuck?" Alex mumbled, still moving, and I grabbed his wrist.

The driver was waving more wildly. But not at anything in the cabin. He was also shouting, but he had the windows rolled up tight, and all I could hear was that he *was* shouting. Not what he was saying.

And overhead, that sound had returned, not so much louder as higher, almost a shriek. The grinding was back, too. Alex and I were halfway between the de-icer truck and our open plane, right at the edge of the tarmac.

It didn't actually sound like grinding, I realized. It seemed too deeply lodged inside my own head for that. It sounded like teeth gnashing.

The lights didn't exactly erupt from the trees. They just slid from behind them, as though they'd been hiding there all along. They hovered at the edge of the forest, coagulating like snow-melt on a windowpane. Forming.

I didn't have to warn Alex. He was already running.

Of course he was decades younger, much faster. Maybe he didn't even see what the lights became, the thing with wings. Or the million smaller things, all of them shining.

They came like a blizzard on a glacier, all at once and from everywhere. I was flat-out sprinting, but knew I wouldn't make it. They were in my hair, ears, eyes, and they *ached*. It was useless to swipe at or fight them, but I was still running anyway, until the first blast from the de-icer blew me straight off my feet. The de-icer didn't stop. It went on pummeling me with fluid, and I started to scream, then shut my mouth tight for fear of what I'd swallow, liquid or light, and tried scrambling back upright. Then I gave that up and crawled.

The lights were screaming. Or I was. Or Alex and Jamie were from the doorway of the plane, both of them soaked, dripping, waving, shouting. I reached the steps, and the gnashing got louder, seemed to clamp down on my spine and chew straight through it, and I sagged bonelessly sideways, feeling light, so light. Then Alex yanked me inside and slammed the door tight.

For one long moment, there was only darkness and silence. Because I hadn't opened my eyes, I realized. Because I was too terrified to open my mouth. I felt a towel on my face, Jamie's gentle hand against the back of my neck. I opened my eyes to find Alex, dripping purple droplets everywhere like a freshly bathed poodle.

"Okay?" he said.

I nodded, trembling. "I think. You?"

He started to laugh. "Holy shit," he said. "Holy crazy Canadian shit."

It wasn't funny. But with Alex there, you couldn't help smiling anyway. Jamie was doing it, too, while pointlessly patting over and over at my face. I took her hand to stop her. Then I just held onto that.

We were back in our seats, our heads wrapped in scratchy airline towels, ears still ringing, hands still shaking but settled firmly on the controls that would guide us either safely back to the terminal or up in the air and as far from Prince Willows Town as this plane's pathetic fuel tanks could carry us, when the cockpit door opened. Alex was the one who turned. Then he said, "Wayne."

I turned, too. Jamie stood in the doorway, face waxy, eyes blank. "He's gone," she said.

"What?" I asked.

"The guy in 2B. The crying guy. He's not on the plane. He didn't go out past me either. He's nowhere."

I stood up, shaking my head. "That's ridiculous. He must have—"

"Wayne," Jamie said, and her eyes filled with tears. "He's gone."

-◦-

It happened only occasionally, Bill told me once, years later, over one final round of Molsons, before both of us left the flying game for good. Only in the dead of winter, on the coldest nights. Mostly not even then. No one really knew when or how the realization had been made about the de-icing fluid. But that seemed to help. Sometimes. To keep them back. Sometimes.

"Always so sad," Bill had said. "Always, always, always."

At least, that's what I thought he'd said. It wasn't until that night, back in my hotel, pouring a drink, that my hands started to shake, and I realized I'd heard him wrong. Not *so* sad. *The* sad. Always the sad.

Was it grief that drew them? Or reacted with something else in that air, in those woods, and created them? Had *my* grief drawn or created them? If so, it wasn't the anti-freeze that saved me. It was the sobbing man. His was fresher.

Had they swallowed him? I like to think he was one of them, now, instead. Reunited, maybe, with what he'd lost. Or at least in company, with the Nimble Men. Sometimes, that thought comforts me.

You can't fly to Prince Willows Town, any more. Not long after that night, they closed the facility, redirecting all traffic to the bigger, better-serviced airport at Sudbury, where the light-towers are numerous and brighter, and the trees keep their distance.

LITTLE AMERICA

DAN CHAON

First of all, here are the highways of America. Here are the states in sky blue, pink, pale green, with black lines running across them. Peter has a children's version of the map, which he follows as they drive. He places an X by the names of towns they pass by, though most of the ones on his old map aren't there anymore. He sits, staring at the little cartoons of each state's products and services. Corn. Oil wells. Cattle. Skiers.

Secondly, here is Mr. Breeze himself. Here he is behind the steering wheel of the long old Cadillac. His delicate hands are thin, reddish as if chapped. He wears a white shirt, buttoned at the wrist and neck. His thinning hair is combed neatly over his scalp, his thin, skeleton head is smiling. He is bright and gentle and lively, like one of the hosts of the children's programs Peter used to watch on television. He widens his eyes and enunciates his words when he speaks.

Third is Mr. Breeze's pistol. It is a Glock 19 nine millimeter compact semi-automatic handgun, Mr. Breeze says. It rests enclosed in the glove box directly in front of Peter, and he imagines that it is sleeping. He pictures the muzzle, the hole where the bullet comes out: a closed eye that might open at any moment.

◄○►

Outside the abandoned gas station, Mr. Breeze stands with his skeleton head cocked, listening to the faintly creaking hinge of an old sign that advertises cigarettes. His face is expressionless, and so is the face of the gas station storefront. The windows are broken and patched with pieces of cardboard, and there is some trash, some paper cups and leaves and such, dancing in a ring on the oil-stained asphalt. The pumps are just standing there, dumbly.

"Hello?" Mr. Breeze calls after a moment, very loudly. "Anyone home?" He lifts the arm of a nozzle from its cradle on the side of a pump and tries it. He pulls the trigger that makes the gas come out of the hose, but nothing happens.

Peter walks alongside Mr. Breeze, holding Mr. Breeze's hand, peering at the road ahead. He uses his free hand to shade his eyes against the low late afternoon sun. A little ways down are a few houses and some dead trees. A row of boxcars sitting on the railroad track. A grain elevator with its belfry rising above the leafless branches of elms.

In a newspaper machine is a *USA Today* from August 6, 2012, which was, Peter thinks, about two years ago, maybe? He can't quite remember.

"It doesn't look like anyone lives here anymore," Peter says at last, and Mr. Breeze regards him for a long moment in silence.

-o-

At the motel, Peter lies on the bed, face down, and Mr. Breeze binds his hands behind his back with a plastic tie.

"Is this too tight?" Mr. Breeze says, just as he does every time, very concerned and courteous.

And Peter shakes his head. "No," he says, and he can feel Mr. Breeze adjusting his ankles so that they are parallel. He stays still as Mr. Breeze ties the laces of his tennis shoes together.

"You know that this is not the way that I want things to be," Mr. Breeze says, as he always does.

"It's for your own good."

Peter just looks at him, with what Mr. Breeze refers to as his "inscrutable gaze."

"Would you like me to read to you?" Mr. Breeze asks. "Would you like to hear a story?"

"No, thank you," Peter says.

⟨o⟩

In the morning, there is a noise outside. Peter is on top of the covers, still in his jeans and T-shirt and tennis shoes, still tied up, and Mr. Breeze is beneath the covers in his pajamas, and they both wake with a start. Beyond the window, there is a terrible racket. It sounds like they are fighting or possibly killing something. There is some yelping and snarling and anguish, and Peter closes his eyes as Mr. Breeze gets out of bed and springs across the room on his lithe feet to retrieve the gun.

"Shhhh," Mr. Breeze says, and mouths silently: "Don't. You. Move." He shakes his finger at Peter: *no no no!* and then smiles and makes a little bow before he goes out the door of the motel with his gun at the ready.

Alone in the motel room, Peter lies breathing on the cheap bed, his face down and pressed against the old polyester bedspread, which smells of mildew and ancient tobacco smoke.

He flexes his fingers. His nails, which were once long and black and sharp, have been filed down to the quick by Mr. Breeze—*for his own good,* Mr. Breeze had said.

But what if Mr. Breeze doesn't come back? What then? He will be trapped in this room. He will strain against the plastic ties on his wrist, he will kick and kick his bound feet, he will wriggle off the bed and pull himself to the door and knock his head against it, but there will be no way out. It will be very painful to die of hunger and thirst, he thinks.

After a few minutes, Peter hears a shot, a dark firecracker echo that startles him and makes him flinch.

Then Mr. Breeze opens the door. "Nothing to worry about," Mr. Breeze says. "Everything's fine!"

⟨o⟩

For a while, Peter had worn a leash and collar. The skin-side of the collar had round metal nubs that touched Peter's neck and would give him a shock if Mr. Breeze touched a button on the little transmitter he carried.

"This is not how I want things to be," Mr. Breeze told him. "I want us to be friends. I want you to think of me as a teacher. Or an uncle!

"Show me that you're a good boy," Mr. Breeze said, "And I won't make you wear that anymore."

In the beginning, Peter had cried a lot, and he had wanted to get away, but Mr. Breeze wouldn't let him go. Mr. Breeze had Peter wrapped up tight and tied in a sleeping bag with just his head sticking out—wriggling like a worm in a cocoon, like a baby trapped in its mother's stomach.

Even though Peter was nearly twelve years old, Mr. Breeze held him in his arms and rocked him and sang old songs under his breath and whispered *shh shhh shhhh.* "It's okay, it's okay," Mr. Breeze said. "Don't be afraid, Peter, I'll take care of you."

⟶o⟵

They are in the car again now, and it is raining. Peter leans against the window on the passenger side, and he can see the droplets of water inching along the glass, moving like schools of minnows, and he can see the clouds with their gray, foggy fingerlings almost touching the ground, and the trees bowed down and dripping.

"Peter," Mr. Breeze says, after an hour or more of silence. "Have you been watching your map? Do you know where we are?"

And Peter gazes down at the book Mr. Breeze had given him. Here are the highways, the states in their pale primary colors. Nebraska. Wyoming.

"I think we're almost halfway there," Mr. Breeze says. He looks at Peter and his cheerful children's-program eyes are careful, you can see him thinking something besides what he is saying. There is a way that an adult can look into you to see if you are paying attention, to see if you are learning, and Mr. Breeze's eyes scope across him, prodding and nudging.

"It's a nice place," Mr. Breeze says. "A very nice place. You'll have a room of your own. A warm bed to sleep in. Good food to eat. And you'll go to school! I think you'll like it."

"Mm," Peter says, and shudders.

They are passing a cluster of houses now, some of them burned and still smoldering in the rain. There are no people left in those houses, Peter knows. They are all dead. He can feel it in his bones; he can taste it in his mouth.

Also, out beyond the town, in the fields of sunflowers and alfalfa, there are a few who are like him. Kids. They are padding stealthily along the rows of crops, their palms and foot soles pressing lightly along the loamy earth, leaving almost no track. They lift their heads, and their golden eyes glint.

◄○►

"I had a boy once," Mr. Breeze says.

They have been driving without stopping for hours now, listening to a tape of a man and some children singing. *B-I-N-G-O*, they are singing. *Bingo was his name-o!*

"A son," Mr. Breeze says. "He wasn't so much older than you. His name was Jim."

Mr. Breeze moves his hands vaguely against the steering wheel.

"He was a rock hound," Mr. Breeze says. "He liked all kinds of stones and minerals. Geodes, he loved. And fossils! He had a big collection of those!"

"Mm," Peter says.

It is hard to picture Mr. Breeze as a father, with his gaunt head and stick body and puppet mouth. It is hard to imagine what Mrs. Breeze must have looked like. Would she have been a skeleton like him, with a long black dress and long black hair, a spidery way of walking?

Maybe she was his opposite: a plump young farm girl, blond and ruddy-cheeked, smiling and cooking things in the kitchen like pancakes.

Maybe Mr. Breeze is just making it up. He probably didn't have a wife or son at all.

"What was your wife's name?" Peter says, at last, and Mr. Breeze is quiet for a long time. The rain slows, then stops as the mountains grow more distinct in the distance.

"Connie," Mr. Breeze says. "Her name was Connie."

◄○►

By nightfall, they have passed Cheyenne—*a bad place*, Mr. Breeze says, *not safe*—and they are nearly to Laramie, which has, Mr. Breeze says, a good, organized militia and a high fence around the perimeter of the city.

Peter can see Laramie from a long way off. The trunks of the light poles are as thick and tall as sequoias, and at their top, a cluster of halogen lights, a screaming of brightness, and Peter knows he doesn't want to go there. His arms and legs begin to itch, and he scratches with his sore, clipped nails, even though it hurts just to touch them to skin.

"Stop that, please, Peter," Mr. Breeze says softly, and when Peter doesn't stop he reaches over and gives Peter a flick on the nose with his finger.

"*Stop.*" Mr. Breeze says. "*Right. Now.*"

There are blinking yellow lights ahead, where a barrier has been erected, and Mr. Breeze slows the Cadillac as two men emerge from behind a structure made of logs and barbed wire and pieces of cars that have been sharpened into points. The men are soldiers of some kind, carrying rifles, and they shine a flashlight in through the windshield at Peter and Mr. Breeze. Behind them, the high chain fence makes shadow patterns across the road as it moves in the wind.

Mr. Breeze puts the car into park and reaches across and takes the gun from its resting place in the glove box. The men are approaching slowly and one of them says very loudly: "STEP OUT OF THE CAR PLEASE SIR," and Mr. Breeze touches his gun to Peter's leg.

"Be a good boy, Peter," Mr. Breeze whispers. "Don't you try to run away, or they will shoot you."

Then Mr. Breeze puts on his broad, bright puppet smile. He takes out his wallet and opens it so that the men can see his identification, so that they can see the gold seal of the United States of America, the glinting golden stars. He opens his door and steps out. The gun is tucked into the waistband of his pants, and he holds his hands up loosely, displaying the wallet.

He shuts the door with a thunk, leaving Peter sealed inside the car.

There is no handle on the passenger side of the car, so Peter cannot open his door. If he wanted to, he could slide across to the driver's seat, and open Mr. Breeze's door, and roll out onto the pavement and try to scramble as fast as he could into the darkness, and maybe he could run fast enough, zig-zagging, so that the bullets they'd shoot would only nip the ground behind him, and he could find his way into some kind of brush or forest and run and run until the voices and the lights were far in the distance.

But the men are watching him very closely. One man is holding his flashlight so that the beam shines directly through the windshield and onto Peter's face, and the other man is staring at Peter as Mr. Breeze speaks and gestures, speaks and gestures like a performer on television who is selling something for kids. But the man is shaking his head no. *No!*

"I don't care what kind of papers you got, mister," the man says. "There's no way you're bringing that thing through these gates."

⟶◦⟵

Peter used to be a real boy.

He can remember it—a lot of it is still very clear in his mind. "I pledge allegiance to the flag" and "Knick knack paddy whack give a dog a bone this old man goes rolling home" and "ABCDEFGHIJKLMNOPQRSTU-VWXYZ now I know my ABCs, next time won't you sing with me?" and "Yesterday . . . all my troubles seemed so far away" and . . .

He remembers the house with the big trees in front, riding a scooter along the sidewalk, his foot pumping and making momentum. The bug in a jar—cicada—coming out of its shell and the green wings. His mom and her two braids. The cereal in a bowl, pouring milk on it. His dad flat on the carpet, climbing on his Dad's back: "Dog pile!"

He can still read. The letters come together and make sounds in his mind. When Mr. Breeze asked him, he found he could still say his telephone number and address, and the names of his parents.

"Mark and Rebecca Krolik," he said. "Two one three four Overlook Boulevard, South Bend, Indiana four six six oh one."

"Very good!" Mr. Breeze said. "Wonderful!"

And then Mr. Breeze said, "Where are they now, Peter? Do you know where your parents are?"

⟶

Mr. Breeze pulls back from the barricade of Laramie and the gravel sputters out from their tires and in the rearview mirror Peter can see the men with their guns in the red taillights and dust.

"Damn it," Mr. Breeze says, and slaps his hand against the dashboard. "Damn it! I knew I should have put you in the trunk!" And Peter says nothing. He has never seen Mr. Breeze angry in this way, and it frightens him—the red splotches on Mr. Breeze's skin, the scent of adult rage—though he is also relieved to be moving away from those big halogen lights. He keeps his eyes straight ahead and his hands folded in his lap, and he listens to the silence of Mr. Breeze unraveling, he listens to the highway moving beneath them, and watches as the yellow dotted lines at the center of the road are pulled endlessly beneath the car. For a while, Peter pretends that they are eating the yellow lines.

After a time, Mr. Breeze seems to calm. "Peter," he says. "Two plus two."

"Four," Peter says softly.

"Four and four."

"Eight."

"Eight and eight."

"Sixteen," Peter says, and he can see Mr. Breeze's face in the bluish light that glows from the speedometer. It is the cold profile of a portrait, like the pictures of people that are on money. There is the sound of the tires, the sound of velocity.

"You know," Mr. Breeze says at last. "I don't believe that you're not human."

"Hm," Peter says.

He thinks this over. It's a complicated sentence, more complicated than math, and he's not sure he knows what it means. His hands rest in his lap, and he can feel his poor clipped nails tingling as if they were still there. Mr. Breeze said that after a while he will hardly remember them, but Peter doesn't think this is true.

"When we have children," Mr. Breeze says, "they don't come out like us. They come out like you, Peter, and some of them even less like us than you are. It's been that way for a few years now. But I have to believe that these children – at least *some* of these children—aren't really so different, because they are a part of us, aren't they? They feel things. They experience emotions. They are capable of learning and reason."

"I guess," Peter says, because he isn't sure what to say. There is a kind of look an adult will give you when they want you to agree with them, and it is like a collar they put on you with their eyes, and you can feel the little nubs against your neck, where the electricity will come out. Of course, he is not like Mr. Breeze, nor the men that held the guns at the gates of Laramie; it would be silly to pretend, but this is what Mr. Breeze seems to want. "Maybe," Peter says, and he watches as they pass a green luminescent sign with a white arrow that says EXIT.

He can remember the time that his first tooth came out, and he put it under his pillow in a tiny bag that his mother had made for him which said "*Tooth Fairy,*" but then the teeth began to come out very quickly after that and the sharp ones came in. Not like Mother or Father's teeth. And the fingernails began to thicken, and the hairs on his forearms and chin and back, and his eyes changed color.

"Tell me," says Mr. Breeze. "You didn't hurt your parents, did you? You loved them, right? Your mom and dad?"

⦿

After that, they are quiet again. They are driving and driving and the darkness of the mountain roads closes in around them. The shadows of pine trees, fussing with their raiments. The grim shadows of solid, staring boulders. The shadows of clouds lapping across the moon.

You loved them, right?

Peter leans his head against the passenger window and closes his eyes for a moment, listening to the radio as Mr. Breeze moves the knob slowly across the dial: Static. Static—static—man crying—static—static very distant Mexican music fading in and out—static—man preaching fervidly—static—static. And then silence as Mr. Breeze turns it off, and Peter keeps his eyes closed, tries to breathe slow and heavy like a sleeping person does.

You loved them, right?

And Mr. Breeze is whispering under his breath. A long stream of whisps, nothing recognizable.

⦿

When Peter wakes, it's almost daylight. They are parked at a rest stop—Peter can see the sign that says "WAGONHOUND REST AREA" sitting in a pile of white rocks, he can see the outlines of the little buildings, one for MEN, one for WOMEN, and there is some graffiti painted against the brick, *FOR GOD SO LOVED THE WOLRD HE GAVE HIS ONLY BEGONTEN SON,* and the garbage cans tipped over and strewn about, the many fast food bags ripped open and torn apart and licked clean, and then the remnants licked again later, hopefully, and the openings of the crushed soda cans tasted, hopefully, and the other detritus examined, sniffed though, scattered.

There is a sound nearby. Sounds. A few of them creeping closer.

An old plastic container is being nosed along the asphalt, prodded for whatever dried bit of sugar might still adhere to the interior. Peter hears it. It rolls—*thok thok thok*—then stops. One has picked it up, one is eying it, the hardened bit of cola at the bottom. He hears the crunch of teeth against the plastic bottle, and then the sound of loud licking and mastication.

And then one is coming near to the car, where he and Mr. Breeze are supposed to be sleeping.

One leaps up onto the front of the Cadillac, naked, on all fours, and lets out a long stream of pee onto the hood of the car. The car bounces as the boy lands on it, and there is the thick splattering sound, and then the culprit bounds away.

That shakes Mr. Breeze awake! He jerks up, scrabbling, and briefly Peter can see Mr. Breeze's real face, hard-eyed and teeth-bared—nothing kindly, nothing from television, nothing like a friendly puppet—and Mr. Breeze clutches his gun and swings it in a circle around the car.

"What the fuck!" Mr. Breeze says.

For a minute, he breathes like an animal, in tight, short gasps. He points his gun at the windows: Front. Back. Both sides. Peter makes himself small in the passenger seat.

Afterward, Mr. Breeze is unnerved. They start driving again right away, but Mr. Breeze doesn't put his gun in the glovebox. He keeps it in his lap and pats it from time to time, like it is a baby he wants to stay asleep.

It takes him a while to compose himself.

"Well!" he says, at last, and he gives Peter his thin lipped smile. "That was a bad idea, wasn't it?"

"I suppose so," Peter says. He watches as Mr. Breeze gives the gun a slow, comforting stroke. *Shhhhhhh. There, there.* Mr. Breeze's friendly face is back on now, but Peter can see how the fingertips are trembling.

"You should have said something to me, Peter," Mr. Breeze says, in a kindly but reproachful voice.

Mr. Breeze raises an eyebrow.

He frowns with mild disappointment.

"You were asleep," Peter says, and clears his throat. "I didn't want to wake you up."

"That was very thoughtful of you," Mr. Breeze says, and Peter glances down at his map. He looks at the dots: Wamsutter. Bitter Creek. Rock Springs. Little America. Evanston.

"How many of them were there, do you think, Peter?" Mr. Breeze says. "A dozen?"

Peter shrugs.

"A dozen means twelve," Mr. Breeze says.

"I know."

"So—do you think there were twelve of them? Or more than twelve of them?"

"I don't know," Peter says. "More than twelve?"

"I should say so," Mr. Breeze says. "I would venture to guess that there were about fifteen of them, Peter." And he is quiet for a little while, as if thinking about the numbers, and Peter thinks about them too. When he thinks about *one dozen,* he can picture a container of eggs. When he thinks about *fifteen,* he can picture a 1 and a 5 standing together, side by side, holding hands like brother and sister.

"You're not like them, Peter," Mr. Breeze whispers. "I know you know that. You're not one of *them.* Are you?"

What is there to say?

Peter stares down at his hands, at his sore, shaved fingernails; he runs his tongue along the points of his teeth; he feels the hard, broad muscles of his shoulders flex, the bristled hairs on his back rubbing uncomfortably against his T-shirt.

"Listen to me," says Mr. Breeze, his voice soft and stern and deliberate. "Listen to me, Peter. You are a special boy. People like me travel all over the country, looking for children just like you. You're different, you know you are. Those *things* back there at the rest stop? You're not like them, you know that, don't you?"

After a time, Peter nods.

You loved them, right? Peter thinks, and he can feel his throat tighten.

He hadn't meant to kill them. Not really.

Most of the time, he forgets that it happened, and even when he *does* remember he can't recall *why* it happened.

It was as if his mind was asleep for a while, and then when he woke up there was the disordered house, as if a burglar had turned over every object, looking for treasure. His father's body was in the kitchen, and his mother's was in the bedroom. A lot of blood, a lot of scratches and bites on her, and he put his nose against her hair and smelled it. He lifted her limp hand and pressed the palm of it against his cheek and made it pet him. Then he made it hit him in the nose and the mouth.

"Bad," he had whispered. "Bad! Bad!"

"It's going to be better once we get to Salt Lake," Mr. Breeze says. "It's a special school for children like you, and I know you're going to enjoy it so much. You're going to make a lot of new friends! And you're going to learn so much, too, about the world! You'll read books and work with a calculator and a computer, and you'll do some things with art and music! And there will be counselors there who will help you with your . . . feelings. Because the feelings are just feelings. They are like weather, they come and go. They're not *you*, Peter. Do you understand what I'm saying?"

"Yes," Peter says. He stares out to where the towering white-yellow butte cliffs have been cut through to make room for the road, and the metal guard rail unreels beside them, and the sky is a glowing, empty blue. He blinks slowly.

If he goes to this school, will they make him tell about his mom and dad?

Maybe it will be all right, maybe he *will* like it there.

Maybe the other children will be mean to him, and the teachers won't like him either.

Maybe he *is* special.

Will his fingernails always hurt like this? Will they always have to be cut and filed?

"Listen," Mr. Breeze says. "We're coming up on a tunnel. It's called the Green River Tunnel. You can probably see it on your map. But I want to tell you that there have been some problems with these tunnels. It's easy to block the tunnels from either end, once a car is inside it, so I'm going to speed up, and I'm going to go very, very fast when we get there. Okay? I just want you to be prepared. I don't want you to get alarmed. Okay?"

"Okay," Peter says, and Mr. Breeze smiles broadly and nods and then without another word they begin to accelerate. The guard rail begins to slip by faster and faster until it is nothing but a silver river of blur, and then the mouths of the tunnels appear before them—one for the left side of the road, one for the right, maybe not mouths but instead a pair of eyes, two black sockets beneath a ridged hill, and Peter can't help himself, he tightens his fingers against his legs even though it hurts.

When they pass beneath the concrete arches, there is a soft *whuff* sound as if they've gone through the membrane of something, and then suddenly there is darkness. He can sense the curved roof of the tunnel over them, a rib cage of dark against dark flicking overhead, and the echo of the car as it speeds up, faster and faster, a long crescendo as the opening in the distance grows wider and wider, and the opening behind them grows smaller.

But even as the car quickens, Peter can feel time slowing down, so that each rotation of tire is like the click of the second hand of a clock. There are kids in the tunnel. Twenty? No, thirty maybe, he can sense the warm bodies of them as they flinch and scrabble up the walls of the tunnel, as they turn and begin to chase after the car's taillights, as they drop stones and bits of metal down from their perches somewhere in the tunnel's concrete rafters. "Yaaah!" they call. "Yaaah!" And their voices make Peter's fingers ache.

In front of them, the hole of daylight spreads open brighter, a corona of whiteness, and Peter can only see the blurry shadow-skeletons of the kids as they leap in front of the car.

They must be going a hundred miles an hour or more when they hit the boy. The boy may be eight or nine, Peter can't tell. There is only the imprint of a contorted face, and the cry he lets out, a thin, wiry body leaping. Then, a heavy thump as the bumper connects with him, and a burst of blood blinds the windshield, and they hear the clunking tumble of the body across the roof of the car and onto the pavement behind them.

Mr. Breeze turns on the windshield wipers, and cleaning fluid squirts up as the wipers squeak across the glass. The world appears through the smeared arcs the wipers make. There is a great expanse of valley and hills and wide open sky.

-◦-

"We're getting very low on gas," Mr. Breeze says, after they've driven for a while in silence.

And Peter doesn't say anything.

"There's a place up ahead. It used to be safe, but I'm not sure if it's safe anymore."

"Oh," Peter says.

"You'll tell me if it's safe, won't you?"

"Yes," Peter says.

"It's called Little America. Do you know why?"

Mr. Breeze looks at him. His eyes are softly sad, and he smiles just a little, wanly, and it's tragic, but it's also okay because that boy wasn't special, not like Peter is special. It is something to be left behind us, says Mr. Breeze's expression.

Peter shrugs.

"It's very interesting," Mr. Breeze says. "Because there once was an explorer named Richard Byrd. And he went into Antarctica, which is a frozen country far to the south, and he made a base on the Ross Ice Shelf, south of the Bay of Whales. And he named his base 'Little America.' And so then later—much much later—they made a motel in Wyoming, and because it was so isolated they decided to call it by the same name. And they used a penguin as their mascot, because penguins are from Antarctica, and when I was a kid there were a lot of signs and billboards that made the place famous."

"Oh," Peter says, and he can't help but think of the kid. The kid saying, "Yaaah!"

They are driving along very slowly, because it is still hard to see out of the windshield, and the windshield wiper fluid has stopped working. It makes its mechanical sound, but no liquid comes out anymore.

⤙⚬⤚

It is a kind of oasis, this place. This Little America. A great, huge parking lot, and many gas pumps, and a store and beyond that a motel, with a green concrete dinosaur standing in the grass, a baby brontosaurus, a little taller than a man.

It is the kind of landscape they like. The long, wide strip-mall buildings with their corridors of shelves; the cave-like concrete passageways of enormous interstate motels, with their damp carpets and moldering beds, the little alcoves where ice machines and tall soda vendors may still be inexplicably running; the parking lots where the abandoned cars provide shelter and hiding places, better than a forest of trees.

"There are a lot of them around here, I think," Mr. Breeze says, as they settle in next to a pump. Above them, there is a kind of plastic-metal canopy, and they sit for a while under its shade. Peter can sense that Mr. Breeze is uncertain.

"How many of them are there, do you think?" Mr. Breeze says, very casually, and Peter closes his eyes.

"More than a hundred?" Mr. Breeze says.

"Yes," Peter says, and he looks at Mr. Breeze's face, surreptitiously, and it is the face of a man who has to jump a long distance, but does not want to.

"Yes," he says. "More than a hundred."

He can feel them. They are peering out from the travel center building and the windows of the boarded-up motel and old abandoned cars in the parking lot.

"If I get out of the car and try to pump gas, will they come?" Mr. Breeze says.

"Yes," Peter says. "They will come very fast."

"Okay," Mr. Breeze says. And the two of them are silent for a long time. The face of Mr. Breeze is not the face of a television man, or a skeleton, or a puppet. It is the elusive face that adults give you when they are telling you a lie, for your own good, they think, when there is a big secret that they are sorry about.

Always remember, Peter's mother said. *I loved you, even . . .*

"I want you to hold my gun," Mr. Breeze says. "Do you think you can do that? If they start coming . . . ?"

And Peter tries to look at his real face. Could it be said that Mr. Breeze loved him, even if . . .

"We won't make it to Salt Lake unless we get gas," Mr. Breeze says, and Peter watches as he opens the door of the car.

Wait, Peter thinks.

Peter had meant to ask Mr. Breeze about his son, about Jim, the rock hound. "You killed him, didn't you?" Peter had wanted to ask, and he expected that Mr. Breeze would have said *yes.*

Mr. Breeze would have hesitated for a while, but then finally he would have told the truth, because Mr. Breeze was that kind of person.

And what about me? Peter wanted to ask. *Would you kill me too?*

And Mr. Breeze would have said yes. *Yes, of course. If I needed to. But you would never put me in that situation, would you, Peter? You aren't like the others, are you?*

Peter thinks of all this as Mr. Breeze steps out of the car. He can sense the other kids growing alert, with their long black nails and sharp teeth, with their swift, jumping muscles and bristling hairs. He can see the soft, slow movement of Mr. Breeze's legs. How easy it would be to think: *Prey.*

How warm and full of pumping juice were his sinews, how tender was his skin, the cheeks of his face like a peach.

He knew that they would converge down upon him so swiftly that there wouldn't be time for him to cry out. He knew that they could not help themselves, even as Peter himself could not help himself. His mom, his dad. *Wait,* he wanted to say, but it happened much faster than he expected.

Wait, he thinks. He wants to tell Mr. Breeze. *I want . . .*

I want?

But there isn't really any time for that. *Oh, Mom, I am a good boy*, he thinks. *I want to be a good boy.*

BLACK AND WHITE SKY

TANITH LEE

I

Almost morning; it is early summer, not quite five o'clock. The sky has a colourless lightness, faintly golden in the east across the fields. In the woods birds sing in pale, clear sprinklings of sound. From a copse one magpie rises. It flies straight upward.

There is a slight visual softness to all distances, perhaps mist, or haze. The air is fresh, but not unwarm.

A second magpie rises, this time not from the copse.

The golden edge of the sky intensifies, begins to dazzle. The sun is nearly free of the horizon.

A third magpie rises.

A fourth magpie rises.

The bird-chorus redoubles, eagerly encouraging the dawn. From the farm over towards the main road, some heavy vehicle or machinery rumbles.

A fifth magpie rises.

The sun rises.

A sixth magpie rises.

The sky floods with shell pink and golden lacquer.

A seventh magpie rises…

It was the day when Alice came to clean Cigarette Cottage. Of course, that was not the cottage's proper name. After it was built in the 1930s someone pastorally minded had christened the place "Woodbine Cottage." And following various renovations, and the removal of the name-plate above the door, "Woodbine" still stuck.

But George Anderton, moving in during 2003, coined his own private version of the name, in memory of those cigarettes he could recall his grandmother puffing at, in the days when smoking was a pleasant habit rather than a capital offence.

George himself had smoked, but no longer did so. He had never really been that serious a smoker. But, although having successfully given it up some twenty years before, he still occasionally missed them. The act perhaps, more than any hit.

"I've counted twenty-four magpies just as I was walking along the lane from the Duck," said Alice, as she put down her bag and accepted a mug of coffee. "What do you think of that?"

"Triple hell," said George, idly.

Alice laughed. She was only about forty, and very attractive. She made no secret of the fact she found George, a man more than ten years older, attractive too. But she was happily married and so would, hopefully, never impinge on George's solitary country life. He had given up London rather as he gave up smoking, missed the act, or *idea* of it, but not constantly. Women he had *not* given up. But there had been plenty—too many, he supposed—in his previous life. To be truly alone at last was restful.

Once a fortnight Alice came in, to dust, hoover and bleach the bathroom and the cooker. Now and then she cleaned the windows unasked. She charged the going rate, damaged nothing, did not get on his nerves, and was out of the house in never more than three hours.

"Triple hell—why's that?"

"The old rhyme," said George. "One for sorrow, two for joy, that stuff. There are several versions. The ones I know all end at nine magpies. And one of them finishes 'Seven's for Heaven, and Eight's for Hell.' So: three times eight equals twenty-four—triple hell."

"And what's nine?"

"The Devil."

"Oh, you," she said, beaming at him and liberating the dusters.

He was a writer; novels, and even some stage plays put on at the Lyric and the Royal Court. Now all he seemed to turn out were short stories, but his reputation, if not major, was not quite non-existent. To Alice, he thought, he was a curiosity, maybe a sort of catch in the cleaning market. The rest of her clients were more usual, weekenders or locals with enough money, plus of course the Duck pub up the lane.

When he went upstairs to his workroom (his study, Alice called it), he glanced from the window. Downstairs by now the trees in the small front garden, and the woods to the back, were thickly leafed, obscuring much of the sky. From the cottage's upper story however, he could see out across the shorter trees to the fields, as far as the farm. So he noticed a magpie fly up at once. And then, about half a minute later, another. And then, approximately equally spaced, several more. They rose singly, each from a different area, from behind the ring of trees on the fields' edge, from the fields themselves, from over the farm, out where the main road to Stantham cut ugly through the curve of the landscape.

Downstairs Alice was gently clinking something. George stood at the window and watched the magpies rising, he thought at first every one from a different spot, yet now and then another one would go up later from the same spot. There seemed always a similar interval, though he did not bother to check it exactly. It was curious. He wondered briefly what had caused it, so many of them, and so regular in rising. But then he told himself to stop prevaricating and go back to the computer. Most writers used almost anything, he knew but too well, to absent themselves from work.

It is midday. The church clock in the village a mile off chimes out twelve. The light is very bright now, metallic and clear. It shines on the hills that rim the distance, and sparks up the windows of the cottage. A woman has cycled away about an hour before. The man is working diligently in the room on the upper story, drinking his fourth mug of coffee now. He is on a roll with the story he writes, does not wish yet to stop for lunch.

A sluggish car lurches along the lane, heading for the pub. Bees buzz, and a few grasshoppers creak in the hedge. A grey squirrel performs acrobatics in the garden trees, then bounds overland for the wood.

A magpie rises.

It is now the most recent example of hundreds. The man in the cottage might have seen, if he had been looking.

It flies straight upwards, straight up into the glare of the zenith sun. Light digests it. It has vanished.

Smaller birds flutter about their business, wood pigeons, finches, a robin, a blackbird. Some are already teaching their young to fly. They quarter the lower air, flit past the oak trees and the now-wild apple that cast its last blossom only a week before. None of these birds heads directly upward. Not even the crow which abruptly wings over, cawing harshly, black as computer ink.

A magpie rises. Half a minute or thereabouts ticks away.

A magpie rises.

Soon after 6:00 p.m., George Anderton backed up the day's work, checked for e-mails—none—and switched off the computer.

Downstairs, lingering over a drink, he made a swift mental foray into the fridge, and promptly decided to visit the Duck for dinner.

At seven he opened the door of Cigarette Cottage, and stood, gazing through the trees into the glowing upper sky. It was blue, and feathered only by faint eddies of cloud, that seemed to foretell a fine tomorrow. The sun was westering towards the hills, visible in gaps, molten yet filmy. At least another hour before it set. This place. He had never regretted coming here. The lack of unnecessary human noise, beyond the intermittent legitimate agricultural sounds from the farm, the birdsong, the notes of various wildlife, the *silences*. Absorbed, he filled his ears with blackbird music, filled his eyes with the light. He had forgotten the magpies.

Then one rose, straight up, from the copse across the lane. Straight up and into the heart of the westered light, vanishing, as if dissolved.

George was startled. He returned to himself, refocussed his eyes, and waited.

Another magpie rose. This one was further over towards the hills, framed in a gap, a small pinpoint of darkness. Perhaps it was not a magpie.

He looked at the hands of his watch, counted off the seconds—lifted his eyes…*I will lift up mine eyes unto the hills*—nothing. No magpie had risen. Crazy, why would it?

Behind him. George turned around, moving almost too fast for himself. He saw this next magpie already high above, in the last moment before the light devoured it.

Had they gone on rising, *continuing* to rise, all day? Why? Where were they going? To the top of the sky?

In the Duck the usual evening crowd was sitting over its drinks. George Anderton had lived here long enough by now that two or three regulars greeted him. In the dining room beyond the front bar, a handful of summer visitors sat, lightly tanned and animated. George scanned them cautiously.

(He had once been trapped here by a mad-ish young-ish woman who was a fan of his work, and had apparently previously met him in London at a book signing. Her recalled London intentions were not strictly literary, but he was then involved elsewhere. Besides she was hardly his type, whatever that really meant. Age had not improved her, or her intentions, or his inclinations. It had been difficult to shake her off without being rude. He had finally only managed to by *telling* her he did not want to be rude, which did the trick.)

Tonight there was no visitor who appeared to recognise him, or care about him in any way.

George went to the bar and ordered his meal and a bottle of Bex.

"What do you think it is, then?" Colly asked him, as he rattled a bottle from the fridge.

"What's that?" George felt curiously oppressed. He knew already what *that* would be. He was correct.

"Them barmy birds."

"Which birds?" My God. George realised he was pretending he had not noticed. Why on earth?

But Colly, handing him a glass, explained, "Bloody magpies. Going up like rockets all the time."

"Are they?"

"I s'pose you ain't seen it, mate," said Colly, who like George hailed from London, and had kept his accent with him though in situ here for more than eighteen years.

"Well, I've seen some flying over. But so what?"

"Here," said Colly to Amethyst, as she came from the kitchen with two plates, "old George ain't bloody seen them magpies going up all day. One every thirty-seven seconds Arnold reckons."

"It's true," said Amethyst, widening her eyes at George through the pleasant steam of one meat and one vegetarian lasagne.

From along the bar a couple of the other men joined in. They told George, and the room in general, how Arnold Weller had timed the darn things. Between thirty-two and thirty-eight seconds. He had counted them for a whole half-hour. Over forty-three magpies, though old Arny had lost count, he thought, by a little—not much—forty or forty-three or even forty-eight. Near enough. And still flying up, one by one. One after another. And all of them from different places, or from the places no other bird was then rising from.

An elderly voice spoke from the corner, under the oil painting of *Ducks in Flight*. "Was on the one o'clock news. I heard it. They made a joke about it. Then someone else came in—some politician. Said he saw 'em too, in Sussex or whatever, that morning, and coming into London all the way."

"Reports all over the country," someone else said.

George turned to Amethyst. "No, thanks. No fries. Just the steak and salad."

"You're, like, clever," said Amethyst. She was in her earliest twenties, bright, respectful, a non-reader who unusually and wrongly seemed to believe writing a novel or play was the act of a wise, well-educated person. "What do you think's causing it?"

"I don't know."

"But it's—like it's *weird,* isn't it?"

"Is it? Maybe not."

"Maybe it's global warming," said one of the dining room visitors, moving in to ask where the gents was. Once told, he added, amused, over one shoulder, "Jude says she saw them from the car when we were driving down. I didn't notice. But Jude's gimlet eye picked them out okay."

"What's a gimlet eye?" Amethyst asked George over the two cooling dinners.

"God knows," he said. "I used to know. Can't remember. Old age," he added, smiling.

"You're not, like, *old,*" Amethyst insisted so vehemently and staring in his eyes with her wide, and certainly un-gimlet-like ones, he felt a hint of random desire. But it passed. It was food he lusted after, he decided, as he walked through into the pub garden.

Dusk was coming now, gradual and inevitable. A moth flew towards him as if in greeting, then on into the lighted pub.

Night falls.

From the farm the lights blaze out, and along the main road the headlamps of the occasional truck, or group of fast cars, spangle up the cats'-eyes like broken glass. A badger crosses, pausing to snuff at the tainted tarmac. A lucky badger, meandering sluggish yet unscathed, in a lacuna of traffic, to the farther side.

A frog croaks from a hidden pool. The night wind stirs softly and brushes through the leaves and grasses.

A magpie rises, blanking out, in passing, the stars, which then reappear.

The moon, almost full, will rise later. It will show far better than the stars the rising magpies, thirty or forty or fifty, that passage upward during every half-hour within the radius of visibility.

The Duck burns like a golden lantern in the darkness. It is almost 11:00 p.m. A couple of vehicles glide down the lane, away to the side-roads that lie north and west of the main one.

Later the more dedicated drinkers emerge, taking various paths homeward. Two cross the fields, a young man and a girl, pausing to kiss among the new-beginning crops, like lovers from Hardy. Behind and sometimes before them, unseen, unnoted, magpies rise one by one, straight up into the stars.

The man who is a writer, and has sat in the pub garden until utter darkness beyond the lights closed up the sky, who afterwards had a vodka at the bar, listening with the publican and a few others to the ten o'clock news, the comments and views of a celebrity, a twitcher, and an eminent ornithologist, leaves the Duck, and himself goes back along the lane. In the doorway of the cottage he stands a moment again, studying the skyscape. Indoors, upstairs, he watches too a while at the workroom window. But he can no longer be certain they are rising. If they are, then not near enough for the lights of his house to catch the white pattern on their wings.

They are like ancient Egyptian birds, he thinks, magpies. Their markings seem primal and elder as the spectacle designs about the eyes of certain snakes.

In the deep hollow of the night, dreamless, he wakes. He hears the eruption of wings leaping at Heaven from the roof above his head. Then he
gets up and crosses through again into his workroom. Against the yellow
three-quarter face of the hot moon, he sees another magpie rise. Another
magpie, more southerly, side-lit, half a minute, or thirty-six seconds after it.
In other areas that the moon can find, presently another. Another. Another.

Back in bed he switches on the radio for the World Service. But all the
BBC will give him now is war, famine and disease; misery, and a tiny bit
of the tune called "Lily Bolero."

He turns it off and falls asleep again, and dreams the young girl from the
pub is stalking him as the mad-ish woman had tried to do. Nevertheless he
lets the pub girl in. Then just inside the doorway, she turns into his cleaning
woman. Before the dream can become properly erotic, unfortunately—or
perhaps actually fortunately—it fades away from him. He does not wake
until the alarm clock sounds at 7:00 a.m.

II

George Anderton no longer bothered regularly to read newspapers. Any
allure they ever had for him had melted away in his forties. Two days after
he saw the first magpie ascending from his window, two nights after hearing
the other magpie clattering up, as if suddenly evolved from the very slates
of the cottage roof, he walked to the village. Orthurst had its point-topped
Saxon church and ancient yews, the scatter of shops and now-defunct post
office, the bus-stop for Stantham Cross, and the other pub, the Cart and
Plough, and some two hundred or so cottages, several dating way back.
There was also the unfinished new estate, virtually builder-abandoned, that
no one had wanted here, and was called the Lavvy.

At Rosie's, now owned and operated by Pam, he bought some butter,
lettuce, pears and bacon, the *Independent* and *Guardian,* and the local
Stantham Spotter.

"It gives me the creeps," said Pam. She was a nice, comfy old thing of
thirty-going-on-sixty-five. "My gran used to tell me they were unlucky.
Ill-omened birds. If you saw one you had to say, 'Good-morrow, Master
Magpie.' Or even, 'Good-Morrow, *Lord* Magpie.' Then it might be all
right. But I tried not to see them, when I was a child. Once one flew right

at me on my bike, when I was only seven, and five minutes after I fell off in a ditch. Broke my little finger. Look. It never came back straight. Doesn't bend like it should, neither."

"Poor you," he said. He refrained from saying gran's scare tactics had freaked Pam out enough that she had been bound to fall off the bike, after a close meeting with a magpie.

"Can't avoid seeing the blessed things now, can I? Nobody can. And the telly news goes on and on about them. They're everywhere. Going up. Did you hear about the plane at Heathrow last night? Yes, of course you did."

But he had not heard, slept solidly last night and through the alarm, missed the news this morning, had only just now seen the Heathrow report, a secondary headline on the *Guardian*'s front page.

It seemed, rather than inhaling a flock of the birds—what usually happened—the Boeing had been struck repeatedly by magpies, rising as if blind and insane, directly in its path, therefore hitting or being hit by fuselage, wings, and next the undercarriage, as the plane descended. The pilot had lost his nerve, many of the passengers too. The co-pilot brought the plane in, but the landing was a bad one, the touchdown heavy, the Boeing slewing across the runway. Three people had died, and seventy were injured, five seriously.

Disliking his own pragmatism, George considered it could have been far worse.

"On *TV Breakfast* they said, in Scotland," went on Pam, unhappy and excitable at once, "one plane there ditched in a loch." She pronounced this "lock," but he nodded. She expanded, "But at Manchester they've grounded them all. They're going to ground all of them, unless they can shoot them out of the sky."

He refrained, now, from asking if she meant the birds or the planes.

"No one can get home, then, except by sea. And they've closed the Chunnel, too. It's on page two in the *Mail*—a train struck so many birds on the approach it had to stop—the wheels and the windows were all…" she hesitated, grimaced. "Black and red."

He had, by then, seen the headline glaring on the *Mail*: WINGED DEATH RISES FROM THE TRACKS. A picture of the stalled train, surrounded by firemen and railway workers, was accompanied by a caption that began: *They seemed to come up out of holes under the line, said driver Ken Rains.*

Pam, shocking him slightly, abruptly started to cry. He had the urge to put an arm around her, tell her everything would be fine and would get sorted out. But he was unsure he himself believed this, going on the general everyday mess. And anyway, he had found out in the not-so-distant past where such gestures might land him.

"Don't worry, Pam," he temporised.

She said, "No, it isn't that. I don't know what it is. My age, I expect."

Poor Pam, he thought again, but did not say it. To be gallant might also be misunderstood. He left the shop having bought the *Mail* as well, the price of an extra paper to appease her. Not much of a consolation.

All the way back, now downhill to the fields and woods, he could watch the magpies rising on all sides, and behind him should he turn round, and off towards the hills those specks which, now, he was sure were magpies too. On his way to the village, going uphill, a single magpie had sprung directly from a bush at the side of the path. And later another from about three metres ahead of him. They might, these two, indeed have been engendered out of holes in the ground. Out of holes in reality.

One minute non-existent, and then—*existing*.

It was overcast today. The patch of fine weather had disintegrated. Well, this was England. High up, cloud had settled, like a pale grey duvet. And the silence. How silent it seemed. Not even the magpies made a sound, beyond the abrupt clapping of their wings, when near enough. That signature rattling chatter of theirs was oddly always absent. There was a fitful, warmish wind. It carried a smell from the farm, he thought, not strong or really unpleasant; animal. Somehow depressing.

It's my age, I expect, George told himself with dry mimicry. He had stuck too on the bloody story.

"Eyewitnesses are mistaken! It is *entirely impossible* that the huge number of birds people are *claiming* to have seen could even be *found* in the *whole* of the British Isles!"

An argument broke out at once between the four guests in the studio. The presenter tried to quieten them in vain.

George switched to another channel. A soap filled the eye and air with over-exaggerated drama that, beside the theatre of the swarming magpies, seemed ludicrous, laughable, and redundant.

The sun was low over the hills.

It had emerged from the duvet of cloud into a swollen vividity, murky orange, more like that of a wintry dawn.

The full moon had not been visible last night.

When the microwave disgorged the frozen pasty, presumably cooked, he started to eat it.

The next news told him, and showed him, men and women interminably shooting at rising magpies. Some birds fell at once. Some fluttered and spiralled away, mutilated and dying. Some, entirely missed, rose on into the overcast of the TV-recorded afternoon.

On the first channel they were still shouting, red in the face under their make-up tans. The presenter, unable to control the verbal fracas, shrugged wryly.

The phone sounded in the front room. George wiped his hands and went to answer it.

"Hi, George, darling. Have you seen the news?"

"Yes." It was Lydia, an actress who had appeared in one of his plays. They had slept together at the time. Lydia was his own age, but beautiful in a way not often seen. He had always liked her voice very much. He found he accordingly tended, during her phone calls, to hear her voice rather than what she said.

"Ah—what, Lydia?"

"Yes, it's an awful line, isn't it. I've heard, half the lines are down."

"How do you mean?" He thought once more he knew. Once more, he did.

"They fly right into them. Poor old birds, all tangled. Then the lines come off those pole things. It's as if they can't see. Or only see one thing—the upper sky. Do you have it there, Georgie?"

"Everyone has it everywhere," he said, "it seems. At least, in Britain."

"Sean told me it just *stops* at the sea."

"What exactly stops at the sea?"

"The—what did he say they called it?—oh, I can't remember. But it's dire, isn't it?"

"I suppose it is."

"*The RSPB,*" someone else said loudly. But it was the television in the other room. The sound for some reason had revved right up, then sunk away.

"...and I just sit at the window and watch them. It's quite hypnotic.

They just go up, straight up, and disappear in the clouds. I wonder why?"

"Yes, I think everyone wonders that."

"I don't think I've ever seen a magpie in central London before. Not here."

"No."

"Everything else. Sparrows, gulls, pigeons—and pelicans and swans in the park. But magpies… None of the other birds are doing it, are they?"

He thought they were not. Then again, he had been noticing, or imagining, the other birds were rather quieter. There was less singing, less of the territorial tweets and cries. The dawn chorus—did that still happen? It was too early in the season for all birdsong to taper off. As for the magpies themselves, they made no sound, as he had been aware for a while. Aside from the flurry of their wings as they rose.

Through the window, in the small front garden, a magpie *evolved* from the rogue apple tree. It lifted straight up into the half-tone upper sky. He could have sworn it had not been there a second before.

"Lydia, are you still—"

"Hello?" she said. "Hello, darling? Oh bugger. I can't hear you. Just a sizzle sort of thing. Never mind. If you can hear *me,* come up to town soon, won't you? We can go to dinner at the Royal."

The light in the other room flickered.

George heard the TV again, the new voice, a woman's, was telling someone that the lower, or upper, stratosphere—he did not take it in—was full of birds, floating, only that, like a fleet at anchor. Updraughts or thermals carrying and supporting it, or them; hundreds, thousands. But when he went back into the room, the pasty, which going by the commandment on its label under no circumstances must anyone reheat, had congealed to a cold, gooey fudge, and the screen was blank. Only the woman's impersonal and rather annoying voice talking of helicopter gunships, or ground-to-air missiles. Another programme then, about Afghanistan, or Pakistan.

George turned off the TV. *Not with a bang,* he thought, as if an alien authoritarian voice was speaking also in his head. *Not with a bang, but with a feather.*

During the night the battery-powered radio, which he had left on, woke him with a blast of between-items noise, some sort of militant jangle now representing the World Service, and obviously designed violently to awaken any insomniac who had managed to fall asleep. So he heard that an Italian plane, approaching Bournemouth airport, had found itself unable to land due to the maelstrom of birds. Having circled for some time, all the while with birds smashing into it, it headed back out to sea. An adjacent bulletin announced the plane had gone down in the water, not a mile out. All passengers and crew were feared dead. On the heels of this, came reports that European and US airlines were refusing to let their craft attempt landing anywhere on British soil, until the avian crisis was resolved. Countless Britons would be stranded. Perhaps they were glad? It seemed the Bird-Blanket, as one commentator called it, was limited to the British Island (also a recent coining), involving only England, Wales and Scotland. The radio then, despite having new batteries, began to fail. He switched it off. That the failure had nothing to do with batteries he understood perfectly.

Morning, noon, evening, night. Time has passed, is passing. Passes. Above the sky, they are to be visualised, the fleets, massed close and massing ever more closely, as more and more of the components rise up to fill them, pack them tight. A black and white expanded and expanding cumulous.

Spy planes have taken photographs. By now the phenomenon is visible from space. Satellites relay batches of curious pictures.

Fighter craft have also risen. They have blasted out gaps in the living, quasi-suspended, fluttering cloud-ceiling. There has been speculation as to what, precisely, keeps the bird cloud in place. Some oblique abnormal thermal, perhaps, some unforetold updraught, maybe created even by the birds' own upward flight. Or else it is all some new facet of pollution, global warming, some scientific experiment that has—of course—misfired, gone wrong…human worthlessness and wickedness in general.

As for the aerial fighters, frequently their planes ingest the half-destroyed bodies of their composite black and white target. Then the planes fall too, like the dead and dying burning birds. Aerial activity is cancelled. And in any event, the endless streams of magpies continue to rise, one bird it has been estimated roughly every half or three-quarter minute. During an hour, a hundred, sometimes one hundred and sixty birds are reckoned to be lifting from every square mile of land. If that is at all conceivable, likely, possible. Eyewitness statements, even those of trained observers, vary precariously.

Beaters plunge for a while through fields, woods, gardens, along hillsides, over moors, by riverbanks, and guns blast like a never-ending soundtrack of war. In towns and cities, citizens are summonarily ordered off the streets, while rapacious bird-dogs and their handlers seek, and always find, their quarry, But for all the birds slaughtered, quick and clean, misjudged and horribly, for all the carnage and the debris and the stink, the pity of it all—poor things, poor things—new birds rise, and keep on rising. Fifty, a hundred, two hundred, to a square mile. They seem to burst from the concrete skin of the streets, the stony ground, the trunks of trees and walls of buildings, out of the impervious world itself, self-perpetuating, ineradicable, inexhaustible.

Feathers lightly, omnipresently, carpet the earth. Feathers are caught in trees, lie along windowsills, drift into offices, houses, shops, stations, subways, alleys and avenues, caves and churches, libraries and reservoirs. Along the side-roads, high streets and motorways the feathers drift, black and white (and red with recent blood), several scorched and many broken. Cars and other vehicles lie tumbled along these thoroughfares too. Broken, some of them also, from multitudinous collisions with the bodies of rising birds which—all dead now and decaying—are plastered against their sides, stuck in their mechanical entrails and between the teeth of their wheels. Feathers drop from the air as well, a thin drizzle of feathers, an autumn of feathers, always falling. Black as ink, white as snow, often sheened mysteriously, mystically blue. Down from the sky that, darkened over now, and made tomb-like after each invisible day's end, reveals no sun, no moon, no single star. The magpie cloud, the blanket, an opaque dome, shuts everything out. Day is dusk, night an upside-down abyss. No more golden mornings, no more ruby settings of the sun.

Sometimes a feeble rain falls too. It is very warm and has a filthy taste, smelling of chickens and giving off a strange, sooty, chemical undertone.

There have been great rushings to and fro on the land, naturally. Flurries of anger and protest, crime and hoarding, as well as the useless bird-war. Then came escapings—towards the nearest coast, where the blanket, the dome, stops, and the fearful ceiling uncannily comes undone. But the road-long deserted ruins of cars and campers, buses and bikes, provide evidence of how few made it there. Or if they did, they will have managed it by other means.

To the majority left inside the trap of Britain, unable to reach any coast, the idea of that exit point is by now nearly a myth. Can it be true that the coast, any coast—is clear?

It is true. All coasts are clear, as glass. Just past the beaches or shingle or stones or rocks or cliffs, the river-mouths, estuaries, bays and sandbanks, the dunes, the spits, the coves—there, where the surf or the big rollers begin; at Eastbourne, Great Yarmouth, Whitby, Berwick-upon-Tweed, at Helmsdale and Melvaig, Aberystwyth, Weston-Super-Mare, and Plymouth—*there*—for *there* "it" finishes. To look up, there, standing in the fringes of the water, is to see suddenly the calmness or disturbance of actual sky, clouds, real weather, light; for there even the night is brilliant again with its stars and moon, with summer lightning, with *distance*. Open heavens. Open, open. And gulls fly over, in a graceful, ordinary way.

And beyond, out across the shining sky-lit sea, the islands. All of them are quite unclosed—the Orkneys, the Hebrides, Wight and Man stand sheer, like miraculous ghosts, like platinum pebbles on a horizon of pure glow, and the hem of Ireland, that too, and the longer strand of France: these are banks of deep blue smoke under a halo of sun-or-moonshine.

What then of the ones who managed an escape, who sped away from Britain's edges, in the racing ferries, fishing boats, speedboats and yachts? Did they, having reached the shining other shores, glance back? Surely they did, surely they still do, for out of Britain now no television picture comes, no telephone call, no e-mail, no text. Britain, robbed of her masts of communication, of a sky through which signals can flow, has grown silent and primitive, secretive and supernatural, as in the ages of darkness. Nor is she to be penetrated, her airways shut, her roads and railway-lines negotiable only on foot, and that with vast difficulty.

And this shutness, this secret, is all that can be seen of her through the satellite cameras, telescopes, and other lenses trained on her, with flat and weary persistence. Not even the straining periscopes of nuclear subs, drawn in from the Atlantic to patrol her shores like voiceless wolves, can determine anything much, beyond her emptied coastline, her immobile interiors veiled by cobwebs of shadow. She is a darkling plain.

Except where, now and then, something surfaces through the dimness, like a fleck of flint in dirty water, a tiny black bubble in poisoned lemonade: a magpie rising, flying straight up. And then another. And then. And then.

III

The pub looked different by now. And, it went without saying, the pub *was* different. In the first weeks the soldiers, initially in multifarious vehicles, then on foot, brought oil, matches, lamps and candles, besides gas canisters to swell the store at the Duck. Out here, in the "heart of the country," only electricity had formerly been available, and the series of chefs at the Duck always preferred, apparently, to cook with gas. Lucky. Electricity now, along with the phone, the TV and the radio, the computer and the World Wide Web, had all become things of the past, a recent past, but one which already seemed to have existed some centuries ago. Tap water was gone too. Reservoirs were polluted with incredible amounts of feathers, even by dilute disseminated bird crap, which had descended into them. For while the magpies had, and did, ascend, their innumerable cast-offs, sometimes including their slaughtered bodies, fell down.

In certain parts of the woodland you came into a stretch where branches were thickly coated in feathers instead of leaves. But the leaves were dying anyway. The woods, the copses, even the fields, deceived by the constipated yet oddly defecating sky, believed winter had suddenly returned. Half the trees were bare, the rest shedding their parched, rusted foliage. The grass was also turning brown. Not much hope of grain or cereal, no promise of fruit; nothing really it seemed could grow.

But for now, some fresh foods persisted. Though the fridges and freezers had long since surrendered, they did not eat too badly at the Duck. Fresh meat—rabbit, chicken, beef and mutton. (They had been lucky there too, those nearer the big cities had had their flocks and herds sequestered by the army early on, before all transportation was understood to be impractical.) Fish, or ordinary low-flying birds, might be contaminated, and were off the menu, however. Tomatoes, salad, even potatoes, all these from hot-houses run off generators, were available. And certain canned, dry, or otherwise less perishable goods, brought from Stantham, currently a two-day trek, aside obviously from any extra time given to bargaining with, fighting off, or else eluding the Stantham locals.

They had boiled the water and put it through filters. Now everyone drank bottled. Alcohol, thank God, George Anderton thought, came with its own indigenous preservatives and antiseptics. He had even relearned a liking for warm beer.

Tonight he was sharing a long table with three of the refugee families now living at the "Lavvy," the unfinished estate at Orthurst. They had been *en route* for the coast when their cars, spattered with birds, gave up the struggle. Some of the estate houses were not in too bad condition, floored, roofed and insulated, with closeable front doors and glazed windows. Their lack of electricity and plumbing hardly mattered either, of course. No one had any.

The refugees were all right, causing little trouble, only grateful not to be cast out. They had already lost their homes. And there had been Draconian rationing in London, and elsewhere, and plans for some type of peculiar military call-up of the young, that seemed to have no purpose. They took to Orthurst as the drowning take to solid land. And each communal evening, the Cart and Plough, like the Duck, did stunning business—if anyone had charged, or paid.

Over by the bar, Amethyst was laughing with one of the two soldiers who had stayed behind, when the rest were force-marched back to Stantham barracks. The young man leant forward and kissed her. An entirely normal scene, it took on instantly a look of utter abnormality.

"What worries me," said Jeremy, from London-and-the-Lavvy, "is the nuclear power stations. How are *they* coping with this? Have they shut down, or are they just…"

"…leaking radiation," concluded Liz from Chatham-and-the-Lavvy.

"I'll tell you one thing," said Dave, Liz's partner, "they'll have taken bloody good care of the oil-rigs off Scotland. Sea's supposed to be clear there, innit. You can bet they've got those rigs well protected."

"Who'd you mean?" asked Jeremy. "The so-called government? They'll have scarpered straight down their bleeding bunkers. And they couldn't run anything anyhow. Couldn't run a piss-up in a toilet."

A trio of children watched, wide-eyed. The eldest was only seven, and Sharron of Reigate-and-the-Lavvy quickly diverted their attention back to the pandas on the special kids' napkins Colly had produced.

"What I miss," said Sharron's boyfriend—Rob, George thought he was called—"is the sport. All had to be stopped, didn't it? Motor racing, rugby—even golf!"

Jeremy said in a light, grieving voice, "And that match—Arsenal versus Brighton—that would have been a cracker."

Jim was plodding by to the bar. "Want another, anybody?"

They did.

It was handy, George thought, the way these people talked about this, regularly skimming their terrors, yet also distracting each other, with the pandas of political complaint, food and drink and company.

He was glad too, that the smell of oil and kerosene, and the candles, some of which were scented, the smell even of people now less-washed and over-deodorised in compensation, helped mask the insidious presence of that metallic chicken stench, that dropped with all else from the sky. But probably too they were all becoming used to it. Soon they would not even notice.

Outside it was a jet-black abyssal night, the only kind, finally. But the pub basked in its pre-electric flame-lit radiance. This was how faces, forms, suddenly moving hands and glasses might have looked in paintings from the Renaissance. Similar at least, he corrected himself, for constructed light was bound to have altered, somehow. You knew, even in the Victorian era, no oil-lamp had cast quite this sort of illumination, or shadow. Everything changed.

And the pub's noise, chatter and clatter, and sometimes a singsong—were also like that. They stood to replace the notes of mobiles, recorded music, radio—and still did not make an elder noise but a modern one, anxiously filling up the void. Beyond which void loomed the agglomeration of silence the magpies had created. The magpies, that themselves no longer chattered or called, that made no sound. How silent then must be the upper skies where they clung or hung. Dumb and deaf, all questions futile, all answers obsolete.

As Jim put the new bottles on the table, George saw Alice come in out of the dark.

She paused a moment to speak to Amethyst, who nodded, while her soldier turned aside to light a roll-up; no one seemed likely to object to it now.

George could see Alice, too, had changed. She had lost weight, become oddly fragile and attenuated, her hair seeming blown about. There was a bruise on her left cheekbone. She put her hand to it absently. Amethyst was pouring Alice a glass of wine. No doubt one of the birds had struck her. In the last weeks that had begun to happen. Before, the birds had seemed, when rushing upward from the ground, or wherever it was they burst from, to strike only inanimate objects. But recently several people had some tale of a magpie springing abruptly past them inches away, the slap of a wing, long scratch of a claw, minor concussion of round body and hollow bones. Old Tim claimed to have seen one bird dash straight upward through the body of a cow that had been grazing on a slope behind the farm. She had not seemed hurt, just frightened. But later a bruised and reddened area had appeared along her ribs. They had decided it best to slaughter her quickly, and then remove the perhaps-contaminated meat when preparing her for eating. But Tim had always romanced, embellished facts. Even something like the thing that now went on might seem worth enhancing, to old Tim.

Alice raised the glass and drank. Her eyes connected with George's. She seemed about twenty, he thought. An infallibly revealing illusion. She smiled a nervous little smile, as if she had never seen him before. But George smiled broadly back, and beckoned, getting to his feet, and Jeremy obligingly shoved himself and family, and their chairs, along the table to make room.

"Oh," said Alice, very low, "I didn't mean to—"

"You're not. It's nice to see you, Alice."

"I'm so sorry I haven't been up to the cottage—"

"Well. Cleaning the house doesn't seem so important, frankly, do you think?"

"I suppose. I don't know. Todd—" Todd was her husband, "always wants everything clean. Or until…" Alice stopped. She drained her glass. She glanced at George under her lashes. Their unexpected meeting had become a liaison of two spies, but what was the espionage Alice had in mind?

"It's fine, Alice."

Jeremy leaned over and refilled her glass. It was the same red wine, or near enough, and everything was free. She thanked Jeremy, but he had already turned tactfully away, leaving the spies to their clandestine conversation in code.

"How are you?" George asked.

This was a fatal, leading question, and he knew it.

She did not answer. Then she softly said, "It's awful, isn't it?"

"Yes, Alice. It's awful."

"I'm—scared," she said.

He saw the oldest child take note, and an expression of fear creep into his face. George smiled broadly again. He said to her, "Why don't we go back to the cottage? Talk there. I can walk you home later. I've even got some spare food."

She too had noticed the child. She brightened, falsely but giving quite an actorly performance. "That would be—yes, let's do that. Why not?"

As they were going out of the door. Colly appeared and handed George another bottle of wine. "Last of the best Merlot. Go on. Have a treat. You know, I knew a feller once, he always wanted a pub. Then he comes into some dosh, buys the pub, gets it done up, cracking, ace cook, full cellar, top class guest-rooms. What d'you think he does then?" George and Alice waited between light and night. A singsong had started, "Oliver's Army" by Elvis Costello. Behind the bar Amethyst was snogging the soldier. "He locks everyone out, and keeps the place to himself, just for him, I mean. Nobody else let in, ever. The Bugle it's called. Up Camden way. What do you think of *that?*"

"This mark on my face—it isn't anything to do with the birds. He hit me. Todd. He hit me."

"Christ. When was this?"

"This morning. He just—did it."

"Had it happened before?"

"No. Not…not really."

"Where is he now?"

"With Pam Boys. You know, from the shop."

They stood still in the lane, in the dark, among the alopecia of the trees, balancing on spent feathers. No car would try to drive through, not any more, and footsteps would be clearly audible. He had turned the torch off, because its batteries were running low. He had had a solar-powered torch too, but it went without saying it was unrechargeable.

He had an urge to touch her, hold her, comfort. But George grasped very well this was not gallantry or outrage—despite the fact that the image of her bastard husband hitting her incensed him. No, it was desire, lust. But then. What else was left? It puzzled George too, the manner in which, above all else, carnality survived, just as biological hunger and thirst, and an extraneous liking for the taste and effect of alcohol. Oh God. The Last bloody Days of Pompeii. Eat, drink and be merry before the volcano exploded, or the circus lions came to tear you limb from limb. Just as in the old "B" movies. But also, be fair, here at least, where some quiet remained, courtesy and camaraderie also persisted, a sort of familial gentleness. Be gentle then.

"I'm so sorry, Alice."

She came into his arms, there in the near-blind blackness of the lane. She was beautiful, smooth and pliant, and her hair curiously rough and savage.

Her mouth was as appetising as he had believed it would be. When they drew apart, she shuddered. "Can we get inside the house—I don't like being out here, in the dark."

He switched the torch back on.

Not until they reached the gate of Cigarette Cottage did it occur to him he had not heard, nor even in the ray of the torch seen, a single magpie. By some fluke they had somehow missed the ones that must have gone on rising all about, as they continually rose, as he had even seen them rising at six this evening. What power sex had, sex, (not love), that drove out fear.

During the night he went to get a bottle of water downstairs, and stood at the window looking out into the front garden. Three foxes grouped there, limned by the light of the candle. All males, he thought, young, healthy enough, but huddled on the wild lawn and staring in at him, exactly as he stared out at them. It was as if they wanted something from him. He wished he could offer something. But maybe what they asked for was what everyone wanted: an answer. Their eyes flamed, all surface, luminous in a spiritless way that made him think of rabies posters from the 1970s—or of demons.

Animals had been behaving oddly for days. You did not notice, then an especially unnatural event made you see, and so recall other incidents. He had first become aware of it with a cluster of robins, nine or ten, then almost twenty of them, a flock almost like that of starlings, flying round and round the copse, before dazzling off through the dirty dreary day-twilight towards the farm. Robins were generally solitary, just as foxes were, out of the mating season. But there had been the cats, too. Each screamed and cried and ran towards you, or from you, still calling. One he had met in the lane. It had a magpie feather in its mouth. The cat hurried up and down, up and down, not dropping the feather, not chewing it, growling low in its throat. Some animals had simply vanished. Consensus opinion had it they were hibernating, misled as were the trees. That—or they had got wise to the idea they also might be shot for food. The absence of all grey squirrel activity, squirrels that even in a real mid-winter were often about, was telling enough. He had not seen or heard any frogs, or pigeons, nor heard a single dog bark or howl for weeks, either. There were no insects. Even the clothes moths had gone away.

George turned from the foxes, collected the water, and went back upstairs. Alice sat up in the bed, no longer sobbing. She had wept after they first made love. Then fallen suddenly asleep against him. Later she woke, and told him she had always wanted him, had fantasies about him. "But you're better." So there had been more sex, rich, brain-flooding orgasm. And then she had begun to sob again, could not stop. She said, "It isn't about him. Sod him. He can fuck off. It's the rest. It—reminds me of that Hitchcock film—"

"From the story by Daphne du Maurier?"

"Was it?"

George did not say that the short story had been far bleaker and more terrible than the film. "But those birds attacked, didn't they," he reminded her instead. "Our magpies—they just fly upward."

"Oh," Alice whispered, "what's going to happen?" She knew he could not tell her, beyond the obvious, which was bad enough.

He said, "It'll be all right, Alice."

"Will it?"

"Yes."

And then she had calmed, knowing, he supposed, (as he did) that either it would or it would not. Out of their hands. Better off also therefore out of their minds.

Now they drank the water.

"Can I stay?" she said, like a child.

"Please do stay."

"I can leave once it gets—once it's lighter. I don't want you to feel—I know you like to be alone."

"How do you know that?" he inquired, playfully.

"So you can write."

"That," he said. He visualised the unfinished story trapped there on the computer screen, now lost in space. Backing up had hardly mattered when the whole bloody lot went. He could have foretold, and printed it. But then, why write stories while Rome burned.

"Do you remember the PM talking, just before Radio 4 went off the air?" she surprised him by saying.

"I didn't listen. He gets—got on my tits, frankly."

"But that night he was so good, he was... It brought out the best in him."

They laughed, bitterly. Then lay down to sleep, back-to-back. How long since he had felt that sumptuous comfort, female flesh against his? And for how much longer? Till the muffled sun rose behind the black and white sky? Until the food and bottled water were all gone? Tears ran also from his eyes. He cried then quietly, not to wake her. The pillow soaked them up, his tears, as eternity soaked up all such flimsy things, weeping, blood, the shells of beasts and men.

In sleep he felt rather than heard a vague amorphous rumbling. Thunder? Some storm created by the choking of the stratos—or a phantom train perhaps, once more enabled to run all those miles off in Stantham. Asleep, he did not care. He was dreaming of Lydia, faithless after all as Alice, (or Todd), Lydia in that hotel in Paris, thirteen years ago.

In the moments before daybreak, or what now passed for it, George's dreams altered into a perfectly coherent recollection of researching magpie legends, which he had done about nine days before. The book was an old one, something he had picked up in London in the 1990s. A writer never knew, he had always maintained, what might or not ultimately be useful.

Birds of Ill-Omen and Evil Luck. This had been the heading. But at the end of the section came a concluding paragraph, with the sub-heading: *Exonerating the Magpie:*

> The Magpie is often badly thought of, as reputedly it refused to don full (black) mourning at the death of Christ. However this would seem to be a misunderstanding of the story. In an older version, the Magpie donned *half* mourning, it is true, to show respect for Christ's suffering and death. But the bird's snow-white feathers were intended to indicate that life continues *after* death, and that indeed Christ *Himself* would rise physically from His tomb. Why else does the Magpie remain with the Zodiac sign of Virgo, the Virgin, which connects directly with the Virgin Mary, the Mother of Christ? At least, apparently, Jesus and Mary were sure that the Magpie was both innocent of all blame, and a witness to the Great Truth. And for that reason the Virgin herself added to his elegant attire the extraordinary sheen of blue, (Mary's own sacred colour), which is to be seen most evidently on his wings.

Almost morning, technically; it is about twenty minutes short of five o'clock. The sky has a colourless darkness, but is strangely faded at a point near the zenith. Gradually this thinning of an upper canopy begins to fill with muffled, dulled, but undeniable light.

In the woods birds do not sing. Then a shrill chorus, not song but warning, surges up, fragments, and ends.

From the copse across the lane no bird rises. No magpie rises. All about nothing stirs. Silence is concrete, now. Stone.

To scan from horizon to horizon is to fail to detect any movement. Not an animal slinks or runs along the earth, let alone takes wing in the lower element of the sky.

No magpie rises.

No magpie rises.

Since 8:00 p.m. yesterday evening, as surprisingly only a very few have noted, nowhere on the landmass of Britain has a single magpie risen, to fly straight upward. Or in any direction.

Above, just east of the zenith, the hole, for so it is, continues dully to grow lighter. Perhaps too it perceptibly widens, just a very little.

Then, to the north, another dim vague thinning seems to be taking place, another occult lightening appears to be wearing through.

Over the fields, miles up it seems, and in some other dimension, a loud indescribable crack bellows through the air. A splintering line, scribbled in silvery radioactive ink, careers across the masked dawn-dusk of the heavens.

A kind of storm, cloudshift and whirlwind, discourages darkness. The episodes of lights brilliantly flash now, knife-like. Then, the sky—is falling.

It is falling everywhere. Far off, near, immediately overhead.

It falls in masonry blocks which, as they descend, drop apart in chunks and waterfalls and tidal waves, and all is blundering and spinning downward. Bodies. The corpses of dead birds. A million million, a trillion trillion. Lifeless and almost weightless yet, in this unthinkable and unavoidable mass, a weight of unguessable and incorrigible proportions.

The air resounds to a type of steely scream. Whether voiced or only a by-product of the avian deluge, it swamps and pierces all and everything.

Death begins to slam against the earth.

The prelude impacts are awesome enough.

Before vision becomes only a mosaic, like scenes from an ancient and damaged film, it is feasible to see whole boughs snapped off from trees, on buildings a slide and tumble of slates and chimneys and TV aerials, satellite dishes, shattering and scattered—smashing with the white-black downpour of death to the ground below.

From the church in the village the clock is silent as its automatic hands approach ten to five, yet the bell in the tower, if barely audible, clangs dolefully. Part of the church roof has been riven open and, cascading by, the dead are striking the bell.

But now the next phase of impact is arriving. To this the prelude was nothing. In the woods the young trees reel, are toppling. Hedgerows and fences crumple and disappear. From the little pool huge gouts of water are displaced—who would have thought it could hold so much?

Whole roofs buckle now. Joists give way. Windows collapse. In the village street shop-fronts disintegrate one after the other as if bombed. The pavement and road are piled high, the gardens. At the half-built estate *all* the building is coming undone. Something is on fire at the farm, smoke curdling upwards, but blotted away almost at once as the rain of the dead pours on—the main road is hidden. Even the stranded cars are covered over. Fields, tracks, hills, landscape—all now under this thick white-black snow…

Through the cacophony of rushing, the whine and shrill of the great lost scream, no individual sound is to be deciphered.

The cottage on the lane is piled high, high as its roof, as if with discoloured sandbags. The pub is only a mound, a sort of heap of unclean washing, featureless and silent, a mashed tree lying against it.

The magpies fall. The ultimate gush of the volcano. They drop and strike and crush and break and are broken. They cover and they bury everything. They load the world like bandaging, like grave-wrappings. And still they are falling. The heads of distant oak trees—drowned. Eradicated.

And the stench, the thunder that seems never likely to end, tempest, tsunami, eruption. Poor things. Poor things. It is 5:00 a.m. The church clock does not chime, even if anyone could hear it.

High, high above the fall, from the widening, shining chasms in the darkness, light foams clear as clean water. And in the east the sun has risen, is visibly rising, like the pitiless eye of Man Himself.

Not for the first time—from an idea by John Kaiine.

THE MONSTER MAKERS

STEVE RASNIC TEM

This is all I can bear of love.

Robert is calling the children in, practically screaming it, how we all need to go, *now*. But I'm too busy gazing at the couple as they talk to the park ranger, the way their ears melt, noses droop, elongating into something else as their hair warps and shifts color, their spines bend and expand, arms and legs crooked impossibly, and their eye sockets migrating across their faces so rapidly they threaten to evict the eye balls.

"Grandpa! Please!" little Evie cries out, but now I look at the park ranger, who has fallen to his knees, his face pale and limbs trembling, mouth struggling to form a word that does not yet exist. Because it isn't the way it is in the movies; human beings cannot accept such change so easily—at some point the mind must shut down and the body lose itself with no one left to tell it what to do. "Please, Grandpa, *now*," Evie wails, and the intensity of her distress finally gets to me, so that I hobble over to the battered old station wagon as fast as I can, which isn't very fast. Because Evie is that special grandchild, you see. Evie has my heart.

The car bucks once as Robert gives it gas too quickly. It rattles, then corrects itself. Alicia is safely in the backseat beside me, but I'm not sure if she ever left. She doesn't move as much as she used to. But it's amazing how young she looks—her long hair is still mostly blonde, even though she's about my age, whatever that might be. We agreed long ago not to keep track anymore. I've loved her as long as I've known her. The trouble is, these days I can't remember how long.

The grandkids are both on the other side of Alicia. They're small, so I can't see all of them, just four skinny legs which barely reach beyond the front edge of the seat, and the occasional equally skinny arm. They kick and wave, thrilled. Despite their fear—they have no understanding of what they've caused, or why—they're quite excited about what's happening to them. I suspect this is the way some addicts or athletes feel—something takes over you, as if it were a spirit or a god, seizing your blood and bones, your muscles—and it makes you run around or die. From this angle, there's no discernible difference between Evie and Tom, but they are not twins, except in spirit. They sing softly as they often do, so softly I can't make out the words, but I've come to believe that their singing is the background music to all my thoughts.

As we leave the park, I can hear the long howls behind me, the humanity disintegrating from those poor people's voices. My grandchildren laugh out loud, giddy from the experience. These changes always seem to happen around certain members of my family, although none of us have precisely understood the relationship or the mechanism. Why did the couple change but not the ranger? I have no idea. Perhaps it is some tendency in the mind, some proclivity of the imagination, or some random, genetic bullet. My grandchildren possess a prodigious talent, but it's not a talent anyone would want to see in action.

Up in the front passenger seat, Jackie pats Robert's shoulder. I don't know if this is meant as encouragement, or if he even needs it. My son has always been sane to a fault. His wife's face looks worried, the skin so tight across her cheeks and chin it's as if she wears a latex mask. But then Jackie always was the nervous sort. She's not of this family; she simply married into it.

"Dad, I thought I asked you not to tell them any more stories." Robert's voice is barely under control.

They're both angry with me, furious. They blame me for all of this. But they try not to show it. I don't think it's because they're careful with my feelings. I think it's because they're somewhat frightened of me. "Telling stories, that's what grandfathers do," I say. "It's how I can communicate with them. The stories of our lives and deaths are secrets even from ourselves. All we are able to share are these substandard approximations. But we still have to try, unless we want to arm ourselves with loneliness. I just tell the children *fairy tales*, Robert. That's all. Stories about monsters. Something they already know about. Monster stories won't turn you into a monster, son. Fairy tales simply tell you something you already knew in a somewhat clever way."

Once upon a time, perhaps gods and monsters walked the earth and a human might choose to be either one. But not anymore. Now people grow and age and die and then are forgotten about. It's the "great circle," or whatever you want to call it. It's sobering information but it can't be helped. I don't tell Robert this—he isn't ready to hear it. He loves his poor, pathetic flesh too much.

"Why couldn't you stop? What will it take to make you stop!" Robert is howling from behind the steering wheel. For just a moment, I think he's about to change, expand, become some sort of wolf thing, but he is simply upset with me. Robert is our only child, and I love him very much, but he has always been vulnerable, frightened by the most mundane of dangers, as if he were unhappy to have been born a mortal human (I'm afraid the only kind there is).

Robert always refused to listen to my bedtime stories, so he's really in no place to evaluate whether they are dangerous or not. The members of our family have been shunned for ages, thought to be witches, demons, and worse. No one wants to hear what we have to say. "Your children simply understand the precariousness of it all. And this is how they express it."

"No more, Dad, okay? No more today."

Whatever my son decides to do, he's likely to keep us all locked up at home from now on. The only reason we went out today was because he knows the children need to get out now and then, and he didn't think we'd run into anybody in that big state park. Besides, it doesn't happen every time, not even every other time. There's no way to predict such things. I've witnessed these transformations again and again, but even I do not understand the agency involved.

I can't blame him, I guess. Sometimes human life makes no sense. We really shouldn't exist at all.

Back at the old farmhouse, I'm suddenly so exhausted I can barely get out of the car. It's as if I've had a huge meal and now all I can manage is sleep. The adrenalin of the previous few hours has come with a cost. I suspect my food must eat me rather than the other way around.

Alicia is even worse than before, and Robert and Jackie each have to pull on an arm to get her to stand. The grandkids push on her butt, giggling, and aren't really helping.

Once inside, they take us up to our room. "I get so exhausted," I tell them.

"I know," Jackie replies. "You should just make it stop. We'd all be happier if you just made it stop."

She's like all the others. She doesn't understand. It happens, but I've never been sure we can make it happen. Perhaps we simply show what has always been. Her children are learning about death. It's a lesson not everyone wants to learn.

She must think that, because I'm an older man, I'm likely to do foolish things. But we have such a limited time on this planet, I want to tell her, why should we avoid the foolish? I feel like that deliverer of bad news whom everyone blames.

Robert is less courteous as he guides us up the stairs, his movements abrupt and careless. He's obviously lost all patience with this—this caring for elderly parents, this endless drama whenever the family goes out. He'll make us all stay home now, planted in front of the television, transfixed by god-knows-what mindless comedy, locked away so that we can't cause any more trouble. But the children have to go out now and then. An active child trapped inside is like a bomb waiting to go off.

Periodically he loses his balance and crashes me into a railing, a wall, the doorframe. Each time he apologizes but I suspect it is intentional. I don't mind especially—each small jolt of pain wakes me up a bit more. You have to stay awake, I think, in order to know which world you're in.

By the time they lay both of us down in the bed, I'm practically blind with fatigue. Almost everything is a dirty yellow smear. It's like a glimpse of an old photograph whose colors have receded into a waxy sheen. Perhaps this is the start of sleep, or the beginning of something else.

Several times during the middle of the night, Alicia crawls beneath the bed. Is this what a nightmare is like? Sometimes I crawl under the bed with her. The floor is gritty, dirty, and uncomfortable to lie on. It's like a taste of the grave. It's what I have to look forward to.

I pat Alicia's arm when she cries. "At least you still have your yellow hair," I tell her. She looks at me so fiercely I back away, far far back under the bed into the shadows where I can hear the winds howl and the insects' mad mutter. I can stay there only a brief while before it sickens me but it still seems safer than lying close to her.

I wake up the next morning with my hand completely numb, sleeping quietly beside my face. I scrape the unfeeling flesh against the rough floorboards until it appears to come back to life. Alicia isn't here; she's wandered off. Although much of the time she is practically immobile, she has these occasional adrenaline-driven spurts in which she moves until she falls down or someone catches her. She is so arthritic, these bouts of intense activity must be agony for her. I can hear the grandchildren laughing outside and there is this note in their tone that drives me to the window to see.

The two darlings have the mail carrier cornered by the garage. We never get mail here and I think how sad it is that this poor man will doubtless lose his life over an erroneous delivery. They chatter away with their monkey-like talk at such a high pitch and speed I cannot follow what they say, but the occasional discrete image floats to the top—screaming heads and bodies in flame. None of these images appears in any of the stories I have told them, although of course Robert will never believe this. What he does not fully appreciate is that out in the real world all heads have the potential for screaming, and all bodies are in fact burning all the time.

On the edge of the yard, I spy Alicia. She has taken off all her clothes again and now scratches about on all fours like some different kind of animal. The Roberts of the world do not wish to admit that humans are animals. We may fancy ourselves better than the beasts because of our language skills, because we possess words in abundance. But all that does is empower us with excuses and equivocations.

The mail carrier has begun to change. He struggles valiantly but to no avail. Already his jaw has lengthened until it disconnects from the rest of his face, wagging back and forth with no muscle to support it. Already his hair drifts away and his fleshier bits have begun to dissolve. These are changes typical, I think, of a body left in the ground for months.

At first Evie laughs as if watching a clown running through his repertoire of shenanigans but now she has begun to cry. Such is the madness of children, but I must do what I can to minimize the damage. I make my way stiffly downstairs with a desperate grip on the banister, my joints like so much broken glass inside my flesh, and as I head for the door I see Robert come up out of the cellar, the axe in his hands. "This has to stop . . . this has to stop," he screams at me. And I very much agree. And if he were coming for *me* with that axe all would be fine—I somehow always understood things might come to this juncture—but he sweeps past me and heads for the front door and my grandchildren outside.

I take a few quick steps, practically falling, and shove him away from the door. I see his hands fumble the axe, but I do not realize the danger until he hits the wall and screams, tumbles backwards, the blade buried in his chest. "Robert!"

It's all I have time to say before Jackie comes out of the kitchen screeching. But it's all I know to say, really, and what good would it do to lose myself now? He would have hated to die from clumsiness, and that's what I take away from this house when I leave.

Out on the lawn, the children are jumping up and down laughing and crying. There is a moment in which time slows down, and I'm heartsick to see their tiny perfect features shift, coarsen, the flesh losing its elasticity and acquiring a dry, plastic filler look, as if they might become puppets, inanimate figures controlled by distant and rapidly-vanishing souls. I see my little Evie's eyes dull into dark marbles, her slackened face and collapsing mouth spilling the dregs of her laughter. I think of Robert dead in the farmhouse—and what a mad and reprehensible thing it is to survive one's child.

But of course I can't tell these children their father has died. Maybe later, but not now, when they are like this. If I told them now they might savage the little that remains of our pitiful world. In fact, I can't tell them anything I feel or know or see.

"Help me find your grandmother!" I shout. "She's gotten away from us, but I'm sure one of you clever children will find her!" And I am relieved when they follow me out of the yard and into the edge of the woods.

I have even more difficulty as I maneuver through the snarled tangle of undergrowth and fallen branches than I thought I would. I'm out of practice, and with every too-wide step to avoid an obstacle, I'm sure I'm going to fall. But the children don't seem to mind our lack of progress; in fact, they already appear to have forgotten why we're out here. They range back and forth, their paths cross as they pretend to be bees or birds or low-flying aircraft. Periodically they deliberately crash into each other, fall back against trees and bushes in dozens of feigned deaths. Sometimes they just break off to babble at each other, point at me, and giggle, sharing secrets in their high-pitched alien language.

Now and then I snatch glimpses of Alicia moving through the trees ahead of us. Her blonde hair, her long legs, and once or twice just a bit of her face, and what might be a smile or a grimace; I can't really tell from this distance. Seeing her in fragments like this, I can almost imagine her as the young athletic woman I met fifty years ago, so quick-witted, who enthralled me and frightened me and ran rings around me in more ways than one. But I know better. I know that that young woman exists more in my mind, now, than in hers. That other Alicia is now like some shattered carcass by the roadside, and what lives, what dances and races and gibbers mindlessly among trees is a broken spirit that once inhabited that same beautiful body. Sometimes the death of who we've loved is but the final act in a grief that has lingered for years.

I think that if Alicia were to embrace me now, she'd have half my face between her teeth before I had time even to speak her name.

As mad as she, the children now shriek on either side of me, slap me on the side of the face, the belly, before they howl and run away. I wonder if they even remember who she is or was to them. How only a few years ago, she made them things and cuddled them and sang them soft songs. But we were never meant to remember everything, I think, and that is a blessing. It seems they have already forgotten about their parents, except as a story they used to know. The young are always more interested in science fiction, those fantasies of days to come, especially if they can be the heroes.

I watch them, or I avoid them, for much of the afternoon. Like a baby sitter who really doesn't want the job. At one point, they begin to fight over a huge burl on a tree about three feet off the ground. It is only the second such tree deformity I've ever seen, and by far the larger of the two. I understand that they come about when the younger tree is damaged and the tree continues to grow around the damage to create these remarkable patterns in the grain.

Their argument is a strange one, although not that different from other arguments they've had. Evie says it'll make a perfect "princess throne" for her after they cut it down. The fact that they have no means to cut it down does not factor into the argument. Tom claims he "saw it first," and although he has no idea what to do with it, the right to decide should be his.

Eventually they come to blows, both of them crying as they continue to pummel each other about the head and face. When they begin to bleed, I decide I have to do something. I have handled this badly, although I can't imagine that anyone else would know better how to handle such a crisis. I stare at them—their flesh is running. Their flesh runs! Their grandmother is gone, and they don't even know that their father is dead. And they dream wide awake and the flesh flows around them.

What do I tell them? Do I reassure them with tales of heaven—that their father is now safe in heaven? Do I tell them that no matter what happens to their poor fragile flesh there is a safe place for them in heaven?

What I want to tell them is that their final destination is not heaven, but memory. And you can make of yourself a memory so profound that it transforms everything it touches.

My Evie screams, her face a mask of blood, and Tom looks even worse—all I can see through the red confusion of his face is a single fixed eye. I try to run, then, to separate them, but I am so awkward and pathetic I fall into the brush and tangle below them, where I sprawl and cry out in sorrow and agony.

Only then do they stop, and they come to me, my grandchildren, to stare down at me silently, their faces solemn. Tom has wiped much of the blood from his face to reveal the scratches there, the long lines and rough shapes like a child's awkward sketch.

This is my legacy, I think. These are the ones who will keep me alive, if only as a memory poorly understood, or perhaps as a ghost too troublesome to fully comprehend.

We try and we try but we cannot sculpt a shape out of what we've done in the world. Our hands cannot touch enough. Our words do not travel far enough. For all our constant waving we still cannot be picked out of a crowd.

My grandchildren approach for the end of my story. I can feel the terrible swiftness of my journey through their short lives. I become a voice clicking because it has run out of sound. I become a tongue silently flapping as it runs out of words. I become motionless as I can think of nowhere else to go.

I become the stone and the plank and the empty field. I am really quite something, the monster made in their image, until I am scattered, and forgotten.

CHAPTER SIX

STEPHEN GRAHAM JONES

They were eighty miles from campus, if miles still mattered.

It had been Dr. Ormon's idea.

Dr. Ormon was Crain's dissertation director. If dissertations still mattered.

They probably didn't.

Zombies. Zombies were the main thing that mattered these days.

Crain lowered his binoculars and turned to Dr. Ormon. "They're still following 95," he said.

"Path of least resistance," Dr. Ormon said back.

The clothes Crain and Dr. Ormon were wearing, they'd scavenged from a home that had had the door flapping, the owners surely scavenged on themselves, by now.

Dr. Ormon's hair was everywhere. The mad professor.

Crain was wearing a paisley skirt as a cape. His idea was to break up the human form, present a less enticing silhouette. Dr. Ormon said that was useless, that the zombies were obviously keying on vibrations in the ground; that was part of why they preferred the cities, and probably had a lot to do with why they were sticking mostly to the asphalt, now: they could hear better through it.

Crain respectfully disagreed. They didn't prefer the cities, it was just that the zombie population was mimicking preplague concentrations. Whether walking or just lying there, you would expect the dead to be pretty much where they died, wouldn't you?

Instead of entertaining the argument, Dr. Ormon ended it by studying the horde through their one pair of binoculars, and noting how, on asphalt, there was no cloud of dust to announce the zombies' presence.

Sophisticated hunting techniques? A rudimentary sense of self and other?

"Do *horde* and *herd* share a root?" Crain asked.

He'd been tossing it back and forth in his head since the last exit.

"We use *horde* for invaders," Dr. Ormon said, in his thinking-out-loud voice. "Mongols, for example."

"While *herd* is for ungulates, generally."

"Herd mentality," Dr. Ormon said, handing the binoculars back. "*Herd* suggests a lack of intelligence, of conscious thought, while *horde* brings with it aggressiveness. Or, at the very least, a danger to the society naming those invaders."

Then no, the two words only sounded similar.

Crain could accept this. Less because he had little invested in a shared etymology, more because the old patterns felt good, felt right: teacher, student, each working toward a common goal.

It was why they were here, eighty miles from campus.

There had been families to return to, of course, but, each being a commuter, their only course of action had been to hole up in the long basement under the anthropology building. The break-room refrigerator could only sustain two people for so long, though.

Crain tried to frame their situation as a return to more primitive times. What the plague was doing, it was resetting humanity. Hunting and gathering were the order of the day, now, not books or degrees on the wall. Survival had become hand-to-mouth again. There was to be no luxury time for a generation or two, there would be no specializing, no social stratification. The idea of a barter economy springing up anytime soon was a lark; tooth and nail was going to be the dominant mode for a while, and only the especially strong would make it through to breed, keep the species going.

Dr. Ormon had taken Crain's musings in as if they were idle ramblings, his eyes cast to the far wall, but then he had emerged from their latrine (the main office, ha) two days later with a decidedly intense cast to his features, his eyes nearly flashing with discovery.

"What?" Crain had said, suddenly sure a window had been breached.

"It does still matter," he said. "All our—this. Our work, our studies, the graduate degrees. It's been a manual, a guide, don't you see?"

Crain studied the map of Paleo-America tacked on the wall and waited.

This was Dr. Ormon's style.

"Your chapter two," Dr. Ormon went on. "That one footnote...it was in the formative part, the foundational prologue. The part I may have said felt straw-mannish."

"The name dropping," Crain filled in.

Now that it was the postapocalypse, they could call things what they were.

"About the available sources of protein."

Crain narrowed his eyes, tried to feel back through his dissertation.

Chapter two had been a textual wrestling match, no doubt.

It was where he had to address all the mutually exclusive claims for why the various and competing contenders for the title of *man* on the African savanna had stood up, gone bipedal.

Crain's thesis was that a lack of body hair, due to the forest's retreat, meant that the mothers were having to carry their infants now, instead of letting them hang on. They had no choice but to stand up.

Part and parcel with this was the supposition that early man—a grand word for a curious ape with new wrist and pelvis morphology—was a persistence hunter, running its prey down over miles and days. Running it to death.

A lifestyle like this would require the whole troop—the proper word for a group of apes was a *shrewdness*, but Crain had always thought that a poor association for gamblers and inventors—to be on the move. No posted guards, no beds to return to, thus no babysitters like jackals had, like meerkats had, like nearly all the other mammalian societies had.

This meant these early would-be humans had to take their babies with them, each chase. They had to hold them close as they ran. Hold them with hands they could no longer devote to running.

It was elegant.

As for how these mutant bipeds were able to persistence hunt so effectively, it was those unheralded, never-seen-before sweat glands, those cavernous lungs, the wide nostrils. What was nice for Crain's argument was that this was all work others had already done. All he had to do was, in chapter two, organize and cite, bow and nod.

But, this being anthropology, and the fossil record being not just sparse but cruelly random, alternate theories of course abounded.

One was the water-ape hypothesis: we got the protein to nourish our growing brains and lengthen our bones from shellfish. Droughts drove us to the shores of Africa, and what initially presented itself as a hurdle became a stepping stone.

Another theory was that our brains grew as self-defense mechanisms against the up-and-down climate. Instead of being allowed to specialize, we had to become generalists, opportunists, our brains having to constantly improvise and consider options, and, in doing so, that accidentally give birth to conceptual thought.

Another theory was that that source of brain-growing protein had been on the savanna all along.

Two days after Dr. Ormon's eureka moment, Crain shouldered open the door to their basement for the last time, and they went in search of a horde.

It didn't take long. As Crain had noted, the preapocalypse population of their part of New Hampshire had already been dense; it stood to reason that it still would be.

Dr. Ormon shrugged it off in that way he had that meant their sample was too limited in scope, that further studies would prove him out.

To his more immediate academic satisfaction, though—Crain could feel it wafting off him—when a horde presented itself on the second day (the smell), the two of them were able to hide not in a closet (vibration-conducting concrete foundation) or under a car (asphalt...), but in a shrub.

The comparatively loose soil saved them, evidently. Hid the pounding of their hearts.

Maybe.

The horde had definitely shuffled past, anyway, unaware of the meal waiting just within arm's reach.

Once it had been gone half a day, Crain and Dr. Ormon rose, scavenged the necessary clothes, and followed.

As Crain had footnoted in chapter two of his dissertation, and as Dr. Ormon had predicted in a way that brooked no objection, the top predators in any ecosystem, they pull all the meat from their prey and move on. Leaving niches to be filled by the more opportunistic.

In Africa, now, that was hyenas, using their powerful jaws to crack into gazelle bones for the marrow locked inside.

Six million years ago, man had been that hyena.

"Skulking at the fringes has its benefits," Dr. Ormon had said.

In this case, those fringes were just far enough behind the horde that the corpses it left behind wouldn't be too far into decay yet.

I-95 was littered with the dead. The dead-dead, Crain christened them. As opposed to the other kind. A field of skeletons scummed with meat and flies, the bones scraped by hundreds of teeth, then discarded.

Crain and Dr. Ormon had stood over corpse after corpse.

Theory was one thing. Practice was definitely another.

And—they talked about it, keeping their voices low—even the ones with enough meat hidden on a buttocks or calf to provide a meal of sorts, still, that meat was more than likely infected, wasn't it?

Their job as survivors, now, it was to go deeper than that infection.

This is how you prove a thesis.

Once it was dark enough that they could pretend not to see, not to know, they used a rock to crack open the tibia of what had once been a healthy man, by all indications. They covered his face with Crain's cape, and then covered it again, with a stray jacket.

"Modern sensibilities," Dr. Ormon narrated. "Our ancestors would have had no such qualms."

"If they were our ancestors," Crain said, something dark rising in his throat.

He tamped it down, just.

The marrow had the consistency of bubble gum meant for blowing bubbles, after you've chewed it through half the movie. There was a granular quality, a warmth, but no real cohesion anymore. Not quite a slurry or a paste. More like an oyster just starting to decompose.

Instead of plundering the bone for every thick, willing drop, they each took a meager mouthful, closed their eyes to swallow.

Neither threw it back up.

Late into the night, then, they talked about how, when man had been living on marrow like this—if he had been, Dr. Ormon allowed, as one meal doesn't an argument prove—this had of course been well before the discovery and implementation of fire. And fire of course was what made the meat they ate easier to digest. Thus their guts had been able to shrink.

"That's what I'm saying," Crain said, piggybacking on what was becoming Dr. Ormon's research. "Persistence hunters."

"You're still attached to the romantic image of them," Dr. Ormon said, studying something under his fingernail, the moonlight not quite playing along. "You have this image of a Zulu warrior, I think. Tall, lean. No, he's Ethiopian, isn't he? What was that Olympic runner's name, who ran barefoot?"

"A lot of them do," Crain said, staring off into the trees. "But can we digest this, do you think?" he said, touching his stomach to show.

"We have to," Dr. Ormon said.

And so they did. Always staying a half day behind the horde, tipping the leg bones up for longer and longer draughts. Drinking from the tanks of toilets they found along the way. Fashioning turbans from scraps.

The smarter among the crows began to follow them, to pick at these splintered-open bones.

"Niches and valleys," Dr. Ormon said, walking backward to watch the big black birds.

"Host-parasite," Crain said, watching ahead, through the binoculars.

"And what do you think we are?" Dr. Ormon called, gleefully.

Crain didn't answer.

⟨◦⟩

The zombies at the back of the horde—Crain still preferred *herd*, in the privacy of his head—he'd taken to naming them. The way a primatologist might name chimpanzees from the troop she was observing.

There was Draggy, and Face B. Gone, and Left Arm. Flannel and Blind Eye and Soup.

By the time they got to the horde's victims, there was rarely anything left but the bones with their precious marrow that Dr. Ormon so needed, to prove Crain's second chapter was in need of overhaul, if not reconception altogether.

That night, over a second tibia he'd taken to holding like a champagne flute—Dr. Ormon somehow affected a cigar with his ulnas—Crain posed the question to Dr. Ormon: "If a species, us, back then, adapts itself to persistence hunting—"

"If," Dr. Ormon emphasized.

"If *we* were adapting like that, then why didn't the prey one-up us?"

Silence from the other side of what would have been the campfire, if they allowed themselves fires. If they needed to cook their food.

These were primitive times, though.

In the darkness, Dr. Ormon's eyes sparked. "Gazelles that can sweat through their skin, you mean," he said. "The better to slip our grasp. The better to run for miles."

"The marathon gazelle," Crain added.

"Do we know they didn't?" Dr. Ormon asked, and somehow in the asking, in the tone, Crain sensed that Dr. Ormon was forever objecting not to him, Crain, or to whatever text he was engaging, whatever panel he was attending, but to someone in his life who called him by his first name, whatever that was. It was an unasked-for insight.

"Mr. Crain?" Dr. Ormon prompted.

This was the classroom again.

Crain nodded, caught up. "What if the gazelles of today are, in comparison to the gazelles of six million years ago, marathon gazelles, right?"

"Excellent."

Crain shook his head what he hoped was an imperceptible bit. "Do you think that's the case?" he asked. "Were we that persistent a hunter?"

"It's your thesis, Mr. Crain."

Crain gathered his words—he'd been running through this argument all day, and Dr. Ormon had stepped right into the snare—said, as if reluctantly, as if only just thinking of this, "You forget that our persistence had rewards, I think."

It had a surely-you-jest rhythm to it that Crain liked. It was like speaking Shakespeare off the cuff, by accident. By natural talent.

"Rewards?" Dr. Ormon asked.

"We persistence hunted until that gave us enough protein to—to develop the necessary brain capacity to communicate. And once we started to communicate, tricks of the trade started to get passed down. Thus was born culture. We graduated out of the gazelle race before the gazelles could adapt."

For long, delicious moments, there was silence from the other side of the noncampfire.

Has the student become the master? Crain said to himself.

Does the old silverback reconsider, in the face of youth?

He was so tired of eating stupid marrow.

Just when it seemed Dr. Ormon must have retreated into sleep, or the understandable pretense of it—this was a new world, requiring new and uncomfortable thinking—he chuckled in the darkness, Dr. Ormon.

Crain bored his eyes into him, not having to mask his contempt.

"Is that how man is, in your estimation?" Dr. Ormon asked. "Or, I should say, is that how man has proven himself to be, over his short tenure at the top of this food chain?"

Crain didn't say anything.

Dr. Ormon didn't need him to. "Say you're right, or in the general area of right. Persistence hunting gave us big brains, which gave us language, which gave us culture."

"Chapter six," Crain said. "When I got to it, I mean."

"Yes, yes, as is always the case. But humor me aloud, if you will. Consider this your defense. Our ancient little grandfathers, able to sweat, lungs made for distance, bipedalistic for efficiency, their infants cradled in arms, not having to grasp at hair like common chimpanzees—"

"I never—"

"Of course, of course. But allowing all this. If we were so successful, evolving in leaps and bounds. Tell me then, why are there still gazelles today? Agriculture and the fabled oryx are still thousands of generations away, here. What's to stop us from plundering the most available food source, unto exhaustion?"

Time slowed for Crain.

"You can't, you can't ever completely—"

"Eradicate a species?" Dr. Ormon completed, his tone carrying the obvious objection. "Not that I disagree about us moving on to other food sources eventually. But only when necessary, Mr. Crain. Only when pressed."

"Chapter six," Crain managed.

"Pardon?"

"I would have addressed this in chapter six."

"Good, good. Perhaps tomorrow you can detail how, for me, if you don't mind."

"Sure, sure," Crain said. And: "Should I just keep calling you doctor?"

Another chuckle, as if this question had already been anticipated as well.

"Able," Dr. Ormon said. "After my father."

"Able," Crain repeated. "Crain and Able."

"Close, close," Dr. Ormon said, dismissing this conversation, and then cleared his throat for sleep as was his practice, and, in his mind's eye, Crain could see the two of them from above, their backs to each other, one with his eyes shut contentedly, the other staring out into the night.

◄○►

Instead of outlining chapter six the next day, Crain kept the binoculars to his face.

If he remembered correctly, 95 crossed another major highway soon.

Would the herd split, wandering down separate ways, or would they mill around indecisively, until some Moses among them made the necessary decision?

It was going to be interesting.

He might write a paper on it, if papers still mattered.

And then they walked up on the most recent group of victims.

They'd been hiding in an RV, it looked like.

It was as good as anywhere, Crain supposed. No hiding place or perfect fortress really worked.

It looked like this group had finally made their big run for it. The RV's front tires were gummed up with zombies. They'd had no choice but to run, really. It was always all that was left, right at the end.

They made it about the usual distance: thirty feet.

They'd been gnawed down to the bone in places, of course.

"If they ever figure out there's marrow in there," Dr. Ormon said, lowering himself to a likely arm, its tendons bare to the sun for the first time.

"They don't have language," Crain said. "It would just be one knowing, not all of them."

"Assuming they speak as you and I do, of course," Dr. Ormon said, wrenching the forearm up.

The harsh creaking sound kickstarted another sound.

In a hiking backpack lying across the center stripe, there was what could only be an infant.

When it cried, it was definitely an infant.

Crain looked to Dr. Ormon, and Dr. Ormon looked ahead of them.

"It's right on the asphalt," Dr. Ormon said, his tone making this an emergency.

"They go by smell," Crain said. "Or sound. Just normal sound, not conductive."

"This is not an argument either of us wants to win," Dr. Ormon said, stepping neatly over to the backpack and leaning forward onto it with both knees.

The crying muffled.

"We're re-enactors," he said, while doing it, while killing this baby. "My brother-in-law was a Civil War soldier on weekends. But this, this is so much more important. An ancient script, you could say. One written by the environment, by biology. Inscribed in our very instincts."

Crain watched, and listened, his own plundered tibia held low along his right leg.

Soon enough, the cries ceased.

"You can test your theory about—about methods of child transport— later," Dr. Ormon said, rising up to drive his knees down one last, terrible time. For emphasis, it seemed.

"That was probably Adam," Crain said, looking down at the quiet lump in the backpack.

"If you believe the children's stories," Dr. Ormon said, casting around for his ulna. He claimed their flavor was slightly headier. That it had something to do with the pendulum motion they'd been subjected to, with a lifetime of walking. That that resulted in more nutrients getting trapped in the lower arms.

Crain didn't care.

He was still staring at the raspy blue fabric of the backpack, and then he looked up the road as well.

Left Arm was watching them.

He'd come back. The sound had traveled along the asphalt ribbon of 95 and found him, bringing up the rear of the horde.

It hadn't been scent or pressure waves in the air, anyway; the wind was in Crain's face, was lifting his ragged cape behind him.

So Ormon was right.

Crain looked across to him, one foot planted on a dead wrist, his chicken elbows cocked back, trying to disinter the ulna from its double-helix soul mate of a radius.

"You're right," Crain said across to him.

Dr. Ormon raised his face, waited for the punch line.

"About how they hear," Crain said, pointing with his chin down 95.

Left Arm was still two or three car lengths from Dr. Ormon.

Dr. Ormon flinched back, tangled in the legs of the woman whose marrow he was plundering.

"I got it," Crain said, and stepped forward, past Dr. Ormon, and, when he was close enough, timing it after a clumsy left-arm swipe, he planted the sole of his boot in Left Arm's chest, sent him tumbling, then stepped in neatly to finish it with the tibia as hammer, as axe, as—as tool.

It made his arm feel floppy and chimp-like, as if unaccustomed, as if only using this long bone from sudden, forgettable inspiration.

"Not very persistent after all, are they?" Dr. Ormon said from his corpse.

Crain looked back to Dr. Ormon about this, and then down to Left Arm.

Right beside him was one of the plundered, the dead, the feasted on. The dead-dead.

Crain lowered himself to this clean corpse, to salvage what he could—pockets first, then the bones, for marrow—and found himself holding Left Arm's left arm. Just to move it away, off.

But then he pulled on it instead.

Because zombies are already decomposing, it came off at the shoulder.

Crain studied it, studied it—*not very persistent, are they?*—and finally nodded to himself, reached through the rancid meat for the bone, liberated it.

The brittle end snapped off under his thumb like a Pez dispenser.

There was still marrow inside.

Crain considered it, considered it *(not very persistent, are they?)*, finally nodded to himself.

"You still into ulnas?" he called across to Dr. Ormon.

"Give them a chance," Dr. Ormon said back, not bothering to turn around.

"Here," Crain said, walking Left Arm's ulna across, careful not to tip the syrupy marrow out. "I broke it already, sorry."

"I really shouldn't," Dr. Ormon said, smiling, taking the ulna between his fingers. "Male or female?" he asked.

He was keeping track. Like it mattered.

"Male," Crain said, loving the truth of it, and watched Dr. Ormon tip the broken end of the bone into his mouth.

Dr. Ormon had already swallowed by the time the taste registered.

He fell to his knees coughing, trying to puke.

Crain pinched his pants up at the thighs to squat down, say it right to Dr. Ormon: "We're not bone suckers, Doctor. We're *persistence* hunters. I think you'll come to agree with me here shortly."

Dr. Ormon tried to respond but could only sputter and gag, swing his arm back and forth for Crain's pants leg.

He was already changing, then.

"This can be chapter six," Crain said. "That sound good to you, sir?"

Dr. Ormon's head bobbed with his regurgitation efforts. With his transformation. With his inevitable acquiescence. Not just to the virus, but to the strength of Crain's argument.

Chapter six, then. It was going to be perfect.

Crain stood, turned to survey his options.

Eighty miles behind him was the campus, with all its vending machines, all its dorm-room toilets to drink from.

All its concrete and asphalt, stretched tight like an eardrum.

The woods, then. Back to the trees.

The soft earth there wouldn't transmit his location to the herd. To any stragglers.

In this particular re-enactment, Crain was to be prey, he knew.

Behind him, the all-too-human horde, exhausting the landscape.

This was his thesis in action. His final proof.

He smiled to himself, if smiles still mattered, and was flipping a coin in his head—*trees to the east, or trees to the west?*—when the blue backpack pulled his attention over.

The lump was gently kicking. A small fist, pushing against the fabric. The baby, more resilient than Dr. Ormon had thought. More human.

Crain turned to Dr. Ormon, already trying to figure out how to stand again, into this new world.

Maybe fifteen seconds, then. Ten to be safe.

Crain ran to the backpack, grabbed the infant up.

A girl.

"Oh, *Eve*," he said, and pulled her to his chest, one of her arms more floppy than it should have been, the ribs on that side dangerously concave. But the other lung was working fine. She mewled, was building to a scream.

Crain chose the side of the road where the trees were closest.

Crossing the ditch, the infant held tight in both arms, because he didn't have close to enough body hair for her to clutch on to with her tiny right hand, Crain shook his head to clear the sweat from his eyes.

The gazelles *did* learn to perspire, he said in his head to Dr. Ormon, shuffling into place behind him, and the race, it was on, it had never really ended, not since those first delicate steps, six million years ago.

IN A CAVERN, IN A CANYON

LAIRD BARRON

Husband number one fondly referred to me as the Good Samaritan. Anything from a kid lost in the neighborhood to a countywide search-and-rescue effort, I got involved. If we drove past a fender-bender, I had to stop and lend a hand or snap a few pictures, maybe do a walk-around of the scene. A major crash? Forget about it—I'd haunt the site until the cows came home or the cops shooed me away. Took the better part of a decade for the light bulb to flash over my hubby's bald head. He realized I wasn't a Samaritan so much as a fetishist. Wore him down in the end and he bailed. I'm still melancholy over that one.

Lucky for him he didn't suffer through my stint with the Park Service in Alaska. After college and the first kid, I finagled my way onto the government payroll and volunteered for every missing person, lost climber, downed plane, or wrecked boat scenario. I hiked and camped on the side. Left my compass and maps at home. I wanted to disappear. Longest I managed was four days. The feds were suspicious enough to send me to a shrink who knew his business. The boys upstairs gave me a generous severance check and said to not let the door hit me in the ass on the way out. Basically the beginning of a long downward slide in my life.

Husband number three divorced me for my fifty-fourth birthday. I pawned everything that wouldn't fit into a van and drove from Ohio back home to

Alaska. I rented a doublewide at the Cottonwood Point Trailer Park near Moose Pass, two miles along the bucolic and winding Seward Highway from Cassie, my youngest daughter.

A spruce forest crowds the back door. Moose nibble the rhododendron hedging the yard. Most folks tuck in for the night by the time Colbert is delivering his monologue.

Cassie drops off my infant granddaughter, Vera, two or three times a week or whenever she can't find a sitter. Single and working two jobs (hardware cashier by day, graveyard security at the Port of Seward Wednesday and Friday), Cassie avoided the inevitability of divorce by not getting married in the first place. She kept the dumb, virile fisherman who knocked her up as baby-daddy and strictly part time squeeze. Wish I'd thought of that. Once I realized that my nanny gig was a regular thing, I ordered a crib and inveigled the handsome (and generally drunken, alas) fellow at 213 to set it up in my bedroom.

On the nanny evenings, I feed Vera her bottle and watch westerns on cable. "Get you started right," I say to her as Bronson ventilates Fonda beneath a glaring sun, or when a cowboy rides into the red-and-gold distance as the credits roll. She'll be a tomboy like her gram if I have any influence. The classic stars were my heroes once upon a time—Stewart, Van Cleef, Wayne, and Marvin. During my youth, I utterly revered Eastwood. I crushed big time on The Man with No Name and Dirty Harry. Kept a poster from *The Good, the Bad and the Ugly* on my bedroom wall. So young, both of us. So innocent. Except for the shooting and murdering, and my lustful thoughts, but you know.

Around midnight, I wake from a nap on the couch to Vera's plaintive cry. She's in the bedroom crib, awake and pissed for her bottle. The last act of *High Plains Drifter* plays in scratchy 1970s Technicolor. It's the part where the Stranger finally gets around to exacting righteous vengeance. Doesn't matter that I've missed two rapes, a horsewhipping, Lago painted red and renamed HELL . . . all those images are imprinted upon my hindbrain. I get the impression the scenes are *always* rolling down there against the screen of my subconscious.

I am depressed to recognize a cold fact in this instant. The love affair with bad boy Clint ended years and years ago, even if I haven't fully accepted the reality. Eyes gummed with sleep, I sit for a few seconds, mesmerized by the stricken faces of the townspeople who are caught between a vicious outlaw gang and a stranger hell-bent on retribution. The Stranger's whip slithers through the saloon window and garrotes an outlaw. I've watched that scene on a dozen occasions. My hands shake and I can't zap it with the remote fast enough.

That solves one problem. I take the formula from the fridge and pop it into the fancy warmer Cassie obtained during a clearance sale. The LED numerals are counting down to nothing when it occurs to me that I don't watch the baby on Sundays.

◄○►

The night in 1977 that my father disappeared, he, Uncle Ned, and I drove north along Midnight Road, searching for Tony Orlando. Dad crept the Fleetwood at a walking pace. My younger siblings, Doug, Shauna, and Artemis, remained at home. Doug was ostensibly keeping an eye on our invalid grandmother, but I figured he was probably glued to the television with the others. That autumn sticks in my memory like mud to a Wellington. We were sixteen, fourteen, eleven, and ten. Babes in the wilderness.

Uncle Ned and I took turns yelling out the window. Whenever Orlando pulled this stunt, Dad swore it would be the last expedition he mounted to retrieve the "damned mutt." I guess he really meant it.

Middle-school classmate Nancy Albrecht once asked me what the hell kind of name was that for a dog, and I said Mom and Dad screwed on the second date to "Halfway to Paradise," and if you laugh I'll smack your teeth down your throat. I have a few scars on my knuckles, for damn sure.

Way back then, we lived in Eagle Talon, Alaska, an isolated port about seventy miles southwest of Anchorage. Cruise ships bloated the town with tourists during spring, and it dried up to around three hundred resident souls come autumn.

Eastern settlers had carved a hamlet from wilderness during the 1920s; plunked it down in a forgotten vale populated by eagles, bears, drunk Teamsters and drunker fishermen. Mountains and dense forest on three sides formed a deep-water harbor. The channel curved around the flank of Eagle Mountain and eventually let into Prince William Sound. Roads were gravel or dirt. We had the cruise ships and barges. We also had the railroad. You couldn't make a move without stepping in seagull shit. Most of us townies lived in a fourteen-story apartment complex called the Frazier Estate. We kids shortened it to Fate. Terra incognita began where the sodium lamplight grew fuzzy. At night, wolves howled in the nearby hills. Definitely not the dream hometown of a sixteen-year-old girl. As a grown woman, I recall it with a bittersweet fondness.

Upon commencing the hunt for Orlando, whom my little brother Doug had stupidly set free from the leash only to watch in mortification as the dog trotted into the sunset, tail furled with rebellious intent, Dad faced a choice—head west along the road, or troll the beach where the family pet sometimes mined for rotten salmon carcasses. We picked the road because it wound into the woods and our shepherd-husky mix hankered after the red squirrels that swarmed during the fall. Dad didn't want to walk if he could avoid it. "Marched goddamned plenty in the Corps," he said. It had required a major effort for him to descend to the parking garage and get the wagon started and pointed in the general direction of our search route. Two bad knees, pain pills for said knees, and a half-pack-a-day habit had all but done him in.

Too bad for Uncle Ned and me, Midnight Road petered out in the foothills. Moose trails went every which way from the little clearing where we'd parked next to an abandoned Winnebago with a raggedy tarp covering the front end and black garbage bags over the windows. Hobos and druggies occasionally used the Winnebago as a fort until Sheriff Lockhart came along to roust them. "Goddamned railroad," Dad would say, despite the fact that if not for the railroad (for which he performed part-time labor to supplement his military checks) and the cruise ships and barges, there wouldn't be any call for Eagle Talon whatsoever.

Uncle Ned lifted himself from the back seat and accompanied me as I shined the flashlight and hollered for Orlando. Dad remained in the station wagon with the engine running and the lights on. He honked the horn every couple of minutes.

"He's gonna keep doing that, huh?" Uncle Ned wasn't exactly addressing me, more like an actor musing to himself on the stage. "Just gonna keep leanin' on that horn every ten seconds—"

The horn blared again. Farther off and dim—we'd come a ways already. Birch and alder were broken by stands of furry black spruce that muffled sounds from the outside world. The black, green, and gray webbing is basically the Spanish moss of the Arctic. Uncle Ned chuckled and shook his head. Two years Dad's junior and a major league stoner, *he'd* managed to keep it together when it counted. He taught me how to tie a knot, paddle a canoe, and gave me a lifetime supply of dirty jokes. He'd also explained that contrary to Dad's Cro-Magnon take on teenage dating, boys were okay to fool around with so long as I ducked the bad ones and avoided getting knocked up. *Which ones were bad?* I wondered. Most of them, according to the Book of Ned, but keep it to fooling around and all would be well. He also clued me in to the fact that Dad's vow to blast any would-be suitor's pecker off with his twelve-gauge was an idle threat. My old man couldn't shoot worth spit even when sober.

The trail forked. One path climbed into the hills where the undergrowth thinned. The other path curved deeper into the creepy spruce where somebody had strung blue reflective tape among the branches—a haphazard mess like the time Dad got lit up and tried to decorate the Christmas tree.

"Let's not go in there," Uncle Ned said. Ominous, although not entirely unusual as he often said that kind of thing with a similar, laconic dryness. *That bar looks rough, let's try the next one over. That woman looks like my ex-wife, I'm not gonna dance with her, uh-uh. That box has got to be heavy. Let's get a beer and think on it.*

"Maybe he's at the beach rolling in crap," I said. Orlando loved bear turds and rotten salmon guts with a true passion. There'd be plenty of both near the big water, and as I squinted into the forbidding shadows, I increasingly wished we'd driven there instead.

Uncle Ned pulled his coat tighter and lit a cigarette. The air had dampened. I yelled "Orlando!" a few more times. Then we stood there for a while in the silence. It was like listening through the lid of a coffin. Dad had stopped leaning on the horn. The woodland critters weren't making their usual fuss. Clouds drifted in and the darkness was so complete it wrapped us in a cocoon. "Think Orlando's at the beach?" I said.

"Well, I dunno. He ain't here."

"Orlando, you stupid jerk!" I shouted to the night in general.

"Let's boogie," Uncle Ned said. The cherry of his cigarette floated in mid-air and gave his narrowed eyes a feral glint. Like Dad, he was middling tall and rangy. Sharp-featured and often wry. He turned and moved the way we'd come, head lowered, trailing a streamer of Pall Mall smoke. Typical of my uncle. Once he made a decision, he acted.

"Damn it, Orlando." I gave up and followed, sick to my gut with worry.

Fool dog would be the death of me, or so I suspected. He'd tangled with a porcupine the summer before and I'd spent hours picking quills from his swollen snout because Dad refused to take him in to see Doc Green. There were worse things than porcupines in these woods—black bears, angry moose, wolves—and I feared my precious idiot would run into one of them.

Halfway back to the car, I glimpsed a patch of white to my left amidst the heavy brush. I took it for a birch stump with holes rotted into the heartwood. No, it was a man lying on his side, matted black hair framing his pale face. By pale, I mean bone-white and bloodless. The face you see on the corpse of an outlaw in those old-timey Wild West photographs.

"Help me," he whispered.

I trained my light on the injured man; he had to be hurt because of the limp, contorted angle of his body, his shocking paleness. He seemed familiar. The lamp beam broke around his body like a stream splits around a large stone. The shadows turned slowly, fracturing and changing him. He might've been weirdo Floyd who swept the Caribou after last call, or that degenerate trapper, Bob-something, who lived in a shack in the hills with a bunch of stuffed moose heads and mangy beaver hides. Or it might've been as I first thought—a tree stump lent a man's shape by my lying eyes. The more I stared, the less certain I became that it was a person at all.

Except I'd heard him speak, raspy and high-pitched from pain; almost a falsetto.

Twenty-five feet, give or take, between me and the stranger. I didn't see his arm move. Move it did, however. The shadows shifted again and his hand grasped futilely, thin and gnarled as a tree branch. His misery radiated into me, caused my eyes to well with tears of empathy. I felt terrible, just terrible, I wanted to mother him, and took a step toward him.

"Hortense. Come here." Uncle Ned said my name the way Dad described talking to his wounded buddies in 'Nam. The ones who'd gotten hit by a grenade or a stray bullet. Quiet, calm, and reassuring was the ticket—and I bet his tone would've worked its magic if my insides had happened to be splashed on the ground and the angels were singing me home. In this case, Uncle Ned's unnatural calmness scared me, woke me from a dream where I heroically tended a hapless stranger, got a parade and a key to the village, my father's grudging approval.

"Hortense, please."

"There's a guy in the bushes," I said. "I think he's hurt."

Uncle Ned grabbed my hand like he used to when I was a little girl, and towed me along at a brisk pace. "Naw, kid. That's a tree stump. I saw it when we went past earlier. Keep movin'."

I didn't ask why we were in such a hurry. It worried me how easy it seemed for him and Dad to slip into warrior mode at the drop of a hat. He muttered something about branches snapping and that black bears roamed the area as they fattened up for winter and he regretted leaving his guns at his house. *House* is sort of a grand term; Uncle Ned lived in a mobile home on the edge of the village. The Estate didn't appeal to his loner sensibilities.

We got to walking so fast along that narrow trail that I twisted my ankle on a root and nearly went for a header. Uncle Ned didn't miss a beat. He took most of my weight upon his shoulder. Pretty much dragged me back to the Fleetwood. The engine ran and the driver side door was ajar. I assumed Dad had gone behind a tree to take a leak. As the minutes passed and we called for him, I began to understand that he'd left. Those were the days when men abandoned their families by saying they needed to grab a pack of cigarettes and beating it for the high timber. He'd threatened to do it during his frequent arguments with Mom. She'd beaten him to the punch and jumped ship with a traveling salesman, leaving us to fend for ourselves. Maybe, just maybe, it was Dad's turn to bail on us kids.

Meanwhile, Orlando had jumped in through the open door and curled into a ball in the passenger seat. Leaves, twigs, and dirt plastered him. A pig digging for China wouldn't have been any filthier. Damned old dog pretended to sleep. His thumping tail gave away the show, though.

Uncle Ned rousted him and tried to put him on Dad's trail. Nothing doing. Orlando whined and hung his head. He refused to budge despite Uncle Ned's exhortations. Finally, the dog yelped and scrambled back into the car, trailing a stream of piss. That was our cue to depart.

⏴⏵

Uncle Ned drove back to the Frazier Estate. He called Deputy Clausen (everybody called him Claws) and explained the situation. Claws agreed to gather a few men and do a walkthrough of the area. He theorized that Dad had gotten drunk and wandered into the hills and collapsed somewhere. Such events weren't rare.

Meanwhile, I checked in on Grandma, who'd occupied the master bedroom since she'd suffered the aneurysm. Next, I herded Orlando into the bathroom and soaked him in the tub. I was really hurting by then.

When I thanked Uncle Ned, he nodded curtly and avoided meeting my eye. "Lock the door," he said.

"Why? The JWs aren't allowed out of the compound after dark." Whenever I got scared, I cracked wise.

"Don't be a smartass. Lock the fuckin' door."

"Something fishy in Denmark," I said to Orlando, who leaned against my leg as I threw the deadbolt. Mrs. Wells had assigned *Hamlet*, *Julius Caesar*, and *Titus Andronicus* for summer reading. "And it's the Ides of August, too."

My brothers and sister sprawled in the living room front of the TV, watching a vampire flick. Christopher Lee wordlessly seduced a buxom chick who was practically falling out of her peasant blouse. Lee angled for a bite. Then he saw, nestled in the woman's cleavage, the teeny elegant crucifix her archaeologist boyfriend had given her for luck. Lee's eyes went buggy with rage and fear. The vampire equivalent to blue balls, I guess. I took over Dad's La-Z-Boy and kicked back with a bottle of Coke (the last one, as noted by the venomous glares of my siblings) and a bag of ice on my puffy ankle.

The movie ended and I clapped my hands and sent the kids packing. At three bedrooms, our apartment qualified as an imperial suite. Poor Dad sacked out on the couch. Doug and Artemis shared the smallest, crappiest room. I bunked with Shauna, the princess of jibber-jabber. She loved and feared me and that made tight quarters a bit easier because she knew I'd sock her in the arm if she sassed me too much or pestered me with one too many goober questions. Often, she'd natter on while I piped Fleetwood Mac and Led Zeppelin through a set of gigantic yellow earphones. That self-isolation spared us a few violent and teary scenes, I'm sure.

Amid the grumbles and the rush for the toilet, I almost confessed the weird events of the evening to Doug. My kid brother had an open mind when it came to the unknown. He wouldn't necessarily laugh me out of the room without giving the matter some real thought. Instead, I smacked the back of his head and told him not to be such a dumbass with Orlando. Nobody remarked on Dad's absence. I'm sure they figured he'd pitched camp at the Caribou like he did so many nights. Later, I lay awake and listened to my siblings snore. Orlando whined as he dreamed of the chase, or of being chased.

From the bedroom, Gram said in a fragile, sing-song tone, "In a cavern, in a canyon, excavatin' for a mine, dwelt a miner forty-niner and his daughter Clementine. In a cavern in a canyon. In a cavern, in a canyon. In a cavern, in a canyon. Clementine, Clementine. Clementine? Clementine?"

⟶

Of the four Shaw siblings I was the eldest, tallest, *and* surliest.

According to Mom, Dad had desperately wanted a boy for his firstborn. He descended from a lineage that adhered to a pseudo-medieval mindset. The noble chauvinist, the virtuous warrior, the honorable fighter of rearguard actions. Quaint when viewed through a historical lens; a real pain in the ass in the modern world.

I was a disappointment. As a daughter, what else could I be? He got used to it. The Shaws have a long, long history of losing. We own that shit. *Go down fighting* would've been our family motto, with a snake biting the heel that crushed its skull as our crest. As some consolation, I was always a tomboy and tougher than either of my brothers—a heap tougher than most of the boys in our hick town, and tougher than at least a few of the grown men. Toughness isn't always measured by how hard you punch. Sometimes, most of the time, it's simply the set of a girl's jaw. I shot my mouth off with the best of them. If nothing else, I dutifully struck at the heels of my oppressors. Know where I got this grit? Sure as hell not from Dad. Oh, yeah, he threw a nasty left hook, and he'd scragged a few guys in the wars. But until Mom had flown the coop she ruled our roost with an iron fist that would've made Khrushchev think twice before crossing her. Yep, the meanness in my soul is pure-D Mom.

Dad had all the homespun apothegms.

He often said, *Never try to beat a man at what he does.* What Dad did best was drink. He treated it as a competitive event. In addition to chugging Molson Export, Wild Turkey, and Absolut, Dad also smoked the hell out of cannabis whenever he could get his hands on some. He preferred the heavy-hitting bud from Mexico courtesy of Uncle Ned. I got my hands on a bag those old boys stashed in a rolled-up sock in a number-ten coffee can. That stuff sent you, all right. Although, judging by the wildness of Dad's eyes, the way they started and stared at the corners of the room after he'd had a few hits, his destination was way different than mine.

Even so, the Acapulco Gold gave me a peek through the keyhole into

Dad's soul in a way booze couldn't. Some blood memory got activated. It might've been our sole point of commonality. He would've beaten me to a pulp if he'd known. For my own good, natch.

Main thing I took from growing up the daughter of an alcoholic? Lots of notions compete for the top spot—the easiest way to get vomit and blood out of fabric, the best apologies, the precise amount of heed to pay a drunken diatribe, when to duck flung bottles, how to balance a checkbook and cook a family meal between homework, dog-walking, and giving sponge baths to Gram. But above all, my essential takeaway was that I'd never go down the rabbit hole to an eternal happy hour. I indulged in a beer here and there, toked some Mary Jane to reward myself for serving as Mom, Dad, Chief Cook and Bottle Washer pro-tem. Nothing heavy, though. I resolved to leave the heavy lifting to Dad, Uncle Ned, and their buddies at the Caribou Tavern.

Randal Shaw retired from the USMC in 1974 after twenty years of active service. Retirement didn't agree with him. To wit: the beer, bourbon, and weed, and the sullen hurling of empties. It didn't agree with Mom either, obviously. My grandmother, Harriet Shaw, suffered a brain aneurysm that very autumn. Granddad passed away the previous winter and Gram moved into our apartment. By day, she slumped in a special medical recliner we bought from the Eagle Talon Emergency Trauma Center. Vivian from upstairs sat with her while I was at school. Gram's awareness came and went like a bad radio signal. Sometimes she'd make a feeble attempt to play cards with Vivian. Occasionally, she asked about my grades and what cute boys I'd met, or she'd watch TV and chuckle at the soaps in that rueful way she laughed at so many ridiculous things. The clarity became rare. Usually she stared out the window at the harbor or at the framed Georgia O'Keeffe knockoff print of a sunflower above the dresser. Hours passed and we'd shoo away the mosquitos while she tunelessly hummed "In a cavern, in a canyon, excavatin' for a mine" on a loop. There may as well have been a VACANCY sign blinking above her head.

After school, and twice daily on weekends, Doug helped bundle Gram into the crappy fold-up chair and I pushed her around the village; took her down to the wharf to watch the seagulls, or parked her in front of the general store while I bought Dad a pack of smokes (and another for myself). By night, Dad or I pushed the button and let the air out and she lay with her eyes fixed on the dented ceiling of the bedroom. She'd sigh heavily and say,

"Nighty-night, nighty-night," like a parrot. It shames me to remember her that way. But then, most of my childhood is a black hole.

⤙

The search party found neither hide nor hair of Dad. Deputy Clausen liked Uncle Ned well enough and agreed to do a bigger sweep in the afternoon. The deputy wasn't enthused. Old Harmon Snodgrass, a trapper from Kobuk, isolated footprints in the soft dirt along the edge of the road. The tracks matched Dad's boots and were headed toward town. Snodgrass lost them after a couple hundred yards.

In Deputy Clausen's professional opinion, Randal Shaw had doubled back and flown the coop to parts unknown, as a certain kind of man is wont to do when the going gets tough. Uncle Ned socked him (the Shaw answer to critics) and Claws would've had his ass in a cell for a good long time, except Stu Herring, the mayor of our tiny burg, and Kyle Lomax were on hand to break up the festivities and soothe bruised egos. Herring sent Uncle Ned home with a *go and sin no more* scowl.

"How's Mom?" Uncle Ned stared at Gram staring at a spot on the wall. He sipped the vilest black coffee on the face of the earth. My specialty. I'd almost tripped over him in the hallway on my way to take Orlando for his morning stroll. He'd spent the latter portion of the night curled near our door, a combat knife in his fist. Normally, one might consider that loony behavior. You had to know Uncle Ned.

"She's groovy, as ever. Why are you lurking?" The others were still zonked, thank God. I hadn't an inkling of how to break the news of Dad's defection to them. I packed more ice onto my ankle. My foot had swollen to the point where it wouldn't fit into my sneaker. It really and truly hurt. "Ow."

"Let's go. Hospital time." He stood abruptly and went in and woke Doug, told him, "Drop your cock and grab your socks. You're man of the house for an hour. Orlando needs a walk—for the love of God, keep him on a leash, will ya?" Then he nabbed Dad's keys and took me straightaway to the Eagle Clinic. Mrs. Cooper, a geriatric hypochondriac, saw the RN, Sally Mackey, ahead of us and we knew from experience that it would be a hell of a wait. So Uncle Ned and I settled into hard plastic waiting room chairs. He lit a cigarette, and another for me, and said, "Okay, I got a story. Don't tell your old man I told you, or he'll kick my ass and then I'll kick yours. Yeah?"

I figured it would be a story of his hippie escapades or some raunchy bullshit Dad got up to in Vietnam. A tale to cheer me up and take my mind off my troubles. Uh-uh. He surprised me by talking about the Good Friday Earthquake of '64. "You were, what? Two, three? You guys lived in that trailer park in Anchorage. The quake hits and your Dad's been shipped to 'Nam. My job was to look over you and your mom. Meanwhile, I'm visiting a little honey out in the Valley. Girl had a cabin on a lake. We just came in off the ice for a mug of hot cocoa and BOOM! Looked like dynamite churned up the bottom muck. Shit flew off the shelves, the earth moved in waves like the sea. Spruce trees bent all the way over and slapped their tops on the ground. Sounded like a train runnin' through the living room. Tried callin' your mom, but the phone lines were down.

"I jumped in my truck and headed for Anchorage. Got part way there and had to stop. Highway was too fucked up to drive on. Pavement cracked open, bridges collapsed. I got stuck in a traffic jam on the Flats. Some cars were squashed under a collapsed overpass and a half-dozen more kind a piled on. It was nine or ten at night and pitch black. Accidents everywhere. The temperature dropped below freezing. Road flares and headlights and flashing hazards made the scene extra spooky. I could taste hysteria in the air. Me and a couple of Hells Angels from Wasilla got together and made sure people weren't trapped or hurt too bad. Then we started pushing cars off the road to get ready for the emergency crews.

"We were taking a smoke break when one of the bikers said to shut up a minute. A big, pot-bellied Viking, at least twice the size of me and his younger pal. Fuckin' enormous. He cocked his head and asked us if we'd heard it too—somebody moaning for help down on the flats. He didn't hang around for an answer. Hopped over the guardrail and was gone. Man on a mission. Guy didn't come back after a few minutes. Me and the younger biker climbed down the embankment and went into the pucker-brush. Shouted ourselves hoarse and not a damned reply. Mist was oozin' off the water and this weird, low tide reek hit me. A cross between green gas from inside a blown moose carcass and somethin' sweet, like fireweed. I heard a noise, reminded me of water and air bubbles gurglin' through a hose. Grace a God I happened to shine my light on a boot stickin' out a the scrub. The skinny biker yelled his buddy's name and ran over there."

Uncle Ned had gotten worked up during the narration of his story. He lit another cigarette and paced to the coffee machine and back. Bernice Monson, the receptionist, glared over her glasses. She didn't say anything. In '77 most folks kept their mouths shut when confronted by foamy Vietnam vets. Bernice, like everybody else, assumed Uncle Ned did a jungle tour as a government employee. He certainly resembled the part with his haggard expression, brooding demeanor, and a partialness for camouflage pants. Truth was, while many young men were blasting away at each other in Southeast Asia, he'd backpacked across Canada, Europe, and Mexico. Or, *went humping foreign broads and scrawling doggerel,* as my dad put it.

Uncle Ned's eyes were red as a cockscomb. He slapped the coffee machine. "I didn't have a perfect position and my light was weak, but I saw plenty. The Viking laid on top of somebody. This somebody was super skinny and super pale. Lots of wild hair. Their arms and legs were tangled so's you couldn't make sense of what was goin' on. I thought he had him a woman there in the weeds and they was fuckin'. Their faces were stuck together. The young biker leaned over his buddy and then yelped and stumbled backward. The skinny, pale one shot out from under the Viking and into the darkness. Didn't stand, didn't crouch, didn't even flip over—know how a mechanic rolls from under a car on his board? Kinda that way, except jittery. Moved like an insect scuttling for cover, best I can describe it. A couple seconds later, the huge biker shuddered and went belly-crawling after the skinny fellow. What I thought I was seeing him do, anyhow. His arms and legs flopped, although his head never lifted, not completely. He just skidded away, Superman style, his face planted in the dirt.

"Meanwhile, the young biker hauled ass toward the road, shriekin' the whole way. My flashlight died. I stood there, in the dark, heart poundin', scared shitless, tryin' to get my brain out a neutral. I wanted to split, hell yeah. No fuckin' way I was gonna tramp around on those flats by myself. I'm a hunter, though. Those instincts kicked in and I decided to play it cool. Your dad always pegged me for a peacenik hippie because I didn't do 'Nam. I'm smarter, is the thing. Got a knife in my pocket and half the time I'm packin' heat too. Had me skinning knife, and lemme say, I kept it handy as I felt my way through the bushes and the brambles. Got most of the way to where I could see the lights of the cars on the road. Somebody whispered, "Help me." Real close and on my flank. Scared me, sure. I probably jumped three feet straight up. And yet, it was the saddest voice I can remember. Woeful, like a lost child, or a wounded woman, or a fawn, or some combination of those cries.

"I might a turned around and walked into the night, except a state trooper hit me with a light. He'd come over the hill lookin' after the biker went bugshit. I think the cop thought the three of us were involved in a drug deal. He sure as hell didn't give a lick about a missing Hells Angel. He led me back to the clusterfuck on the highway and I spent the rest of the night shivering in my car while the bulldozers and dump trucks did their work." He punched the coffee machine.

"Easy, killer!" I said and gave an apologetic smile to the increasingly agitated Bernice. I patted the seat next to me until he came over and sat. "What happened to the biker? The big guy."

Uncle Ned had sliced his knuckles. He clenched his fist and watched the blood drip onto the tiles. "Cops found him that summer in the inlet. Not enough left for an autopsy. The current and the fish had taken him apart. Accidental death, they decided. I saw the younger biker at the Gold Digger. Must a been five or six years after the Good Friday Quake. He acted like he'd forgotten what happened to his partner until I bought him the fifth or sixth tequila. *He* got a real close look at what happened. Said that to him, the gurglin' was more of a slurpin'. An animal lappin' up a gory supper. Then he looked me in the eye and said his buddy got snatched into the darkness by his own guts. They were comin' out a his mouth and whatever it was out there gathered' em up and reeled him in."

"Holy shit, Uncle Ned." Goose pimples covered my arms. "That's nuts. Who do you think was out there?"

"The boogeyman. Whatever it is that kids think is hidin' under their bed."

"You tell Dad? Probably not, huh? He's a stick in the mud. He'd never buy it."

"Well, you don't either. Guess that makes you a stick in the mud too."

"The apple, the tree, gravity . . ."

"Maybe you'd be surprised what your old man knows." Uncle Ned's expression was shrewd. "I been all over this planet. Between '66 and '74, I roamed. Passed the peace pipe with the Lakota; ate peyote with the Mexicans; drank wine with the Italians; and smoked excellent bud with a whole lot of other folks. I get bombed enough, or stoned enough, I ask if anybody else has heard of the Help Me Monster. What I call it. The Help Me Monster."

The description evoked images of Sesame Street and plush toys dancing on wires. "Grover the Psycho Killer!" I said, hoping he'd at least crack a smile. I also hoped my uncle hadn't gone around the bend.

He didn't smile. We sat there in one of those long, awkward silences while Bernice coughed her annoyance and shuffled papers. I was relieved when Sally Mackey finally stuck her head into the room and called my name.

The nurse wanted to send me to Anchorage for X-rays. No way would Dad authorize that expense. No veterinarians and no doctors; those were ironclad rules. When he discovered Uncle Ned took me to the clinic, he'd surely blow his top. I wheedled a bottle of prescription-strength aspirin, and a set of cheapo crutches on the house, and called it square. A mild ankle sprain meant I'd be on the crutches for days. I added it to the tab of Shaw family dues.

Dad never came home. I cried, the kids cried. Bit by bit, we moved on. Some of us more than others.

⟶

I won't bore you with the nightmares that got worse and worse with time. You can draw your own conclusions. That strange figure in the woods, Dad's vanishing act, and Uncle Ned's horrifying tale coalesced into a witch's brew that beguiled me and became a serious obsession.

Life is messy and it's mysterious. Had my father walked away from his family or had he been taken? If the latter, then why Dad and not me or Uncle Ned? I didn't crack the case, didn't get any sense of closure. No medicine man or antiquarian popped up to give me the scoop on some ancient enemy that dwells in the shadows and dines upon the blood and innards of good Samaritans and hapless passersby.

Closest I came to solving the enigma was during my courtship with husband number two. He said a friend of a friend was a student biologist on a research expedition in Canada. His team and local authorities responded to a massive train derailment near a small town. Rescuers spent three days clearing out the survivors. On day four, they swept the scattered wreckage for bodies.

This student, who happened to be Spanish, and three fellow countrymen were way out in a field after dark, poking around with sticks. One of them heard a voice moaning for help. Of course, they scrambled to find this wretched soul. Late to the scene, a military search-and-rescue helicopter flew overhead, very low, its searchlight blazing. When the chopper had gone, all fell silent. The cries didn't repeat. Weird part, according to the Spaniard, was that in the few minutes they'd frantically tried to locate the injured person, his voice kept moving around in some bizarre acoustical illusion. The survivor switched from French, to English, and finally to Spanish. The biologist claimed he had nightmares of the incident for years afterward. He dreamed of his buddies separated in a dark field, each crying for help, and he'd stumble across their desiccated corpses, one by one. He attributed it to the guilt of leaving someone to die on the tundra.

My husband-to-be told me that story while high on coke and didn't mention it again. I wonder if that's why I married the sorry sonofabitch. Just for that single moment of connectedness, a tiny and inconstant flicker of light in the wilderness.

⟵◦⟶

High noon on a Sunday night.

Going on thirty-eight haunted years, I've expected this, or something like this, even though the entity represents, with its very jack-in-the-box manifestation, a deep, dark mystery of the universe. What has drawn it to me is equally inexplicable. I've considered the fanciful notion that the Shaws are cursed and Mr. Help Me is the instrument of vengeance. Doesn't feel right. I've also prayed to Mr. Help Me as if he, or it, is a death god watching over us cattle. Perhaps it is. The old gods wanted blood, didn't they? Blood and offerings of flesh. That feels more on the mark. Or, it could be the simplest answer of them all—Mr. Help Me is an exotic animal whose biology and behavior defy scientific classification. The need for sustenance is the least of all possible mysteries. I can fathom *that* need, at least.

A window must be open in my bedroom. Cool night air dries the sweat on my cheeks as I stand in the darkened hall. The air smells vaguely of spoiled meat and perfume. A black, emaciated shape lies prone on the floor, halfway across the bedroom threshold. Long, skinny arms are extended in a swimmer's pose. Its face is a smudge of white and tilted slightly upward to regard me. It is possible that these impressions aren't accurate, that my eyes are interpreting as best they can.

I slap a switch. The light flickers on, but doesn't illuminate the hall or the figure sprawled almost directly beneath the fixture. Instead, the glow bends at a right angle and gathers on the paneled wall in a diffuse cone.

"Help me," the figure says. The murmur is so soft it might've originated in my own head.

I'm made of sterner stuff than my sixteen-year-old self. I resist the powerful compulsion to approach, to lend maternal comfort. My legs go numb. I stagger and slide down the wall into a seated position. Everybody has had the nightmare. The one where you are perfectly aware and paralyzed and an unseen enemy looms over your shoulder. Difference is, I can see my nemesis, or at least its outline, at the opposite end of the hall. I can see it coming for me. It doesn't visibly move except when I blink, and then it's magically two or three feet closer. My mind is in overdrive. What keeps going through my mind is that predator insects seldom stir until the killing strike.

"Oh my darlin', oh my darling, oh my darlin' Clementine. You are lost and gone forever, dreadful sorry Clementine." I hum tunelessly, like Gram used to after her brain softened into mush. I'm reverting to childhood, to a time when Dad or Uncle Ned might burst through the door and save the day with a blast of double-aught buckshot.

It finally dawns upon me that I'm bleeding, am sitting in a puddle of blood. Where the blood is leaking from, I've not the foggiest notion. Silly me, *that's* why I'm dead from the waist down. My immobility isn't a function of terror, pheromones, or the occult powers of an evil spirit. I've been pricked and envenomed. Nature's predators carry barbs and stings. Those stings deliver anesthetics and anticoagulants. Have venom, will travel. I chuckle. My lips are cold.

"Help me," it whispers as it plucks my toes, testing my resistance. Even this close, it's an indistinct blob of shadowy appendages.

"I have one question." I enunciate carefully, the way I do after one too many shots of Jager. "Did you take my dad on August 15th, 1977? Or did that bastard skip out? Me and my brother got a steak dinner riding on this."

"Help me." The pleading tone descends into a lower timbre. A satisfied purr.

One final trick up my sleeve, or in my pocket. Recently, while browsing a hardware store for a few odds and ends, I'd come across a relic of my youth—a black light. Cost a ten spot, on special in a clearance bin. First it made me smile as I recalled how all my childhood friends illuminated their funkadelic posters, kids as gleeful as if we'd rediscovered alchemy. Later, in college, black light made a comeback on campus and at the parties we attended. It struck a chord, got me thinking, wondering . . .

Any creature adapted to distort common light sources might be susceptible to *uncommon* sources. Say infrared or black light. I hazard a guess that my untutored intuition is on the money and that thousands of years of evolution hasn't accounted for a twenty-dollar device used to find cat piss stains in the carpet.

I raise the box with the black light filter in my left hand and thumb the toggle. For an instant, I behold the intruder in all its malevolent glory. It recoils from my flashlight, a segmented hunter of soft prey retreating into its burrow. A dresser crashes in the bedroom, glass shatters, and the trailer rocks slightly, and then it's quiet again. The moment has passed, except for the fresh hell slowly blooming in my head.

The black light surprised it and nothing more. Surprised and amused it. The creature's impossibly broad grin imparted a universe of corrupt wisdom that will scar my mind for whatever time I have left. Mr. Help Me's susurrating chuckle lingers like a psychic stain. Sometimes the spider cuts the fly from its web. Sometimes nature doesn't sink in those red fangs; sometimes it chooses not to rend with its red claws. A reprieve isn't necessarily the same weight as a pardon. Inscrutability isn't mercy.

We Shaws are tough as shoe leather. Doubtless, I've enough juice left in me to crawl for the phone and signal the cavalry. A quart or two of type-O and I'll be fighting fit with a story to curl your toes. The conundrum is whether I really want to make that crawl, or whether I should close my eyes and fall asleep. *Did you take my father?* I've spent most of my life waiting to ask that question. Is Dad out there in the dark? What about those hunters and hikers and kids who walk through the door and onto the crime pages every year?

I don't want to die, truly I don't. I'm also afraid to go on living. I've seen the true, unspeakable face of the universe; a face that reflects my lowly place in its scheme. And the answer is yes. Yes, there are hells, and in some you are burned or boiled or digested in the belly of a monster for eternity. Yes, what's left of Dad abides with a hideous mystery. He's far from alone.

What would Clint Eastwood do? Well, he would've plugged the fucker with a .44 Magnum, for starters. I shake myself. Mid-fifties is too late to turn into a mope. I roll onto my belly, suck in a breath, and begin the agonizing journey toward the coffee table where I left my purse and salvation. Hand over hand, I drag my scrawny self. It isn't lost on me what I resemble as I slather a red trail across the floor.

Laughing hurts. Hard not to, though. I begin to sing the refrain from "Help." Over and over and over.

ALLOCHTHON

LIVIA LLEWELLYN

"Taking definite form toward the middle of the century, comes the revival of romantic feeling—the era of new joy in Nature, and in the radiance of past times, strange scenes, bold deeds, and incredible marvels. We feel it first in the poets, whose utterances take on new qualities of wonder, strangeness, and shuddering."

—H. P. Lovecraft, *Supernatural Horror in Literature*

On this planet, in this universe, geology is geology—the land simply *is*, and it is nothing else. Mountain ranges and forests and "Nature" in its entirety are not sentient, they have no wisdom or knowledge to impart upon the world, and whatever emotional expectations each individual traveler draws from their journeys into the wild is of their making alone—the landscape "speaks" to us, but it's only we who are doing the talking. Or so we say we believe—I myself am not quite as certain, and I suspect many of us feel the same. Lovecraft certainly didn't believe this to be the truth of our world. "There was a . . . cosmic beauty in the hypnotic landscape through which we climbed and plunged fantastically," Lovecraft wrote in "The Whisperer in the Darkness," "and I seemed to find in its necromancy a thing I had innately known or inherited and for which I had always been vainly searching."

Time and time again, he wrote of the land around us as alive in ways we barely comprehend, watching us, calling out to us, drawing us in. How, then, can we really know for certain that the conversation is so one-sided, that those resplendent and horrifying feelings of *mysterium tremendum et fascinans* that the supernal wilderness of the world draws from us aren't the cosmic answers to questions we instinctively ask? Living as we do today, in cities and suburbs subtly crafted as if to seem once removed from unstoppable Nature, we forget that we came from the land; we are wet mortal ghost-slivers of the geologic forces out of which every living thing evolved. The land is always with us, because it *is* us. And when, in ways wondrous and strange, we are called home, we have no choice but to go.

North Bonneville, 1934

Ruth sits in the kitchen of her company-built house, slowly turning the pages of her scrapbook. The clock on the bookcase chimes ten. In the next room, the only other room, she hears her husband getting dressed. He's deliberately slow on Sundays, but he's earned the right. Something about work, he's saying from behind the door. Something about the men. Ruth can't be bothered to listen. She stares at the torn magazine clipping taped to a page. It's a photo of an East Coast socialite vacationing somewhere in the southern tropics: a pretty young woman in immaculate white linens, lounging on a bench that encircles the impossibly thick trunk of a palm tree. All around the woman and the tree, a soft manicured lawn flows like a velvet sea, and the skies above are clear and dry. Ruth runs her free hand across the back of her neck, imagining the heat in the photo, the lovely bite and sear of an unfiltered sun. Her gaze wanders up to the ceiling. Not even a year old, and already rain and mold have seeped through the shingled roof, staining the cream surface with hideous blossoms. It's supposed to be summer, yet always the overcast skies in this part of the country, always the clouds and the rain. She turns the page. More photos and ephemera, all the things that over the years have caught her eye. But all she sees is the massive palm, lush and hard and tall, the woman's back curved into it like a drowsy lover, the empty space around them, above and below, as if they are the only objects that have ever existed in the history of time.

Henry walks into the room and grabs his coat, motioning for her to do the same. Ruth clenches her jaw and closes the scrapbook. Once again, she's made a promise she doesn't want to keep. But she doesn't care enough to speak her mind, and, anyway, it's time to go.

Their next-door neighbor steers his rusting car down the dirt road, past the edges of the town and onto the makeshift highway. His car is one of many, a caravan of beat-up trucks and buggies and jalopies. Ruth sits in the back seat with a basket of rolls on her lap, next to the other wife. It started earlier in the week as an informal suggestion over a session of grocery shopping and gossip by some of the women, and now almost forty people are going. A weekend escape from the routine of their dreary lives to a small park farther down the Columbia River, far from the massive construction site for the largest dam in the world, which within the decade will throttle the river's power into useful submission. The wives will set up the picnic, a potluck of whatever they can afford to offer, while they gossip and look after the children. The men will eat and drink, complain about their women and their jobs and the general rotten state of affairs across the land, and then they'll climb a trail over eight hundred feet high, to the top of an ancient volcanic core known as Beacon Rock.

The company wife speaks in an endless paragraph, animate and excited. Billie or Betty or Becky, some childish, interchangeable name. She's four months pregnant and endlessly, vocally grateful that her husband found work on a WPA project when so many in the country are doing without. Something about the Depression. Something about the town. Something about schools. Ruth can't be bothered. She bares her teeth, nods her head, makes those ridiculous clucking sounds like the other wives would, all those bitches with airs. Two hours of this passes, the unnatural rattle and groan of the engines, the monotonous roll of pine-covered hills. The image of the palm tree has fled her mind. It's only her on the lawn, alone, under the unhinged jaw of the sky. Something about dresses. Something about the picnic. Something about a cave—

Ruth snaps to attention. There is a map in her hands, a crude drawing of what looks like a jagged-topped egg covered in zigzagging lines. This is the trail the men are going to take, the wife is explaining. Over fifty switchbacks. A labyrinth, a maze. The caravan has stopped. Ruth rubs her eyes. She's used to this, these hitches of lost time. Monotonous life, gloriously washed away in the backwater tides of her waking dreams. She stumbles out of the car, swaying as she clutches the door. The world has been reduced to an iron gray bowl of silence and vertigo, contained yet infinite. Mountains and space and sky, all around, with the river diminished to a soft mosquito's whine. Nausea swells at the back of her throat, and a faint, pain-tinged ringing floods her ears. She feels drunk, unmoored. Somewhere, Henry is telling her to turn, to look. There it is, he's saying, as he tugs her sleeve like a child. Ruth spirals around, her tearing eyes searching, searching the horizon, until finally she—

Something about—

◄○►

—the rock.

Ruth lifts her head. She's sitting at her kitchen table, a cup of lukewarm coffee at her hand. The scrapbook is before her, open, expectant, and her other hand has a page raised, halfway through the turn. On the right side of the book, the woman in the southern tropics reclines at her palm in the endless grass sea, waiting.

Henry stands before her, hat on head, speaking.

—Ruthie, quit yer dreamin' and get your coat on. Time to go.

—Go where.

—Like we planned. To Beacon Rock.

The clock on the bookcase chimes ten.

Outside, a plane flies overhead, the sonorous engine drone rising and falling as it passes. Ruth rubs her eyes, concentrating. Every day in this colorless town at the edge of this colorless land is like the one before, indistinguishable and unchanging. She doesn't remember waking up, getting dressed, making coffee. And there's something outside, a presence, an all-consuming black static wave of sound, building up just beyond the wall of morning's silence, behind the plane's mournful song. She furrows her brow, straining to hear.

Henry speaks, and the words sound like the low rumble of avalanching rock as they fall away from his face. It's language, but Ruth doesn't know what it means.

—Gimme a moment, I'm gonna be sick, Ruth says to no one in particular as she pushes away from the table. She doesn't bother to close the front door as she walks down the rickety step into warm air and a hard gray sun. Ruth stumbles around the house to the back, where she stops, placing both hands against the wooden walls as she bends down, breathing hard, willing the vomit to stay down. Gradually, the thick sticky feeling recedes, and the tiny spots of black that dance around the corners of her vision fade and disappear. She stands, and starts down the dusty alley between the rows of houses and shacks.

Mountains, slung low against the far horizon of the earth, shimmering green and gray in the clear quiet light. Ruth stops at the edge of the alley, licking her lips as she stands and stares. Her back aches. Beyond the wave and curve of land, there is... Ruth bends over again, then squats, cupping her head in her hands, elbows on knees. This day, this day already happened. She's certain of it. They drove, they drove along the dirt highway, the woman beside her, mouth running like a hurricane. They hung to the edges of the wide river, and then they rounded the last curve and stopped, and Ruth pooled out of the car like saliva around the heavy shaft of a cock, and she looked up, and, and, and.

And now some company brat is asking her if she's ok, hey lady are you sick or just taking a crap, giggling as he speaks. Ruth stands up, and slaps him, crisp and hard. The boy gasps, then disappears between the houses. Ruth clenches her jaw, trying not to cry as she heads back around the house. Henry stands beside the open car door, ruin and rage dancing over his face. Her coat and purse and the basket of rolls have been tossed in the back seat, next to the wife. She's already talking up a storm, rubbing her belly while she stares at Ruth's, her eyes and mouth all smug and smarmy in that oily sisterly way, as if she knows. As if she could know anything at all.

The sky above is molten lead, bank after bank of roiling dark clouds vomiting out of celestial foundries. Ruth cranks the window lever, presses her nose against the crack. The air smells vast and earthen. The low mountains flow past in frozen antediluvian waves. Something about casseroles, the company bitch says. Something about gelatin and babies. Something about low tides. Ruth touches her forehead, frowns. There's a hole in her memory, borderless and black, and she feels fragile and small. Not that she hates the feeling. Not entirely. Her hand rises up to the window's edge, fingers splayed wide, as if clawing the land aside to reveal its piston-shaped core. The distant horizon undulates against the dull light, against her flesh, but fails to yield. It's not its place to. She knows she's already been to Beacon Rock. Lost deep inside, a trace remains. She got out of the car and she turned, and the mountains and the evergreens and thrusting up from the middle, a geologic eruption, a disruption hard and wide and high and then: nothing. Something was there, some thing was there, she knows she saw it, but the sinkhole in her mind has swallowed all but the slippery edges.

Her mouth twists, silent, trying to form words that would describe what lies beyond that absence of sound and silence and darkness and light, outside and in her head. As if words like that could exist. And now they are there, the car is rounding the highway's final curves before the park. She rolls down the window all the way, and sticks her head and right arm out. A continent behind, her body is following her arm, like a larva wriggling and popping out of desiccated flesh, out of the car, away from the shouting, the ugly engine sounds, into the great shuddering static storm breaking all around. She saw Beacon Rock, then and now. The rest, they all saw the rock, but she saw beyond it, under the volcanic layers she saw *it*, and now she feels it, now she hears, and it hears her, too.

Falling, she looks up as she reaches out, and—

-◦-

The clock on the bookcase chimes ten. Her fingers, cramping, slowly uncurl from a cold coffee cup. Henry is in the other room, getting dressed. Ruth hears him speaking to her, his voice tired water dribbling over worn gravel. Something about the company picnic. Something about malformed, moldering backwaters of trapped space and geologic time. Something about the rock.

Tiny spattering sounds against paper make her stare up to the ceiling, then down at the table. Droplets of blood splash against the open page in her scrapbook. Ruth raises her hand to her nose, pinching the nostrils as she raises her face again. Blood slides against the back of her throat, and she swallows. On the clipping, the young socialite's face disappears in a sudden crimson burst, like a miniature solar flare erupting around her head, enveloping her white-teethed smile. Red coronas everywhere, on her linen-draped limbs, on the thick bark of the palm, on the phosphorus-bright velvet lawn. Somewhere outside, a plane drones overhead, or so it sounds like a plane. No, a plain, a wide expanse of plain, a moorless prairie of static and sound, all the leftover birth and battle and death cries of the planet, jumbled into one relentless wave streaming forth from some lost and wayward protrusion at the earth's end. Ruth pushes the scrapbook away and wipes her drying nose with the edges of her cardigan and the backs of her hands. Her lips open and close in silence as she tries to visualize, to speak the words that would describe what it is that's out there, what waits for her, high as a mountain and cold and alone. What is it that breathes her name into the wind like a mindless burst of radio static, what pulses and booms against each rushing thrust of the wide river, drawing her body near and her mind away? She saw and she wants to see it again and she wants to remember, she wants to feel the ancient granite against her tongue, she wants to rub open-legged against it until it enters and hollows her out like a mindless pink shell. She wants to fall into it, and never return here again.

—Not again, she says to the ceiling, to the walls, as Henry opens the door.

—Not again, not again, not again.

He stares at her briefly, noting the red flecks crusting her nostrils and upper lip.

—Take care of that, he says; grabbing his coat, he motions at the kitchen sink. Always the same journey, and the destination never any closer. Ruth quickly washes her face, then slips out the door behind him into the hot, sunless morning. The company wife is in the back, patting the seat next to her. Something about the weather, she says, her mouth spitting out the words in little squirts of smirk while her eyes dart over Ruth's wet red face. She thinks she knows what that's all about. Lots of company wives walk into doors. Something about the end of Prohibition. Something about the ghosts of a long-ago war. Ruth sits with her head against the window, eyes closed, letting the one-sided conversation flow out of the woman like vomit. Her hand slips under the blue-checked dish towel covering the rolls, and she runs her fingers over the flour-dusted tops. Like cobblestones. River stones, soft water-licked pebbles, thick gravel crunching under her feet. She pushes a finger through the soft crust of a roll, digging down deep into its soft middle. That's what it's doing to her, out there, punching through her head and thrusting its basalt self all through her, pulverizing her organs and liquefying her heart. The car whines and rattles as it slams in and out of potholes, gears grinding as the company man navigates the curves. Eyes still shut, Ruth runs a fingertip over each lid, pressing in firm circles against the skin, feeling the hard jelly mounds roll back and forth at her touch until they ache. The landscape outside reforms itself as a negative against her lids, gnarled and blasted mountains rimmed in small explosions of sulfur-yellow light. She can see it, almost the tip of it, pulsating with a monstrous beauty in the distance, past the last high ridges of land. Someone else must have known, and that's why they named it so. A wild perversion of nature, calling out through the everlasting sepulcher of night, seeking out and casting its blind gaze only upon her—

The company wife is grabbing her arm. The car has stopped. Henry and the man are outside, fumbling with the smoking engine hood. Ruth wrests her arm away from the woman's touch, and opens the door. The rest of the caravan has passed them by, rounded the corner into the park. Ruth starts down the side of the road, slow, nonchalant, as if taking in a bit of air. As if she could. The air has bled out, and only the pounding static silence remains, filling her throat and lungs with its hadal-deep song.

—I'm coming, she says to it.

—I'm almost here. She hears the wife behind her, and picks up her pace.

—You gals don't wander too far, she hears the company man call out.

—We should have this fixed in a jiffy.

Ruth kicks her shoes off and runs. Behind her, the woman is calling out to the men. Ruth drops her purse. She runs like she used to when she was a kid, a freckled tomboy racing through the wheat fields of her father's farm in North Dakota. She runs like an animal, and now the land and the trees and the banks of the river are moving fast, slipping past her piston legs along with the long bend of the road. Her lungs are on fire and her heart is all crazy and jumpy against her breasts and tears streak into her mouth and nose and it doesn't matter because she is so close and it's calling her with the hook of its song and pulling her reeling her in and Henry's hand is at the back of her neck and there's gravel and the road smashing against her mouth and blood and she's grinding away and kicking and clawing forward and all she has to do is lift up her head just a little bit and keep her eyes shut and she will finally see—

-‹o›-

Ruth's hands are clasped tight in her lap. Scum floats across the surface of an almost empty cup of coffee. A sob escapes her mouth, and she claps her hand over it, hitching as she pushes it back down. This small house. This small life. This cage. She can't do it anymore. The clock on the bookcase chimes ten.

—I swear, this is the last time, Ruth says, wiping the tears from her cheeks. The room is empty, but she knows who she's speaking to. It knows, too.

—I know how to git to you. I know how to see you. This is the last god-damn day.

On the kitchen table before her is the scrapbook, open to her favorite clipping. Ruth peels it carefully from the yellowing page and holds it up to the light. Somewhere in the southern tropics: a pretty young woman in stained white linens, lounging on a bench that encircles the impossibly thick trunk of a tree that has no beginning or end, whose roots plunge so far beyond the ends of earth and time that, somewhere in the vast cosmic oceans above, they loop and descend and transform into the thick fronds and leaves that crown the woman's head with dappled shadow. All around the woman and the tree, drops of dried blood are spattered across the paper like the tears of a dying sun. The woman's face lies behind one circle of deep brown, earth brown, wood brown, corpse brown. She is smiling, open-eyed, breathing it all in. Ruth balls the clipping up tight, then places it in her mouth, chewing just a bit before she swallows. There is no other place the woman and the palm have been, that they will ever be. Alone, apart, removed, untouched. All life here flows around them, utterly repelled. They cannot be bothered. It is of no concern to them. What cycle of life they are one with was not born in this universe.

In the other room, Henry is getting dressed. If he's talking, she can't hear. Everywhere, black static rushes through the air, strange equations and latitudes and lost languages and wondrous geometries crammed into a silence so old and deep that all other sounds are made void. Ruth closes the scrapbook and stands, wiping the sweat from her palms on her Sunday dress. There is a large knife in the kitchen drawers, and a small axe by the fireplace. She chooses the knife. She knows it better, she knows the heft of it in her hand when slicing into meat and bone. When he finally opens the door and steps into the small room, she's separating the rolls, the blade slipping back and forth through the powdery grooves. Ruth lifts one up to Henry, and he takes it. It barely touches his mouth before she stabs him in the stomach, just above the belt, where nothing hard can halt its descent. He collapses, and she falls with him, pulling the knife out and sitting on his chest as she plunges it into the center of his chest, twice because she isn't quite sure where his heart is, then once at the base of his throat. Blood, like water gurgling over river stones, trickling away to a distant, invisible sea. That, she can hear. Ruth wipes the blade on her dress as she rises, then places it on the table, picks up the basket and walks to the front door. She opens it a crack.

—Henry's real sick, she says to the company man. We're gonna stay home today. She gives him the rolls, staring hard at the company wife in the back seat as he walks back to his car. The wife looks her over, confused. Ruth smiles and shuts the door. That bitch doesn't know a single thing.

Ruth slips out the back, through the window of their small bedroom. The caravan of cars is already headed toward the highway, following the Columbia downstream toward Beacon Rock. They'll never make it to their picnic. They'll never see it. They never do. She moves through the alley, past the last sad row of company houses and into the tall evergreens that mark the end of North Bonneville. With each step into the forest, she feels the weight of the town fall away a little, and something vast and leviathan burrows deeper within, filling up the unoccupied space. When she's gone far and long enough that she no longer remembers her name, she stops, and presses her fingers deep into her sockets, scooping her eyes out and pinching off the long ropes of flesh that follow them out of her body like sticky yarn. What rushes from her mouth might be screaming or might be her soul, and it is smothered in the indifferent silence of the wild world.

And now it sees, and it moves in the way it sees, floating and darting back and forth through the hidden phosphorescent folds of the lands within the land, darkness punctured and coruscant with unnamable colors and light, its dying flesh creeping and hitching through forests petrified by the absence of time, past impenetrable ridges of mountains whose needle-sharp peaks cut whorls in the passing rivers of stars. A veil of flies hovers about the caves of its eyes and mouth, rising and falling with every rotting step, and bits of flesh scatter and sink to the earth like barren seeds next to its pomegranate blood. If there is pain, it is beyond such narrow knowledge acknowledge-ment of its body. There is only the bright beacon of light and thunderous song, the sonorous ringing of towering monolithic basalt breathing in and out, pushing the darkness away. There is, finally, past the curvature of the overgrown wild, a lush grass plain of emerald green, ripe and plump under a fat hot sun, a wide bench of polished wood, and a palm tree pressing in a perfect arc against its small back, warm and worn and hard like ancient stone. When it looks up, it cannot see the tree's end. Its vision rises blank and wondrous with branches as limitless as its both their dreams, past all the edges of all time, and this is the way it should be.

SHEPHERDS' BUSINESS

STEPHEN GALLAGHER

Picture me on an island supply boat, one of the old Clyde Puffers seeking to deliver me to my new post. This was 1947, just a couple of years after the war, and I was a young doctor relatively new to General Practice. Picture also a choppy sea, a deck that rose and fell with every wave, and a cross-current fighting hard to turn us away from the isle. Back on the mainland I'd been advised that a hearty breakfast would be the best preventative for seasickness and now, having loaded up with one, I was doing my best to hang onto it.

I almost succeeded. Perversely, it was the sudden calm of the harbour that did for me. I ran to the side and I fear that I cast rather more than my bread upon the waters. Those on the quay were treated to a rare sight; their new doctor, clinging to the ship's rail, with seagulls swooping in the wake of the steamer for an unexpected water-borne treat.

The island's resident Constable was waiting for me at the end of the gangplank. A man of around my father's age, in uniform, chiselled in flint and unsullied by good cheer. He said, "Munro Spence? Doctor Munro Spence?"

"That's me," I said.

"Will you take a look at Doctor Laughton before we move him? He didn't have too good a journey down."

There was a man to take care of my baggage, so I followed the Constable to the Harbourmaster's house at the end of the quay. It was a stone building, square and solid. Doctor Laughton was in the Harbourmaster's sitting room behind the office. He was in a chair by the fire with his feet on a stool and a rug over his knees and was attended by one of his own nurses, a stocky red-haired girl of twenty or younger.

I began, "Doctor Laughton. I'm . . ."

"My replacement, I know," he said. "Let's get this over with."

I checked his pulse, felt his glands, listened to his chest, noted the signs of cyanosis. It was hardly necessary; Doctor Laughton had already diagnosed himself, and had requested this transfer. He was an old-school Edinburgh-trained medical man, and I could be sure that his condition must be sufficiently serious that 'soldiering on' was no longer an option. He might choose to ignore his own aches and troubles up to a point, but as the island's only doctor he couldn't leave the community at risk.

When I enquired about chest pain he didn't answer directly, but his expression told me all.

"I wish you'd agreed to the aeroplane," I said.

"For my sake or yours?" he said. "You think I'm bad. You should see your colour." And then, relenting a little, "The airstrip's for emergencies. What good's that to me?"

I asked the nurse, "Will you be travelling with him?"

"I will," she said. "I've an Aunt I can stay with. I'll return on the morning boat."

Two of the men from the Puffer were waiting to carry the doctor to the quay. We moved back so that they could lift him between them, chair and all. As they were getting into position Laughton said to me, "Try not to kill anyone in your first week, or they'll have me back here the day after."

I was his locum, his temporary replacement. That was the story. But we both knew that he wouldn't be returning. His sight of the island from the sea would almost certainly be his last.

Once they'd manoeuvred him through the doorway, the two sailors bore him with ease toward the boat. Some local people had turned out to wish him well on his journey.

As I followed with the nurse beside me, I said, "Pardon me, but what do I call you?"

"I'm Nurse Kirkwood," she said. "Rosie."

"I'm Munro," I said. "Is that an island accent, Rosie?"

"You have a sharp ear, Doctor Spence," she said.

She supervised the installation of Doctor Laughton in the deck cabin, and didn't hesitate to give the men orders where another of her age and sex might only make suggestions or requests. A born Matron, if ever I saw one. The old salts followed her instruction without a murmur.

When they'd done the job to her satisfaction, Laughton said to me, "The latest patient files are on my desk. Your desk, now."

Nurse Kirkwood said to him, "You'll be back before they've missed you, Doctor," but he ignored that.

He said, "These are good people. Look after them."

The crew were already casting off, and they all but pulled the board from under my feet as I stepped ashore. I took a moment to gather myself, and gave a pleasant nod in response to the curious looks of those well-wishers who'd stayed to see the boat leave. The day's cargo had been unloaded and stacked on the quay and my bags were nowhere to be seen. I went in search of them and found Moodie, driver and handyman to the island hospital, waiting beside a field ambulance that had been decommissioned from the military. He was chatting to another man, who bade good day and moved off as I arrived.

"Will it be much of a drive?" I said as we climbed aboard.

"Ay," Moodie said.

"Ten minutes? An hour? Half an hour?"

"Ay," he agreed, making this one of the longest conversations we were ever to have.

⟶

The drive took little more than twenty minutes. This was due to the size of the island and a good concrete road, yet another legacy of the Army's wartime presence. We saw no other vehicle, slowed for nothing other than the occasional indifferent sheep. Wool and weaving, along with some lobster fishing, sustained the peacetime economy here. In wartime it had been different, with the local populace outnumbered by spotters, gunners, and the Royal Engineers. Later came a camp for Italian prisoners of war, whose disused medical block the Highlands and Islands Medical Service took over when the island's cottage hospital burned down. Before we reached it we passed the airstrip, still usable, but with its gatehouse and control tower abandoned.

The former prisoners' hospital was a concrete building with a wooden barracks attached. The Italians had laid paths and a garden, but these were now growing wild. Again I left Moodie to deal with my bags, and went looking to introduce myself to the Senior Sister.

Senior Sister Garson looked me over once and didn't seem too impressed. But she called me by my title and gave me a briefing on everyone's duties while leading me around on a tour. It was then that I learned my driver's name. I met all the staff apart from Mrs. Moodie, who served as cook, housekeeper, and island midwife.

"There's just the one six-bed ward," Sister Garson told me. "We use that for the men and the officers' quarters for the women. Two to a room."

"How many patients at the moment?"

"As of this morning, just one. Old John Petrie. He's come in to die."

Harsh though it seemed, she delivered the information in a matter-of-fact manner.

"I'll see him now," I said.

Old John Petrie was eighty-five or eighty-seven. The records were unclear. Occupation, shepherd. Next of kin, none—a rarity on the island. He'd led a tough outdoor life, but toughness won't keep a body going for ever. He was now grown so thin and frail that he was in danger of being swallowed up by his bedding. According to Doctor Laughton's notes he'd presented with no specific ailment. One of my teachers might have diagnosed a case of TMB, Too Many Birthdays. He'd been found in his croft house, alone, half-starved, unable to rise. There was life in John Petrie's eyes as I introduced myself, but little sign of it anywhere else.

We moved on. Mrs. Moodie would bring me my evening meals, I was told. Unless she was attending at a birth, in which case I'd be looked after by Rosie Kirkwood's mother who'd cycle up from town.

My experience in obstetrics had mainly involved being a student and staying out of the midwife's way. Senior Sister Garson said, "They're mostly home births with the midwife attending, unless there are complications and then she'll call you in. But that's quite rare. You might want to speak to Mrs. Tulloch before she goes home. Her baby was stillborn on Sunday."

"Where do I find her?" I said.

The answer was, in the suite of rooms at the other end of the building. Her door in the women's wing was closed, with her husband waiting in the corridor.

"She's dressing," he explained.

Sister Garson said, "Thomas, this is Doctor Spence. He's taking over for Doctor Laughton."

She left us together. Thomas Tulloch was a young man, somewhere around my own age but much hardier. He wore a shabby suit of all-weather tweed that looked as if it had outlasted several owners. His beard was dark, his eyes blue. Women like that kind of thing, I know, but my first thought was of a wall-eyed collie. What can I say? I like dogs.

I asked him, "How's your wife bearing up?"

"It's hard for me to tell," he said. "She hasn't spoken much." And then, as soon as Sister Garson was out of earshot, he lowered his voice and said, "What was it?"

"I beg your pardon?"

"The child. Was it a boy or a girl?"

"I've no idea."

"No one will say. Daisy didn't get to see it. It was just, your baby's dead, get over it, you'll have another."

"Her first?"

He nodded.

I wondered who might have offered such cold comfort. Everyone, I expect. It was the approach at the time. Infant mortality was no longer the commonplace event it once had been, but old attitudes lingered.

I said, "And how do you feel?"

Tulloch shrugged. "It's nature," he conceded. "But you'll get a ewe that won't leave a dead lamb. Is John Petrie dying now?"

"I can't say. Why?"

"I'm looking after his flock and his dog. His dog won't stay put."

At that point the door opened and Mrs. Tulloch—Daisy—stood before us. True to her name, a crushed flower. She was pale, fair, and small of stature, barely up to her husband's shoulder. She'd have heard our voices though not, I would hope, our conversation.

I said, "Mrs. Tulloch, I'm Doctor Spence. Are you sure you're well enough to leave us?"

She said, "Yes, thank you, Doctor." She spoke in little above a whisper. Though a grown and married woman, from a distance you might have taken her for a girl of sixteen.

I looked to Tulloch and said, "How will you get her home?"

"We were told, the ambulance?" he said. And then, "Or we could walk down for the mail bus."

"Let me get Mister Moodie," I said.

◄◦►

Moodie seemed to be unaware of any arrangement, and reluctant to comply with it. Though it went against the grain to be firm with a man twice my age, I could see trouble in our future if I wasn't. I said, "I'm not discharging a woman in her condition to a hike on the heath. To your ambulance, Mister Moodie."

Garaged alongside the field ambulance I saw a clapped-out Riley Roadster at least a dozen years old. Laughton's own vehicle, available for my use.

As the Tullochs climbed aboard the ambulance I said to Daisy, "I'll call by and check on you in a day or two." And then, to her husband, "I'll see if I can get an answer to your question."

My predecessor's files awaited me in the office. Those covering his patients from the last six months had been left out on the desk, and were but the tip of the iceberg; in time I'd need to become familiar with the histories of everyone on the island, some fifteen hundred souls. It was a big responsibility for one medic, but civilian doctors were in short supply. Though the fighting was over and the Forces demobbed, medical officers were among the last to be released.

I dived in. The last winter had been particularly severe, with a number of pneumonia deaths and broken limbs from ice falls. I read of frostbitten fishermen and a three-year-old boy deaf after measles. Two cases had been sent to the mainland for surgery and one emergency appendectomy had been performed, successfully and right here in the hospital's theatre, by Laughton himself.

Clearly I had a lot to live up to.

Since October there had been close to a dozen births on the island. A fertile community, and dependent upon it. Most of the children were thriving, one family had moved away. A Mrs. Flett had popped out her seventh, with no complications. But then there was Daisy Tulloch.

I looked at her case notes. They were only days old, and incomplete. Laughton had written them up in a shaky hand and I found myself wondering whether, in some way, his condition might have been a factor in the outcome. Not by any direct failing of his own, but Daisy had been thirty-six hours in labour before he was called in. Had the midwife delayed calling him for longer than she should? By the time of his intervention it was a matter of no detectable heartbeat and a forceps delivery.

I'd lost track of the time, so when Mrs. Moodie appeared with a tray I was taken by surprise.

"Don't get up, Doctor," she said. "I brought your tea."

I turned the notes face-down to the desk and pushed my chair back. Enough, I reckoned, for one day.

I said, "The stillbirth, the Tullochs. Was it a boy or a girl?"

"Doctor Laughton dealt with it," Mrs. Moodie said. "I wasn't there to see. It hardly matters now, does it?"

"Stillbirths have to be registered," I said.

"If you say so, Doctor."

"It's the law, Mrs. Moodie. What happened to the remains?"

"They're in the shelter for the undertaker. It's the coldest place we have. He'll collect them when there's next a funeral."

I finished my meal and, leaving the tray for Mrs. Moodie to clear, went out to the shelter. It wasn't just a matter of the Tullochs' curiosity. With no note of gender, I couldn't complete the necessary registration. Back then the bodies of the stillborn were often buried with any unrelated female adult. I had to act before the undertaker came to call.

The shelter was an air raid bunker located between the hospital and the airfield, now used for storage. And when I say storage, I mean everything from our soap and toilet roll supply to the recently deceased. It was a series of chambers mostly buried under a low, grassy mound. The only visible features above ground were a roof vent and a brick-lined ramp leading down to a door at one end. The door had a mighty lock, for which there was no key.

Inside I had to navigate my way through rooms filled with crates and boxes to find the designated mortuary with the slab. Except that it wasn't a slab; it was a billiard table, cast in the ubiquitous concrete (by those Italians, no doubt) and repurposed by my predecessor. The cotton-wrapped package that lay on it was unlabelled, and absurdly small. I unpicked the wrapping with difficulty and made the necessary check. A girl. The cord was still attached and there were all the signs of a rough forceps delivery. Forceps in a live birth are only meant to guide and protect the child's head. The marks of force supported my suspicion that Laughton had been called at a point too late for the infant, and where he could only focus on preserving the mother's life.

Night had all but fallen when I emerged. As I washed my hands before going to make a last check on our dying shepherd, I reflected on the custom of slipping a stillbirth into a coffin to share a stranger's funeral. On the one hand, it could seem like a heartless practice; on the other, there was something touching about the idea of a nameless child being placed in the anonymous care of another soul. Whenever I try to imagine eternity, it's always long and lonely. Such company might be a comfort for both.

John Petrie lay with his face toward the darkened window. In the time since my first visit he'd been washed and fed, and the bed remade around him.

I said, "Mister Petrie, do you remember me? Doctor Spence."

There was a slight change in the rhythm of his breathing that I took for a yes.

I said, "Are you comfortable?"

Nothing moved but his eyes. Looking at me, then back to the window.

"What about pain? Have you any pain? I can help with it if you have."

Nothing. So then I said, "Let me close these blinds for you," but as I moved, he made a sound.

"Don't close them?" I said. "Are you sure?"

I followed his gaze.

I could see the shelter mound from here. Only the vague shape of the hill was visible at this hour, one layer of deepening darkness over another. Against the sky, in the last of the fading light, I could make out the outline of an animal. It was a dog, and it seemed to be watching the building.

I did as John Petrie wished, left the blinds open, and him to the night.

My accommodation was in the wooden barracks where the prisoners had lived and slept. I had an oil lamp for light and a ratty curtain at the window. My bags had been lined up at the end of a creaky bunk. The one concession to luxury was a rag rug on the floor.

I could unpack in the morning. I undressed, dropped onto the bed, and had the best sleep of my life.

◄◦►

With the morning came my first taste of practice routine. An early ward round, such as it was, and then a drive down into town for weekday Surgery. This took place in a room attached to the Library and ran on a system of first come, first served, for as long as it took to deal with the queue. All went without much of a hitch. No doubt some people stayed away out of wariness over a new doctor. Others had discovered minor ailments with which to justify their curiosity. Before Surgery was over, Rosie Kirkwood joined me fresh from the boat. Doctor Laughton had not enjoyed the voyage, she told me, and we left it at that.

After the last patient (chilblains) had left, Nurse Kirkwood said, "I see you have use of Doctor Laughton's car. Can I beg a lift back to the hospital?"

"You can," I said. "And along the way, can you show me where the Tullochs live? I'd like to drop by."

"I can show you the way," she said. "But it's not the kind of place you can just 'drop by.'"

I will not claim that I'd mastered the Riley. When I described it as clapped-out, I did not exaggerate. The engine sounded like a keg of bolts rolling down a hill and the springs gave us a ride like a condemned fairground. Rosie seemed used to it.

Passing through town with the harbour behind us, I said, "Which one's the undertaker?"

"We just passed it."

"The furniture place?"

"Donald Budge. My father's cousin. Also the Coroner and cabinet maker to the island."

Two minutes later, we were out of town. It was bleak, rolling lowland moor in every direction, stretching out to a big, big sky.

Raising my voice to be heard over the whistling crack in the windshield, I said, "You've lived here all your life?"

"I have," she said. "I saw everything change with the war. We thought it would go back to being the same again after. But that doesn't happen, does it?"

"Never in the way you expect," I said.

"Doctor Laughton won't be coming back, will he?"

"There's always hope."

"That's what we say to patients."

I took my eyes off the road for a moment to look at her.

She said, "You can speak plainly to me, Doctor. I don't do my nursing for a hobby. And I don't always plan to be doing it here." And then, with barely a change in tone, "There's a junction with a telephone box coming up."

I quickly returned my attention to the way ahead. "Do I turn?"

"Not there. The next track just after."

It was a rough track, and the word boneshaking wouldn't begin to describe it. Now I understood why the Riley was falling apart, if this was the pattern for every home visit. The track ran for most of a mile and finally became completely impassable, with still a couple of hundred yards to go to reach the Tullochs' home.

Their house was a one-storey crofter's cottage with a sod roof and a barn attached. The cottage walls were lime washed, those of the barn were of bare stone. I took my medical bag from the car and we walked the rest of the way.

When we reached the door Nurse Kirkwood knocked and called out, "Daisy? It's the Doctor to see you."

There was movement within. As we waited, I looked around. Painters romanticise these places. All I saw was evidence of a hard living. I also saw a dog tethered some yards from the house, looking soulful. It resembled the one I'd seen the night before, although, to be honest, the same could be said of every dog on the island.

After making us wait as long as she dared for a quick tidy of the room and herself, Daisy Tulloch opened the door and invited us in. She was wearing a floral print dress, and her hair had been hastily pinned.

She offered tea; Nurse Kirkwood insisted on making it as we talked. Although Daisy rose to the occasion with the necessary courtesy, I could see it was a struggle. The experience of the last week had clearly hit her hard.

"I don't want to cause any fuss, Doctor," was all she would say. "I'm tired, that's all."

People respect a doctor, but they'll talk to a nurse. When I heard sheep and more than one dog barking outside, I went out and left the two women conferring. Tulloch was herding a couple of dozen ewes into a muddy pen by the cottage; a mixed herd, if the markings were anything to go by. Today he wore a cloth cap and blue work pants with braces. I realised that the tweeds I'd taken for his working clothes were actually his Sunday best.

I waited until the sheep were all penned, and then went over.

I told him, "It would have been a girl. But . . ." And I left it there, because what more could I add? But then a thought occurred and I said, "You may want to keep the information to yourself. Why make things worse?"

"That's what Doctor Laughton said. Chin up, move on, have yourself another. But she won't see it like that."

I watched him go to the barn and return with a bucket of ochre in one hand and a stick in the other. The stick had a crusty rag wrapped around its end, for dipping and marking the fleeces.

I said, "Are those John Petrie's sheep?"

"They are," he said. "But someone's got to dip 'em and clip 'em. Will he ever come back?"

"There's always hope," I said. "What about his dog?"

He glanced at the tethered animal, watching us from over near the house. "Biddy?" he said. "That dog's no use to me. Next time she runs off, she's gone. I'm not fetching her home again."

—◦—

"A dog?" Nurse Kirkwood said. She braced herself against the dash as we bumped our way back onto the road. "Senior Sister Garson will love you."

"I'll keep her in the barracks," I said. "Senior Sister Garson doesn't even need to know."

She turned around to look at Biddy, seated in the open luggage hatch. The collie had her face tilted up into the wind and her eyes closed in an attitude of uncomplicated bliss.

"Good luck with that," she said.

That night, when the coast was clear, I sneaked Biddy into the ward.

"John," I said, "you've got a visitor."

—◦—

I began to find my way around. I started to make home visits and I took the time to meet the island's luminaries, from the priest to the postman to the secretary of the Grazing Committee. Most of the time Biddy rode around with me in the back of the Riley. One night I went down into town and took the dog into the pub with me, as an icebreaker. People were beginning to recognise me now. It would be a while before I'd feel accepted, but I felt I'd made a start.

Senior Sister Garwood told me that Donald Budge, the undertaker, had now removed the infant body for an appropriate burial. She also said that he'd complained to her about the state in which he'd found it. I told her to send him to me, and I'd explain the medical realities of the situation to a man who ought to know better. Budge didn't follow it up.

The next day in town Thomas Tulloch came to morning surgery, alone. "Mister Tulloch," I said. "How can I help you?"

"It's not for me," he said. "It's Daisy, but she won't come. Can you give her a tonic? Anything that'll perk her up. Nothing I do seems to help."

"Give her time. It's only been a few days."

"It's getting worse. Now she won't leave the cottage. I tried to persuade her to visit her sister but she just turns to the wall."

So I wrote him a scrip for some Parrish's, a harmless red concoction of sweetened iron phosphate that would, at best, sharpen the appetite, and at worst do nothing at all. It was all I could offer. Depression, in those days, was a condition to be overcome by 'pulling oneself together'. Not to do so was to be perverse and most likely attention-seeking, especially if you were a woman. I couldn't help thinking that, though barely educated even by the island's standards, Tulloch was an unusually considerate spouse for his time.

Visits from the dog seemed to do the trick for John Petrie. I may have thought I was deceiving the Senior Sister, but I realise now that she was most likely turning a blind eye. Afterwards his breathing was always easier, his sleep more peaceful. And I even got my first words out of him when he beckoned me close and said into my ear:

"*Ye'll do.*"

After this mark of approval I looked up to find the Constable waiting for me, hat in his hands as if he were unsure of the protocol. Was a dying man's bedside supposed to be like a church? He was taking no chances.

He said, "I'm sorry to come and find you at your work, Doctor. But I hope you can settle a concern."

"I can try."

"There's a rumour going round about the dead Tulloch baby. Some kind of abuse?"

"I don't understand."

"Some people are even saying it had been skinned."

"Skinned?" I echoed.

"I've seen what goes on in post-mortems and such," the Constable persisted. "But I never heard of such a thing being called for."

"Nor have I," I said. "It's just Chinese whispers, David. I saw the body before Donald Budge took it away. It was in poor condition after a long and difficult labour. But the only abuse it suffered was natural."

"I'm only going by what people are saying."

"Well for God's sake don't let them say such a thing around the mother."

"I do hear she's taken it hard," the Constable conceded. "Same thing happened to my sister, but she just got on. I've never even heard her speak of it."

He looked to me for permission, and then went around the bed to address John Petrie. He bent down with his hands on his knees, and spoke as if to a child or an imbecile.

"A'right, John?" he said. "Back on your feet soon, eh?"

◦

Skinned? Who ever heard of such a thing? The chain of gossip must have started with Donald Budge and grown ever more grotesque in the telling. According to the records Budge had four children of his own. The entire family was active in amateur dramatics and the church choir. You'd expect a man in his position to know better.

I was writing up patient notes at the end of the next day's town Surgery when there was some commotion outside. Nurse Kirkwood went to find out the cause and came back moments later with a breathless nine-year-old boy at her side.

"This is Robert Flett," she said. "He ran all the way here to say his mother's been in an accident. "

"What kind of an accident?"

The boy looked startled and dumbstruck at my direct question, but Rosie Kirkwood spoke for him. "He says she fell."

I looked at her. "You know the way?"

"Of course."

We all piled into the Riley to drive out to the west of the island. Nurse Kirkwood sat beside me and I lifted Robert into the bag hatch with the dog, where both seemed happy enough.

At the highest point on the moor Nurse Kirkwood reckoned she spotted a walking figure on a distant path, far from the road.

She said, "Is that Thomas Tulloch? What could he be doing out here?" But I couldn't spare the attention to look.

⋅◦⋅

Adam Flett was one of three brothers who, together, were the island's most prosperous crofter family. In addition to their livestock and rented lands they made some regular money from government contract work. With a tenancy protected by law, Adam had built a two-storey home with a slate roof and laid a decent road to it. I was able to drive almost to the door. Sheep scattered as I braked, and the boy jumped out to join with other children in gathering them back with sticks.

It was only a few weeks since Jean Flett had borne the youngest of her seven children. The birth had been trouble-free but the news of a fall concerned me. Her eldest, a girl of around twelve years, let us into the house. I looked back and saw Adam Flett on the far side of the yard, watching us.

Jean Flett was lying on a well-worn old sofa and struggled to rise as we came through the door. I could see that she hadn't been expecting us. Despite the size of their family, she was only in her thirties.

I said, "Mrs. Flett?" and Nurse Kirkwood stepped past me to steady our patient and ease her back onto the couch.

"This is Doctor Spence," Nurse Kirkwood explained.

"I told Marion," Jean Flett protested. "I told her not to send for you."

"Well, now that I'm here," I said, "let's make sure my journey isn't wasted. Can you tell me what happened?"

She wouldn't look at me, and gave a dismissive wave. "I fell, that's all."

"Where's the pain?"

"I'm just winded."

I took her pulse and then got her to point out where it hurt. She winced when I checked her abdomen, and again when I felt around her neck.

I said, "Did you have these marks before the fall?"

"It was a shock. I don't remember."

Tenderness around the abdomen, a raised heart rate, left side pain, and what appeared to be days-old bruises. I exchanged a glance with Nurse Kirkwood. A fair guess would be that the new mother had been held against the wall and punched.

I said, "We need to move you to the hospital for a couple of days."

"No!" she said. "I'm just sore. I'll be fine."

"You've bruised your spleen, Mrs. Flett. I don't think it's ruptured but I need to be sure. Otherwise you could need emergency surgery."

"Oh, no."

"I want you where we can keep an eye on you. Nurse Kirkwood? Can you help her to pack a bag?"

I went outside. Adam Flett had moved closer to the house but was still hovering. I said to him, "She's quite badly hurt. That must have been some fall."

"She says it's nothing." He wanted to believe it, but he'd seen her pain and I think it scared him.

I said, "With an internal injury she could die. I'm serious, Mister Flett. I'll get the ambulance down to collect her." I'd thought that Nurse Kirkwood was still inside the house, so when she spoke from just behind me I was taken by surprise.

She said, "Where's the baby, Mister Flett?"

"Sleeping," he said.

"Where?" she said. "I want to see."

"It's no business of yours or anyone else's."

Her anger was growing, and so was Flett's defiance. "What have you done to it?" she persisted. "The whole island knows it isn't yours. Did you get rid of it? Is that what the argument was about? Is that why you struck your wife?" I was aware of three or four of his children now standing at a distance, watching us.

"The Flett brothers have a reputation, Doctor," she said, lowering her voice so the children wouldn't hear. "It wouldn't be the first time another man's child had been taken out to the barn and drowned in a bucket."

He tried to lunge at her then, and I had to step in.

"Stop that!" I said, and he shook me off and backed away. He started pacing like an aggrieved wrestler whose opponent stands behind the referee. Meanwhile his challenger was showing no fear.

"Well?" Rosie Kirkwood said.

"You've got it wrong," he said. "You don't know anything."

"I won't leave until you prove the child's safe."

And I said, "Wait," because I'd had a sudden moment of insight and reckoned I knew what must have happened.

I said to Rosie, "He's sold the baby. To Thomas Tulloch, in exchange for John Petrie's sheep. I recognise those marks. I watched Tulloch make them." I looked at Flett. "Am I right?"

Flett said nothing right away. And then he said, "They're Petrie's?"

"I suppose Thomas drove them over," I said. "Nurse Kirkwood spotted him heading back on the moor. Is the baby with him?"

Flett only shrugged.

"I don't care whether the rumours are true," I said. "You can't take a child from its mother. I'll have to report this."

"Do what you like," Flett said. "It was her idea." And he walked away.

I couldn't put Jean Flett in the Riley, but nor did I want to leave her unattended as I brought in the ambulance. "I'll stay," Nurse Kirkwood said. "I'll come to no harm here."

On the army highway I stopped at the moorland crossroads, calling ahead from the telephone box to get the ambulance on its way. It passed me heading in the opposite direction before I reached the hospital.

There I made arrangements to receive Mrs. Flett. My concern was with her injury, not her private life. Lord knows how a crofter's wife with six children found the time, the opportunity, or the energy for a passion, however brief. I'll leave it to your H. E. Bateses and D. H. Lawrences to explore that one, with their greater gifts than mine. Her general health seemed, like so many of her island breed, to be robust. But a bruised spleen needs rest in order to heal, and any greater damage could take a day or two to show.

Biddy followed at my heels as I picked up a chair and went to sit with John Petrie. He'd rallied a little with the dog's visits, though the prognosis was unchanged. I opened the window eighteen inches or so. Biddy could be out of there like a shot if we should hear the Senior Sister coming.

"I know I can be straight with you, John," I said. "How do you feel about your legacy giving a future to an unwanted child?"

They were his sheep that had been traded, after all. And Jean Flett had confirmed her wish to see her child raised where it wouldn't be resented. As for Daisy's feelings, I tried to explain them with Tulloch's own analogy of a ewe unwilling to leave its dead lamb, which I was sure he'd understand. John Petrie listened and then beckoned me closer.

What he whispered then had me running to the car.

I'd no way of saying whether Thomas Tulloch might have reached his cottage yet. My sense of local geography wasn't that good. I didn't even know for sure that he was carrying the Flett baby.

I pushed the Riley as fast as it would go, and when I left the road for the bumpy lane I hardly slowed. How I didn't break the car in two or lose a wheel, I do not know. I was tossed and bucketed around but I stayed on the track until the car could progress no farther, and then I abandoned it and set myself to fly as best I could the rest of the way.

I saw Tulloch from the crest of a rise, at the same time as the cottage came into view. I might yet reach him before he made it home. He was carrying a bundle close to his chest. I shouted, but either he didn't hear me or he ignored my call.

I had to stop him before he got to Daisy.

It was shepherds' business. In the few words he could manage John Petrie had told me how, when a newborn lamb is rejected by its mother, it can be given to a ewe whose own lamb has died at birth. But first the shepherd must skin the dead lamb and pull its pelt over the living one. Then the new mother might accept it as her own. If the sheep understood, the horror would be overwhelming. But animals aren't people.

I didn't believe what I was thinking. But what if?

I saw the crofter open his door and go inside with his bundle. I was only a few strides behind him. But those scant moments were enough.

When last I'd seen Daisy Tulloch, she'd the air of a woman in whom nothing could hope to rouse the spirit, perhaps ever again.

But the screaming started from within the house, just as I was reaching the threshold.

DOWN TO A SUNLESS SEA

NEIL GAIMAN

The Thames is a filthy beast: it winds through London like a snake or a sea serpent. All the rivers flow into it, the Fleet and the Tyburn and the Neckinger, carrying all the filth and scum and waste, the bodies of cats and dogs and the bones of sheep and pigs down into the brown water of the Thames, which carries them east into the estuary and from there into the North Sea and oblivion.

It is raining in London. The rain washes the dirt into the gutters, and it swells streams into rivers, rivers into powerful things. The rain is a noisy thing, splashing and pattering and rattling the rooftops. If it is clean water as it falls from the skies, it only needs to touch London to become dirt, to stir dust and make it mud.

Nobody drinks it, neither the rain water nor the river water. They make jokes about Thames water killing you instantly, and it is not true. There are mudlarks who will dive deep for thrown pennies then come up again, spout the river water, shiver, and hold up their coins. They do not die, of course, or not of that, although there are no mudlarks over fifteen years of age.

The woman does not appear to care about the rain.

She walks the Rotherhithe docks, as she has done for years, for decades: nobody knows how many years, because nobody cares. She walks the docks, or she stares out to sea. She examines the ships, as they bob at anchor. She must do something, to keep body and soul from dissolving their partnership, but none of the folk of the dock have the foggiest idea what this could be.

You take refuge from the deluge beneath a canvas awning put up by a sailmaker. You believe yourself to be alone under there, at first, for she is statue-still and staring out across the water, even though there is nothing to be seen through the curtain of rain. The far side of the Thames has vanished.

And then she sees you. She sees you and she begins to talk, not to you, oh no, but to the grey water that falls from the grey sky into the grey river. She says, "My son wanted to be a sailor," and you do not know what to reply or how to reply. You would have to shout to make yourself heard over the roar of the rain, but she talks, and you listen. You discover yourself craning and straining to catch her words.

"My son wanted to be a sailor.

"I told him not to go to sea. I'm your mother, I said. The sea won't love you like I love you, she's cruel. But he said, Oh Mother, I need to see the world. I need to see the sun rise in the tropics, and watch the Northern Lights dance in the Arctic sky, and most of all I need to make my fortune and then, when it's made, I will come back to you and build you a house, and you will have servants, and we will dance, mother, oh how we will dance . . .

"And what would I do in a fancy house? I told him. You're a fool with your fine talk. I told him of his father, who never came back from the sea—some said he was dead and lost overboard, while some swore blind they'd seen him running a whore-house in Amsterdam.

"It's all the same. The sea took him.

"When he was twelve years old, my boy ran away, down to the docks, and he shipped on the first ship he found, to Flores in the Azores, they told me.

"There's ships of ill-omen. Bad ships. They give them a lick of paint after each disaster, and a new name, to fool the unwary.

"Sailors are superstitious. The word gets around. This ship was run aground by its captain, on orders of the owners, to defraud the insurers; and then, all mended and as good as new, it gets taken by pirates; and then it takes shipment of blankets and becomes a plague ship crewed by the dead, and only three men bring it into port in Harwich . . .

"My son had shipped on a stormcrow ship. It was on the homeward leg of the journey, with him bringing me his wages—for he was too young to have spent them on women and on grog, like his father—that the storm hit.

"He was the smallest one in the lifeboat.

"They said they drew lots fairly, but I do not believe it. He was smaller than them. After eight days adrift in the boat, they were so hungry. And if they did draw lots, they cheated.

"They gnawed his bones clean, one by one, and they gave them to his new mother, the sea. She shed no tears and took them without a word. She's cruel.

"Some nights I wish he had not told me the truth. He could have lied.

"They gave my boy's bones to the sea, but the ship's mate—who had known my husband, and known me too, better than my husband thought he did, if truth were told—he kept a bone, as a keepsake.

"When they got back to land, all of them swearing my boy was lost in the storm that sank the ship, he came in the night, and he told me the truth of it, and he gave me the bone, for the love there had once been between us.

"I said, you've done a bad thing, Jack. That was your son that you've eaten.

"The sea took him too, that night. He walked into her, with his pockets filled with stones, and he kept walking. He'd never learned to swim.

"And I put the bone on a chain to remember them both by, late at night, when the wind crashes the ocean waves and tumbles them on to the sand, when the wind howls around the houses like a baby crying."

The rain is easing, and you think she is done, but now, for the first time, she looks at you, and appears to be about to say something. She has pulled something from around her neck, and now she is reaching it out to you.

"Here," she says. Her eyes, when they meet yours, are as brown as the Thames. "Would you like to touch it?"

You want to pull it from her neck, to toss it into the river for the mudlarks to find or to lose. But instead you stumble out from under the canvas awning, and the water of the rain runs down your face like someone else's tears.

THE MAN FROM THE PEAK

ADAM GOLASKI

The sun left tatters in shades of red across the sky; tatters that shriveled through purple, indigo—to black. The stars didn't come out. Instead, oil-gray clouds. I kept the car going, up, steering around the worst ruts and rocks in the road. I drove under the no trespassing sign, kept driving up. The forest around me was thick—the leaves had come in, hearty and wet: spring. I wondered if this would be the last time I'd make the drive up to Richard's. I thought so. Richard was leaving. Moving east. So, a farewell bash. Sarah would be there, too. With a sound like marbles clicking, or teeth, the wine bottle and the whisky bottle on the passenger seat bumped against each other.

Richard's house stood in the shadow of the mountain's peak. I turned off the car and sat, let my eyes adjust to the darkness, listened to cooling engine skitter. The walk to Richard's was lined with paper lanterns—no doubt Sarah's touch. I grabbed the bottles, set them on the roof of the car, lit a cigarette and looked up the peak. I heard people talking—some of the voices outside, from the hot tub, no doubt, and muted voices from the house. There were a dozen cars parked in front of my own. I opened the back door of the car and took out a small package—a book for Sarah, a collection of short stories she and I had talked about the last time the three of us—Richard, Sarah and I—had been together. I tucked the book under my arm, took the bottles and walked up to the house. I rang the bell and a woman wearing a bikini opened the door. She looked at me—looked me up and down as if I were wearing a bikini—laughed a little and brushed past me. As she passed, she asked, "Did you bring your suit?"

The house was long and narrow. To my left was the guest room, to my right a kitchen and a television room/bar. Michael, an old friend of Richard's who I'd come to like, was busy mixing drinks. He'd explained to me once that he took up the role of bartender at parties so he could get to know all the women. I approached the bar and said, "I'd say the hot tub is where you want to be tonight." Michael nodded, ruefully. I handed Michael the bottles I'd brought. "Good stuff," he said. "Good to see you," he said. I shook his hand and patted his shoulder. "What'll you have?" he asked. "A glass of that whiskey," I said. He said, "Try this instead," and poured from an already open bottle. I put my cigarette out in a red-glass ashtray by the bar and had a sip. I nodded my appreciation. "I should announce myself," I said, and backed away.

The living room: a large, open space dominated by a fat couch and a grand piano (Richard didn't play). Sarah was on the couch drinking wine. When she saw me, she stood, crossed the room with a quick, woozy stride and put her arms around me.

"Watch the wine," I said.

She stepped back from me, a wounded expression on her face. I took her glass and rested it on the piano. She put her arms around me again and said, "I get so excited when you come. I always do. It's so silly. I always am so excited to see you."

"It's good to see you too." We kissed, as we did whenever we saw each other; I'm not sure how this greeting got started, but our kisses were long and on the lips; she'd been dating Richard as long as I'd known her.

"Have you seen Richard yet?" she asked.

"I just got here."

"Can I?" She tapped the cigarette box in my breast pocket. She slipped her fingers into the pocket and smiled at me. "You always have the best cigarettes." As she lit up, she eyed the wrapped package under my arm.

"It's for you," I said.

She unwrapped my gift, dropped the brown paper to the floor. "You found a copy," she said. She opened the book, careful with the spine, a delicate touch on the yellow edge of each page she turned over. "You're the only one who ever gets me books." She tapped her necklace: an elegant, expensive silver knot. "Richard always buys me jewelry," she said, with a frown.

We caught up, a little; a little about Richard's preparations for leaving, though we skirted the issue of whether or not she'd be going. We would have that conversation later. I needed to drink a little more, to meet everyone. I looked past Sarah, at the women on the couch. Sarah said, "That one's Carmilla—she's a stunning bore—and that's Kat—fun, fun, fun. They're friends of Richard's. From where, I do not know. Come, I need more wine." We left her glass on the piano, made our way up to the bar. She fell into a conversation with Michael. I walked off—I didn't feel like standing around while Sarah and Michael talked.

Richard was in the yard, beer in hand, talking with someone I didn't know. Just behind him was the hot tub. The woman who'd answered the door was in the tub with a couple of guys. Before Richard spotted me, the woman said, "You should come in, it's perfect, cold outside, warm in here." She giggled. One of the guys leaned over and whispered to her. She pushed him away.

"David, you made it," Richard said.

"I wouldn't miss it."

"Well I'm glad, you know."

He introduced me to his friend, and to the guys in the tub. He didn't know the woman's name and she didn't supply it. "Come on and sit," he said to me.

I sat on a cooler. Richard and his friend were talking about Boston, where Richard was moving. I'd never been to Boston, I told them, though I'd heard it was like San Francisco. We talked about San Francisco, Seattle, Portland.

The woman in the hot tub interrupted us and asked me to get her a beer. I got up to get a beer from the cooler. She stood. She was very thin, no hips, but gifted with significant breasts. She leaned forward—bent at the waist without bending her knees—and brought her bosom to my face. Freckles swirled into the dark line of her cleavage. "Thank you so much," she said, and took the beer. The guys in the tub were happily gazing up at her tiny bottom—those men were nothing to her, made to carry her bags and perform rudimentary tasks while she gazed off in other, more interesting directions. I'd met women like her many times before. "My name's Prudence," she said.

"Of course it is," I said.

"You really ought to join."

"You know I'm not going to."

She did know, too, and smiled a wide, long smile.

"But I'll be here all night," I said.

She settled back into her pool.

I lit a cigarette; for a moment, a flame cupped in my hand; I drew my hand away, and looked up to the peak. A man, briefly illuminated by moonlight before the clouds closed up, appeared at the top, moved toward the house. I said to Richard, "Does someone live up there?" Richard told me he didn't think so. I tried to point out the man—who I could still see, as a dark shape on a dark background—but Richard couldn't find him. "I'm going to go in, get a real drink," I said. Richard said he'd be in shortly. I shrugged and walked around to the front of the house—an eye on the man walking down the mountain.

Most of the people at Richard's party weren't attractive. They might be fit and many were dressed in expensive clothes, but most of his friends looked average and, upon getting to know them, were. The exceptions were notable. Michael, a transplant from the coast, a man of style; Kat and Carmilla—just beautiful; Prudence—a manipulator I appreciated; and Sarah. Kat and Carmilla were seated on a small couch in the guest room, surrounded by four or five guys and one unfortunate looking girl (pasty, a large, flat nose and hair forced into a strange shade of red). They were all watching a movie—Kat spotted me in the doorway, shifted on the couch, shoved at one of the guys, and gestured for me to sit beside her. They were watching *The Man Who Fell To Earth*, that beautiful David Bowie film—

I let myself get drawn into the movie. Kat ran her hand in a circle on my back. When the unfortunate girl sneezed, breaking my mood, I excused myself and walked down the hall to the bar. I passed the front door just as there was a knock; the door was answered and I heard, "What, you need a formal invitation? Sure come on in, you are welcome to come in." Sarah joined me at the bar and took my arm. We collected drinks and Michael and I went out onto the back patio. Mercifully, the three of us were there alone.

Sarah stole a cigarette and complained about Richard's friends—"Present company excluded."

Michael then brought up the subject Sarah and I had danced around once already: "What's in Boston for you? I mean, I know Richard has a great job, but what are you going to do?"

Sarah looked at the floor for a moment, took a drag and a drink and said, "That's just the thing, Michael."

I was eager to hear her explain to Michael just what that thing was—I thought I knew but I wanted her to say it—but instead she stared past Michael, back into the house. I turned and Michael turned and we all watched a very ugly man walk past the back patio door toward the bar.

"Who the hell was that?" I asked.

Sarah said, "I don't know, but—" then drifted past me into the hall. Michael and I looked at each other, then followed—I dropped my cigarette on the patio floor.

The ugly man wasn't at the bar by the time we stepped into the hall—no one was.

He was in the living room, behind the piano, playing the adagio from the *Moonlight Sonata* on Richard's out-of-tune grand—the result was not lulling or melancholic, as the adagio is, but dissonant and eerie.

No one else seemed to share my evaluation of the music. Everyone—the whole party except Prudence and her men—were gathered around the piano watching the ugly man play, laughing when he made an exaggerated flourish over the keyboard, but rapt, totally caught up—so that they all jumped when he moved into the more upbeat allegretto. I wanted to jump too—each out-of-tune note grated on my nerves.

I stared at the ugly man as he played. He was bald. His head was long and boney, his eyes lost in shadow. His skin was a dark brown—not like Michael's, no, he didn't look African—the ugly man was black all right, but his skin was waxy and all over there was a patina of green—the green of rotten beef. I couldn't help but imagine what it would be like to touch his skin—my finger, I was sure, would sink in, as it would in a pool of congealed fat. His ears were large and pointed. His mouth was small—pursed as he played—and his teeth were too large for his tiny mouth. His two front teeth were the worst: jagged, yellow, buck-teeth.

I was greatly relieved to see that Sarah did not appear to be under his spell. She stood in the corner watching not the ugly man, but the crowd—and Richard, who stood with a stupid open-mouthed expression on his face, clapping like a little girl every time the ugly man crossed his hands over the keyboard. I could hear, barely audible, David Bowie's voice in the guest room.

The ugly man stopped playing the piano then, and it dawned on me that he must be the man I'd seen coming down from the peak. He waved his hands in the air, and this seemed to release everyone. There was some applause, and people returned to what they had been doing. I watched Kat and Carmilla walk back toward the guest room, Michael made a bee-line for the bar, and Sarah and Richard walked over to me. I noticed the pasty girl with the bad dye-job standing next to the ugly man, looking down at him as he caressed her hand. The perfect couple, I thought. I led Sarah and Richard to the bar and insisted that Michael open the whisky I'd brought—a far better whisky than what he'd served me when I'd arrived.

I asked who the ugly man was.

Sarah said she didn't know. Michael and Richard acted as if I hadn't asked the question. I put my hand on Richard's arm and asked again, and he said, "Which ugly man?"

I took Richard's response to be a joke and gave him a forced, weak chuckle. My whisky was a relief. I needed a moment alone with Sarah—I wanted her to have a chance to finish what she'd been saying earlier, I wanted her to tell me that there was nothing for her in Boston, that she had no intention of ever joining Richard in Boston and was only pretending so as not to break his heart before his big trip.

I felt a hand on my shoulder. I was certain it was the ugly man's; I was surprised—relieved—that the hand belonged to Prudence. "I'm out of the tub," she whispered.

Sarah and Richard were talking; I asked Prudence what she wanted to drink and she held up a beer. "I'm all set in that department. Did you know they're watching a movie in the guest room?"

"Yes," I said. I followed Prudence down the hall. She'd put on a dress over her wet suit—somehow, with the bands of wet, clingy material around her waist and her chest, she seemed more naked than she had before. I'd catch up with Sarah later, catch her when Richard was off chatting up one of his boring friends.

Prudence and I entered the room—*The Man Who Fell to Earth* was still on—had Bowie yet revealed his alien identity? Kat and Carmilla were on the couch, and to my satisfaction, Kat shot Prudence a nasty look and beckoned me to a spot beside her. Prudence, first in the guest room, took that spot. Small as her hips were, there was no more room left on the couch. When she saw this, she slid off the couch, onto the floor, and offered me the spot Kat had already offered. Regardless of the outcome of my conversation with Sarah, I knew I would not leave the party alone; I considered, even, the possibility that Prudence and Kat's attentions would prove useful in gaining Sarah's attention.

Kat stroked my hair; Prudence my leg. The other men in the room couldn't help but glance away from the television to look first at the women, then at me, wishing themselves in my position.

Just before the movie ended—a sad, pale scene—I'd been lulled by all the petting—the ugly man, the man from the peak, walked past the guest room. I caught a glimpse of him, just as he walked out of sight. Except for Prudence, the people in the guest room left: the guys, Carmilla and Kat. Before I could dwell on this much, Prudence was on the couch beside me, hand on the inside of my thigh, mouth drifting toward my face. I knew that face, drifting sleepily, a drunk woman about to kiss me. I let her kiss me. We kissed. Her tongue darted in and out of my own mouth. Her open hand pressed against my erection. My hand on the damp cloth covering her right breast, my hand on the damp cloth at the small of her back.

I broke off our kissing. I said, "Let's get something more to drink." Though she gave me a petulant look, I knew she would do as I asked and I thought—for a moment—this woman actually knows what I'm doing, understands, would have ended the kiss herself, shortly, if I hadn't. In that moment I preferred Prudence to Sarah. The moment was fleeting.

The ugly man had been speaking—addressing the entire party, it seemed. When Prudence and I stepped into the living room, he waved his hand as he'd done before, and the crowd dispersed as it had before. Everyone left the room except for one person, one of the guys who'd been in the hot tub with Prudence—I watched her watch him talk to the ugly man and Prudence said, "I knew he was gay." I wasn't sure who she was referring to at first—I didn't think the ugly man was gay—and then I realized who she meant.

"Who is that man?" I asked.

"I don't know. I've been outside all night."

"Didn't you see him come down from the peak?"

"From the peak? There's nothing up there. I'm going to get another drink."

She left me. I lit a cigarette and went out onto the patio. Richard and Sarah were out there, though Richard was talking with one of his friends and Sarah was just standing around, looking bored. She brightened when she saw me. I gave her a cigarette.

"Why don't we go outside a while," Sarah said.

We left the enclosed patio. We heard voices, coming from the direction of the hot tub. We walked out into the dark yard, toward the woods.

"What was that guy talking about?" I asked.

"Which guy?"

"The ugly guy. They guy with the buck teeth."

Sarah turned up a confused expression. When she pulled on her cigarette, her face was illuminated. She had, I thought, the most perfect face. Between her eyebrows, just above the bridge of her nose was a circular patch of skin very smooth and brighter white than the rest of her face. I wanted to put my fingertip on that spot. I did. She scrunched her face up and giggled, brushing my finger away.

"So that's what that button does," I said. "So," I said. "You didn't finish what you were saying earlier."

She didn't answer me, but pointed, and I forgot what I'd asked when I saw what she was pointing out. The man from the peak walked across the lawn—on a line parallel with our own course, maybe twenty feet away—with the guy he'd been talking to in the living room. They walked toward the edge of the wood, where a woman—the woman with the bad dye-job—lay on the ground.

"What is going on over there?" Sarah asked.

I said, "I'm sure we don't want to know."

"Do you think she's all right?"

"She looks fine to me," I said, though there was no way I could actually judge, from where we stood. "We should leave them be," I said, but I asked, "Who is that guy anyhow? I saw him come down from the peak."

"Which guy?" Sarah asked.

"The bald guy." Right when I said that, he was out of sight, he'd stepped into a shadow that made him all but invisible. So I said never mind.

On the patio, we finished our drinks. Sarah took another cigarette. She looked around—there were other guests on the patio, but none we knew more than just in passing. Richard had gone inside. Sarah said, "I'm not putting any pressure on you, David, but I'm not going to Boston."

Sarah seemed like herself when she said that, more than she had all night, and I was glad, I'd known it, known she would leave Richard for me if I'd wanted, and I did want that, and I hadn't been wrong.

All the voices on the porch seemed to rise in volume—there was a scream—I decided from inside the house—but no one paid any attention.

⊸◦⊳

Several hours later, I stood in front of Richard's house, trying to figure out why there were twelve cars, not including my own, in the driveway. The party had started to die about an hour before; people had slipped out one-by-one. I realized, as I stood in front of Richard's house smoking, sipping a cheap glass of whisky, that I hadn't heard a single car go. Even if people had carpooled, had designated a driver, there were still too many cars in the driveway.

My thoughts weren't adding up in any significant way. I was in a haze of drunk and sleepiness—not so far gone that I wouldn't be able to collect Sarah and leave soon, but dull enough that my lines of thought were short.

I stared for a while at the mountaintop. There were no houses, that I could see, higher than Richard's. If the man from the peak lived up there, he must have walked from the other side of the peak, and that looked to me like a hell of a walk.

I coughed, caught a coughing fit, felt a hand on my back.

"Prudence?" I managed, still bent over.

"No, not Prudence."

The voice was a voice I hadn't heard once that night, but I knew whose voice it was.

"Taking in the air?" the man from the peak asked.

I saw a laugh on his face; he was laughing at me.

"Smoke?" I asked. "Whisky?" I held out my drink and my cigarette.

He held up a hand—his fingers were long, his nails were long.

"You don't drink," I said.

He just grinned his stupid ugly grin, a set of teeth crooked and misshapen. That his speech wasn't impeded by his malformed mouth was a wonder—indeed, his voice was the most soothing voice I'd ever heard. "So who are you?" I asked.

He said, "I'm an invited guest," and I remembered what I'd overheard earlier that night.

I said, "I watched you come down from the peak. Are there houses up there?"

He looked at the peak, followed its upward rise with his head until he'd found the very tip and said, "No, there are no houses."

I thought maybe he lived in a tent or a trailer home and was just having fun with me, making me ask my questions just so. Normally, when I think someone's doing that, some cute girl who thinks she's coy or some clever boy trying to impress, I walk away without so much as a fuck you and that puts them out, and then they beg me for my attention. Normally, that's what I'd do. But I said, "But do you live on the peak? In a tent? In a trailer? In a mobile home?" I gave that ugly man from the peak all the options I could because I was desperate to hear his answer. For some reason: I was desperate to know.

He said, "I live in the peak."

I didn't know what he meant by "in the peak," but I smiled—I felt that dumb smile spread on my face—I smiled and nodded as if "in the peak" made all the sense in the world.

I asked, "So what is it you're doing in the backyard?"

He gave me a straight answer. An awful answer. And for a moment I could see him exactly as he was; all of a sudden I could see him, see that his clothes—from pant cuff to shirt collar—were drenched in blood and gore. Blood dripped off his shirt sleeves, blood was pooled around his feet, there was blood on the top of his bald head and there was blood all around his mouth. The blood around his mouth was the most horrible, smeared around like finger-paint. Before I became hysterical, I couldn't see the blood anymore. He looked ugly, but his clothes were clean. His pant cuffs flapped in the breeze. His bright white shirt sleeves were rolled up just below his elbows.

I wondered, if he could do that, why he didn't make himself look handsome to me. I think he knew my thought, because he said, "Charisma. You know what I mean."

I laughed. He walked back into the house. I stood shaking my head, enjoying for a moment the great joke. Then a wave of nausea passed through me and I vomited—all spit and whisky—and my head was clear. I rushed into the house—for Sarah, I thought, where is Sarah? The guest room was empty. No one was at the bar. Richard was seated on the piano bench next to the man from the peak, and they were playing "Heart and Soul." The man from the peak playing the chords, Richard plinking out the simple tune with a single finger, laughing like an idiot.

I ran into Prudence out on the patio. She was drunk, but when she looked at me I knew she was still in control: I'd known from the moment she brushed past me at the front door that the big breasts and the flirty girl-voice were all for show, plumage that got Prudence what she wanted. I'd known that she was like me in that way, and admired her for it. So instead of just ignoring her for Sarah I stopped and told her that we were all in a lot of trouble.

"I'd sort of picked up on that," she said, pointing with her thumb toward the backyard. Her calm was wrong, a part of all that was wrong that night. She said, "I was just leaving. My car's blocked though. I was trying to find someone—"

"So go out to my car—it's silver, it's the last one in the driveway. Go out to my car and wait for me. I'm going to get Sarah."

She said, "Sarah? Fuck Sarah. What do you need Sarah for?" I sensed her control was limited, or running low, and so she obeyed me, started toward the driveway. Better to do as I said, than to do what the man from the peak asked her to do. I went through the near-empty rooms, finally went into the backyard, where I knew everyone must be.

I tried not to understand too much of what I saw. Since there was no moonlight, no stars, I couldn't make out the exact details anyhow. But the yard was lined with bodies. Many stripped of their clothes, all flat on their back. The bodies, piled like sandbags, formed a wall along the edge of the woods. They were neatly stacked but for a few strays—I saw Michael's body, not five feet from where I stood.

And then I saw Sarah, on her feet, wandering in a daze. I became aware that "Heart and Soul" had stopped. I could hear Sarah's feet brush through the grass.

I couldn't speak—had no impulse to. I ran to Sarah, put my arm around her and guided her toward the side of the house, away from the patio door which was opening, away from Richard, who staggered out into the yard, singing, "Heart and Soul." He fell in love, he sang, "madly."

Prudence was not in the driveway, and I thought fine, if he has her, that'll buy me and Sarah some time, and I'm going to live, and Sarah, too. I pushed Sarah along the driveway, dragged her. I opened the car and put Sarah into the passenger seat, then started the car and backed up to turn around. In the headlights, the car still facing the wrong way, toward the house—I saw Prudence, on her back. Her body must have been just out of sight, just under the front bumper. She jerked, once. I couldn't help watching her breasts: a spray of freckles that vanished into her cleavage.

The mountain road was so rutted, I couldn't go fast, not without taking the chance of breaking an axle.

We were close. Very close to the bottom of the mountain when I heard the bang from the inside of the trunk. I jumped on the accelerator and I could feel a heavy weight shift. Sarah stared calmly ahead, as if we were on a day-trip. There was another bang, and the trunk burst open. I couldn't see anything out the rear-view mirror—just the silver trunk lid. I drove, swerving around boulders, bouncing in and out of pot holes, cursing each time the front end of the car ground into the dirt, until, incredibly, the man from the peak stared at me through the windshield. He clung to the hood on all fours, his arms and legs wide apart, face inches from the glass. He wasn't hiding himself: his teeth were bared and he was filthy with blood, dribbling blood onto the glass, foaming blood from his nostrils.

I felt, suddenly, quite serene. I brought the car to an easy stop. Sarah and I stepped out.

The man from the peak hid himself again. He hopped off the hood with a single, graceful flex of his legs. I heard stones crunch under his shoes as he walked up to Sarah. He looked at me while he put a hand on her right shoulder. And she relaxed completely—I wasn't sure what kept her from collapsing. He grabbed her hair and yanked, forcing her head to the side. She winked at me as if she were about to get a treat she'd been waiting for all day.

Did I make a move to stop him? No. His eyes locked onto mine. And any desire for survival I'd had, any wish for Sarah to live, just slipped away—was leeched from my thoughts. I reached into my breast pocket, slowly removed my cigarette pack, took a cigarette, tamped it against the box, lit it and smoked. I stood, smoked, watched as he tore a chunk of flesh from Sarah's throat with those stupid buck teeth of his and opened his mouth to the jet of blood that burst from her artery. I watched him and he watched me and was he grinning while he drank? Oh, surely he was and I smiled back at him, smiled and smoked my cigarette, smoked so hard the filter flared up before I finally dropped my cigarette and stamped it dead.

I looked up after watching my own foot twist a cigarette butt out on the dirt road and they were gone. He and Sarah were gone. I stared up at the top of the mountain. Stood for at least an hour. Finally, I was released.

Trembling, I slid into the driver's seat and drove down off the mountain into Rattlesnake Valley, as blue light crept across the sky.

◄o►

I listened to the radio for three days. I had the dial somewhere between stations. Sometimes one came in stronger, sometimes the other. I heard news, I heard a minister Bible-teaching, organ music, chants—when both stations grew weak I heard a murkier broadcast: two voices, disharmonious music, swamp-static. I'd ordered all my meals by delivery for the last few days. Greasy wax paper curled in on itself; half-eaten sandwiches, flat soda, Styrofoam. I spent the day in a leather arm chair. I slept there—I woke often to be sure that all my windows were fastened, that the bolts on the door had been shot—that I hadn't been careless after a delivery boy had come by, though, each time I closed the door on a delivery, I locked up, leaned against the door and double-checked the locks. I worried the skin around my fingers and smoked—I'd found a stale pack in my bedroom; not my brand, someone else's cigarettes, some woman I'd brought here had left her cigarettes. I tried to think of ways that I could have stopped what happened from happening, but there was nothing I could've done. I could've done little things differently—not waited so long to take Sarah away (not sent Prudence on her own). Yet, even these small acts seemed out of the realm of possibility to me—that I couldn't have behaved any way other than the way I behaved. My own personality, my own desires, took on monstrous shapes in my mind.

On the third day I remembered the book that I gave to Sarah—that slim collection of short stories. An image of that book popped into my head, completely unbidden. And once that image was there, I couldn't shake it—try as I might. As if the image of that book were being broadcast directly into my head. The book must still have been at Richard's house. I could picture it in each room: on the bar next to a clear, empty bottle; in the guest room on the couch; etc. The book, then the empty room all around it. My thoughts returned incessantly to the book. The book as object. The book as icon. The book as literature—how did those stories tie in with the events of that night? At times, just as sleep would come over me, the stories in that book would seem clearly prophetic—how could I, having read the book, not have known what was going to happen at Richard's party?

I left my apartment to retrieve the book. A small part of my brain screamed at me not to, pointed out that going anywhere near Richard's house was lunacy. I drove up the mountain, tapped the steering wheel, chewed on the end of an unlit cigarette and drove under the no trespassing sign to Richard's. I would get the book and leave. I would have the book. The sun was high and bright, there was nothing at all to going into Richard's house and getting the book and then leaving with it, set on the passenger seat or, perhaps, on my lap. Once I had the book, I would be able to settle back into my rational life.

Prudence's body wasn't in the driveway. I remembered the wall of corpses the man from the peak had made.

I was glad there was still a mess from the party—bottles, ash trays full of butts, objects displaced, leftover dip, etc. If the man from the peak had taken the time to clean the house—that might have made me crazy—if the house had looked as it did on the occasions I'd come to visit Sarah when Richard was away, I'd've been greatly disturbed. There had been a party. The man from the peak had come.

The moment I touched the book I knew that I hadn't come for it after all, and that I hadn't come of my own will.

The peak was a black spike surrounded by sun. I climbed toward the peak. I sweated heavily in my dark clothes—if someone had stood at Richard's front door, would they have been able to see me at all? Just shy of the boulders that crowned the mountain, I found the crevasse I knew was home to the man from the peak. "I live in the peak," he'd said.

I sat down at the edge of the crevasse. A jagged, open crescent, as if a sliver of the moon had burned its impression onto the side of the mountain. When I leaned over, I felt a gust of wet air, like breath; it reeked of ammonia and dirt. I'd smoke until my cigarettes were gone and by then there wouldn't be much light left. I didn't want to be here but I found that it was impossible to leave.

IN PARIS,
IN THE MOUTH OF KRONOS

JOHN LANGAN

I

"You know how much they want for a Coke?"

"How much?" Vasquez said.

"Five euros. Can you believe that?"

Vasquez shrugged. She knew the gesture would irritate Buchanan, who took an almost pathological delight in complaining about everything in Paris, from the lack of air conditioning on the train ride in from De Gaulle to their narrow hotel rooms, but they had an expense account, after all, and however modest it was, she was sure a five-euro Coke would not deplete it. She didn't imagine the professionals sat around fretting over the cost of their sodas.

To her left, the broad Avenue de la Bourdonnais was surprisingly quiet; to her right, the interior of the restaurant was a din of languages: English, mainly, with German, Spanish, Italian, and even a little French mixed in. In front of and behind her, the rest of the sidewalk tables were occupied by an almost even balance of old men reading newspapers and young-ish couples wearing sunglasses. Late afternoon sunlight washed over her surroundings like a spill of white paint, lightening everything several shades, reducing the low buildings across the Avenue to hazy rectangles. When their snack was done, she would have to return to one of the souvenir shops they had passed on the walk here and buy a pair of sunglasses. Another expense for Buchanan to complain about.

"*M'sieu? Madame?*" Their waiter, surprisingly middle-aged, had returned. "*Vous êtes—*"

"You speak English," Buchanan said.

"But of course," the waiter said. "You are ready with your order?"

"I'll have a cheeseburger," Buchanan said. "Medium-rare. And a Coke," he added with a grimace.

"Very good," the waiter said. "And for Madame?"

"*Je voudrais un crêpe de chocolat,*" Vasquez said, "*et un café au lait.*"

The waiter's expression did not change. "*Très bien, Madame. Merçi,*" he said as Vasquez passed him their menus.

"A cheeseburger?" she said once he had returned inside the restaurant.

"What?" Buchanan said.

"Never mind."

"I like cheeseburgers. What's wrong with that?"

"Nothing. It's fine."

"Just because I don't want to eat some kind of French food—ooh, *un crêpe, s'il vous-plait.*"

"All this," Vasquez nodded at their surroundings, "it's lost on you, isn't it?"

"We aren't here for 'all this,'" Buchanan said. "We're here for Mr. White."

Despite herself, Vasquez flinched. "Why don't you speak a little louder? I'm not sure everyone inside the café heard."

"You think they know what we're talking about?"

"That's not the point."

"Oh? What is?"

"Operational integrity."

"Wow. You pick that up from the *Bourne* movies?"

"One person overhears something they don't like, opens their cellphone and calls the cops—"

"And it's all a big misunderstanding officers, we were talking about movies, ha ha."

"—and the time we lose smoothing things over with them completely fucks up Plowman's schedule."

"Stop worrying," Buchanan said, but Vasquez was pleased to see his face blanch at the prospect of Plowman's displeasure.

For a few moments, Vasquez leaned back in her chair and closed her eyes, the sun lighting the inside of her lids crimson. *I'm here*, she thought, the city's presence a pressure at the base of her skull, not unlike what she'd felt patrolling the streets of Bagram, but less unpleasant. Buchanan said, "So you've been here before."

"What?" Brightness overwhelmed her vision, simplified Buchanan to a dark silhouette in a baseball cap.

"You parlez the français pretty well. I figure you must've spent some time—what? In college? Some kind of study abroad deal?"

"Nope," Vasquez said.

"'Nope,' what?"

"I've never been to Paris. Hell, before I enlisted, the farthest I'd ever been from home was the class trip to Washington senior year."

"You're shittin me."

"Uh-uh. Don't get me wrong: I wanted to see Paris, London—everything. But the money—the money wasn't there. The closest I came to all this were the movies in Madame Antosca's French 4 class. It was one of the reasons I joined up: I figured I'd see the world and let the Army pay for it."

"How'd that work out for you?"

"We're here, aren't we?"

"Not because of the Army."

"No, precisely because of the Army. Well," she said, "them and the spooks."

"You still think Mr.—oh, sorry—*You-Know-Who* was CIA?"

Frowning, Vasquez lowered her voice. "Who knows? I'm not even sure he was one of ours. That accent... he could've been working for the Brits, or the Aussies. He could've been Russian, back in town to settle a few scores. Wherever he picked up his pronunciation, dude was not regular military."

"Be funny if *he* was on Stillwater's payroll."

"Hysterical," Vasquez said. "What about you?"

"What about me?"

"I assume this is your first trip to Paris."

"And there's where you would be wrong."

"Now you're shittin me."

"Why, because I ordered a cheeseburger and a Coke?"

"Among other things, yeah."

"My senior class trip was a week in Paris and Amsterdam. In college, the end of my sophomore year, my parents took me to France for a month." At what she knew must be the look on her face, Buchanan added, "It was an attempt at breaking up the relationship I was in at the time."

"It's not that. I'm trying to process the thought of you in college."

"Wow, anyone ever tell you what a laugh riot you are?"

"Did it work—your parents' plan?"

Buchanan shook his head. "The second I was back in the US, I knocked her up. We were married by the end of the summer."

"How romantic."

"Hey." Buchanan shrugged.

"That why you enlisted, support your new family?"

"More or less. Heidi's dad owned a bunch of McDonald's; for the first six months of our marriage, I tried to assistant manage one of them."

"With your people skills, that must have been a match made in Heaven."

The retort forming on Buchanan's lips was cut short by the reappearance of their waiter, encumbered with their drinks and their food. He set their plates before them with a, "*Madame*," and, "*M'sieu*," then, as he was distributing their drinks, said, "Everything is okay? *Ça va?*"

"*Oui*," Vasquez said. "*C'est bon. Merçi.*"

With the slightest of bows, the waiter left them to their food.

While Buchanan worked his hands around his cheeseburger, Vasquez said, "I don't think I realized you were married."

"*Were*," Buchanan said. "She wasn't happy about my deploying in the first place, and when the shit hit the fan…" He bit into the burger. Through a mouthful of bun and meat, he said, "The court martial was the excuse she needed. Couldn't handle the shame, she said. The humiliation of being married to one of the guards who'd tortured an innocent man to death. What kind of role model would I be for our son?

"I tried—I tried to tell her it wasn't like that. It wasn't that—you know what I'm talking about."

Vasquez studied her neatly-folded crêpe. "Yeah." Mr. White had favored a flint knife for what he called *the delicate work*.

"If that's what she wants, fine, fuck her. But she made it so I can't see my son. The second she decided we were splitting up, there was her dad with money for a lawyer. I get a call from this asshole—this is right in the middle of the court martial—and he tells me Heidi's filing for divorce—no surprise—and they're going to make it easy for me: no alimony, no child support, nothing. The only catch is, I have to sign away all my rights to Sam. If I don't, they're fully prepared to go to court, and how do I like my chances in front of a judge? What choice did I have?"

Vasquez tasted her coffee. She saw her mother, holding open the front door for her, unable to meet her eyes.

"Bad enough about that poor bastard who died—what was his name? If there's one thing you'd think I'd know…"

"Mahbub Ali," Vasquez said. *What kind of a person are you?* her father had shouted. *What kind of person is part of such things?*

"Mahbub Ali," Buchanan said. "Bad enough what happened to him; I just wish I'd know what was happening to the rest of us, as well."

They ate the rest of their meal in silence. When the waiter returned to ask if they wanted dessert, they declined.

II

Vasquez had compiled a list of reasons for crossing the Avenue and walking to the Eiffel Tower, from, *It's an open, crowded space: it's a better place to review the plan's details*, to, *I want to see the fucking Eiffel Tower once before I die, okay?* But Buchanan agreed to her proposal without argument; nor did he complain about the fifteen euros she spent on a pair of sunglasses on the walk there. Did she need to ask to know he was back in the concrete room they'd called the Closet, its air full of the stink of fear and piss?

Herself, she was doing her best not to think about the chamber under the prison's sub-basement Just-Call-Me-Bill had taken her to. This was maybe a week after the tall, portly man she knew for a fact was CIA had started spending every waking moment with Mr. White. Vasquez had followed Bill down poured concrete stairs that led from the labyrinth of the basement and its handful of high-value captives in their scattered cells (not to mention the Closet, whose precise location she'd been unable to fix), to the sub-basement, where he had clicked on the large yellow flashlight he was carrying. Its beam had ranged over brick walls, an assortment of junk (some of it Soviet-era aircraft parts, some of it tools to repair those parts, some of it more recent: stacks of toilet paper, boxes of plastic cutlery, a pair of hospital gurneys). They had made their way through that place to a low doorway that opened on carved stone steps whose curved surfaces testified to the passage of generations of feet. All the time, Just-Call-Me-Bill had been talking, lecturing, detailing the history of the prison, from its time as a repair center for the aircraft the Soviets flew in and out of here, until some KGB officer decided the building was perfect for housing prisoners, a change everyone who subsequently held possession of it had maintained. Vasquez had struggled to pay attention, especially as they had descended the last set of stairs and the air grew warm, moist, the rock to either side of her damp. *Before*, the CIA operative was saying, *oh, before. Did you know a detachment of Alexander the Great's army stopped here? One man returned.*

The stairs had ended in a wide, circular area. The roof was flat, low, the walls no more than shadowy suggestions. Just-Call-Me-Bill's flashlight had roamed the floor, picked out a symbol incised in the rock at their feet: a rough circle, the diameter of a manhole cover, broken at about eight o'clock. Its circumference was stained black, its interior a map of dark brown splotches. *Hold this*, he had said, passing her the flashlight, which had occupied her for the two or three seconds it took him to remove a plastic baggie from one of the pockets of his safari vest. When Vasquez had directed the light at him, he was dumping the bag's contents in his right hand, tugging at the plastic with his left to pull it away from the dull red wad. The stink of blood and meat on the turn had made her step back. *Steady, specialist.* The bag's contents had landed inside the broken circle with a heavy, wet smack. Vasquez had done her best not to study it too closely.

A sound, the scrape of bare flesh dragging over stone, from behind and to her left, had spun Vasquez around, the flashlight held out to blind, her sidearm freed and following the light's path. This section of the curving wall opened in a black arch like the top of an enormous throat. For a moment, that space had been full of a great, pale figure. Vasquez had had a confused impression of hands large as tires grasping either side of the arch, a boulder of a head, its mouth gaping amidst a frenzy of beard, its eyes vast, idiot. It was scrambling towards her; she didn't know where to aim—

And then Mr. White had been standing in the archway, dressed in the white linen suit that somehow always seemed stained, even though no discoloration was visible on any of it. He had not blinked at the flashlight beam stabbing his face; nor had he appeared to judge Vasquez's gun pointing at him of much concern. Muttering an apology, Vasquez had lowered gun and light immediately. Mr. White had ignored her, strolling across the round chamber to the foot of the stairs, which he had climbed quickly. Just-Call-Me-Bill had hurried after, a look on his bland face that Vasquez took for amusement. She had brought up the rear, sweeping the flashlight over the floor as she reached the lowest step. The broken circle had been empty, except for a red smear that shone in the light.

That she had momentarily hallucinated, Vasquez had not once doubted. Things with Mr. White already had raced past what even Just-Call-Me-Bill had shown them, and however effective his methods, Vasquez was afraid that she—that all of them had finally gone too far, crossed over into truly bad territory. Combined with a mild claustrophobia, that had caused her to fill the dark space with a nightmare. However reasonable that explanation, the shape with which her mind had replaced Mr. White had plagued her. Had she seen the Devil stepping forward on his goat's feet, one red hand using his pitchfork to balance himself, it would have made more sense than that giant form. It was as if her subconscious was telling her more about Mr. White than she understood. Prior to that trip, Vasquez had not been at ease around the man who never seemed to speak so much as to have spoken, so that you knew what he'd said even though you couldn't remember hearing him saying it. After, she gave him still-wider berth.

Ahead, the Eiffel Tower swept up into the sky. Vasquez had seen it from a distance, at different points along hers and Buchanan's journey from their hotel towards the Seine, but the closer she drew to it, the less real it seemed. It was as if the very solidity of the beams and girders weaving together were evidence of their falseness. *I am seeing the Eiffel Tower*, she told herself. *I am actually looking at the goddamn Eiffel Tower.*

"Here you are," Buchanan said. "Happy?"

"Something like that."

The great square under the Tower was full of tourists, from the sound of it, the majority of them groups of Americans and Italians. Nervous men wearing untucked shirts over their jeans flitted from group to group—street vendors, Vasquez realized, each one carrying an oversized ring strung with metal replicas of the Tower. A pair of gendarmes, their hands draped over the machine guns slung high on their chests, let their eyes roam the crowd while they carried on a conversation. In front of each of the Tower's legs, lines of people waiting for the chance to ascend it doubled and redoubled back on themselves, enormous fans misting water over them. Taking Buchanan's arm, Vasquez steered them towards the nearest fan. Eyebrows raised, he tilted his head towards her.

"Ambient noise," she said.

"Whatever."

Once they were close enough to the fan's propeller drone, Vasquez leaned into Buchanan. "Go with this," she said.

"You're the boss." Buchanan gazed up, a man debating whether he wanted to climb *that* high.

"I've been thinking," Vasquez said. "Plowman's plan's shit."

"Oh?" He pointed at the Tower's first level, three hundred feet above.

Nodding, Vasquez said, "We approach Mr. White, and he's just going to agree to come with us to the elevator."

Buchanan dropped his hand. "Well, we do have our... persuaders. How do you like that? Was it cryptic enough? Or should I have said, 'Guns'?"

Vasquez smiled as if Buchanan had uttered an endearing remark. "You really think Mr. White is going to be impressed by a pair of .22s?"

"A bullet's a bullet. Besides," Buchanan returned her smile, "isn't the plan for us not to have to use the guns? Aren't we relying on him remembering us?"

"It's not like we were BFFs. If it were me, and I wanted the guy, and I had access to Stillwater's resources, I wouldn't be wasting my time on a couple of convicted criminals. I'd put together a team and go get him. Besides, twenty grand a piece for catching up to someone outside his hotel room, passing a couple of words with him, then escorting him to an elevator: tell me that doesn't sound too good to be true."

"You know the way these big companies work: they're all about throwing money around. Your problem is, you're still thinking like a soldier."

"Even so, why spend it on us?"

"Maybe Plowman feels bad about everything. Maybe this is his way of making it up to us."

"Plowman? Seriously?"

Buchanan shook his head. "This isn't that complicated."

Vasquez closed her eyes. "Humor me." She leaned her head against Buchanan's chest.

"What have I been doing?"

"We're a feint. While we're distracting Mr. White, Plowman's up to something else."

"Like?"

"Maybe Mr. White has something in his room; maybe we're occupying him while Plowman's retrieving it."

"You know there are easier ways for Plowman to steal something."

"Maybe we're keeping Mr. White in place so Plowman can pull a hit on him."

"Again, there are simpler ways to do that that would have nothing to do with us. You knock on the guy's door, he opens it, pow."

"What if we're supposed to get caught in the crossfire?"

"You bring us all the way here just to kill us?"

"Didn't you say big companies like to spend money?"

"But why take us out in the first place?"

Vasquez raised her head and opened her eyes. "How many of the people who knew Mr. White are still in circulation?"

"There's Just-Call-Me-Bill—"

"You think. He's CIA. We don't know what happened to him."

"Okay. There's you, me, Plowman—"

"Go on."

Buchanan paused, reviewing, Vasquez knew, the fates of the three other guards who'd assisted Mr. White with his work in the Closet. Long before news had broken about Mahbub Ali's death, Lavalle had sat on the edge of his bunk, placed his gun in his mouth, and squeezed the trigger. Then, when the shitstorm had started, Maxwell, on patrol, had been stabbed in the neck by an insurgent who'd targeted only him. Finally, in the holding cell awaiting his court martial, Ruiz had taken advantage of a lapse in his jailers' attention to strip off his pants, twist them into a rope, and hang himself from the top bunk of his cell's bunkbed. His guards had cut him down in time to save his life, but Ruiz had deprived his brain of oxygen for sufficient time to leave him a vegetable. When Buchanan spoke, he said, "Coincidence."

"Or conspiracy."

"Goddammit." Buchanan pulled free of Vasquez, and headed for the long, rectangular park that stretched behind the Tower, speedwalking. His legs were sufficiently long that she had to jog to catch up to him. Buchanan did not slacken his pace, continuing his straight line up the middle of the park, through the midst of bemused picnickers. "Jesus Christ," Vasquez called, "will you slow down?"

He would not. Heedless of oncoming traffic, Buchanan led her across a pair of roads that traversed the park. Horns blaring, tires screaming, cars swerved around them. *At this rate*, Vasquez thought, *Plowman's motives won't matter.* Once they were safely on the grass again, she sped up until she was beside him, then reached high on the underside of Buchanan's right arm, not far from the armpit, and pinched as hard as she could.

"Ow! Shit!" Yanking his arm up and away, Buchanan stopped. Rubbing his skin, he said, "What the hell, Vasquez?"

"What the hell are you doing?"

"Walking. What did it look like?"

"Running away."

"Fuck you."

"Fuck you, you candy-ass pussy."

Buchanan's eyes flared.

"I'm trying to work this shit out so we can stay alive. You're so concerned about seeing your son, maybe you'd want to help me."

"Why are you doing this?" Buchanan said. "Why are you fucking with my head? Why are you trying to fuck this up?"

"I'm—"

"There's nothing to work out. We've got a job to do; we do it; we get the rest of our money. We do the job well, there's a chance Stillwater'll add us to their payroll. That happens—I'm making that kind of money—I hire myself a pit bull of a lawyer and sic him on fucking Heidi. You want to live in goddamn Paris, you can eat a croissant for breakfast every morning."

"You honestly believe that."

"Yes I do."

Vasquez held his gaze, but who was she kidding? She could count on one finger the number of stare-downs she'd won. Her arms, legs, everything felt suddenly, incredibly heavy. She looked at her watch. "Come on," she said, starting in the direction of the Avenue de la Bourdonnais. "We can catch a cab."

III

Plowman had insisted they meet him at an airport café before they set foot outside De Gaulle. At the end of those ten minutes, which had consisted of Plowman asking details of their flight and instructing them how to take the RUR to the Metro to the stop nearest their hotel, he had passed Vasquez a card for a restaurant, where, he had said, the three of them would reconvene at 3:00 pm local time to review the evening's plans. Vasquez had been relieved to see Plowman seated at a table outside the café. Despite the ten thousand dollars gathering interest in her checking account, the plane ticket that had been Fed-Ex'd to her apartment, followed by the receipt for four nights' stay at the Hôtel Resnais, she had been unable to shake the sense that none of this was as it appeared, that it was the set up to an elaborate joke whose punchline would come at her expense. Plowman's solid form, dressed in a black suit whose tailored lines announced the upward shift in his pay grade, had confirmed that everything he had told her the afternoon he had sought her out at Andersen's farm had been true.

Or true enough to quiet momentarily the misgivings that had whispered ever-louder in her ears the last two weeks, to the point that she had held her cell open in her left hand, the piece of paper with Plowman's number on it in her right, ready to call him and say she was out, he could have his money back, she hadn't spent any of it. During the long, hot train ride from the airport to the Metro station, when Buchanan had complained about Plowman not letting them out of his sight, treating them like goddamn kids, Vasquez had found an explanation on her lips. *It's probably the first time he's run an operation like this*, she had said. *He wants to be sure he dots all his i's and crosses all his t's.* Buchanan had harrumphed, but it was true: Plowman obsessed over the minutiae; it was one of the reasons he'd been in charge of their detail at the prison. Until the shit had buried the fan, that attentiveness had seemed to forecast his steady climb up the chain of command. At his court martial, however, his enthusiasm for exact strikes on prisoner nerve clusters, his precision in placing arm restraints so that a prisoner's shoulders would not dislocate when he was hoisted off the floor by his bonds, his speed in obtaining the various surgical and dental instruments Just-Call-Me-Bill requested, had been counted liabilities rather than assets, and he had been the only one of their group to serve substantial time at Leavenworth, ten months.

Still, the Walther Vasquez had requested had been waiting where Plowman had promised it would be, wrapped with an extra clip in a waterproof bag secured inside the tank of her hotel room's toilet. A thorough inspection had reassured her that all was in order with the gun, its ammunition. If he were setting her up, would Plowman have wanted to arm her? Her proficiency at the target range had been well-known, and while she hadn't touched a gun since her discharge, she had no doubts of her ability. Tucked within the back of her jeans, draped by her blouse, the pistol was easily accessible.

That's assuming, of course, that Plowman's even there tonight. But the caution was a formality. Plowman being Plowman, there was no way he was not going to be at Mr. White's hotel. Was there any need for him to have made the trip to West Virginia, to have tracked her to Andersen's farm, to have sought her out in the far barns, where she'd been using a high-pressure hose to sluice pig shit into gutters? An e-mail, a phone call would have sufficed. Such methods, however, would have left too much outside Plowman's immediate control, and since he appeared able to dunk his bucket into a well of cash deeper than any she'd known, he had decided to find Vasquez and speak to her directly. (He'd done the same with Buchanan, she'd learned on the flight over, tracking him to the suburb of Chicago where he'd been shift manager at Hardee's.) If the man had gone to such lengths to persuade them to take the job, if he had been there to meet them at the Charles de Gaulle and was waiting for them even now, as their taxi crossed the Seine and headed towards the Champs-Élysées, was there any chance he wouldn't be present later on?

Of course, he wouldn't be alone. Plowman would have the reassurance of God-only-knew-how-many Stillwater employees, which was to say, mercenaries (no doubt, heavily-armed and armored) backing him up. Vasquez hadn't had much to do with the company's personnel; they tended to roost closer to the center of Kabul, where the high-value targets they guarded huddled. Iraq: that was where Stillwater's bootprint was the deepest; from what Vasquez had heard, the former soldiers riding the reinforced Lincoln Navigators through Baghdad not only made about five times what they had in the military, they followed rules of engagement that were, to put it mildly, less robust. While Paris was as far east as she was willing to travel, she had to admit, the prospect of that kind of money made Baghdad, if not appealing, at least less unappealing.

And what would Dad have to say to that? No matter that his eyes were failing, the center of his vision consumed by Macular Degeneration, her father had lost none of his passion for the news, employing a standing magnifier to aid him as he pored over the day's *New York Times* and *Washington Post*, sitting in his favorite chair listening to *All Things Considered* on WVPN, even venturing online to the BBC using the computer whose monitor settings she had adjusted for him before she'd deployed. Her father would not have missed the reports of Stillwater's involvement in several incidents in Iraq that were less shoot-outs than turkey-shoots, not to mention the ongoing Congressional inquiry into their policing of certain districts of post-Katrina and Rita New Orleans, as well as an event in Upstate New York last summer, when one of their employees had taken a camping trip that had left two of his three companions dead under what could best be described as suspicious circumstances. She could hear his words, heavy with the accent that had accreted as he'd aged: *Was this why I suffered in the Villa Grimaldi? So my daughter could join the* Caravana de la Muerte? The same question he'd asked her the first night she'd returned home.

All the same, it wasn't as if his opinion of her was going to drop any further. *If I'm damned*, she thought, *I might as well get paid for it.*

That said, she was in no hurry to certify her ultimate destination, which returned her to the problem of Plowman and his plan. You would have expected the press of the .22 against the small of her back to have been reassuring, but instead, it only emphasized her sense of powerlessness, as if Plowman were so confident, so secure, he could allow her whatever firearm she wanted.

The cab turned onto the Champs-Élysées. Ahead, the Arc de Triomphe squatted in the distance. Another monument to cross off the list.

IV

The restaurant whose card Plowman had handed her was located on one of the sidestreets about halfway to the Arc; Vasquez and Buchanan departed their cab at the street's corner and walked the hundred yards to a door flanked by man-sized plaster Chinese dragons. Buchanan brushed past the black-suited host and his welcome; smiling and murmuring, *"Padonnez, nous avons un rendez-vous içi,"* Vasquez pursued him into the dim interior. Up a short flight of stairs, Buchanan strode across a floor that glowed with pale light—glass, Vasquez saw, thick squares suspended over shimmering aquamarine. A carp the size of her forearm darted underneath her, and she realized that she was standing on top of an enormous, shallow fishtank, brown and white and orange carp racing one another across its bottom, jostling the occasional slower turtle. With one exception, the tables supported by the glass were empty. Too late, Vasquez supposed, for lunch, and too early for dinner. Or maybe the food here wasn't that good.

His back to the far wall, Plowman was seated at a table directly in front of her. Already, Buchanan was lowering himself into a chair opposite him. *Stupid*, Vasquez thought at the expanse of his unguarded back. Her boots clacked on the glass. She moved around the table to sit beside Plowman, who had exchanged the dark suit in which he'd greeted them at De Gaulle for a tan jacket over a cream shirt and slacks. His outfit caught the light filtering from below them and held it in as a dull sheen. A metal bowl filled with dumplings was centered on the tablemat before him; to its right, a slice of lemon floated at the top of a glass of clear liquid. Plowman's eyebrow raised as she settled beside him, but he did not comment on her choice; instead, he said, "You're here."

Vasquez's, "Yes," was overridden by Buchanan's, "We are, and there are some things we need cleared up."

Vasquez stared at him. Plowman said, "Oh?"

"That's right," Buchanan said. "We've been thinking, and this plan of yours doesn't add up."

"Really." The tone of Plowman's voice did not change.

"Really," Buchanan nodded.

"Would you care to explain to me exactly how it doesn't add up?"

"You expect Vasquez and me to believe you spent all this money so the two of us can have a five-minute conversation with Mr. White?"

Vasquez flinched.

"There's a little bit more to it than that."

"We're supposed to persuade him to walk twenty feet with us to an elevator."

"Actually, it's seventy-four feet three inches."

"Whatever." Buchanan glanced at Vasquez. She looked away. To the wall to her right, water chuckled down a series of small rock terraces through an opening in the floor into the fishtank.

"No, not 'whatever,' Buchanan. Seventy-four feet, three inches," Plowman said. "This is why the biggest responsibility you confront each day is lifting the fry basket out of the hot oil when the buzzer tells you to. You don't pay attention to the little things."

The host was standing at Buchanan's elbow, his hands clasped over a pair of long menus. Plowman nodded at him and he passed the menus to Vasquez and Buchanan. Inclining towards them, the host said, "May I bring you drinks while you decide your order?"

His eyes on the menu, Buchanan said, "Water."

"*Moi aussi*," Vasquez said. "*Merçi.*"

"Nice accent," Plowman said when the host had left.

"Thanks."

"I don't think I realized you speak French."

Vasquez shrugged. "Wasn't any call for it, was there?"

"Anything else?" Plowman said. "Spanish?"

"I understand more than I can speak."

"You folks were from—where, again?"

"Chile," Vasquez said. "My Dad. My Mom's American, but her parents were from Argentina."

"That's useful to know."

"For when Stillwater hires her," Buchanan said.

"Yes," Plowman answered. "The company has projects underway in a number of places where fluency in French and Spanish would be an asset."

"Such as?"

"One thing at a time," Plowman said. "Let's get through tonight, first, and then you can worry about your next assignment."

"And what's that going to be," Buchanan said, "another twenty K to walk someone to an elevator?"

"I doubt it'll be anything so mundane," Plowman said. "I also doubt it'll pay as little as twenty thousand."

"Look," Vasquez started to say, but the host had returned with their water. Once he deposited their glasses on the table, he withdrew a pad and pen from his jacket pocket and took Buchanan's order of crispy duck and Vasquez's of steamed dumplings. After he had retrieved the menus and gone, Plowman turned to Vasquez and said, "You were saying?"

"It's just—what Buchanan's trying to say is, it's a lot, you know? If you'd offered us, I don't know, say five hundred bucks apiece to come here and play escort, that still would've been a lot, but it wouldn't—I mean, *twenty thousand dollars*, plus the air fare, the hotel, the expense account. It seems too much for what you're asking us to do. Can you understand that?"

Plowman shook his head yes. "I can. I can understand how strange it might appear to offer this kind of money for this length of service, but..." He raised his drink to his lips. When he lowered his arm, the glass was half-drained. "Mr. White is... to say he's high-value doesn't begin to cover it. The guy's been around—he's been around. Talk about a font of information: the stuff this guy's forgotten would be enough for a dozen careers. What he remembers will give whoever can get him to share it with them permanent tactical advantage."

"No such thing," Buchanan said. "No matter how much the guy says he knows—"

"Yes, yes," Plowman held up his hand like a traffic cop. "Trust me. He's high value."

"But won't the spooks—what's Just-Call-Me-Bill have to say about this?" Vasquez said.

"Bill's dead."

Simultaneously, Buchanan said, "Huh," and Vasquez, "What? How?"

"I don't know. When my bosses greenlighted me for this, Bill was the first person I thought of. I wasn't sure if he was still with the Agency, so I did some checking around. I couldn't find out much—goddamn spooks keep their mouths shut—but I was able to determine that Bill was dead. It sounded like it might've been that chopper crash in Helmand, but that's a guess. To answer your question, Vasquez, Bill didn't have a whole lot to say."

"Shit," Buchanan said.

"Okay," Vasquez exhaled. "Okay. Was he the only one who knew about Mr. White?"

"I find it hard to believe he was," Plowman said, "but thus far, no one's nibbled at any of the bait I've left out. I'm surprised: I'll admit it. But it makes our job that much simpler, so I'm not complaining."

"All right," Vasquez said, "but the money—"

His eyes alight, Plowman leaned forward. "To get my hands on Mr. White, I would have paid each of you ten times as much. That's how important this operation is. Whatever we have to shell out now is nothing compared to what we're going to gain from this guy."

"Now you tell us," Buchanan said.

Plowman smiled and relaxed back. "Well, the bean counters do appreciate it when you can control costs." He turned to Vasquez. "Well? Have your concerns been addressed?"

"Hey," Buchanan said, "I was the one asking the questions."

"Please," Plowman said. "I was in charge of you, remember? Whatever your virtues, Buchanan, original thought is not among them."

"What about Mr. White?" Vasquez said. "Suppose he doesn't want to come with you?"

"I don't imagine he will," Plowman said. "Nor do I expect him to be terribly interested in assisting us once he is in our custody. That's okay." Plowman picked up one of the chopsticks alongside his plate, turned it in his hand, and jabbed it into a dumpling. He lifted the dumpling to his mouth; momentarily, Vasquez pictured a giant bringing its teeth together on a human head. While he chewed, Plowman said, "To be honest, I hope the son of a bitch is feeling especially stubborn. Because of him, I lost everything that was good in my life. Because of that fucker, I did time in prison—fucking *prison*." Plowman swallowed, speared another dumpling. "Believe me when I say, Mr. White and I have a lot of quality time coming."

Beneath them, a half-dozen carp that had been floating lazily, scattered.

V

Buchanan was all for finding Mr. White's hotel and parking themselves in its lobby. "What?" Vasquez said. "Behind a couple of newspapers?" Stuck in traffic on what should have been the short way to the Concorde Opera, where Mr. White had the Junior Suite, their cab was full of the reek of exhaust, the low rumble of the cars surrounding them.

"Sure, yeah, that'd work."

"Jesus—and I'm the one who's seen too many movies?"

"What?" Buchanan said.

"Number one, at this rate, it'll be at least six before we get there. How many people sit around reading the day's paper at night? The whole point of the news is, it's new."

"Maybe we're on vacation."

"Doesn't matter. We'll still stick out. And number two, even if the lobby's full of tourists holding newspapers up in front of their faces, Plowman's plan doesn't kick in until eleven. You telling me no one's going to notice the same two people sitting there, doing the same thing, for five hours? For all we know, Mr. White'll see us on his way out and coming back."

"Once again, Vasquez, you're overthinking this. People don't see what they don't expect to see. Mr. White isn't expecting us in the lobby of his plush hotel, ergo, he won't notice us there."

"Are you kidding? This isn't 'people.' This is Mr. White."

"Get a grip. He eats, shits, and sleeps same as you and me."

For the briefest of instants, the window over Buchanan's shoulder was full of the enormous face Vasquez had glimpsed (hallucinated) in the caves under the prison. Not for the first time, she was struck by the crudeness of the features, as if a sculptor had hurriedly struck out the approximation of a human visage on a piece of rock already formed to suggest it.

Taking her silence as further disagreement, Buchanan sighed and said, "All right. Tell you what: a big, tony hotel, there's gotta be all kinds of stores around it, right? Long as we don't go too far, we'll do some shopping."

"Fine," Vasquez said. When Buchanan had settled back in his seat, she said, "So. You satisfied with Plowman's answers?"

"Aw, no, not this again…"

"I'm just asking a question."

"No, what you're asking is called a leading question, as in, leading me to think that Plowman didn't really say anything to us, and we don't know anything more now than we did before our meeting."

"You learned something from that?"

Buchanan nodded. "You bet I did. I learned that Plowman has a hard-on for Mr. White the size of your fucking Eiffel Tower, from which, I deduce that anyone who helps him satisfy himself stands to benefit enormously." As the cab lurched forward, Buchanan said, "Am I wrong?"

"No," Vasquez said. "It's—"

"What? What is it, now?"

"I don't know." She looked out her window at the cars creeping along beside them.

"Well that's helpful."

"Forget it."

For once, Buchanan chose not to pursue the argument. Beyond the car to their right, Vasquez watched men and women walking past the windows of ground-level businesses, tech stores and clothing stores and a bookstore and an office whose purpose she could not identify. Over their wrought-iron balconies, the windows of the apartments above showed the late-afternoon sky, its blue deeper, as if hardened by a day of the sun's baking. *Because of him, I lost everything that was good in my life. Because of that fucker, I did time in prison—fucking prison.* Plowman's declaration sounded in her ears. Insofar as the passion on his face authenticated his words, and so the purpose of their mission, his brief monologue should have been reassuring. And yet, and yet…

In the moment before he drove his fist into a prisoner's solar plexus, Plowman's features, distorted and red from the last hour's interrogation, would relax. The effect was startling, as if a layer of heavy makeup had melted off his skin. In the subsequent stillness of his face, Vasquez initially had read Plowman's actual emotion, a clinical detachment from the pain he was preparing to inflict that was based in his utter contempt for the man standing in front of him. While his mouth would stretch with his screams to the prisoner to *Get up! Get the fuck up!* in the second after his blow had dropped the man to the concrete floor, and while his mouth and eyes would continue to express the violence his fists and boots were concentrating on the prisoner's back, his balls, his throat, there would be other moments, impossible to predict, when, as he was shuffle-stepping away from a kick to the prisoner's kidney, Plowman's face would slip into that non-expression and Vasquez would think that she had seen through to the real man.

Then, the week after Plowman had brought Vasquez on board what he had named the White Detail, she'd found herself sitting through a Steven Seagal double-feature—not her first or even tenth choice for a way to pass three hours, but it beat lying on her bunk thinking, *Why are you so shocked? You knew what Plowman was up to—everyone knows.* An hour into *The Patriot*, the vague sensation that had been nagging at her from Seagal's first scene crystallized into recognition: that the blank look with which the actor met every ebb and flow in the drama was the same as the one that Vasquez had caught on Plowman's face, was, she understood, its original. For the remainder of that film and the duration of the next (*Belly of the Beast*), Vasquez had stared at the undersized screen in a kind of horrified fascination, unable to decide which was worse: to be serving under a man whose affect suggested a sociopath, or to be serving under a man who was playing the lead role in a private movie.

How many days after that had Just-Call-Me-Bill arrived? No more than two, she was reasonably sure. He had come, he told the White Detail, because their efforts with particularly *recalcitrant* prisoners had not gone unnoticed, and his superiors judged it would be beneficial for him to share his knowledge of enhanced interrogation techniques with them—and no doubt, they had some things to teach him. His back ramrod straight, his face alight, Plowman had barked his enthusiasm for their collaboration.

After that, it had been learning the restraints that would cause the prisoner maximum discomfort, expose him (or occasionally, her) to optimum harm. It was hoisting the prisoner off the ground first without dislocating his shoulders, then with. Waterboarding, yes, together with the repurposing of all manner of daily objects, from nail files to pliers to dental floss. Each case was different. Of course you couldn't believe any of the things the prisoners said when they were turned over to you, their protestations of innocence. But even after it appeared you'd broken them, you couldn't be sure they weren't engaged in a more subtle deception, acting as if you'd succeeded in order to preserve the truly valuable information. For this reason, it was necessary to keep the interrogation open, to continue to revisit those prisoners who swore they'd told you everything they knew. *These people are not like you and me*, Just-Call-Me-Bill had said, confirming the impression that had dogged Vasquez when she'd walked patrol, past women draped in white or slate *burqas*, men whose *pokool* proclaimed their loyalty to the *mujahideen*. *These are not a reasonable people. You cannot sit down and talk to them*, Bill went on, *come to an understanding with them. They would rather fly an airplane into a building full of innocent women and men. They would rather strap a bomb to their daughter and send her to give you a hug. They get their hands on a nuke, and there'll be a mushroom cloud where Manhattan used to be. What they understand is pain. Enough suffering, and their tongues will loosen.*

Vasquez could not pin down the exact moment Mr. White had joined their group. When he had shouldered his way past Lavalle and Maxwell, his left hand up to stop Plowman from tilting the prisoner backwards, Just-Call-Me-Bill from pouring the water onto the man's hooded face, she had thought, *Who the hell?* And, as quickly, *Oh—Mr. White.* He must have been with them for some time for Plowman to upright the prisoner, Bill to lower the bucket and step back. The flint knife in his right hand, its edge so fine you could feel it pressing against your bare skin, had not been unexpected. Nor had what had followed.

It was Mr. White who had suggested they transfer their operations to the Closet, a recommendation Just-Call-Me-Bill had been happy to embrace. Plowman, at first, had been noncommittal. Mr. White's… call it his taking a more active hand in their interrogations, had led to him and Bill spending increased time together. Ruiz had asked the CIA man what he was doing with the man whose suit, while seemingly filthy, was never touched by any of the blood that slicked his knife, his hands. *Education,* Just-Call-Me-Bill had answered. *Our friend is teaching me all manner of things.*

As he was instructing the rest of them, albeit in more indirect fashion. Vasquez had learned that her father's stories of the Villa Grimaldi, which he had withheld from her until she was fifteen, when over the course of the evening after her birthday she had been first incredulous, then horrified, then filled with righteous fury on his behalf, had little bearing on her duties in the Closet. Her father had been an innocent man, a poet, for God's sake, picked up by Pinochet's *Caravana de la Muerte* because they were engaged in a program of terrorizing their own populace. The men (and occasional women) at whose interrogations she assisted were terrorists themselves, spiritual kin to the officers who had scarred her father's arms, his chest, his back, his thighs, who had scored his mind with nightmares from which he still fled screaming, decades later. They were not like you and me, and that difference authorized and legitimized whatever was required to start them talking.

By the time Mahbub Ali was hauled into the Closet, Vasquez had learned other things, too. She had learned that it was possible to concentrate pain on a single part of the body, to the point that the prisoner grew to hate that part of himself for the agony focused there. She had learned that it was preferable to work slowly, methodically— religiously, was how she thought of it, though this was no religion to which she'd ever been exposed. This was a faith rooted in the most fundamental truth Mr. White taught her, taught all of them, namely, that the flesh yearns for the knife, aches for the cut that will open it, relieve it of its quivering anticipation of harm. As junior member of the Detail, she had not yet progressed to being allowed to work on the prisoners directly, but it didn't matter. While she and Buchanan sliced away a prisoner's clothes, exposed bare skin, what she saw there, a fragility, a vulnerability whose thick, salty taste filled her mouth, confirmed all of Mr. White's lessons, every last one.

Nor was she his best student. That had been Plowman, the only one of them to whom Mr. White had entrusted his flint knife. With Just-Call-Me-Bill, Mr. White had maintained the air of a senior colleague; with the rest of them, he acted as if they were mannequins, placeholders. With Plowman, though, Mr. White was the mentor, the last practitioner of an otherwise-dead art passing his knowledge on to his chosen successor. It might have been the plot of a Steven Seagal film. And no Hollywood star could have played the eager apprentice with more enthusiasm than Plowman. While the official cause of Mahbub Ali's death was sepsis resulting from improperly tended wounds, those missing pieces of the man had been parted from him on the edge of Mr. White's stone blade, gripped in Plowman's steady hand.

VI

Even with the clotted traffic, the cab drew up in front of the Concorde Opera's three sets of polished wooden doors with close to five hours to spare. While Vasquez settled with the driver, Buchanan stepped out of the cab, crossed the sidewalk, strode up three stairs, and passed through the center doors. The act distracted her enough that she forgot to ask for a receipt; by the time she remembered, the cab had accepted a trio of middle-aged women, their arms crowded with shopping bags, and pulled away. She considered chasing after it, before deciding that she could absorb the ten euros. She turned to the hotel to see the center doors open again, Buchanan standing in them next to a young man with a shaved head who was wearing navy pants and a cream tunic on whose upper left side a name tag flashed. The young man pointed across the street in front of the hotel and waved his hand back and forth, all the while talking to Buchanan, who nodded attentively. When the young man lowered his arm, Buchanan clapped him on the back, thanked him, and descended to Vasquez.

She said, "What was that about?"

"Shopping," Buchanan said. "Come on."

The next fifteen minutes consisted of them walking a route Vasquez wasn't sure she could retrace, through clouds of slow-moving tourists stopping to admire some building or piece of public statuary; alongside briskly-moving men and women whose ignoring those same sights marked them as locals as much as their *chic* haircuts, the rapid-fire French they delivered to their cellphones; past upscale boutiques and the gated entrances to equally upscale apartments. Buchanan's route brought the two of them to a large, corner building whose long windows displayed teddy bears, model planes, dollhouses. Vasquez said, "A toy store?"

"Not just 'a' toy store," Buchanan said. "This is *the* toy store. Supposed to have all kinds of stuff in it."

"For your son."

"Duh."

Inside, a crowd of weary adults and overexcited children moved up and down the store's aisles, past a mix of toys Vasquez recognized—Playmobil, groups of army vehicles, a typical assortment of stuffed animals—and others she'd never seen before—animal-headed figures she realized were Egyptian gods, replicas of round-faced cartoon characters she didn't know, a box of a dozen figurines arranged around a cardboard mountain. Buchanan wandered up to her as she was considering this set, the box propped on her hip. "Cool," he said, leaning forward. "What is it, like, the Greek gods?"

Vasquez resisted a sarcastic remark about the breadth of his knowledge; instead, she said, "Yeah. That's Zeus and his crew at the top of the mountain. I'm not sure who those guys are climbing it…"

"Titans," Buchanan said. "They were monsters who came before the gods, these kind of primal forces. Zeus defeated them, imprisoned them in the underworld. I used to know all their names: when I was a kid, I was really into myths and legends, heroes, all that shit." He studied the toys positioned up the mountain's sides. They were larger than the figures at its crown, overmuscled, one with an extra pair of arms, another with a snake's head, a third with a single, glaring eye. Buchanan shook his head. "I can't remember any of their names, now. Except for this guy," he pointed at a figurine near the summit, "I'm pretty sure he's Kronos."

"Kronos?" The figure was approximately that of a man, although its arms, its legs, were slightly too long, its hands and feet oversized. Its head was surrounded by a corona of gray hair that descended into a jagged beard. The toy's mouth had been sculpted with its mouth gaping, its eyes round, idiot. Vasquez smelled spoiled meat, felt the cardboard slipping from her grasp.

"Whoa." Buchanan caught the box, replaced it on the shelf.

"Sorry," Vasquez said. *Mr. White had ignored her, strolling across the round chamber to the foot of the stairs, which he had climbed quickly.*

"I don't think that's really Sam's speed, anyway. Come on," Buchanan said, moving down the aisle.

When they had stopped in front of a stack of remote-controlled cars, Vasquez said, "So who was Kronos?" Her voice was steady.

"What?" Buchanan said. "Oh—Kronos? He was Zeus's father. Ate all his kids because he'd heard that one of them was going to replace him."

"Jesus."

"Yeah. Somehow, Zeus avoided becoming dinner and overthrew the old man."

"Did he—did Zeus kill him?"

"I don't think so. I'm pretty sure Kronos wound up with the rest of the Titans, underground."

"Underground? I thought you said they were in the underworld."

"Same diff," Buchanan said. "That's where those guys thought the underworld was, someplace deep underground. You got to it through caves."

"Oh."

In the end, Buchanan decided on a large wooden castle that came with a host of knights, some on horseback, some on foot, a trio of princesses, a unicorn, and a dragon. The entire set cost two hundred and sixty euros, which struck Vasquez as wildly overpriced but which Buchanan paid without a murmur of protest—the extravagance of the present, she understood, being the point. Buchanan refused the cashier's offer to gift-wrap the box, and they left the store with him carrying it under his arm.

Once on the sidewalk, Vasquez said, "Not to be a bitch, but what are you planning to do with that?"

Buchanan shrugged. "I'll think of something. Maybe the front desk'll hold it."

Vasquez said nothing. Although the sky still glowed blue, the light had begun to drain out of the spaces among the buildings, replaced by a darkness that was almost granular. The air was warm, soupy. As they stopped at the corner, Vasquez said, "You know, we never asked Plowman about Lavalle or Maxwell."

"Yeah, so?"

"Just—I wish we had. He had an answer for everything else, I wouldn't have minded hearing him explain that."

"There's nothing to explain," Buchanan said.

"We're the last ones alive—"

"Plowman's living. So's Mr. White."

"Whatever—you know what I mean. Christ, even Just-Call-Me-Bill is dead. What the fuck's up with that?"

In front of them, traffic stopped. The walk signal lighted its green man. They joined the surge across the street. "It's a war, Vasquez," Buchanan said. "People die in them."

"Is that what you really believe?"

"It is."

"What about your freakout before, at the Tower?"

"That's exactly what it was, me freaking out."

"Okay," Vasquez said after a moment, "okay. Maybe Bill's death was an accident; maybe Maxwell, too. What about Lavalle? What about Ruiz? You telling me it's normal two guys from the same detail try to off themselves?"

"I don't know." Buchanan shook his head. "You know the Army isn't big on mental health care. And let's face it, that was some pretty fucked-up shit went on in the Closet. Not much of a surprise if Lavalle and Ruiz couldn't handle it, is it?"

Vasquez waited another block before asking, "How do you deal with it, the Closet?" Buchanan took one more block after that to answer: "I don't think about it."

"You don't?"

"I'm not saying the thought of what we did over there never crosses my mind, but as a rule, I focus on the here and now."

"What about the times the thought does cross your mind?"

"I tell myself it was a different place with different rules. You know what I'm talking about. You had to be there; if you weren't, then shut the fuck up. Maybe what we did went over the line, but that's for us to say, not some panel of officers don't know their ass from a hole in the ground, and damn sure not some reporter never been closer to war than a goddamn showing of *Platoon*." Buchanan glared. "You hear me?"

"Yeah." How many times had she used the same arguments, or close enough, with her father? He had remained unconvinced. *So only the criminals are fit to judge the crime?* he had said. *What a novel approach to justice.* She said, "You know what I hate, though? It isn't that people look at me funny—*Oh, it's her*—it isn't even the few who run up to me in the supermarket and tell me what a disgrace I am. It's like you said, they weren't there, so fuck 'em. What gets me are the ones who come up to you and tell you, 'Good job, you fixed them Ay-rabs right,' the crackers who wouldn't have anything to do with someone like me, otherwise."

"Even crackers can be right, sometimes," Buchanan said.

VII

Mr. White's room was on the sixth floor, at the end of a short corridor that lay around a sharp left turn. The door to the Junior Suite appeared unremarkable, but it was difficult to be sure, since both the bulbs in the wall-sconces on either side of the corridor were out. Vasquez searched for a light switch and, when, she could not find one, said, "Either they're blown, or the switch is inside his room."

Buchanan, who had been unsuccessful convincing the woman at the front desk to watch his son's present, was busy fitting it beneath one of the chairs to the right of the elevator door.

"Did you hear me?" Vasquez asked.

"Yeah."

"Well?"

"Well what?"

"I don't like it. Our visibility's fucked. He opens the door, the light's behind him, in our faces. He turns on the hall lights, and we're blind."

"For like, a second."

"That's more than enough time for Mr. White to do something."

"Will you listen to yourself?"

"You saw what he could do with that knife."

"All right," Buchanan said, "how do you propose we deal with this?"

Vasquez paused. "You knock on the door. I'll stand a couple of feet back with my gun in my pocket. If things go pear-shaped, I'll be in a position to take him out."

"How come I have to knock on the door?"

"Because he liked you better."

"Bullshit."

"He did. He treated me like I wasn't there."

"That was the way Mr. White was with everyone."

"Not you."

Holding his hands up, Buchanan said, "Fine. Dude creeps you out so much, it's probably better I'm the one talking to him." He checked his watch. "Five minutes till showtime. Or should I say, 'T-minus five and counting,' something like that?"

"Of all the things I'm going to miss about working with you, your sense of humor's going to be at the top of the list."

"No sign of Plowman, yet." Buchanan checked the panel next to the elevator, which showed it on the third floor.

"He'll be here at precisely eleven ten."

"No doubt."

"Well…" Vasquez turned away from Buchanan.

"Wait—where are you going? There's still four minutes on the clock."

"Good: it'll give our eyes time to adjust."

"I am so glad this is almost over," Buchanan said, but he accompanied Vasquez to the near end of the corridor to Mr. White's room. She could feel him vibrating with a surplus of smart-ass remarks, but he had enough sense to keep his mouth shut. The air was cool, floral-scented with whatever they'd used to clean the carpet. Vasquez expected the minutes to drag by, for there to be ample opportunity for her to fit the various fragments of information in her possession into something like a coherent picture; however, it seemed practically the next second after her eyes had adapted to the shadows leading up to Mr. White's door, Buchanan was moving past her. There was time for her to slide the pistol out from under her blouse and slip in into the right front pocket of her slacks, and then Buchanan's knuckles were rapping the door.

It opened so quickly, Vasquez almost believed Mr. White had been positioned there, waiting for them. The glow that framed him was soft, orange, an adjustable light dialed down to its lowest setting, or a candle. From what she could see of him, Mr. White was the same as ever, from his unruly hair, more gray than white, to his dirty white suit. Vasquez could not tell whether his hands were empty. In her pocket, her palm was slick on the pistol's grip.

At the sight of Buchanan, Mr. White's expression did not change. He stood in the doorway regarding the man, and Vasquez three feet behind him, until Buchanan cleared his throat and said, "Evening, Mr. White. Maybe you remember me from Bagram. I'm Buchanan; my associate is Vasquez. We were part of Sergeant Plowman's crew; we assisted you with your work interrogating prisoners."

Mr. White continued to stare at Buchanan. Vasquez felt panic gathering in the pit of her stomach. Buchanan went on, "We were hoping you would accompany us on a short walk. There are matters we'd like to discuss with you, and we've come a long way."

Without speaking, Mr. White stepped into the corridor. The fear, the urge to sprint away from here as fast as her legs would take her, that had been churning in Vasquez's gut, leapt up like a geyser. Buchanan said, "Thank you. This won't take five minutes—ten, tops."

Behind her, the floor creaked. She looked back, saw Plowman standing there, and in her confusion, did not register what he was holding in his hand. Someone coughed, and Buchanan collapsed. They coughed again, and it was as if a snowball packed with ice struck Vasquez's back low and to the left.

All the strength left her legs. She sat down where she was, listing to her right until the wall stopped her. Plowman stepped over her. The gun in his right hand was lowered; in his left, he held a small box. He raised the box, pressed it, and the wall sconces erupted in deep purple—black light, by whose illumination Vasquez saw the walls, the ceiling, the carpet of the short corridor covered in symbols drawn in a medium that shone pale white. She couldn't identify most of them: she thought she saw a scattering of Greek characters, but the rest were unfamiliar, circles bisected by straight lines traversed by short, wavy lines, a long, gradual curve like a smile, more intersecting lines. The only figure she knew for sure was a circle whose thick circumference was broken at about the eight o'clock point, inside which Mr. White was standing and Buchanan lying. Whatever Plowman had used to draw them made the symbols appear to float in front of the surfaces on which he'd marked them, strange constellations crammed into an undersized sky.

Plowman was speaking, the words he was uttering unlike any Vasquez had heard, thick ropes of sound that started deep in his throat and spilled into the air squirming, writhing over her eardrums. Now Mr. White's face showed emotion: surprise, mixed with what might have been dismay, even anger. Plowman halted next to the broken circle and used his right foot to roll Buchanan onto his back. Buchanan's eyes were open, unblinking, his lips parted. The exit wound in his throat shone darkly. His voice rising, Plowman completed what he was saying, gestured with both hands at the body, and retreated to Vasquez.

For an interval of time that lasted much too long, the space where Mr. White and Buchanan were was full of something too big, that had to double over to cram itself into the corridor. Eyes the size of dinner plates stared at Plowman, at Vasquez, with a lunacy that pressed on her like an animal scenting her with its sharp snout. Amidst a beard caked and clotted with offal, a mouth full of teeth cracked and stained black formed sounds Vasquez could not distinguish. Great pale hands large as tires roamed the floor beneath the figure—Vasquez was reminded of a blind man investigating an unfamiliar surface. When the hands found Buchanan, they scooped him up like a doll and raised him to that enormous mouth.

Groaning, Vasquez tried to roll away from the sight of Buchanan's head surrounded by teeth like broken flagstones. It wasn't easy. For one thing, her right hand was still in her pants pocket, its fingers tight around the Walther, her wrist and arm bent in at awkward angles. (She supposed she should be grateful she hadn't shot herself.) For another thing, the cold that had struck her back was gone, replaced by heat, by a sharp pain that grew sharper still as she twisted away from the snap and crunch of those teeth biting through Buchanan's skull. *God.* She managed to move onto her back, exhaling sharply. To her right, the sounds of Buchanan's consumption continued, bones snapping, flesh tearing, cloth ripping. Mr. White—what had been Mr. White—or what he truly was—that vast figure was grunting with pleasure, smacking its lips together like someone starved for food given a gourmet meal.

"For what it's worth," Plowman said, "I wasn't completely dishonest with you." One leg to either side of hers, he squatted over her, resting his elbows on his knees. "I do intend to bring Mr. White into my service; it's just the methods necessary for me to do so are a little extreme."

Vasquez tried to speak. "What... is he?"

"It doesn't matter," Plowman said. "He's old—I mean, if I told you how old he is, you'd think...." He looked to his left, to the giant sucking the gore from its fingers. "Well, maybe not. He's been around for a long time, and he knows a lot of things. We—what we were doing at Bagram, the inter-rogations, they woke him. I guess that's the best way to put it; although you could say they called him forth. It took me a while to figure out everything, even after he revealed himself to me. But there's nothing like prison to give you time for reflection. And research.

"That research says the best way to bind someone like Mr. White is—actually, it's pretty complicated." Plowman waved his pistol at the symbols shining around them. "The part that will be of most immediate interest to you is the sacrifice of a man and woman who are in my command. I apologize. I intended to put the two of you down before you knew what was happening; I mean, there's no need to be cruel about this. With you, however, I'm afraid my aim was off. Don't worry. I'll finish what I started before I turn you over to Mr. White."

Vasquez tilted her right hand up and squeezed the trigger of her gun. Four pops rushed one after the other, blowing open her pocket. Plowman leapt back, stumbled against the opposite wall. Blood bloomed across the inner thigh of his trousers, the belly of his shirt. Wiped clean by surprise, his face was blank. He swung his gun towards Vazquez, who angled her right hand down and squeezed the trigger again. The top of Plowman's shirt puffed out; his right eye burst. His arm relaxed, his pistol thumped on the floor, and, a second later, he joined it.

The burn of suddenly hot metal through her pocket sent Vasquez scrambling up the wall behind her before the pain lodged in her back could catch her. In the process, she yanked out the Walther and pointed it at the door to the Junior Suite—

—in front of which, Mr. White was standing, hands in his jacket pockets. A dark smear in front of him was all that was left of Buchanan. *Jesus God...* The air reeked of black powder and copper. Across from her, Plowman stared at nothing through his remaining eye. Mr. White regarded her with something like interest. *If he moves, I'll shoot*, Vasquez thought, but Mr.

White did not move, not the length of time it took her to back out of the corridor and retreat to the elevator, the muzzle of the pistol centered on Mr. White, then on where Mr. White would be if he rounded the corner. Her back was a knot of fire. When she reached the elevator, she slapped the call button with her left hand while maintaining her aim with her right. Out of the corner of her eye, she saw Buchanan's gift for his son, all two hundred and sixty euros worth, wedged under its chair. She left it where it was. A faint glow shone from the near end of the corridor: Plowman's black-lighted symbols. Was the glow changing, obscured by an enormous form crawling towards her? When the elevator dinged behind her, she stepped into it, the gun up in front of her until the doors had closed and the elevator had commenced its descent.

The back of her blouse was stuck to her skin; a trickle of blood tickled the small of her back. The interior of the elevator dimmed to the point of disappearing entirely. The Walther weighed a thousand pounds. Her legs wobbled madly. Vasquez lowered the gun, reached her left hand out to steady herself. When it touched, not metal, but cool stone, she was not as surprised as she should have been. As her vision returned, she saw that she was in a wide, circular area, the roof flat, low, the walls no more than shadowy suggestions. The space was lit by a symbol incised on the rock at her feet: a rough circle, the diameter of a manhole cover, broken at about eight o'clock, whose perimeter was shining with cold light. Behind and to her left, the scrape of bare flesh dragging over stone turned her around. This section of the curving wall opened in a black arch like the top of an enormous throat. Deep in the darkness, she could detect movement, but was not yet able to distinguish it.

As she raised the pistol one more time, Vasquez was not amazed to find herself here, under the ground with things whose idiot hunger eclipsed the span of the oldest human civilizations, things she had helped summon. She was astounded to have thought she'd ever left.

For Fiona.

THE MORAINE

SIMON BESTWICK

The mist hit us suddenly. One moment we had the peak in sight; the next, the white had swallowed up the crags and was rolling down towards us.

"Shit," I said. "Head back down."

For once, Diane didn't argue.

Trouble was, it was a very steep climb. Maybe that was why we'd read nothing about this mountain in the guidebooks. Some locals in the hotel bar the night before had told us about it. They'd warned us about the steepness, but Diane liked the idea of a challenge. All well and good, but now it meant we had to descend very slowly; one slip and you'd go down the mountainside, arse over apex.

That was when I saw the faint desire-line that led off, almost at right angles to the main path, running sideways and gently downwards.

"There, look," I said, pointing. "What do you reckon?"

Diane hesitated, glancing down the main path then up at the fast-falling mist. "Let's try it."

So we did.

"Look out," I said. Diane was lagging a good four or five yards behind me. "Faster."

"I'm going as fast as I bloody can, Steve."

I didn't rise to the bait, just turned and jogged on. The gentler slope meant we could run, but even so, we weren't fast enough. Everything went suddenly white.

"Shit," Diane said. I reached out for her hand—she was just a shadow in the wall of white vapour—and she took it and came closer. The mist was cold, wet and clinging, like damp cobwebs.

"What now?" Diane said. She kept her voice level, but I could tell it wasn't easy for her. And I couldn't blame her.

Don't be fooled by Lakeland's picture-postcard scenery; its high mountains and blue tarns, the boats on Lake Windermere, the gift shops and stone-built villages. You come here from the city to find the air's fresher and cleaner, and when you look up at night you see hundreds, thousands more stars in the sky because there's no light pollution. But by the same token, fall on a slope like this and there'll be no-one around, and your mobile won't get a signal. And if a mist like this one comes down and swallows you up and you don't know which way to go—it doesn't take that long, on a cold October day, for hypothermia to set in. These fells and dales claimed lives like ours each year.

I took a deep breath. "I think..."

"You OK?" she asked.

"I'm fine." I was a little nettled she'd thought otherwise; she was the one who'd sounded in need of reassurance, but I wasn't going to start bickering now. It occurred to me—at the back of my head, and I'd have denied it outright if anyone had suggested it to me—that this might be a blessing in disguise; if I could stay calm and lead us to safety, I could be a hero in her eyes. "We need to get to some lower ground."

"Yes, I *know*," she said, as if I'd pointed out the stupidly obvious. Well, perhaps I had. I was just trying to clarify the situation. Alright, I wanted to impress her, to look good. But I wanted to do the right thing as well. Honestly.

So I pointed down the trail—the few feet of it we could see where it disappeared into the mist. "Best off keeping on. Keep our heads and go slowly."

"Yes, I worked that bit out as well." I recognised her tone of voice; it was the one she used to take cocky students down a peg. There'd been a time when I used to slip into her lectures, even though I knew nothing, then or now, about Geology; I just liked hearing her talk about her favoured subject. I couldn't remember ever seeing her in any of *my* lectures—not that she was interested in Music. Maybe it had never been what I'd thought it was. Maybe it had never been for either of us.

Not an idea I liked, but one I'd kept coming back to far too often lately. As had Diane. Hence this trip, which was looking less and less like a good idea all the time. We'd spent our honeymoon here; I suppose we'd hoped to recapture something or other, but there's no magic in places. Only people, and precious little of that; less and less the older you get.

And none of that was likely to get us safely out of here. "OK then," I said. "Come on."

◄○►

Diane caught the back of my coat and pulled. I wheeled to face her and swayed, off-balance. Loose scree clattered down into the mist; the path had grown rockier underfoot. She caught my arm and steadied me. I yanked it free, thoroughly pissed off. "What?"

"Steve, we're still walking."

"I noticed. Well, actually, we're not just now, since you just grabbed me."

She folded her arms. "We've been walking nearly twenty minutes." I could see she was trying to stop her teeth chattering. "And I don't think we're much closer to ground level. I think we might be a bit off course."

I realised my teeth had started chattering too. It was hard to be sure, but I thought she might have a point; the path didn't look like it was sloping down any longer. If it'd levelled off, we were still halfway up the damned mountain. "Shit."

I felt panic threatening, like a small hungry animal gnawing away inside my stomach, threatening to tear its way up through my body if I let it. I wouldn't. Couldn't. Mustn't. If we panicked we were stuffed.

At least we hadn't come completely unprepared. We had Kendal Mint Cake and a thermos of hot tea in our backpacks, which helped, but they could only buy a little more time. We either got off this mountain soon, or we never would.

We tried our mobiles, but it was an exercise; there was no reception out here. They might as well have been bits of wood. I resisted the temptation to throw mine away.

"Should've stayed on the main path," Diane said. "If we'd taken it slow we'd have been OK."

I didn't answer. She glanced at me and rolled her eyes.

"What?"

"Steve, I wasn't having a go at you."

"Fine."

"Not everything has to be about that."

"I said, fine."

But she wouldn't leave it. "All I said was that we should've stuck to the main path. I wasn't saying this was all your fault."

"*Okay.*"

"I wasn't. If I'd seen that path I would've probably done the same thing. It looked like it'd get us down faster."

"Right."

"I'm just saying, looking back, we should've gone the other way."

"Okay. Alright. You've made your point." I stood up. A sheep bleated faintly. "Can we just leave it now?"

"*Okay.*" I saw her do the eye roll again, but pretended not to. "So now what? If we backtrack…"

"Think we can make it?"

"If we can get back to the main path, we should be able to find our way back from there."

If we were very lucky, perhaps; our hotel was a good two miles from the foot of this particular peak, and chances were the mist would be at ground level too. Even off the mountain we'd be a long way from home and dry, but it seemed the best choice on offer. If only we'd taken it sooner; we might not have heard the dog bark.

But we did.

We both went still. Diane brushed her dark hair back from her eyes and looked past me into the mist. I looked too, but couldn't see much. All I could see was the rocky path for a few feet ahead before it vanished into the whiteout.

The sheep bleated again. A few seconds later, the dog barked.

I looked at Diane. She looked back at me. A sheep on its own meant nothing—most likely lost and astray, like us. But a dog—a dog most likely had an owner.

"Hello?" I called into the mist. "Hello?"

"Anybody down there?" Diane called.

"Hello?" A voice called back.

"Thank god for that," Diane whispered.

We started along the rattling path, into the mist. "Hello?" called the voice. "Hello?"

"Keep shouting," I called back, and it occurred to me that we were the ones who sounded like rescuers. Maybe we'd found another fell-walker, caught out in the mists like us. I hoped not. What with the dog barking as well, I was pinning my hopes on a shepherd out here rounding up a lost sheep, preferably a generously-disposed one with a warm, nearby cottage complete with a fire and a kettle providing hot cups of tea.

Scree squeaked and rattled underfoot as we went. I realised the surface of the path had turned almost entirely into loose rock. Not only that, but it was angling sharply down after all. Diane caught my arm. "Careful."

"Yeah, okay, I know." I tugged my arm free and tried to ignore the long sigh she let out behind me.

The mist cleared somewhat as we reached the bottom. We could see between twenty-five and thirty yards ahead, which was a vast improvement, although the whiteout still completely hid everything beyond that point. The path led down into a sort of shallow ravine between our peak and its neighbour. The bases of the two steep hillsides sloped gently downwards to a floor about ten yards wide. It was hard to be certain as both the floor and those lower slopes were covered in a thick layer of loose stone fragments.

The path we'd followed petered out, or more into accurately disappeared into that treacherous surface. Two big, flat-topped boulders jutted out of the scree, one about twenty yards down the ravine floor, the other about fifteen yards on from that, at the mouth of a gully that gaped in the side of our peak.

The mist drifted. I couldn't see any sign of man or beast. "Hello?" I called.

After a moment, there was a click and rattle somewhere in the ravine. Rocks, pebbles, sliding over one another, knocking together.

"Bollocks," I said.

"Easy," Diane said. "Looks like we've found some low ground anyway."

"That doesn't mean much. We've lost our bearings."

"There's somebody around here. We heard them. Hello?" She shouted the last—right down my earhole, it felt like.

"Ow."

"Sorry."

"Forget it."

There was another click and rattle of stone. And the voice called out "Hello?" again.

"There," said Diane. "See?"

"Yeah. Okay."

There was a bleat, up and to our left. I looked and sure enough there was the sheep we'd heard, except it was more of a lamb, picking its unsteady way over the rocks on the lower slopes of the neighbouring peak.

"Aw," said Diane. "Poor little thing." She's one of those who goes all gooey over small furry animals. Not that it stops her eating them; I was nearly tempted to mention the rack of lamb in red wine jus she'd enjoyed so much the night before. Nearly.

The lamb saw us, blinked huge dark eyes, bleated plaintively again.

In answer, there were more clicks and rattles, and an answering bleat from further down the ravine. The lamb shifted a bit on its hooves, moving sideways, and bleated again.

After a moment, I heard the rocks click again, but softly this time. It lasted longer too, this time. Almost as if something was moving slowly, as stealthily as the noisy terrain allowed. The lamb was still, looking silently up the ravine. I looked too, trying to see past where the scree faded into the mist.

The rocks clicked softly, then were silent. And then a dog barked, twice.

The lamb tensed but was still.

Click click click, went the rocks, and the dog barked again.

The lamb bleated. A long silence.

Diane's fingers had closed round my arm. I felt her draw breath to speak, but I turned and shushed her, fingers to her lips. She frowned; I touched my finger back to my own lips and turned to look at the lamb again.

I didn't know why I'd done all that, but somehow knew I'd had to. A moment later we were both glad of it.

The click of shifting rocks got louder and faster, almost a rustle, like grass parting as something slid through it. The lamb bleated and took a few tottering steps back along the slope. Pebbles clattered down. The rock sounds stopped. I peered into the mist, but I couldn't see anything. Then the dog barked again. It sounded very close now. More than close enough to see, but the ravine floor was empty. I looked back at the lamb. It was still. It cocked its head.

A click of rocks, and something bleated.

The lamb bleated back.

Rocks clattered again, deafeningly loud, and Diane made a strangled gasp that might have been my name, her hand clutching my arm painfully, and pointed with her free hand.

The ravine floor was moving. Something was humped beneath the rocks, pushing them up as it went so they clicked and rattled in its wake. It was like watching something move underwater. It raced forward, arrowing towards the lamb.

The lamb let out a single terrified bleat and tried to turn away, but it never stood a chance. The humped shape under the scree hurtled towards it, loose stone rattling like dice in a shaken cup, and then rocks sprayed upwards like so much kicked sand where the lamb stood. Its bleat became a horrible squealing noise—I'd no idea sheep could make sounds like that. The shower of rubble fell back to earth. The lamb kept squealing. I could only see its head and front legs; the rest was buried under the rock. The front legs kicked frantically and the head jerked about, to and fro, the lips splaying back horribly from the teeth as it squealed out its pain. And then a sudden, shocking spray of blood spewed out from under the collapsing shroud of rocks like a scarlet fan. Diane clapped a hand to her mouth with a short, shocked cry. I think I might have croaked 'Jesus', or something along those lines, myself.

The lamb's squeals hit a new, jarring crescendo that hurt the ears, like nails on a blackboard, then choked and cut off. Scree clattered and hissed down the slope and came to rest. The lamb lay still. Its fur was speckled red with blood; its eyes already looked fixed and unblinking, glazing over. The rocks above and around it glistened.

With any luck it was beyond pain. I hoped so, because in the next moment the lamb's forequarters were yanked violently, jerked further under the rubble, and in the same instant the scree seemed to surge over it. The heaped loose rock jerked and shifted a few times, rippled slightly and was still. Even the stones splashed with blood were gone, rolled under the surface and out of sight. A few glistening patches remained, furthest out from where the lamb had been, but otherwise there was no sign that it'd even existed.

"Fuck." I definitely said it this time. "Oh fucking hell."

There was a moment of silence; I could hear Diane drawing breath again to speak. And then there was that now-familiar click and rattle as something moved under the scree. And from where the lamb had been a voice, a low, hollow voice called "Hello?"

⊰◦⊱

Diane put her hand over my mouth. "Stay quiet," she whispered.

"I know that," I whispered back, muffled by her hand.

"It hunts by sound," she whispered. "Must do. Vibration through the rocks."

There was a slight, low hump where the lamb had been killed; you had to look hard to see it, and know what it was you were trying to spot. A soft clicking sound came from it. Rock on rock.

"It's under the rocks," she whispered.

"I can *see* that."

"So if we can get back up onto solid ground, we should be okay."

"Should."

She gave me an irritated look. "Got any better ideas?"

"Okay. So we head back?"

"Hello?" called the voice again.

"Yes," whispered Diane. "And very, very slowly, and carefully and quietly." I nodded.

The rocks clicked and shifted, softly. Diane raised one foot, moved it upslope, set it slowly, gently down again. Then the other foot. She turned and looked at me, then reached out and took my hand. Or I took hers, as you prefer.

I followed her up the slope. We climbed in as near silence as we could manage, up towards the ravine's entrance, towards the solidity of the footpath. Rocks slid and clicked underfoot. As if in answer, the bloodied rocks where the lamb had died clicked too, knocking gently against one another as something shifted under them.

"Hello?" I heard again as we climbed. And then again: "Hello?"

"Keep going," Diane whispered.

The rocks clicked again. With a loud rattle, a stone bounced down to the ravine floor. "John?" This time it was a woman's voice. Scottish, by the accent. "John?"

"Fucking hell," I muttered. Louder than I meant to and louder than I should have, because the voice sounded again. "John? John?"

Diane gripped my hand so tight I almost cried out. For a moment I wondered if that was the idea– make me cry out, then let go and run, leave the unwanted partner as food for the thing beneath the rocks while she made her getaway, kill two birds with one stone. But it wasn't, of course.

"Shona?" This time the voice was a man's, likewise Scottish-accented. "Shona, where are ye?"

Neither of us answered. A cold wind blew. I clenched my teeth as they tried to start chattering again. I heard the wind whistle and moan. Shrubs flapped and fluttered in the sudden gale and the surrounding terrain became a little clearer, though not much. Then the wind dropped again, and a soft, cold whiteness began to drown the dimly-glimpsed outlines of trees and higher ground again.

Stones clicked. A sheep's bleat sounded. Then a cow lowed.

Diane tugged my hand. "Come on," she said, "let's go."

The dog barked two, three times as we went, sharp and sudden, startling me a little and making me sway briefly for balance. I looked at Diane, smiled a little, let out a long breath.

We were about nine feet from the top when a deafening roar split the silence apart. I don't know what the hell it was, what kind of animal sound—but even Diane cried out, and I stumbled, and sending a mini-landslide slithering back down the slope.

The broken slate heaved and rattled, and then surged as something flew across, under, *through* the ravine floor towards us.

"Run!" I heard Diane yell, and I tried, we both did, but the shape was arrowing past us. We saw that at the last moment; it was hurtling past us to the edge of the scree, the point where it gave way to the path.

Diane was already starting back down, pushing me behind her, when the ground erupted in a shower of stone shrapnel. I thought I glimpsed something, only for the briefest of moments, moving in the hail of broken stone, but when it fell back into place there was no sign of anything—except, if you looked, a low humped shape.

Diane shot past me, still gripping my hand, pelting along the ravine. Behind us I heard the stones rattle as the thing gave chase. Diane veered towards the nearest of the boulders—it was roughly the size of a small car, and looked like pretty solid ground.

"Come on!" Diane leapt—pretty damned agile for a woman in her late thirties who didn't lead a particularly active life—onto the boulder, reached back for me. "Quick!"

The shape was hurtling towards us, slowing as it neared us. Its bow-wave of loose stones thickened, widened; it was gathering speed. I could see what was coming; I grabbed Diane and pushed her down flat on the boulder. She didn't fight, so I'm guessing she'd reached the same conclusions as me.

There was a muffled thud and the boulder shook. For a moment I thought we'd both be pitched onto the scree around it, but the boulder held, too deeply rooted to be torn loose. Rocks rained and pattered down on us; I tucked my head in.

I realised I was clinging on to Diane, and that she was doing the same to me. I opened my eyes and looked at her. She looked back. Neither of us said anything.

Behind us, there were clicks and rattles. I turned slowly, sliding off Diane. We both sat up and watched.

There was a sort of crater in the layer of loose rocks beside the boulder, where the thing had hit. The scree at the bottom was heaving, shifting, rippling. The crater walls trembled and slid. After a moment, the whole lot collapsed on itself. The uneven surface rippled and heaved some more, finally stopped when it looked as it had before—undisturbed, except of course for the low humped shape beneath it.

Click went the stones as it shifted in its tracks, taking stock. Click click as it moved and began inching its way round the boulder. "John? Shona? Hello?" All emerged from the shifting rocks, each of those different voices. Then the bleat. Then the roar. I swear I felt the wind of it buffet me.

"Christ," I said.

The rocks clicked, softly, as the humped shape began moving, circling slowly round the boulder. "Christ," my own voice answered me. Then another voice called, a child's. "Mummy?" Click click click. "Shona?" Click. "Oh, for God's sake, Marjorie," came a rich, fruity voice which sounded decidedly pre-Second World War. If not the First. "For God's sake."

Click. Then silence. The wind keened down the defile. Fronds of mist drifted coldly along. Click. A high, thin female voice, clear and sweet, began singing 'The Ash Grove.' Very slowly, almost like a dirge. *"Down yonder green valley where streamlets meander…"*

Diane clutched my wrist tightly.

Click, and the song stopped, as if a switch had been thrown. Click click. And then there was a slow rustling and clicking as the shape began to move away from the boulder, moving further and further back. Diane gripped me tighter. The mist was thickening and the shape went slowly, so that it was soon no longer possible to be sure exactly where it was. Then the last click died away and there was only the silence and the wind and the mist.

—◦—

Time passed.

"It's not gone far," Diane whispered. "Just far enough that we've got some freedom of movement. It wants us to make a move, try to run for it. It knows it can't get us here."

"But we can't stay here either," I pointed out in the same whisper. My teeth were already starting to chatter again, and I could see hers were too. "We'll bloody freeze to death."

"I know. Who knows, maybe it does too. Either way, we'll have to make a break for it, and sooner rather than later. If we leave it much longer we won't stand a chance."

"What the hell do you think it is?" I asked.

She scowled at me. "You expect me to know? I'm a geologist, not a biologist."

"Don't suppose you've got the number for a good one on your mobile?"

She stopped and stared at me. "We're a pair of fucking idiots," she said, and dug around in the pocket of her jeans. Out came her mobile. "Never even thought of it."

"There's no signal."

"There wasn't before. It's worth a try."

Hope flared briefly, but not for long; it was the same story as before.

"Okay," I said. "So we can't phone a friend. Let's think about this then. What do we know about it?"

"It lives under the rocks," Diane said. "Moves under them."

"Likes to stay under them, too," I said. "It was right up against us before. *That* far from us. It could've attacked us easily just by coming up out from under, but it didn't. It'd rather play it safe and do the whole waiting game thing."

"So maybe it's weak, if we can get it out of the rocks. Vulnerable." Diane took off her glasses, rubbed her large eyes. "Maybe it's blind. It seems to hunt by sound, vibration."

"A mimic. That's something else. It's a mimic, like a parrot."

"Only faster," she said. "It mimicked you straight away, after hearing you once."

"Got a good memory for voices, too," I whispered back. "Some of those voices…"

"Yes, I think so too. And that roar it made. How long's it been since there was anything roaming wild in this country, could make a noise like that?"

"Maybe a bear," I offered, "or one of the big sabre-toothed cats."

Diane looked down at the scree. "Glacial till," she said.

"What?"

"Sorry. The stones here. It's what's called glacial till—earth that's been compressed into rock by the pressure of the glaciers coming through here." She looked up and down the ravine.

"So?"

The look she gave me was equal parts hurt and anger. "So... nothing much, I suppose."

Wind blew.

"I'm sorry."

She shrugged. "S'okay."

"No. Really."

She gave me a smile, at least, that time. Then frowned, looked up at the way we'd come in—had it only been in the last hour? "Look at that. You can see it now."

"See what?"

She pointed. "This is a moraine."

"A what?"

"Moraine. It's the debris—till and crushed rock—a glacier leaves behind when it melts. All this would've been crushed up against the mountainsides for god knows how long..."

I remembered Diane telling me about the last Ice Age, how there'd have been two miles of ice above the cities we'd grown up in. How far down would all this have been? And would—*could*—anything have lived in it?

I was willing to bet any of our colleagues in the Biology Department would have snorted at the idea. But even so... life is very tenacious, isn't it? It can cling on in places you'd never expect it to.

Maybe some creatures had survived down here in the Ice Age, crawling and slithering between the gaps in the crushed rock. And in every food chain, something's at the top—something that hunted blindly by vibration and lured by imitation. Something that had survived the glaciers' melting, even prospered from it, growing bigger and fatter on bigger, fatter prey.

The lost lamb had saved us by catching its attention. Without that, we'd

have had no warning and would've followed that voice—no doubt belonging to some other, long-dead victim—into the heart of the killing ground.

Click click click, went the rocks in the distance, as the creature shifted
and then grew still.

And Diane leant close to me, and breathed in my ear: "We're going to
have to make a move."

—◇—

To our left was the way we'd come, the scree-thick path sloping up before
blending with the moraine. Twenty yards. It might as well have been ten
miles.

The base of the peak was at our backs. It wasn't sheer, not quite, but it
may as well have been. The only handholds were the occasional rock or root;
even if the fall didn't kill you, you'd be too stunned or injured to stand a
chance. The base of the opposite peak—even if we *could* have got past the
creature—was no better.

To our right, the main body of the ravine led on, thick with rubble, before
vanishing into the mist. Running along that would be nothing short of suicide, but there was still the gully we'd seen before. From what I could see the
floor of it was thickly littered with rubble, but it definitely angled upwards,
hopefully towards higher ground of solid earth and grass, where the thing
from the moraine couldn't follow. Better still, there was that second boulder
at the gully mouth, as big and solidly rooted-looking as this one, if not bigger. If we could make it that far—and we might, with a little luck—we had
a chance to get out through the gully.

I looked at the boulder and back to Diane. She was still studying it. "What
do you reckon?" I breathed.

Click click click, came softly, faintly, gently in answer.

Diane glanced sideways. "The bastard thing's fast," she whispered back.
"It'll be a close thing."

"We could distract it," I suggested. "Make a noise to draw it off."

"Like what?"

I nodded at the rocks at the base of the boulder. "Pick a spot and lob a few
of them at it. Hopefully it'll think it's another square meal."

She looked dubious. "S'pose it's better than nothing."

"If you've got a better idea..."

She looked hurt rather than annoyed. "Hey…"

"I'm sorry." I was, too. I touched her arm. "We've just got to make that boulder."

"And what then?"

"We'll think of something. We always do."

She forced a smile.

Reaching down to pick up the bits of rubble and rock wasn't pleasant, mainly because the thing had gone completely silent and there was no knowing how close it might be now. Every time my hands touched the rocks I was convinced they'd explode in my face before something grabbed and yanked me under them.

But the most that happened was that once, nearby, the rocks clicked softly and we both went still, waiting, for several minutes before reaching down again after a suitable pause. At last we were ready with half a dozen good-sized rocks apiece.

"Where do we throw them?" Diane whispered. I pointed to the footpath; we'd be heading, after all, in the opposite direction. She nodded.

"Ready?"

Another nod.

I threw the first rock. We threw them all, fast, within a few seconds, and they cracked and rattled on the slate. The slate nearby rattled and hissed as something moved.

"Go," Diane said; we jumped off the boulder and ran for the gully mouth.

Diane'd often commented on my being out of condition, so I was quite pleased that I managed to outpace her. I overtook easily, and was soon a good way ahead. The boulder was two more strides away, three at most, and then—

The two sounds came together; a dismayed cry from Diane, and then that hiss and click and rattle of displaced scree, rising to a rushing roar as a bow wave of broken rocks rose up behind Diane and bore down on her.

I screamed at her to run, covering the rest of the distance to the boulder and leaping onto it, turning, holding my hands out to her, as if that was going to help. But what else could I have done? Running back to her wouldn't have speeded her up, and—

Oh. Yes. I could've tried to draw it off. Risked my own life, even sacrificed it, to save hers. Yes, I could've done that. Thanks for reminding me.

It got to her as I turned. There was an explosion of rubble, a great spray of it, and she screamed. I threw up my hands to protect my face. A piece of rock glanced off my forehead and I stumbled, swayed, losing balance, but thank God I hadn't ditched my backpack—the weight dragged me back and I fell across the boulder.

Rubble rained and pattered about us as I stared at Diane. She'd fallen face-down on the ground, arms outstretched. Her pale hands, splayed out on the earth, were about three feet from the boulder.

I reached out a hand to her, leaning forward as far as I dared. I opened my mouth to speak her name, and then she lifted her head and looked up. Her glasses were askew on her pale face, and one lens was cracked. In another moment I might have jumped off the boulder and gone to her, but then she screamed and blood sprayed from the ground where her feet were covered by a sheet of rubble. Her back arched; a fingernail split as she clawed at the ground. Red bubbled up through the stones, like a spring.

Diane was weeping with pain; she tried to twist round to see what was being done to her, but jerked, shuddered and cried out before she could complete it. She twisted back to face me, lips trembling, still crying.

I leant forward, hands outstretched, but couldn't reach. Then I remembered the backpack and struggled out of it, loosening the straps to give the maximum possible slack, gripping one and holding the backpack as far out as I could, so that the other dangled closer to her. "Grab it," I whispered. "I'll pull you in."

She shook her head hard. "No," she managed at last. "Don't you get it?"

"What?" We weren't whispering anymore. Didn't seem much point. Besides, her voice was ragged with pain.

"It wants you to try. Don't you see? Otherwise it would've dragged me straight under by now."

I stared at her.

"Steve… it's using me as bait." Her face tightened. She bit her lips and fresh tears leaked down her pale cheeks. Her green eyes squeezed shut. When they opened again, they were red and bloodshot. "Oh God. What's it done to my legs? My feet?"

"I don't know," I lied.

"Well, that's it, don't you see?" She was breathing deeply now, trying to get the agony under control. "I've had it. Won't get far, even if it did let me go to chase after you. Can't get at you up there. So stay put."

"But… but…" Dimly I realised I was crying too. This was my wife. My *wife*, for Christ's sake.

Diane forced a smile. "Just stay put. Or try… make a getaway."

"I'm not leaving you."

"Yes, you are. It'll go after you. Might be able… drag myself there." She nodded at the boulder. "You could go get help. Help me. Might stand a chance."

I looked at the blood still bubbling up from the stones. She must have seen the expression on my face. "Like that, is it?"

I looked away. "I can try." My view of the gully was still constricted by my position. I could see the floor of it sloping up, but not how far it ultimately went. If nothing else, I could draw it away from her, give her a chance to get to the boulder.

And what then? If I couldn't find a way out of the gully? If there wasn't even a boulder to climb to safety on, I'd be dead and the best Diane could hope for was to bleed to death.

But I owed her a chance of survival, at least.

I put the backpack down, looked into her eyes. "Soon as it moves off, start crawling. Shout me when you're here. I'll keep making a racket, try and keep it occupied."

"Be careful."

"You too." I smiled at her and refused to look at her feet. We met at University, did I tell you? Did I mention that? A drunken discussion about politics in the Student Union bar. More of an argument really. We'd been on different sides but ended up falling for each other. That pretty much summed up our marriage, I supposed. "Love you," I managed to say at last.

She gave a tight, buckled smile. "You too," she said back.

That was never something either of us had said easily. Should've known it'd take something like this. "Okay, then," I muttered. "Bye."

I took a deep breath, then jumped off the boulder and started to run.

⤙⟶

I didn't look back, even when Diane let out a cry, because I could hear the rattle and rush of slate behind me as I pelted into the gully and knew the thing had let her go—let her go so that it could come after me.

The ground's upwards slope petered out quite quickly and the walls all around were a good ten feet high, sheer and devoid of handholds, except for at the very back of it. There was an old stream channel—only the thinnest trickle of water made it out now, but I'm guessing it'd been stronger once, because a mix of earth and pebbles, lightly grown over, formed a slope leading up to the ground above. A couple of gnarled trees sprouted nearby, and I could see their roots breaking free of the earth—thick and twisted, easy to climb with. All I had to do was reach them.

But then I noticed something else; something that made me laugh wildly. Only a few yards from where I was now, the surface of the ground changed from a plain of rubble to bare rock. Here and there earth had accumulated and sprouted grass, but what mattered was that there was no rubble for the creature to move under.

I chanced one look behind me, no more than that. It was hurtling towards me, the huge bow-wave of rock. I ran faster, managed the last few steps, and then dived and rolled across blessed solid ground.

Rubble sprayed at me from the edge of the rubble and again I caught the briefest glimpse of something moving in there. I couldn't put any kind of name to it if I tried, and I don't think I want to.

The rubble heaved and settled. The stones clicked. I got up and started backing away. Just in case. Click, click, click. Had anything ever got away from it before? I couldn't imagine anything human doing so, or men would've come back here with weapons, to find and kill it. Or perhaps that survivor hadn't been believed. Click. Click, click. Click, click, click.

Click. A sheep bleated.

Click. A dog barked.

Click. A wolf howled.

Click. A cow lowed.

Click. A bear roared.

Click. "John?"

Click. "Shona? Shona, where are ye?"

Click. "Mummy?"

Click. "Oh, for God's sake, Marjorie. For God's sake."

Click. "*Down yonder green valley where streamlets meander…*"

Click. "Christ." My voice. "Christ."

Click. "Steve? Get help. Help me." Click. "Steve. Help me."

I turned and began to run, started climbing. I looked back when I heard stones rattling. I looked back and saw something, a wide shape, moving under the stones and heading away, back towards the mouth of the gully.

"Diane?" I shouted. "Diane?"

There was no answer.

⭑

I've been walking now, according to my wristwatch, for a good half-hour. My teeth are chattering and I'm tired and all I can see around me is the mist.

Still no signal on the mobile. They can trace your position from a mobile call these days. That'd be helpful. I've tried to walk in a straight line, so that if I find help I can just point back the way I came, but I doubt I've kept to one.

I tell myself that she must have passed out—passed out from the effort and pain of dragging herself onto that boulder. I tell myself that the cold must have slowed her circulation down to the point where she might still be alive.

I do not think of how much blood I saw bubbling out from under the stones.

I do not think of hypothermia. Not for her. I'm still going, so she still must have a chance there too, surely?

I keep walking. I'll keep walking for as long as I can believe Diane might still be alive. After that, I won't be able to go on, because it won't matter anymore.

I'm crawling, now.

We came out here to see if we still worked, the two of us, under all the clutter and the mess. And it looks like we still did.

There's that cold comfort, at least.

AT THE RIDING SCHOOL

CODY GOODFELLOW

ONE

"**C**ome quick," she said, in a voice so leaden each word took a year off my life. "Bring the black bag... There's been an accident."

The call woke me up, and I knocked over a water bottle getting out of bed. For an instant, the glimmer of my ex-husband's terrified countenance flashed through my murky thoughts. Shaking his horrible visage off, I realized that the cabin was freezing, then I began to worry about what really mattered: getting to Madame fast enough...

I had only been in town six months, struggling to make a name for myself when Madame Dioskilos had called the first time. I had already heard that she owned a large barn and twenty-four horses, but that she was a rather difficult client, and stingy. She and her charges did all the routine medical work, and she'd had the same blacksmith since opening the Academy.

I found her to be demanding, but fair; I kept her secrets, and she—so far—kept mine.

I was all packed before I woke Tonio. He had only been with me for a few months, and I was afraid of spooking him, but he got dressed and helped me load the truck, then climbed in with his sketchpad and box of colored pencils. I told him only that we were going to see a sick animal. A ward of the state for almost all of his ten years, he was well trained to follow directions. I knew Madame Dioskilos would become irate about the boy—no men were allowed on the estate after dark, unless sent for—but I was more worried about him waking up alone in an empty house.

Anyway, it was time, if this was what I thought it was, for Madame to see—

I brought my special kit bag, though I doubted if it would do any good. She would have the only sure cure loaded and propped beside the stable door, like always.

We didn't pass any cars going through town to the coast road. My windshield was frosted over, and it was freakishly cold for Big Sur, even in winter. The lights were out at the Yogic Retreat at the end of Main Street and the few streetlamps lit only coronas of sleet, but I had to keep myself from driving too fast. The road spilled out of the trees and clove to the sheer cliffs over the Pacific, surfing the uneasy edge of the land for sixty unlit white-knuckle miles. The state hadn't replaced the guardrail where the last car had gone over, only a week before. Nearly ten years prior, I'd learned, Greta Spivak, a local vet who'd worked for Madame Dioskilos before me, drove over the edge during a winter storm. They found no body in the truck, and it was blithely assumed that the sharks got her before she could drown.

Tonio fell asleep, rocked by the swaying, serpentine highway. I turned the radio on as loud as I dared to keep myself from thinking.

Only four other emergencies had called me up to Madame Dioskilos's house after dark in the whole seven years that I had worked for her. That first time, she had explained our situation: she had found me out, and we both understood that her leverage meant that I could be trusted with what I must do.

There are many veterinarians between Big Sur and Monterey who would have done the work and had no qualms about it—bitter, middle-aged divorcees; born-again pagans; misanthropic bull-dykes... but, they were all too clean for her. Just as I needed her, she needed someone like me.

The entrance to her estate is nestled in one of the box canyons that the highway wanders into, seeking an escape from the sea, only to veer away in a panicky hairpin turn. The gate itself is formidable, shrouded in veils of coastal live oak and laurels, wrought-iron barbs ten feet high, a press conference's worth of cameras fixed on the road.

I always paused to look at the sculpture in the grove, just outside the gate. Most thought it was a modern piece, the angular severity shaming the mathematical fascism of the Italian Futurists; but the sculpture was symptomatic of Madame Dioskilos herself: so easy to completely misread. Like her, it came from the Cyclades Islands, and was a forgotten relic before Athens had erected its first temple.

It depicted a lithe blade of a human figure—somehow, undeniably a girl—riding the back of a rampant chimerical beast Madame told the curious was a centaur, though its hindquarters seemed to be broken off and lost to posterity. It might have been Nessus's abduction of Alcmene, the bride of Hercules, but when you got to know Madame Dioskilos, you figured it out. The centaur was not broken, and it wasn't a centaur, and the myth depicted was not in any storybooks.

The gates were swinging open as I turned up the drive, braking cagily on the slippery driveway, one arm out to brace Tonio. They'd let me adopt him with no problems, glad to empty a bed at the struggling group home in Oakland where we met. Though they did a thorough background check, the authorities never found any red flags in the short, happy life of Ruth Wyeth. Of course, they hadn't dug half as diligently as she had…

TWO

Artemisia Dioskilos, Madame's mother, was a fiery vamp and celebrated equestrian from a tiny Greek island. She married an ancient Italian Count who died in WWI, then fled to California with his wealth and title. The Countess ran a riding school in the Hollywood hills until 1926, when she retreated from society under a shameful cloud and purchased an estate on the Central Coast of California to raise her only daughter, Scylla. No inquiry was ever made into the identity of the child's father.

Alone on the estate with her mother and servants, the young Scylla Dioskilos must have pined for friends as a child. When her mother died in 1960, she went back to the Old Country to live for three years. When she returned, Scylla opened a new private school.

For forty years now, she'd run the Delos Academy, and if there were occasional problems with the state, no one had ever raised an eyebrow. She boarded no more than twelve children at a time, taught them to read, do sums, and shoot arrows at deer from the back of a horse. She could have charged ten thousand a semester to the snots in Carmel and gotten it, but she didn't need money, and she avoided publicity like the plague.

She selected abandoned and orphaned girls from Bay Area cities, and she didn't discriminate by race, so they tried to stuff kids into the trunk of her Rolls Royce as she drove away. They were all smart, strong little girls; the rest she could make over.

A certified teacher educated the girls, who had only each other for society. Most stayed through puberty, and came out fearless, aglow with eerie confidence and destined for bright futures. The whole West Coast was peppered with Madame's prodigies; a sorority that had helped girls obtain scholarships and entry into ivy-league schools, interviews with Fortune 500 companies, and even temporary financial assistance once they graduated university. Counted among the Delos alumni were many powerful women: one of San Francisco's most successful defense attorneys; a sitting Assemblywoman in Sacramento; even a U.S. junior Senator. They also help keep the secret. Madame Dioskilos wanted no awards, no media attention; most people in town didn't even know about the riding school.

THREE

I rolled up the drive and past the whitewashed Cretan villa with its showcase equestrian stables, over the ridge at the top of the canyon and around the front of the austere pine-log hunting lodge. The garage was locked down, motion-detector lights and security cameras triggering each other. Seeing no lights on, I drove on down into a stand of oaks, where I knew she would be, in the other stables…

I parked under the awning and told Tonio to stay in the truck. I gave him my cell phone and told him what to do if it rang, then got out and stumbled through the dark to the golden glow of a lantern over the stable door.

Only the oldest girls at the school came anywhere near here, the ones who had been initiated into what Madame called "the Mysteries." I didn't pretend to know what she meant, but I sensed what lay at the root of her fanaticism.

I pushed open the stable door and stepped into Mediterranean heat and the awesome stink of Madame Dioskilos's steeds.

"Ms. Wyeth?" Her voice, from the tack room. I responded and went to the little door beside the corridor that led to the indoor arena. If there'd been an accident at this hour, it would have happened there. I didn't see the shotgun anywhere about, and was both more and less uneasy as I ducked into the tack room.

Madame sat in a rocking chair in a corner of the tack room, beside a mountain of dusty blankets. She was wiry and much stronger than I was for her age and size. Her hands clutched each other, shaking.

"What happened?"

"An accident," Madame Dioskilos murmured, "an ill omen."

"Which one was it?"

"I was a fool to trust her with him! I thought, in her, I saw something... Ah! Actaeon," her wounded voice faltered, and I felt my own heart race with distress. Her prized stallion—

"Well, where is he? What can I do for him here?"

"He is... unharmed. I will deal with him later, myself. But I need your help with another matter... It is not for him, that I call you." She leaned forward as if to get up again, and pulled back the top blanket from the pile.

A girl lay curled up on her side with her knees tight against her chest, and bound up by her arms. She wore a few rags of the short white chitins that the girls always wore when riding. Blood smeared the inside of her legs down to her knees, soaking the blanket under her.

"Oh God! What do you want me to do?" I felt sick to my stomach with the tragedy of it; I say tragedy, because it was so inevitable.

Clearly, she'd already been sedated, or was in shock; her eyes half-lidded, her tongue protruding from her teeth. She was twelve, maybe thirteen, with caramel skin, and straight, shiny black hair in a boyish bob. Her elbows and knees were torn and blotted with sawdust, her lip split, and bruises bloomed on her neck and shoulders. The horrible wound between her legs still bled. She was ready for an ambulance—

One had to look very long and hard to see her breathe.

I wasn't breathing at all. "He—he did this?"

"Trista is a vigorous rider, a natural hunter... When her first bloodletting came, she embraced the Mysteries, and hunted the hunter. She rode Minos like a high priestess—but she trained too hard. Such girls, one cannot always see it, they are wanton..."

"Where is he now?" I demanded. It was only for the girl's sake that I didn't shout. "Where is the shotgun?"

The other ones had never done anything like this, but the others were all geldings. They'd only wounded each other or been lamed in accidents. Although they were bred for the steep terrain and rocky cliffs of Greece, there were other dangers here. One was bitten by a rattlesnake; another snarled in razor wire. Madame always went back to Greece and got more, though how she got them into the country always puzzled me.

The lights were dim in the arena, but I heard him, snorting and pawing the muddy turf. I couldn't find the shotgun, but I wasn't to be denied: I found a shovel.

In the Greek myths, Actaeon was a hunter who stumbled on Diana bathing in a sacred pool. For stealing a glance at her divine nakedness, the hunter was transformed into a stag, and ripped to shreds by his own dogs.

I went into the dark faster than I could see through it, with the shovel cocked over my shoulder. I followed the wall of the big round arena, wary of the hidden obstacles the girls jumped to train for the Hunt.

I heard him before I saw him, chains rattling as he came charging out of the shadows, but it gave me no advantage. The chains ran back to stout rings in the wall, giving him more than enough slack to get me. I swung the shovel as hard as I could, but he ducked under it and drove his head and massive shoulder into my gut. I fell hard on my back and lost the shovel.

I curled into a sobbing ball, with no breath to do anything else. His eyes reflected the moon glow from the skylight as he looked me over, trying to decide what he wanted most.

He was still saddled. His bridle was twisted around so it hung from his muzzle, which he'd already half-chewed through. His silver fighting spurs glittered in the moonlight.

A whip cracked between us, the tip raking his face so he leapt back and barked, submissive.

"Is not his fault!" she cried. "Trista rode him too hard... Her sisters say there is—carnality—in her, but I pay no heed; they are jealous, naturally. She rides him too hard on the course, driving with her hips, but with ulterior motivations: she pleasures herself upon the saddle! Such girls often break their maidenhood on the pommel, and this she did... nature ran away with them both. It is not his fault—the blood—"

"Well, what the fuck did you expect, Madame?" She looked as if she'd never been yelled at before, so I resolved to make it memorable for her. "He's a man, for God's sake!"

"No!" She shouted, and crossed her arms in negation between us.

"Not a man: a beast..."

"All men are beasts," I said. And most women, I thought.

"Let me tell you," she growled, and approached Actaeon. He shifted from foot to foot and studied us both. They'd always been sedated or sequestered when I came before. I had no problem killing them. I did not see their faces in my dreams. Thanks to them, I hardly ever dreamed about my husband.

Madame Dioskilos coiled the whip taut around one gloved fist as she spoke. "When my ancestors came to the island of Dioskilos three thousand years ago, they were set upon by beasts in the shape of men, who killed and ate our men, and raped our women. The drunken gods often rutted with animals, and sired monsters such as these, here and there in the dark corners of the earth.

"The goddess Diana heard our prayers and appeared to the girls of the tribe, who alone could tame them, so long as they remained chaste. And they did tame them, Mrs. Slabbert, but they have ever been beasts."

Throwing my real name in my face, Madame untangled Actaeon's reins and tugged his huge anvil of a head down to the dirt. He bowed with a snort, one sturdy knee extended out, and Madame stepped up on it, swung her leg over the saddle and sat erect with her boots in the stirrups. At a clipped shout from Madame, Actaeon rose to his full height. His hooded eyes leered at me over his bloody muzzle.

She could make a good argument for her case without words. Though he stood on two legs and had hands, he had no thumbs, whether from selective breeding or post-natal surgery, I didn't care to guess. His barrel torso was rudely muscled, covered in sleek black hair like a goat's, and his shoulders were broad enough to carry a full-grown woman up a mountain on the elaborate saddle perched upon his slightly hunched back. That those mighty shoulders produced such puny, almost flipper-like arms screamed selective breeding over hundreds of centuries from proto-human stock, perhaps even the last Neanderthals. A Greek myth that Bulfinch left out, for better or worse, though Madame's ancestors might've been the grain of sand that grew so many pearls: the Amazons, who made impotent slaves of their men; Circe, who made pigs and asses of Odysseus's crew; satyrs and centaurs—

"This one, you will not kill." From the saddle, Madame reclaimed her regal bearing. The whip uncoiled, now, for me. "It is his nature."

"How many girls will you let him rape?"

"This has never happened before… It will never happen again. The girls will be trained—"

I raised the shovel. "Get down off him, Madame—"

"When you kill them, Phyllis, do you imagine that they are your husband?"

That stopped me cold, but I didn't take the bait. I could see where she was leading this, and I brought it back. "What's to become of the girl? When's the ambulance due?"

Actaeon took a few hopping steps, stalking in a lazy, tightening spiral around me. He balanced himself and Madame effortlessly on the balls of his feet—splayed, talon-tipped toes like a mountain lion, the heels augmented with curved bronze stiletto spurs, like a gamecock; and, peeking out of the blood-matted black thicket between his powerful legs—the weapon. He couldn't have gotten his chastity belt off by himself—nature ran away with them both…His monstrous appendage bobbed and lengthened visibly as he circled; slavering and twitching to have done with Madame's games.

She dug her heels into his scarred flanks and tracked my eyes with hers, stroking the back of his head. "She ran away from us, went back to the city, where—small surprise—she was attacked. We will be heartbroken, but resolute. She brought this upon herself. The heart of it is the truth."

"So I—you want me—" It was beneath words. "But when she talks—"

"You are not to hurry, Mrs. Slabbert."

Actaeon gave a gibbering gurgle from deep in his throat and strained with his stunted forelegs to stroke his cock, still crusted with Trista's blood. I tried to stare him down. Menopause makes you think you can pull shit like that.

He shook his head. His muzzle slipped off. He grinned at me. Each yellow tooth was the size of a big man's toenail, and the moray eel of his tongue lurking behind them. His breath raised welts on my skin.

I still had the shovel. "Hey, cut this shit out! I am not going to help you kill that girl!"

"Of course not, but you are going to get yourself out of what we are both in, no?" She snapped the reins and Actaeon reared up, his spurred feet kicking in the air, flinging sod and sweat. He bent down low, craning his neck until his head was between his knees to sniff my crotch. Madame dismounted to stand between us. "I know that what you have done for me in the past was not wholly out of necessity. You knew how others would judge you. You are a part of the Mysteries, now."

I stepped around her and reached out to stroke Actaeon's bristly black mane. He twitched and unfolded warily from his rigid dismounting stance, and an alarmingly powerful musky scent suddenly filled the arena. Madame gripped his reins in one hand, the whip in the other.

I scratched behind his ears and the base of his skull, where all animals like it. His jaw went slack, but his eyes never left mine. I leaned in closer, holding my breath. I knew what I'd find, but it was the least dangerous way into the subject.

"What do you do?" Madame Dioskilos demanded, jerking his head back by the reins.

"Nothing… I was only counting his teeth. You told me once that they have four more than us—"

Actaeon obliged by baring his fierce dentition. The extra bicuspids and molars were there. Along with the outsized mandible muscles and projecting palate, they were made to crack open seeds, shellfish and bones. I wondered who had given him his four gold fillings.

"Like jackals," Madame said and led Actaeon away from me. She didn't know where this was going, and so it had to stop.

"Eskimos and American Indians have different dentition from Europeans. How much 'less human' does that make them?" I should have gone to the girl. Madame trusted me to let her die, it would have been so easy to save her and deliver her to the hospital, and we would both get what we deserved. But first, I had to show her—

She flicked her whip at me by way of dismissal and led Actaeon to the grooming stalls. I went to look at the girl. Her breathing was shallow, pulse shocky, and she still bled. If I dumped her out in the cold somewhere up the coast, like Madame ordered me to, she'd never revive. Madame would never dirty her patrician mind with an explicit request that I help her along, but when you work for someone long enough, you learn to read them.

Cruel, surely, but in Madame's world, nature was a serial rapist, and unfit children were left out for the wolves.

I tried not to think about it. I had treated Madame Dioskilos's livestock—her men—for seven years, and put down four of them, and I knew that what I did wasn't the worst of it. I knew about the High Hunt at the vernal and autumnal equinoxes, and what they hunted. Drifters, illegal aliens, men nobody missed. Anybody with a gun would have killed all of her creatures because they were less than human, but I had let her use me to kill only the useless ones, because they were men.

Madame's school—the Hunt and the Mysteries—made these cast-off girls into women the rest of the world respected, envied. It empowered them to reach for undreamed of heights, and liberated them from ever becoming a man's creature. And I guess I was one of them, from the day I killed my husband.

We had a thriving vet practice in Maryland—clients in Chevy Chase, contracts with stables that bred Triple Crown contenders. For such a smart man, Dan Slabbert got very, very stupid around money. He did things for it, just to get close to it, to dream of belonging to it. They let him think he could someday be one of them, so he started doping horses for them. Whatever they promised him was enough that, eventually, he killed a champion thoroughbred for them. Insurance paid off, and Dan must've got a healthy cut in a hidden account. He started getting consultant work across the country from rich friends who could afford to fly in a witch doctor to see to their sick investments.

He killed three more before I found out, but I didn't do anything. I found out he was fucking call girls the clients threw his way, but I said nothing. Then I found out what they'd promised him, in return for becoming their equine hit man: they were going to make him a rich widower.

I confronted him with the insurance policies and the rest of it, and he took it like a man; he tried to kill me himself. We fought; I won.

I left the country, laying a convincing trail to nowhere, then quietly snuck back in under an assumed name I'd bought with Dan's blood money. I knew my new identity wasn't airtight when somebody deposited fifty thousand dollars into Ruth Wyeth's new checking account. I suppose, in the end, I did the horsey set a favor.

In Big Sur, I was just another dumpy misfit who had sublimated her miserable lack of sex appeal into a gift for animal husbandry. I thought I could start over. It took Madame Dioskilos to show me how fucking mad I still was, how many times I still wanted to kill him.

I packed surgical gauze into Trista's wound and wrapped her up in a blanket. I left the tack room and found Madame locking her prize stallion in his stable. I hit the speed dial on the spare cell phone in my coat pocket and went to meet her.

"I'm ready to take her," I said.

The barn door creaked and a solemn ten-year-old black girl in a spotless white tracksuit slipped in through the crack, a big flashlight in one hand, my phone ringing in the other. Looking back at someone outside, she bowed and whispered, "Madame, there's a boy—"

Madame Dioskilos hissed in outrage and reached for the bullwhip coiled on the wall. I moved to stop her.

"He's mine, he's just a little boy. I adopted him. Leave him alone—" The girl swung the flashlight at me. It smashed my forearm and the arm went limp.

"A boy, here?" Madame Dioskilos spat, eyes locked imperiously on mine until I looked away. "And on this night, of all nights!"

"I didn't know I'd be dumping a—" He was on the other side of the barn door. I begged, "Oh God, let me see him, please!"

"You know my rules!"

"You must've rubbed off on me," I pleaded. "I took him in to have somebody to teach the trade… I couldn't leave him at home, could I?"

"If you have taken in a boy, you have learned nothing from me." Her strong-gloved fingers worried at the silver lunular clasp holding her long white hair. She never looked so old to me before. I thought it was fear over what happened; it had never occurred to me she was disappointed in me.

"Let him come in, please, Madame. I want you to see him."

The door opened wider and Tonio crept in, hugging his pad and pencils to his chest. He looked scared to death, and I started to cry, but when I went to him, the girl brandished the flashlight. A little little Latina girl came in with a bow stretched and a silver-tipped hunting arrow nocked.

I screamed at them to back off. Tonio cried, and I hugged him. "Tonio, it's okay, honey, you scared them as bad as they scared you."

I turned him around to face the old woman. "Tonio, I want you to meet Madame Scylla Dioskilos. She's one of the ladies whose horses I take care of. She runs a school for girls, kind of like a foster group home, but… nicer. Madame, this is Tonio. Smile big for the nice lady, Tonio."

Scared, Tonio yet managed a thin smile at Madame Dioskilos, who barely glanced at him. "Hi," he whispered.

"Show her your drawings, honey," I said, but he only hugged the pad tighter.

Madame scowled and made some ancient cursing gesture with her fingers.

"You see, Tonio was born with severe cognitive disabilities, so bad that his mother surrendered him to the state. He grew up in a special group home in Oakland. I had a hard time tracking him down. There are so many, many children that nobody wants. I wanted you to meet him—"

"You have defiled my house with this—"

"They're beasts, then, and can never be more?" I demanded, and Madame nodded.

"What is your point?" she snapped.

"Please, Tonio, show her your drawings, I want her to see what a good artist you are."

Tonio looked warily around the barn, then slowly unclenched and opened the pad. Shy, slow, autistic, whatever the ignorant might call him, he could draw. Horses leapt across the pages like a storm, filling and spilling off the paper, rendered in every color in his box, and some others he'd cleverly blended by smudging them with his little fingers.

"So you were wrong," I started, "and you lied to me before…"

Madame made a gesture of water flowing off her face. "You did the right thing bringing him," Madame said. "You must be made to see." She advanced on Tonio until she stood between him and me. Something she took out of her belt made him scream.

From somewhere in the barn came an answer. The lowing roar and crash of wood and metal froze the room. My heart leapt into my mouth. The jaundiced whites of Madame's eyes gleamed all around her violet irises. The knife flashed in her hand.

"Chandra, go and see to the beasts!" Madame ordered. "Marina, shoot her if she moves." The black girl edged around the awkward scene and stalked into the stables. The girl behind Tonio aimed the arrow at me and drew the string back. Tonio sank to the ground, took out a pencil and began to draw.

Madame hovered over Tonio, the knife behind her back, intrigued. "You adopted this boy? Do not tell me lies, Phyllis Slabbert."

"You lied to me, when you said this had never happened, before…"

Madame blinked at me. Tonio whimpered and sketched. The bowstring creaked.

"Look at him, Madame: I want you to count his teeth."

Madame whirled on me and brought the knife up to my chin so quickly I couldn't even flinch. "What is this game?"

My muscles locked up and I just stared at her. "Actaeon's done it before, hasn't he? Maybe you even let it happen, part of the 'rituals,' or a breeding experiment? And you made Greta Spivak, your old vet, dump the girl—"

"Who is this? I know no one by this name!" Madame's wounded innocence was silent movie acting at its finest.

"Bullshit! She worked for you! I think it was because you both knew the girl was pregnant—"

"You lie!" The knife slashed at my face. I ducked away, but the edge flayed my scalp. A big flap of skin with hair on it came away in my hand as I cradled the wound.

Sobs of pain welled up in my throat, but I gagged them back. Whether or not I could go on, it had to come out. "The girl was only twelve, you remember? She couldn't keep him, so they put him up for adoption, but nobody wanted him. He'd retreat and draw on everything, then have violent fits of rage. His hormones are all screwed up and no one's ever tried to reach him, let alone love him, but he's a sweet, sensitive little boy."

Madame looked from Tonio to the bloody knife in her hand. "Look at his teeth, Madame. He's a strange little boy, no doubt, but is he an animal? Do you want to put a saddle on him?"

Madame bent down and took Tonio's jaw, almost tenderly, in her gloved hand. Tonio was too far gone to resist her. Still looking into his mouth as the silence dragged on, she called out, "Chandra, come here."

In the stables, a metal pail hit the ground. The stable door groaned as it swung open. The darkness beyond yawned, absolute. Marina's fingers grew sweaty and tired on the bowstring, and she lowered it. Blood stung my eyes, soaking my hand when I wiped it away. I needed to lie down. I had to get Tonio out of there. I wanted to show her, but I never meant for things to get so out of hand—

Madame seemed, all of a sudden, to decide. She rose and turned on Tonio with the knife out: he didn't see it coming.

I dove after her, screaming. I grabbed her arm, but she slipped out of my blood-slick grip to stab him.

The knife scythed through Tonio's down parka and came out amid a flurry of feathers. I'd spoiled her attack, but she cocked her arm to stab him in the throat. I stepped inside her reach and shoved her as hard as I could. Tonio rolled away shrieking and threw his pad at her. Marina shouted, "Madame!" and raised her bow, loosed her arrow.

It never hit me. Sailing past my eyes, it hit Actaeon in the shoulder, but didn't slow him down.

He came so fast I could only fall before him. Leaping over me, he dealt Marina a brutal kick to the chest. The girl slammed into the barn door and slumped to the ground. Almost in the same movement, he lunged after Madame who, in turn, dove after Tonio. His jaws snapped at her and she hung, howling, in mid-air, caught by his teeth in her long white hair.

Tonio crab-walked backwards into a corner between two walls of hay bales. Hanging by her hair, Madame roared commands in Greek, but Actaeon stood frozen, unable to parse the sticky situation with the stunted brute mind his mistress had given him.

Sounds of shuffling feet behind me made me turn, and I gasped. The rest of them had broken loose, and skulked out of the dark like madhouse inmates on Judgment Day, knees skinned and spurs bloodied from kicking down their stable doors. Their big black eyes rolled and they began to hoot, deep in their barrel chests, nostrils flared as they scented blood on the air.

Tonio's blood. A trickle stood out on his green parka, studded with white down feathers, radioactive in its effect.

I knew, then, why Madame Dioskilos had always had someone else treat and put down her beasts. The smell of their own blood, the sounds of their pain, drove them mad. I thought, then, that I would die, and I laid still as death on the ground, but I did not exist for them. They stampeded over me and converged on Madame Dioskilos.

I got up, pointedly not looking at them as I crawled along the wall to Tonio. He pressed his face against the wall and chewed his lips, too scared to make a sound as I bundled him up in my arms and shuffled with my eyes closed for a thousand years to the barn door.

I raced home and packed bags in a panic. Tonio had fallen asleep in the truck. I was ready to flee again, when exhaustion set in. I had enough strength to bring Tonio into the house and lay him in his bed, before I passed out myself.

I awakened at dawn, and no sirens wailed, no police broke down the door. We would leave, but not in a hurry, not as fugitives. I couldn't understand how the world couldn't sense something so wrong happening, but then, how could it not have sensed how wrong things had been, all along? The sisterhood would smother it in secrecy, and that would be best. No one needed to know—

I only went back once, that morning. Of the beasts there was no sign, nor of any of the girls. Trista was gone, and there were opened pill packets and gauze bandage wrappers on the floor of the tack room. I still worry about them, but I think they will make out all right. After her fashion, Madame Dioskilos prepared them well to face the world.

I won't detail what they did to her body, or where I found the head. The bloody paintings they made on the walls of the barn, in their stables, in the chapel of the Goddess at the barn's heart, were what I will always remember. Though they had only one color to work in, the delicacy of the shapes of centaurs, satyrs and nymphs sporting across, filling and spilling off the cedar beam walls, spoke as no words could of what they might have been, in another life.

I burned the place down. I buried what I could find of Madame Dioskilos under the laurel tree behind the hunting lodge. I said a prayer for her, after I counted her teeth. Her extra bicuspids were filed down and the jaw surgically rebuilt, but she still had too many molars to pass for human, in her own book. I hope God sees it differently.

CARGO

E. MICHAEL LEWIS

I dreamt of cargo. Thousands of crates filled the airplane's hold, all made of unfinished pine, the kind that drives slivers through work gloves. They were stamped with unknowable numbers and bizarre acronyms that glowed fiercely with dim red light. They were supposed to be jeep tires, but some were as large as a house, others as small as a spark plug, all of them secured to pallets with binding like straitjacket straps. I tried to check them all, but there were too many. There was a low shuffling as the boxes shifted, then the cargo fell on me. I couldn't reach the interphone to warn the pilot. The cargo pressed down on me with a thousand sharp little fingers as the plane rolled, crushing the life out of me even as we dived, even as we crashed, the interphone ringing now like a scream. But there was another sound too, from inside the crate next to my ear. Something struggled inside the box, something sodden and defiled, something that I didn't want to see, something that wanted *out*.

It changed into the sound of a clipboard being rapped on the metal frame of my crew house bunk. My eyes shot open. The airman—new in-country, by the sweat lining his collar—stood over me, holding the clipboard between us, trying to decide if I was the type to rip his head off just for doing his job. "Tech Sergeant Davis," he said, "they need you on the flight line right away."

I sat up and stretched. He handed me the clipboard and attached manifest: a knocked-down HU-53 with flight crew, mechanics, and medical support personnel bound for… somewhere new.

"Timehri Airport?"

"It's outside Georgetown, Guyana." When I looked blank, he went on, "It's a former British colony. Timehri used to be Atkinson Air Force Base."

"What's the mission?"

"It's some kind of mass med-evac of ex-pats from somewhere called Jonestown."

Americans in trouble. I'd spent a good part of my Air Force career flying Americans out of trouble. That being said, flying Americans out of trouble was a hell of a lot more satisfying than hauling jeep tires. I thanked him and hurried into a clean flight suit.

I was looking forward to another Panamanian Thanksgiving at Howard Air Force Base—eighty-five degrees, turkey and stuffing from the mess hall, football on Armed Forces Radio, and enough time out of flight rotation to get good and drunk. The in-bound hop from the Philippines went by the numbers and both the passengers and cargo were free and easy. Now this.

Interruption was something you grew accustomed to as a Loadmaster. The C-141 StarLifter was the largest freighter and troop carrier in the Military Air Command, capable of carrying seventy thousand pounds of cargo or two hundred battle-ready troops and flying them anywhere in the world. Half as long as a football field, the high-set swept-back wings drooped bat-like over the tarmac. With an upswept T-tail, petal-doors, and a built-in cargo ramp, the StarLifter was unmatched when it came to moving cargo. Part stewardess and part moving man, my job as a Loadmaster was to pack it as tight and as safe as possible.

With everything onboard and my weight and balance sheets complete, the same airman found me cussing up the Panamanian ground crew for leaving a scuffmark on the airframe.

"Sergeant Davis! Change in plans," he yelled over the whine of the forklift. He handed me another manifest.

"More passengers?"

"New passengers. Med crew is staying here." He said something unintelligible about a change of mission.

"Who are these people?"

Again, I strained to hear him. Or maybe I heard him fine and with the sinking in my gut, I wanted him to repeat it. I wanted to hear him wrong.

"Graves registration," he cried.

That's what I'd thought he'd said.

—◦—

Timehri was your typical third-world airport—large enough to squeeze down a 747, but strewn with potholes and sprawling with rusted Quonset huts. The low line of jungle surrounding the field looked as if it had been beaten back only an hour before. Helicopters buzzed up and down and US servicemen swarmed the tarmac. I knew then that things must be bad.

Outside the bird, the heat rising from the asphalt threatened to melt the soles of my boots even before I had the wheel chocks in place. A ground crew of American GIs approached, anxious to unload and assemble the chopper. One of them, bare-chested with his shirt tied around his waist, handed me a manifest.

"Don't get comfy," he said. "As soon as the chopper's clear, we're loading you up." He nodded over his shoulder.

I looked out over the shimmering taxiway. Coffins. Rows and rows of dull aluminum funerary boxes gleamed in the unforgiving tropical sun. I recognized them from my flights out of Saigon six years ago, my first as Loadmaster. Maybe my insides did a little flip because I'd had no rest, or maybe because I hadn't carried a stiff in a few years. Still, I swallowed hard. I looked at the destination: Dover, Delaware.

—◦—

The ground crew loaded a fresh comfort pallet when I learned we'd have two passengers on the outbound flight.

The first was a kid, right out of high school by the look of it, with bristle-black hair, and too-large jungle fatigues that were starched, clean, and showed the rank of Airman First Class. I told him, "Welcome aboard," and went to help him through the crew door, but he jerked away, nearly hitting his head against the low entrance. I think he would have leapt back if there had been room. His scent hit me, strong and medicinal—Vicks VapoRub.

Behind him a flight nurse, crisp and professional in step, dress, and gesture, also boarded without assistance. I regarded her evenly. I recognized her as one of a batch I had flown regularly from Clark in the Philippines to Da Nang and back again in my early days. A steel-eyed, silver-haired lieutenant. She had been very specific—more than once—in pointing out how any numbskull high school dropout could do my job better. The name on her uniform read Pembry. She touched the kid on his back and guided him to the seats, but if she recognized me, she said nothing.

"Take a seat anywhere," I told them. "I'm Tech Sergeant Davis. We'll be wheels up in less than half an hour so make yourself comfortable."

The kid stopped short. "You didn't tell me," he said to the nurse.

The hold of a StarLifter is most like the inside of a boiler room, with all the heat, cooling, and pressure ducts exposed rather than hidden away like on an airliner. The coffins formed two rows down the length of the hold, leaving a center aisle clear. Stacked four high, there were one hundred and sixty of them. Yellow cargo nets held them in place. Looking past them, we watched the sunlight disappear as the cargo hatch closed, leaving us in an awkward semi-darkness.

"It's the fastest way to get you home," she said to him, her voice neutral. "You want to go home, don't you?"

His voice dripped with fearful outrage. "I don't want to see them. I want a forward facing seat."

If the kid would have looked around, he could have seen that there were no forward facing seats.

"It's okay," she said, tugging on his arm again. "They're going home, too."

"I don't want to look at them," he said as she pushed him to a seat nearest one of the small windows. When he didn't move to strap himself in, Pembry bent and did it for him. He gripped the handrails like the oh-shit bar on a roller coaster. "I don't want to think about them."

"I got it." I went forward and shut down the cabin lights. Now only the twin red jump lights illuminated the long metal containers. When I returned, I brought him a pillow.

The ID label on the kid's loose jacket read "Hernandez." He said, "Thank you," but did not let go of the armrests.

Pembry strapped herself in next to him. I stowed their gear and went through my final checklist.

-⟨o⟩-

Once in the air, I brewed coffee on the electric stove in the comfort pallet. Nurse Pembry declined, but Hernandez took some. The plastic cup shook in his hands.

"Afraid of flying?" I asked. It wasn't so unusual for the Air Force. "I have some Dramamine…"

"I'm not afraid of flying," he said through clenched teeth. All the while he looked past me, to the boxes lining the hold.

Next the crew. No one bird was assigned the same crew, like in the old days. The MAC took great pride in having men be so interchangeable that a flight crew who had never met before could assemble at a flight line and fly any StarLifter to the ends of the Earth. Each man knew my job, like I knew theirs, inside and out.

I went to the cockpit and found everyone on stations. The second engineer sat closest to the cockpit door, hunched over instrumentation. "Four is evening out now, keep the throttle low," he said. I recognized his hangdog face and his Arkansas drawl, but I could not tell from where. I figured after seven years of flying StarLifters, I had flown with just about everybody at one time or another. He thanked me as I set the black coffee on his table. His flightsuit named him Hadley.

The first engineer sat in the bitchseat, the one usually reserved for a "Black Hatter"—mission inspectors were the bane of all MAC aircrews. He asked for two lumps and then stood and looked out the navigator's dome at the blue rushing past.

"Throttle low on four, got it," replied the pilot. He was the designated Aircraft Commander, but both he and the co-pilot were such typical flight jocks that they could have been the same person. They took their coffee with two creams each. "We're trying to outfly some clear air turbulence, but it won't be easy. Tell your passengers to expect some weather."

"Will do, sir. Anything else?"

"Thank you, Load Davis, that's all."

"Yes, sir."

Finally time to relax. As I went to have a horizontal moment in the crew berth, I saw Pembry snooping around the comfort pallet. "Anything I can help you find?"

"An extra blanket?"

I pulled one from the storage cabinet between the cooking station and the latrine and gritted my teeth. "Anything else?"

"No," she said, pulling a piece of imaginary lint from the wool. "We've flown together before, you know."

"Have we?"

She raised an eyebrow. "I probably ought to apologize."

"No need, ma'am," I said. I dodged around her and opened the fridge. "I could serve an in-flight meal later if you are…"

She placed her hand on my shoulder, like she had on Hernandez, and it commanded my attention. "You do remember me."

"Yes, ma'am."

"I was pretty hard on you during those evac flights."

I wished she'd stop being so direct. "You were speaking your mind, ma'am. It made me a better Loadmaster."

"Still…"

"Ma'am, there's no need." Why can't women figure out that apologies only make things worse?

"Very well." The hardness of her face melted into sincerity, and suddenly it occurred to me that she wanted to talk.

"How's your patient?"

"Resting." Pembry tried to act casual, but I knew she wanted to say more.

"What's his problem?"

"He was one of the first to arrive," she said, "and the first to leave."

"Jonestown? Was it that bad?"

Flashback to our earlier evac flights. The old look, hard and cool, returned instantly. "We flew out of Dover on White House orders five hours after they got the call. He's a Medical Records Specialist, six months in the service, he's never been anywhere before, never saw a day of trauma in his life. Next thing he knows, he's in a South American jungle with a thousand dead bodies."

"A thousand?"

"Count's not in yet, but it's headed that way." She brushed the back of her hand against her cheek. "So many kids."

"Kids?"

"Whole families. They all drank poison. Some kind of cult, they said. Someone told me the parents killed their children first. I don't know what could make a person do that to their own family." She shook her head. "I stayed at Timehri to organize triage. Hernandez said the smell was unimaginable. They had to spray the bodies with insecticide and defend them from hungry giant rats. He said they made him bayonet the bodies to release the pressure. He burned his uniform." She shuffled to keep her balance as the bird jolted.

Something nasty crept down the back of my throat as I tried not to visualize what she said. I struggled not to grimace. "The AC says it may get rough. You better strap in." I walked her back to her seat. Hernandez's mouth gaped as he sprawled across his seat, looking for all the world like he'd lost a bar fight—bad. Then I went to my bunk and fell asleep.

❧

Ask any Loadmaster: after so much time in the air, the roar of engines is something you ignore. You find you can sleep through just about anything. Still, your mind tunes in and wakes up at the sound of anything unusual, like the flight from Yakota to Elmendorf when a jeep came loose and rolled into a crate of MREs. Chipped beef everywhere. You can bet the ground crew heard from me on that one. So it should not come as a shock that I started at the sound of a scream.

On my feet, out of the bunk, past the comfort pallet before I could think. Then I saw Pembry. She was out of her seat and in front of Hernandez, dodging his flailing arms, speaking calmly and below the engine noise. Not him, though.

"I heard them! I heard them! They're in there! All those kids! All those kids!"

I put my hand on him—hard. "Calm down!"

He stopped flailing. A shamed expression came over him. His eyes riveted mine. "I heard them singing."

"Who?"

"The children! All the…" He gave a helpless gesture to the unlighted coffins.

"You had a dream," Pembry said. Her voice shook a little. "I was with you the whole time. You were asleep. You couldn't have heard anything."

"All the children are dead," he said. "All of them. They didn't know. How could they have known they were drinking poison? Who would give their own child poison to drink?" I let go of his arm and he looked at me. "Do you have kids?"

"No," I said.

"My daughter," he said, "is a year-and-a-half old. My son is three months. You have to be careful with them, patient with them. My wife is really good at it, y'know?" I noticed for the first time how sweat crawled across his forehead, the backs of his hands. "But I'm okay too, I mean, I don't really know what the fuck I'm doing, but I wouldn't hurt them. I hold them and I sing to them and—and if anyone else tried to hurt them…" He grabbed me on the arm that had held him. "Who would give their child poison?"

"It isn't your fault," I told him.

"They didn't know it was poison. They still don't." He pulled me closer and said into my ear, "I heard them singing." I'll be damned if the words he spoke didn't make my spine shiver.

"I'll go check it out," I told him as I grabbed a flashlight off the wall and started down the center aisle.

There was a practical reason for checking out the noise. As a Load-master, I knew that an unusual sound meant trouble. I had heard a story about how an aircrew kept hearing the sound of a cat meowing from somewhere in the hold. The Loadmaster couldn't find it, but figured it'd turn up when they off-loaded the cargo. Turns out the "meowing" was a weakened load brace that buckled when the wheels touched runway, freeing three tons of explosive ordnance and making the landing very interesting. Strange noises meant trouble, and I'd have been a fool not to look into it.

I checked all the buckles and netting as I went, stooping and listening, checking for signs of shifting, fraying straps, anything out of the ordinary. I went up one side and down the other, even checking the cargo doors. Nothing. Everything was sound, my usual best work.

I walked up the aisle to face them. Hernandez wept, head in his hands. Pembry rubbed his back with one hand as she sat next to him, like my mother had done to me.

"All clear, Hernandez." I put the flashlight back on the wall.

"Thanks," Pembry replied for him, then said to me, "I gave him a Valium, he should quiet down now."

"Just a safety check," I told her. "Now, both of you get some rest."

I went back to my bunk to find it occupied by Hadley, the second engineer. I took the one below him but couldn't fall asleep right away. I tried to keep my mind far away from the reason that the coffins were in my bird in the first place.

Cargo was the euphemism. From blood plasma to high explosives to secret service limousines to gold bullion, you packed it and hauled it because it was your job, that was all, and anything that could be done to speed you on your way was important.

Just cargo, I thought. But whole families that killed themselves... I was glad to get them the hell out of the jungle, back home to their families— but the medics who got there first, all those guys on the ground, even my crew, we were too late to do any more than that. I was interested in having kids in a vague, unsettled sort of way, and it pissed me off to hear about anyone harming them. But these parents did it willingly, didn't they?

I couldn't relax. I found an old copy of the *New York Times* folded into the bunk. Peace in the Middle East in our lifetimes, it read. Next to the article was a picture of President Carter and Anwar Sadat shaking hands. I was just about to drift off when I thought I heard Hernandez cry out again.

I dragged my ass up. Pembry stood with her hands clutched over her mouth. I thought Hernandez had hit her, so I went to her and peeled her hands away, looking for damage.

There was none. Looking over her shoulder, I could see Hernandez riveted to his seat, eyes glued to the darkness like a reverse color television.

"What happened? Did he hit you?"

"He—he heard it again," she stammered as one hand rose to her face again. "You—you ought to go check again. You ought to go check..."

The pitch of the plane shifted and she fell into me a little, and as I steadied myself by grabbing her elbow she collapsed against me. I met her gaze matter-of-factly. She looked away. "What happened?" I asked again.

"I heard it too," Pembry said.

My eyes went to the aisle of shadow. "Just now?"

"Yes."

"Was it like he said? Children singing?" I realized I was on the verge of shaking her. Were they both going crazy?

"Children playing," she said. "Like—playground noise, y'know? Kids playing."

I wracked my brain for some object, or some collection of objects, that when stuffed into a C-141 StarLifter and flown thirty-nine thousand feet over the Caribbean, would make a sound like children playing.

Hernandez shifted his position and we both brought our attention to bear on him. He smiled a defeated smile and said to us, "I told you."

"I'll go check it out," I told them.

"Let them play," said Hernandez. "They just want to play. Isn't that what you wanted to do as a kid?"

I remembered my childhood like a jolt, endless summers and bike rides and skinned knees and coming home at dusk to my mother saying, "Look how dirty you are." I wondered if the recovery crews washed the bodies before they put them in the coffins.

"I'll find out what it is," I told them. I went and got the flashlight again. "Stay put."

I used the darkness to close off my sight, give me more to hear. The turbulence had subsided by then, and I used my flashlight only to avoid tripping on the cargo netting. I listened for anything new or unusual. It wasn't one thing—it had to be a combination—noises like that just don't stop and start again. Fuel leak? Stowaway? The thought of a snake or some other jungle beast lurking inside those metal boxes heightened my whole state of being and brought back my dream.

Near the cargo doors, I shut off my light and listened. Pressurized air. Four Pratt and Whitney turbofan engines. Fracture rattles. Cargo straps flapping.

And then, something. Something came in sharp after a moment, at first dull and sweeping, like noise from the back of a cave, but then pure and unbidden, like sounds to a surprised eavesdropper.

Children. Laughter. Like recess at grade school.

I opened my eyes and flashed my light around the silver crates. I found them waiting, huddled with me, almost expectant.

Children, I thought, *just children*.

I ran past Hernandez and Pembry to the comfort pallet. I can't tell you what they saw in my face, but if it was anything like what I saw in the little mirror above the latrine sink, I would have been at once terrified and redeemed.

I looked from the mirror to the interphone. Any problem with the cargo should be reported immediately—procedure demanded it—but what could I tell the AC? I had an urge to drop it all, just eject the coffins and call it a day. If I told him there was a fire in the hold, we would drop below ten thousand feet so I could blow the bolts and send the whole load to the bottom of the Gulf of Mexico, no questions asked.

I stopped then, straightened up, tried to think. *Children*, I thought. *Not monsters, not demons, just the sounds of children playing. Nothing that will get you. Nothing that* can *get you.* I tossed off the shiver that ran through my body and decided to get some help.

At the bunk, I found Hadley still asleep. A dog-eared copy of a paperback showing two women locked in a passionate embrace lay like a tent on his chest. I shook his arm and he sat up. Neither of us said anything for a moment. He rubbed his face with one hand and yawned.

Then he looked right at me and I watched his face arch into worry. His next action was to grab his portable oxygen. He recovered his game face in an instant. "What is it, Davis?"

I groped for something. "The cargo." I said. "There's a... possible shift in the cargo. I need a hand, sir."

His worry snapped into annoyance. "Have you told the AC?"

"No sir," I said. "I—I don't want to trouble him yet. It may be nothing."

His face screwed into something unpleasant and I thought I'd have words from him, but he let me lead the way aft. Just his presence was enough to revive my doubt, my professionalism. My walk sharpened, my eyes widened, my stomach returned to its place in my gut.

I found Pembry sitting next to Hernandez now, both together in a feigned indifference. Hadley gave them a disinterested look and followed me down the aisle between the coffins.

"What about the main lights?" he asked.

"They don't help," I said. "Here." I handed him the flashlight and asked him, "Do you hear it?"

"Hear what?"

"Just listen."

Again, only engines and the jetstream. "I don't..."

"Shhh! Listen."

His mouth opened and stayed there for a minute, then shut. The engines quieted and the sounds came, dripping over us like water vapor, the fog of sound around us. I didn't realise how cold I was until I noticed my hands shaking.

"What in the hell is that?" Hadley asked. "It sounds like…"

"Don't," I interrupted. "That can't be it." I nodded at the metal boxes. "You know what's in these coffins, don't you?"

He didn't say anything. The sound seemed to filter around us for a moment, at once close, then far away. He tried to follow the sound with his light. "Can you tell where it's coming from?"

"No. I'm just glad you hear it too, sir."

The engineer scratched his head, his face drawn, like he swallowed something foul and couldn't lose the aftertaste. "I'll be damned," he drawled.

All at once, as before, the sound stopped, and the roar of the jets filled our ears.

"I'll hit the lights." I moved away hesitantly. "I'm not going to call the AC."

His silence was conspiratorial. As I rejoined him, I found him examining a particular row of coffins through the netting.

"You need to conduct a search," he said dully.

I didn't respond. I'd done midair cargo searches before, but never like this, not even on bodies of servicemen. If everything Pembry said was true, I couldn't think of anything worse than opening one of these caskets.

We both started at the next sound. Imagine a wet tennis ball. Now imagine the sound a wet tennis ball makes when it hits the court—a sort of dull THWAK—like a bird striking the fuselage. It sounded again, and this time I could hear it inside the hold. Then, after a buffet of turbulence, the thump sounded again. It came clearly from a coffin at Hadley's feet.

Not a serious problem, his face tried to say. We just imagined it. *A noise from one coffin can't bring a plane down*, his face said. *There are no such things as ghosts.*

"Sir?"

"We need to see," he said.

Blood pooled in my stomach again. *See*, he had said. *I didn't want to see.*

"Get on the horn and tell the AC to avoid the chop," he said. I knew at that moment he was going to help me. He didn't want to, but he was going to do it anyway.

"What are you doing?" Pembry asked. She stood by as I removed the cargo netting from the row of caskets while the engineer undid the individual straps around that one certain row. Hernandez slept head bowed, the downers having finally taken effect.

"We have to examine the cargo," I stated matter-of-factly. "The flight may have caused the load to become unbalanced."

She grabbed my arm as I went by. "Was that all it was? A shifting load?"

There was a touch of desperation in her question. *Tell me I imagined it*, the look on her face said. *Tell me and I'll believe you, and I'll go get some sleep.*

"We think so," I nodded.

Her shoulders dropped and her face peeled into a smile too broad to be real. "Thank God. I thought I was going crazy."

I patted her shoulder. "Strap in and get some rest," I told her. She did.

Finally, I was doing something. As Loadmaster, I could put an end to this nonsense. So I did the work. I unstrapped the straps, climbed the other caskets, shoved the top one out of place, carried it, secured it, removed the next one, carried it, secured it, and again. The joy of easy repetition.

It wasn't until we got to the bottom one, the noisy one, that Hadley stopped. He stood there watching me as I pulled it out of place enough to examine it. His stance was level, but even so it spoke of revulsion, something that, among swaggering Air Force veterans and over beers, he could conceal. Not now, not to me.

I did a cursory examination of the deck where it had sat, of the caskets next to it, and saw no damage or obvious flaws.

A noise sounded—a moist "thunk." From inside. We flinched in unison. The engineer's cool loathing was impossible to conceal. I suppressed a tremble.

"We have to open it," I said.

The engineer didn't disagree, but like me, his body was slow to move. He squatted down and, with one hand firmly planted on the casket lid, unlatched the clasps on his end. I undid mine, finding my fingers slick on the cold metal, and shaking a little as I pulled them away and braced my hand on the lid. Our eyes met in one moment that held the last of our resolve. Together, we opened the casket.

⟶⟵

First, the smell: a mash of rotten fruit, antiseptic, and formaldehyde, wrapped in plastic with dung and sulfur. It stung our nostrils as it filled the hold. The overhead lights illuminated two shiny black body bags, slick with condensation and waste. I knew these would be the bodies of children, but it awed me, hurt me. One bag lay unevenly concealing the other, and I understood at once that there was more than one child in it. My eyes skimmed the juice-soaked plastic, picking out the contour of an arm, the trace of a profile. A shape coiled near the bottom seam, away from the rest. It was the size of a baby.

Then the plane shivered like a frightened pony and the top bag slid away to reveal a young girl, eight or nine at the most, half in and half out of the bag. Wedged like a mad contortionist into the corner, her swollen belly, showing stab wounds from bayonets, had bloated again, and her twisted limbs were now as thick as tree limbs. The pigment-bearing skin had peeled away everywhere but her face, which was as pure and as innocent as any cherub in heaven.

Her face was really what drove it home, what really hurt me. Her sweet face.

My hand fixed itself to the casket edge in painful whiteness, but I dared not remove it. Something caught in my throat and I forced it back down.

A lone fly, fat and glistening, crawled from inside the bag and flew lazily towards Hadley. He slowly rose to his feet and braced himself, as if against a body blow. He watched it rise and flit a clumsy path through the air. Then he broke the moment by stepping back, his hands flailing and hitting it—I heard the slap of his hand—and letting a nauseous sound escape his lips.

When I stood up, my temples throbbed and my legs weakened. I held onto a nearby casket, my throat filled with something rancid.

"Close it," he said like a man with his mouth full. "Close it."

My arms went rubbery. After bracing myself, I lifted one leg and kicked the lid. It rang out like an artillery shot. Pressure pounded into my ears like during a rapid descent.

Hadley put his hands on his haunches and lowered his head, taking deep breaths through his mouth. "Jesus," he croaked.

I saw movement. Pembry stood next to the line of coffins, her face pulled up in sour disgust. "What—is—that—smell?"

"It's okay." I found I could work one arm and tried what I hoped looked like an off-handed gesture. "Found the problem. Had to open it up though. Go sit down."

Pembry brought her hands up around herself and went back to her seat.

I found that with a few more deep breaths, the smell dissipated enough to act. "We have to secure it," I told Hadley.

He looked up from the floor and I saw his eyes as narrow slits. His hands were in fists and his broad torso stood fierce and straight. At the corner of his eyes, wetness glinted. He said nothing.

It became cargo again as I fastened the latches. We strained to fit it back into place. In a matter of minutes, the other caskets were stowed, the exterior straps were in place, the cargo netting draped and secure.

Hadley waited for me to finish up, then walked forwards with me. "I'm going to tell the AC you solved the problem," he said, "and to get us back to speed."

I nodded.

"One more thing," he said. "If you see that fly, kill it."

"Didn't you..."

"No."

I didn't know what else to say, so I said, "Yes, sir."

Pembry sat in her seat, nose wriggled up, feigning sleep. Hernandez sat upright, eyelids half open. He gestured for me to come closer, bend down.

"Did you let them out to play?" he asked.

I stood over him and said nothing. In my heart, I felt that same pang I did as a child, when summer was over.

When we landed in Dover, a funeral detail in full dress offloaded every coffin, affording full funeral rights to each person. I'm told as more bodies flew in, the formality was scrapped and only a solitary Air Force chaplain met the planes. By week's end I was back in Panama with a stomach full of turkey and cheap rum. Then it was off to the Marshall Islands, delivering supplies to the guided missile base there. In the Military Air Command, there is no shortage of cargo.

E. Michael Lewis says: "Of the nine hundred people who died in the Jonestown Massacre, nearly a third of them were under the age of eighteen. This story is dedicated to the families who lost loved ones at Jonestown, and to the servicemen and -women who brought them home."

TENDER AS TEETH

STEPHANIE CRAWFORD AND DUANE SWIERCZYNSKI

"**I**s it true that the cure made all of you vegetarians?" Carson asked.

Justine was staring at the road ahead, but could see him toying with his digital recorder in her peripheral vision. He was asking a flurry of questions, but at the same time, avoiding The Big Question. She wished he'd just come out with it already.

"Why are you asking me?" she replied. "I'm not the mouthpiece for every single survivor."

Carson stammered a little before Justine glanced over and gave him a wide grin.

"Oh yes, I referred to former zombies as survivors. Make sure to include that. Your readers will love it."

As they drove across the desert the sun was pulling the sky from black to a gritty blue-grey. The rented compact car held a thirty-three-year-old man named Carson with enough expensive camera equipment to crowd up the backseat, and Justine, a woman two years younger, who kept her own small shoulder bag between her feet.

The rest of her baggage was invisible.

—◇—

Some said as far as apocalyptic plagues went, it could have been a lot worse.

The dead didn't crawl out of their graves. Society didn't crumble entirely. The infection didn't spread as easily as it did in the movies—you had to either really *try* to get infected, or be genetically predisposed to it.

Justine happened to be one of the latter.

After work one night, Justine was nursing a Pabst at her local generic, suburban sports bar while half-listening to the news about a virus that would probably quiet down like H1N1 and texting her late friend Gina. She was just raising the bottle's mouth to her lips when a thick, dead weight fell against her and knocked her out of her bar stool and onto the sticky, peanut shell covered floor. Too fucking enraged to wait for a good Samaritan to jump up and give a *Hey, Pal*, Justine started blindly kicking out her heels and thrusting out fists at the drunk bastard. That's how it played out until the drunk started gnawing at her fists until his incisors connected with the actual bone of her fingers while his mouth worked to slurp up and swallow the shredded meat of her knuckles. After that, Justine remembered little until the cure hit her bloodstream.

That had been six months after the attack in the bar. And in the meantime . . .

⟶⟨○⟩⟶

Carson tried to look at Justine without full-on *staring* at her. Like much of the time he'd spent with her so far, he was fairly certain he was failing miserably. The miracle vaccine seemed to have left Justine with little more damage than a scarred face, a lean-muscled body that bordered on emaciation, and an entire planet filled with people who actively wanted her dead. That was called "being one of the lucky ones."

Keep her talking, he reminded himself. Carson asked, "I understand your mom paid for the cure?"

Justine kicked the glove compartment while crossing her legs. "Sadly, yes. I guess she meant well."

"Aren't you glad to be alive?"

"If you call this living."

"Better than being dead."

She turned to face him, squinting and twisting her lips into a pout. "Is it?"

Asking questions was the problem, Carson decided. He wasn't a real journalist. He'd only brought the digital recorder to please his editor, who couldn't afford to send both a photographer *and* a reporter.

Just keep her talking as much as possible, the editor had said. *We'll make sense of it later.*

But most important, his editor added, *we want her to talk about what it's like.*

What what *is like?* Carson had asked.

His editor replied: *What it's like to go on living.*

A year ago today he'd been out in Las Vegas for one of the most inane reasons of all: a photo shoot for a celebrity cookbook. The celebrity in question was a borderline morbidly obese actor known for both his comedic roles as well as his darker turns in mob flicks. Right before he'd left on that trip the first outbreaks had been reported, but the virus seemed to be contained to certain parts of the country, and Carson thought he'd come to regret it if he turned down the assignment over the latest health scare. Especially if that would leave him stuck in his Brooklyn apartment for months on end while this thing ran its course. They were saying it could be as bad as the 1918 flu pandemic.

Oh, if he had only known.

The outbreak had happened mid-shoot. A pack of zombies had burst in just as the food stylist had finished with the chicken scarpariello. They weren't interested in the dish. They wanted the celebrity chef instead. Carson kept snapping photos before he quite realized what was happening. He escaped across Vegas, continuing to take photos as the city tore itself apart.

And then he saw Justine, though he didn't know her name then.

Back then, she was just . . .

Carson heard his editor's impatient reminder in his head:

Keep her talking.

Yeah.

Not talking was the reason he'd become a photographer. He preferred to keep the lens between himself and the rest of the world, speaking to subjects only when he absolutely *had* to.

He was struggling to formulate a new inane question when she spoke up.

"Do you remember the exact place?"

Carson nodded.

"So where was it?" Justine asked.

That surprised him. He assumed she would have just . . . known. Maybe not when she was in that state, because the former zombies—the *survivors*— were supposed to have blanked memories. The photo, though . . . surely she had to have seen the photo at some point.

Or did she?

"Outside of Vegas. Almost near Henderson."

"Huh," Justine said. "Makes sense."

"Does it?"

"That's not far from where I used to live. So come on. Where did you . . . um, *encounter* me?"

Carson pulled onto the 5, which would take them out of the Valley and out through the desert. "I'm hoping I'll be able to find it again once we're out there," he said.

"Don't count on it, buddy boy," she said. "My mom tells me they've razed a lot of the old neighborhood. There's even been talk of abandoning Vegas altogether. Clear everyone out, then drop an H-bomb directly on it. Wipe the slate clean."

Carson, still fumbling, heard the question tumble out of his mouth before he could stop himself.

"Have you, um, *seen* the photo?"

⟶⟵

Justine had woken up in the hospital, still spoiling for a fight. After about a minute her eyes registered that she was in a hospital bed, and she felt her mom squeezing her hand through layers of aching pain and a wooziness that could only be coming from the IV attached to her arm—so she'd assumed. So the bastard actually put her in the hospital?

Justine's first lucid words were spent reassuring her mom, who herself looked like she'd been put through the wringer.

"Hey ma, it's alright . . . you should see the other guy."

That's what she attempted to say, at any rate. It came out sounding more like "ACK-em, aight . . . shouldas . . . other guy." Her voice sounded cracked and enfeebled . . . almost as if her actual esophagus was bruised and coated in grime.

Her mother teared up and went in for the most delicate hug Justine could remember ever having experienced.

"Thank God . . . He finally showed up. Thank God you're back, and thank Him that you don't remember."

It was only then that Justine noticed that the doctors and nurses surrounding her had what could only be taken as unprofessional looks of pure, barely disguised looks of disgust on their faces. All this for a fucking bar fight she didn't even start?

Before Justine could ask what exactly was going on, her mom cupped her palm against her daughter's cheek: Justine couldn't help realizing how hollowed out it felt against her mom's warm hand.

"Sweetie . . . I have a lot I need to tell you. It's not when you think it is, and you're not exactly who you think you are anymore. The world got infected and wormed you worse than anyone. You're going to need to prepare yourself. Just know I love you, always."

And then her mom told her what the world had been up to.

-o-

Justine stared at the passing power lines with an interest they didn't exactly warrant. "Is this professional curiosity?"

"No," Carson said. "I'd really like to know."

Justine glanced over at Carson, who gave her a tight-lipped smile. She had done her research on him, and she was almost personally insulted by what she found. A small part of her was hoping she'd get a gonzo journalist-type that would end the interview with him trying to hunt her in a "most dangerous game" scenario. Carson was, at best, a mid-level photog—his writing credits adding up to captions under his glossy photos of celebrities she had never heard of. There were a few dashes of pretension, but he was clearly paying the bills.

Except for those unexpected, dramatic moments every photographer lives for. He had a few absorbing shots.

The main one starring her ownself.

"My mom kept it from me for as long as possible. She acted a bit as if seeing it would trigger me, somehow. But . . . eh."

Justine started absently gnawing on a fingernail with more vigor that she realized.

"I'll see little thumbnails on Google and squint my eyes to blur it out. I've been told about it enough that my taste to see the actual money shot has long been sated."

Justine glanced over at Carson to see how that landed. She was sleep deprived and barely knew the guy, but he somehow looked . . . puzzled.

-o-

Was she serious? How could she have not looked?

Carson knew he'd created that photo by pure accident. Even the framing and lighting and composition were a happy accident—a trifecta of the perfect conditions, snapped at exactly the right moment. He admitted it. He'd lucked into it. He couldn't even claim to have created that photo. He'd merely been the one holding the camera, his index finger twitching. That image wanted to exist; he was simply the conduit.

The photo wasn't his fault, just like her . . . sickness . . . wasn't her fault. They were like two car accident victims, thrown together by chance, and left to deal with the wreckage.

He got all that.

Still . . . how could she *not* want to see? How could you ever hope to recover if you didn't confront it head-on?

"Pull over," she said suddenly.

"Are you okay?"

"Unless you want to clean chunks of puke out of this rental, pull over now. Please."

Carson was temporarily desert-blind. He couldn't tell where the edge of the broken road ended and the dead, dry earth began. Blinking, he slowly edged to the right as Justine's hands fumbled at the door handle. He saw— *felt*—her entire body jolt. He applied the brake, kicking up a huge plume of dust. Justine flew out of the passenger seat even before the car had come to a complete halt. She disappeared into the dust. Within seconds, Carson could hear her heaving.

He knew this was what the Cure did to you. It took away the zombie, but left you a very, very sick person.

Should he get out? Did she maybe want a little water, or her privacy? He didn't know. For a moment, Carson sat behind the wheel, watching the dust settle back down. There were a lot of dust storms out here, he'd read. The Southwest hadn't seen them this bad since the 30s Dust Bowl days. Some people thought it was nature's way of trying to wipe the slate clean, one sharp grain of sand at a time.

All was quiet; she'd stopped heaving.

"Justine?" he called out. "You okay?"

He opened the door just as the truck pulled up behind them. Damnit. Probably a good Samaritan, thinking they needed help.

"Justine?"

Car doors slammed behind Carson. He turned off the ignition, pulled the keys from the steering column, pushed open the door with his foot, stepped out into the hot, dry air. There were three people standing there. Carson was struck at first by how familiar they looked, but couldn't immediately place them. Not until one of them said,

"Where's the babykiller?"

Fuck me, he thought. It was the protesters.

They'd followed them out into the desert.

◄◦►

When Carson arrived at Justine's Burbank apartment just a few hours earlier, he was stunned to see them there, carrying placards and pacing up and down the front walkway. They must have been at it all night, and towards the end of some kind of "shift," because they look tired, haggard and vacant eyed. Ironically enough, they kind of looked like you-know-whats.

Carson was equally stunned by the things coming out of their mouths, the sheer hate painted on their signs.

An Abomination Lives Here.

That Baby Had A Future.

Kill Yourself Justine.

Delusional people who had to seize on something, he supposed. There was a whole "Disbelief in the Cure" movement going on now, with a groundswell of people who brought out these pseudo-scientists claiming that the Cure was only temporary, that at any moment, thousands of people could revert to flesh-eating monsters again. There was not a lick of scientific evidence to back this up, mind you. But when has that stopped zealots before?

Carson had parked the car a block away, in the rubble of a lot in front of an old 50s-style motel that had promptly gone out of business a year ago during the chaos. He wiped the sweat from his brow—wasn't California supposed to be cooler this time of year? At first he grabbed his small digital camera and locked everything else in the trunk, figuring that if he tried to run that gauntlet with his full gear there was a strong chance he'd be molested. Carson was prepared for anything, but wasn't in the mood to lose ten grand worth of gear that he *knew* the paper wouldn't replace.

But then again, when the going gets weird, the weird turn pro . . . wasn't that what Hunter S. Thompson said? Carson donned his vest (he hated it, but people associated it with being a pro, so . . .) and walked right up to the nutcases, smiling. That's right, he thought. Just a happy photojournalist on assignment, here to take your picture.

That's the thing: you don't ask. You keep your camera low and just start shooting. Ask, and there's a strong chance they'll think, Hey, wait a minute, maybe I shouldn't agree to this. But if you act like God Himself sent you down here to record the moments for posterity, most people will step out of your way and let you do His Holy Work. Carson snapped away from waist level. Sometimes you want that feeling of looking up from a child's POV, right up into the faces of these lunatics, the sun bouncing from their hand-painted signs. Carson was feeling good about the assignment when something hard slammed into the center of his back and he tumbled forward into someone's fist.

These things happen so fast—your ass getting kicked. In the movies there's always an explanation. Your antagonists go to great pains to tell you exactly *why* you're going to receive a brutal beating right before the beating actually happens. Not in reality. When a mob attacks you, and blood's filling your mouth, and someone's kicking you in the back and you can feel your internal organs convulsing . . . there there are no explanations.

But Carson heard one thing. The most chilling thing he could possibly hear, actually. And that was his name.

They know who I am, he thought. *They know I'm the one who had made Zombie Chick famous.*

Which was when said Zombie Chick saved Carson from hospitalization.

She didn't rush down and start growling at the crowd, asking for brains. She merely opened her window and stared down at them. Carson didn't notice it at first; all he sensed was that the kicks came slower, and then tapered off entirely.

The crowd backed away from Carson and focused on her, up in her window. Cursing at her. Gesturing at her. Spitting. Picking up tiny chunks of broken sidewalk and hurling them at her. Only then did she duck inside and slide the window shut.

Carson wanted to get the hell out of there . . . *pronto.* But then he imagined stepping into his boss's office empty-handed, without a single photo. That simply wasn't an option. Not if he wanted to eat. So he pushed himself, ribs and legs screaming, and took advantage of the temporary distraction, jogging right up through the center of the crowd, pushing his way past them, blasting through the front door of the apartment complex. By the time they noticed, it was too late—Carson had flipped the deadbolt behind him. As he scanned the mailboxes with the call buzzers he could hear them yelling, threatening to kill him for real . . .

Looked like they wanted to make good on that promise now, out here in an empty stretch of desert, with no one to interrupt them.

⤙◦⤚

Justine looked down at what she evacuated, noting it was pretty much pure water. She started to straighten up but stopped herself when she noticed the long shadows stumble over themselves.

"Shit."

Justine stayed bent over, hands on her knees, mind racing. She could hear muffled angry voices and some half-hearted pounding on a car. She figured it was road warriors, insanely persistent Latter-Day Saints missionaries, or they were being followed by her own personal Raincoat Brigade. Whoever it was, she was going to need a decent-sized rock at the very least, and she needed to look as fucked up as possible. The latter was covered, and her eyes scanned quickly for the former.

Jackpot.

Eyes up. Take it slow.

Most of the brigade (biggest bunch of vultures this desert has ever produced, Justine thought) was standing back from the car, attempting to look casual but barely pulling off "vaguely gassy." There were three men in their mid-forties actually on the car. One was playing the lean-against-the-windshield cop move, with the other two settling for leaning against the side.

Justine crouched in the warm dirt, obscured by a large grouping of banana yucca. If Carson had left the passenger seat unlocked she could probably jump in, he could floor it and ride like hell until they got to a gas station.

Fake cop had just cocked some kind of gun. Seriously? Fuck this. Fuck all of it. She should have never agreed to this interview. She was probably going to be one of those survivors who ended up dead—for real this time—at the hands of a frightened mob.

Unless she could use their fear against them.

Justine stood up, stretched . . . and moaned. Moaned like some kind of unholy undead piece of hell would yawn after centuries of hungry slumber—or whatever these assholes believed.

"There she is!"

"Why didn't anyone see her get out?"

"Weren't you supposed to be watching that patch, Dana?"

"There's the babykiller! I bet they don't prosecute in Nevada and he's smuggling her!"

But the crowd quickly lost interest in Carson and his compact car, and moved en masse towards Justine. Just a yard down was a van with a flat tire facing the road.

Clever dumb bastards, Justine thought. That'll keep the passing cars moving.

"I'd ask if you didn't have anything better to do," Justine called out. "But after watching you all for months out my window I know you don't."

Justine found bravado sometimes worked when the rocks weren't up to snuff.

One of the guys leaning against the car gave a grimace that bordered on a grin at Justine.

"You have served no jail time for killing the most innocent of our Savior's creations. We just want to . . . talk to you about it. Maybe get you to turn yourself in. There's no reason for you to get your bowels in an uproar."

Some of the gang nodded in agreement, others just eyed Justine as if she was about to leap out like a cat in a closet in a bad slasher movie. Fake Cop kept his fingers moving on the gun that he was holding close to his thigh.

Justine glanced over to the car. Carson was standing there quietly. Now that their little "freak" was front and center, nobody bothered to keep an eye on him. He had his cell phone in his hand. He made eye contact and gave a short nod.

Please, Justine thought. *Don't come to my rescue, photo boy. From the looks of you, you've got the muscle strength of warm butter.*

Moving her eyes back to the group, Justine took a deep breath and tried to make eye contact with as many as possible.

"Look, I really understand. I hate myself too," Justine said. "But I really, truly was not myself when that happened, and believe me they would have found out if I was. I'm cured now and my life is a living hell, so can you just leave me alone to fester it out, please? You guys will just go to jail and I'm really not worth it."

"Maybe we can just shoot 'er here," one of them said.

Another: "Shut up. Just shut up. You weren't even invited here, you dumb psycho."

Fake Cop and the one that had been talking had a tension between them that made Justine more nervous than the pure hatred that was being leveled at her.

The man turned back to her.

"I'm sorry, this was stupid. My name is Mike. How about you let your friend leave, and you come with us and we can talk to my brother—he's a police officer—and we can get you right. . . ."

Mike stopped himself. Justine could see that he had just spotted the phone in Carson's hand.

"Well shit, son," Mike said. "I really wish you hadn't done that."

Justine, strangely enough, wished the same thing.

◄○►

For an awful moment there, Carson thought that Justine's "cure" hadn't fully taken.

His fevered imagination put together the sequence of events this way:

She's riding along, in the sun, next to a living human being. She doesn't get out much. She's not around people much. Something in her breaks down. She senses the flesh, the blood beating through his veins. It's all too much. It makes her sick. She thinks she has to puke. She asks him to pull over and she scrambles from the car when it hits her. She can't help it, can't control it. Suddenly she's acting like a zombie again. . . .

Because suddenly, she *was.*

A zombie again.

Forcing this unholy sound out of her throat, clawing at invisible enemies, eyes rolling up in the back of her head . . .

The protest mob jolted, taking a step away from each other, as if collectively hoping the crazy baby-killing zombie bitch would attack the person standing next to them. Carson jolted, too, from the shock of it, but also the thought that just a few minutes ago, he'd been inside a speeding car with this woman. *Thing.*

He instantly regretted that it was a cell phone in his hand and not his camera, which was still packed up in the backseat. He hated himself for even thinking it, but . . . c'mon! The impact of a photo like that would be seismic. Proof that the cure doesn't work! As shown by its most infamous poster child. . . .

But those fantasies were dashed the moment he heard Justine scream, in perfect English:

"Carson—the car—NOW!"

◄◦►

The best Justine could hope for was not getting shot.

She dove into the crowd and just started shoving. There was no telling how many other guns were hiding in this group, but she was counting on the stark raving fear factor and element of surprise to keep the men from using them. For a few seconds at least. Until fucking Carson got the car revved up. . . .

"Carson, goddamnit!'

She couldn't keep herself from picturing how, if Carson wasn't here, she'd probably just have gone for it. Her anger and annoyance were burning so hot that she could easier have chosen this day as her last—as long as she took these assholes out along with her.

Baby-Eating Zombie Desert Rampage; 8 Dead!

Justine smiled at the imagined headline; she should have been the journalist.

But no, Justine felt oddly protective towards Carson. He wasn't much, but right at this moment he was the only one listening. One last blind elbow to what felt like a butt, and Justine scrammed it to the passenger door.

"GO GO GO!" she screamed at Carson as she locked her door, screaming in laughter as Carson fishtailed it out of there with white knuckles. "All we need is some banjo chase music, compadre!"

Once they'd cleared the first quarter mile, Justine patted the shoulder of the poor, shaking Carson.

"The fuck," Carson sputtered. "The fuck was that?"

"The usual," Justine said.

"Are you okay? I mean . . . shit, did they . . ."

Justine looked behind them, seeing only a random semi-truck. "I'm fine. Actually, no. I'm not fine. I'm hungry. *Starving* even."

Carson looked at her, wide-eyed. Justine noticed the stare also contained a bit of apprehension. "What?"

"And in an answer to your earlier question," she said, "no. I'm not a vegetarian."

◄○►

Justine had Carson stop at a roadside barbecue joint a handful of miles outside Barstow. She assured him it was the best obscure, outdoor barbecue you could get in the southwest, not to mention that she was pretty sure the owner was a Hell's Angel and therefore coated the area with a kind of grimy aura of protection.

Carson sat at a picnic table while Justine ordered them two orders of the works. She had put on a pair of large-framed glasses and affected an uneven Texan drawl, claiming it was a disguise while Carson suspected it was mostly to amuse herself.

Roughly half an hour had passed since they were accosted, but in that short span of time Justine had seemed to come alive. Bouncing in her seat, looking behind them in her sun visor's mirror and squeezing his shoulder every few minutes—she was as enthusiastic as he imagined she might have been on a regular road trip in her life before infection had made her somber and shifty-eyed. Her skin also seemed to take on what he could only describe as a glow, and her stone grey eyes seemed to skew closer to silver.

"How much for one rib?"

Carson sat up straight and turned to see Justine laughing with the barbecue proprietor before shaking her head and walking to their table. She smiled at him before laying down a stack of white sandwich bread and two Styrofoam boxes in front of him.

"Is everything ok? Did you need more money?" Carson asked while he peeked under one of the lids.

"What? Are you not familiar with the comedic stylings of Chris Rock?" Justine was still putting on her weird drawl, which was toeing the line between cute and unsettling pretty aggressively. "*I'm Gonna Git You Sucka?* No? Boy, we need to hook you up with a movie marathon."

Justine took the bench across from Carson, popped open her lid, and proceeded to stare at the meat. The only motion she made was to follow in the tradition of countless customers before her in leisurely picking at the peeling red paint of the table with a fingernail. Carson couldn't help indulging himself in a mouthful of brisket before asking her if everything was okay.

Justine sighed.

"No. Sure. Everything is fine. This is the first time I had even the desire to eat meat since you-know-what, let alone actually ate the stuff. Before that I was a stone cold carnivore."

She never took her eyes off her meal, but had worked up to poking it around with her spork.

Carson raised his eyebrows and took a long sip of his lukewarm Mountain Dew. He became aware of a weird undercurrent that had seemed to sit itself at their table, but couldn't place it.

Justine stabbed at a piece of pork until the weak teeth of the spork finally speared it enough to lift. He eyed the meat and her mouth, wishing he had his camera out. She caught him staring. He flashed her a quick, reassuring half smile when their eyes met. Justine saluted him with her spork full of pork, and took it in one bite.

She chewed. Carson took another mouthful of his meal in camaraderie. He waited until they both swallowed and took sips of their respective drinks before asking her how it was.

"Tastes good, but just that one bite already made my jaw ache."

"Does eating hurt?"

"Aren't you forward? But no; the little I eat just sits with me funny and makes my tongue feel coated in something like wax. I probably brush my teeth about 10 times a day. I don't care enough about my check-ups with the therapist or doctor to find out if it's mostly in my head or if human veal just forever fucked up my stomach."

Carson coughed in surprise, choking a bit as Justine's words hit him. She gave him a sad shrug and continued eating the meat.

"This is good though. No coated-tongue feeling, either."

"Maybe you just needed time. Just try to take it slow."

Carson took out his camera, nodded as if to ask, Is this okay? Justine paused for a moment before nodding in return. He snapped a few photos of her eating with the large, faded MOOSE'S BBQ sign behind her.

Suddenly he noticed a man moving at a leaden pace a few feet behind Justine. Carson lowered his camera. The man was gaunt, with gnarled hands reminiscent of arthritic joints and old tree branches. He worked his mouth around hungrily; almost like an infant eyeing a nipple just out of reach. Only when he noticed the old, slow-shambling man pull out a Black & Mild cigar and chomp it between his grinning teeth did he relax.

"I'll be right back," Justine said, and put a hand on his shoulder as she passed. Carson thought she might be feeling sick again, but when he glanced across the way a few minutes later he saw that she was on her cell phone.

◂◦▸

They rode in mostly companionable silence for about ninety more minutes, until the suburban sprawl of Henderson appeared. Carson felt a thrumming work its way up his spine, plucking at his nerves until his skin physically itched. Here was the moment he'd been dreading: setting up a shot where you ask someone to hunker down in a place where they'd experienced the darkest moment of their life.

"You, uh, feeling okay?" Carson asked.

Justine rustled a bit in her seat, looking tiny and weird from the corner of Carson's eye.

"Yeah. Was worried about all that food I ate, but it's staying down."

Carson cleared his throat, and Justine hurried over the sound. "I know that's not what you're asking about, but I'm putting off any reaction to this as long as I can. Is that okay with you?"

Carson nodded as he squeezed his hands tighter around the wheel. Justine crammed some more gum into her mouth. She had told him that with her stomach working with rarely any food in it had given her "death breath." He hadn't noticed any of it personally, but when she also divulged how often and obsessively she brushed her teeth, he understood that the situation went a little deeper than oral hygiene.

Carson fumbled at the radio dials until he heard Sam Cooke's voice. He told himself to stop feeling guilty. Everyone in this car was there by choice, right? Of course they were.

Except they really weren't.

Carson had been there by chance.

Justine had been there because of a fluke of a disease. She didn't know what she was doing, where she'd gone, who she'd hurt.

And it was only because Carson happened to be there, with his camera, that Justine—and the rest of the world—knew that while she'd been a zombie, she had eaten an infant child.

→o→

The area had been cleaned up more than Carson expected. Imported palm trees stood perfectly distanced from each other, as pretty and welcoming as well-trained showgirls. As they pulled into the parking lot of the grocery store, his memory replaced the newly built structures with the way he remembered the place looking the last time he was here—a looted out, broken shell of a place crawling with cops, zombies and "reporters" like himself. There was a rumor that the area was harboring a building full of people who had taken over a grocery store after raiding a gun store, but the virus had gotten in there with them. Carson had been unable to confirm any of this at the time. He was mostly walking around in the area in a horrified daze, snapping photos to give himself a sense of purpose in all of the chaos.

"So, where were you?" Justine asked.

Carson shook himself mentally into the present. "I was walking around the barricades at the back of the lot. I guess luckily nobody was paying much attention to me. My editor just told me to snap anything interesting or fucked up that might pop out."

Justine turned to him. "And then out I popped, all interesting and fucked up with bells on?"

Carson tried to smile. "Yeah."

Justine laughed in surprise but it quickly died in her throat.

They slowly pulled themselves out of the car, groaning and stretching as they squinted into the sun. A nervous and false jovial energy permeated the air between them, as if they decided by an unspoken vote to act as if they were here to recreate a photo from a first date rather than an amnesiac murder.

Justine wandered the half-full parking lot while Carson started gathering and preparing his gear. Once he was fully kitted up he inhaled deeply and started towards her.

Keeping her back to him, she said, "I thought maybe standing here there'd be . . . something. A fragment of memory. But no."

"In all honesty it's almost hard to remember it happening myself. It happened so quickly and there was so much chaos . . ."

"Did anyone try to stop me? Did you?"

Carson stopped fidgeting before answering.

"Stop? I mean . . . the cops tackled you. The thing is, I think the baby was already dead. I didn't hear crying."

"How did I get it?"

"Uh . . ." Carson wished for a cigarette more than he had wished for anything else in the entirety of his life. "There was a huge crush of people running out of the shopping center when the police smoked them out. They think the baby was inside, and got . . . trampled. There was a broken stroller nearby."

It was, in fact, in the photograph.

He heard Justine exhale shakily.

"Fuck me, fuck you, and fuck this. What's the point of us being here? I'd want me dead, too. Let's just get this done so I can crawl back to my hole."

Carson silently worked his mouth open and closed, platitudes at the ready on his tongue. They didn't want to come out, though; every fiber of his being fully agreed with her that being here was wrong. In for a penny, in for a pound, though. The texts he had been getting from his editor were becoming increasingly insistent.

"Yeah, alright."

The photojournalist considered the parking lot around them, trying to avoid looking at the photo again on his iPhone and going solely by memory.

"The pile of rubble . . . I'm pretty sure it was over there."

He pointed at a grouping of empty parking spaces, completely indistinguishable from any other in the world. Apparently not everything required a plaque.

They made their way over, the cloud of unease silencing them. Everything was so generic and bright around them that it the entire assignment the feel of some kind of ill-planned playacting. The only piece of reality that didn't seem a part of their make-believe was a small murder of crows nearby that were effectively edging any pigeons out of their territory.

It seemed easier to just mumble and gesture the whole thing. In the back of his mind Carson supposed he had hoped returning here might summon up at least an emotional memory for Justine, but it was clear that whatever breakthrough he had been hoping for was doomed to die the quiet death of simply going through the motions.

Carson pointed and shot, getting the majority of his pictures framing

Justine in front of the rapidly setting sun. She crouched, stood and even sat in a few, looking pensive and disconnected in each one. The stark contrast of a traumatized woman in a new parking lot made the whole thing feel a dust-in-the-blood kind of dirty to Carson. The look in her eyes, though . . .

"Alright, I think we got it. We can go."

She didn't move.

"What's wrong?" Carson asked.

"Aren't you going to ask me?"

"Ask you what?"

"All this time together, and you're too timid to ask the question. I know you want to ask. It's been all over your face since we met."

Carson opened his mouth, then closed it and shook his head.

"Go ahead," Justine said, hands on her hips. "Ask me, how can I possibly go on living after something like that? How can I make jokes and drop stupid pop culture references and eat ribs and laugh and listen to music? Isn't that what you want to know? Isn't that what you've been dying to ask me this whole time?"

Carson didn't know how to respond, mainly because she was dead right. It was the question he'd wanted to ask ever since he'd heard the news a month ago that the Famous Baby Eater—the subject of a photo that had won him fame he didn't want and acclaim he didn't deserve—was still alive.

How *do* you go on living after something like that?

Justine sighed and walked past him, muttering: "Let's get to a hotel with a bar."

⊸o⊳

"Thanks for being less of a dick about this than I thought you'd be," she said.

They were sitting at the bar in some sports-themed joint on the ground floor of a chain hotel on the edge of Henderson, knees almost touching. Carson stared into his beer, already thinking about the new set of photos he'd just made. Wondering if it was going to do more harm than good. Of course he'd sold it to Justine as a way to show the world that she wasn't a monster, that the Cure *did* work. But now he wasn't so sure.

Justine laid her hand over his and gave a gentle squeeze. Her other hand fiddled with her cell phone on the bar top.

"Hey."

Carson met her gaze. Said nothing. What could he say? That he was about to ruin her life all over again?

The photo of Justine eating ribs alone . . . ugh. She had no idea what she'd agreed to.

"Look, I'm serious," Justine said. "You've been good to me, despite everything. Which is why I feel bad about doing this."

"Doing what?"

Without warning she leaned forward and pressed her lips to his.

To a passerby it would have looked like a couple doing a parody of a cover of a historical romance novel, except with the man in the submissive stance. Right in the thick of it, however, was a demented sincerity. Justine used her tongue to pry open his lips. What the hell was she doing?

Justine didn't have "death breath." He could taste peppermint and beer; her lips were warm. But still, all he could think about was where her lips had been, and about the chunks of flesh her tongue had once licked away from her teeth . . .

Before he could break the embrace he heard the sound of a fake camera shutter snapping closed.

Oh God, Carson thought as his eye popped open and saw the cell in her hand. *She's taken a photo of her own.*

"Wait," he said. "Please . . ."

But Justine's fingers were already working the keypad, and the photo was already on its way to a wireless cell tower, and from there... who knew? She glanced up at him.

"Sorry, I grabbed your boss's number when you left your cell alone at the BBQ place. He's just one, though. I guess I could have sold this as an exclusive, but that felt a little tacky."

Carson pulled back from the table and just stared. His eyes felt feverish as they flitted from Justine's face to the phone, to the staring bar patrons surrounding them.

"You want to know what it was like, to have your worst moment broadcast to the world?" Justine asked. "Buddy, you're about to find out."

She smiled, and reached back to hold his shaking hand. "But at least we have each other, right?"

WILD ACRE

NATHAN BALLINGRUD

Three men are lying in what will someday be a house. For now it's just a skeleton of beams and supports, standing amid the foundations and frames of other burgeoning houses in a large, bulldozed clearing. The earth around them is a churned, orange clay. Forest abuts the Wild Acre development site, crawling up the side of the Blue Ridge Mountains, hickory and maple hoarding darkness as the sky above them shades into deepening blue. The hope is that soon there will be finished buildings here, and then more skeletons and more houses, with roads to navigate them. But now there are only felled trees, and mud, and these naked frames. And three men, lying on a cold wooden floor, staring up through the roof beams as the sky organizes a nightfall. They have a cooler packed with beer and a baseball bat.

Several yards away, mounted in the back of Jeremy's truck, is a hunting rifle.

Jeremy watches stars burn into life: first two, then a dozen. He came here hoping for violence, but the evening has softened him. Lying on his back, balancing a beer on the great swell of his belly, he hopes there will be no occasion for it. Wild Acre is abandoned for now, and might be for a long time to come, making it an easy target. Three nights over the past week, someone has come onto the work site and committed small but infuriating acts of vandalism: stealing and damaging tools and equipment, spray painting vulgar images on the project manager's trailer, even taking a dump on the floor of one of the unfinished houses. The project manager complained to the police, but with production stalled and bank accounts running dry, angry subcontractors and prospective homeowners consumed most of his attention. The way Jeremy saw things, it was up to the trade guys to protect the site. He figured the vandals for environmental activists, pissed that their mountain had been shaved for this project; he worried that they'd soon start burning down his frames. Insurance would cover the developer, but he and his company would go bankrupt. So he's come here with Dennis and Renaldo – his best friend and his most able brawler, respectively – hoping to catch them in the act and beat them into the dirt.

"They're not coming tonight," says Renaldo.

"No shit," says Dennis. "You think it's 'cause you talk too loud?" Dennis has been with Jeremy ten years now. For a while, Jeremy thought about making him partner, but the man just couldn't keep his shit together, and Jeremy privately nixed the idea. Dennis is forty-eight years old, ten years older than Jeremy. His whole life is invested in this work: he's a carpenter and nothing else. He has three young children, and talks about having more. This work stoppage threatens to impoverish him. "Bunch of goddamn Green Party eco-fucking-terrorist mother*fuckers*," Dennis says.

Jeremy watches him. Dennis is moving his jaw around, working himself into a rage. That would be useful if he thought anybody was going to show tonight; but he thinks they've screwed it all up. They got here too early, before the sun was down, and they made too much noise. No one will come now.

"Dude. Grab yourself a beer and mellow out."

"These kids are fucking with my *life*, man! You tell me to mellow *out?*"

"Dennis, man, you're not the only one." A breeze comes down the mountain and washes over them. Jeremy feels it move through his hair, deepening his sense of easy contentment. He remembers feeling that rage just this afternoon, talking to that asshole from the bank, and he knows he'll feel it again. He knows he'll have to. But right now it's as distant and alien as the full moon, catching fire unknown miles above them. "But they're not here. 'Naldo's right, we blew it. We'll come back tomorrow night." He looks into the forest crowding against the development site, and wonders why they didn't think to hide themselves there. "And we'll do it right. So for tonight? Just chill."

Renaldo leans over and claps Dennis on the back. "Mañana, amigo. Mañana!"

Jeremy knows that Renaldo's optimism is one of the reasons Dennis resents him, but the young Mexican wouldn't be able to function in this all-white crew without it. He gets a lot of crap from these guys and just takes it. When work is this hard to come by, pride is a luxury. Nevertheless Jeremy is dismayed at Renaldo's easy manner in the face of it all. A man can't endure that kind of diminishment, he thinks, and not release anger somewhere.

Dennis casts Jeremy a defeated look. The sky retains a faint glow from twilight, but darkness has settled over the ground. The men are black shapes. "It's not the same for you, man. Your wife works, you know? You got another income. My wife don't do *shit*."

"That's not just her fault, though, Dennis. What would you do if Rebecca told you she was getting a job tomorrow?"

"I'd say it's about goddamned time!"

Jeremy laughs. "Bullshit. You'd just knock her up again. If that woman went out into the world you'd lose your mind, and you know it."

Dennis shakes his head, but a sort of smile breaks through.

The conversation has undermined whatever small good the beer has done for him tonight: all the old fears are stirring. He hasn't been able to pay these men for three weeks now, and even an old friend like Dennis will have to move on eventually. The business hasn't paid a bill in months, and Tara's teacher's salary certainly isn't enough to support them by itself. He realizes that their objective tonight is mostly just an excuse to vent some anger; cracking some misguided kids' heads isn't going to get the bank to stop calling him, and it isn't going to get the bulldozers moving again. It isn't going to let him call his crew and tell them they can come back to work, either.

But he won't let it get to him tonight. Not this beautiful, moonlit night on the mountain, with bare wood lifting skyward all around them. "Fuck it," he says, and claps his hands twice, a reclining sultan. "Naldo! Más cervesas!"

Renaldo, who has just settled onto his back, slowly folds himself into a sitting position. He climbs to his feet and heads to the cooler without complaint. He's accustomed to being the gofer.

"Little Mexican bastard," Dennis says. "I bet he's got fifty cousins packed into a trailer he's trying to support."

"Hablo fucking ingles, motherfucker," Renaldo says.

"What? Speak English! I can't understand you."

Jeremy laughs. They drink more beer, and the warmth of it washes through their bodies until they are illuminated, three little candles in a clearing, surrounded by the dark woods.

-‹o›-

Jeremy says, "I gotta take a piss, dude." The urge has been building in him for some time, but he's been lying back on the floor, his body filled with a warm, beery lethargy, and he's been reluctant to move. Now it manifests as a sudden, urgent pain, sufficient to propel him to his feet and across the red clay road. The wind has risen and the forest is a wall of dark sound, the trees no longer distinct from each other but instead a writhing movement, a grasping energy which prickles his skin and hurries his step. The moon, which only a short while ago seemed a kindly lantern in the dark, smolders in the sky. Behind him, Dennis and Renaldo continue some wandering conversation, and he holds onto the sound of their voices to ward off a sudden, inexplicable rising fear. He casts a glance back toward the house. The ground inclines toward it, and at this angle he can't see either of them. Just the cross-gables shouldering into the sky.

He steps into the tree line, going back a few feet for modesty's sake. Situating himself behind a tree, he opens his fly and lets loose. The knot of pain in his gut starts to unravel.

Walking around has lit up the alcohol in his blood, and he's starting to feel angry again. If I don't get to hit somebody soon, he thinks, I'm going to snap. I'm going to unload on somebody that doesn't deserve it. If Dennis opens his whining mouth one more time it might be him.

Jeremy feels a twinge of remorse at the thought; Dennis is one of those guys who has to talk about his fears, or they'll eat him alive. He has to give a running commentary on every grim possibility, as if by voicing a fear he'd chase it into hiding. Jeremy relates more to Renaldo, who has yet to utter one frustrated thought about how long it's been since he's been paid, or what their future prospects might be. He doesn't really know Renaldo, knows his personal situation even less, and something about that strikes him as proper. The idea of a man keening in pain has always embarrassed him.

When Jeremy has weak moments, he saves them for private expression. Even Tara, who has been a rock of optimism throughout all of this, isn't privy to them. She's a smart, intuitive woman, though, and Jeremy recognizes his fortune in her. She assures him that he is both capable and industrious, and that he can find work other than hammering nails into wood, should it come down to it. She's always held the long view. He feels a sudden swell of love for her, as he stands there pissing in the woods: a desperate, childlike need. He blinks rapidly, clearing his eyes.

He's staring absently into the forest as he thinks this all through, and so it takes him a few moments to focus his gaze and realize that someone is staring back at him.

It's a young man—a kid, really—several feet deeper into the forest, obscured by low growth and hanging branches and darkness. He's skinny and naked. Smiling at him. Just grinning like a jack-o-lantern.

"Oh, *shit!*"

Jeremy lurches from the tree, yanking frantically at his zipper, which has caught on the denim of his pants. He staggers forward a step, his emotions a snarl of rage, excitement, and humiliation. "What the fuck!" he shouts. The kid bounds to his right and disappears, soundlessly.

"Dennis? *Dennis!* They're here!"

He turns but he can't see up the hill. The angle is bad. All he can see through the trees is the pale wooden frame standing out against the sky like bones, and he's taking little hopping steps as he wrestles with his zipper. He trips over a root and crashes painfully to the ground.

He hears Dennis's raised voice.

He climbs awkwardly to his feet. The zipper finally comes free and Jeremy yanks it up, running clumsily through the branches while fastening his fly. As he ascends the small incline and crosses the muddy road he can discern shapes wrestling between the wooden support struts; he hears them fighting, hears the brute explosions of breath and the heavy impact of colliding meat. It sounds like the kid is putting up a pretty good fight; Jeremy wants to get in on the action before it's all over. He's overcome by instinct and violent impulse.

He's exalted by it.

A voice breaks out of the tumult and it's so warped by anguish that it takes him a moment to recognize it as Dennis's scream.

Jeremy jerks to a stop. He burns crucial seconds trying to understand what he's heard.

And then he hears something else: a heavy tearing, like ripping canvas, followed by a liquid sound of dropped weight, of moist, heavy objects sliding to the ground. He catches a glimpse of motion, something huge and fast in the house and then an inverted leg standing out suddenly like a dark rip in the bright flank of stars, and then nothing. A high, keening wail—ephemeral, barely audible—rises from the unfinished house like a wisp of smoke.

Finally he reaches the top of the hill and looks inside.

Dennis is on his back, his body frosted by moonlight. He's lifting his head, staring down at himself. Organs are strewn to one side of his body like beached, black jellyfish, dark blood pumping slowly from the gape in his belly and spreading around him in a gory nimbus. His head drops back and he lifts it again. Renaldo is on his back too, arms flailing, trying to hold off the thing bestride him: huge, black-furred, dog-begotten, its man-like fingers wrapped around Renaldo's face and pushing his head into the floor so hard that the wood cracks beneath it. It lifts its shaggy head, bloody ropes of drool swinging from its snout and arcing into the moonsilvered night. It peels its lips from its teeth. Renaldo's screams are muffled beneath its hand.

"Shoot it," Dennis says. His voice is calm, like he's suggesting coffee. "Shoot it, Jeremy."

The house swings out of sight and the road scrolls by, lurching and violently tilting, and Jeremy realizes with some dismay that he is running. His truck, a small white pickup, is less than fifty feet away. Parked just beyond it is Renaldo's little import, its windows rolled down, rosary beads hanging from the rearview mirror.

Jeremy runs fill-tilt into the side of his truck, rebounding off it and almost falling to the ground. He opens the door and is inside with what feels like unnatural speed. He slides across to the driver's side and digs into his pocket for the keys, fingers grappling furiously through change and crumpled receipts until he finds them.

He can feel the rifle mounted on the rack behind his head, radiating a monstrous energy. It's loaded; it's always loaded.

He looks through the passenger window and sees something stand upright inside the frames, looking back at him. He sees Renaldo spasming beneath it. He sees the dark forested mountains looming behind this stillborn community with a hostile intelligence. He guns the engine and slams down the accelerator, turning the wheel hard to the left. The tires spray mud in huge arcs until they find traction, and he speeds down the hill toward the highway.

The truck bounces hard on the rough path and briefly goes airborne. The engine screams, the sound of it filling his head.

⟶⟨○⟩⟶

"What the hell are you *look*ing at?"

"What?" Jeremy blinked, and looked at his wife.

Breakfast time at the Blue Plate was always busy, but today the noise and the crowd were unprecedented. People crowded on the bench by the door, waiting for a chance to sit down. Short order cooks and servers hollered at each other over the din of loud customers, boiling fryers, and crackling griddles. He knew that Tara hated it here, but on bad days—and he's had plenty of bad days in the six months since the attack—he needed to be in places like this. Even now, wedged into a booth too narrow for him, with the table's edge pressing uncomfortably into his gut, he did not want to leave.

His attention was drawn by the new busboy. He was young and gangly, lanky hair swinging over his lowered face. He scurried from empty table to empty table, loading dirty plates and coffee mugs into his gray bus tub. He moved with a strange grace through the crowd, like someone well practiced at avoidance. Jeremy was bothered that he couldn't get a clear view of his face.

"Why do you think he wears his hair like that?" he said. "He looks like a drug addict or something. I'm surprised they let him."

Tara rolled her eyes, not even bothering to look. "The busboy? Are you serious?"

"What do you mean?"

"Are you even *listening* to me?"

"What? Of course. Come on." He forced his attention back where it belonged. "You're talking about that guy who teaches the smart kids. What's his name. Tim."

Tara let her stare linger a moment before pressing on. "Yeah, I mean, what an asshole, right? He *knows* I'm married!"

"Well, that's the attraction."

"The fact that I'm married to you is why he wants me? Oh my God, and I thought *he* had an ego!"

"No, I mean, you're hot, he'd be into you anyway. But the fact that you belong to somebody just adds another incentive. It's a challenge."

"Wait."

"Some guys just like to take what isn't theirs."

"Wait. I *belong* to you now?"

He smiled. "Well . . . yeah, bitch."

She laughed. "You are so lucky we're in a public place right now."

"You're not scary."

"Oh, I'm pretty scary."

"Then how come you can't scare off little Timmy?"

She gave him an exasperated look. "Do you think I'm not trying? He just doesn't *care*. I think he thinks I'm flirting with him or something. I want him to see you at the Christmas party. Get all alpha male on him. Squeeze his hand really hard when you shake it or something."

A waitress arrived at their table and unloaded their breakfast: fruit salad and a scrambled egg for Tara, a mound of buttery pancakes for Jeremy. Tara cast a critical eye over his plate and said, "We gotta work on that diet of yours, big man. There's a new year coming up. Resolution time."

"Like hell," he said, tucking in. "This is my fuel. I need it if I'm going to defeat Tim in bloody combat."

The sentence hung awkwardly between them. Jeremy found himself staring at her, the stupid smile on his face frozen into something miserable and strange. His scalp prickled and he felt his face go red.

"Well, that was dumb," he said.

She put her hand over his. "Honey."

He pulled away. "Whatever." He forked some of the pancakes into his mouth, staring down at his plate.

He breathed in deeply, taking in the close, burnt-oil odor of the place, trying to displace the smell of blood and fear which welled up inside him as though he was on the mountain again, half a year ago, watching his friends die in the rearview mirror. He looked around again to see if he could get a look at that creepy busboy's face, but he couldn't spot him in the crowd.

◄◦►

The coroner had decided that a wolf had killed Dennis and Renaldo. It was a big story in the local news for a week or so; there weren't supposed to be any wolves in this part of North Carolina. Nevertheless, the bite marks and the tracks in the mud were clear. Hunting parties had ranged into the woods; they'd bagged a few coyotes, but no wolves. The developer of Wild Acre filed for bankruptcy: buyers who had signed conditional agreements refused to close on the houses, and the banks gave up on the project, locking their coffers for good. Wild Acre became a ghost town of empty house frames and mud. Jeremy's outfit went under too. He broke the news to his employees and began the dreary process of appeasing his creditors. Tara still pulled down her teacher's salary, but it was barely enough to keep pace, let alone catch them up. They weren't sure how much longer they could afford their own house.

Within a month of the attack, Jeremy discovered that he was unemployable. Demand for his services had dried up. The framing companies were streamlining their payrolls, and nobody wanted to add an expensive ex-owner to their rosters.

He never told his wife what really happened that night. Publicly, he corroborated the coroner's theory, and he tried as best he could to convince himself of it, too. But the thing that had straddled his friend and then stared him down had not been a wolf.

He could not call it by its name.

◀◦▶

In the middle of all that were the funerals.

Renaldo's had been a small, cheap affair. He'd felt like an imposter there, too close to the tumultuous emotion on display. Renaldo's mother filled the room with her cries. Jeremy felt alarmed and even a little appalled at her lack of self-consciousness, which was so at odds with her late son's unflappable nature. Everyone spoke in Spanish, and he was sure they were all talking about him. On some level he knew this was ridiculous, but he couldn't shake it.

A young man approached him, late teens or early twenties, dressed in an ill-fitting, rented suit, his hands hanging stiffly at his sides.

Jeremy nodded at him. "Hola," he said. He felt awkward and stupid.

"Hello," the man said. "You were his boss?"

"Yeah, yeah. I'm, um . . . I'm sorry. He was a great worker. You know, one of my best. The guys really liked him. If you knew my guys, you'd know that meant something." He realized he was beginning to ramble, and made himself stop talking.

"Thank you."

"Were you brothers?"

"Brothers-in-law. Married to my sister?"

"Oh, of course." Jeremy didn't know Renaldo had been married. He looked across the gathered crowd, thinking for one absurd moment that he might know her by sight.

"Listen," the man said, "I know you're having some hard times. The business and everything."

Well, here it comes, Jeremy thought. He tried to cut him off at the pass. "I still owed some money to Renaldo. I haven't forgotten. I'll get it to you as soon as I can. I promise."

"To Carmen."

"Of course. To Carmen."

"That's good." He nodded, looking at the ground. Jeremy could sense there was more coming, and he wanted to get away before it arrived. He opened his mouth to express a final platitude before taking his leave, but the young man spoke first. "Why didn't you shoot it?"

He felt something grow cold inside him. "What?"

"I know why you were there. Renaldo told me what was happening. The vandals? He said you had a rifle."

Jeremy bristled. "Listen, I don't know what Renaldo thought, but we weren't going up there to shoot anybody. We were going to scare them. That's all. The gun's in my truck because I'm a hunter. I don't use it to threaten kids."

"But it wasn't kids on the mountain that night, was it?"

They stared at each other for a moment. Jeremy's face was flushed, and he could hear the laboring of his own breath. By contrast the young man seemed entirely at ease; either he didn't really care about why Jeremy didn't shoot that night or he already knew that the answer wouldn't satisfy him.

"No, I guess it wasn't."

"It was a wolf, right?"

Jeremy was silent.

"A wolf?"

He had to moisten his mouth. "Yeah."

"So why didn't you shoot it?"

" . . . It happened really fast," he said. "I was out in the woods. I was too late."

Renaldo's brother-in-law gave no reaction, holding his gaze for a few more moments and then nodding slightly. He took a deep breath, turned to look behind him at the others gathered for the funeral, some of whom were staring in their direction. Then he turned back to Jeremy and said, "Thank you for coming. But maybe now, you know, you should go. It's hard for some people to see you."

"Yeah. Okay. Of course." Jeremy backed up a step, and said, "I'm really sorry."

"Okay."

And then he left, grateful to get away, but nearly overwhelmed by shame. He'd removed the rifle from his truck the day after the attack, stowing it in the attic. Its presence was an indictment. Despite what he'd told Renaldo's brother-in-law, he didn't know why he hadn't taken the gun, climbed back out of the truck, and blown the wolf to hell. Because that's all it had been. A wolf. A stupid animal. How many animals had he killed with that very rifle?

Dennis's funeral had been different. There, he was treated like family, if a somewhat distant and misunderstood relation. Rebecca, obese and unemployed, looked doomed as she stood graveside with her three children, completely unanchored from the only person in the world who had cared about her fate, or the fates of those stunned boys at her side. He wanted to apologize to her but he didn't know precisely how, so instead he hugged her after the services and shook the boys' hands and said, "If there's anything I can do."

She wrapped him in a hug. "Jeremy," she said.

⟨○⟩

The boy is skinny and naked. Smiling at him, his teeth shining like cut crystal. Jeremy's pants are unfastened and loose around his hips. He's afraid that if he runs they'll fall and trip him up. The kid can't even be out of high school yet: Jeremy knows he can break him in half if he can just get his hands on him in time. But it's already too late; terror pins him there, and he can only watch. The kid's body begins to shake, and what he thought was a smile is only a rictus of pain – his mouth splits along his cheeks and something loud breaks inside him, cracking like a tree branch. The boy's bowels spray blood and his body convulses like he's in the grip of a seizure.

"Jeremy!"

He opened his eyes. He was in their bedroom, with Tara standing over him. The light was on. The bed felt warm and damp.

"Get out of bed. You had a nightmare."

"Why is the bed all wet?"

She pulled him by his shoulder. She had a strange expression: distracted, pinched. "Come on," she said. "You had an accident."

"What?" He sat up, smelling urine. "What?"

"Get out of bed, please. I have to change the sheets."

He did as she asked. His legs were sticky, his boxers soaked.

Tara began yanking the sheets off the bed as quickly as she could. She tugged the mattress pad off too, and cursed quietly when she saw that the stain had already bled down to the mattress itself.

"Let me help," he said.

"You should get in the shower. I'll take care of this."

" . . . I'm sorry."

She turned on him. For a moment he saw the anger and the impatience there, and he was conscious of how long she had been putting up with his stoic routine, of the extent to which she had fastened down her own frustration for the sake of his wounded ego. It threatened to finally spill over, but she pulled it back, she sucked it in for him one more time. Her expression softened. She touched his cheek. "It's okay, baby." She pushed the hair from his forehead, turning the gesture into a caress. "Go ahead and get in the shower, okay?"

"Okay." He headed for the bathroom.

He stripped and got under the hot water. Six months of being without work had caused him to get even heavier, a fact he was acutely conscious of as he lowered himself to the floor and wrapped his arms around his knees. He did not want Tara to see him. He wanted to barricade the door, to wrap barbed wire around the whole room. But fifteen minutes later she joined him there, putting her arms around him and pulling him close, resting her head against his.

⬦

Two months after the funeral, Dennis's wife had called and asked him to come over. He arrived at her house—a single-story, three-bedroom bungalow—later that afternoon, and was dismayed to see boxes in the living room and the kitchen. The kids, ranging in age from five to thirteen, moved ineffectively among them, piling things in with no regard to maximizing their space or gauging how heavy they might become. Rebecca was a dervish of industry, sliding through the mazes of boxes and furniture with a surprising grace, barking orders at her kids and even at her herself. When she saw him through the screen door, standing on her front porch, she stopped, and in doing so seemed to lose all of her will to move. The boys stopped too, and followed her gaze out to him.

"Becca, what's going on?"

"What's it look like? I'm packing boxes." She turned her back to him and moved through an arch into the kitchen. "Come on in, then," she called.

Sitting across from her at the table, glasses of orange soda between them, he was further struck by the disorganized quality of the move. The number of boxes seemed sadly inadequate to the task, and it seemed like things were being packed piecemeal: some dishes were wrapped in newspaper and stowed, while others were still stacked in cupboards or piled, dirty, in the sink; drawers hung open, partially disemboweled.

Before Jeremy could open his mouth, Rebecca said, "They's foreclosing on us. We got to be out by the weekend."

For a moment he was speechless. ". . . I . . . Jesus, Becca."

She sat there and watched him. He could think of nothing to say, so he just said, "I had no idea."

"Well, Dennis ain't been paid for a long time before he was killed, and he sure as shit hadn't been paid *since* then, so I guess anybody ought to of seen this comin."

He felt like he'd been punched in the gut. He didn't know if she'd meant it as an accusation, but it felt like one. It didn't help that it was true. He looked at the orange soda in the glass, a weird dash of cheerful color in all this gloom. He couldn't take his eyes off it. "What are you gonna do?"

"Well," she said, staring at her fingers as they twined around each other, "I don't really know, Jeremy. My mama lives out by Hickory but that's a ways away, and she don't have enough room in her house for all of us. Dennis ain't spoke with his family in years. These boys don't even *know* their grandparents on his side."

He nodded. In the other room, the boys were quiet, no doubt listening in.

"I need some money, Jeremy. I mean I need it real bad. We got to be out of here in four days and we don't have nowhere to go." She looked up at the clock on the wall, a big round one with Roman numerals, a bright basket of fruit painted in the center. "I'm gonna lose all my things," she said. She wiped at the corner of an eye with the inside of her wrist.

Jeremy felt the twist in his gut, like his insides were being spooled on a wheel. He had to close his eyes and ride it out.

He'd sat at this table many times while Rebecca cooked for Dennis and for him; he'd been sitting here sharing a six pack with Dennis when the call came from the hospital that their youngest had come early. "Oh, Becca," he said.

"I just need a little so we can stay someplace for a few weeks. You know, just until we can figure something out."

"Becca, I don't have it. I just don't have it. I'm so sorry."

"Jeremy, we got nowhere to go!"

"I don't have anything. I got collection agencies so far up my ass . . . Tara and I put the house up, Becca. The bank's threatening us too. We can't stay where we are. We're borrowing just to keep our heads above water."

"*I can fucking sue you!*" she screamed, slapping her hand on the table so hard that the glasses toppled over and spilled orange soda all over the floor. "*You owe us! You never paid Dennis , and you owe us! I called a lawyer and he said I can sue your ass for every fucking cent you got!*"

The silence afterward was profound, broken only by the pattering of the soda trickling onto the linoleum floor.

The outburst broke a dam inside her; her face crumpled, and tears spilled over. She put a hand over her face and her body jerked silently. Jeremy looked toward the living room and saw one of the boys, his blonde hair buzzed down to his scalp, staring into the kitchen in shock.

"It's okay, Tyler," he said. "It's okay, buddy."

The boy appeared not to hear him. He watched his mother until she pulled her hand from her face and seemed to suck it all back into herself; without looking to the doorway she fluttered a hand in the boy's direction. "It's fine, Tyler," she said. "Go help your brothers."

The boy retreated.

Jeremy reached across the table and clasped her hands in his own. "Becca," he said, "you and the boys are like family to me. If I could give you some money I would. I swear to God I would. And you're right, I do owe it to you. Dennis didn't get paid towards the end. Nobody did. So if you feel like you gotta sue me, then do it. Do what you have to do. I don't blame you. I really don't."

She looked at him, tears beading in her eyes, and said nothing.

"Shit, if suing me might keep you in your house a little while longer—if it'll keep the bank away, or something—then you *should* do it. I *want* you to do it."

Rebecca shook her head. "It won't. It's too late for that now." She rested her head on her arm, her hands still clasped in Jeremy's. "I ain't gonna sue you, Jer. It ain't your fault."

She pulled her hands free and got up. She grabbed a roll of paper towels and tore off a great handful, setting to work on the spill. "Look at this damn mess," she said.

He watched her for a moment. "I have liens on those houses we built," he said. "They can't sell them until they pay us first. The minute they do, you'll get your money."

"They won't ever finish those houses, Jer. Ain't nobody gonna want to buy them. Not after what happened."

He stayed quiet, because he knew she was right. He had privately given up on seeing that money long ago.

"A man from the bank come by last week and put that notice on the door. He had a sheriff with him. Can you believe that? A sheriff come to my house. Parked right in my driveway, for everybody to see." She paused in her work. "He was so rude," she said, her voice quiet and dismayed. "The both of them were. He told me I had to get out of my own house. My boys were standing right by me, and they just bust out crying. He didn't give a damn. Treated me like I was dirt. Might as well of called me white trash to my face."

"I'm so sorry, Becca."

"And he was such a *little* man," she said, still astonished at the memory of it. "I kept thinking how if Dennis was here that man would of *never* talked to me like that. He wouldn't of *dared!*"

Jeremy stared at his hands. Large hands, built for hard work. Useless now. Rebecca sat on the floor, fighting back tears. She gave up on the orange soda, seeming to sense the futility of it.

⟨◦⟩

It was a week before Christmas, and Tara was talking to him from inside the shower. The door was open and he could see her pale shape behind the curtain, but he couldn't make out what she was saying. He sat on the bed in his underwear, his clothes for the evening laid out beside him. It was the same suit he'd worn to the funerals, and he dreaded putting it on again.

Outside the short wintertime afternoon was giving way to evening. The Christmas lights strung along the eaves and wound into the bushes still had to be turned on. The neighbors across the street had already lit theirs; the colored lights looked like glowing candy, turning their home into a gingerbread house from a fairy tale. The full moon was resplendent.

Jeremy supposed that a Christmas party full of elementary school professionals might be the worst place in the world. He would drift among them helplessly, like a grizzly bear in a roomful of children, expected not to eat anyone.

He heard the squeak of the shower faucet and suddenly his wife's voice carried to him. "—time it takes to get there," she said.

"What?"

She slid the curtain open and pulled a towel from the shelf. "Have you been listening to me?"

"I couldn't hear you over the water."

She went to work on her hair. "I've just had a very lively conversation with myself, then."

"Sorry."

"Are you going to get dressed?" she said.

He loved to watch her like this, when she was naked but not trying to be sexy, when she was just going about the minor business of being a human being. Unselfconscious and miraculous.

"Are *you?*" he said.

"Very funny. You were in that same position when I started my shower. What's up?"

"I don't want to go."

She turned the towel into a blue turban and wrapped another around her body. She crossed the room and sat beside him, leaving wet footprints in the carpet, her shoulders and her face still glistening with beaded water.

"You'll catch cold," he said.

"What are you worried about?"

"I'm obese. I'm a fricking spectacle. I'm not fit to be seen in public."

"You're my handsome man."

"Stop it."

"Jeremy," she said, "you can't turn into a shut-in. You have to get out. It's been six months, and you've totally disengaged from the world. These people are safe, okay? They're not going to judge you. They're my friends, and I want them to be your friends too."

"They're going to look at me and think, that's the guy that left *his* friends on a mountain to die."

"You're alive," Tara said, sharply, and turned his head so he had to look at her. "You're alive because you left. I still have a husband because you left. So in the end I don't give a shit what people think." She paused, took a steady breath, and let him go. "And not everyone's thinking bad things about you. Sometimes you have to take people at face value, Jeremy. Sometimes people really are what they say they are."

He nodded, chastened. He knew she was right. He'd been hiding in this house for months. It had to stop.

She touched his cheek and smiled at him. "Okay?"

"Yeah. Okay."

She got up and headed back to the bathroom, and he fell back on the bed. "Okay," he said.

"Besides," she called back happily, "don't forget about Tim! Someone has to keep the beast at bay!"

A sudden, coursing heat pulsed through him. He *had* forgotten Tim. "Oh yeah," he said, sitting up. He watched her dress, her body incandescent with water and light, and felt something like hope move inside him.

◄ο►

The house was bigger than Jeremy had been expecting. It was in an upscale subdivision, where all the houses had at least two stories and a basement. The front porch shed light like a fallen star, and colored Christmas bulbs festooned the neighborhood. "Jesus," he said, turning into the parking lot already full of cars. "Donny lives *here?*"

Donny Winn was the vice-principal of the school: a rotund, pink-faced man who sweated a lot and always seemed on the brink of a nervous breakdown. Jeremy had only met him once or twice, but the man made an impression like a damp cloth.

"His wife's a physical therapist," Tara said. "She works with the Carolina Panthers or something. Trust me, she's the money."

The house was packed. Jeremy didn't recognize anybody. A table in the dining room had been pushed against a wall and its wings extended, turning it into a buffet table loaded with an assortment of holiday dishes and confections. Bowls of spiked eggnog anchored each end of the table. Donny leaned against a wall nearby, alone but smiling. His wife worked the crowd like a politician, steering newly-arrived guests toward the table and bludgeoning them with good will.

Christmas lights were strung throughout the house, and mistletoe hung in every doorway. Andy Williams crooned from speakers hidden by the throng.

Jeremy wended his way through the mill of people behind Tara, who guided him to the table. Within moments they were armed with booze and ready for action. Jeremy spoke into Tara's ear. "Where's Tim?"

She craned her neck and looked around, then shook her head. "I can't see him. Don't worry. He'll find us!"

"You mean he'll find *you*," he said.

She smiled and squeezed his hand.

He measured time in drinks, and then he lost track of it. The lights and the sounds were beginning to blur into a candy-hued miasma that threatened to drown him. He'd become stationary in the middle of the living room, people and conversations revolving around him like the spokes of some demented Ferris wheel. Tara was beside him, nearly doubled over in laughter, one hand gripping his upper arm in a vise as she talked to a gaunt, heavily made-up woman whose eyes seemed to reflect light like sheets of ice.

"He's evil!" The woman had to shout to be heard. "His parents should have strangled him at birth!"

"Jesus," Jeremy said, trying to remember what they were talking about.

"Oh my God, Jeremy, you don't know this kid," Tara said. "He's got like—this *look*. I'm serious! Totally dead."

The woman nodded eagerly. "And the other day? I was looking through their daily journals? I found a picture of a severed head."

"What? No way!"

"The neck was even drawn with jagged red lines, to show it was definitely cut off. To make sure I knew it!"

"Somebody should do something," Jeremy said. "We're gonna be reading about this little monster someday."

Tara shook her head. "Nobody wants to know anymore. 'Boys will be boys,' right?"

The woman arched an eyebrow. "People are just fooled by the packaging," she said. "Kids shouldn't be drawing severed heads!"

Tara laughed. "But it's okay for grown-ups to?"

"Nobody should draw them," the woman said gravely.

"Excuse me," Jeremy said, and moved away from them both. He felt Tara's hand on his arm but he kept going. The conversation had rattled him.

Severed heads. What the fuck!

He slid clumsily through the crowd, using his weight to help along the people who were slow in getting out of his way. He found himself edging past the hostess, who smiled at him and said "Merry Christmas," her eyes sliding away from him before the words were even out of her mouth. He was briefly overwhelmed by a spike of outrage at her blithe manner—at the whole apparatus of entitlement and assumption this party suddenly represented to him, with its abundance and its unapologetic stink of money. "I'm Jewish," he said, and felt a happy thrill when she whipped her head around as he pressed further into the crowd.

He stationed himself by the fireplace, which was, at the moment, free of people. He set his drink on the mantel and turned his back to the crowd, looking instead at the carefully arranged manger scene on display there. The ceramic pieces were old and chipped; it had clearly been in the family for a long time. He looked past the wise men and the shepherds crouched in reverent awe, and saw the baby Jesus at the focal point, his little face rosy pink, his mouth a gaping oval, one eye chipped away. Jeremy's flesh rippled and he turned away.

And then he saw Tim approaching through the crowd. Tim was a slight man, with thinning hair and a pair of silver-rimmed glasses. Jeremy decided he looked like a cartoonist's impression of an intellectual. He stared at him as he approached.

This was what he had come for. He felt the blood start to move in his body, slowly, like a river breaking through ice floes. He felt some measure of himself again. It was just as intoxicating as the liquor.

Tim held out his hand, still closing the distance, and Jeremy took it.

"Hey. Jeremy, right? Tara's husband?"

"Yeah. I'm sorry, you are?"

"Oh I'm Tim Duckett, we met last year, at that teachers' union thing?"

"Oh yeah. Tim, hey."

"I just saw you over here by yourself and I thought, that guy is frickin lost. You know? Totally out of his element."

Jeremy bristled. "I think you made a mistake."

"Really? I mean, look at these people." He shifted to stand beside Jeremy so they could look out over the crowd together. "Come on. *Tea*chers? This is hell for *me!* I can only imagine how you must feel."

"I feel just fine."

Tim touched his glass to Jeremy's. "Well here's to you then. I feel like I'm about to fucking choke." He took a deep drink. "I mean, look at that guy over there. The fat one?" Jeremy flushed but held his tongue. These people didn't think. "That's Shane Mueller," Tim continued. "Laughing like he's high or something. He can afford to laugh because he's got the right friends, you know what I mean? Goddamn arrogant prick. Not like her."

He gestured at the woman Jeremy had been talking to just a few moments ago. Where was Tara?

"Word is she's not coming back next year. She won't be the only one, either. Everybody here's scared shitless. The fucking legislature's throwing us to the wolves. Who cares about education, right? Not when there's dollars at stake." He took a drink. "*English?* Are you kidding me?"

Tim sidled up next to him, so that their arms brushed. Jeremy gave a small push with his elbow and Tim surrendered some ground, seeming not to notice.

"I always kind of envied you, you know?" he was saying.

". . . what?"

"Oh yeah. Probably freaks you out, right? This guy you barely even know? But Tara talks about you in the lounge sometimes, and it got to where I felt like I kind of knew you a little bit."

"So you like to talk to Tara, huh?"

"Oh yeah man, she's a great girl. Great girl. But what you do is real work. You hang out with grown men and build things. With your *hands*." He held out his own hands, as though to illustrate the concept. "I hang out with kids, man." He gestured at the crowd. "A bunch of goddamn kids."

Jeremy took a drink. He peered into his glass. The ice had almost completely melted, leaving a murky, diluted puddle at the bottom. "Things change," he said.

Tim gave him a fierce, sympathetic look. "Yeah, you've been through some shit, haven't you?"

Jeremy looked at him, dimly amazed, feeling suddenly defensive. This guy had no boundaries. "What?"

"Come on, man, we all know. It's not like it's a secret, right? That fucking wolf?"

"You don't know shit."

"Now that's not fair. If you don't want to talk about it, okay, I get that. But we were all here for Tara when it happened. She's got a lot of friends here. It's not like we're totally uninvested."

Jeremy turned on him, a sudden wild heat burning his skin from the inside. He pressed his body against Tim's and backed him against the fireplace. Tim nearly tripped on the hearth and grabbed the mantel to keep his balance. "I said you don't know *shit.*"

Tim's face was stretched in surprise. "Holy shit, Jeremy, are you gonna hit me?"

Jeremy felt a hand on his shoulder, and he heard his wife's voice. "What's going on here?"

He backed off, letting her pull him away, and allowing Tim to regain his balance. Tim stared at the two of them, looking more bemused now than worried or affronted.

Tara laced her hand into her husband's. "Do you boys need a time out?"

Tim made a placating gesture. "No, no, we're just talking about—"

"Tim's just running his mouth," Jeremy said. "He needs to learn to shut it."

Tara squeezed his hand and leaned against him. He could feel the tension in her body. "Why don't we get some fresh air?" she said.

"What?"

"Come on. I want to see the lights outside."

"Don't you try to placate me. What's the matter with you?"

Tim said, "Whoa, whoa, let's all calm down a little bit."

"Why don't you shut the fuck up."

The sound of the party continued unabated, but Jeremy could sense a shift in the atmosphere around him. He didn't have to turn around to know that he was beginning to draw attention.

"Jeremy!" Tara's voice was sharp. "What the hell has gotten into you?"

Tim touched her arm. "It's my fault. I brought up the wolf thing."

Jeremy grabbed his wrist. "If you touch my wife one more time I'll break your goddamn arm." His mind flooded with images of operatic violence, of Tim's guts garlanding all the expensive furniture like Christmas bunting. He rode the crest of this wave with radiant joy.

Astonishingly, Tim grinned at him. "What the fuck, man?"

Jeremy watched Tim's lips pull back, saw the display of teeth, and surrendered himself to instinct. It was like dropping a chain; the freedom and the relief that coursed through his body was almost religious in its impact. Jeremy hit him in the mouth as hard as he could. Something sharp and jagged tore his knuckles. Tim flailed backwards, tripping on the hearth again but this time falling hard. His head knocked the mantel on the way down, leaving a bloody postage stamp on the white paint. Manger pieces toppled over the side and bounced off him.

Someone behind him shrieked. Voices rose in a chorus, but it was all just background noise. Jeremy leaned over and hit him again and again, until several hands grabbed him from behind and heaved him backward, momentarily lifting him off his feet. He was grappled by a cluster of men, his arms twisted behind him and immobilized. The whole mass of them lurched about like some demented monster, as Jeremy tried to break free.

The room had gone quiet. "Silver Bells" went on for another few seconds until someone rushed to the stereo and switched it off. All he could hear was his own heavy breathing.

He resumed a measure of control over himself, though his blood still galloped through his head and his muscles still jerked with energy. "Okay," he said. "Okay."

He found himself at the center of the crowd, most of them standing well back and staring agape. Someone was crouched beside Tim, who was sitting on the hearth, his face pale; his hands cupped beneath his bloody mouth. One eye was already swelling shut.

Tara stood to one side, her face red with anger, or humiliation, or both. She marched forward and grabbed him forcibly by the bicep, and yanked him behind her. The men holding him let him go.

"Should we call the police?" someone said.

"Oh *fuck you!*" Tara shouted.

She propelled him through the front door and out into the cold air. She did not release him until they arrived at the truck. The night arced over them both, and the world was bespangled with Christmas-colored constellations. Tara sagged against the truck's door, hiding her face against the window. He stood silently, trying to grasp for some feeling here, for some appropriate mode of behavior. Now that the adrenaline was fading, it was starting to dawn on him how bad this was.

Tara stood up straight and said, without looking at him, "I have to go back inside for a minute. Wait here."

"Do you want me to go with you?"

"Just wait here."

He did. She went up to the front door and rang the bell, and after a moment she was let inside. He stood there and let the cold work its way through his body, banking the last warm embers of the alcohol. After a while he got behind the wheel of the truck and waited. Soon, the front door opened again, and she came out. She walked briskly to the truck, her breath trailing behind her, and opened his door. "Move over," she said. "I'm driving."

He didn't protest. Moments later she started the engine and pulled onto the road. She drove them slowly out of the neighborhood, until the last big house receded into the darkness behind them, like a glittering piece of jewelry dropped into the ocean. She steered them onto the highway and they eased onto the long stretch home.

"He's not going to call the police," she said at last. "Small miracle."

He nodded. "I thought you wanted me to confront him," he said, and regretted it immediately.

She didn't respond. He stole a glance at her: her face was unreadable. She drew in a deep breath. "Did you tell Mrs. Winn that we're Jewish?"

" . . . yeah."

"Why? Why would you do that?"

He just shook his head and stared out the window. Lights streaked by, far away.

Tara sobbed once, both hands still clutching the steering wheel. Her face was twisted in misery. "You have to get a hold of yourself," she said. "I don't know what's happening to you. I don't know what to do."

He leaned his head back and closed his eyes. He felt his guts turn to stone. He knew he had to say something, he had to try to explain himself here, or someday she would leave. Maybe someday soon. But the fear was too tight; it wouldn't let him speak. It would barely let him breathe.

◄○►

When they get home the fight is brief and intense, and Jeremy escapes in the truck, making a trip to the attic before he leaves. Now he's speeding down a winding two-lane blacktop, going so fast he can't stay in his lane. If anyone else appears on this road, everybody's fucked. He makes a fast right when he comes to the turn-in for Wild Acre, the truck hitting the bumps in the road too hard and smashing its undercarriage into the dirt. He pushes it up the hill, the untended dirt road overgrown with weeds. The truck judders around a bend, something groaning under the hood. The wheel slips out of his hands and the truck slides into a ditch, coming to a crunching halt and slamming Jeremy's face into the steering wheel.

The headlights peer crookedly into the dust-choked air, illuminating the house frames, which look like huge, drifting ghosts behind curtains of raised dirt and clay. He leans back in his seat, gingerly touching his nose, and his vision goes watery. The full moon leaks silver blood into the sky. Something inside him buckles, and acid fills his mouth. He puts a hand over it, squeezes his eyes shut, and thinks, Don't you do it, don't you fucking do it.

He doesn't do it. He swallows it back, burning his throat.

He slams his elbow into the door several times. Then he rests his head on the steering wheel and sobs. These are huge, body-breaking sobs, the kind that leave him gasping for breath, the kind he hasn't suffered since he was a little kid. They frighten him a little. He is not meant to sound like this.

After a few moments he stops, lifts his head, and stares at the closest house frame, bone-colored in the moonlight. The floor is covered in dark stains. The forest is surging behind it. In a scramble of terror he wrenches the rifle from its rack, opens the door and jumps into the road.

The gun is slippery in his hands. He strides into the house frame and raises the gun to his chin, aiming it into the dark forest, staring down the sight. The world and its sounds retreat into a single point of stillness. He watches, and waits.

"Come on!" he screams. "Come on! *Come on!*"

But nothing comes.

THE CALLERS

RAMSEY CAMPBELL

Mark's grandmother seems barely to have left the house when his grandfather says "Can you entertain yourself for a bit? I could do with going to the pub while I've got the chance."

Mark wonders how much they think they've entertained him, but he only says "Will grandma be all right coming home on her own?"

"Never fret, son. They can look after theirselves." The old man's hairy caterpillar eyebrows squirm as he frowns at Mark and blinks his bleary eyes clear. "No call for you to fetch her. It's women's stuff, the bingo." He gives the boy's shoulder an unsteady squeeze and mutters "You're a good sort to have around."

Mark feels awkward and a little guilty that he's glad he doesn't have to meet his grandmother. "Maybe I'll go to a film."

"You'd better have a key, then." His grandfather rummages among the contents of a drawer of the shaky sideboard—documents in ragged envelopes, rubber bands so desiccated they snap when he takes hold of them, a balding reel of cotton, a crumpled folder stuffed with photographs—and hauls out a key on a frayed noose of string. "Keep hold of that for next time you come," he says.

Does he mean Mark will be visiting by himself in future? Was last night's argument so serious? His mother objected when his grandfather offered him a glass of wine at dinner, and then her mother accused her of not letting Mark grow up. Before long the women were shouting at each other about how Mark's grandmother had brought up her daughter, and the men only aggravated the conflict by trying to calm it down. It continued after Mark went to bed, and this morning his father informed him that he and Mark's mother were going home several days early. "You can stay if you like," she told Mark.

Was she testing his loyalty or hoping he would make up for her behaviour? While her face kept her thoughts to itself his father handed him the ticket for the train home like a business card, one man to another. Mark's mother spent some time in listing ways he shouldn't let anyone down, but these didn't include going to the cinema. Wearing his coat was among the requirements, and so he takes it from the stand in the hall. "Step out, lad," his grandfather says as Mark lingers on the pavement directly outside the front door. "You don't want an old crock slowing you down."

At the corner of the street Mark glances back. The old man is limping after him, resting a hand on the roof of each car parked with two wheels on the pavement. Another narrow similarly terraced street leads into the centre of the small Lancashire town, where lamps on scalloped iron poles are stuttering alight beneath a congested late April sky. Many of the shops are shuttered, and some are boarded up. Just a few couples stroll past deserted pristine kitchens and uninhabited items of attire. Most of the local amusements have grown too childish for Mark, though he might still enjoy bowling or a game of indoor golf if he weren't by himself, and others are years out of bounds—the pubs, the clubs waiting for the night crowds while doormen loiter outside like wrestlers dressed for someone's funeral. Surely the cinema won't be so particular about its customers. More than one of Mark's schoolmates has shown him the scene from *Facecream* on their phones, where the girl gets cream squirted all over her face.

As he hurries past the clubs he thinks a doorman is shouting behind him, but the large voice is down a side street full of shops that are nailed shut. At first he fancies that it's chanting inside one of them, and then he sees an old theatre at the far end. While he can't distinguish the words, the rhythm makes it clear he's hearing a bingo caller. Mark could imagine that all the blank-faced doormen are determined to ignore the voice.

The Frugoplex is beyond the clubs, across a car park for at least ten times as many vehicles as it presently contains. The lobby is scattered with popcorn, handfuls of which have been trodden into the purple carpet. A puce rope on metal stilts leads the queue for tickets back and forth and twice again on the way to the counter. When Mark starts to duck under the rope closest to the end of the queue, a man behind the counter scowls at him, and so he follows the rope all the way around, only just heading off two couples of about his own age who stoop under. He's hoping to avoid the disgruntled man, but the queue brings Mark to him. "*Facecream*, please," Mark says and holds out a ten-pound note.

"Don't try it on with me, laddie," the man says and turns his glare on the teenagers who have trailed Mark to the counter. "And your friends needn't either."

"He's not our friend," one of the boys protests.

"I reckon not when he's got you barred."

Mark's face has grown hot, but he can't just walk away or ask to see a film he's allowed to watch. "I don't know about them, but I'm fifteen."

"And I'm your sweet old granny. That's it now for the lot of you. Don't bother coming to my cinema." The manager tells his staff at the counter "Have a good look at this lot so you'll know them."

Mark stumbles almost blindly out of the multiplex. He's starting across the car park when somebody mutters behind him "He wants his head kicked in."

They're only words, but they express his feelings. "That's what he deserves," Mark agrees and turns to his new friends.

It's immediately clear that they weren't thinking of the manager. "You got us barred," says the girl who didn't speak.

"I didn't mean to. You oughtn't to have stood so close."

"Doesn't matter what you meant," she says, and the other girl adds "We'll be standing a lot closer. Standing on your head."

Mark can't take refuge in the cinema, but running would look shameful and invite pursuit as well. Instead he tramps at speed across the car park. His shadow lurches ahead, growing paler as it stretches, and before long it has company, jerking forward to catch up on either side of him. He still stops short of bolting but strides faster. He's hoping passers-by will notice his predicament, but either they aren't interested or they're determined not to be. At last he reaches the nightclubs, and is opening his mouth to appeal to the nearest doorman when the fellow says "Keep walking, lad."

"They're after me."

The doorman barely glances beyond Mark, and his face stays blank. "Walk on."

It could be advice, though it sounds like a dismissal. It leaves Mark feeling that he has been identified as an outsider, and he thinks the doormen's impassive faces are warning him not to loiter. He would make for the police station if he knew where it is. He mustn't go to his grandparents' house in case they become scapegoats as well, and there's just one sanctuary he can think of. He dodges into the side street towards the bingo hall.

The street looks decades older than the main road and as though it has been forgotten for at least that long. Three streetlamps illuminate the cracked roadway bordered by grids that are clogged with old leaves. The glow is too dim to penetrate the gaps between the boards that have boxed up the shopfronts, because the lanterns are draped with grey cobwebs laden with drained insects. The only sign of life apart from a rush of footsteps behind Mark is the amplified voice, still delivering its blurred chant. It might almost be calling out to him, and he breaks into a run.

So do his pursuers, and he's afraid that the bingo hall may be locked against intruders. Beyond the grubby glass of three pairs of doors the foyer is deserted; nobody is in the ticket booth or behind the refreshment counter. His pursuers hesitate as he sprints to the nearest pair of doors, but when neither door budges, the gang closes in on him. He nearly trips on the uneven marble steps as he stumbles along them. He throws all his weight, such as it is, against the next set of doors, which give so readily that he almost sprawls on the threadbare carpet of the foyer.

The caller seems to raise his voice to greet him. "Sixty-three," he's announcing, "just like me." The pursuers glare at Mark from the foot of the shallow steps. "You can't stay in there," one girl advises him, and the other shouts "Better not try."

All the gang look determined to wait for him. If they don't tire of it by the time the bingo players go home, surely they won't dare to let themselves be identified, and so Mark shuts the doors and crosses the foyer. The entrance to the auditorium is flanked by old theatrical posters, more than one of which depicts a plump comedian with a sly schoolboyish face. Mark could imagine they're sharing a joke about him as he pushes open the doors to the auditorium.

The theatre seats have been cleared out, but the stage remains. It faces a couple of dozen tables, most of which are surrounded by women with score cards in front of them and stumpy pencils in their hands. The stage is occupied by a massive lectern bearing a large transparent globe full of numbered balls. Mark might fancy that he knows why the posters looked secretly amused, because the man in them is behind the lectern. He looks decades older, and the weight of his face has tugged it piebald as well as out of shape, but his grin hasn't entirely lost its mischief, however worn it seems. Presumably his oversized suit and baggy shirt are meant to appear comical rather than to suggest a youngster wearing cast-off clothes. He examines a ball before returning it to the globe, which he spins on its pivot. "Three and three," he says as his eyes gleam blearily at Mark. "What do you see?" he adds, and all the women eye the newcomer.

At first Mark can't see his grandmother. He's distracted by a lanky angular woman who extends her speckled arms across the table nearest to him. "Lost your mammy, son?" she cries. "There's plenty here to tend to you."

For an uneasy moment he thinks she has reached for her breast to indicate how motherly she is, but she's adjusting her dress, her eagerness to welcome him having exposed a mound of wrinkled flesh. Before he can think of an answer his grandmother calls "What are you doing here, Mark?"

She's at a table close to the stage. He doesn't want to make her nervous for him if there's no need, and he's ashamed of having run away. The uncarpeted floorboards amplify every step he takes, so that he feels as if he's trying to sound bigger than he is. All the women and the bingo caller watch his progress, and he wonders if everybody hears him mutter "I went to the cinema but they wouldn't let me see the film."

As his grandmother makes to speak one of her three companions leans forward, flattening her forearms on the table to twice their width. "However old are you, son?"

"Mark's thirteen," says his grandmother.

Another of her friends nods vigorously, which she has been doing ever since Mark caught sight of her. "Thirteen," she announces, and many of the women coo or hoot with enthusiasm.

"Looks old enough to me," says the third of his grandmother's tablemates, who is sporting more of a moustache than Mark has achieved. "Enough of a man."

"Well, we've shown you off now," Mark's grandmother tells him. "I'll see you back at home."

This provokes groans throughout the auditorium. The woman who asked his age raises her hands, and her forearms sag towards the elbows. "Don't keep him to yourself, Lottie."

The nodding woman darts to grab a chair for him. "You make this the lucky table, Mark."

He's disconcerted to observe how frail his grandmother is by comparison with her friends, though they're at least as old as she is. The bingo caller gives him a crooked grin and shouts "Glad to have another feller here. Safety in numbers, lad."

Presumably this is a joke of some kind, since quite a few women giggle. Mark's grandmother doesn't, but says "Can he have a card?"

This prompts another kind of laughter, and the nodding woman even manages to shake her head. "It's the women's game, lad," the caller says. "Are you ladies ready to play?"

"More than ever," the moustached woman shouts, which seems somehow to antagonise Mark's grandmother. "Sit down if you're going to," she says. "Stop drawing attention to yourself."

He could retort that she has just done that to him. He's unable to hide his blazing face as he crouches on the spindly chair while the bingo caller elevates the next ball from the dispenser. "Eighty-seven," he reads out. "Close to heaven."

The phrase earns mirth and other noises of appreciation as the women duck in unison to their cards. They chortle or grunt if they find the number, grimacing if they fail. Nobody at Mark's table has located it when the man at the lectern calls "Number forty, old and naughty."

"That's us and no mistake," the moustached woman screeches before whooping at the number on her card.

"Number six, up to tricks."

"That's us as well," her friend cries, but all her nodding doesn't earn her the number.

"Forty-nine, you'll be fine."

The third woman crosses out the number, and flesh cascades down her arm as she lifts the pencil. "He's that with bells on," she says, favouring Mark with a wink.

He has to respond, though the smile feels as if his swollen lips are tugging at his hot stiff face. "Three and twenty," the man at the lectern intones. "There'll be plenty."

Mark's grandmother hunches over the table. He could think she's trying to evade the phrase or the coos of delight it elicits from the rest of the players, but she's marking the number on her card. She seems anxious to win, staying bent close to the card as the bingo caller consults the next ball. "Six and thirty," he says, and a roguish grin twists the left side of his mouth. "Let's get dirty."

He pokes at the grin with a finger as if he wants to push the words back in, although they've raised appreciative squeals throughout the auditorium. The fleshy woman falls to her card so eagerly that every visible part of her wobbles. "That'll do me," she cries.

Presumably she means his suggestion, since she hasn't completed her card. Mark sees his grandmother glance nervously at it and then stare at her own as though striving to conjure up a number. "Four and four," the caller says and almost at once "There's the door."

The moustached woman rubs her upper lip so hard that Mark fancies he hears the hairs crackle. "Never mind that," she tells the caller.

He blinks at her and stares around the hall. Mark feels more out of place than ever, as though he's listening to jokes too old for him—beyond his comprehension, at any rate. The caller's drooping face grows defiant as he identifies the next ball. "Ninety-five," he says. "Leave alive."

This brings no laughter, just a murmur that falls short of words. At least Mark's grandmother has found the number on her card. She needs three more to win, and he's surprised by how much he hopes she will. He puts the wish into his eyes as he gazes up at the stage. "Number fifty," the caller says in a tone that seems almost as mechanical as the dispenser. "He'll be nifty."

"Aye," several women respond, and the quivering woman gives Mark another wink.

"Eighty-one, nearly done."

"That's me," the nodding woman agrees, bowing to her card as if the motion of her head has overtaken the rest of her.

Perhaps she means her age, since the irregular cross she makes doesn't finish off the card. "Twenty-nine," the caller says, keeping his eyes on the ball he's raised between the fingertips of both hands. "See the sign."

If the players do so, they keep quiet about it, not even greeting the number or bemoaning their luck. The caller displays the next ball like a magician and puts a finger to the edge of a grin that's meant to appear mysterious. "Sixty-three," he says. "Time to flee."

The murmur this provokes is unamused, and he concentrates on the ball that rolls out of the dispenser. "Twenty-four," he says. "Can't do more."

His gaze is drifting towards Mark when the fleshy woman emits a shriek that jabs deep into the boy's ears. "We're done," she cries. "It's mine."

The caller shuts the globe and extends a hand. "Give us a look."

As she mounts the steps to the stage a series of tremors passes through her body, starting at her veinous legs. Having checked her numbers against those that came up, the caller says "We've a winner."

She snatches the card and plods back to the table, where Mark sees how the crosses resemble sketches of gravestones, at least until she turns the card the right way up. She lowers herself onto her creaking chair and says "I claim the special."

The caller doesn't look at her or anywhere near her. "It's not time yet," he tells whoever needs to hear.

While he leans on the lectern to say so he puts Mark in mind of a priest in a pulpit, though the comparison seems wrong in some way Mark doesn't understand. He's distracted by his grandmother, who lays down her pencil next to the card scattered with the kind of crosses all the women have been drawing. "I'll do without my luck tonight," she says and grasps his arm to help her stand up. "Time someone was at home."

"Don't be like that," the fleshy woman says. "You can't just go running off."

"I won't be running anywhere." As Mark wonders whether that's defiance or the painful truth his grandmother says "I'll see you all another night."

"See us now and see yourself." The speaker nods so violently that her words grow jagged. "You're still one of us."

"I'm not arguing," Mark's grandmother says and grips his arm harder. "Come along now, Mark."

He doesn't know how many women murmur as she turns towards the exit. While he can't make out their words, they sound unhappy if not worse, and all of them are closer than the exit. Nobody moves as long as he can see them, and he finds he would rather not look back. His grandmother has almost led him out, clutching his arm so tightly that it throbs, when the lanky woman who first greeted him plants a hand on her breast again. Though she could be expressing emotion, Mark has the unwelcome fancy that she's about to bare the wizened breast to him. His grandmother hurries him past, and the doors to the foyer are lumbering shut behind them when a woman says "We aren't done."

Mark hopes she's addressing the man on the stage—urging him to start the next game—but he hasn't heard the caller by the time he and his grandmother emerge onto the steps. The street is deserted, and he suspects that the couples who followed him from the cinema are long gone. Outside the clubs the doormen keep their faces blank at the sight of him and his escort, who is leaning on him as much as leading him. She's quiet until they reach the shops, where she mutters "I wish you hadn't gone there tonight, Mark. We're meant to be responsible for you."

He feels guiltier than he understands. She says nothing more while they make their increasingly slow way home. She's about to ring the doorbell with her free hand when Mark produces the key. "Isn't he in?" she protests.

"He went to the pub."

"Men," she says so fiercely that Mark feels sentenced too. She slams the door by tottering against it and says "I think you should be in your bed."

He could object that it isn't his bedtime—that he doesn't know what offence he's committed—but perhaps he isn't being punished, in which case he isn't sure he wants to learn her reason for sending him to his room. He trudges up the narrow boxed-in stairs to the decidedly compact bathroom, where every item seems too close to him, not least the speckled mirror that frames his uneasy face. The toothpaste tastes harsher than usual, and he does his best to stay inaudible while spitting it into the sink. As he dodges into the smaller of the two front bedrooms he sees his grandmother sitting at the bottom of the stairs. He retreats under the quilt of the single bed against the wall beneath the meagre window and listens for his grandfather.

He doesn't know how long he has kept his eyes shut by the time he hears the front door open below him. His grandmother starts to talk at once, and he strains to catch her words. "Did you send Mark to fetch me tonight?"

"I told him to stay clear," Mark's grandfather says not quite as low. "What did he see?"

"It isn't what he saw, it's what they did."

"Are you still up to that old stuff? Makes you all feel powerful, does it?"

"I'll tell you one thing, Len—you don't any more." Just as righteously she says "I don't remember you crying about it too much when it was your turn."

"Well, it's not now."

"It shouldn't be our house at all." This sounds accusing, especially when she adds "If there's any talking to be done you can do it."

Apparently that's all. Mark hears his grandparents labour up the stairs and take turns to make various noises in the bathroom that remind him how old they are. He finds himself wondering almost at random whether they'll take him to the celebrations tomorrow on the town green; they have on other May Days. The prospect feels like a reward if not a compensation for some task. The door of the other front bedroom shuts, and he hears a series of creaks that mean his grandparents have taken to their bed.

For a while the night is almost quiet enough to let him drift into sleep, except that he feels as if the entire house is alert. He's close to dozing when he hears a distant commotion. At first he thinks a doorman outside a club is shouting at someone, perhaps a bunch of drunks, since several people respond. There's something odd about the voice and the responses too. Mark lifts his head from the lumpy pillow and strives to identify what he's hearing, and then he realises his efforts are unnecessary. The voice and its companions are approaching through the town.

Mark does his best to think he's misinterpreting what he hears. The voices sound uncomfortably close by the time he can't mistake them. "Seventy-four," the leader calls, and the ragged chorus answers "Knock on his door." Mark is additionally disconcerted by recognising that the caller isn't the man who was on the stage. However large and resonant it is, it's a woman's voice.

"Number ten," it calls, and the chant responds "Find the men." The chorus is nearly in unison now, and the performance puts Mark in mind of a priest and a congregation—some kind of ritual, at any rate. He kicks the quilt away and kneels on the yielding mattress to scrag the curtain and peer through the window. Even when he presses his cheek against the cold glass, all of the street that he can see is deserted. His breath swells up on the pane and shrinks as the first voice cries "Sweet thirteen" and the rest chant "While he's green."

They sound surer of themselves with every utterance, and they aren't all that troubles Mark. Although he knows that the houses opposite are occupied, every window is dark and not a single curtain stirs. Is everyone afraid to look?

Why are his grandparents silent? For a few of Mark's breaths the nocturnal voices are too, but he can hear a muffled shuffling—the noise of a determined march. Then the caller announces "Pair of fives," and as her followers chant "We're the wives" the procession appears at the end of the road.

It's led by the fleshy woman. As she advances up the middle of the street she's followed by her moustached friend and the nodding one, and then their fellow players limp or trot or hobble in pairs around the corner. The orange glow of the streetlamp lends them a rusty tinge like an unnatural tan. Mark doesn't need to count them to be certain that the parade includes everybody from the bingo hall except the man who was onstage and Mark's grandmother. As his grip on the windowsill bruises his fingers the fleshy woman declares "Ninety-eight."

She has a handful of bingo cards and is reading out the numbers. "We're his fate," the procession declares with enthusiasm, and Mark sees eyes glitter, not only with the streetlight. The moustached woman wipes her upper lip with a finger and thumb while her partner in the procession nods so eagerly that she looks in danger of succumbing to a fit. "Eighty-nine," their leader intones as if she's reading from a missal, and the parade almost as long as the street chants "He'll be mine."

They're close enough for Mark to see the fleshy woman join in the response. He sees her quivering from head to foot with every step she takes towards him, and then his attention is caught by the lanky woman in the middle of the procession. She's by no means alone in fumbling at a breast as though she's impatient to give it the air. That's among the reasons why Mark lets go of the curtain and the windowsill to huddle under the quilt. Once upon a time he might have believed this would hide him, but it doesn't even shut out the voices below the window. "Twenty-four," the caller shouts and joins in the chant of "Here's the door."

This is entirely too accurate for Mark's liking. It's the number of the house. As he hugs his knees with his clasped arms and grinds his spine against the wall he hears a muffled rumble close to him. Someone has opened the window of the next bedroom. Mark holds his breath until his grandfather shouts "Not here. Like Lottie says, you've been here once."

"That was a long time ago, Len." Mark can't tell whether this is reminiscent or dismissive, but the tone doesn't quite leave the fleshy woman's voice as she says "It's either you or him."

After a pause the window rumbles shut, and Mark finds it hard to breathe. He hears footsteps padding down the stairs—whose, he doesn't know—and the front door judders open. This is followed by an outburst of shuffling, first in the street and almost at once to some extent inside the house. As it begins to mount the stairs Mark hears the caller's voice, though it's little more than a whisper. "Number one," she prompts, and a murmuring chorus responds "Let's be mum." Is it proposing a role to play or enjoining secrecy? Mark can't judge, even when the procession sets about chanting in a whisper "Mum, mum, mum . . ." The repetition seems to fill the house, which feels too small for it, especially once the front door closes behind the last of the procession. The chorus can't blot out the shuffling, which sounds like the restlessness of an impatient queue. All Mark can do is squeeze his eyes so tight that the darkness throbs in time with his pulse, and he manages not to look until he hears a door creep open.

THIS STAGNANT BREATH OF CHANGE

BRIAN HODGE

B easley had died three times within the last month alone. Each time, they'd brought him back, and each time, it got harder.

The first was a simple heart attack, which they'd fought off by jump-starting him with the defibrillator; later, balloon angioplasty.

That opened the door to human error. Beasley's vitals were normal, until, without warning, he flatlined. They'd traced that to a bag of potassium solution with too high a concentration, and got his pulse going again by shooting him up with insulin and glucose, along with intravenous calcium and inhalations of albuterol.

This last scare was the worst, a line infection that would've begun small, as they always did, then swamped him with tidal waves of bacteria before anyone realized what was happening. That was the insidious thing about line infections. Once one line was compromised, it was all but guaranteed to spread to the rest. And he was hooked up to so many.

They got him through the worst of it, and once it looked as if Donald Beasley would survive another day, they stood down. By now, his room here at Good Sam was an ICU unto itself.

And by now, the routine was familiar enough that Bethany knew what to expect once it was over: *Hello, adrenaline crash, my old friend. Hello, relief, you seductive lie.*

As she always did, once the crisis was averted, the inevitable pushed back a little farther, she retreated to the hall in her green scrubs to shake out the stress and peer out the nearest window to search the sky for signs. Retreating storm clouds, maybe, or a fading giant wisp of faces from years of bad dreams. There was no rational reason it had to be the sky, only that it seemed as good a source as any to unleash . . .

Well, whatever was going to happen the day they *couldn't* bring him back.

"How long can we keep this up?" Bethany asked the attending physician, who was prone to de-stressing in his own way.

Cavendish, his name, but most here just called him Doctor Richard. He puffed at a cigarette as if it were the only thing keeping him upright. He was one of those doctors who continued to smoke in spite of knowing every reason not to. It would never catch up with him. That was the problem. His, hers, and everyone else's.

"How much more can that withered old body of his take?"

"As much as we can force on it," Dr. Richard said. "I'll crack his chest open and crawl in there and stay if I have to."

"Heroics aside," she said. "Just be honest."

He'd been on staff here long enough to have treated her the summer she was eight, after she and her bicycle lost a minor altercation with a car. Today, he looked every year of it.

"If we're having this same conversation a month from now, I'll consider that a miracle." Richard chained another cig off the first. "Honest enough for you?"

A few hours later, when her shift was over, she dropped by Donald Beasley's room to reassure herself that she could leave with a clear conscience. Another post-crisis habit. Like driving past a leaky dam to make sure the cracks hadn't widened. One of the off-duty nurses was sitting in a chair by the bed, watching him. Somebody was always watching him.

The cycles of death and restoration had taken their toll. According to Beasley's charts, he was seventy-six now, but he looked at least a hundred.

He was still unconscious, but would come around again eventually, and she didn't want to be here when that happened. She'd done her time.

Beasley might talk jabbering nonsense. Then again, he might be cognizant of everything, and resume begging for them to let him die. Either option was its own brand of unnervingly awful. He would tug at the restraints holding his wrists to the bed rails, feeble and mewling, and somehow, his desiccated body would find enough moisture for tears. They lived in fear of him thinking to bite through his tongue in an effort to drown in his own blood.

The watch-nurse glanced back over one heavy, rounded shoulder and nodded a dead-eyed hello. They'd gone to high school together, sort of. Janet Swain had been a senior when Bethany had come in as an undersized freshman, no boobs to speak of, and invisible.

They'd all gone to high school together here in Tanner Falls.

"If we can't save him, and we know it, say he's got a little time left, just not long, what would you want to do?" Janet said. "Would you give him what he deserves?"

Bethany squeezed her eyes closed. "Don't ask me something like that."

"I would. I mean, why not? Last chance, why waste the opportunity? It's only what everybody in the whole town has wanted to do to him for years. If we announced it, there'd be a line ten thousand people long. We should raffle off chances while we still can."

"Is that really what you'd want to be thinking of at the end?"

"I'd start with his eyes. Somebody going for your eyes, that's some scary business, right there. I'd leave him one, though, so he could see what I do to the rest of him."

Talk. Bethany tried to dismiss it as empty talk, no risk. They all needed to vent sometimes.

"Even old men are still attached to their ding-dongs." Janet smacked her hand on the bed rail and addressed Beasley directly. "You think that catheter was painful going in, you old buzzard? You have no idea."

If they got it out of their systems this way, maybe it would be enough, and they wouldn't lose control over the urge to act.

"And yeah, that *is* what I'll be thinking of at the end." Janet said this with a glare, almost an accusation. "That's the kind of thing you get to think of when you don't have anybody, and know you never will."

She made companionship sound like a comfort she was denied, but really, was it? Maybe Janet was the lucky one here, and would see it that way when the time came. When not dying alone meant having to watch someone you love die next to you, who really wanted that?

They could all die alone, together.

◄◦►

Bethany walked home after her shift, because she could. All the first-stringers on the Beasley team lived close enough for a shoe leather commute. Call it hospital policy, and plain old good sense. They wanted to be able to assemble the top tier crash team in minutes, any time of day or night, regardless of how much rain or snow or wind or ice might get in the way.

The plan had gone into effect years ago, before the old man's health started to decline. It had begun early, as soon as the first of the city fathers from a generation ago died. They would all be sick old men one day. Some of them were already old. Others were already sick middle-aged men. Over time, they'd all done what sick old men do, eventually overcoming each and every extraordinary measure to prolong their selfish lives, until Donald Beasley was the last man standing, however unsteadily.

Children used to sing about him, years ago, and maybe still would, if only there were enough kids around to pass the song down to, the way these things used to work. But after a generation, birth rates had fallen so low, by choice, that children were now a rarity in Tanner Falls. Even they knew something was wrong, in this place where their future had been taken from them before they were born.

"Old Mad Donald had a town,
iä iä oh!
And in that town he had a goat,
iä iä oh!"

Horrible little song. You had to marvel at how jubilantly children could sing of terrible things without appreciating what they were actually about. Yet she still missed the sound of it.

There was a time when Tanner Falls had been a great place to grow up. That was how she'd experienced it. You could roam all day here, under the radar of adults. Even within town, there were pockets of woodland that felt so much farther from civilization than they really were, centuries of trees grown up around ponds and laced together by streams and paths worn smooth by bicycle tires. There were fish to catch and frogs to race. There were railroad tracks to explore, wondering where they led, hunting for treasures that might have fallen from passing trains, and if you couldn't find anything, at least there were plenty of targets daring you to throw rocks at them.

And in the city park, the concrete bandshell always seemed to smell faintly of pee—a phenomenon explained by the shards of brown glass that always seemed to reappear—but it projected your voice in a most wonderful way, especially when you bunched together with your friends to see how loudly all of you could shriek together, so that even the old people who lived by the park came out on their porches to scowl.

And when you grew old enough for four wheels instead of two, you had the drive-in theater on the edge of town, and the A&W, where carhops on skates brought trays to hang on your door, loaded with burgers and onion rings and frosted mugs of root beer. And that was good for a while, as well, until it all started to seem too small, and boredom became an enemy that could only be outrun by going anywhere else but here.

Bethany didn't have to work to remember the town that way. Because it was still the same. It was all exactly the same, as immutably fixed as the old spoke-wheeled cannon on the courthouse lawn, commemorating a war no one alive had even fought in.

Like the shop on the corner over there, Stewart Drug & Sundries. *Sundries*—who even used the word anymore? Here, they did. Across the street and down the block? Where would you even expect to find something called Franklin's Dime Store today, in this, the post-Reagan years of George Bush? But here it was, unchanged from the pictures she'd seen when her parents were children. In any direction you looked where houses stood, you would see a skyline bristling with towering TV aerials, as if no one had heard of cable. They had . . . but it had never come here.

Bethany knew enough of the world beyond to realize you were meant to remember such things fondly because they were no longer around. That was how nostalgia was supposed to work—mourning defunct businesses and outmoded ways and untamed land lost to bulldozers sent by developers who called it progress. Recalling them with a golden luster because they had meant enough to your heart once to crowd out memories of all the uglier things better off forgotten.

Like that sign painted on the huge brick side of the Tanner Hotel, smack in the heart of downtown:

Nigger, Don't Let The Sun Set On You Here

Nobody wanted it. Nobody liked what it had to say, or what it said now about the town. They could scarcely bring themselves to look at it. It repelled the eye, yet resisted all efforts to erase its existence. Whitewash it, paint over it, paper over it, hang a banner across it from the roof—whatever went up wouldn't last the night. Sandblasting just made a gritty mess. Even attempts at demolition were plagued by mechanical failure.

It had been more than fifteen years since they'd given up trying.

And Tanner Falls stayed just as it was in 1969.

The hotel's insistence on cleaving to the status quo was one of the first bits of evidence that something was wrong here, early proof that someone had done a terrible thing to them all.

People change. People grow. Those who can't, die off, and with luck their worst notions die with them. Nobody wanted that hateful sign anything other than gone.

Except, maybe, for Donald Beasley and the fellow town fathers from a generation ago who had beat him to the grave.

There was a time when Tanner Falls had seemed like a great place to grow up.

What an unlikely thing to have doomed it.

⟵⬥⟶

Matt was already home when she got there, his back-support belt hanging from its peg by the side door. His shift had an hour to go yet, and by the look of things he'd been home long enough for three cans of Iron City already. Matt was the first person she was aware of who'd figured out that once you had a job in Tanner Falls, it was impossible to lose it, a fact of life he exploited with heedless impunity. Termination was change, and hey, they couldn't have that.

So there he was, still moving the same furniture in the same warehouse that had paid him for fifteen hours a week after school in 1969, so he could save up to buy his first real guitar.

He didn't notice her, such was his focus, so for a while she watched him play. Watched him go somewhere else, the only way left to him.

He was a leftie, and so was his Les Paul. Even Bethany, who had assisted while surgeons' hands worked wonders, could never figure out how Matt could be so dexterous as to play three parts at once: rhythms on the bottom two strings, melodies on the top two, and harmony and counterpoint in the middle. The effects pedals between the guitar and amp made it even more expansive, a swirling, psychedelic storm front of thunder and squalls that climbed and plunged, that promised hope and delivered heartache.

Every generation in every town had its Matt Meadows: the guy who could've really done something, gone places, if only he'd left.

He noticed her, finally, and brought the spaceship in for a landing, the last ripple of arpeggios echoing into the sonic horizon, until the only sound left in the hush of the house was the hum of his amp.

And in every town, every girl had her own potential Matt: the guy she ended up marrying because she hadn't left either.

"That good a day, huh?" he said.

Later, they went for a walk, meandering through the neighborhood, then straying west, as she sensed he might, through neighborhoods where the houses got bigger and farther apart. He had a homing instinct, and Bethany knew where they were going to end up long before they did: a pocket of undeveloped woodland tucked alongside a tributary upstream of the falls that gave the town its name. Matt had a need to torture himself with this place, and all it had taken from them.

She regarded this the way she regarded the beer he brought with him, even on a stroll: didn't like it, but didn't object. Let Matt be Matt. Let him have what he needs to get by, because without it, it could be so much worse. Everything would be worse soon enough.

The trees were not packed tightly here, except for a few small, compact groves. It was mostly an open field, with thickets enclosing the sides like walls, and a stream ran through it. Matt and his friends used to put on safety goggles and thick sweatshirts and have BB gun fights here. Nobody had ever lost an eye, a tooth. Welts were as bad as it got. No wonder they'd gotten the idea they were blessed.

They were boys and, for a time, invincible.

In some other life, in some other town, she might have had a son just like that. She would've welcomed the prospect of fretting over every little injury and wound that, in the puzzling way of boys, grounded him with pride and meaning. She would've welcomed a daughter like this just the same.

Only once had the Ortho-Novum failed. She'd kept the procedure quiet, kept Matt in the dark altogether. Nothing good could have come of him knowing. It wasn't that he would have disagreed with her decision; more that she didn't want to give him one more thing to regret.

The hoofprints. Once here, Matt always went for the hoofprints.

It was what people called them, anyway—a row of inches-deep depressions striding along the broadest clearing in the field. They hadn't filled in during the twenty-two years they'd been there, as if something about their creation had seared them in place for all time. Life shunned them. Not even the most opportunistic weeds grew in them, or anywhere close.

Honestly, Bethany didn't know if they were hoof prints or not. They were the right shape, cloven, like mirrored images of half-moons. Then again, each one was as big around as a truck tire.

She'd been a child when the event had happened, not yet ten, and although she hadn't witnessed it, she'd heard so many stories that it felt as if she had. Not that the stories were necessarily trustworthy. People were liars, even if they didn't mean to be. By now the strands of folklore had wound so inextricably around fact that it was impossible to twist them apart and get to the truth of things.

Under the black watch of a springtime new moon, the town had been lit for an instant by a flash of light. It wasn't lightning, though—no account ever mentioned a storm. It was more like reports describing the bright death of a meteorite. Nor was it white. Blue, some said. Others insisted it was green, while still others couldn't pin down a color at all, only that they didn't find it natural.

A fearsome wind had kicked up, too, and that lasted longer. Residents in the north of town swore it blew south, while those in the south swore it blew north. On the east side, they said it swept in toward the west, and here on the west side, the direction depended on how far out people were. They couldn't all be right, unless something had punched a hole in the night, like knocking out a window in an airliner that sucked the air in from everywhere at once.

Maybe it had.

People said that something appeared through the trees that night, big enough to have appeared above even the tallest ones. Some reported a churning cloud, while others swore they witnessed vast legs striding through the woods, coarse with bristling black hair and cloven hooves. A cloud with legs? Oh, why not. Something had changed the fundamentals of reality here.

She couldn't recall the first time she heard someone, in a low voice, speak of the Black Goat of the Woods with a Thousand Young. It was just one of those things you grew up with, like Santa Claus and the Tooth Fairy.

"You think it'll come back, right here?" Matt said. "Is that the way it's supposed to happen?"

"I don't know," she said.

"Beasley, any of them, they've never said anything about what to expect? Not even at the end, or when they were doped out on the good meds?"

"No."

He looked at her in a way that made it feel like they were strangers. He was just thirty-two, and already his face was too lined. "You'd tell me, wouldn't you? You wouldn't keep it to yourself just to spare me?"

Briefly, she wondered if he knew about the abortion after all, how she'd suctioned out the life they'd created rather than see it born into a short, cruel existence as chattel.

"Most of those guys," she said, "I think they were in denial about what they did. They wouldn't admit they'd done anything at all, much less speculate about what the consequences were going to be like. Not to us, anyway. Why would they? They knew by the time it happened, they weren't going to be around to worry about it."

"Yeah, but . . . they had kids, grandkids."

"Denial can cover a lot of ground when you're determined."

They walked and he drank and they pondered issues whose understanding would forever be denied them.

"How does something like that even get started in a town like this?" Matt said. "I bet they didn't even mean it."

"I don't know about that. Whatever happened here, it didn't happen because they were half-assed about it."

"At first, I mean, when they first started. I'll bet it was like some small town, good old boy version of the Hellfire Clubs."

"Hellfire Clubs?" This was a new one. "That sounds ominous enough to me."

"It wasn't. They were just something a bunch of upper crust English and Irish politicians and other outwardly pious types did for a lark. An excuse for them to get together to frolic with whores and feel like bad boys." Matt looked at her, and couldn't have missed her puzzled expression, how this was in his storehouse of knowledge. "I used to read up on stuff like that. When I was a kid, once I got to a certain point, all my favorite bands and musicians, they seemed like there was something dangerous about them. You'd hear how they were *into* things. Secret things. It seemed like maybe they knew stuff nobody else did. It seemed like it should be true. How else could they be so good at what they did? But eventually you realize it's just an image."

"That must've been disappointing," she said.

"I don't know what was worse." He threw his empty can to the ground, because who cared anymore. "Deciding it's all bullshit? Or realizing there's something to it after all, and these goobers here were the ones who figured it out."

⊸⊹⊱

Beasley remained stable over the days to come, but word of his condition had spread. There was no way of keeping a thing like that quiet. Everyone in Tanner Falls had a vested interest in his health, and its insistence on declining set off a fresh wave of subdued panic.

One would think they'd gotten it out of their systems years ago. But no.

At the sound of a daybreak ruckus on her day off, Bethany looked out to see the Hendersons, across the street and three houses down, stuffing their sedan with as much as it could hold. Middle-aged husband, middle-aged wife, twenty-something son still living with them because job prospects were dim. They loaded and argued, squabbled and hurried, and then, in a streak of taillights, they were gone.

As if nobody had ever thought of this before.

If it was happening on their block, she assumed that fear had pushed others across town into trying it, too, hopes bolstered by the mantra of the desperate: *Maybe this time will be different.*

Yeah, good luck with that.

Nearly everyone able-bodied enough to do it had attempted at least once over the last two decades to get away. Failed efforts, all. The early, unsuspecting ones were those who simply had normal, greener-pastures reasons to move along. The later refugees fled in terror, compelled by the very inability of others to leave, and the rumors that had started to spread about why the town shrugged off every attempt at modernity and change.

They'd tried everything from moving vans to impulse exits with little more than the clothes on their backs. They'd driven cars, taken buses, ridden motorcycles. The more adventurous ones had attempted it on foot, as if to steal away with no more noise than what their shoes made would let them pass beneath the notice of what waited and watched, ready to corral them like straying livestock.

Everyone, it seemed, had to prove it for themselves, and often more than once.

They would be back.

The Hendersons would be back.

‹•›

While Matt slept, she made coffee and set up watch from the porch that night, all cool air and the creaking of crickets. How more normal a night could anyone ask for? Except for the first aid kit by her chair, just in case.

The moon had arced halfway across the sky before things started to happen, when the streetlights flickered and dimmed. However these entities moved, it seemed to create electromagnetic disturbances. It seemed more than a simple factor of visibility. Dimensions, some speculated. They moved in and out of different dimensions.

Bethany had no recollection of the experience herself.

One moment they weren't there, and the next they were, like full-grown trees sprouted on the Hendersons' lawn. But trees didn't scuttle from one place to another, or wield their branches like arms. They were visible only for a few moments, more shadows than details. Far too tall to fit in the house, the three of them simply smashed a pair of second-story windows with their crowns of appendages and jammed their cargo through, then scuttled away from the house and faded from view as if they'd never been there at all.

Had they been aware of her watching them? One seemed to pause and turn her way, but nothing about them remotely suggested that they had faces, much less eyes.

Surprisingly few people had seen them, even though most had been carried by them. These, the general consensus went, were but a few of the Thousand Young, left behind to enforce the pact.

She grabbed her bag and hurried for the Hendersons' house. She wondered how far they'd gotten, and where the car was, if they'd ever see it again, or the possessions they'd deemed important enough to carry. If they would even care. In maintaining the status quo, vehicles didn't seem to matter. People were paramount.

They'd locked their front door when they left this morning, but had overlooked the back, so she let herself into the house that way. It was as silent as it was dark, until she blindly slapped a light switch in the kitchen, then heard them overhead as they started to awaken. They got louder as she made her way up the stairs—the weeping, the sounds on the verge of screams, as if they hadn't yet processed what had happened. These were not cries of physical pain. She was intimately familiar with those. These were worse, in a way. Pain could be managed. Hopelessness and despair came from a deeper place than nerve endings.

She found them lying huddled in the shards of their windows. Cuts, bruises, scrapes—that was the worst of it. She could treat those. The trauma might take a lot longer to get over.

More likely, Old Mad Donald would be dead before they had a chance.

◂◦▸

As went the Hendersons, so went the rest of Tanner Falls.

Few things were more contagious than panic, and few people were in a better position to gauge it than hospital staff. The accident rate spiked again, the way it did whenever fresh fears arose over Donald Beasley's mortality, and those prone to dulling their fears with drink did what drunks often do.

Had Beasley and the others foreseen *this*, in their selfishness?

The suicide rate spiked, too . . . or rather, attempted suicides. It never worked. They were brought in by paramedics and frantic families, and occasionally they came in under their own ghastly power—people who should've been dead, bodies broken, veins opened, brains exposed, yet somehow life had been refused exit. There was nothing worse to treat than screaming people who should've been in the morgue, and knew it; who wanted to be there, and were denied it.

Had Beasley and the rest meant for *this* to happen, in trying to preserve the town they'd claimed to love?

All along, townsfolk had continued to die of natural causes, but cheating was not allowed. Which didn't keep the desperate from trying anyway. They learned the folly of it no better than those who tried to flee, but at least the runners weren't shattering their bodies in the process. In trying to kill themselves, they had instead been slowly killing her sense of compassion, which made it all the easier for Bethany to hate them for it.

The adults, anyway.

It wasn't in her—not yet—to hate today's casualty. Allison, the girl's name. She'd hung from her back yard noose all night, and by the time her father discovered her this morning, her slim neck was stretched by inches. This soon, it was impossible to say if she would ever hold her head upright again. She was fifteen years old.

You did what you could. You made them comfortable. You tried not to contract their despair.

This was no way to live. For anyone.

And as she needed to do more and more, once a crisis was over, Bethany retreated into the hospital hall to shake it out. Soon there followed the smell of cigarette smoke. She'd come to welcome the stink of it, for these little moments of decompression with Dr. Richard.

"There's no meaning in this anymore," said the man who, two weeks ago, vowed to crawl inside Beasley's chest before letting him die.

For the first time in her life, she wished she smoked too, because if she did, that was exactly what she would be doing now. She pointed to the fuming stick between his fingers. "Those things'll kill you, you know."

"If only." He seemed to contemplate snuffing it out, then didn't. "That's been the idea. But I don't think cancer likes me."

"The ones who die naturally . . . do you really think they've escaped what's coming?" she asked. "Or did they just get scooped up earlier than the rest of us?"

He shrugged. "A moot point for me. It was worth a try."

The hallway windows overlooked a stretch of parking lot, and beyond that stood a neighborhood of grand old houses, and beyond that the buildings of downtown, most prominently the Tanner Hotel, with that hateful sign they could never be rid of. It was the tallest thing around. They all lived under it, no matter where their homes were.

"You know, I've never believed in life at all costs. I've been called a heretic for it. Just not by anybody whose good opinion of me mattered," Richard told her. "I could never see the value of using extraordinary measures to squeeze day after day of life out of a patient when the only thing we're accomplishing is prolonging suffering. Quality of life always seemed the better benchmark to me. Somehow I got away from that."

As they stared out the window, from somewhere beyond view came the sound of another siren.

"Is this *really* quality of life?"

"Matt, my husband, says we should go out to Route Fifteen and repaint the *Welcome to Tanner Falls* sign to read *Death Row*," she said. "But of course, that would be change."

"Can't have that." Richard clucked disapproval. "Don't most patients, when it's terminal, want to be the ones to choose when they die? I think they do."

"It's the last decision they can control. At least, it should be."

"Exactly," he said. "I think I'll have a word with the mayor."

She felt the weight of responsibility bearing down from above, from Donald Beasley's room on the second floor. How nice to be rid of it.

"Are you getting at what I think you are?" she asked.

"Probably."

So it had come to this. After a moment's shock, she was surprisingly at peace with it. Then thought of her fellow nurse, Janet, sitting watch over the most hated man in the town's history. *I'd start with his eyes . . .*

"You need to offer people more than just a choice." She couldn't believe the words coming out of her. But it had come to this. "You need to offer them participation."

◂•▸

On the day of the special election, she took another turn as watch-nurse, sitting at Donald Beasley's bedside, listening to the reassuring beep of the cardiac monitor, watching the rise and fall of his chest. Machines hummed and puffed. His face and arms were a topography of wrinkles and tubes.

He was awake, even cognizant. He studiously avoided her, preferring instead to look straight ahead at the far wall, until, after an hour of being ignored, Bethany scooted her chair close enough to lean on the bed rail, and to smell the dry musty odor of him, so he couldn't pretend her away any more.

"I get it," she told him. "I really do. How scared you all must have been. That's the last word any of you would've used with each other, or with yourselves, but that's exactly what you were. Scared. Grown men as scared as little boys when the bully shows up to take a toy truck away."

The more she had to say, the more he creaked his head away from her, toward the window and its view of the town that despised him.

"No, I get it. The whole world must've looked like it was changing all at once back then, and none of it into a place you wanted to go. Guys like my husband, they grew their hair out and started playing music you couldn't understand. Girls like me, they got birth control pills and started realizing there could be a life beyond the kitchen and the crib. We discovered drugs you shot-and-a-beer types never dreamed of."

Now that she'd started, she couldn't turn it off.

"And black people, there was no keeping them to the back of the bus anymore, was there? It didn't matter how many of their leaders bigots like you shot, or how many dogs or firehoses you turned on them, they were going to keep coming no matter what, and that must've scared you most of all."

Under his sheet, Beasley quivered with what she hoped was impotent rage.

"You armchair patriots, you had a war the country was turning against, and deep down, maybe you even suspected that the men who wanted to keep it going were lying to you whenever it fit their agenda, only you were too dug in to admit it."

She wanted tears from him. Maybe he was finally too dried out to weep.

"The world was leaving you behind. You cowards. Everything was slipping away from you. You were probably afraid someone like Charles Manson was going to show up any day, if you didn't do something. *I get it.* So if you couldn't stop the rest of the world from moving on, you wanted to stay hunkered down here in Mayberry while it did. And I can't blame you for that, for being cowards, because that's what cowards do. It's the nature of the beast to cringe."

Under the sheet, his shallow breath had visibly quickened, and the cardiac monitor pulsed more rapidly.

"But how do you go from that to sacrificing everybody else's lives just to sustain your own illusions a little longer? That's a whole different level of greed. A bunch of goddamn sociopaths, the lot of you."

If he had a massive heart attack now, that would be the most merciful thing for him. But he didn't. Good.

"How much could you all *really* have loved your town when you bargained it away to something that shouldn't even exist? Just to keep it the way it was, until the last of your little group was dead, and then to hell with the rest of us, because we were only . . . what, bargaining chips?"

At last, with effort, Beasley rolled his head back to face her.

"The Goat," he whispered, slowly, with a sound like dry reeds. "The Black Goat . . . we never thought she would answer."

Maybe Matt was right. Maybe this whole unconscionable situation began as a stupid lark. Sad little men, still frolicking with whores and pretending to be bad boys, desperate to hold onto what was theirs a little longer, a little longer.

"Here's something else you never thought of." She shouldn't have been telling him, but it seemed important that he experience dread, the same as the rest of them. "Ever since people started to figure this out, the only thing that's kept you alive and whole is their fear of what will happen when you die. But even something like that runs its course. So you may not get off as easily as you thought. You know what's happening right now? The entire town is voting on what to do with you. To see if they're willing to trade these last few days, weeks, whatever we have . . . whatever *you* have . . . for the satisfaction of making you suffer."

And there—there it was. The terror in his eyes. It was what they all needed.

"I already voted before I came to work," she said. "I voted in favor of it."

⟵⟶

To the surprise of few, the special ballot initiative passed: 3,658 in favor, 2,077 against, and another 5,100 or so who didn't bother turning out one way or another.

Judgment Day, people were calling it, and preachers argued against it with all the effectiveness of street corner lunatics. The town wanted blood now. There was no divine intervention coming, so they would take what they could get.

It happened in the town square. Thousands filled the streets, while thousands more stayed home. On the courthouse lawn, they erected the platform used for speeches on Veterans Day, Memorial Day, a half-dozen different kinds of parade days.

The mayor was there to officiate, and police officers to keep order, and when Donald Beasley was brought in an ambulance, the crowd parted like water to let it through. His care team was down to just two: one physician, Dr. Richard, and one nurse, her colleague, Janet Swain. Even though they were overseeing his death, their job was still the same: to keep him alive as long as possible.

And Janet got her wish. She drew first blood, taking Beasley's left eye. He'd been strapped to a gurney that was propped upright, so the crowd could see it happen, and a roaring cheer went up at the sight of the emptied socket.

He may have been seventy-six years old, and looked at least a hundred, but he squealed like a feeble child.

Out in the crowd, a few rows away, Bethany averted her gaze to the ground and squirmed her hand into Matt's, to hold tight for as long as they had remaining.

"Do you want to leave?" he asked.

She shook her head. "If you vote for something like this, you should be prepared to see it through."

Anyone who wished it got to take a turn, ushered into a line that filed up the steps on one side of the platform, descended on the other, and as far as what happened in the middle, that was up to them. Some were content to curse Beasley, others to spit on him. The rest were not so easily sated. They slapped him, sliced him, pried off nails with pliers. They took his ears. They knocked out teeth. They ground cigarettes into his forehead, and drizzled trenches into his skin with droppers full of acid.

The cheering quit long before the line was through.

People stayed, people left, people sobbed with a thousand different sorrows. Some were sick. Others wanted to get back in the line again. A few started laughing and never stopped.

Bethany reminded herself that there was a time when Tanner Falls had been a great place to grow up. Scrape the veneer away, though, and this was what you got.

The line kept advancing even after Beasley was pronounced dead, and why not. He may have cheated them out of tomorrow, but they weren't about to let him cheat them out of one last chance to take it out on his corpse.

They had an hour, give or take, before the sky pulsed with a single flash of light—green, perhaps, or blue, or maybe it was no color in the known spectrum. A fearsome wind kicked up, blowing west, pulled toward the source of the flash. They had felt this wind before.

She clutched Matt's hand so hard it had to hurt him. Had to.

All around them, their neighbors shrieked and scattered by the hundreds, and though they were buffeted from all sides, she and Matt decided not to bother. When had running *ever* worked?

"I had this dream last night," he told her, his voice starting to shake. "It felt so real. As real as life. I dreamed I was given some sort of pipe to play for God in the chaos at the heart of the universe."

Soon it became visible over distant trees and rooftops, dark and boiling, as mercurial in appearance as a storm cloud. So this was what they had summoned, called up, bargained with . . . this, the Black Goat of the Woods with a Thousand Young. It was a deity from nightmares still seeking its hold in the world, and in the east, the north, the south, wherever people had fled, they all soon found reason to shriek there, as well. Tanner Falls resounded with it. A thousand young could round up a lot of stragglers.

"So maybe we'll be okay," Matt said.

Closer, and closer still, it rent the air with a screech as if lightning could speak. It churned with mouths that opened and closed and reappeared elsewhere in the anarchy of its form.

"Why," she said, "would you ever think that?"

Three blocks away, it detoured toward the hospital, passing by it, passing *through* it, this warehouse of failed suicides, and timeless moments later the sky disgorged a furious rain of meat and blood.

"What if it could've had us all along?" Matt said. "But waited anyway?"

It was coming.

"Why would it have done that?"

Coming for the town square.

"Maybe it was curious. Maybe it wanted to see what we would do."

It was coming, as ground and pavement alike steamed beneath its pile-driver hooves.

"And maybe now, here, today," Matt said, "some of us finally became . . . worthy."

Bethany shut her eyes as tightly as her hand held Matt's, as it bore down on them with the sound and fury of a cyclone.

At last. At last. At long, elusive last . . .

It was time to leave home.

GRAVE GOODS

GEMMA FILES

Put the pieces back together, fit them against each other chip by chip and line by line, and they start to sing. There's a sort of tone a skeleton gives off; Aretha Howson can feel it more than hear it, like it's tuned to some frequency she can't quite register. It resonates through her in layers: skin, muscle, cartilage, bone; whispers in her ear at night, secret, liquid. Like blood through a shell.

The site they're working on is probably Early Archaic—6,500 B.P. or so, going strictly by contents, thus beating out the recent Bug River find by almost 2,000 years. Up above the water-line, too, which makes it *incredibly* unlikely; most people lived in lakeshore camps back then, right when the water levels were at their lowest after the remnant ice mass from the last glacial advance lying across the eastern outlet of Lake Superior finally wasted away, causing artificially high lake levels to drop over a hundred metres. Then isostatic rebound led to a gradual return, which is why most sites dating between the end of the Paleo-Indian and 4,000 years ago are largely under water.

Not this one, though: it's tucked up under a ridge of granite, surrounded by conifer old growth so dense they had to park the vehicles a mile away and cut their way in on foot, trying to disturb as little as possible. Almost a month later—a hideously cold, rainy October, heading straight for

Hallowe'en—the air still stinks of sap, stumps bleeding like wounds. Dr. Anne-Marie Begg's people hauled the trunks out one by one, cross-cut the longest ones, then loaded them up and took them back to the Reserve, where they'll be planed in the traditional manner and used for rebuilding. Always a lot of home improvement projects on the go, over that way; that's what Anne-Marie—Dr. Begg—says.

Though Canadian ethics laws largely forbid excavations, once Begg brought Dr. Elyse Lewin in to consult, even the local elders had to agree this particular discovery merited looking into. They've been part of the same team practically since Begg was Lewin's favourite TA, operating together out of Lakehead University, Thunder Bay; Lewin's adept at handling funding and expedition planning, while Begg handles both tribal liaison duties and general PR, plus almost anything else to do with the media. It was Begg who sowed excitement about "Pandora's Box," as the pit's come to be called, on account of the flat slab of granite—lightly incised with what look like ancestral petroglyphs similar to those found on Qajartalik Island, in the Arctic—stoppering it like a bottle. Incised on top *and* below, as Aretha herself discovered when they pried it apart, opening a triangular gap large enough to let her jump in; shone the flashlight downwards first, just far enough to check her footing before she landed—down on one knee, a soggy crouch, too cramped to straighten fully—then automatically reversed it, revealing those square-cut, coldly eyeless faces set in silent judgement right above her head.

"How'd they get it here?" Morgan, the other intern, asks Lewin, who shrugs and glances at Begg before letting her answer.

"The slab itself, that's found, not made—shaped a little, probably. More than enough rockfall in this area for that, post-glacial shear. Then they'd have made an earthwork track like at Stonehenge, dug underneath—" Begg uses her hands to sketch the movements in midair. "—then piled in front, put down logs overtop, used them like rollers. Get enough people pushing and pulling, you're golden."

Lewin nods. "Yes, exactly. Once the grave was dug, there'd be no particular problem fitting it overtop; just increase the slope 'til they had a hill and push it up over the edge, down-angled so one side touched the opposite lip, before dismantling the hill to lay it flat again."

"Mmm." Morgan turns slightly, indicating: "What're the carvings for, though? Like . . . what do they mean?"

"Votive totems," Begg replies, with confidence.

The forensics expert—Dr. Tatiana Huculak—just shakes her head. "No way to know," she counters. "Told us yourself they don't look like any of the ritual marks you grew up with, remember? So it's like a sign in Chinese, for all of us—just as likely to say 'fuck you' as 'God bless,' unless you know Pinyin."

Begg's already opening her mouth to argue when Lewin sees Aretha's hand go up; she shushes them both. "Oh dear, you don't have to do *that*!" she exclaims. "Just sing out, if an idea's struck you."

Aretha hesitates, eyes flicking to Morgan, who nods. Courage in hand, she replies—

"Uh, maybe. I mean—even when you don't know the language, there's still a lot you can get from context, right? Well . . ." She hauls herself up, far enough past the slab to tap its top, nails grating slightly over rough-edged stone. "'Keep out,' that'd be my guess," she concludes. "'Cause it's up here."

Lewin nods, as Huculak and Begg exchange glances. "Logical. And down there? On the underside?"

Here Aretha shrugs, uncomfortably unanonymous for once, pinned beneath the full weight of all three professors' eyes.

". . . 'stay in?'" she suggests, finally.

◄◦►

Working this dig with Lewin's team was supposed to be the best job placement ever, a giddy dream of an archaeological internship—government work with her way paid up front, hands-on experience, the chance to literally uncover something unseen since thousands of years BCE. By the end of the first week, however, Aretha was already beginning to dream about smothering almost everyone else in their sleep or hanging herself from the next convenient tree, and the only thing that's improved since then is that she's now far too exhausted to attempt either.

Doesn't help that the rain which greeted them on arrival still continues, cold and constant, everything covered in mud, reeking of pine needles. Sometimes it dims to a fine mist, penetrating skin-deep through Aretha's heaviest raincoat; always it chills, lighting her bone-marrow up with sharp threads of ache, air around her so cold it hurts to inhale through an open mouth. Kneeling here in the mud, she sees her breath boil up as cones fall down through the dripping, many-quilled branches, their sticky impacts signalled with rifle-shot cracks, and every day starts the same, ends the same: wood mould burning in her eyes and sinuses like smoke, impossible to ward off, especially since the Benadryl ran out.

"Jesus," Morgan suddenly exclaims, like she just hasn't noticed it before, "that's one hell of a cold you've got there, Ree. Does Lewin know?"

Aretha shrugs, droplets scattering; hard to do much else, when she's up to her elbows in grave-gunk. And: "Uh, well . . . yeah, sure," she replies, vaguely. "Can't see how she wouldn't."

"Close quarters, and all? You're probably right. But who knows, huh? I mean . . ." Here Morgan trails off, eyes sliding back to the main tent—over which two very familiar voices are starting to rise, yet again—before returning to the task at hand. ". . . she's kinda—distracted, these days, with . . . everything. I guess."

"Guess so."

Inside the main tent, Begg and Huculak are going at each other like ideological hammer and tongs, as ever—same shit, different day, latest instalment in an infinite series. It's been a match made in hell, pretty much since the beginning; Huculak's specialization makes her view all human remains as an exploitable resource, while Begg's tribal band liaison status puts her in charge of making sure everything that could conceivably once have been a person gets put right back where it was found after cataloguing, with an absolute minimum of ancestral disrespect. Of course, Begg's participation is basically the only reason they're all here in the first place, as Lewin makes sure to keep reminding Huculak—but from Huculak's point of view, just because she knows it's true doesn't mean she has to pretend to like it.

"I'll point out, yet again," Huculak's saying right now, teeth audibly gritted, "that the *single easiest way* we could get a verifiable date on this site continues to be if we could take some of the bones back and carbon-date them, in an honest-to-Christ lab . . ."

Aretha can almost see Begg curtly shaking her head, braids swinging—the way she does about fifty times a day, on average—as she replies. "Carbon-date the grave goods, then, Tat, to your heart's content—carbon-date the *shit* out of them, okay? Grind them down to paste, you want to; burn them, smoke the fucking ashes. But the bones, themselves? *Those* stay here."

"Oh, 'cause one of 'em might share maybe point-one out of a hundred-thousandth part of their genetic material with yours? Bitch, please."

Lewin's voice here, smooth and placatory as ever: "Ladies! Let's be civil, shall we? We all have to work together, after all, for a good month more . . ."

"Unfortunately," Huculak snaps back, probably making Begg puff up like a porcupine. Hurling, back in her turn—

"Hey, don't denigrate my spirituality just because you don't share it, is that so hard? Say we were in Africa, digging up Rwandan massacre dumps—things'd be different *then,* right?"

"You know, funny thing about that, Anne-Marie: not really. They'd be the same way anyplace, for me, because I am a *scientist,* first and foremost. Full friggin' stop."

"And I'm not, is what you mean."

"Well . . . if the moccasin fits."

At that, Aretha whips her head around sharply, only to meet Morgan's equally-disbelieving gaze halfway. The both of them staring at each other, like: *seriously?* Holy cultural slap-fight with potential impending fisticuffs, Batman. *Wow.*

"Knock-down drag-out by six, seven at the latest," Morgan mutters, sidelong. "I'm callin' it now—fifty on Tat to win, unless Anne-Marie puts her down with the first punch. You in, or what?"

Aretha hisses out something that can't quite be called a laugh. "Pass, thanks."

Morgan shrugs, then turns back to her designated task, head shaking slightly. "Your loss."

Going by her initial pitch, Lewin genuinely seems to have thought hiring only female associates and students would guarantee this little trip going far more smoothly than most, as though removing all traces of testosterone from the equation would create some sort of paradisical meeting of hearts and minds: cycles synched, hands kept busy, no muss, no fuss. The principle, however, was flawed from its inception: *just 'cause they ain't no peckers don't mean ain't no peckin' order,* as Aretha's aunties have often been heard to remark, 'round the all-gal sewing circle they run after hours out of their equally all-girl cleaning service's head office. It frankly amazes Aretha how Lewin could ever have gotten the idea that women never bring such divisive qualities as ambition, wrath, or lust to the metaphorical table, when she's spent the bulk of her career teaching at all-girl facilities across the U.S., before finally ranging up over the border—

But whatever. Maybe Lewin's really one of those evo-psych nuts underneath the Second Wave feminist frosting, forever hell-bent on mistaking biology for destiny no matter the context. Just as well she's apparently never thought to wonder exactly what those pills Aretha keeps choking down each day are, if so.

On puberty blockers since relatively early diagnosis, thank Christ, so she never did reach the sort of giveaway heights her older brothers have, and her voice hasn't changed all that much, either; that, plus no Adam's apple, facial and body hair kept chemically downy as any natal female in her immediate family, even if the other team-members felt inclined to body-police. But the plain fact is, they've none of them seen each other in any sort of disarray since they left base-camp—it's too cold to strip for sleep, let alone to shower, assuming they even had one.

This is typical paranoia, though, and she knows it; the reason everyone here knows her as Aretha is because she *is*. That's the name under which she entered university, legally, and it'll be the name with which she graduates, just like from high school. She's a long damn way away from where she was born at this point, both literally and figuratively.

Looks back up to find Morgan still looking at her and blushes, sniffing liquid, with nothing handy even halfway clean enough to wipe the result away on. "Sorry," she manages, after a second. "*So* gross, I know, I really do. I just—sorry, *God*."

Morgan laughs. "Dude, it's fine. Who knew, right?"

"Yeah." A pause. "Think it would've been okay, probably, it just hadn't rained the whole fucking time."

"And yet."

". . . and yet."

Morgan has a great smile, really; Aretha'd love to see it closer up sometime, under different circumstances. But right now, little moment of connection under pressure already had, the only thing either of them can really think to do about it is just shrug a little and drift apart once more—Morgan back towards the generator array, which is starting to make those worrying pre-brownout noises yet again, while Aretha heaves herself up out of the pit and stamps sloshily towards the tent itself, planning to sluice her gloved hands under the tarp's overflowing gutter. This brings her so close to the ongoing argument she can finally see what the various players are actually doing, through that space where the tent's ill-laid side gapes open: Begg and Huculak squaring off, with Lewin playing referee. It's not quite at the cat-fight stage yet, but if Morgan's placing bets, Aretha's at least setting her watch.

"Look, Anne-Marie . . ." Huculak says, finally, "I know you want to think these are your people outside, in the grave—but I've been studying them hands-on for weeks now, and I just don't think they were, at all. I don't think these were *anybody's* 'people.'"

"Jesus, Tat! What the hell kind of Othering, colonialist bullshit—"

"No, but seriously. *Seriously.*" Huculak points to a pelvic arrangement, a crushed-flat skull, as much of the spinal column as they've been able to find. "Pelvis slung backwards, like a *bird*, not a mammal. Orbital sockets fully ten ml larger than usual, and side-positioned, not to the front; these people were barely binocular—probably had to cock their heads just to look at something in front of them. Twice as many teeth, half of them canines, back ones serrated: this is a meat-eater, exclusively. And that's not even getting into the number of vertebrae, projection processes to the front and rear of each, locking them together like a snake's . . ."

"You've got three bodies to look at, barely, and you're already pushing taxonomic boundaries? Phylogenetic analysis by traits is a slanted system, makes it too easy by far to mistake clades or haplogroups for whole separate species—"

Ooh, bad move, Dr. Begg, Aretha thinks, even as that last sentence starts, and indeed, by its end Huculak's eyes have widened so far her smile-lines disappear completely. "Oh really, *is* it?" she all but spits. "Golly gee, I didn't *know* that, please tell me more! Hottentot Venus what?"

"You know what I'm saying."

"I know *exactly* what you're saying, yes; do you know what *I'm* saying? Or did you just start shoving your fingers in your ears and singing *lalalala I can't HEEEEAR yooou* the minute I started talking, like usual?"

Begg snorts, explosively. "You've seen the dig, every damn day for a month—it's a *grave*, Tat, you just used the word yourself. Full of grave goods. Animals don't *do* that, if that's what you're implying."

"Of course I'm not saying what's in there is animals, for shit's sake; an offshoot of humanity, maybe—some evolutionary dead end. Like Australopithecus."

"You telling me Australopithecus had snake-spines?"

"*No.* But just because we haven't found something yet doesn't mean it never existed."

"Good line, Agent Mulder."

"Oh *fuck you*, you condescending, indigenocentrist *fuck*—"

Lewin raises her hands, goes to interpose between them, but they ignore her roundly—both wider as well as darker, more built for the long haul, able to shrug her off like a charley-horse. Huculak glares up as Begg stares down, hands on hips and braids still swinging, and demands: "Seriously, is that what we're down to, right now? The black girl and the Indian, calling each other out as racists?"

Huculak twitches like she's about to start throwing elbows, trying to divert the urge to punch first and answer questions later; the movement's actually violent enough to rock Begg back a micro-step, make her start to flinch involuntarily, right before she catches herself.

"You first," is all Huculak replies, finally, voice flat.

And: "*Ladies,*" Lewin puts in again, a tad more frantically. "We're scientists here, yes? Professionals. We can differ, even quarrel, but with *respect*—always respect. This is all simply theory, for now."

Now it's Huculak's turn to snort. "For*ever*, she gets her way," she replies. "And she will."

"Bet your ass," Begg agrees. "'Cause this is Kitchenuhmaykoosib Inninuwug First Nation land, and that's *not* a theory, so those bones go right on back in the ground where we found them, just like your government promised. No debate."

Lewin looks at Huculak. Huculak looks away.

"Never actually thought there would be," she mutters, under her breath.

⤙◦⤚

The grave goods Huculak finds so uninteresting are typical Early Archaic: a predominance of less extensively flaked stone tools with a distinct lack of pottery and smoking pipes, new-style lanceolate projectile points with corner notches and serration along the side of the blades suitable to a mixture of coniferous and deciduous forests, increased reliance on local chert sources. What's odd about it, however, is the sheer size of the overall deposit—far more end scrapers, side scrapers, crude celts, and polished stone *atl-atl* weight-tubes than seem necessary for a mere family burial, which is what the three bodies Begg talked about would indicate: one male, one female, one sexually indistinct adolescent (its pelvis missing, possibly scavenged by animals before the cap-stone was laid).

Folded beneath a blanketing layer of grave goods so large it almost appears to act as a secondary grounding weight, the three bodies nevertheless take pride of place, traces of red ochre still visible on and around all three rather than just the male skeleton, as would be customary. Weirder yet, on closer examination, the same sort of ochre appears to have been painstakingly applied not only to the flensed bones themselves but also to all the grave goods as well, before they were piled on top.

In burials from pre-dynastic Egypt to prehistoric Britain, Aretha knows, red ochre was used to symbolize blood; skeletons were flensed and decorated with it as both a sign of respect and of propitiation, a potential warding off of vampiric ghosts: *take this instead, leave us ours.* With no real sense of an afterlife, the prehistoric dead in general were thought to be eternally jealous, resentful of and predatory towards the living . . . but particularly so if they'd died young, or unjustly, and thus been cheated of everything more they might have accomplished while alive. Like the Lady of Cao, Aretha thinks, or the so-called "Scythian Princess," both of whom died in their twenties, both personages of unusual power (the former the first high-status woman found in Moché culture, the latter actually a Siberian priestess buried in silk and fur and gold), and both of whose tombs also contained the most precious grave good of all, startlingly common across cultures from Mesoamerican to Hindu to Egyptian to Asian: more corpses, often showing signs of recent, violent, *sacrificial* death.

Retainer sacrifice, that's what they call it, Aretha thinks, her head spinning slightly, skull gone hot and numb under its cold, constantly wet cap of skin. *Like slaughtering horses so they can draw the princess's chariot into the underworld, except with people: concubines, soldiers, servants, slaves—maybe chosen by lots, maybe volunteers. Killing for company on that final long day's journey into whatever night comes next. In Egypt, eventually, they started substituting* shawabti *figures instead, magic clay dolls incised with spells swapped in for actual corpses; an image of a thing, just as good as the thing itself. Unless it's not.*

Text taking shape behind her eyes, wavering: she can almost see it on her laptop's screen or maybe even a page somewhere, whatever reference-method she first encountered this information through. How in Mound 72 at Cahokia, largest site of the Mississippian culture (800 to 1600 CE, located near moden St. Louis, Missouri), pits were found filled with mass burials—53 young women, strangled and neatly arranged in two layers; 39 men, women and children, unceremoniously dumped, with several showing signs of not having been fully dead when buried, of having tried to claw their way back out. Another group of four individuals was neatly arranged on litters made of cedar poles and cane matting, arms interlocked, but heads and hands removed.

Most spectacular is the "Birdman," a tall man in his forties, thought to have been an important early Cahokian ruler. He was buried on an elevated platform, covered by a bed of more than 20,000 marine-shell disc beads arranged in the shape of a falcon with the bird's head appearing beneath the man's head, its wings and tail beneath his arms and legs. Below the Birdman another corpse was found, buried facing downward, while surrounding him were piles of elaborate grave goods . . . .

Cahokia was a trade centre, of course, the apex of an empire; makes sense they'd do things big, lay on the bling. This, meanwhile . . . this is different: smaller, meaner. The faces of the three prime skeletons have been smashed, deliberately, as if in an attempt to make them unrecognizable, a spasm of disgust or desecration; God knows, Aretha's spent more than enough time piecing them back together to know how effective that first attack was, how odd that it should be followed up with what reads as an almost equally violent avalanche of reverence. But then there's the cap-stone, the lid, the flensing and the ochre, plus the ochre-saturated grave goods pile itself—all added later, at what had to be great cost to the givers. Like a belated apology.

No retainers, though. Not here.

Not where anybody's thought to look, as yet.

This last thought jolts Aretha out of half-sleep at last, making her sit up so sharply she almost falls over, a blinding surge of pain stitching temple to temple; holds herself still on her sleeping bag, breathing slowly as possible to thwart nausea. She presses her fingers up against the edge of her eyesockets until white dots flicker behind her eyelids, forcing the pain back by pressure and sheer will, until—gradually—the agony recedes. The minute she's able, she slips her boots back on, grabs her excavation spade and trowel and ducks out of her tent.

The mist, cool on her flushed face, brings a moment's relief. Not sure if her giddiness is inspiration or fever, Aretha heads for the grave pit as fast as she can.

The light is dimming; she won't have long. Can't see anybody working, which suggests they're at dinner, in the chow tent. But no, not all of them, it turns out. Because as she pauses by the main tent, she can hear Dr. Begg arguing with someone yet again—over the sat-phone, this time. Who?

Curiosity gets the better of her. She edges up to the tent's outer wall, holding her breath.

". . . don't know *who* she knows, is my point, *Gammé*," Begg says. Aretha frowns, translating: *Gammé* for grandmother, the elder who helped swing the tribal council towards permitting this dig in the first place; Aretha's never heard Begg sound this uncomfortable with her. "But if it's somebody with enough clout, somebody who decides they don't want to honour the arrangement any more—" She stops; sighs. "Might be more money involved, sure. Maybe not. And maybe money's not what we should be thinking about, right now."

A longer pause. "Well, you saw the pictures, right? Yeah, they're the ones Tat already sent. So if people start agreeing with her—" A beat. "Okay, what? No, I'm not going to do that. *No.* Because this is *science*, not story-time, that's why, and by those standards, what Tat says makes *sense*. Muddying the waters with mythology isn't going to—hey, you there? Hello? *Hello?*"

No reply, obviously; the receiver slams down, *bang.* Sometimes the phone cuts out for no reason, even with satellite help—vagaries of location, technology, all that. So: "Oh, fuck *me*," Begg mutters, and goes trudging away, still swearing at herself under her breath.

Mythology?

There was a moment, back in Week One . . . yes, she remembers it now. Sitting around the one smoking camp-fire they'd ever risked as the tarp above dipped and sloshed, Lewin asking Begg to fill in the tribal history of this particular area and Begg replying, slightly snappish, that there wasn't one, as such: *Lots of stories, that's all; heroes and monsters, that kind of shit.* "We don't go up there much, that place, 'cause of the—"

—and a word here, something Aretha'd never heard before, clipped and odd: *buack, paguk, baguck.* Something like that.

(*bakaak*)

Bakaak in *Ojibwe*, pakàk in *Algonquin*, a version of Begg's voice corrected, from somewhere deep inside. *It's an Anishinaabe* aadizookaan, *a fairytale. They split the difference, usually, and call it Baykok.*

Like the Windigo, Morgan suggested, but Begg shook her head. The point of the Windigo, she replied, was that a Windigo started out human, while the Baykok never was.

It's a bunch of puns stuck together. Bakaak *means "skeleton," "bones draped in skin"; thus* bakaakadozo, *to be thin, skinny, poor. Or* bakaakadwengwe, *to have a thin face*—bekaakadwaabewizid, *an extremely thin being. Not to mention how it yells shrilly in the night,* bagakwewewin, *literally clear or distinct cries, and beats warriors to death with a club,* baagaakwaa'ige. *Flings its victim's chest open,* baakaakwaakiganezh, *to eat their liver . . . .*

Why the liver? Aretha asked, but Begg just shrugged.

Why any damn thing? It's a boogeyman, so it has to do something gross. Like giants grinding bones to make their bread.

You could do that, you know, as long as you added flour, Huculak put in, from the fire-pit's far side. *Just a flatbread, though. Bone-meal won't bond with yeast.*

Thank you, Martha Stewart.

Is that what Begg's grandmother just said, over the 'phone? That the skeletons look like Baykok—Baykoks? That Huculak's right, and also wrong? That Begg—

Oh, but Aretha's head is burning now, bright and hot, like the Windigo's legendary feet of fire. So hot the raindrops should sizzle on her skin, except they don't; just keep on falling, soft-sharp, solid points of cold pocking down through the sodden, pine-scented air. And the pit gaping open for her at her feet, a toothless, mud-filled mouth.

She drops to her knees, scrambles over the lip, slides down messily inside.

By the time Morgan comes by it's . . . well, later. Aretha doesn't know by how much, but the light's just about completely gone, and she's long since been reduced to scraping blindly away at the grave's interior walls with her gloved fingers. Looks up to see Morgan blinking down at her through a flashlight beam, and smiles—or thinks she does; her face is far too rigid-numb at this point for it to be any sort of certainty.

"'Lo, Morgan," she calls up, not stopping. "How was dinner?"

"Uh, okay. What . . . what're you *doing* down there, Ree? Exactly?"

"I have to dig."

"Yeah, I can see that. Are you okay? You don't look okay."

"I *feel* okay, though. Mainly. I mean—" Aretha takes a second to shake her head, almost pausing; the pit-walls blur on either side of her, heave dangerously, like they're breathing. Then: "It doesn't matter," she concludes, mainly to herself, and goes back to her appointed task.

"Um, all right." Morgan steps back, raising her voice incrementally with each new name: "Tat, Dr. Huculak, c'mon over here for a minute, will you . . . like, right now? Anne-*Marie? Dr. Lewin!*"

They cluster 'round the edge like flies on a wound, staring in as Aretha just keeps on keeping on, almost up to her wrists now in muck. "Aretha," Dr. Lewin begins, at last, "you do know we mapped out that area already, yes? Since a week ago."

"I remember, doctor."

"You took the measurements, as I recall."

"I remember."

"Okay, so *stop*, damnit," Huculak orders. "You hear me? Look at what you're *doing*, for Christ's sake! Anne-Marie—"

Begg, however, simply shakes her head, hunkering down. "Shut up, Tat," she says, without turning. To Aretha: "Howson, Ree . . . it's Aretha, right?" Aretha nods. "Aretha, did you maybe hear me, before? Up there, on the sat-phone?"

"Yes, Dr. Begg."

"Uh huh; shit. Look . . . the Baykok's just a story, Ree. It's folklore. You're not gonna find a, what—separate bunch of human bones in there, is that what you're thinking? Like a larder?"

Still scratching: "I'm not thinking that, no."

"Then what *are* you thinking?"

Aretha wipes mud off on her cheek, gets some in her mouth, spits brown. "Sacrifice," she answers, once her lips are clear again. "Like at Cahokia; slaves for the underworld, not food. But then again, who knows? Might've been both."

"Uh *huh*. How long you been down there, Ree?"

"I don't know. How long did they co-exist, Neanderthals and Homo habilis? 'Cause they did, right? I'm right about that. Lived long enough to share the same lands, even interbreed, enough so some people have Neanderthal DNA . . . ."

"That's the current theory," Lewin agrees, sharing a quick, dark look with Begg. But: "The hell's she saying?" Huculak demands of Lewin, at almost the same time. "Elyse, don't you *vet* your damn volunteers? We need to get her out, back to the Rez at least, get her airlifted somewhere—"

"Just shut *up*, Tat," Begg repeats, still not turning. "Morgan, you're her friend—on my count, okay? One . . . two . . . ."

But that, precisely, is when the wall of the grave-pit finally gives way. Releases a sudden avalanche of half-liquid earth that sweeps Aretha back, pins her under, crowns and crushes her alike on a swift, dark flood of roots and stones and bones, bones, bones.

Here they are, I was right, she barely has time to think, reeling delirious, her arms full of trophies, struggling to raise them high. *See? See? I was right, they're here, we're*

(*here*)

But who's that, back a little further beyond her team's shocked rim-ring, peering down on her as well? That tall, thin figure with its cocked head, its burning, side-set eyes? Its featureless face carved from jet-black stone?

She hears its scream in her mind, thin but distinct, a far-flung cry. The wail of every shattered skull-piece laid back together and set ringing, tuned to some distant tone: shell-bell, blood-hiss. Words made flesh, at long last.

(*here, yes*)

(*as we always have been*)

(*as we always will*)

◁◦▷

Aretha comes back to herself slowly, lying on a cot in the main tent, pain-paralyzed: hurt all over, inside and out. The out is mainly bruises, scrapes, a general wrenched ache, but the inside—that's something different. Like the world's worst yeast infection, a spike through her bladder, pithing her up the middle and watching her writhe; whole system clenched at once against her own core, a furled agony-seed, forever threatening to bloom.

She'd whimper, even weep, but she can barely bear to breathe. Which at least makes it easy—easi*er*—to keep quiet while the other talk around her, above her, about her.

"Baykok, huh?" Dr. Huculak's saying, while Dr. Begg makes a weird snorting noise. "Looks more like a damn prehistoric serial killer's dump-site, to me. And how'd she know where to dig, anyhow?"

Morgan: "She said she had a dream. Whispered it, when I was taking her vitals."

Dr. Lewin sounds worried; Aretha wishes she thought it was for the right reasons. "Yes, as to that. How bad's her damage?"

"That's one way to put it," Huculak mutters, as Morgan draws a breath, then replies: "Well . . . she's fine, I guess, believe it or not. Physically, anyway."

"What about the—"

Morgan's voice gets harder. "Those scars are old, not fresh. Surgical. And none of our business."

Lewin sighs. "If they mean what I think they mean, I'm not happy with . . . 'her' choice to misrepresent 'herself,' on the project application form."

"Can we not use bullshit scare-quotes, please?" Morgan asks. "I mean— check the University rules and regs, doc. Pronouns are up to the individual, these days."

"Is biology? Aretha is—is female, just because 'she' says 'she' is?"

"Uh, yeah, Dr. L, that's *exactly* what that means. Just like a multiracial person's black if they say they are, or anybody's a Christian if they say so, even if they don't go to church." The fierceness in Morgan's voice puts a lump in Aretha's throat. She cracks her eyes open, tries to find words to thank her with, but her lips won't work; all that comes out is a dry clicking, some insect clearing its throat from inside her mouth.

But Huculak's already moved into the pause anyhow, adding: "Like those things in the pit'd be human, if they could say so."

At this, Begg turns, confronting her. "Excuse me, *things*? We're back there again? What the fuck happened to parallel evolution?"

"Oh, I don't know—tell me again how your elders think of them as ancestors, Anne-Marie. Tell me they *don't* call them monsters."

"Sure, okay: this is Baykok country, like I said that first week, which is why somebody non-tribal—some hiker from Toronto—literally had to stumble over the cap-stone for us to even know it was here, and why we had to cut our way in, after. But all that proves is that superstition's a powerful thing. My *Gammé*'s in her eighties, and frankly, when it comes to archaeology, she doesn't know what she's talking about."

Huculak scoffs. "Yeah, and Schliemann never found eight different versions of Troy by looking where Homer said to, either."

"Oh, so what—folktales are fact disguised, is that the song we're singing? Schliemann using *The Iliad* as a guidebook was the exception, not the rule; he got lucky, and what he found was *not* what he'd been looking for, either. Which is exactly what's happened here, all over."

"A pile of bones that don't look human, with a much larger pile of bones attached which do," says Huculak, voice heavy with sarcasm. "Yeah, sure, no big mystery *there*."

"Well, in point of fact, no. You heard Aretha: retainer sacrifice, like in a hundred other places, and do you really think we need monsters for that?" For once, Begg sounds more exhausted than angry. "It's classic Painted

Bird syndrome, Tat. Whatever makes a person different enough from the herd to be rendered . . . pariah, alien, monstrous: this little family with their wide-spaced eyes and their snake-spines, or my *Gammé* when she came back from Residential School, hair cut and wearing white kid clothes, barely able to speak her own language anymore. Or Aretha here, for that matter, once Elyse got a look at her chest . . . ."

Lewin lifts her hands. "Don't bring me into this, please."

"But you're already *in* it. We all are." Now it's Huculak's turn to sound uncharacteristic, all her usual snark gone. With some difficulty, Aretha turns her head, sees the woman bent down over something long, greyish-brown and filthy: one of the fresh-dug bones, plucked from a teetery, cross-stacked pyramid of such, off the gurney she stands next to. "I mean, I'd need to do a full lab workup to verify, but some of these remains—they still have flesh on them, under the muck. Like, non-mummified flesh."

Dr. Lewin, blinking: "You mean they're—"

"Recent. Yeah."

"But they were buried. How—?"

"You tell me. Anne-Marie?"

Begg opens and closes her mouth. "Well," she starts, "that's obviously—um. Okay. I mean, that's . . ." She deflates, slumping. "I don't know what that is," she says at last, near-inaudibly.

You'd think Huculak would be proud to have thrown her chief rival off so thoroughly, but no; she looks equally taken aback, almost scared. Lewin just stands there, studying the tent's tarp floor, like she's misplaced something; above, rain drums the roof, incessant, a dull cold tide. Morgan's gaze flicks from one to the next as the silence stretches ever more thin, disbelieving, 'til it finally falls on Aretha, and her eyes widen. "Shit—Ree! You're awake!" She hurries over to the cot and kneels down, stroking Aretha's forehead. "How you feeling, babe?"

Babe. In Morgan's mouth, the word sounds good enough to make Aretha cry, or want to.

"Hurts," she husks instead, through chapped lips. "All through my groin, lower abdomen . . ." She tries to move and hisses, agony spiking her joints. "Elbows and knees, ankles, too."

Morgan puts the inside of one wrist to Aretha's forehead, then takes her pulse; Aretha's creeped out by how pale her own wrist looks when hefted slackly in the tent's lantern-light, its veins slightly distended and purpled. "Fever feels like it's gone down, at least," Morgan tells her, attempting an unconvincing smile. "But since that's as far as my Girl Guide first aid training goes, all I can tell you beyond that is you need a hospital, like *now*. Dr. Begg, is the sat-phone working again?"

"Um, no, not yet."

"Fine. You know what? It's half an hour back to the access road; give me that damn thing and I'll get it to where it can get a signal out, then call an airlift to get her down to Thunder Bay."

Lewin puts a hand to her mouth, Victorian as all hell. "Oh dear, not at night, in this rain! What if you get lost, slip and fall, or—?"

"Ma'am, I'll be fine, my boots are hiking-rated. Seriously."

But: "No, Morgan, trust me, bad *bad* idea," Huculak says, Begg nodding agreement. "Wait for daybreak, for the weather to clear, that'll free up the signal link—"

Both stop as Morgan, already bent to lace her boots tighter, slashes one hand across the air.

"I have a compass and a map," she tells them, not looking up, "a flashlight, a knife, and I'm not gonna melt. Plus it's safer on foot than trying to drive, when it's like this. Anybody wants to go instead of me, I'm amenable, but you better speak now or forever hold your peace: Ree's my friend, and I'm not putting her through one second more of this than we have to."

Straightening, she glares 'round, hands on hips, but no one objects. So she stuffs the blocky sat-phone away and ducks down with a shrug instead, planting a swift kiss on Aretha's forehead—too light to fully track, here and then gone, almost hallucinatory. Like a promise.

"See you soon," she murmurs, swinging her knapsack onto her back.

But: *no,* that same voice hisses, from inside Aretha's mind. *I—*

(we)

—think not.

⟡

Aretha doesn't remember falling asleep. When she wakes, the pain has diminished astonishingly; not gone, still twinging through her hips and knees when she swings herself into a tentative sitting position, but so much less it's near-euphoric. She feels light-headed, insubstantial; even the forest's damp pine-reek doesn't burn the way it used to. For a few moments, she simply enjoys breathing with something like her normal ease.

Then she sees the light, or lack thereof. The similar lack of company. No sat-phone on the table, just dirt and bones. No Morgan.

Shit.

Wrapping the sleeping bag around her like a puffy cloak, she stumbles out into open air, for once blessedly free of rain; no visible sky between the trees, but there's less sinus-drag, cueing a possible shift in air pressure. Lewin, Begg and Huculak are huddled around a Coleman stove maybe ten feet away, clustered gnats and moths flying up like sparks; Lewin turns as Aretha nears, almost smiling as she recognizes her, which is . . . odd, but welcome. Things *must* be bad.

"Aretha!" she calls out, voice only a little strained on the up-note. "You look—better. Than you did."

Aretha clears her throat, even as the other two shoot Lewin looks whose subtext both clearly read *are you fucking kidding me?* ". . . thanks," she manages, finally. Then: "Morgan?"

Lewin sighs. "No, dear. Not yet."

"How—long?"

"Two hours, maybe three," Huculak replies. "Anne-Marie went out looking, but—"

"I didn't find her," Begg says, a bit too quickly, too flat. "Not her."

Aretha nods, swallows again. No spit.

"What *did* you find?" she asks.

Tracks, that's the answer; about five minutes' walk from the camp. They're narrow but deep, as if carved, each a slipper full of dark liquid, welling up from underground. The soil is saturated here, Aretha can only suppose, after a solid four and a half weeks of precipitation—but there's something about the marks, both familiar and un-. They look . . . wrong, somehow. Turned upside-down.

"They're backwards," she observes, at last. Bends closer, just a bit, and wavers, not trusting herself to be able to crouch; the water throws back light, Huculak's beam crossing Lewin's as Begg hovers next to them, holding back, waiting to see if Aretha can eventually identify that particular winey shade without prompting.

"Not water," Aretha says, throat clicking drier yet, and Begg shakes her head. "No," she confirms, and Aretha dips further, sniffing hard. Smells rust, and rot, and meat.

Blood.

Lewin recoils, almost tripping, but Huculak stands her ground, demanding: "And you didn't think to tell us? The *fuck,* Anne-Marie!"

Begg stays where she is, rooted fast, as though every ounce of protest in her has long since drained out through her heels. Doesn't even bother shrugging.

"Not much point," she says, simply. "You'd've found out eventually too, once either of you thought to ask. But Aretha here's been a whole lot better at that than most of us throughout, hasn't she? Which is sort of interesting, in context."

"How so?"

"Things my *Gammé* told me over the years, that's all, about this area. Stuff I discounted automatically, pretty much, because—well, *you* know why, Tat: because science. Empirical data vs. subjective belief, all that. Because I've tried so fucking hard to never be *that* sort of Indian, if I can help it." She pauses here, takes a ragged breath. "But what do you know, huh? Sometimes, a monster isn't a metaphor for prejudice at all, plus or minus power. Sometimes, it's just a monster."

Huculak stares at her, like she's grown another head. "What?" she asks, yet again.

"What I just said, Tat. We should probably get going, if we're going to."

"Going to—?" Lewin apparently can't help prompting, carefully.

Begg sighs, windily, as though about to deflate. "Try, that's what I mean," she says, after a long moment's pause. "To leave, I mean. Before they get here."

"'They,'" Lewin repeats. "They . . . who?"

Now it's Begg's turn to stare, even as Huculak—possibly just a tad swifter on the uptake, or simply paranoid enough to connect the dots without being asked—draws a sudden in-breath, a choked half-gasp; hugs herself haphazardly, grasping for comfort, but finding none. While Lewin just stands there, visibly baffled: it doesn't make sense to her, any of it, and *can't,* really. Not in any *scientific* way.

"They were here first, that's what *Gammé* always told me," Dr. Begg—Anne-Marie—remarks, softly, as if to herself. "Hunted us like animals when we came into their territory, because that's what we must have seemed like to them, the same way *they* did, to us; things with some qualities of people, not people who just happen to look like things. So we fought back, because that's what we do, but there were more of them, and they were—stronger, fought harder. Started out taking us for food, then for slaves, then for breeding stock. Changed so they could hide, everywhere. Hide inside of *us*."

"Neanderthals," Aretha says. "And *Homo habilis*."

Begg smiles, slightly. "The current theory," she replies, echoing Lewin. Not looking 'round as she does, even to watch how Lewin—her cognitive refusal suddenly punctured, sharp and clean and quick—begins, at last, to buckle under her own words' weight.

Behind them, the grave-site still gapes uncovered, rain-filled, ochre seeping. From above, Aretha muses, the unearthed cache of grave goods must look like a huge, slightly layered blood-blotch, all that remains of some unspeakably old crime. An apology made on literally bended knees, pot sweetened with a pile of tools and corpses, yet left forever unaccepted.

Huculak—Tat—clears her throat, knuckles still knit and paling on either elbow. Complains, voice weak: "But . . . we didn't know."

"I did."

"You never *said*, though."

"No, 'course not, because I didn't want to think it was true. I mean, c'mon, Tat; seriously, now. Would *you?*"

"Well . . ."

(No.)

Deep twilight, now, under the trees, overlaid with even deeper silence. Deep enough Aretha can finally start to hear it once more, rising the same way her pain does, threading itself through her system: the song of the bones, set shiver-thrumming in every last wet, cold part of her; that note, that tone, so thin and distinct, a faraway cry drawing ever nearer. Like blood through some fossilized shell.

And oh, oh: *Anne-Marie was right, not to want to,* she thinks, faintly, as she feels her knees start to give way—as she droops, drops, ends up on hands and knees in the mud, the blood-smelling earth. *I'm not even Native, and I don't like that story much, either. Not at all.*

Not at all.

"Who's that?" Aretha can hear Lewin—Elyse—call out, faintly, squinting past her, into the darkness. Adding, hopefully, as she does: "Morgan? I—is that you, dear?"

To which Anne-Marie just shakes her head, while Tat begins to sob. And Aretha, looking up—seeing those familiar features hanging flat against the thickening curtain of night, mouth slack-hung and eyes empty, set every-so-slightly askew—doesn't even have to wait to hear the bones' answer to know the trick of it already, to her sorrow: that skeletal shadow poised behind, head cocked, holding Morgan's skin up like an early Hallowe'en mask with the scent of fresh-eaten liver on its breath. That line of similar shadows fanned behind, making their stealthy, back-footed way towards them all, with claws outstretched.

Don't worry, the bones' song tells her, from the inside out, as the Baykok sweep in. *This darkness is yours as much as ours, after all: a legacy, passed down hand to hand, from our common ancestors. Where we are, and were, and have been. Where you are, now, and always.*

The only place any of us have left to be.

Not so different, then, after all: cold comfort at best, and none at all, at worst. Not that it really matters, either way.

Every grave is our own, that's the very last thing Aretha Howson has time to think, before the earth opens up beneath her. Before she falls headlong, wondering who will find her bones, and when—what tales they'll tell, when dug free . . . what songs they'll sing, when handled . . . .

How long it'll be, this time, before anyone stops to listen.

THE BALLAD OF
BALLARD AND SANDRINE

PETER STRAUB

1997

"So, do we get lunch again today?" Ballard asked. They had reached the steaming, humid end of November.

"We got fucking lunch yesterday," replied the naked woman splayed on the long table: knees bent, one hip elevated, one boneless-looking arm draped along the curves of her body, which despite its hidden scars appeared to be at least a decade younger than her face. "Why should today be different?"

After an outwardly privileged childhood polluted by parental misconduct, a superior education, and two failed marriages, Sandrine Loy had evolved into a rebellious, still-exploratory woman of forty. At present, her voice had a well-honed edge, as if she were explaining something to a person of questionable intelligence.

Two days before joining Sandrine on this river journey, Ballard had celebrated his sixty-fifth birthday at a dinner in Hong Kong, one of the cities where he conducted his odd business. Sandrine had not been invited to the dinner and would not have attended if she had. The formal, ceremonious side of Ballard's life, which he found so satisfying, interested her not at all.

Without in any way adjusting the facts of the extraordinary body she had put on display, Sandrine lowered her eyes from the ceiling and examined him with a glance brimming with false curiosity and false innocence. The glance also contained a flicker of genuine irritation.

Abruptly and with vivid recall, Ballard found himself remembering the late afternoon in 1969 when, nine floors above Park Avenue, upon a carpet of almost unutterable richness in a room hung with paintings by Winslow Homer and Albert Pinkham Ryder, he had stood with a rich scapegrace and client named Lauritzen Loy, his host, to greet Loy's daughter on her return from another grueling day at Dalton School, then observed the sidelong, graceful, slightly miffed entrance of a fifteen-year-old girl in pigtails and a Jackson Brown sweatshirt two sizes too large, met her gray-green eyes, and felt the very shape of his universe alter in some drastic way, either expanding a thousand times or contracting to a pinpoint, he could not tell. The second their eyes met, the girl blushed, violently.

She hadn't liked that, not at all.

"I didn't say it was going to be different, and I don't think it will." He turned to look at her, making sure to meet her gaze before letting his eye travel down her neck, over her breasts, the bowl of her belly, the slope of her pubis, the length of her legs. "Are you in a more than ordinarily bad mood?"

"You're snapping at me."

Ballard sighed. "You gave me that *look*. You said, 'Why should today be different?'"

"Have it your way, old man. But as a victory, it's fucking pathetic. It's hollow."

She rolled onto her back and gave her body a firm little shake that settled it more securely onto the steel surface of the table. The metal, only slightly cooler than her skin, felt good against it. In this climate, nothing not on ice or in a freezer, not even a corpse, could ever truly get cold.

"Most victories are hollow, believe me."

Ballard wandered over to the brass-bound porthole on the deck side of their elaborate, many-roomed suite. Whatever he saw caused him momentarily to stiffen and take an involuntary step backwards.

"What's the view like?"

"The so-called view consists of the filthy Amazon and a boring, muddy bank. Sometimes the bank is so far away it's out of sight."

He did not add that a Ballard approximately twenty years younger, the Ballard of, say, 1976, dressed in a handsome dark suit and brilliantly white shirt, was leaning against the deck rail, unaware of being under the eye of his twenty-years-older self. Young Ballard, older Ballard observed, did an excellent job of concealing his dire internal condition beneath a mask of deep, already well-weathered urbanity: the same performance, enacted day after day before an audience unaware of being an audience and never permitted backstage.

Unlike Sandrine, Ballard had never married.

"Poor Ballard, stuck on the *Endless Night* with a horrible view and only his aging, moody girlfriend for company."

Smiling, he returned to the long steel table, ran his mutilated right hand over the curve of her belly, and cupped her navel. "This is exactly what I asked for. You're wonderful."

"But isn't it funny to think—everything could have been completely different."

Ballard slid the remaining fingers of his hand down to palpate, lightly, the springy black shrub-like curls of her pubic bush.

"Everything is completely different right now."

"So take off your clothes and fuck me," Sandrine said. "I can get you hard again in a minute. In thirty seconds."

"I'm sure you could. But maybe you should put some clothes *on*, so we could go into lunch."

"You prefer to have sex in our bed."

"I do, yes. I don't understand why you wanted to get naked and lie down on this thing, anyhow. Now, I mean."

"It isn't cold, if that's what you're afraid of." She wriggled her torso and did a snow angel movement with her legs.

"Maybe this time we could catch the waiters."

"Because we'd be early?"

Ballard nodded. "Indulge me. Put on that sleeveless white French thing."

"Aye, aye, *mon capitaine.*" She sat up and scooted down the length of the table, pushing herself along on the raised vertical edges. These were of dark green marble, about an inch thick and four inches high. On both sides, round metal drains abutted the inner side of the marble. At the end of the table, Sandrine swung her legs down and straightened her arms, like a girl sitting on the end of a diving board. "I know why, too."

"Why I want you to wear that white thing? I love the way it looks on you."

"Why you don't want to have sex on this table."

"It's too narrow."

"You're thinking about what this table is for. Right? And you don't want to combine sex with *that*. Only I think that's exactly why we *should* have sex here."

"Everything we do, remember, is done by mutual consent. Our Golden Rule."

"Golden Spoilsport," she said. "Golden Shower of Shit."

"See? Everything's different already."

Sandrine levered herself off the edge of the table and faced him like a strict schoolmistress who happened momentarily to be naked. "I'm all you've got, and sometimes even I don't understand you."

"That makes two of us."

She wheeled around and padded into the bedroom, displaying her plush little bottom and sacral dimples with an absolute confidence Ballard could not but admire.

Although Sandrine and Ballard burst, in utter defiance of a direct order, into the dining room a full nine minutes ahead of schedule, the unseen minions had already done their work and disappeared. On the gleaming rosewood table two formal place settings had been laid, the plates topped with elaborately chased silver covers. Fresh irises brushed blue and yellow filled a tall, sparkling crystal vase.

"I swear, they must have a greenhouse on this yacht," Ballard said.

"Naked men with muddy hair row the flowers out in the middle of the night."

"I don't even think irises grow in the Amazon basin."

"Little guys who speak bird-language can probably grow anything they like."

"That's only one tribe, the Piraha. And all those bird-sounds are actual words. It's a human language." Ballard walked around the table and took the seat he had claimed as his. He lifted the intricate silver cover. "Now what is that?" He looked across at Sandrine, who was prodding at the contents of her bowl with a fork.

"Looks like a cut-up sausage. At least I hope it's a sausage. And something like broccoli. And a lot of orangey-yellowy goo." She raised her fork and licked the tines. "Um. Tastes pretty good, actually. But...."

For a moment, she appeared to be lost in time's great forest.

"I know this doesn't make sense, but if we ever did this before, *exactly* this, with you sitting over there and me here, in this same room, well, wasn't the food even better, I mean a *lot* better?"

"I can't say anything about that," Ballard said. "I really can't. There's just this vague…." The vagueness disturbed him far more than seemed quite rational. "Let's drop that subject and talk about bird language. Yes, let's. And the wine." He picked up the bottle. "Yet again a very nice Bordeaux," Ballard said, and poured for both of them. "However. What you've been hearing are real birds, not the Piraha."

"But they're talking, not just chirping. There's a difference. These guys are saying things to each other."

"Birds talk to one another. I mean, they sing."

She was right about one thing, though: in a funky, down-home way, the stew-like dish was delicious. He thrust away the feeling that it should have been a hundred, a thousand times more delicious: that once it, or something rather like it, had been paradisal.

"Birds don't sing in sentences. Or in paragraphs, like these guys do."

"They still can't be the Piraha. The Piraha live about five hundred miles away, on the Peruvian border."

"Your ears aren't as good as mine. You don't really hear them."

"Oh, I hear plenty of birds. They're all over the place."

"Only we're not talking about *birds*," Sandrine said.

1982

On the last day of November, Sandrine Loy, who was twenty-five, constitutionally ill-tempered, and startlingly good-looking (wide eyes, long mouth, black widow's peak, columnar legs), formerly of Princeton and Clare College, Cambridge, glanced over her shoulder and said, "Please tell me you're kidding. I just showered. I put on this nice white frock you bought me in Paris. And I'm *hungry*." Relenting a bit, she let a playful smile warm her face for nearly a second. "Besides that, I want to catch sight of our invisible servants."

"I'm hungry, too."

"Not for food, unfortunately." She spun from the porthole and its ugly view—a mile of brown, rolling river and low, muddy banks where squat, sullen natives tended to melt back into the bushes when the *Sweet Delight* went by—to indicate the evidence of Ballard's arousal, which stood up, darker than the rest of him, as straight as a flagpole.

"Let's have sex on this table. It's a lot more comfortable than it looks."

"Kind of defeats the fucking purpose, wouldn't you say? Comfort's hardly the point."

"Might as well be as comfy as we can, I say." He raised his arms to let his hands drape from the four-inch marble edging on the long steel table. "There's plenty of space on this thing, you know. More than in your bed at Clare."

"Maybe you're not as porky as I thought you were."

"Careful, careful. If you insult me, I'll make you pay for it."

At fifty Ballard had put on some extra weight, but it suited him. His shoulders were still wider far than his hips, and his belly more nascent than actual. His hair, longer than that of most men his age and just beginning to show threads of gray within the luxuriant brown, framed his wide brow and executive face. He looked like an actor who had made a career of playing senators, doctors, and bankers. Ballard's real profession was that of fixer to an oversized law firm in New York with a satellite office in Hong Kong, where he had grown up. The weight of muscle in his arms, shoulders, and legs reinforced the hint of stubborn determination, even perhaps brutality in his face: the suggestion that if necessary he would go a great distance and perform any number of grim deeds to do what was needed. Scars both long and short, scars like snakes, zippers, and tattoos bloomed here and there on his body.

"Promises, promises," she said. "But just for now, get up and get dressed, please. The sight of you admiring your own dick doesn't do anything for me."

"Oh, really?"

"Well, I do like the way you can still stick straight up into the air like a happy little soldier—at your age! But men are so soppy about their penises. You're all queer for yourselves. You more so than most, Ballard."

"Ouch," he said, and sat up. "I believe I'll put my clothes on now, Sandrine."

"Don't take forever, all right? I know it's only the second day, but I'd like to get a look at them while they're setting the table. Because someone, maybe even two someones, does set that table."

Ballard was already in the bedroom, pulling from their hangers a pair of white linen slacks and a thick, long-sleeved white cotton T-shirt. In seconds, he had slipped into these garments and was sliding his sun-tanned feet into rope-soled clogs.

"So let's move," he said, coming out of the bedroom with a long stride, his elbows bent, his forearms raised.

From the dining room came the sharp, distinctive chirping of a bird. Two notes, the second one higher, both clear and as insistent as the call of a bell. Ballard glanced at Sandrine, who seemed momentarily shaken.

"I'm not going in there if one of those awful jungle birds got in. They have to get rid of it. We're paying them, aren't we?"

"You have no idea," Ballard said. He grabbed her arm and pulled her along with him. "But that's no bird, it's *them*. The waiters. The staff."

Sandrine's elegant face shone with both disbelief and disgust.

"Those chirps and whistles are how they talk. Didn't you hear them last night and this morning?"

When he pulled again at her arm, she followed along, reluctance visible in her stance, her gait, the tilt of her head.

"I'm talking about birds, and they weren't even on the yacht. They were on shore. They were up in the air."

"Let's see what's in here." Six or seven minutes remained until the official start of dinner time, and they had been requested never to enter the dining room until the exact time of the meal.

Ballard threw the door open and pulled her into the room with him. Silver covers rested on the Royal Doulton china, and an uncorked bottle of a distinguished Bordeaux stood precisely at the mid-point between the two place settings. Three inches to its right, a navy-blue-and-royal-purple orchid thick enough to eat leaned, as if languishing, against the side of a small square crystal vase. The air seemed absolutely unmoving. Through the thumb holes at the tops of the plate covers rose a dense, oddly meaty odor of some unidentifiable food.

"Missed 'em again, damn it." Sandrine pulled her arm from Ballard's grasp and moved a few steps away.

"But you have noticed that there's no bird in here. Not so much as a feather."

"So it got out—I know it was here, Ballard."

She spun on her four-inch heels, giving the room a fast 360-degree inspection. Their dining room, roughly oval in shape, was lined with glassed-in bookshelves of dark-stained oak containing perhaps five hundred books, most of them mid-to-late nineteenth and early twentieth century novels ranked alphabetically by author, regardless of genre. The jackets had been removed, which Ballard minded, a bit. Three feet in front of the bookshelves on the deck side, which yielded space to two portholes and a door, stood a long wooden table with a delicately inlaid top—a real table, unlike the one in the room they had just left, which was more like a work station in a laboratory. The real one was presumably for setting out buffets.

The first door opened out onto the deck; another at the top of the oval led to their large and handsomely-furnished sitting room, with reading chairs and lamps, two sofas paired with low tables, a bar with a great many bottles of liquor, two red lacquered cabinets they had as yet not explored, and an air of many small precious things set out to gleam under the parlor's low lighting. The two remaining doors in the dining room were on the interior side. One opened into the spacious corridor that ran the entire length of their suite and gave access to the deck on both ends; the other revealed a gray passageway and a metal staircase that led up to the Captain's deck and cabin and down into the engine room, galley, and quarters for the yacht's small, unseen crew.

"So it kept all its feathers," said Sandrine. "If you don't think that's possible, you don't know doodly-squat about birds."

"What isn't possible," said Ballard, "is that some giant parrot got out of here without opening a door or a porthole."

"One of the waiters let it out, dummy. One of those handsome *Spanish-speaking* waiters."

They sat on opposite sides of the stately table. Ballard smiled at Sandrine, and she smiled back in rage and distrust. Suddenly and without warning, he remembered the girl she had been on Park Avenue at the end of the sixties, gawky-graceful, brilliantly surly, her hair and wardrobe goofy, claiming him as he had claimed her, with a glance. He had rescued her father from ruinous shame and a long jail term, but as soon as he had seen her he understood that his work had just begun, and that it would demand restraint, sacrifice, patience, and adamantine caution.

"A three-count?" he asked.

She nodded.

"One," he said. "Two." They put their thumbs into the round holes at the tops of the covers. "Three." They raised their covers, releasing steam and smoke and a more concentrated, powerful form of the meaty odor.

"Wow. What is that?"

Yellow-brown sauce or gravy covered a long, curved strip of foreign matter. Exhausted vegetables that looked a little like okra and string beans but were other things altogether lay strewn in limp surrender beneath the gravy.

"All of a sudden I'm really hungry," said Sandrine. "You can't tell what it is, either?"

Ballard moved the strip of unknown meat back and forth with his knife. Then he jabbed his fork into it. A watery yellow fluid oozed from the punctures.

"God knows what this is."

He pictured some big reptilian creature sliding down the riverbank into the meshes of a native net, then being hauled back up to be pierced with poison-tipped wooden spears. Chirping like birds, the diminutive men rioted in celebration around the corpse, which was now that of a hideous insect the size of a pony, its shell a poisonous green.

"I'm not even sure it's a mammal," he said. "Might even be some organ. Anaconda liver. Crocodile lung. Tarantula heart."

"You first."

Ballard sliced a tiny section from the curved meat before him. He half-expected to see valves and tubes, but the slice was a dense light brown all the way through. Ballard inserted the morsel into his mouth, and his taste buds began to sing.

"My god. Amazing."

"It's good?"

"Oh, this is way beyond 'good.'"

Ballard cut a larger piece off the whole and quickly bit into it. Yes, there it was again, but more sumptuous, almost floral in its delicacy and grounded in some profoundly satisfactory flavor, like that of a great single-barrel bourbon laced with a dark, subversive French chocolate. Subtlety, strength, sweetness. He watched Sandrine lift a section of the substance on her fork and slip it into her mouth. Her face went utterly still, and her eyes narrowed. With luxuriant slowness, she began to chew. After perhaps a second, Sandrine closed her eyes. Eventually, she swallowed.

"Oh, yes," she said. "My, my. Yes. Why can't we eat like this at home?"

"Whatever kind of animal this is, it's probably unknown everywhere but here. People like J. Paul Getty might get to eat it once a year, at some secret location."

"I don't care what it is, I'm just extraordinarily happy that we get to have it today. It's even a little bit sweet, isn't it?"

A short time later, Sandrine said, "Amazing. Even these horrible-looking vegetables spill out amazing flavors. If I could eat like this every day, I'd be perfectly happy to live in a hut, walk around barefoot, bathe in the Amazon, and wash my rags on the rocks."

"I know exactly what you mean," said Ballard. "It's like a drug. Maybe it is a drug."

"Do the natives really eat this way? Whatever this animal was, before they serve it to us, they have to hunt it down and kill it. Wouldn't they keep half of it for themselves?"

"Be a temptation," Ballard said. "Maybe they lick our plates, too."

"Tell me the truth now, Ballard. If you know it. Okay?"

Chewing, he looked up into her eyes. Some of the bliss faded from his face. "Sure. Ask away."

"Did we ever eat this stuff before?"

Ballard did not answer. He sliced a quarter sized piece off the meat and began to chew, his eyes on his plate.

"I know I'm not supposed to ask."

He kept chewing and chewing until he swallowed. He sipped his wine. "No. Isn't that strange? How we know we're not supposed to do certain things?"

"Like see the waiters. Or the maids, or the Captain."

"Especially the Captain, I think."

"Let's not talk anymore, let's just eat for a little while."

Sandrine and Ballard returned to their plates and glasses, and for a time made no noise other than soft moans of satisfaction.

When they had nearly finished, Sandrine said, "There are so many books on this boat! It's like a big library. Do you think you've ever read one?"

"Do you?"

"I have the feeling… well, of course that's the reason I'm asking. In a way, I mean in a *real* way, we've never been here before. On the Amazon?

Absolutely not. My husband, besides being continuously unfaithful, is a total asshole who never pays me any attention at all unless he's angry with me, but he's also tremendously jealous and possessive. For me to get here to be with you required an amazing amount of secret organization. D-Day didn't take any more planning than this trip. On the other hand, I have the feeling I once read at least one of these books."

"I have the same feeling."

"Tell me about it. I want to read it again and see if I remember anything."

"I can't. But… well, I think I might have once seen you holding a copy of *Little Dorrit*. The Dickens novel."

"I went to Princeton and Cambridge, I know who wrote *Little Dorrit*," she said, irritated. "Wait. Did I ever throw a copy of that book overboard?"

"Might've."

"Why would I do that?"

Ballard shrugged. "To see what would happen?"

"Do you remember that?"

"It's tough to say what I remember. Everything's always different, but it's different *now*. I sort of remember a book, though—a book from this library. *Tono-Bungay*. H. G. Wells. Didn't like it much."

"Did you throw it overboard?"

"I might've. Yes, I actually might have." He laughed. "I think I did. I mean, I think I'm throwing it overboard right now, if that makes sense."

"Because you didn't—don't—like it?"

Ballard laughed and put down his knife and fork. Only a few bits of the vegetables and a piece of meat the size of a knuckle sliced in half remained on his plate. "Stop eating and give me your plate." It was almost exactly as empty as his, though Sandrine's plate still had two swirls of the yellow sauce.

"Really?"

"I want to show you something."

Reluctantly, she lowered her utensils and handed him her plate. Ballard scraped the contents of his plate onto hers. He got to his feet and picked up a knife and the plate that had been Sandrine's. "Come out on deck with me."

When she stood up, Sandrine glanced at what she had only briefly and partially perceived as a hint of motion at the top of the room, where for the first time she took in a dun-colored curtain hung two or three feet before the end of the oval. What looked to be a brown or suntanned foot, smaller than a normal adult's and perhaps a bit grubby, was just now vanishing behind the curtain. Before Sandrine had deciphered what she thought she had seen, it was gone.

"Just see a rat?" asked Ballard.

Without intending to assent, Sandrine nodded.

"One was out on deck this morning. Disappeared as soon as I spotted it. Don't worry about it, though. The crew, whoever they are, will get rid of them. At the start of the cruise, I think there are always a few rats around. By the time we really get in gear, they're gone."

"Good," she said, wondering: *If the waiters are these really, really short Indian guys, would they hate us enough to make us eat rats?*

She followed him through the door between the two portholes into pitiless sunlight and crushing heat made even less comfortable by the dense, invasive humidity. The invisible water saturating the air pressed against her face like a steaming washcloth, and moisture instantly coated her entire body. Leaning against the rail, Ballard looked cool and completely at ease.

"I forgot we had air conditioning," she said.

"We don't. Vents move the air around somehow. Works like magic, even when there's no breeze at all. Come over here."

She joined him at the rail. Fifty yards away, what might have been human faces peered at them through a dense screen of jungle—weeds with thick, vegetal leaves of a green so dark it was nearly black. The half-seen faces resembled masks, empty of feeling.

"Remember saying something about being happy to bathe in the Amazon? About washing your clothes in the river?"

She nodded.

"You never want to go into this river. You don't even want to stick the tip of your finger in that water. Watch what happens, now. Our native friends came out to see this, you should, too."

"The Indians knew you were going to put on this demonstration? How could they?"

"Don't ask me, ask them. *I* don't know how they do it."

Ballard leaned over the railing and used his knife to scrape the few things on the plate into the river. Even before the little knuckles of meat and gristle, the shreds of vegetables, and liquid strings of gravy landed in the water, a six-inch circle of turbulence boiled up on the slow-moving surface. When the bits of food hit the water, the boiling circle widened out into a three-foot, thrashing chaos of violent little fish tails and violent little green shiny fish backs with violent tiny green fins, all in furious motion. The fury lasted about thirty seconds, then disappeared back under the river's sluggish brown face.

"Like Christmas dinner with my husband's family," Sandrine said.

"When we were talking about throwing *Tono-Bungay* and *Little Dorrit* into the river to see what would happen—"

"The fish ate the books?"

"They'll eat anything that isn't metal."

"So our little friends don't go swimming all that often, do they?"

"They never learn how. Swimming is death, it's for people like us. Let's go back in, okay?"

She whirled around and struck his chest, hard, with a pointed fist. "I want to go back to the room with the table in it. *Our* table. And this time, you can get as hard as you like."

"Don't I always?" he asked.

"Oh," Sandrine said, "I like that 'always.'"

"And yet, it's always different."

"I bet *I'm* always different," said Sandrine. "You, you'd stay pretty much the same."

"I'm not as boring as all that, you know, " Ballard said, and went on, over the course of the long afternoon and sultry evening, to prove it.

After breakfast the next morning, Sandrine, hissing with pain, her skin clouded with bruises, turned on him with such fury that he gasped in joy and anticipation.

1976

End of November, hot sticky muggy, a vegetal stink in the air. Motionless tribesmen four feet tall stared out from the overgrown bank over twenty yards of torpid river. They held, seemed to hold, bows without arrows, though the details swam backward into the layers of folded green.

"Look at those little savages," said Sandrine Loy, nineteen years old and already contemplating marriage to handsome, absurdly wealthy Antonio Barban, who had proposed to her after a chaotic Christmas dinner at his family's vulgar pile in Greenwich, Connecticut. That she knew marriage to

Antonio would prove to be an error of sublime proportions gave the idea most of its appeal. "We're putting on a traveling circus for their benefit. Doesn't that sort of make you detest them?"

"I don't detest them at all," Ballard said. "Actually, I have a lot of respect for those people. I think they're mysterious. So much gravity. So much *silence*. They understand a million things we don't, and what we do manage to get they know about in another way, a more profound way."

"You're wrong. They're too stupid to understand anything. They have mud for dinner. They have mud for brains."

"And yet...." Ballard said, smiling at her.

As if they knew they had been insulted and seemingly without moving out of position, the river people had begun to fade back into the network of dark, rubbery leaves in which they had for a long moment been framed.

"And yet what?"

"They knew what we were going to do. They wanted to see us throwing those books into the river. So out of the bushes they popped, right at the time we walked out on deck."

Her conspicuous black eyebrows slid nearer each other, creating a furrow. She shook her beautiful head and opened her mouth to disagree.

"Anyway, Sandrine, what did you think of what happened just now? Any responses, reflections?"

"What do I think of what happened to the books? What do I think of the fish?"

"Of course," Ballard said. "It's not *all* about us."

He leaned back against the rail, communicating utter ease and confidence. He was forty-four, attired daily in dark tailored suits and white shirts that gleamed like a movie star's smile, the repository of a thousand feral secrets, at home everywhere in the world, the possessor of an understanding it would take him a lifetime to absorb. Sandrine often seemed to him the center of his life. He knew exactly what she was going to say.

"I think the fish are astonishing," she said. "I mean it. Astonishing. Such concentration, such power, such complete *hunger*. It was breathtaking. Those books didn't last more than five or six seconds. All that thrashing! My book lasted longer than yours, but not by much."

"*Little Dorrit* is a lot longer than *Tono-Bungay*. More paper, more thread, more glue. I think they're especially hot for glue."

"Maybe they're just hot for Dickens."

"Maybe they're speed readers," said Sandrine. "What do we do now?"

"What we came here to do," Ballard said, and moved back to swing open the dining room door, then froze in mid-step.

"Forget something?"

"I was having the oddest feeling, and I just now realized what it was. You read about it all the time, so you think it must be pretty common, but until a second ago I don't think I'd ever before had the feeling that I was being watched. Not really."

"But now you did."

"Yes." He strode up to the door and swung it open. The table was bare, and the room was empty.

Sandrine approached and peeked over his shoulder. He had both amused and dismayed her. "The great Ballard exhibits a moment of paranoia. I think I've been wrong about you all this time. You're just another boring old creep who wants to fuck me."

"I'd admit to being a lot of things, but paranoid isn't one of them." He gestured her back through the door. That Sandrine obeyed him seemed to take both of them by surprise.

"How about being a boring old creep? I'm not really so sure I want to stay here with you. For one thing, and I know this is not related, the birds keep waking me up. If they are birds."

He cocked his head, interested. "What else could they be? Please tell me. Indulge a boring old creep."

"The maids and the waiters and the sailor guys. The cook. The woman who arranges the flowers."

"You think they belong to that tribe that speaks in bird calls? Actually, how did *you* ever hear about them?"

"My anthropology professor was one of the people who first discovered that tribe. The Piranhas. Know what they call themselves? The tall people. Not very observant, are they? According to the professor, they worshiped a much older tribe that had disappeared many generations back—miracle people, healers, shamans, warriors. The Old Ones, they called them, but the Old Ones called themselves **We**, you always have to put it in boldface. My professor couldn't stop talking about these tribes—he was so full of himself. *Sooo* vain. Kept staring at me. Vain, ugly, and lecherous, my favorite trifecta!"

The memory of her anthropology professor, with whom she had clearly gone through the customary adoration-boredom-disgust cycle of student-teacher love affairs, had put Sandrine in a sulky, dissatisfied mood.

"You made a lovely little error about thirty seconds ago. The tribe is called the Piraha, not the Piranhas. Piranhas are the fish you fell in love with."

"Ooh," she said, brightening up. "So the Piraha eat piranhas?"

"Other way around, more likely. But the other people on the *Blinding Light* can't be Piraha, we're hundreds of miles from their territory."

"You *are* tedious. Why did I ever let myself get talked into coming here, anyhow?"

"You fell in love with me the first time you saw me—in your father's living room, remember? And although it was tremendously naughty of me, in fact completely wrong and immoral, I took one look at your stupid sweatshirt and your stupid pigtails and fell in love with you on the spot. You were perfect—you took my breath away. It was like being struck by lightning."

He inhaled, hugely.

"And here I am, thirty-eight years of age, height of my powers, capable of performing miracles on behalf of our clients, exactly as I pulled off, not to say any more about this, a considerable miracle for your father, plus I am a fabulously eligible man, a tremendous catch, but what do you know, still unmarried. Instead of a wife or even a steady girlfriend, there's this succession of inane young women from twenty-five to thirty, these Heathers and Ashleys, these Morgans and Emilys, who much to their dismay grow less and less infatuated with me the more time we spend together. 'You're always so distant,' one of them said, 'you're never really *with* me.' And she was right, I couldn't really be with her. Because I wanted to be with you. I wanted us to be *here*."

Deeply pleased, Sandrine said, "You're such a pervert."

Yet something in what Ballard had evoked was making the handsome dining room awkward and dark. She wished he wouldn't stand still; there was no reason why he couldn't go into the living room, or the other way, into the room where terror and fascination beckoned. She wondered why she was waiting for Ballard to decide where to go, and as he spoke of seeing her for the first time, was assailed by an uncomfortably precise echo from the day in question.

Then, as now, she had been rooted to the floor: in her family's living room, beyond the windows familiar Park Avenue humming with the traffic she only in that moment became aware she heard, Sandrine had been paralyzed. Every inch of her face had turned hot and red. She felt intimate with Ballard before she had even begun to learn what intimacy meant. Before she had left the room, she waited for him to move between herself and her father, then pushed up the sleeves of the baggy sweatshirt and revealed the inscriptions of self-loathing, self-love, desire and despair upon her pale forearms.

"You're pretty weird, too. You'd just had your fifteenth birthday, and here you were, gobsmacked by this old guy in a suit. You even showed me your arms!"

"I could tell what made *you* salivate." She gave him a small, lop-sided smile. "So why were you there, anyhow?"

"Your father and I were having a private celebration."

"Of what?"

Every time she asked this question, he gave her a different answer. "I made the fearsome problem of his old library fines disappear. *Poof*, no more late-night sweats." Previously, Ballard had told her that he'd got her father off jury duty, had cancelled his parking tickets, retroactively upgraded his B- in Introductory Chemistry to an A.

"Yeah, what a relief. My father never walked into a library, his whole life."

"You can see why the fine was so great." He blinked. "I just had an idea." Ballard wished her to cease wondering, to the extent this was possible, about the service he had rendered for her father. "How would you like to take a peek at the galley? Forbidden fruit, all that kind of thing. Aren't you curious?"

"You're suggesting we go down those stairs? Wasn't *not* doing that one of our most sacred rules?"

"I believe we were given those rules in order to make sure we broke them." Sandrine considered this proposition for a moment, then nodded her head. *That's my girl,* he thought.

"You may be completely perverted, Ballard, but you're pretty smart." A discordant possibility occurred to her. "What if we catch sight of our extremely discreet servants?"

"Then we know for good and all if they're little tribesmen who chirp like bobolinks or handsome South American yacht bums. But that won't happen. They may, in fact they undoubtedly do, see us, but we'll never catch sight of them. No matter how brilliantly we try to outwit them."

"You think they watch us?"

"I'm sure that's one of their main jobs."

"Even when we're in bed? Even when we... you know."

"Especially then," Ballard said.

"What do we think about that, Ballard? Do we love the whole idea, or does it make us sick? You first."

"Neither one. We can't do anything about it, so we might as well forget it. I think being able to watch us is one of the ways they're paid—these tribes don't have much use for money. And because they're always there, they can step in and help us when we need it, at the end."

"So it's like love," said Sandrine.

"Tough love, there at the finish. Let's go over and try the staircase."

"Hold on. When we were out on deck, you told me that you felt you were being watched, and that it was the first time you'd ever had that feeling."

"Yes, that was different—I don't *feel* the natives watching me, I just assume they're doing it. It's the only way to explain how they can stay out of sight all the time."

As they moved across the dining room to the inner door, for the first time Sandrine noticed a curtain the color of a dark camel hair coat hanging up at the top of the room's oval. Until that moment, she had taken it for a wall too small and oddly shaped to be covered with bookshelves. The curtain shifted a bit, she thought: a tiny ripple occurred in the fabric, as if it had been breathed upon.

There's one of them now, she thought. *I bet they have their own doors and their own staircases.*

For a moment, she was disturbed by a vision of the yacht honeycombed with narrow passages and runways down which beetled small red-brown figures with matted black hair and faces like dull, heavy masks. Now and then the little figures paused to peer through chinks in the walls. It made her feel violated, a little, but at the same time immensely proud of the body that the unseen and silent attendants were privileged to gaze at. The thought of these mysterious little people watching what Ballard did to that body, and she to his, caused a thrill of deep feeling to course upward through her body.

"Stop daydreaming, Sandrine, and get over here." Ballard held the door that led to the gray landing and the metal staircase.

"You go first," she said, and Ballard moved through the frame while still holding the door. As soon as she was through, he stepped around her to grasp the gray metal rail and begin moving down the stairs.

"What makes you so sure the galley's downstairs?"

"Galleys are always downstairs."

"And why do you want to go there, again?"

"One: because they ordered us not to. Two: because I'm curious about what goes on in that kitchen. And three: I also want to get a look at the wine cellar. How can they keep giving us these amazing wines? Remember what we drank with lunch?"

"Some stupid red. It tasted good, though."

"That stupid red was a '55 Chateau Petrus. Two years older than you."

Ballard led her down perhaps another dozen steps, arrived at a landing, and saw one more long staircase leading down to yet another landing.

"How far down can this galley be?" she asked.

"Good question."

"This boat has a bottom, after all."

"It has a hull, yes."

"Shouldn't we actually have gone past it by now? The bottom of the boat?"

"You'd think so. Okay, maybe this is it."

The final stair ended at a gray landing that opened out into a narrow gray corridor leading to what appeared to be a large, empty room. Ballard looked down into the big space, and experienced a violent reluctance, a mental and physical refusal, to go down there and look further into the room: it was prohibited by an actual taboo. That room was not for him, it was none of his business, period. Chilled, he turned from the corridor and at last saw what was directly before him. What had appeared to be a high gray wall was divided in the middle and bore two brass panels at roughly chest height. The wall was a doorway.

"What do you want to do?" Sandrine asked.

Ballard placed a hand on one of the panels and pushed. The door swung open, revealing a white tile floor, metal racks filled with cast-iron pans, steel bowls, and other cooking implements. The light was a low, diffused dimness. Against the side wall, three sinks of varying sizes bulged downward beneath their faucets. He could see the inner edge of a long, shiny metal counter. Far back, a yellow propane tank clung to a range with six burners, two ovens, and a big griddle. A faint mewing, a tiny *skritch skritch skritch* came to him from the depths of the kitchen.

"Look, is there any chance…?" Sandrine whispered.

In a normal voice, Ballard said "No. They're not in here right now, whoever they are. I don't think they are, anyhow."

"So does that mean we're supposed to go inside?"

"How would I know?" He looked over his shoulder at her. "Maybe we're not *supposed* to do anything, and we just decide one way or the other. But here we are, anyhow. I say we go in, right? If it feels wrong, smells wrong, whatever, we boogie on out."

"You first," she said.

Without opening the door any wider, Ballard slipped into the kitchen. Before he was all the way in, he reached back and grasped Sandrine's wrist.

"Come along now."

"You don't have to drag me, I was right behind you. You bully."

"I'm not a bully, I just don't want to be in here by myself."

"All bullies are cowards, too."

She edged in behind him and glanced quickly from side to side. "I didn't think you could have a kitchen like this on a yacht."

"You can't," he said. "Look at that gas range. It must weigh a thousand pounds."

She yanked her wrist out of his hand. "It's hard to see in here, though. Why is the light so fucking weird?"

They were edging away from the door, Sandrine so close behind that Ballard could feel her breath on his neck.

"There aren't any light fixtures, see? No overhead lights, either."

He looked up and saw, far above, only a dim white-gray ceiling that stretched away a great distance on either side. Impossibly, the "galley" seemed much wider than the *Blinding Light* itself.

"I don't like this," he said.

"Me, neither."

"We're really not supposed to be here," he said, thinking of that other vast room down at the end of the corridor, and said to himself, *That's what they call the "engine room", we absolutely can't even glance that way again, can't can't can't, the "engines" would be way too much for us.*

The mewing and skritching, which had momentarily fallen silent, started up again, and in the midst of what felt and tasted to him like panic, Ballard had a vision of a kitten trapped behind a piece of kitchen equipment. He stepped forward and leaned over to peer into the region beyond the long counter and beside the enormous range. Two funny striped cabinets about five feet tall stood there side by side.

"Do you hear a cat?" he asked.

"If you think that's a cat…" Sandrine said, a bit farther behind him than she had been at first.

The cabinets were cages, and what he had seen as stripes were their bars. "Oh," Ballard said, and sounded as though he had been punched in the stomach.

"Damn you, you started to bleed through your suit jacket," Sandrine whispered. "We have to get out of here, fast."

Ballard scarcely heard her. In any case, if he were bleeding, it was of no consequence. They knew what to do about bleeding. Here on the other hand, perhaps sixty feet away in this preposterous "galley," was a phenomenon he had never before witnessed. The first cage contained a thrashing beetle-like insect nearly too large for it. This gigantic insect was the source of the mewing and scratching. One of its mandibles rasped at a bar as the creature struggled to roll forward or back, producing noises of insect-distress. Long smeary wounds in the wide middle area between its scrabbling legs oozed a yellow ichor.

Horrified, Ballard looked hastily into the second cage, which he had thought empty but for a roll of blankets, or towels, or the like, and discovered that the blankets or towels were occupied by a small boy from one of the river tribes who was gazing at him through the bars. The boy's eyes looked hopeless and dead. Half of his shoulder seemed to have been sliced away, and a long, thin strip of bone gleamed white against a great scoop of red. The arm half-extended through the bars concluded in a dark, messy stump.

The boy opened his mouth and released, almost too softly to be heard, a single high-pitched musical note. Pure, accurate, well defined, clearly a word charged with some deep emotion, the note hung in the air for a brief moment, underwent a briefer half-life, and was gone.

"What's that?" Sandrine said.

"Let's get out of here."

He pushed her through the door, raced around her, and began charging up the stairs. When they reached the top of the steps and threw themselves into the dining room, Ballard collapsed onto the floor, then rolled onto his back, heaving in great quantities of air. His chest rose and fell, and with every exhalation he moaned. A portion of his left side pulsing with pain felt warm and wet. Sandrine leaned against the wall, breathing heavily in a less convulsive way. After perhaps thirty seconds, she managed to say, "I trust that was a bird down there."

"Um. Yes." He placed his hand on his chest, then held it up like a stop sign, indicating that he would soon have more to say. After a few more great heaving lungfuls of air, he said, "Toucan. In a big cage."

"You were that frightened by a kind of parrot?"

He shook his head slowly from side to side on the polished floor. "I didn't want them to catch us down there. It seemed dangerous, all of a sudden. Sorry."

"You're bleeding all over the floor."

"Can you get me a new bandage pad?"

Sandrine pushed herself off the wall and stepped toward him. From his perspective, she was as tall as a statue. Her eyes glittered. "Screw you, Ballard. I'm not your servant. You can come with me. It's where we're going, anyhow."

He pushed himself upright and peeled off his suit jacket before standing up. The jacket fell to the floor with a squishy thump. With blood-dappled fingers, he unbuttoned his shirt and let that, too, fall to the floor.

"Just leave those things there," Sandrine said. "The invisible crew will take care of them."

"I imagine you're right." Ballard managed to get to his feet without staggering. Slow-moving blood continued to ooze down his left side.

"We have to get you on the table," Sandrine said. "Hold this over the wound for right now, okay?"

She handed him a folded white napkin, and he clamped it over his side. "Sorry. I'm not as good at stitches as you are."

"I'll be fine," Ballard said, and began moving, a bit haltingly, toward the next room.

"Oh, sure. You always are. But you know what I like about what we just did?"

For once he had no idea what she might say. He waited for it.

"That amazing food we loved so much was Toucan! Who would've guessed? You'd think Toucan would taste sort of like chicken, only a lot worse."

"Life is full of surprises."

In the bedroom, Ballard kicked off his shoes, pulled his trousers down over his hips, and stepped out of them.

"You can leave your socks on," said Sandrine, "but let's get your undies off, all right?"

"I need your help."

Sandrine grasped the waistband of his boxers and pulled them down, but they snagged on his penis. "Ballard is aroused, surprise number two." She unhooked his shorts, let them drop to the floor, batted his erection down, and watched it bounce back up. "Barkis is willin', all right."

"Let's get into the workroom," he said.

"Aye aye, *mon capitaine*." Sandrine closed her hand on his erection and said, "Want to go there on-deck, give the natives a look at your magnificent manliness? Shall we increase the index of penis envy among the river tribes by a really big factor?"

"Let's just get in there, okay?"

She pulled him into the workroom and only then released his erection.

A wheeled aluminum tray had been rolled up beside the worktable. Sometimes it was not given to them, and they were forced to do their work with their hands and whatever implements they had brought with them. Today, next to the array of knives of many kinds and sizes, cleavers, wrenches, and hammers lay a pack of surgical thread and a stainless steel needle still warm from the autoclave.

Ballard sat down on the worktable, pushed himself along until his heels had cleared the edge, and lay back. Sandrine threaded the needle and, bending over to get close to the wound, began to do her patient stitching.

1982

"Oh, here you are," said Sandrine, walking into the sitting room of their suite to find Ballard lying on one of the sofas, reading a book whose title she could not quite make out. Because both of his hands were heavily bandaged, he was having some difficulty turning the pages. "I've been looking all over for you."

He glanced up, frowning. "All over? Does that mean you went down the stairs?"

"No, of course not. I wouldn't do anything like that alone, anyhow."

"And just to make sure…. You didn't go up the stairs, either, did you?"

Sandrine came toward him, shaking her head. "No, I'd never do that, either. But I want to tell you something. I thought *you* might have decided to take a look upstairs. By yourself, to sort of protect me in a way I never want to be protected."

"Of course," Ballard said, closing his book on an index finger that protruded from the bulky white swath of bandage. "You'd hate me if I ever tried to protect you, especially by doing something sneaky. I knew that about you when you were fifteen years old."

"When I was fifteen, you did protect me."

He smiled at her. "I exercised an atypical amount of restraint."

His troublesome client, Sandrine's father, had told him one summer day that a business venture required him to spend a week in Mexico City. Could he think of anything acceptable that might occupy his daughter during that time, she being a teenager a bit too prone to independence and exploration? Let her stay with me, Ballard had said. The guest room has its own bathroom and a TV. I'll take her out to theaters at night, and to the Met and Moma during the day when I'm not doing my job. When I *am* doing my job, she can bat around the city by herself the way she does now. Extraordinary man you are, the client had said, and allow me to reinforce that by letting you know that about a month ago my daughter just amazed me one morning by telling me that she liked you. You have no idea how god-damned fucking unusual that is. That she talked to me at all is staggering, and that she actually announced that she liked one of my friends is stupefying. So yes, please, thank you, take Sandrine home with you, please do, escort her hither and yon.

When the time came, he drove a compliant Sandrine to his house in Harrison, where he explained that although he would not have sex with her until she was at least eighteen, there were many other ways they could express themselves. And although it would be years before they could be naked together, for the present they would each be able to be naked before the other. Fifteen-year-old Sandrine, who had been expecting to use all her arts of bad temper, insult, duplicity, and evasiveness to escape ravishment by this actually pretty interesting old guy, responded to these conditions with avid interest. Ballard announced another prohibition no less serious, but even more personal.

"I can't cut myself any more?" she asked. "Fuck you, Ballard, you loved it when I showed you my arm. Did my father put you up to this?" She began looking frantically for her bag, which Ballard's valet had already removed to the guest rooms.

"Not at all. Your father would try to kill me if he knew what I was going to do to you. And you to me, when it's your turn."

"So if I can't cut myself, what exactly happens instead?"

"*I* cut you," Ballard said. "And I do it a thousand times better than you ever did. I'll cut you so well no one ever be able to tell it happened, unless they're right on top of you."

"You think I'll be satisfied with some wimpy little cuts no one can even see? Fuck you all over again."

"Those cuts no one can see will be incredibly painful. And then I'll take the pain away, so you can experience it all over again."

Sandrine found herself abruptly caught up by a rush of feelings that seemed to originate in a deep region located just below her ribcage. At least for the moment, this flood of unnamable emotions blotted out her endless grudges and frustrations, also the chronic bad temper they engendered.

"And during this process, Sandrine, I will become deeply familiar, profoundly familiar with your body, so that when at last we are able to enjoy sex with each other, I will know how to give you the most amazing pleasure. I'll know every inch of you, I'll have your whole gorgeous map in my head. And you will do the same with me."

Sandrine had astonished herself by agreeing to this program on the spot, even to abstain from sex until she turned eighteen. Denial, too, was a pain she could learn to savor. At that point Ballard had taken her upstairs to her the guest suite, and soon after down the hallway to what he called his "workroom."

"Oh my God," she said, taking it in, "I can't believe it. This is real. And you, you're real, too."

"During the next three years, whenever you start hating everything around you and feel as though you'd like to cut yourself again, remember that I'm here. Remember that this room exists. There'll be many days and nights when we can be here together."

In this fashion had Sandrine endured the purgatorial remainder of her days at Dalton. And when she and Ballard at last made love, pleasure and pain had become presences nearly visible in the room at the moment she screamed in the ecstasy of release.

"You dirty, dirty, dirty old man," she said, laughing.

Four years after that, Ballard overheard some Chinese bankers, clients of his firm for whom he had several times rendered his services, speaking in soft Mandarin about a yacht anchored in the Amazon Basin; he needed no more.

"I want to go off the boat for a couple of hours when we get to Manaus," Sandrine said. "I feel like getting back in the world again, at least for a little while. This little private bubble of ours is completely cut off from everything else."

"Which is why—"

"Which is why it works, and why we like it, I understand, but half the time I can't stand it, either. I don't live the way you do, always flying off to interesting places to perform miracles…"

"Try spending a rainy afternoon in Zurich holding some terminally anxious banker's hand."

"Not that it matters, especially, but you don't mind, do you?"

"Of course not. I need some recuperation time, anyhow. This was a little severe." He held up one thickly bandaged hand. "Not that I'm complaining."

"You'd better not!"

"I'll only complain if you stay out too late—or spend too much of your father's money!"

"What could I buy in Manaus? And I'll make sure to be back before dinner. Have you noticed? The food on this weird boat is getting better and better every day?"

"I know, yes, but for now I seem to have lost my appetite," Ballard said. He had a quick mental vision of a metal cage from which something hideous was struggling to escape. It struck an oddly familiar note, as of something half-remembered, but Ballard was made so uncomfortable by the image in his head that he refused to look at it any longer.

"Will they just know that I want to dock at Manaus?"

"Probably, but you could write them a note. Leave it on the bed. Or on the dining room table."

"I have a pen in my bag, but where can I find some paper?"

"I'd say, look in any drawer. You'll probably find all the paper you might need."

Sandrine went to the little table beside him, pulled open its one drawer and found a single sheet of thick, cream-colored stationery headed *Sweet Delight*. An Omas roller-ball pen, much nicer than the Pilot she had liberated from their hotel in Rio, lay angled atop the sheet of stationery. In her formal, almost italic handwriting, Sandrine wrote *Please dock at Manaus. I would like to spend two or three hours ashore.*

"Should I sign it?"

Ballard shrugged. "There's just the two of us. Initial it."

She drew a graceful, looping S under her note and went into the dining room, where she squared it off in the middle of the table. When she returned to the sitting room, she asked, "And now I just wait? Is that how it works? Just because I found a piece of paper and a pen, I'm supposed to trust this crazy system?"

"You know as much as I do, Sandrine. But I'd say, yes, just wait a little while, yes, that's how it works, and yes, you might as well trust it. There's no reason to be bitchy."

"I have to stay in practice," she said, and lurched sideways as the yacht bumped against something hard and came to an abrupt halt.

"See what I mean?"

When he put the book down in his lap, Sandrine saw that it was *Tono-Bungay*. She felt a hot, rapid flare of irritation that the book was not something like *The Women's Room*, which could teach him things he needed to know: and hadn't he already read *Tono-Bungay*?

"Look outside, try to catch them tying us up and getting out that walkway thing."

"You think we're in Manaus already?"

"I'm sure we are."

"That's ridiculous. We scraped against a barge or something."

"Nonetheless, we have come to a complete halt."

Sandrine strode briskly to the on-deck door, threw it open, gasped, then stepped outside. The yacht had already been tied up at a long yellow dock at which two yachts smaller than theirs rocked in a desultory brown tide. No crewmen were in sight. The dock led to a wide concrete apron across which men of European descent and a few natives pushed wheelbarrows and consulted clipboards and pulled on cigars while pointing out distant things to other men. It looked false and stagy, like the first scene in a bad musical about New Orleans. An avenue began in front of a row of warehouses, the first of which was painted with the slogan MANAUS AMAZONA. The board walkway with rope handrails had been set in place.

"Yeah, okay," she said. "We really do seem to be docked at Manaus."

"Don't stay away too long."

"I'll stay as long as I like," she said.

The avenue leading past the facades of the warehouses seemed to run directly into the center of the city, visible now to Sandrine as a gathering of tall office buildings and apartment blocks that thrust upwards from the jumble of their surroundings like an outcropping of mountains. The sky-scrapers were blue-gray in color, the lower surrounding buildings a scumble of brown, red, and yellow that made Sandrine think of Cezanne, even of Seurat: dots of color that suggested walls and roofs. She thought she could walk to the center of the city in no more than forty-five minutes, which left her about two hours to do some exploring and have lunch.

Nearly an hour later, Sandrine trudged past the crumbling buildings and broken windows on crazed, tilting sidewalks under a domineering sun. Sweat ran down her forehead and cheeks and plastered her dress to her body. The air seemed half water, and her lungs strained to draw in oxygen. The office buildings did not seem any nearer than at the start of her walk. If she had seen a taxi, she would have taken it back to the port, but only a few cars and pickups rolled along the broad avenue. The dark, half-visible men driving these vehicles generally leaned over their steering wheels and stared at her, as if women were rare in Manaus. She wished she had thought to cover her hair, and was sorry she had left her sunglasses behind.

Then she became aware that a number of men were following her, how many she could not tell, but more than two. They spoke to each other in low, hoarse voices, now and then laughing at some remark sure to be at Sandrine's expense. Although her feet had begun to hurt, she began moving more quickly. Behind her, the men kept pace with her, neither gaining nor falling back. After another two blocks, Sandrine gave in to her sense of alarm and glanced over her shoulder. Four men in dark hats and shapeless, slept-in suits had ranged themselves across the width of the sidewalk. One of them called out to her in a language she did not understand; another emitted a wet, mushy laugh. The man at the curb jumped down into the street, trotted across the empty avenue, and picked up his pace on the sidewalk opposite until he had drawn a little ahead of Sandrine.

She felt utterly alone and endangered. And because she felt in danger, a scorching anger blazed up within her: at herself for so stupidly putting herself at risk, at the men behind her for making her feel frightened, for ganging up on her. She did not know what she was going to have to do, but she was not going to let those creeps get any closer to her than they were now. Twisting to her right, then to her left, Sandrine removed her shoes and rammed them into her bag. They were watching her, the river scum; even the man on the other side of the avenue had stopped moving and was staring at her from beneath the brim of his hat.

Literally testing the literal ground, Sandrine walked a few paces over the paving stones, discovered that they were at any rate not likely to cut her feet, gathered herself within, and, like a race horse bursting from the gate, instantly began running as fast as she could. After a moment in which her pursuers were paralyzed with surprise, they too began to run. The man on the other side of the street jumped down from the curb and began sprinting toward her. His shoes made a sharp *tick-tick* sound when they met the stony asphalt. As the ticks grew louder, Sandrine heard him inhaling great quantities of air. Before he could reach her, she came to a cross street and wheeled in, her bag bouncing at her hip, her legs stretching out to devour yard after yard of stony ground.

Unknowingly, she had entered a slum. The structures on both sides of the street were half-collapsed huts and shanties made of mismatched wooden planks, of metal sheeting, and tarpaper. She glimpsed faces peering out of greasy windows and sagging, cracked-open doors. Some of the shanties before her were shops with soft drink cans and bottles of beer arrayed on the window sills. People were spilling from little tarpaper and sheet-metal structures out into the street, already congested with abandoned cars, empty pushcarts, and cartons of fruit for sale. Garbage lay everywhere. The women who watched Sandrine streak by displayed no interest in her plight.

Yet the slum's chaos was a blessing, Sandrine thought: the deeper she went, the greater the number of tiny narrow streets sprouting off the one she had taken from the avenue. It was a feverish, crowded warren, a *favela*, the kind of place you would never escape had you the bad luck to have been born there. And while outside this rat's nest the lead man chasing her had been getting dangerously near, within its boundaries the knots of people and the obstacles of cars and carts and mounds of garbage had slowed him down. Sandrine found that she could dodge all of these obstacles with relative ease. The next time she spun around a corner, feet skidding on a slick pad of rotting vegetables, she saw what looked to her like a miracle: an open door revealing a hunched old woman draped in black rags, beckoning her in.

Sandrine bent her legs, called on her youth and strength, jumped off the ground, and sailed through the open door. The old woman only just got out of the way in time to avoid being knocked down. She was giggling, either at Sandrine's athleticism or because she had rescued her from the pursuing thugs. When Sandrine had cleared her doorway and was scrambling to avoid ramming into the wall, the old woman darted forward and slammed her door shut. Sandrine fell to her knees in a small room suddenly gone very dark. A slanting shaft of light split the murk and illuminated a rectangular space on the floor covered by a threadbare rug no longer of any identifiable color. Under the light, the rug seemed at once utterly worthless and extraordinarily beautiful.

The old woman shuffled into the shaft of light and uttered an incomprehensible word that sounded neither Spanish nor Portuguese. A thousand wayward wrinkles like knife cuts, scars, and stitches had been etched into her white, elongated face. Her nose had a prominent hook, and her eyes shone like dark stones at the bottom of a fast, clear stream. Then she laid an upright index finger against her sunken lips and with her other hand gestured toward the door. Sandrine listened. In seconds, multiple footsteps pounded past the old woman's little house. Leading the pack was *tick tick tick.* The footsteps clattered up the narrow street and disappeared into the ordinary clamor.

Hunched over almost parallel to the ground, the old woman mimed hysterical laughter. Sandrine mouthed *Thank you, thank you,* thinking that her intention would be clear if the words were not. Still mock-laughing, her unknown savior shuffled closer, knitting and folding her long, spotted hands. She had the ugliest hands Sandrine had ever seen, knobbly arthritic fingers with filthy, ragged nails. She hoped the woman was not going stroke her hair or pat her face: she would have to let her do it, however nauseated she might feel. Instead, the old woman moved right past her, muttering what sounded like *Munna, munna, num.*

Outside on the street, the ticking footsteps once again became audible. Someone began knocking, hard, on an adjacent door.

Only half-visible at the rear of the room, the old woman turned toward Sandrine and beckoned her forward with an urgent gesture of her bony hand. Sandrine moved toward her, uncertain of what was going on.

In an urgent, raspy whisper: *Munna! Num!*

The old woman appeared to be bowing to the baffled Sandrine, whose sense of peril had begun again to boil up within her. A pane of greater darkness slid open behind the old woman, and Sandrine finally understood that her savior had merely bent herself more deeply to turn a doorknob.

Num! Num!

Sandrine obeyed orders and *nummed* past her beckoning hostess. Almost instantly, instead of solid ground, her foot met a vacancy, and she nearly tumbled down what she finally understood to be a staircase. Only her sense of balance kept her upright: she was grateful she still had all of her crucial toes. Behind her, the door slammed shut. A moment later, she heard the clicking of a lock.

⟶⟨○⟩⟵

Back on the yacht, Ballard slipped a bookmark into *Tono-Bungay* and for the first time, at least for what he thought was the first time, regarded the pair of red lacquered cabinets against the wall beside him. Previously, he had taken them in, but never really examined them. About four feet high and three feet wide, they appeared to be Chinese and were perhaps moderately valuable. Brass fittings with latch pins held them closed in front, so they were easily opened.

The thought of lifting the pins and opening the cabinets aroused both curiosity and an odd dread in Ballard. For a moment, he had a vision of a great and forbidden room deep in the bowels of the yacht where enormous spiders ranged across rotting, heaped-up corpses. (With wildly variant details, visions of exactly this sort had visited Ballard ever since his adolescence.) He shook his head to clear it of this vision, and when that failed, struck his bandaged left hand against the padded arm of the sofa. Bright, rolling waves of pain forced a gasp from him, and the forbidden room with its spiders and corpses zipped right back to wherever had given it birth.

Was this the sort of dread he was supposed to obey, or the sort he was supposed to ignore? Or if not ignore, because that was always unwise and in some sense dishonorable, acknowledge but persist in the face of anyway? Cradling his throbbing hand against his chest, Ballard let the book slip off his lap and got to his feet, eyeing the pair of shiny cabinets. If asked to inventory the contents of the sitting room, he would have forgotten to list them. Presumably that meant he was supposed to overlook his foreboding and investigate the contents of these vertical little Chinese chests. *They* wanted him to open the cabinets, if *he* wanted to.

Still holding his electrocuted left hand to his chest, Ballard leaned over and brought his exposed right index finger in contact with the box on the left. No heat came from it, and no motion. It did not hum, it did not quiver, however delicately. At least six or seven coats of lacquer had been applied to the thing—he felt as though he were looking into a deep river of red lacquer.

Ballard hunkered and used his index finger to push the brass latch pin up and out of the ornate little lock. It swung down on an intricate little cord he had not previously noticed. The door did not open by itself, as he had hoped. Once again, he had to make a choice, for it was not too late to drop the brass pin back into its latch. He could choose not to look; he could let the *Sweet Delight* keep its secrets. But as before, Ballard acknowledged the dread he was feeling, then dropped his hip to the floor, reached out, and flicked the door open with his fingernail. Arrayed on the cabinet's three shelves were what appeared to be photographs in neat stacks. Polaroids, he thought. He took the first stack of photos from the cabinet and looked down at the topmost one. What Ballard saw there had two contradictory effects on him. He became so light-headed he feared he might faint; and he almost ejaculated into his trousers.

ᐧ◦ᐧ

Taking care not to tumble, Sandrine moved in the darkness back to the top of the staircase, found the door with her fingertips, and pounded. The door rattled in its frame but did not give. "Open up, lady!" she shouted. "Are you *kidding*? Open this door!" She banged her fists against the unmoving wood, thinking that although the old woman undoubtedly did not speak English, she could hardly misunderstand what Sandrine was saying. When her fists began to hurt and her throat felt ragged, the strangeness of what had just happened opened before her: it was like… like a fairy tale! She had been duped, tricked, flummoxed; she had been trapped. The world had closed on her, as a steel trap snaps shut on the leg of a bear.

"Please!" she yelled, knowing it was useless. She would not be able to beg her way out of this confinement. Here, the Golden Shower of Shit did not apply. "Please let me out!" A few more bangs of her fist, a few more shouted pleas to be set free, to be *let go*, *released*. She thought she heard her ancient captor chuckling to herself.

Two possibilities occurred to her: that her pursuers had driven her to this place and the old woman was in league with them; and that they had not and she was not. The worse by far of these options was the second, that to escape her rapists she had fled into a psychopath's dungeon. Maybe the old woman wanted to starve her to death. Maybe she wanted to soften her up so she'd be easy to kill. Or maybe she was just keeping her as a snack for some monstrous get of hers, some overgrown looney-tunes son with pinwheel eyes and horrible teeth and a vast appetite for stray women.

More to exhaust all of her possibilities than because she imagined they possessed any actual substance, Sandrine turned carefully around, planted a hand on the earthen wall beside her, and began making her way down the stairs in the dark. It would lead to some spider-infested cellar, she knew, a foul-smelling hole where ugly, discarded things waited thug-like in the seamless dark to inflict injury upon anyone who entered their realm. She would grope her way from wall to wall, feeling for another door, for a high window, for any means to escape, knowing all the while that earthen cellars in shabby slum dwellings never had separate exits.

Five steps down, it occurred to Sandrine that she might not have been the first woman to be locked into this awful basement, and that instead of broken chairs and worn-out tools she might find herself knocking against a ribcage or two, a couple of femurs, that her foot might land on a jawbone, that she might step on somebody's forehead! Her body of a sudden shook, and her mind went white, and for a few moments Sandrine was on the verge of coming unglued: she pictured herself drawn up into a fetal ball, shuddering, weeping, whimpering. For a moment this dreadful image seemed unbearably tempting.

Then she thought, *Why the FUCK isn't Ballard here?*

Ballard was one hell of a tricky dude, he was full of little surprises, you could never really predict what he'd feel like doing, and he was a brilliant problem-solver. That's what Ballard did for a living, he flew around the world mopping up other people's messes. The only reason Sandrine knew him at all was that Ballard had materialized in a New Jersey motel room where good old Dad, Lauritzen Loy had been dithering over the corpse of a strangled whore, then caused the whore to vanish, the bloody sheets to vanish, and for all she knew the motel to vanish also. Two hours later a shaken but sober Lauritzen Loy reported to work in an immaculate and spotless Armani suit and Brioni tie. (Sandrine had known the details of her father's vile little peccadillo for years.) Also, and this quality meant that his presence would have been particularly valuable down in the witch-hag's cellar, although Ballard might have looked as though he had never picked up anything heavier than a briefcase, he was in fact astonishingly strong, fast, and smart. If you were experiencing a little difficulty with a dragon, Ballard was the man for you.

While meditating upon the all-round excellence of her longtime lover and wishing for him more with every fresh development of her thought, Sandrine had been continuing steadily on her way down the stairs. When she reached the part about the dragon, it came to her that she had been on these earthen stairs far longer than she had expected. Sandrine thought she was now actually beneath the level of the cellar she had expected to enter. The fairy tale feeling came over her again, of being held captive in a world without rational rules and orders, subject to deep patterns unknown to or rejected by the daylit world. In a flash of insight, it came to her that this fairytale world had much in common with her childhood.

To regain control of herself, perhaps most of all to shake off the sense of gloom-laden helplessness evoked by thoughts of childhood, Sandrine began to count the steps as she descended. Down into the earth they went, the dry firm steps that met her feet, twenty more, then forty, then fifty. At a hundred and one, she felt light-headed and weary, and sat down in the darkness. She felt like weeping. The long stairs were a grave, leading nowhere but to itself. Hope, joy, and desire had fled, even boredom and petulance had fled, hunger, lust, and anger were no more. She felt tired and empty. Sandrine leaned a shoulder against the earthen wall, shuddered once, and realized she was crying only a moment before she fled into unconsciousness.

In that same instant she passed into an ongoing dream, as if she had wandered into the middle of a story, more accurately a point far closer to its ending. Much, maybe nearly everything of interest, had already happened. Sandrine lay on a mess of filthy blankets at the bottom of a cage. The Golden Shower of Shit had sufficiently relaxed, it seemed, as to permit the butchering of entire slabs of flesh from her body, for much of the meat from her right shoulder had been sliced away. The wound reported a dull, wavering ache that spoke of those wonderful objects, Ballard's narcotic painkillers. So close together were the narrow bars, she could extend only a hand, a wrist, an arm. In her case, an arm, a wrist, and a stump. The hand was absent from the arm Sandrine had slipped through the bars, and someone had cauterized the wounded wrist.

The Mystery of the Missing Hand led directly to Cage Number One, where a giant bug-creature sat crammed in at an angle, filling nearly the whole of the cage, mewing softly, and trying to saw through the bars with its remaining mandible. It had broken the left one on the bars, but it was not giving up, it was a bug, and bugs don't quit. Sandrine was all but certain that when in possession of both mandibles, that is to say before capture, this huge *thing* had used them to saw off her hand, which it had then promptly devoured. The giant bugs were the scourge of the river tribes. However, the Old Ones, the Real People, the Cloud Huggers, the Tree Spirits, the archaic Sacred Ones who spoke in birdsong and called themselves **We** had so shaped the River and the Forest, which had given them birth, that the meat of the giant bugs tasted exceptionally good, and a giant bug guilty of eating a person or parts of a person became by that act overwhelmingly delicious, like manna, like the food of paradise for human beings. **We** were feeding bits of Sandrine to the captured bug that it might yield stupendous meals for the Sandrine and Ballard upstairs.

Sandrine awakened crying out in fear and horror, scattering tears she could not see.

Enough of that. Yes, quite enough of quivering; it was time to decide what to do next. Go back and try to break down the door, or keep going down and see what happens? Sandrine hated the idea of giving up and going backwards. She levered herself upright and resumed her descent with stair number one hundred and two.

At stair three hundred she passed through another spasm of weepy trembling, but soon conquered it and moved on. By the four hundredth stair she was hearing faint carnival music and seeing sparkly light-figments flit through the darkness like illuminated moths. Somewhere around stair five hundred she realized that the numbers had become mixed up in her head, and stopped counting. She saw a grave that wasn't a grave, merely darkness, and she saw her old tutor at Clare, a cool, detached Don named Quentin Jester who said things like, "If I had a lifetime with you, Miss Loy, we'd both know a deal more than we do at present," but she closed her eyes and shook her head and sent him packing.

Many stairs later, Sandrine's thigh muscles reported serious aches, and her arms felt extraordinarily heavy. So did her head, which kept lolling forward to rest on her chest. Her stomach complained, and she said to herself, *Wish I had a nice big slice of sautéed giant bug right about now*, and chuckled at how crazy she had become in so short a time. Giant bug! Even good old Dad, old LL, who often respected sanity in others but wished for none of it himself, drew the line at dining on giant insects. And here came yet another proof of her deteriorating mental condition, that despite her steady progress deeper and deeper underground, Sandrine could almost sort of half-persuade herself that the darkness before her seemed weirdly less dark than only a moment ago. This lunatic delusion clung to her step after step, worsening as she went. She said to herself, I'll hold up my hand, and if I think I see it, I'll know it's good-by, real world, pack Old Tillie off to Bedlam. She stopped moving, closed her eyes, and raised her hand before her face. Slowly, she opened her eyes, and beheld... her hand!

The problem with the insanity defense lay in the irrevocable truth that it was really her hand before her, not a mad vision from Gothic literature but her actual, entirely earthly hand, at present grimy and crusted with dirt from its long contact with the wall. Sandrine turned her head and discovered that she could make out the wall, too, with its hard-packed earth showing here and there the pale string of a severed root, at times sending in her direction a little spray or shower of dusty particulate. Sandrine held her breath and looked down to what appeared to be the source of the illumination. Then she inhaled sharply, for it seemed to her that she could see, dimly and a long way down, the bottom of the stairs. A little rectangle of light burned away down there, and from it floated the luminous translucency that made it possible for her to see.

Too shocked to cry, too relieved to insist on its impossibility, Sandrine moved slowly down the remaining steps to the rectangle of light. Its warmth heated the air, the steps, the walls, and Sandrine herself, who only now registered that for most of her journey she had been half-paralyzed by the chill leaking from the earth. As she drew nearer to the light, she could finally make out details of what lay beneath her. She thought she saw a strip of concrete, part of a wooden barrel, the bottom of a ladder lying on the ground: the intensity of the light surrounding these enigmatic objects shrank and dwindled them, hollowed them out even as it drilled painfully into her eyes. Beneath her world existed another, its light a blinding dazzle.

When Sandrine had come within thirty feet of the blazing underworld, her physical relationship to it mysteriously altered. It seemed she no longer stepped downward, but moved across a slanting plane that leveled almost imperceptibly off. The dirt walls on either side fell back and melted to ghostly gray air, to nothing solid, until all that remained was the residue of dust and grime plastered over Sandrine's white dress, her hands and face, her hair. Heat reached her, the real heat of an incendiary sun, and human voices, and the clang and bang and underlying susurrus of machinery. She walked toward all of it, shading her eyes as she went.

Through the simple opening before her Sandrine moved, and the sun blazed down upon her, and her own moisture instantly soaked her filthy dress, and sweat turned the dirt in her hair to muddy trickles. She knew this place; the dazzling underworld was the world she had left. From beneath her shading hand Sandrine took in the wide concrete apron, the equipment she had noticed all that harrowing time ago and the equipment she had not, the men posturing for the benefit of other men, the sense of falsity and stagecraft and the incipient swelling of a banal unheard melody. The long yellow dock where on a sluggish umber tide three yachts slowly rocked, one of them the *Sweet Delight*.

In a warm breeze that was not a breeze, a soiled-looking scrap of paper flipped toward Sandrine over the concrete, at the last lifting off the ground to adhere to her leg. She bent down to peel it off and release it, and caught a strong, bitter whiff, unmistakably excremental, of the Amazon. The piece of paper wished to cling to her leg, and there it hung until the second tug of Sandrine's dirty fingers, when she observed that she was gripping not a scrap of paper but a Polaroid, now a little besmudged by contact with her leg. When she raised it to her face, runnels of dirt obscured portions of the image. She brushed away much of the dirt, but could still make no sense of the photograph, which appeared to depict some pig-like animal.

In consternation, she glanced to one side and found there, lounging against bollards and aping the idleness of degenerates and river louts, two of the men in shabby suits and worn-out hats who had pursued her into the slum. She straightened up in rage and terror, and to confirm what she already knew to be the case, looked to her other side and saw their companions. One of them waved to her. Sandrine's terror cooled before her perception that these guys had changed in some basic way. Maybe they weren't idle, exactly, but these men were more relaxed, less predatory than they had been on the avenue into Manaus.

They had their eyes on her, though, they were interested in what she was going to do. Then she finally got it: they were different because now she was where they had wanted her to be all along. They didn't think she would try to escape again, but they wanted to make sure. Sandrine's whole long adventure, from the moment she noticed she was being followed to the present, had been designed to funnel her back to the dock and the yacht. The four men, who were now smiling at her and nodding their behatted heads, had pushed her toward the witch-hag, for they were all in it together! Sandrine dropped her arms, took a step backward, and in amazement looked from side to side, taking in all of them. It had all been a trick; herded like a cow, she had been played. Falsity again; more stagecraft.

One of the nodding, smiling men held his palm up before his face, and the man beside him leaned forward and laughed into his fist, as if shielding a sneeze. Grinning at her, the first man went through his meaningless mime act once again, lifting his left hand and staring into its palm. Grinning even more widely, he pointed at Sandrine and shouted, "*Munna!*"

The man beside him cracked up, *Munna!*, what a wit, then whistled an odd little four note melody that might have been a birdcall.

Experimentally, Sandrine raised her left hand, regarded it, and realized that she was still gripping the dirty little Polaroid photograph of a pig. Those two idiots off to her left waved their hands in ecstasy. She was doing the right thing, so *Munna!* right back atcha, buddy. She looked more closely at the Polaroid and saw that what it pictured was not actually a pig. The creature in the photo had a head and a torso, but little else. The eyes, nose, and ears were gone. A congeries of scars like punctuation marks, like snakes, like words in an unknown language, decorated the torso.

I know what Munna *means, and* Num, thought Sandrine, and for a moment experienced a spasm of stunning, utterly sexual warmth before she fully understood what had been given her: that she recognized the man in the photo. The roar of oceans, of storm-battered leaves, filled her ears and caused her head to spin and wobble. Her fingers parted, and the Polaroid floated off in an artificial, wind-machine breeze that spun it around a couple of times before lifting it high above the port and winking it out of sight, lost in the bright hard blue above the *Sweet Delight.*

Sandrine found herself moving down the yellow length of the long dock.

Tough love, Ballard had said. To be given and received, at the end perfectly repaid by that which she had perhaps glimpsed but never witnessed, the brutal, exalted, slow-moving force that had sometimes rustled a curtain, sometimes moved through this woman her hair and body now dark with mud, had touched her between her legs, Sandrine, poor profane lost deluded most marvelously fated Sandrine.

1997

From the galley they come, from behind the little dun-colored curtain in the dining room, from behind the bookcases in the handsome sitting room, from beneath the bed and the bloodstained metal table, through wood and fabric and the weight of years, **We** come, the Old Ones and Real People, the Cloud Huggers, **We** process slowly toward the center of the mystery **We** understand only by giving it unquestioning service. What remains of the clients and patrons lies, still breathing though without depth or force, upon the metal work-table. It was always going to end this way, it always does, it can no other. Speaking in the high-pitched, musical language of birds that **We** taught the Piraha at the beginning of time, **We** gather at the site of these ruined bodies, **We** worship their devotion to each other and the Great Task that grew and will grow on them, **We** treat them with grave tenderness as we separate what can and must be separated. Notes of the utmost liquid purity float upward from the mouths of **We** and print themselves upon the air. **We** know what they mean, though they have long since passed through the realm of words and gained again the transparency of music. **We** love and accept the weight and the weightlessness of music. When the process of separation is complete, through the old sacred inner channels **We** transport what the dear, still-living man and woman have each taken from the other's body down down down to the galley and the ravening hunger that burns ever within it.

Then. Then. With the utmost tenderness, singing the deep tuneless music at the heart of the ancient world, **We** gather up what remains of Ballard and Sandrine, armless and legless trunks, faces without features, their breath clinging to their mouths like wisps, carry them (in our arms, in baskets, in once-pristine sheets) across the deck and permit them to roll from our care, as they had always longed to do, and into that of the flashing furious little river-monarchs. **We** watch the water boil in a magnificence of ecstasy, and **We** sing for as long as it lasts.

MAJORLENA

JANE JAKEMAN

She scared the hell out of me.

We never did find out where she came from, before she found us.

After the explosions, three of us scrambled out, away from the road, over the ridge. There was a rocky overhang on the other side. I had the map they'd showed us still in my head. We were bang in the middle of real thick hostiles territory, like jelly in a doughnut.

"Fuck it, man, we stay right here," hissed Leroy.

"You ain't in charge," said Schulz.

"We stay on the ridge," I said.

The explosion had taken out the lead trucks. If we hadn't been straggling, we'd have been gone as well.

There was no movement on the road except for flames. Then came black smoke and a stink. Strange, I knew what it was right away. Like in my mom's kitchen when she made us taffy, stirring away in a boiling-hot saucepan.

"Man comin' up!" shouted Leroy. Then he added, "Jeez, maybe it's a female!"

A helmet outlined above the ridge, then a small figure, hands high, coming up slowly in regulation desert boots, skidding on the sand and shale. People think the Iraqi desert is smooth sand like the beach, but there's places where it's all little stones slipping under your feet. When I think of Major Lena now, and I try not to do that, it's what I remember: the air full of black smouldering stuff and the smell of burning sugar.

We hadn't thought anyone else was alive, but she came from the direction of the road. She was dead cautious, waited, lay on the ground, let Schulz take her rifle and fumble all over her.

"Clean!" he shouted.

She had dog-tags, ID, but it was her voice, more than anything, that was ranking US female military. Though, like I said, we never did find out exactly where she was from. She had a kit-bag and Schulz pushed his hand in it.

"No weapons here," he said.

This was just after dawn and we was stuck there in the desert. Go back down onto the road—no way! A beat-up old wagon came along the road as we were sitting under that ridge; it was full of rag-heads, their rifles all sticking out at odd angles. They didn't spot us. We might have taken them, four of us now, all armed. But something a damned sight more powerful had taken out the trucks—a rocket-launcher, maybe—and whoever fired that might still be around.

This bunch nudged through the smouldering debris with their rifles. It looked like the metal was still too hot to touch—one of them put a hand to a door and drew it back like he'd been scorched. They didn't hang around.

We took a good look at ourselves. Two privates, Leroy and Schulz. Me, the sergeant. And the woman, Major Lena. I guess she had a surname but I don't remember one. Whenever I think of her, which is as little as possible, it's all run together like it was one name—Majorlena. Sounds like a fancy name someone might give a girl. Anyway, that's what we called her. "Yes, Majorlena! Sure, Majorlena! Show us your boobs, Majorlena!"

No, not that. We'd never have dared.

"I'm taking charge here, Sergeant," she said in that voice, slow scraping on steel, flashing her white teeth (that's another reason we was sure she was genuine US of A) but not in any real smile.

She had brown eyes, huge, but not pretty.

"Yes, sir!" I said.

"We'll assess the situation."

We assessed.

Stuck in the middle of a fucking desert surrounded by terrorists, that was our situation.

And no food or water.

Choppers circled above the roadkill like great buzzing flies, and I said, "Sir, we could spread out our shirts or wave something at them."

"Yeah, they're bound to see us," said Leroy. "They're real low."

He ran to the top of the ridge of rock, pulled his shirt off and waved it. There was a burst of machine-gun fire. They had lousy aim. Leroy came running back and we all crowded under the overhang.

"Private Leroy, you take your orders from me," said Majorlena. "Don't move without my say-so. We have to sit it out under the ridge till nightfall. Then we can go down and maybe find some water and ammo." I saw she was eyeing Leroy's bare chest as she talked. He was a good-looking guy, one of them tall, slim blacks.

I forgot about sex. By noon, my eyes felt like they was eggs frying in a pan. I felt like I'd never been in the country before, though I'd been in Iraq for two months. But never really in it, if you see what I mean. Never like this, without iced drinks or showers. I found out you don't rightly sweat when it gets that hot, if you ain't got no water to sweat out of you. Any little trickle off your skin dries instantly. Kind of comfortable after a while, except your head feels like it's in a furnace. Schulz had a shaved head, like a lot of the Pennsylvania boys, unprotected.

We got some shade from the overhang. But my mouth was parching like it was full of sand and when evening was coming I knew we had to get water or we was going to die right there.

Majorlena had been assessing the road situation.

"Sergeant, you and I will go down to the road," she said. "The third truck hasn't been too badly hit. There may be some water, or even a radio."

"That the one you was in, sir?" No one could have survived from the two front trucks. They was nothing but metal frames with charred lumps in the drivers' seats.

"Why, yes, Sergeant," she said. "That's right. I've been travelling with this army."

The melted sugar had poured down the sides of the trucks. There was all kinds of flies and insects there, drawn to the sweetness, I guess. You don't usually get those big fat things in the middle of the desert. It's mostly hard little flies that choke you up when the wind blows a swarm in your face. Majorlena and I were brushing juicy ones off as we got to the third truck. I didn't like the way they flew into my mouth when I opened it.

"Check the tanks and see if you can find some containers," she said.

She climbed up into the cabin. The driver hadn't been burned to cinders. I could see the fire hadn't hit so bad here, though his hair and face was scorched.

Going to unscrew the caps, I went round the side of the truck and looked up. She was there right next to the driver, with her head bent down towards him, when she realised I was watching her. She made a sudden jerking arm movement. Getting down out of the cabin, she showed me something in her hand.

"Got his tags. Give his family closure."

Poor bastard had closure all right. But I still wasn't sure what she'd been doing.

I managed to drain water from the radiator into some big cans, US army property we found in the truck. They was full of coffee. We emptied it into the sand, where it blew away like darker smoke against the dusk.

Before we got back to the top of the ridge, we heard shots.

Schulz was dragging Leroy back up.

"Stupid asshole tried to make a break. They got night-sights."

Majorlena put her hand over Leroy's mouth to stop his screams. They gradually went down to whimpering. He died near dawn. We scrabbled a place for him in the sand and tipped it over him with our hands, then Schulz said some prayers.

‹◦›

The hunger was like real pain. We had a little water left, tasting of metal and coffee.

"We got to figure a way off here." Schulz was clutching his belly as if he were trying to press it smaller.

"We stay near the vehicles," said Majorlena. She was walking 'round. She didn't look sunk-eyed, not like she had spent the night out in the open with no food or water.

"Yeah," I said, "I know that's official. But there's exceptions."

"There may be some of that melted sugar we could break off," said Majorlena, like she was making a concession.

"I'll go down to the trucks when it gets dark," I said. Just the thought of filling my mouth with that real sweet taste near drove me crazy.

They let me go alone. I figured I would be entitled to extra sugar.

The driver's body was stinking. Stars and moon were bright as electric, so I was afraid I'd be seen by snipers. But nothing. Got to the back of the truck and there was like smooth icicles hanging down. I broke one off and took a suck. Damn me if it wasn't as sweet as candy at a fair. I felt the sugar running through me, its energy coming up in my blood.

When I scrabbled back to the top of the ridge, sending some shale skidding under me, the Major was waiting.

I gave her a piece of sugar.

"Where's Schulz?"

"Getting some sleep down there."

But he was next to Leroy's body and when I shook him he didn't wake up. I called softly for Majorlena to come down.

"What is it?"

She rolled Schulz over towards her and his face was cold and still in the moonlight, his eyes staring up at the stars.

"Jesus! How the hell?—he was okay when I went down." I looked across and saw that Leroy's body was partly uncovered, down to about the waist. Saw what had happened to that smooth skin.

"You reckon Schulz did that?" I said.

"Must have, unless it was wild dogs or something, but I've been keeping watch all the time you were down there. I didn't hear anything."

"Maybe Schulz went a bit crazy, didn't know what he was doing."

"Yeah, sunstroke, heat exhaustion." She sat back. "I'll have to make a report on it when we get picked up."

It was the coldest night I have ever spent. There was no cloud cover. I didn't sleep any, just sat up with my back against the rock. Majorlena was a little ways off, kind of hunched over. I closed my eyes at one point and then opened them a few moments later. She seemed to have shifted a little towards me.

"I ain't going to get no sleep tonight," I said.

Was I warning her or asking her? I still don't know.

But I did go to sleep, and when I woke up, something was moving over Leroy's body. It was a big mass of stuff, like a long beard trailing down from his neck. I stared for a few moments trying to make sense of it, rolling over so I could get a better look. There was a fluttering and crawling going on nonstop over Leroy's chest.

I couldn't see his face. It looked to be moving and heaving, and that was a big swarm of fat blowflies crawling over it and down his body. They glistened, their sticky bodies shifting and pushing, some flying a bit and then settling. In the wounds on his chest, there were flies right in the bloody furrows, twisting round and fluttering like whores in a jacuzzi.

Lying a few feet away, like she and Leroy was in a bed, was Majorlena. And then the flies was coming off Leroy in this black stream, climbing and hopping and flying towards her.

I took a step towards her, thinking she was asleep. I was going to warn her. Then I saw she was awake.

Worse than awake. Her mouth was open and the flies were crawling up over her body and she was saying things. I got closer and heard her whispering.

"Come on my little ones, Mamma's thirsty, Mamma's hungry. You know what she wants. She needs you now."

And the flies were crawling into her dark wet open mouth, scrambling and fluttering over her lips, and she was chawing down on them.

The charred dead in their trucks down on the road was better than that. I sat there all night.

A patrol coming along the road picked me up next day. I told them to look for three more up on the ridge, but they only found two bodies.

I guess she's still travelling with the army.

THE DAYS OF OUR LIVES

ADAM L. G. NEVILL

The ticking was much louder on the first floor and soon after the ticking began I heard Lois moving upstairs. Floorboards groaned as she made unsteady progress through areas made murky by curtains not opened for a week. She must have come up inside our bedroom and staggered into the hall, passing herself along the walls with her thin hands. I hadn't seen her for six days but could easily imagine her aspect and mood: the sinewy neck, the fierce grey eyes, a mouth already downcast, and the lips atremble at grievances revived upon the very moment of her return. But I also wondered if her eyes and nails were painted. She had beautiful eyelashes. I went and stood at the foot of the stairs and looked up.

Even on the unlit walls of the stairwell a long and spiky shadow was cast by her antics above. Though I could not see Lois, the air was moving violently, as were parts of her shadow, and I knew she was already batting the side of her face with her hands and then throwing her arms into the air above her scruffy grey head. As expected, she'd woken furious.

The muttering began and was too quiet for me to clearly hear all of what she was saying, but the voice was sharp, the words sibilant and near spat out, so I could only assume she had woken thinking of me. "I told you . . . how many times! . . . and you wouldn't listen . . . for God's sake . . . what is wrong with you? . . . why must you be so difficult? . . . all the time . . . you have been told . . . time after time . . ."

I'd hoped for a better mood. I had cleaned the house over two days, thoroughly but hurriedly for when she next arose. I'd even washed the walls and ceilings, had moved all of the furniture to sweep, dust and vacuum. I had brought no food indoors but loaves of cheap white bread, eggs, plain biscuits, and baking materials that would never be used. I had scalded and boiled the house of dirt and rid the building of its pleasures, with the exception of the television that she enjoyed and the little ceramic radio in the kitchen that only picked up Radio Two from 1983. Ultimately, I had bleached our rented home of any overt signifier of joy, as well as those things she was not interested in, or anything that remained of myself that I forgot about as soon as it was gone.

The last handful of books that intrigued me, anything of any colour or imagination that enabled me to pass this great expanse of time, that burned my chest and internal organs as if my body was pressed against a hot radiator, I finally removed from the shelves yesterday and donated to charity shops along the seafront. Only the ancient knitting patterns, gardening books, antique baking encyclopaedias, religious pamphlets, old socialist diatribes, completely out-of-date versions of imperial history, and indigestible things of that nature, remained now. Faded spines, heavy paper smelling of unventilated rooms, leprous-spotted, migraine-inducing reminders of what, her time? Though Lois never looked at them, I'm pretty sure those books never had anything to do with me.

I retreated from the stairs and moved to the window of the living room. I opened the curtains for the first time in a week. Without any interest in the flowers, I looked down at the artificial iris in the green glass vase to distract my eyes from the small, square garden. Others had also come up since the ticking began, and I didn't want to look at them. A mere glance out back had been sufficient and had revealed the presence of a mostly rotten, brownish snake; one still writhing and showing its paler underbelly on the lawn beneath the washing line. Two wooden birds with ferocious eyes pecked at the snake. Inside the sideboard beside me, the ornaments of the little black warriors that we bought from a charity shop began to beat their leather drums with their wooden hands. On the patio and inside the old kennel, that had not seen a dog in years, I glimpsed the pale back of a young woman. I knew it was the girl with the bespectacled face that suited newsprint and a garish headline above a picture of a dismal, wet field beside an A road. I'd seen this young woman last week from a bus window and looked away from her quickly to feign interest in the plastic banner strung across the front of a pub. Too late, though, because Lois had been sat beside me and had noticed my leering. She angrily ripped away the foil from a tube of Polo mints and I knew that girl by the side of the road was in trouble deep.

"I saw you," was all that Lois said. She'd not even turned her head.

I wanted to say, "Saw what?" but it would do me no good and I couldn't speak for the terrible, cold remorse that seemed to fill my throat like a potato swallowed whole. But I could now see that the girl had been strangled with her own ivory-toned tights and stuffed inside the kennel in our garden. The incident must have been the cause of Lois's distress and the reason why she'd withdrawn from me to lie down for a week.

But Lois was coming down the stairs now, on her front, and making the sound of a large cat coughing out fur because she was eager to confront me with those displeasures lingering from the last time she was around.

The ticking filled the living room, slipping inside my ears and inducing the smell of a linoleum floor in a preschool that I had attended in the nineteen seventies. In my memory, a lollipop lady smiled as I crossed a road with a leather satchel banging against my side. I saw the faces of four children I'd not thought of in decades. For a moment, I remembered all of their names before forgetting them again.

Reflected upon the glass of the window, Lois's tall, thin silhouette with the messy head swayed from side to side as she entered the living room. When Lois saw me she stopped moving and said, "You," in a voice exhausted by despair and panted out with disgust. And then she rushed in quickly and flared up behind me.

I flinched.

⟶

In the café on the pier I cut a small dry cake in half, a morsel that would have failed to satisfy a child. I carefully placed half of the cake on a saucer before Lois. One of her eyelids flickered as if in acknowledgement, but more from displeasure, as if I was trying to win her over and make her grateful.

What I could see of her eyes still expressed detachment, anger and a morbid loathing. Tense and uncomfortable, I continued to mess with the tea things.

We were the only customers. The sea beyond the windows was grey and the wind flapped the pennants and the plastic coverings on idle bumper cars. Our mugs held watery, unsweetened tea. I made sure that I did not enjoy mine.

Inside her vinyl, crab-coloured handbag the ticking was near idle, not so persistent, but far below the pier, in the water, I was distracted by a large, dark shape that might have been a cloud shadow. It appeared to flow beneath the water before disappearing under the pier, and for a moment I could smell the briny wet wood under the café and hear the slop of thick waves against the uprights. A swift episode of vertigo followed and I remembered a Christmas tree on red and green carpet that reminded me of chameleons, and a lace cloth on a wooden coffee table with pointy legs similar to the fins on old American cars, and a wooden bowl of nuts and raisins, a glass of sherry, and a babysitter's long shins in sheer, dark tights that had a wet sheen by the light of a gas fire. Legs that I couldn't stop peeking at, even at that age, and I must have been around four years old. I'd tried to use the babysitter's shiny legs as a bridge for a Matchbox car to pass under, so that I could get my face closer. The babysitter's pale skin was freckled under her tights. And right up close her legs smelled of a woman's underwear drawer and the material of her tights was just lots of little fabric squares that transformed into a smooth, second skin as I moved my face away again. One thing then another thing. So many ways to see everything. One skin and then another skin. It had made me squirm and squirt.

Across the table, in the café on the pier, Lois smiled and her eyes glittered with amusement. "You'll never learn," she said, and I knew that she wanted to hit me hard. I shivered in the draught that came under the door from off the windswept pier, and my old hands looked so veiny and bluish upon the laminate table top.

Slipping the gauzy scarf around her head, she indicated that she wanted to leave. As she rose her spectacles caught the light from the fluorescent strip, a shimmer of fire above sharp ice.

There was no one outside the café, or on the pier, or the grassy area behind the esplanade, so she hit me full in the face with a closed fist and left me dazed and leaning against a closed ice-cream concession. Blood came into my mouth.

I followed her for ten minutes, sulking, then pulled up alongside her and we trudged up and down the near-empty grey streets of the town and looked in shop windows. We bought some Christmas cards, a pound of potatoes we'd boil fluffy and eat later with tasteless fish, and carrots from a tin. From the pound shop we picked up a small box of Scottish shortbread. In a charity shop she bought a pencil skirt without trying it on, and two satin blouses. "I have no idea when I'll be able to wear anything nice again."

As we passed Bay Electrics I saw a girl's face on two big television screens. Local news too, showing a pretty girl with black-framed glasses who never made it to work one morning just over a week ago. It was the girl inside the kennel.

"Is that what you like?" Lois whispered in a breathless voice beside me. "Is that what you fancy?"

Increasing her pace, she walked in front of me, head down, all the way back to the car, and she never spoke during the drive home. At our place, she sat and watched a television quiz show that I hadn't seen since the seventies. It could not have been scheduled, possibly never even recorded by ITV either, but it's what she wanted and so it appeared and she watched it.

She couldn't bear the sight of me, I could tell, and she didn't want me watching her quiz show either, so I removed my clothes and went and lay in the basket under the kitchen table. I tried to remember if we'd ever had a dog, or if it was my teeth that had made those marks on the rubber bone.

An hour after I lay down and curled up, Lois began screaming in the lounge. I think she was on the telephone and had called a number she'd recalled from years, or even decades, long gone. "Is Mr. Price there? What do you mean I have the wrong number? Put him on immediately!" God knows what they made of the call at the other end of the line. I just stayed very still and kept my eyes clenched shut until she hung up and began to sob.

Inside the kitchen the ticking lulled me to sleep amongst vague odours of lemon disinfectant, the dog blanket and cooker gas.

◄○►

Lois was doing a one-thousand-piece jigsaw puzzle; the one with the painting of a mill beside a pond. The puzzle was spread across a card table and her legs passed beneath the table. I sat before her, naked, and stayed quiet. Her toes were no more than a few inches from my knees and I dared not shuffle any closer. She was wearing her black brassiere, a nylon slip, and very fine tights. She had painted her toenails red and her legs whisked when she rubbed them together. The rollers had come out of her hair now too and her silver hair shimmered beside the fairy lights. Her eye makeup was pink and gloriously alluring around her cold iron-coloured eyes. When she wore makeup she looked younger. A thin gold bracelet circled her slender wrist and the watch attached to the metal strap ticked quietly. The watch face was so tiny I could not see what the time was. Gone midnight, I guessed.

Until she'd finished the puzzle she only spoke to me once, in a quiet, hard voice. "If you touch it, I'll have it straight off."

I let my limp hands fall back to the floor. My whole body was aching from sitting still for so long.

She mostly remained calm and disinterested for the remainder of the time it took her to finish her puzzle, so I didn't have many memories. I only recall things when she is agitated and I forget them when she calms down. When she is enraged I am flooded.

Lois began to drink sherry from a long glass and to share unflattering reminiscences and observations about our courtship. Things like, "I don't know what I was thinking back then? And now I'm stuck. Ha! Look at me now, ha! Hardly The Ritz. Promises, promises. I'd have been much better off with that American chappy. That one you were friendly with . . ." Increasingly roused, she padded back and forth through the living room, so long, thin and silky with her thighs susurrating together. I could smell her lipstick, perfume and hairspray, which usually excited me, particularly as her mood changed to something ugly and volatile. And as I sensed the vinegar of spite rising up through her I began to remember . . . I think . . . a package that arrived in a small room where I had lived, years before. Yes, I've remembered this before, and many times, I think.

The padded envelope had once been addressed to a doctor, but someone had written NO LONGER AT THIS ADDRESS on the front, and then written my address as the correct postal address. Only it wasn't addressed to me, or anyone specifically, but was instead addressed to "You," and then "A Man," and "Him," and all on the same line above my postal address. There were no details of the sender, so I'd opened the parcel. And it had contained an old watch, a ladies wristwatch, with a thin, scuffed bracelet that smelled of perfume, and so strongly that I received an impression of slim white wrists when I held the watch. Within the cotton wool was a mass-produced paper flier advertising a "literary walk," organised by something called "The Movement."

I went along to this walk, but only, I think, to return the watch to the sender. It was a themed walk on a wet Sunday: something to do with three gruesome paintings in a tiny church. The triptych of paintings featured an ugly antique wooden cabinet as their subject. There was some kind of connection between the cabinet and a local poet who had gone mad. I think. There were drinks after the tedious walk too, I am sure, in a community centre. I'd asked around the group on the walk, trying to establish to whom the watch belonged. Everyone I asked had said, "Ask Lois. That looks like one of hers." Or, "Speak to Lois. That's a Lois." Maybe even, "Lois, she's looking. She's due."

I'd eventually identified and approached this Lois, spoken to her, and complemented her on her fabulous eye makeup. She'd looked wary, but appreciated the remark with a nod and tight smile that never extended to her eyes. She said, "You're from that building where the down-and-outs live? I was hoping you were going to be that other chap that I've seen going inside." And she'd taken the watch from me, and sighed resignedly. "But all right then," as if accepting an invitation from me. "At least you returned it. But it's not going to be what you think, I'm afraid." I remember being confused.

That afternoon I'd not been able to stop staring at her beautiful hands either, or thinking of her wearing nothing but the tight leather boots she'd worn on the walk. So I was glad that the watch had a connection to this woman called Lois. I think my attentions made her feel special but also irritable, as if I were a pest. I wasn't sure how old she was, but she had clearly tried to look older with the grey coat and headscarf and A-line tweed skirts.

From a first sighting she had made me feel uncomfortable, but intrigued and aroused also, and at the time I had been lonely and unable to get the cold, unfriendly woman out of my mind, so I had gone to the community centre again knowing that is where the strange group of people, The Movement, met monthly. This dowdy, plain and depressing building was the centre of their organisation, and had pictures painted by children covering the walls. On my second visit plastic chairs had been set out in rows. They were red. There was a silver urn with tea and biscuits on a paper plate too: Garibaldis, Lemon Puffs, and stale Iced Gems. I was nervous and didn't really know anyone well, and those that I thought might recognise me from the walk seemed unwilling to converse.

When something was about to occur on the stage, I sat in the row behind Lois. She was wearing a grey coat that she didn't take off indoors. Her head was covered by a scarf again, but her eyes were concealed by red-tinted glasses. She'd worn those boots again too, but had seemed indifferent to me, even after I'd returned the watch and she'd suggested some kind of enigmatic agreement had been made between us the first time we met. I did suspect that she was unstable, but I was lonely and desperate. I found it all very bewildering too, but my bafflement was only destined to increase.

To replicate the image in one of the hideous paintings that I had seen on the literary walk, a picture responsible for sending a local poet mad, a motionless elderly woman had sat in a chair on the low stage. She was draped in black and wore a veil. One of her legs was contained inside a large wooden boot. Beside her chair was a curtained cabinet, the size of a wardrobe but deeper, the sort of thing budget magicians used. On the other side of her was a piece of navigational equipment; naval, I had assumed, and all made from brass with what looked like a clock face on the front. A loud ticking had issued from the brass device.

Another woman with curly black hair, who was overweight and dressed like a little girl, came onto the stage too . . . I think she wore very high heels that were red. When the woman in the red shoes read poems from a book, I felt uneasy and thought that I should go; just get up and leave the hall quickly. But I lingered for fear of drawing attention to myself by scraping a chair leg across the floor, while everyone else at the meeting was so enraptured by the performance on the stage.

After the reading, the woman dressed like a little girl withdrew from the stage and the hall darkened until the building was solely lit by two red stage lights.

Something inside the cupboard on the stage began to croak and the sound made me think of a bullfrog. It must have been a recording, or so I had thought at the time. The ticking from the brass clock grew louder and louder too. Some people stood up and shouted things at the box. I felt horrified, embarrassed for the shouters, uncomfortable, and eventually I panicked and made to leave.

Lois had turned round then and said, "Sit back down!" It was the first time she'd even acknowledged me that evening and I returned to my seat, though I wasn't sure why I obeyed her. And the others near me in the hall had looked at me too, expectantly. I had shrugged and cleared my throat and asked, "What?"

Lois had said, "It's not what, it's who and when?"

I didn't understand.

On the stage, the elderly woman with the false leg spoke for the first time. "One can go," she'd said, her frail voice amplified through some old plastic speakers above the stage.

Chairs were knocked aside or even upturned in the undignified scrabble toward the stage that was made by at least four female members of the group. They'd all held pocket watches in the air too, as they stumbled to the stage. Lois got there first, her posture tense with a childlike excitement, and had looked up at the elderly woman expectantly.

The old veiled head above her had nodded and Lois had risen up the stairs to the stage. On her hands and knees, with her head bowed, she then crawled inside the curtained cabinet. As she moved inside, kind of giggling, or maybe it was whimpering, the elderly woman in the chair had beaten Lois on the back, buttocks and legs, quite mercilessly, with a walking stick.

The stage lights went out, or failed, and the congregation fell silent in the darkness. All I could hear was the clock ticking loudly until a sound like a melon being split apart came wetly from the direction of the stage.

"That time is over," the amplified voice of the elderly woman announced.

The lights came on and the people in the hall started to talk to each other in quiet voices. I couldn't see Lois and wondered if she was still inside the cabinet. But I'd seen enough of a nonsensical and unpleasant tradition, or ritual, connected to those paintings, and some kind of deeper belief system that I cannot remember much about, and couldn't even grasp back then, and so I left hurriedly. No one tried to stop me.

I think . . . that's what might have happened. It might have been a dream, though. I never really know if I can trust what appears in my head like memories. But I've recalled that scene before, I am sure, on another evening like this one as Lois bemoaned our coming together. Maybe this was as recent as last month? I don't know, but all of this feels so familiar.

Lois began calling me after the night she entered the cabinet on the stage of the community hall. On the telephone she would be abusive. I remember standing by the communal phone, to receive the calls in the hallway of the building in which I had rented a bedsit. Her voice had sounded as if it were many miles away and struggling to be heard in a high wind. I then told the other residents of the lodging to tell all callers that I was not home and the phone calls soon stopped.

I met someone else not long after my brush with Lois and The Movement . . . Yes, a very sweet woman with red hair. But I didn't know her for long because she was murdered; she was found strangled and her remains had been put inside a rubbish skip.

Not long after that Lois came for me in person.

I think . . .

Yes, and there was a brief ceremony soon after, in the back of a charity shop. I remember wearing a suit that was too small for me. It had smelled of someone else's sweat. And I was on my knees beside a pile of old clothes that needed sorting, while Lois stood beside me in a smart suit and her lovely boots, with her fabulous eye makeup, and her silver hair freshly permed.

We had been positioned before the wooden cabinet that I had seen at the community centre, and in the odd paintings inside the chapel on the literary walk. And someone had been struggling to breathe inside the box, like they were asthmatic. We could all hear them on the other side of the purple curtain.

A man, and I think he was the postman in that town, held a pair of dress-maker's scissors under my chin, to make sure I said the words that were asked of me. But there had been no need of the scissors because even though our courtship was short, by that time I was so involved with Lois that I was actually beside myself with excitement whenever I saw her, or heard her voice on the phone. At the charity shop wedding service, as we all recited a poem from the poet that went mad, Lois held up the ladies wristwatch with the very loud tick that had once been sent to my address, though intended for someone else.

We were married.

She was given a garish bouquet of artificial flowers, and I had a long wooden rule broken over my shoulders. The pain had been withering.

There was a wedding breakfast too, with Babycham and cheese footballs, salmon sandwiches, round lettuces, sausage rolls. And there was a lot of sex on the wedding night too; the kind of thing I had never imagined possible.

At least I think it was sex, but I can only remember a lot of screaming in the darkness around a bed, while someone kind of coughed and hiccupped in between lowing like a bullock. I know I was beaten severely with a belt by the witnesses, who were also in the bedroom at a Travelodge that had been rented for the occasion.

Or was that Christmas?

I'm not sure she's ever allowed me to touch her since, though she takes her pleasures upstairs with what I can only assume was inside that box in the community centre and at our wedding. I may be her spouse, but I believe she is wedded to another who barks with a throat full of catarrh, and she cries out with pleasure, or grunts, and finally she weeps.

The betrayals used to upset me and I would cry in the dog basket downstairs, but in time you can get used to anything.

—◦—

On Thursday Lois killed another young woman, this time with a house brick, and I knew we'd have to move on again.

The disagreement culminated in a lot of hair pulling and kicking behind some beach huts because I had said hello to the attractive woman who'd been walking her dogs past our picnic blanket. Lois went after the dogs too and I had to look away and out to sea when she caught up with the spaniel.

I got Lois home, up through the trees when it was dark, wrapped in our picnic blanket. Shivering, all stained down the front, she talked to herself the whole way home, and she had to lie down the following day with a mask over her face. The episode had been building for days and Lois detested younger women.

While she convalesced I read Ceefax alone—I had no idea that channel was still on the telly—and I thought about where we should go next.

When Lois came downstairs two days later, she wore lots of eye makeup and her tight, shiny boots and was nice to me, but I remained subdued. I was unable to get the sound of the frightened dog on the beach out of my mind; the yelp and the coconut sound and then the splashing.

"We'll have to move again. That's two in one place," I'd said wearily.

"I never liked this house," was her only response.

She relieved me into a thick bath towel, using both of her hands, kissed me and then spat in my face.

I didn't see her again for three weeks. By then I had found a terraced house two hundred miles away from where she'd done the killing of two fine girls. And in the new place I'd begun to hope that she'd never return to me. Vain and futile to wish for such a thing, I know, because before Lois vanished at the seaside, she'd slowly and provocatively wound up her golden wristwatch while staring into my eyes, so that my hopes for a separation would be wishful thinking and nothing else. The only possible severance between me and Lois would involve my throat being placed over an ordinary washbasin in a terraced house and her getting busy with the dressmaker's scissors as I masturbated. That's how she rid herself of the last two: some painter in Soho in the sixties and a surgeon she'd been with for years. Either a quick divorce with the scissors over vintage porcelain, or I could be slaughtered communally in a charity shop on a Sunday afternoon. Neither option particularly appealed to me.

In the new town there is evidence of The Movement. They've set themselves up in two rival organisations: a migratory bird society that meets above a legal high shop only open on a Wednesday, and an M. L. Hazzard study group that meets in an old Methodist church. No one in their right mind would want an involvement in either group, and I suspected each would convulse with schisms until they faded away. There are a few weddings, though, and far too many young people are already missing in the town. But I hoped the proximity of the others of Lois's faith would calm her down or distract her.

Lois eventually came up in the spare bedroom of the new house, naked save for the gold watch, bald and pinching her thin arms. It took me hours with the help of a hot bath and lots of watery tea to bring her round and to make the ticking in the house slow down and quieten, and for the leathery snakes with dog faces to melt into shitty stains on the carpet. She'd been through torments while away from me, I could see that, and she just wanted to hurt herself on arrival. But across several days I brought Lois back to a semblance of what we could recall of her, and she began to use a bit of lippy and do her hair and wear underwear beneath her housecoat.

Eventually we went out, just to the end of the road, then to the local shops to treat her to new clothes, then down and along the seafront, where we'd eat child-size vanilla ice creams and sit on the benches to watch the misty grey horizon. We'd not been down to the sea much before a drunken, unkempt man asked her to do something rude and frightened her, and then another dirty youth in a grimy tracksuit on a bike followed us for half a mile and tried to tug her hair from behind.

That second time, while I pumped two-pence pieces into an arcade machine to win some Swan Vesta matches and Super King cigarettes tied up in a five-pound note, Lois got away from me. I ran the length of the pier and shore looking for her and only found her after following the sound of what I thought was someone stamping in a puddle in the public toilets. And then I saw the bicycle outside.

She'd lured the lad who'd yanked her hair on the promenade inside the ladies toilets and been thorough with him in the end cubicle. When I finally dragged her out of there, little was left of his face, that I could see, and the top of his head had come off like pie crust. When I got her home I had to put her best boots in a dustbin and her tights were ruined.

Two people from The Movement came and saw us at home after the incident and told me not to worry because hardly anything like that was investigated anymore, and besides the police had already charged two men. Apparently, the smashed-up lad was always knocking about with them and they had form for stamping on people in the grimy streets. The visitors from The Movement also invited us to be witnesses at a wedding, which I instantly dreaded despite hungering to see Lois all dressed up again.

The wedding was held in the storeroom of a Sea Scout hut that smelled of bilge and in there, within minutes, Lois met someone else: a fat, bald man who did little but leer at her and sneer at me. She also did her best to lose me in the crowd, and there were a lot of people there to whip the bridegroom with leather belts, but I kept my eyes on her. At the wedding breakfast I saw the fat man feeding her the crisps that come with a sachet of salt inside the bag. He wasn't married and wasn't in The Movement either, so I was appalled by the fact that they let single men attend an event like that. At one point, as I hid below Lois's eyeline, I even caught her slipping the fat man our telephone number. All of the other women felt sorry for me.

I barely recognised Lois after the wedding in the Sea Scout hut. For days she was euphoric and acted as if I wasn't even there, and then she was enraged because I was there and clearly preventing her from pursuing another opportunity.

The fat man even approached me in the street when I was out shopping and spoke down to me and said that I may as well give up on Lois, as our relationship was dead, and that he intended to marry her within weeks.

"Is that what you think?" I said, and he slapped my face.

I writhed beneath the kitchen table for three days after the incident with the fat man, before getting up and dressing in Lois's clothes, which made me giddy. When I got the eye-shadow just right, my knees nearly gave way. But I still managed to leave the house in the early hours to pay a visit to the fat man. Lois ran into the street after me, shouting, "Don't you touch him! Don't you touch my Richey!" When some of the neighbours started looking out of windows, she retreated indoors, sobbing.

Well aware that Lois was absolutely forbidden from making such an overture to a new partner, without my voluntary participation in a divorce, Richey hadn't been able to restrain himself from making a move on her. Through the spyhole in the door of his flat he saw me with my face all made up and he thought that I was Lois. He couldn't get the door open fast enough. Then he stood in the doorway smiling, with his gut pushing out his dressing gown like a big shiny pouch, and I went into that bulb of guts with a pair of sharp scissors, my arm going really fast. He didn't even have a chance to get his hairy hands up, and into his tubes and tripes I cut deep.

We cannot have oafs in The Movement. Everyone knows that. I found out later that he'd only been let in because the woman in the bird migrating group, the one who always wore her raincoat hood up indoors, had her eye on "Richey" and had believed that she was in with a chance. She was only one week from crossing over too, but I think I saved her a few decades of grief. Later, for sorting out Richey, she even sent me a packet of Viscount biscuits and a card meant for a nine-year-old boy with a racing car on the front.

Anyway, right along the length of the hall of his flat, I went through Richey like a sewing machine and I made him bleat. I'd worn rubber washing-up gloves because I knew my hands would get all slippery on the plastic handles of the scissors. In and out, in and out, in and out! And as he slowed and half collapsed down the wall of the hall, before falling into his modest living room, I put the scissors deep into his neck from the side, and then closed the door of the lounge until he stopped coughing and wheezing.

Heavy, stinky bastard, covered in coarse black hair on the back like a goat, with a big, plastic, bully face that had once bobbed and grinned, but I took him apart to get him out of his flat piecemeal. Unbelievably, as I de-jointed his carcase in the bath, he came alive for a bit and scared me half to death. He didn't last for long, though, and I finished up with some secateurs that were good on meat. I found them under the sink in the kitchen.

Took me three trips: one to the old zoo that should have been closed years ago where I threw bits into the overgrown cassowary enclosure (they had three birds); one trip to where the sea gulls fight by the drainage pipe; and one trip to the Sea Scout hall with the head, which I buried beside the war memorial so that Richey could always look upon the place where he got the ball rolling.

When I got home, I shut Lois in the loft and took down the smoke alarms and burned all of her clothes, except for the best party tights, in the kitchen sink with the windows open. I went through the house and collected up all of her things and what I didn't dump in the council rubbish bins I gave to charity.

Before I left her growling like a cat, up in the loft amongst our old Christmas decorations, I told Lois that I might see her in our new place when I found it. I went downstairs and put her ladies' watch on my wrist and listened to it tick rapidly, like a heart fit to burst. Inside the sideboard, the little black warriors began to beat their leather drums with their wooden hands.

Lois was still clawing at the plywood loft hatch when I left the house with only one suitcase.

YOU CAN STAY ALL DAY

MIRA GRANT

The merry-go-round was still merry-going, painted horses prancing up and down while the calliope played in the background, tinkly and bright and designed to attract children all the way from the parking lot. There was something about the sound of the calliope that seemed to speak to people on a primal level, telling them "the fun is over here," and "come to remember how much you love this sort of thing."

Cassandra was pretty sure it wasn't the music that was attracting the bodies thronging in the zoo's front plaza. It was the motion. The horses were still dancing, and some of them still had riders, people who had become tangled in their safety belts when they fell. So the dead people on the carousel kept flailing, and the dead people who weren't on the carousel kept coming, and—

They were dead. They were all dead, and they wouldn't stay down, and none of this could be happening. None of this could be real.

The bite on her arm burned with the deep, slow poison of infection setting in, and nothing was real anymore. Nothing but the sound of the carousel, playing on and on, forever.

—◦—

Morning at the zoo was always Cassandra's favorite time. Everything was bright and clean and full of possibility. The guests hadn't arrived yet, and so the paths were clean, sparkling in the sunlight, untarnished by chewing gum and wadded-up popcorn boxes.

It was funny. People came to the zoo to goggle at animals they'd never seen outside of books, but it was like they thought that alone was enough to conserve the planet: just paying their admission meant that they could litter, and feed chocolate to the monkeys, and throw rocks at the tigers when they weren't active enough to suit their sugar-fueled fantasies.

Nothing ruined working with animals like the need to work with people at the same time. But in the mornings, ah! In the mornings, before the gates opened, everything was perfect.

Cassandra walked along the elegant footpath carved into the vast swath of green between the gift shop and the timber wolf enclosure—people picnicked here in the summer, enjoying the great outdoors, sometimes taking in an open-air concert from the bandstand on the other side of the carefully maintained field—and smiled to herself, content with her life choices.

One of the other zookeepers strolled across the green up ahead, dressed in khakis like the rest of the staff. The only thing out of place was the thick white bandage wrapped around his left bicep. It was an excellent patch job, and yet . . .

"Michael!"

He stopped at the sound of his name, and turned to watch as she trotted to catch up with him. His face split in a smile when she was halfway there.

"Cassie," he said. "Just the girl I was hoping to see."

"What did you do to yourself this time?" she asked, trying to make the question sound as light as she could. Michael worked with their small predators, the raccoons and otters and opossums. It wasn't outside the realm of possibility that one of them could have bitten him. If he reported it, it would reflect poorly on him, and on the zoo. If he didn't, and it got infected . . .

There were things that could kill or cripple a zoo. An employee failing to report an injury was on the list.

"No," he said, and grimaced sheepishly. "It was my roommate."

"What?"

"My roommate, Carl. He was weird this morning. Not talking, just sort of wandering aimlessly around the front room. I thought he was hungover again. I figured I'd help him back to bed—but as soon as he realized I was there, he lunged for me and he bit me." Michael shook his head. "Asshole. I'm going to tell him I'm through with this shit when I get home tonight. He's never been late with his share of the rent, but enough's enough, you know?"

"I do," said Cassandra, with another anxious glance at the bandage. "You want me to take over your feedings for the morning?"

"Please. I cleaned it out and wrapped it up as best I could. I did a pretty decent job, if I do say so myself. There's still a chance the smell of blood could get through the gauze, and well . . ."

"We don't need to exacerbate a human bite with a bunch of animal ones, even though the animal bites would be cleaner." Cassandra frowned. "You're sure it's cleaned out? I can take a look, if you want."

"No, really, I'm good. I just wanted to ask about the feedings, and it turned out I didn't need to." Michael's grin seemed out of place on the face of a man who'd just been assaulted. "That's our oracle."

"Ha ha," said Cassandra. "Get to work. I'll do your feedings after I finish mine."

"Yes, ma'am," said Michael, and resumed his progress across the green, seemingly no worse for wear. Cassandra frowned. It was entirely like him to brush off something as unusual and traumatic as being bitten by his own roommate, and it wasn't her place to get involved. At the same time, the situation wasn't right. People didn't just start biting.

"Classic Cassandra," she muttered. "If you can't find a catastrophe, you'll invent one. Get over yourself."

She started walking again, trying to shake the feeling that some of the brightness had gone out of the day. The sky was clear; the sun was shining; one little bit of human weirdness shouldn't have been enough to dampen her enthusiasm. But it was. It always was. Humans were strange. Animals made sense.

A tiger would always act like a tiger. It might do things she didn't expect, might bite when she thought it was happy to see her, or scratch when it had no reason to be threatened, but those times were on her, the human: she was the one who'd been trained on how to interact with wild animals, how to read the signs and signals that they offered. There was no class for tigers, to tell them how to deal with the strange, bipedal creatures who locked them in cages and refused to let them out to run. Tigers had to figure everything out on their own, and if they got it wrong sometimes, who could blame them? They didn't know the rules.

People, though . . . people were supposed to know the rules. People weren't supposed to bite each other, or treat each other like obstacles to be defeated. Michael was a good guy. He cared about the animals he was responsible for, and he didn't slack off when he had duties to attend to. He wasn't like Lauren from the aviary, who smoked behind the lorikeet feeding cage sometimes, and didn't care if the birds were breathing it in. He wasn't like Donald from the African safari exhibit, either, who liked to flirt with female guests, talking to their breasts when he should have been watching to be sure that little kids didn't jab sticks at the giraffes. Michael was a good guy.

So why was she so unsettled?

Cassandra walked a little faster. Work would make things better. Work always did.

◄◦►

The big cats were uneasy when Cassandra let herself into the narrow hall that ran back behind their feeding cages. They should have been in the big enclosures by this hour of the morning, sunning themselves on the rocks. Instead, they were pacing back and forth, not even snarling at each other, although her big male lion normally snarled at anything else feline that got close enough for him to smell. Cassandra stopped, the feeling of wrongness that had arrived with Michael blossoming into something bigger and brighter.

"What's wrong with you?" she asked.

The big cats, unable to answer her, continued to pace. She walked over to the first cage, where her female tiger, Andi, was prowling. She pressed the palm of her hand against the bars. That should have made Andi stop, made her come over to sniff at Cassandra's fingers, checking them for interesting new smells. Instead, Andi kept pacing, grumbling to herself in the low tones of a truly distressed tiger.

"You're not going to delight many families today if you keep hanging out back here," said Cassandra, trying to cover her concern with a quip. It was a small coping mechanism, but one that had served her well over the years: her therapist said that it was a means of distancing herself from situations she didn't want to be a part of.

It was funny how her therapist never suggested anything better. Surely there were situations that no one wanted to be a part of. What were people supposed to do then?

"All right," said Cassandra. "I'll go see what's going on. You stay where you are." She pressed the button that would close the tigers in their feeding cages, keeping them from venturing into the larger enclosure. Then she counted noses.

It was unlikely that she would ever mistake three tigers for four tigers, but it only took once. No matter how much they liked her, no matter how often she fed them, they would still be tigers, and she would still be a human being. They would eat her as soon as look at her if she caught them in the wrong mood, and then they would be put down for the crime of being exactly what nature intended them to be. So she counted noses, not to save herself, but to save them.

Always to save them.

The door to the main tiger enclosure was triple-locked, secured with two keys and a deadbolt. It had always seemed a bit extreme to Cassandra, especially since there was the concern that some zoo visitor—probably a teenager; it was always a teenager, on the news—would climb over the wall and scale the moat in order to try to pet a tiger. The number of locks involved would just keep any zookeeper who saw the incident from getting to the fool in time.

But maybe that, too, was part of the point. All it took was one mauling a decade to keep people out of the enclosures. It could be seen as a necessary sacrifice, letting the animals devour the one for the sake of the many who would be spared.

Even if that was true, Cassandra didn't want the sacrifice to involve her charges. Let some other zoo pay the price. Her tigers had done nothing wrong. They didn't deserve to die as an object lesson.

The day had only gotten prettier while she was inside, and stepping into the tiger enclosure—a place where tourists never got to litter, where snotty little children never got to chase the peacocks and squirrels into the trees, where the air smelled of big cat and fresh grass—made everything else seem trivial and small. She paused to take a deep breath, unbothered by the sharp, animal odor of tiger spoor clinging to the rocks. They had to mark their territory somehow.

The smell of rotting flesh assaulted her nostrils. She coughed, choking on her own breath, and clapped a hand over her nose. It wasn't enough to stop the scent from getting through. Whatever had died here, it had somehow managed to go unnoticed by the groundskeepers long enough to start to truly putrefy, turning the air septic. No wonder the tigers hadn't wanted to be outside. This was bad enough that *she* didn't want to be outside, and her nose was nowhere near as sensitive as theirs.

Hand still clasped over her nose, Cassandra started toward the source of the smell. It seemed to be coming from the moat that encircled the enclosure, keeping the tigers from jumping out. That made a certain amount of sense. Raccoons and opossums could fall down there, and the tigers couldn't get to them. If it had fallen behind a rock or something, that might even explain how it had gone unnoticed by the groundskeepers. They worked hard and knew their jobs, but they were only human.

So was the source of the smell.

Cassandra stopped at the edge of the moat, eyes going wide and hand slowly dropping from her mouth to dangle by her side as shock overwhelmed revulsion. There was a man at the bottom of the moat.

He wore the plain white attire of the night groundskeepers, who dressed that way to make themselves visible from a distance. He was shambling in loose, uncoordinated circles, bumping against the walls of the moat and reorienting himself, staggering off in the next direction. He must have been drunk, or under the influence of something less than legal, because he didn't seem to know or care where he was going: he just went, a human pinball, perpetually in motion.

From the way his left arm dangled, Cassandra was willing to bet that it was broken. Maybe he wasn't drunk. Maybe he was just in shock.

"Hey!" she called, cupping her hands around her mouth to make her voice carry further. "Are you all right down there?"

The man looked up, turning toward the sound of her voice. His face was smeared with long-dried blood. Staring at her, he drew back his lips and snarled before walking into the wall again and again, like he could somehow walk through it to reach her. His gaze never wavered. He didn't blink.

Cassandra stumbled backward, clasping her hands over her mouth again, this time to stop herself from screaming.

She had been a zookeeper for five years. Before that, she had been a biology student. She had worked with animals for her entire adult life. She knew dead when she saw it.

That man was dead.

◄O►

"Now Cassandra, be reasonable," said the zoo administrator. He was a smug, oily man who smiled constantly, like a smile would be enough to chase trouble away. "I believe that something has fallen into the moat of the tiger enclosure, and I'm dispatching a maintenance crew to deal with it, but it's not a dead man. It's certainly not a dead man who keeps walking around. Did you get enough sleep last night? Is it possible that this is the stress speaking?"

"I always get enough sleep," she said, voice tight. "It's not safe to work with tigers if you're not sleeping. I slept, I ate, I drank water and coffee with breakfast, and I know what I saw. There's a man in the moat. He doesn't blink. He doesn't breathe. He's dead."

"But he's still walking. Cassandra, have you listened to yourself? You have to hear how insane this sounds."

Cassandra stiffened. "I'm not insane."

"Then maybe you shouldn't say things that make you sound like you are." The administrator's walky-talky crackled. He grabbed it, depressing the button as he brought it to his mouth. "Well? Is everything taken care of?"

"Dan, we've got a problem." The response was faint, and not just because of the walky-talky: the speaker sounded like he was on the verge of passing out. "She was right."

Dan blanched. "What do you mean, she was right?"

"There's a man in the moat."

"A dead man?"

"That's biologically impossible. He's up and walking, if non-responsive to questions. Angela thinks it's Carl from the night crew. She's going to get his shift supervisor. But he doesn't answer when we call his name, and he keeps snarling at us when we try to offer down a hook. I don't think it's safe for people to approach him. I think he might get violent."

Dan glared at Cassandra as he asked his next question: "But he's not dead."

"That wouldn't make any sense. Dead men don't walk."

"Roger. Deal with it. I'll order the path shut down. Call me as soon as you know what's going on." Dan put the walky-talky aside. "So you were right about the man in the moat. That's an unexpected twist."

"Wait." Cassandra shook her head, staring at him. "You can't be serious."

"About what?"

"About shutting the path to the tiger enclosures. People always get around the barricades. They want to see blood. You have to shut down that whole portion of the zoo. Or wait—we haven't opened yet. Can't we just . . . not open? For a little while?"

"Not open. Are you sure that's what you want to recommend?" Dan stood. "I can keep people away from that area. I can protect the innocent eyes of children. But admission fees are what pay your salary and feed your precious cats. Do you really want to risk that?"

"No," admitted Cassandra. "But the man in the moat . . . something's really wrong with him. We shouldn't let anyone in until we know what it is."

"Everything will be fine. Go back to work." Dan walked to the door and opened it, holding it for her in clear invitation. After a moment's pause, Cassandra walked out of his office.

The day seemed less beautiful now, tainted somehow, as if the stranger in her moat had cast a pall over the entire sky. Cassandra walked quickly back toward the tigers, intending to help the rescue crew, and paused when she saw a familiar figure staggering across the grass. Michael was walking surprisingly slowly for a man who had never met a path he didn't want to jog on. He looked sick. Even from a distance, he looked sick.

"Michael?" she called, taking a step in his direction. "Are you all right?"

He turned to fully face her, lips drawing back. Cassandra paused, eyes widening. His eyes . . . they were like the eyes of the man in the moat.

He was her friend. She should help him. She should stay, and she should help him.

She turned, and she ran.

◄◦►

The tigers were still locked in their feeding pens, prowling back and forth and snarling at each other. They were restless. Even for big cats trapped temporarily in small cages, they were restless. It was like they could smell the taint in the air, warning them of trials yet to come.

"Sorry, guys," said Cassandra, stopping in the aisle between cages, well out of the reach of questing paws. The tigers didn't want to hurt her. She was almost certain of that. They still would. She was absolutely certain of that.

Humans had intelligence, and thought, and the ability to worry about the future. It made them great at things like "building zoos" and "taking over the world," and it made them terrible at being predators. Humans could plan. Humans could think about consequences. Tigers, though . . .

Tigers existed to hunt, and feed, and make more tigers. They existed for the sake of existence, without needing to care about whether tomorrow was going to come. She envied them sometimes. No one ever told a tiger that it didn't know how to be what it was. No one ever said "you must be mistaken," or implied that there was something wrong with a tiger because it didn't want to spend its time with confusing, contradictory humans.

One of the tigers yawned, showing her a vast array of fine, sharp teeth. Cassandra smiled.

"No, I'm not going to feed you early just because you're locked in the feeding cage," she said. "We'll have you out in the enclosure in no time, and you know the guests get cranky when you spend the whole day asleep and digesting. Be good, and this will all be over soon."

As if to put an immediate lie to her words, someone outside screamed.

Cassandra was running before she realized it. A large metal hook on a pole hung on the wall next to the door, intended to be used to remove snakes from the visitor paths and animal enclosures. She grabbed it without thinking. Something about that scream spoke to the need for weapons, the vital necessity of self-defense. Whatever was happening out there, she didn't want to race into it unarmed.

The smell of decay hit her as soon as she was outside the tiger run. It was thinner than it had been on the edge of the moat. It was stronger at the same time, like it was coming from more than one source. The person screamed again. Cassandra kept running.

The tiger exhibits had their own "island" in the zoo's design, dividing the public-facing portion of a large oval structure between themselves. Cassandra came around the curve of the wall and froze, grasp tightening on the snake hook as her eyes went wide, trying to take in every aspect of the scene.

The man from the moat was no longer in the moat. The security crew dispatched to help him had obviously done so, using their own, larger versions of Cassandra's snake hook. Those big hooks were on the ground, discarded. The security team had bigger things to worry about, like the man who was even now sinking his teeth into the throat of one of their own.

She had been screaming, when he first started biting her. She wasn't screaming anymore. Instead, she was dangling limply in his arms while the other security people struggled to pull him away. For a dead man—and he was a dead man, he must have been a dead man; nothing living could smell so bad, or have skin so sallow and tattered, like he had slid down the side of the moat without so much as lifting his hands to defend himself—he had a remarkably strong grip. It took three security men to finally pull him off her.

He didn't go without a prize. The front of her throat came away with him, clasped firmly between his teeth. As Cassandra watched in horror, the security woman hit the ground, and the man chewed at his prize, still staring mindlessly ahead of himself.

This was not predation. Her tigers were predators, would eat a raccoon or a foolish zoo peacock as soon as they would look at it, but they were aware of what they were doing. There was a beautiful intelligence in their eyes, even when their muzzles were wet with blood and their shoulders were hunched in preemptive defense of their prey. Tigers knew. They might not understand the morality of their kills, but they knew.

This man . . . he didn't know. His eyes were blank, filmed over with a scrimshaw veil of decay. His jaws seemed to work automatically, inhaling the scrap of flesh he had ripped from the security woman.

The screaming hadn't stopped. It was just more dismay and anger now, as the security guards who weren't restraining the dead man tried to help their fallen coworker.

Then the man whipped around, faster than should have been possible, moving like he didn't care whether he dislocated his shoulders or broke his arms, and buried his teeth in the neck of the guard who was restraining him.

Then the woman without a throat opened her eyes and lunged for the person closest to her, biting down on their wrist. The screaming resumed, taking on a whole new edge of agony and horror. Cassandra's eyes got wider still. This was wrong. Everything about this was wrong, and she couldn't stay here any longer, she couldn't, this was wrong and unnatural and she needed to go, she needed to—

When she turned, Michael was standing right behind her.

He couldn't have been there for long; she had been working with predators for too long to be the kind of person who could be snuck up on. The same smell of putrefaction and decay that she had gotten from the man in the moat was coming off of him. Faint, as yet, but there; undeniably there. His eyes were filmed over, unseeing, unblinking.

"Please don't," she whispered.

He struck.

⋯

Everything was a blur after that. Cassandra didn't know how she'd been able to escape; only that she had, because it was like she had blinked and been standing in front of the tiger habitat first aid station, with the door firmly closed behind her and the tigers snarling down the hall, still confined in their feeding pens, growing slowly angrier and angrier. Blood had been sheeting down her arm from the deep bite in her shoulder, painting everything in red. The marks of human teeth were unmistakable.

Even if they hadn't been, the fact that Michael had left one of his crowns behind would have made it impossible to pretend that she had been bitten by anything other than a human being. Gritting her own teeth, she used the tweezers to extract the small piece of white porcelain from her flesh. It was jagged where it had snapped off, and had probably done almost as much damage to Michael as he had to her. But he hadn't seemed to notice. He hadn't seemed to care.

He had been gone. Impossible as it was to contemplate, sometime between asking her to take care of his charges and their encounter outside the tiger enclosures, he had died, and kept on walking.

"No," said Cassandra. She grabbed for the hydrogen peroxide bottle and emptied it over the wound. It foamed and bubbled and stung like anything, like it was supposed to, but the feeling of rotten wrongness remained, worming its way down toward the bone. "No, no, no. No."

No amount of denial would heal the wound in her arm, or chase the smell of decay from her arm. Time seemed to jump again, taking her along with it: this time, when the haze cleared, she was applying butterfly clips to the gauze encircling her arm, sealing the bite marks out of sight. They continued to throb. Out of sight was not out of mind.

"No," said Cassandra, somewhat more firmly. She shook her head, trying to prevent another jump. What was this?

Think about it logically. Think about it like a biologist. Yes: that was the ticket. Think about it like she was back in class, like the worst that could come from getting the answer wrong was a bad grade.

Michael's roommate had been acting strange this morning. Michael had come to work with a bite from that roommate fresh on his arm. Michael had been behaving normally. Now Michael was acting like the man from the moat, and he had bitten her. Michael smelled of decay.

The man in the moat had smelled of decay when she had found him; her first impression had been that he was dead, yet somehow still standing. He was wearing the uniform of the night groundskeepers. She had seen wounds on him, but they had all been consistent with sliding down the side of the rocky wall between the fence line and the ground. What if nothing had bitten him? What if he'd just . . . fallen? It was always a risk, especially when the staff had to lean over the low retaining wall to retrieve something from the moat's edge. There had been falls before.

The woman, the security guard . . . the man from the moat had bitten her. He had torn her throat out with her teeth, and she had died. Cassandra had no doubt at all that the woman had died. She'd seen it. But after dying, she had started moving again, attacking another member of her team. So what if . . .

What if the man in the moat had died, only to come back again as something that wasn't quite human anymore? Sometime dead and terrible, that looked like a human being but smelled like the grave, and only wanted to . . . what? Feed? Bite?

Pass the . . . curse, infection, whatever it was along?

Cassandra turned to look at the bandage on her own arm. Michael hadn't died. Not like the woman. Michael had been fine. Human mouths were filthy things, but a bite wouldn't be enough to kill a healthy man, not under ordinary circumstances. She could feel the hot pulsing buried deep in her flesh, telling her that something was very, very wrong. Whatever had been in him, it was in her now too. Hurting her. Maybe killing her.

"Okay," she said, as much to hear her own voice as for any other reason. "I need to get out of here." Michael's mistake had been coming to work instead of going to the doctor. Doctors could flush the wound, could make things better. Could fix it.

She had long since accepted the fact that one mistake at her job could put her in the ground. But she wasn't going to die like this.

Feeling better now that she had a plan, Cassandra started for the door. She needed to get to the locker room, to retrieve her purse and her car keys. She would tell Dan that it didn't matter whether he closed the zoo today, because she wouldn't be here either way. She would be at the doctor's office, getting the flesh on her arm debrided and patched up, until the hot pulsing from within stopped. Until she wasn't scared anymore.

The tigers paced and muttered in their deep feline voices as she passed them, expressing their displeasure with the whole situation. Cassandra smiled wanly.

"I need to be sure the dead man isn't in front of your enclosure anymore before I let you out," she said. "If he fell back in, that would only upset you. I'll make sure someone comes to open the gates, I promise."

The tigers didn't speak English, but she had been their handler for years. Most stopped grumbling and just looked at her, staring with their wide amber eyes. They trusted her, as much as one apex predator could trust another.

"I promise," Cassandra said again, and opened the door to the outside.

The smell of decay was like an assault. Behind her, the tigers roared and snarled, protesting this invasion. She couldn't see anyone, but that didn't have to mean anything: not when she could smell them.

The zoo grounds had never seemed so claustrophobic before, so crowded with thick bushes and copses of trees. How many dead people could be lurking in there?

This couldn't be happening. This couldn't be happening. This couldn't be happening. She would get to the locker room, get her purse, and drive herself to the hospital. Maybe stop long enough to make a few phone calls, to make sure that whatever was going on at the zoo was only going on at the zoo. Michael's roommate was confined to their apartment, right? And Michael could have been exposed here, at work, picking up some . . . some novel parasite or tropical disease from one of the animals. Spillover diseases didn't always look the same in people as they did in their original hosts. This could be, could be a flu, or a respiratory illness, or something, that behaved in a new, terrifying way when it got into a human being. It could be—

Cassandra crested the hill and froze, getting her first look at the zoo's entry plaza.

They had opened the gates after all. Sometime between her leaving Dan's office and coming to in the back hall of the big cat building, someone had turned on the carousel and opened the gates, letting the public—letting the dead—come to the zoo one last time. Bodies thronged around the admin buildings, moving with that same odd, graceless hitch that she had seen in Michael, before he had attacked her. Whatever this was, it was spreading with horrific speed. Based on what she'd seen in front of the tiger enclosure, it wasn't unreasonable to think that it was spreading to everyone who was bitten.

Including her. She had been bitten. It was spreading—it had spread—to her.

Maybe that would protect her. If this was a disease, they might not attack someone who had already been infected. There was no sense in taking chances: if she got killed, who would take care of the tigers? They were trapped, penned in their little cages, without even the freedom of their enclosures to enjoy. She needed to make it back to them, now more than ever. But she also needed to see. She had to.

Carefully, Cassandra crept closer, sticking to the edges of the underbrush, where she might be ambushed, but she was less likely to be seen. When she came to one of the staff gates in the fence, she opened it and slipped through, relieved to see that the path was clear. These pathways were mostly used to transport things—food, equipment, sick animals—during the day; until the crowds got thick around noon, even the most privacy-loving zookeepers would tend to stick to the public side of the zoo. Maybe she could get to the gates without further incident.

Maybe it wouldn't matter.

The throbbing from her arm was getting worse and worse, reminding her with every step that this was how it had started for Michael. Whatever this was, it spread through the bites. If she didn't get medical help soon, she was going to become like them: dead, but still moving, still standing. Still biting. She was going to become a dangerous predator, something both more than animal and less than human.

The path ended at a slatted gate looking out over the zoo's front plaza. The merry-go-round was running, the painted horses dancing up and down in their eternal slow ballet. Cassandra stopped a few feet back, looking silently at the crowd that pressed around the classic amusement. They swayed and shambled, eyes glazed over and focusing on nothing. The smell that rose from their bodies was thick and undeniable, the smell of death, the smell of things decaying where they stood.

There had been people riding the merry-go-round when . . . whatever had happened here had happened. Some of them were still tangled in their safety belts, dangling from their painted horses, unable to free themselves as they pawed mindlessly at the air. Cassandra's stomach churned, bile rising in the back of her throat.

Soon that will be me, she thought. Soon I will be one of them.

What would happen to her tigers then? What would happen to Michael's otters, or Betsy's zebras, or any of the other animals in the zoo? Some of them were already doomed, unable to survive in this ecosystem, but others . . .

She could see the parking lot from her current position. There were dead, shambling people moving there, too. As she watched, a group of them caught up with a screaming man and drove him to the ground, where he vanished beneath a hail of bodies. This wasn't contained to the zoo. This could never have been contained.

Cassandra turned her back on the scene in the front plaza. She had work to do.

◄►

Any disease that hit this hard and spread this exponentially was going to overwhelm the city in a matter of hours: that was just simple math. One was bad; two was worse; four was a disaster. The numbers kept climbing from there, until she reached the point where the dead outnumbered the living, and there was nothing left to do but die.

If she hadn't been bitten, she might have tried to find another way. The big cat house, especially, had hundreds of pounds of raw meat stored in the freezers, just in case, and doors that were designed to stand up to a raging male lion. She could have locked herself inside with her beloved cats. She could have tried to wait it out.

But her arm burned, throbbing with every heartbeat, and she was starting to feel . . . bad. Feverish. Like she wanted nothing more than to lay down for a nap, to close her eyes and let her body finish the transition it was clearly aching to undergo. She needed to act quickly, before she was no longer equipped to act at all.

She began with the herbivores. She opened doors and propped gates, leaving the avenues of escape open for anything that wanted to take them. By the time she made her way to the aviary, there were zebras cropping at the lawn, ears flicking wildly back and forth as they scanned for danger. A kangaroo went bounding away down a side path, all but flying in its haste to get away. If there were dead people lurking in the bushes, they weren't fast enough to catch it.

The birds knew something was wrong. As she opened their cages, they flew away, wings clawing at the air, and were gone. Some of them would make it. Some of them had to make it.

Slowly, almost shambling now, she made her way back to the big cat house. The smell of decay was less noticeable now, maybe because she was adding to it. Maybe because her nose was dying with the rest of her.

There were so many doors she hadn't opened. There were so many cages she hadn't unlocked. But there wasn't time, and she didn't want to endanger her animals. Not in the end. Not when the burning in her arm had become nothing more than a dull and distant throb, like the nerves were giving up.

The tigers stopped their pacing when she came into view, staring at her silently. Cassandra pulled out her keys.

"Try . . . not to eat me, okay?" she rasped, and started down the line of cages. One by one, she unlocked them, leaving them standing open. When she finished with the tigers, she began releasing the lions, the cheetahs, until she was at the end of the hallway with a dozen massive predators between her and freedom. They looked at her. She looked at them.

One by one, they turned and walked away, heading for the open door; heading for freedom. Cassandra followed them until she reached the main door to the tiger enclosure. Her fingers didn't want to cooperate, didn't want to work the key or let her turn the lock. She fought through the numbness, until the bolt clicked open and she stepped through, into the open air on the other side.

The door, unbraced, swung shut and locked itself behind her. Cassandra didn't care.

Stumbling, she walked across the uneven ground to the rock where her big male liked to sun himself during the hottest hours of the day. She sat down. She closed her eyes. In the distance, the merry-go-round played on, a soft counterpart to the slowing tempo of her heart.

Cassandra stayed where she was, and waited for the music to stop.

NO MATTER WHICH WAY WE TURNED

BRIAN EVENSON

No matter which way we turned the girl, she didn't have a face. There was hair in front and hair in the back—only saying which was the front and which was the back was impossible. I got Jim Slip to look on one side and I looked from the other and the other members of the lodge just tried to hold her gently or not so gently in place, but no matter how we looked or held her the face just wasn't there. Her mother was screaming, blaming us, but what could we do about it? We were not to blame. There was nothing we could have done.

It was Verl Kramm who got the idea of calling out to the sky, calling out after the lights as they receded, to tell them to come and take her. *You've taken half of her*, he shouted. *You've taken the same half of her twice. Now goddam have the decency to take the rest of her.*

Some of the others joined in, but *they* didn't come back, none of them. They left and left us with a girl who, no matter how you looked at her, you saw her from the back. She didn't eat or if she did, did so in a way we couldn't see. She just kept turning in circles, walking backwards and knocking into things, trying to grab things with the backs of her hands. She was a whole girl made of two half girls, but wrongly made, of two of the same halves.

After a while we couldn't hardly bear to look at her. In the end we couldn't think what to do with her except leave her. At first her mother protested and bit and clawed, but in the end she didn't want to take her either—she just wanted to feel better about letting her go, to have the blame rest on us.

We nailed planks across the door and boarded up the windows. At Verl's request, we left the hole in the roof in the hopes they would come back for her. For a while we posted a sentry outside the door, who reported to the lodge on the sound of her scrabbling within, but once the noise stopped we gave that up as well.

◄o►

Late at night, I dreamed of her, not the doubled half of the girl we had, but the doubled half we didn't. I saw her, miles above us, in air rarefied and thin, not breathable by common means at all, floating within their vessel. There she was, a girl who, no matter where you turned, always faced you. A girl who bared her teeth and stared, stared.

NESTERS

SIOBHAN CARROLL

They killed the last calf that morning. Ma wanted to hold off, give the poor thing a chance, but Pa said it were cruel to let a body live like that. He cracked the hammer on its head—a sick, sad sound. Later he slit the calf open and showed Sally the animal's stomach, choked with dust. "Suffocated from the inside," he said.

Sally cried, or would have cried, but her face was too caked with dirt. The Vaseline in her nostrils couldn't keep it out. She wondered how much dirt was in her stomach and whether her body was already full of it, like the calf, her tears and blood just rivers of dust. But when she asked, Ma said, "Jaisus, quit nattering and help the bairn." So Sally did, even though her baby brother was curled up like the calf had been, under a skin of dust that never went away no matter how they cleaned.

Sally followed Ma round the dugout, stuffing rags into the cracks where the dust had trickled through. Alice toddled after her. Ben watched from the bed, his feverish eyes glistening. At fourteen, he was taller than Sally and better at reaching the upper cracks. But what could be done? The dust-lung had him. If Ben were to move, Ma said it would be to her sister's place in Topeka, away from the land that was killing him. Better still, Ma said, would be to head out to California, where there was still work to be had.

But Pa had heard about the cities. Many who went there came home poorer than before. They told tales of Hoover camps, the shame of being spat on by city-dwellers. At least here they suffered together. At least here they had the land.

To lose your land was to lose yourself, her father had warned her and Ben. This was in the early years, when folks still thought next year would bring the rains back.

"This here's the first thing our family's ever owned in this country," he'd said, showing Sally the dark soil between his fingers. "Mackay land." His eyes had shone with the wonder of it.

Now the earth was hard and brown and dusters turned the sky the same color, choking and fierce. "Still," said Pa, "we have the land. We lost it once to the English. We won't lose it to the wind."

◦

Two strangers were at the gate. Sally could see right off they weren't farmers. Too pale. Too well-fed.

The taller man leaned forward, dangling his hands into the yard in a way Sally didn't like. "Your father at home, sweetheart?"

Sally looked the stranger up and down, the starving chickens pecking at her feet. "You from Washington?" There was talk of Mr. Roosevelt sending folk to tell the Nesters how to run their farms. This man, with his clean suit, seemed like he could be one of them.

A glance from the leaning man to his companion. "What d'ya think, Bill? Are we from Washington?"

The older man looked like a schoolteacher, one of the impatient ones who rapped kids' knuckles. "We're on official business," he said. "We're looking for the man of the house."

Sally knew Ma would scold her if she let a government man pass by, even rude ones. There might be a dime in it, and a dime could buy bread.

"I'll fetch him then," she said. "Best come out of the blow."

At the dugout's entrance, Ma's face already showed the strain of a smile. Sally knew Ma was thinking of rusted cans of water instead of tea, the assistance bread gone hard by week's end. At least they had some milk to offer, thanks to the dead calf. Still, it was as much her mother's smile as the need to fetch her father that made her run so quickly.

She found Pa fixing up the old John Deere D, trying to get work done while the air was clear.

"Government men come."

Pa nodded and wiped his hands, reluctant to leave a task half-done. "You take over here."

Sally took Pa's place as he strode off. She checked the front tires for cuts, wiping off a grease splatter with a gasoline-damped rag. Everything on the farm depended on the tractor. If it broke, they'd be beat.

Sally thought instead about the government men. Maybe they brought work with them. Maybe it'd be a good day after all.

◂◦▸

Stepping inside the dugout, Sally realized something was wrong. Ma stood stiffly in a corner. Pa sat beside the older man, his shoulders squared. The younger government man looked at Sally as she entered, then back at Pa.

The older man spoke, an edge to his voice. "Did no one go out to the farm to look for him?"

Pa's face was closed. He shook his head.

"Why not?"

Pa glanced at Ma, who folded her arms tightly against her chest. Reluctantly, Pa said, "They say the Dubort place's cursed." Pa shrugged as if to remind them he didn't hold with superstitions.

The Dubort place! Sally watched the strangers with new interest. The abandoned farm was the only site for miles with greenery to spare. Tom Hatchett said if you passed too close to the Devil's Garden—what the kids called it—one of the monsters living there'd gobble you up. Tom Hatchett was a liar, but still.

The man flipped through his notebook. If he was trying to frighten Pa with that flapping paper, he didn't know nothing. "Stories of strange vegetation? Odd lights and noises? Animals disappearing? That kind of thing?"

Pa's gaze was stony. He shrugged again.

"And all this happened after the meteor fell?"

"I don't know nothing about no meteor," Pa said. "One of Dubort's fields caught fire. We went to fight it, like good neighbors. Some folk said a falling star started it. Don't know more than that."

"Good neighbors," the government man said. "But nobody went looking when Frank Dubort disappeared?"

Pa blinked. Looked away. "Place got a bad reputation," he said. "No one wanted to borrow trouble. It was a wrong thing," he admitted, quietly, to himself.

Rage blossomed in Sally. Couldn't these men see how tired Pa was? He had enough to deal with, without these men asking him to feel bad for a stranger, a weekend farmer who couldn't take the hard times.

But Sally remembered that day at Ted Howser's farm, the man scuttling out of the barn on his back, like an upside-down beetle. Mr. Howser had put his hand over his mouth. Sally's Pa had stared like he hoped what he saw wasn't true. Sally thought the scrabbler looked like Howser's neighbor, Mr. Dubort—or like some hobo wearing one of Mr. Dubort's famous blue-checked shirts, all stained and tore-up. But Pa stood in front of her, blocking her view.

Pa told her and Ben to go home. He'd stayed behind to talk to Mr. Howser about what needed to be done. What *had* they done? Pa had refused to speak of it. He'd said it was settled, and to ask no questions.

Dread crept through Sally. She wondered what had happened to bring these government men here.

"We'd like to go out there, Mr. Mackay," the government man said, "To have a look around. Your name was mentioned as one who could take us there."

Sally wanted to know who'd given them Pa's name. She suspected Pa did too. But the less said to these folk, the better.

"There's money in it." The younger man pronounced the words carefully, as though he knew the effect they'd have in this dusty, coughing dugout. "Fifteen dollars, for a guided trip, there and back." He smiled at their astonishment. "We're . . . scientific men, Mr. Mackay," he said reassuringly, "We need to see this site close up."

Sally thought the older man might be angry with his companion for offering money straight off, but he seemed to be taking Pa's measure.

"If we find Frank, that'll put this thing to rest." The young man added, slyly, "It's the right thing to do."

Pa's face was tight. His gaze slid over to Ma. But Ma didn't know what to do either, Sally saw. She was caught between fear and worry and the promise of fifteen dollars.

"Alright then," Pa said. "But you pay upfront."

The older man got up from the table. "Five now, the rest later."

"Ten." There was a determined glitter in Pa's eyes. The government man flicked a bill onto the table. Ten whole dollars.

"We appreciate your help." The younger man smirked, like he'd known how this was going to go all along.

Sally hated him, she decided. She hated them both. She itched to give the nearest one a kick on his shins as he passed. It was the sort of thing she'd have done last year, never mind the manners. But she thought of Ma and the remaining five dollars. She let the men go.

Pa glanced down at Sally as he put his hat on. "Take care of your Ma." He patted her head, messing up Sally's hair. Sally smoothed it back as she watched Pa leave.

It was a funny thing to say, she thought. Ma was the one who took care of everyone else. The strangeness of this kept her standing there, while the men got in the car and drove off.

◄○►

The duster rolled in a few hours later. Sally crouched into the grating wind and kept one hand on the guide rope, the other over her eyes as she traced her path back from the chicken coop. She struggled along blindly, feeling her bare skin scraped raw. She tried not to think of Pa out in this duster, guiding strangers on someone else's land.

In the dugout, they huddled together with cloths over their faces. There was no point in burning the kerosene lamp. No light would get through. They sat silently, trying not to breathe in too much of the dust, while the wind raged outside.

The duster lasted the rest of the day. When its blackness cleared, the night was there to take over, and the cold. They lit the lamp and looked at each other, her and Ben and Alice and Ma.

Ma said, "Let's clean up," and so they did. Sally tried not to wonder about Pa. He'd have to see the government men back to town. He'd probably stayed there.

But in the morning, Pa still wasn't back. Sally forced the door open and trudged to the chicken coop to count the survivors. There were two dead, dust-choked. She took the bodies out, feeling the lightness of their scrawny bodies. They needed more food.

It was Sunday and Sunday meant church. Pa wouldn't miss church, Sally was sure. She put on her "nice" dress—still made out of feed sacks, but cleaner than the others—while Ma got Alice ready.

Ben's eyes opened when Ma put a hand on his forehead. "Keep an eye on the bairn. And if you see Pa, make sure you tell him to stay put till we get back." Ben closed his eyes. Sally wasn't sure if he'd heard them.

But Pa wasn't at church. Sally kept turning around, scanning the pews. Ma pinched her arm to make her stop, but Ma kept glancing backwards too, every time they had to stand up.

The service was one of the usual ones, about the end times and how the dusters were the Nesters' fault for ignoring the Lord's will. Inwardly Sally was having none of it. It was a pretty poor God who visited misery on folk for drinking too much and taking his name in vain now and then. Maybe it was true what the ranch hands said, that they'd done wrong by taking the grassland from the Injuns and turning it to the plow. But even so, where was the good in little kids dying? If that was God's will, then she hated him, Sally thought, and felt a flash of fear.

After the service Ma caught Ted Howser by the arm. "I need to talk to you about Pat."

Sally wanted to hear the rest of it, but Ma told her to mind Alice didn't hurt herself. Sure enough, Alice took a spill. The dust cushioned her so she wasn't even crying when she looked up. Well, that's one thing it's good for, Sally thought, offering the toddler her fingers to grab.

She looked back. Ma was at the center of a ring of old ranch hands and farmwives, their faces grave.

"Come on," she said, tugging at Alice's hand. "Back this way."

"Paddy's a good man and I'd walk to hell for him," Jake Hardy was saying, "but if the wind stirred something up, we'd best not get too close."

Someone else snorted. "Walk to hell but wouldn't go in it, would you?"

"Facts are," Mr. Howser said, "the Dubort place is off-limits. Pat knew that when he headed out there." He looked round the circle. "You saw what it did to Frank. We can't go there. Can't let anyone go there," he said, looking back at Sally's Ma. "Who knows where it'd end?"

"He's probably holed up at another farm," Dan Giss said. "Roads are tough. Duster's closed a lot of 'em. He's probably holed up with Schmitt, minding those damn fool government men."

Sally's Ma seemed to sway on her feet. Sally let go of Alice to run towards her.

Margie Fisher, the schoolteacher, reached Ma first. She put an arm around the younger woman.

"There now," she said, glaring at Ted Howser. "We need to organize a search party. Knock on every door. Chances are, Pat's not the only one who could use a hand."

Sally heard a wail behind her. She turned to see the abandoned Alice sitting in the dust, blood running down her forehead. Somehow the toddler had found the only uncovered rock in the yard and fallen smack into it. Of course she had. And it was Sally's fault for leaving her.

"Shush," Sally pleaded, stroking the toddler's sweat-damp hair. "It'll be okay." But it wouldn't be, Sally knew, the dread rising in her. It wouldn't be.

◄○►

Ma and Mrs. Fisher would search along the road, Mr. Howser would take a horse up Fincher's lot. Jake and Dan would go to the Dubort place. Everyone was worried about this plan, but Jake and Dan swore they'd leave right quick if they felt they were stirring things up.

Stirring things up, Sally thought, remembering the giant vegetables Mr. Dubort had brought to town. Turnip skins so bright they hurt your eyes, apples that glistened like they'd been dipped in water, and huge! One turnip was as big as Ben's head—he'd put it on the table so Sally could measure before Pa had slapped them away.

"Don't you do that," Pa had said, angrier than Sally had ever seen him. "Don't you touch those things, no matter what."

Sure enough, when Mr. Dubort sliced the turnip open, dark gray powder crumbled out.

"Must be some kind of blight," Mr. Dubort had said, pushing his hat back on his head. He was a city man, unused to farming. "Have you seen anything like this before?"

The Nesters said nothing. Their silence hung around them like a sky empty of rain, waiting for the dust to roll through.

Now Sally walked behind Alice as the toddler clung to Mrs. Fisher's furniture. Mrs. Fisher had a proper house, with tablecloths and everything. Sally noted the dirty film on Mrs. Fisher's table with satisfaction. She reckoned it must take a lot of sweeping to get dust out of a place this size.

The tick-tocks of Mrs. Fisher's clock reverberated through the house. Each one felt like a burning pin pushed into Sally's flesh. Why couldn't someone else watch the babies? If Ben was here, she reckoned they'd let him go.

She imagined herself wandering across the dust-dunes, finding Pa in a place no one had thought to look. Not hurt, of course. Her mind shied away from that. No, Pa would be fine but helping one of the government men, who'd gotten his fool self hurt. The younger one, Sally decided, viciously. She imagined Pa's grin when she clambered up the dune that hid them from the road. "I knew I could trust you to figure it out," he'd say. And the government men would pay them thirty whole dollars for the trouble they'd caused. And—

There was a noise outside.

"Stay there," Sally told Alice. She didn't want to pull away the sheets the Fishers had nailed over the windows, so she headed to the door instead.

There was a scramble of people in the yard. Jake was trying to hold a flailing man by the shoulders. "Don't let him go!" Mr. Fisher, the mortician, grabbed the man's other arm.

It took Sally a moment to recognize the flailing figure, all covered in dust. It was the older government man. He lips were pulled back from his teeth, his eyes rolled to the sky. As Sally watched he arched his back and howled, a long hard sound that raised all the hairs on her scalp. A string of gibberish babbled out of him: *grah'n h'mglw'nafh fhthagn-ngah* . . .

She shut the door, closing out the sight. It was as though God had heard Sally's foolish dream of finding Pa and had sent the government man back to punish her vanity. *Please, please,* she thought frantically, hushing Alice, *please let them have found Pa, please let him be all right—*

When Ma came back her face was strange. "Make sure you thank Mrs. Fisher for letting you stay here."

Sally obediently repeated the words, even though Mrs. Fisher was standing right there. Ma and Mrs. Fisher stared at each other like they were having a silent conversation above Sally's head. Normally Sally would hate that. Now it made her more scared than ever, because something was really wrong if nobody was talking about Pa.

-◦-

Ma's silence carried them back to the dugout. It filled the air there when Ben tried to gasp out a question.

"Others are seeing to that," Ma said shortly. And, "Jaisus, get the broom, will you?"

Sally got the broom and swept the dust about the place, while Ben wheezed and the babies coughed and Ma tried not to cry. *If only the dust would leave the place, they'd be alright*, Sally thought wildly, knowing it wasn't true.

Next morning, Sally was up before cockcrow. Her head was buzzing as she cast the hard, dried-up corn into her bucket and went out to face the chickens.

"I'm going to school," she told Ma at the door. Ma hesitated, then nodded. Ma was always on at Sally and Ben to keep up their lessons. In truth, Sally doubted there'd be any kids in the school. The morning had that hard-light look to it that threatened dusters, and there was too much work to do just to get some food through the door.

But today Sally had other things on her mind. If there was a duster coming, she needed to move fast and early.

She packed her water and the scrap of hard-bread that Mam set aside for her. She'd also take the shovel from the back of the tumble-down barn, in case she needed to dig her way out. That's what Pa would do.

Ben watched her tie the strings up on the rucksack, his eyes angry. He knew what she was doing.

"Just . . . don't say nothing. Unless I'm not back by sundown," Sally whispered. Then she threw the rucksack on and left, before Ben could muster the air to call her back, before anyone changed her mind about what needed to be done.

-◦-

The sky above her was blue, blue, blue, dotted with the occasional cloud. No point trying the local road over to Dubort—that would be drifted over. She'd cut across land, avoiding the big drifts except when it came time to climb the fences.

It was hard going. Sally's feet sank into the sand, her boots filling with grit. *Mackay land,* she thought, *turned against us.* The spade was heavy on her shoulder.

About halfway to the Dubort place she started to feel she'd made a mistake. The sun was fully up now. In its glare she could see the green strip of land away in the distance. The Devil's Garden, some called it. It'd been so long since there'd been green in these parts, Sally couldn't tell if it was the drought or whether there was actually something wrong with the color.

The animal-sounds dropped away as she approached the Dubort place. You'd think the jackrabbits and birds would flock here, given that no one hunted at the farm. But the air out here was stiller than the desert.

Sally walked along the side of the giant dune that had piled up over Dubort's old fence. She saw the white bones of some animal poking through. Probably a starved cow, tangled in wire and Russian thistle. Beyond the bones was a place where the dune dipped a little. As good as any spot for a crossing, she thought, and waded up.

It was strange being surrounded by green again. Sally remembered the color from the old days, but here it was everywhere. Dubort's fruit trees had grown large and tangled. Between them, vines draped and alien flowers gaped at the sky. A nearby bush dangled huge, glossy fruit. They looked like they would quench the thirst that was beginning to rasp her throat. Sally looked away, remembering the powdery vegetables.

The lurid greenery stretched everywhere on the Dubort-side. There was nothing for it. "Pa!" she shouted. "Pa!"

Silence. Sally took a swig from her bottle and kept walking.

The Dubort house stood on the northern part of the property, close to Mr. Daverson's fence. Surely, if Pa was in trouble—if a duster was bearing down on them—that's where he'd head. For shelter. And he hadn't had the shovel that now ground into her skinny shoulder. They could be stuck in there, underneath the grit.

At a certain point the trees thinned and she saw a hard-pack section where nothing grew, a burned-looking hole at its center. She figured that must be where the rock had hit. There was something blue standing by the crater—a human color.

Sally didn't want to walk into the clearing—it seemed strange to her somehow—but she figured if she were looking for Pa, she had to check out every clue. So she walked quietly over to the blue thing. A couple cans of gasoline and a man's hat, filmed with dust.

Sally tested the weight on the gas cans. They were full. The young man had been wearing a hat.

A screeching sound jerked her head up. It was probably some kind of buzzard, she told herself, walking quickly back to the dune line. She had the uncomfortable feeling something was watching her, its gaze focused just between her shoulder blades. It was a relief when she left that clearing behind her.

She knew she should yell for Pa again, but after the screech she couldn't work up the nerve. Pa had to be at the house. The sooner she got there, the better everything would be.

When she finally reached Dubort's house, her stomach sank. It didn't look like a house at all these days—more like a sandy hill, with a strange gray vine growing up its side. As with the clearing, the forest that had claimed the rest of the property seemed to have left this part alone.

Sally circled the house, afraid of what she'd do if it was empty. She saw a dark square opening in the leeward wall. The black square of a window, or door. Someone had recently been inside.

Sally lowered the shovel. "Pa?" She tried the word out, scared of speaking too loud. "You there?" The air itself seemed to be listening to her.

Sally closed her eyes, thinking of Pa and his tobacco smell and his graceful fingers as he patched up a gunny sack. She had to see.

She walked slowly up to the dark square and peered inside.

◂◦▸

The first thing that hit Sally was the smell. It was horrible, and faintly familiar, as though she'd encountered it many years before. It was the smell of rot, the kind of thing you might find in a wet place, not here on the plains.

She stared hard at the darkness, trying to make it form shapes. She had matches in her pocket, swiped from the old kerosene lamp. She struck one, but a faint stir of wind guttered it out too quickly. She needed to do better than that.

She slung her leg over the windowsill, gulping what clean air she could. The wooden sill moved beneath her hands. *You're doing a dumb thing,* she thought, and slipped inside.

The ground was soft sand. Grimacing, she put her hand up against the wall. She'd follow the wall around, in the dark. Figure out how far she could go.

But she hadn't gone very far at all when she heard the breathing.

Sally froze. She wanted to believe she was imagining things. She held her breath, to prove it. A wheeze in. A wheeze out. Too regular to be the wind.

Fear pressed on her. She didn't want to call for her father. If he hadn't heard her earlier, he wouldn't hear her now. And if it was something else there breathing, she didn't want to know.

Don't try to solve all the problems at once, Pa always said. *Break them up. Deal with each one in order.*

So Sally groped her way back to the window, with its bright patch of light. She was glad, now, to see the lurid green outside. She fumbled the matches out, holding them in the light. Ten left. *I am going to do this,* she thought, *I am.*

She struck the match.

At first she could see nothing in the orange circle of light. She cupped the flame and extended her arms. There was one shadow that was stranger than all the others, taller than any man should be. Something was there.

Sally moved forward. She had to get the circle of light closer before the match went out. The soles of her feet crunched onto uneven sand piles, miniature dunes that hissed out of place as she stepped on them.

Yes, there was definitely something there, in the jumping flame. A line of vine, of leaves, a reassuringly normal shape. The vines fed into the bulky mass growing out of the wall, a

> *—gaping incomprehension of seeds and veins and flesh and interiors that were exteriors yawning backwards into dark [consumed] the dirt the air the vine the stone the bird the man the the—*

It had her father's face.

It used that face as a hand, reaching for her, sensing maybe the kinship between them. It reached for her with its

> *—fused body that bulked vegetable animal a cuff link from the other agent still on its cuff oh god the—*

Sally ran. Quick as sight, she was out the window, her disconnected self not feeling the stones that slammed and cut her knees and saved her life because the father-thing stopped to drink her blood, the jeweled red pools that clustered in the stone—

Sally ran, feeling her body again when the evil not-vegetation tried to clutch her legs her arms but she was an arrow loosed from a bow. She thought of those crusts of bread her mother had saved *eat this you must stay strong,* and here was why, this flight this stumble towards sand, the sand would save her. Even the *gnaiih*-thing behind her could not grow in the dust the choking otherness would slow it down while she, a Nester, fleet, could reach the fence, could stagger *ch'*it while *h'*followed her on what kind of legs? Dear god *h'ah'olna'ftaghu*—

She was over the fence, running across the dust to the end of the horizon.

When her legs gave out, Sally forced herself to look back towards the house. This was maybe the bravest thing she'd done, because she knew if [it] was coming for her, there was nothing she could do but watch her death walk up. Not death, no: [it] was worse than that, her father's face absorbed into some amalgamation of life and used as a tool to probe the world. At least [it] didn't look human, because if [it] did—

But [it] didn't. She hoped [it] never did. She hoped that along with those pieces of her father and the government man, [it] had not taken their memories: the pattern of her mother's dress, the creak of the old well, the words the government man had used to get her father, oh, her father, to come trudging out here to die.

Except he wasn't dead.

Sally understood now what the screaming government man had tried to tell them,

—the exterior turned interior the reaching dark the—

and knew also there was no words to contain [it]. She had to force her mind back, to here, to the soil on her hands and the gleam of life that was Sally because

—the howling light a rage of knowing—

if she didn't, she would become like one of those wizened stock, tangled in the wire. No. She was a Nester. She would not die like that.

But her Pa.

If she told, they would come out here. If she lied and said she'd found nothing, they might come anyway.

She'd lost the shovel, dropped it somewhere. That wouldn't do. A fire. She remembered the red can of gasoline by the crater.

I've cracked, she thought, brushing her face. But that was all right.

When her legs started working again, she got up and went back to the clearing.

⟶

Sally struggled over the dunes, the sun high in the sky. No birds, no clouds, only infinity staring her down.

When she was actually at Dubort's fence, seeing again the drift, the body of the cow ominously absent, she felt fear thrill through her. It was that fear that finally brought her back to herself, no longer one with the sky and the—

down in the dark, in the deep

—but back in her shaking, dry-throated body.

She didn't want to die. She was sure the calf hadn't wanted to die either, no matter how its stomach hurt or how short its life would be. It had struggled even as the hammer came down, with Sally's fear reflected in its eyes.

It's like riding a horse, she thought. *Like riding a horse somewhere it doesn't want to go.* With that in mind she coaxed a foot forward. Then another one. And another.

She watched her feet. If this was all she saw, maybe it wouldn't be so bad.

But it was bad. The hideous green jangled her mind. The wind breathed wrong, whispering things. Why had she come, after all? Why had she come?

There was a stubbornness in Sally that went down through the soil and past that, through the rock and its layers of time. She was a Nester, wasn't she? She belonged here, or at least—(remembering the Comanche, remembering the English with their guns)—at least she *was* here, and she would not easily be moved.

It was a long hot way. She had to keep switching the gas can from one arm to another when the pull got too much. As she walked she became more and more herself, these tired muscles lugging a sloshing burden through an ugly glare of green. She should have brought Ben. If Ben could walk, he would have helped her. But then he would see the thing and she did not want anyone else in her family to see [it]. That would be too much.

At last the house swam into the tunnel of her vision. She expected her legs to balk again, but they didn't. It was as though, having crossed the fence, all of her options were gone.

She did not bother wasting a match outside this time. She slung her leg over, and stepped inside.

⟶

When she lit the match, she saw only awful greenery. The father thing had vanished.

[It] couldn't have gone far, she thought. Of course she wasn't sure if that was true or not. Maybe the thing was faster than it seemed. Maybe [it] was already advancing through the township, swallowing stray passersby into its madness.

No. The thing was here. Somewhere.

Perhaps [it] was deeper in the house.

The hairs on the nape of her neck rose. Of course the house had more rooms. It was a wealthy house. Now that the outgrowth on the wall had torn itself away, she could even see the gap where the door had been. Might not that be a sign, then? That something had gone through?

Between her and the door was a mess of tangled growth. It was dangerous to step through, and not just because of the smell of rot that rose with every step. She had the notion that the vines and [it] were all connected. She was like an ant walking on [its] arm letting [it] know where she was.

If [it] found her, she could kill it faster, she reminded herself. She walked through the door.

◄◦►

The air inside this room was moist and sweet-smelling. The rot-stench was thick here, and something else, something indescribable, and bitter-edged.

She struck a match. There was a dark square in the floor. A rusted ladder curled out.

Sally peered into the black hole and thought about dropping the match. But what would happen if the flame lit on part of [it]? The thing would know what she intended.

So she blew out the match. In darkness she found the creaking, terrifyingly mobile rungs of the cellar ladder. She climbed down.

◄◦►

At last Sally had come to the end. She knew that even before she opened her eyes, before she struck the second match. She could hear the breathing around her. Synchronized, from many points. A sucking in and out.

She stepped down. Fumbled the cap off the gasoline.

A puff of air on her leg. She carefully pulled that leg away, trying to stand close to the ladder. They were all around her.

And they were.

The jumping orange light revealed twisted bodies—humans, cows, birds, plants, all merged together. Bird wings fanned air around the room. Human faces twisted on vine stems. A flower opened around an eye. She placed the match carefully on the ladder, letting it burn.

The antenna/vines/fingers quested forward. She looked for her father's face. That was the only one that mattered. The prickle down her leg told her that one of the vines had caught her, was latching on.

Then she saw Pa. It helped that he didn't look like her father anymore, but like a sack that had been stretched over a different shape. Something appeared to be growing under his eyelids.

She hurled the gasoline at him. It missed, soaking a good portion of the vine-wall instead. Heart clutching, she felt the slight slosh of some remaining gasoline. Nothing to do but this. She strode forward and poured, the awful, wonderful smell of gasoline filling her nostrils.

She could feel the latch of the vines on her arms and hands, could feel them burrowing into her skin. But what mattered, what truly mattered, was that she get the other match free, and out, and—stepping back, despite the tearing pain at her legs—struck.

The whoosh of flame knocked her backwards. Now there was heat to get away from and the screams of [it] as flowers, vines, hands stretched up in pain and terror. She stumbled away from the father-thing, crawling with flame. Her hand found the cold rungs of the ladder. Up.

Eyes streaming Sally stumbled towards the thin light of the window—a different window this time, she'd come out wrong. The house was filling with smoke and blackness, like a duster. She didn't want to die like this. She tore vines away from the old window frame, pushed her way through the rotten wood. She fell outside, into the sunshine and the merciful air.

Sally choked on the ground. There was not enough air in the whole world for her. The sun dazzled overhead, a hot stare, and black trekked above her in a column of smoke. Behind her, the vines were screaming.

Let them scream. Sally rolled on her side, scrabbled blindly away from the noise, going somewhere else.

◄o►

They found her on the road. Her mother grabbed Sally, a relief of human skin pressing against hers. "Sally what happened to you, your face—my God—"

All of these words were tiresome. Sally leaned her smarting face against her mother's shoulder, breathing in the smell of flour. One of the adult men was shouting but Sally ignored him. "It's okay Ma," she tried to say. The words came out as a croak.

"Hold on, Sally," Ma said, "You hold on." And Sally lowered her head as though Ma's words would keep her safe.

◄◦►

Later, when the doctors finally let Sally come home, she helped Ma look for dimes. The funeral had come and gone when Sally was in her fever. About it, all Ma said was, "Your Pa was a good man." She added, staring at the pile of bills, "He would have wanted us to stay here."

Sally knew Ma was talking about the hardware men who were calling in their debts, and who Ma refused to look at when they were in town. It wasn't fair of Ma, really, Sally thought. What choice did the hardware men have about eating? They needed the money.

But something seemed to have changed for Ma, since the day Sally had come stumbling back to them on the road. She didn't care so much about politeness now. That part of Ma seemed to have been lost somewhere. Sally missed it.

Ben, on the bed, was trying to do his part. He held up the coin he'd found—or hidden, Sally thought, a long time ago.

"Found one," he gasped. He looked away from them. Ma added it to the small pile on the table. Sally remembered the ten dollar bill sitting there and turned her head away. That money was long spent.

"Are we going to be okay, Ma?" Ben couldn't see the coins from where he lay. He didn't know how few there were.

Baby Alasdair snuffled in his box, his breathing low and ragged. Ma adjusted his blanket, then scooped up Alice, who was getting underfoot as always. She went over to Ben and sat on the bed beside him, motioning Sally to join her. Sally sat gingerly on the end of the bed. Sometimes she thought she could still feel the vines squirming under her skin, and then she was afraid to let folk touch her.

"Now you listen, all of you," her mother said. "This is Mackay land. We've worked for it and we're going to keep working for it." She squeezed Ben's hand and threw a hard, half hug around Alice and Sally. Sally found herself returning the painful embrace, as though she was hanging on to her family as they slid off the face of the world.

"We won't be moved," her mother repeated into Alice's hair, like it was true.

From the nick of her eye, Sally could see the future coming for them: baby Alasdair dead from dust pneumonia by year's end, the land foreclosed, her mother half-mad at losing another loved one in a land not even good for graves any more. They'd be moved, alright, the way you had to move, when the only other choice was to die.

Sally felt that future and it terrified her more than the thing she'd seen at Dubort's. But she said nothing. Instead, she reached out and took hold of Ben's arm, like it really could work, like they really could make it.

Head bowed, she told the lie that was asked of her.

"We'll hold on, Ma," she agreed. "You'll see."

BETTER YOU BELIEVE

CAROLE JOHNSTONE

> *Maybe true*
> *Maybe not true*
> *Better you believe*
> —Old Sherpa Saying

t's all downhill on a descent. The oldest climbing joke of the lot, but only because it's true. If I like any bit of it at all, it could never be that slow, painful climb down from the highs of before and the bone-deep exhaustion of after. People make mistakes on a descent because everything's against them: altitude, time, their bodies. And always their mind. No one gets excited about survival—not like they do about standing on the top of the world. And no one gets a good write-up in *Nat Geo* or *Time* for managing to get back down a bloody mountain in one piece. Unless they're Jean-Christophe Lafaille, I guess.

The air is raw, thin, dry. Acke Holmberg's cough is worse; when ice walls throw up rare shelter, I can hear it rattle up from his lungs hard enough to start doing damage. Nick likes to tell me about the gross stuff when we're in bed, warm and lazy, blissed out. One guy he climbed with ruptured his esophagus on Nanga Parbat, a few thousand feet above base camp. The blood spray froze in mid-air, Nick said with a grin, before pulling me back under the covers and him.

The wind is a demented banshee. *Only fifty k*, Nick said maybe twelve hours ago; on the summit it beat around our heads so hard we had to crouch. Some of the Swedes were convinced they were going to be yanked off into the swirling white void. *As if they'd be fuckin wheeched off*, Nick said with usual scorn. *As if* it had never happened, when I know just how many dozens of times it has on this peak alone. But he's earned the right to be scathing, I guess. Until today, Annapurna was the only eight-thousander he hadn't summited.

But things are different now—I know that without being able to either see or hear him, somewhere further down the Lafaille line and attached to the same fixed rope. It's dark and growing darker. It's too late—much too late—I can barely see the low sun beyond Gangapurna's peak, some 7,000 meters above the Marsyangdi River. The weather is moving. And the mountain is getting jittery; I feel its hackles under my frozen feet, like we're ticks that just won't quit. We've been inside the Death Zone for too long, but we're too slow, too tired, and have too far to go.

Bad Things, I think, in Nick's lesser spotted concerned voice, as I battle on down through the white and the wind, putting one boot in front of the other in the kind of trance that's both helpful and dangerous. Bad Things are about to happen.

◄o►

By the time they do, I've managed to convince myself they won't. The wind has died again; the flag cloud west of the summit tilts up and sharp against the dying sun. Up is good, flat is bad, down is fucked. I remember the big poster tacked alongside prayer flags in the med tent, and Nick laughing with one of the American doctors that it was a far more reliable indicator than any other base camp forecast. The mountains make their own weather, and it's rarely kind.

Even though I'm still descending through the French Couloirs, the snowpack is harder, the incline less steep. I'm surprisingly warm, but I know much of that is a cocktail of O and illusion—I last felt my feet at Camp IV. I don't feel bad, I don't feel good. I don't feel much of anything at all. Not even afraid.

There's a subtle but sudden shift in the air around me, like a hush, a breath too close to my ear; my heart stutters a little to feel it through my hood and balaclava. And then Jakub Hornik appears from the gloom behind and above—maybe ten feet east, no more—face-first and flat on his belly, anchored to nothing. He doesn't flail or shout as he slides down the snowfield; he makes no sound at all save the fast friction of his suit against ice. And he makes no attempt at self-arrest either, even though he's holding his ice axe up like any moment he's going to let it fall. His eyes are wild. They find my light and grow wilder, wider—holding onto it right up to the moment that the gloom swallows him back down and I'm left alone, literally frozen, the dropping wind washing out my mouth.

There's a tug on the rope from below. Nick. *Are you all right?*

Not really, not at all, but what use is there in saying so; in being either one or the other up here? I'll still be up here. I'll still be needing to get down fucking there. A big shudder goes through me, it cricks my neck and finds a home in my belly. It's never a good idea to puke more than halfway up a mountain. I think of Jakub's eyes, his silent slide. I remember Kate renaming him The Horn, after he spent the whole first month at base camp trying to hit on her. My belly squeezes hard again.

Bad Things.

Because they're never ever singular.

◆

The last Bad Thing was Felix Garcia. There are always deaths on a climb. Climbing seasons are short, summit windows shorter; at any one time there can be dozens of teams within a few hundred meters of each other. But the threat of actually seeing someone die is surprisingly low, as easily dismissed as the threat of dying yourself. You hear about them, on the short wave or the satellite phone, or when you reach a camp: falls, accidents, strokes, disappearances. People go crazy. People get the shitty end of the stick. People just die. There are lots of ways to do it. And pretty soon those muttered summations become nearly routine, like all the frozen landmarks and trig points that used to be people. *Red Legs. Green Boots. North Col.*

Felix was different. Mountains attract arseholes; eight-thousanders attract Olympic-level arseholes. He and Nick clashed before we even left Everest base camp. Felix was a solo-climber, and that's pretty hard to do on a mountain as rammed as Everest. Nick doesn't like taking them on because they're glory hounds and crappy team players, but he's had to get a lot less picky now that he's competing with Nepali companies for business. It was to be my third summit, Nick's seventh, but we didn't even get close before the weather doubled down and Pasang advised Nick to turn us all back and fast. Felix suffered the final indignity of being geared up with me and three Koreans on the snow fields at the foot of the Lhotse Face as we scrambled over crevasses on shrieking ladders, a snow storm blinding us, deafening us, making us stupid.

By the time I heard his scream, I was already being dragged so fast along the ice I couldn't get my axe free. Our belaying had been too clumsy, the Koreans behind too quick, the rope too slack—Felix plummeted so hard and so fast down the hidden crevasse that by the time anyone managed to arrest our screaming progress along the glacier, I was flying over its edge too. The pain I didn't feel. The horror of all that silent blue dark after howling white space, I did. I looked down at a still screaming Felix and didn't see him, only the hard tight swing of the rope between us vanishing into black. The air prickled against my skin like blunted pins. I looked up at the shouting beyond the ice-rimmed circle of white, and I thought, *they can't hold us both. They can't save us both.*

And they didn't.

I feel another yank on my harness. I've been standing still for too long; the fixed rope is taut, impatient. The wind has grown high again. The darkening sky looks heavy with snow, and when I squint west, I can't see the flag cloud any more. I start moving.

Nick won't have told the other Slovaks about Jakub. They were last to leave the summit, despite Nick and Pasang's warnings about the time. They're far too far behind us to attempt any kind of rescue, but they'd want us to try because the four of them were tight: Jakub and Hasan were as close as brothers. They wouldn't accept that there's no point; that at the edge of this snowfield is a short rock buttress and then a drop of over a thousand feet. I don't want to think about that: about Jakub's wild eyes staring at my light as he slid away from me toward the plummet of black, empty space that he must have known was coming.

Jakub's silence; Felix's high screams. Dark, cold yawns of nothing. What it feels like to fall, to be alone, to feel it coming, to *know*. I can't think about shit like that. We're still nearly a thousand feet inside the Death Zone— thinking about shit like that is for messy Khukuri rum nights in Pokhara or

Kathmandu. Or if you're Nick, never. Easier just to pretend things didn't happen at all.

—◇—

The snow starts heavy and doesn't stop. It slows my efforts to catch up to Nick. Even though I know he's already got his hands full with the Chinese couple who arrived at The Sanctuary with no equipment at all, and the always determined Tomie Nà from Hong Kong, who started showing signs of altitude sickness as low as Camp II. And Kate, of course. Following him around like a bad smell. Nick always does the babysitting, while Pasang rounds up the stragglers, the hardcore *just-another-five-minuters*. It's always been this way, even though Pasang is the tolerant one, and Nick couldn't be patient if he tried. But Pasang is the better climber too; certainly, he's the better guide. Nick is the guy in charge, the guy people write the checks to, and even if that's the kind of responsibility he'd sooner shirk than have to suffer, it lets him climb mountains. For that he'd babysit an entire busload of Sunday hikers and Olympic-level arseholes.

I wonder what he'll tell Jakub's family. I remember an evening in The Sanctuary, one of those rare pre-climb nights of excitement and camaraderie not yet spoiled by the reality of weeks of acclimatizing in close, cold quarters. Pavol and Hasan were drunk and red-cheeked, laughing about Jakub's wife, and how pissed off she'd be when she found out how much their trip was costing. That Nick will be the one to tell her what has happened, I have no doubt, but he won't say how it really was: how long Jakub suffered knowing he was going to die on that hard, fast slide; that we were all still on that mountain, but he was already lost, already gone before he was gone.

Climbers have their own rules, their own language, their own religion. And these take years to earn, to learn, to understand. Climbers believe in dreams, as long as those dreams have a purpose, a summit. They believe in God, if God is a mountain, because they worship nothing but the climb—the endless, soulless, merciless demand of it. They believe in trying to help, in trying to save, until they can't. Until they don't. They believe in the individual: in their own strength, their own will, their own survival. And they also believe that mountains can hate, that the weather can be cajoled, that the spirits of those long dead can provide comfort to the dying and lead the living to safety. Even Nick believes—scornful, pragmatic, ever practical Nick—like a liar crossing his fingers, or a fisherman never setting sail on a Friday, or like Pasang leaving offerings to the mountain at the end of every day, while muttering low to the friends whom he has lost.

I trip on a rock under growing drifts of snow and stumble against the fixed line. It's too much snow too fast. Anything over an inch an hour is bad news, and this is much, much more. Visibility is getting worse: I can no longer see the setting sun at all, and my headlight shines through a kaleidoscope of dense monochrome. I'm starting to wonder if we'll make it back down to Camp IV today at all, and that is bad—worse than bad. Bivouacking in the Death Zone is never a good idea, but on the South Face of Annapurna, it's pretty much suicide. I try not to think of all the stats that Nick—and so many other climbers—take such solemn glee in. The summit-to-death ratio on Everest is one in twenty-six. *On Annapurna*, he said, sliding a cool palm down my naked back and along my flank, making me shiver even though then I was warm, *it's one in three*.

The first stirrings of real fear find me then, and it's followed by a strange, slow sense of unreality. I should *already* be frightened. I should have been frightened when the Slovaks weren't ready to leave Camp IV at midnight, or when we finally summited at 5 p.m. instead of 3. I should have been frightened when Nick started moving folk back down the mountain so fast there was barely any time to celebrate our victory; when Acke started sounding like he was coughing up a lung; when the wind, then the night, then the snow started closing in, the mountain began trying to buck us off, and our descent became a disordered, scattered scramble. And I should have been *shitting* myself when Jakub slid past me on the way to his silent death.

Denial. A mountain climber's best and worst friend.

Acke, I think. Acke should be behind me, higher up, but not so far that I can't hear him. Only I can't remember the last time I did hear him; the last time I remembered that I *should* be able to hear him.

"Acke?"

The wind screams back at me.

"Acke! Are you there?"

Maybe I hear him, I don't know. Something hits my face: a stone or some ice carried on the rising wind, and when I press a glove against my cheek, it hurts; the balaclava sticks warm and wet to my skin. "Acke!"

Though I don't want to, I start back up. Not far, I won't go far. Just far enough to ascertain that he's still there, still alive, still descending. In this direction, the wind batters at me hard enough to nearly drop me to my knees.

"Acke!"

There are different kinds of numb in the Death Zone, and denial is only one. Is my heart rate and breathing fast because of altitude or fear? Or because of cerebral oedema? Are my actions, my responses still rational? Do I *think* they are? Climbing above 7,500 meters is the same slow asphyxiation suffered in the *Nightmare-Age* of heavy-curtained four-poster beds. When we climb, we have night terrors, paranoia, depression. When we descend, the euphoria of returning oxygen levels can just as quickly cause psychosis. We're not supposed to function up here; we're not *designed* to function up here. Nick once saw a man launch himself off the Hillary Step like he was dive-bombing the deep end of a swimming pool.

I nearly stumble over Acke before I see him. He's sitting in the snow, legs splayed out, trying to take off his gloves.

"Don't!"

He stills, lifts up his face, winces against the wind and flying debris, but what he says is in Swedish; the only word I recognize is *allena*. Alone.

"You can't stop. You have to get up. Where's Bosse? Is he still behind you? Acke!" I'm shouting hard enough to hurt my throat now. "We *can't* stay here."

He shakes his head, resumes the removal of his gloves, and once he's done that, his frostbitten fingers move to the carabiner connecting him to the fixed line.

"Acke, no!"

He pays me no mind. There's a ring of blood around his mouth like old lipstick, and a brighter slash of it running into his frozen beard. And if he already has pulmonary oedema, then he's probably not too far behind dive-bombing the deep end of a swimming pool either. Because disengaging from the line in a snowstorm is what you do if you're crazy. It's what you do if you want to die.

He grins and his teeth are bloody. "Stay with me," he says. Shouts. But he's not looking at me, he's looking all around me—at the stone, the snow, the nearly night sky.

And then I hear it. The worst Bad Thing. The thing I've been trying the hardest not to think about on our painfully slow descent down this 2,500 meter gulley in a snowstorm; this funnel for spindrift and debris and worse.

By the time Acke hears it, I'm already turned around and running. *Trying* to run. The noise is terrific. My heart thunders in my ears, as I try to seek out somewhere—anywhere—to hide. But there's nothing, nowhere. Because there never is. You're fucked or you're lucky, and that's it.

I know when it's about to hit me because Acke screams high and short, and I feel a cold wall of air rushing against my back, shoving me forward with invisible hands. An impossibly high shadow that eclipses even my own light. I think of Jakub. Dark, cold yawns of nothing. I think of Nick.

And then the avalanche steals away any sense I have left.

◄◦►

Climbing is lonely. You think it won't be. You imagine that the endeavor will be mutually achieved, an ordeal always shared, but the truth is, on some sections, particularly on a disorganized descent, you can go a whole day without setting eyes on another soul. I've learned if not to love, then to appreciate the stark, stripped isolation of those days. The very opposite of the long, crowded intimacy of lower camp life, or the breath-stealing wonder of the summit—whether your vista is the golden curve of Earth and low, white mountain peaks in a sea of clouds, or a whiteout of raging wind and snow. But that other isolation—that other *allena*—is what you dread while never allowing yourself to think of it. It's the realization that you're fucked. Like Jakub. That you're still alive, still on the mountain, but suddenly you're on the other side of a two-way mirror and you won't ever be coming back. *That* is the worst Bad Thing. The only one. Whichever way it happens.

When I open my eyes, I think I'm inside that terrible crevasse again; the horror of all that silent blue dark after howling white space. Blunted pins and the hard tight swing of the rope vanishing into black. An echo of *they can't hold us both. They can't save us both.*

The cold is too cold to feel. I'm not in the crevasse because I can't move. My limbs are folded tight and trapped; my lungs struggle to find space enough to breathe. Too much weight presses down on me. Panic starts crushing me from the inside out. Not this. Not this.

The circle of my arms around my head has allowed for a small air pocket, but it won't last long. My wrist strap has snapped; my ice axe has gone. I think of Nick's face: the dimple in his left cheek, the chip in his right incisor, the always paler circles of skin around his eyes. I think of *his* weight on me, pressing me down, filling me up, and it calms me a little. It calms me enough.

I breathe. I breathe. And then I spit. It dribbles down my cheek along the length of my right eyebrow. Upside down. Maybe 160, 170 degrees. I don't know how deep I am, and the small space I have left isn't enough to find out. Slowly, slowly, I burrow my hands down toward my torso. The snow is like cement. By the time my knuckles bump against the axe, I'm already hyperventilating again. I have cobalt blue boots, I think. The legs of my suit are black with red stripes.

I make myself remember the night we first met in a dark tavern off the main Kathmandu drag in Thamel. Me, pissed on Mustang Coffee and home-brewed Raksi, dancing among dozens of other sweaty gap year tits just like me. And Nick, sitting in a darker corner, disinterested, his mouth curled into a routine sneer until I asked him if he'd dance with me too. The first time we fucked, he gripped me tight enough to leave bruises and told me that he'd never come so hard in his life. The first time we summited—close to the end of season on the Northeast Ridge of Everest—he swung me up to that golden curve of Earth and told me that he loved me; laughed when I said I was on top of the world.

I make myself think of the warm flat of his hands against my skin; the low and steady timbre of his voice, whether he's talking about clove hitches and belay points, or about those spirits that save only people like us: explorers on the edge of the world. Stroking my hair and reading aloud from Ernest Shackleton's *South*: the treacherous glaciers, icy slopes, and snow fields of his doomed Trans-Antarctic expedition; the fog, the dark, the blank map; the exhaustion, starvation, hopelessness. And the spirit—the voiceless, faceless Third Man—that had led him down to the safety of the whaling station on Stromness. Nick's solemn eyes, his slow smile; quoting T. S. Eliot in a tickling whisper against my ear—

Who is the third who walks always beside you?

Where is my *third*? I wonder now, and my eyes sting. Where the hell is the bloody spirit that's going to lead *me* down to safety? My tears feel hot and my throat tries to close up. I stop trying to think of anything at all.

Me. Just me. My own strength, my own will. I am all that can save me.

Slowly, slowly, I manage to turn around now, to bring the axe around. At first I can only twist and shimmy it against the hard-packed snow; I choke and try to turn my face away from what little I manage to hollow out. I feel panic rising again. I don't want to be on the other side of that mirror. I don't want to be a frozen landmark. A trig point. I don't want people to take selfies next to my frozen corpse. My cobalt blue boots. My red-striped suit.

When the way becomes abruptly easier, I nearly sob with relief. I choke more as my axe excavates more, but now I don't care. I'm reaching out of that dark blue echoing silence, up toward that ice-rimmed circle of white. I can nearly taste the mountain's thin air; see its clear, starry sky.

But in the instant before I break through—in the instant before I know I'm *going* to break through, I hear Acke's scream. No longer high and short, but long and horrified. And oh God, so, so much deeper. I have enough room now to clasp my left hand hard over my mouth. I can't feel the press of its glove against my lips, my skin, my teeth.

And then I'm free. The snowstorm has died. My headlight is dead. The only remaining light comes from a half-crescent moon, hanging low over the Nilgiri Himal range to the northwest. I shuffle onto my knees, pushing away from my already collapsing escape shaft. After moving no more than ten feet, I look down at the hard-packed snow between my hands and knees. Acke. *Acke.* I don't shout his name, don't even say it out loud. If he hears me, he might think that I can save him.

Two months ago, in a trekkers' lodge close to the edge of The Sanctuary, he laughed and sang along to Fernando while mixing terrible Brännvin cocktails. He had a boyfriend in the Swedish navy who'd bought him a house, but wouldn't tell anyone he existed. He struggled to grow a beard, always trying: every morning he'd roll his eyes and tug on it, *still sexy ass fluff, my friends.*

So I stay. In the disorientating white-dark, I kneel in the snow over where I think Acke is, and I keep him silent company. I hear him coughing again. Maybe he'll drown instead of suffocate; which is worse, I don't know—don't *want* to know. I reach round for my O. I don't know when I last drank or ate something either. These are the things you must fight: numbness, confusion, lethargy. Mercy. What good will staying here do? How can Acke know he's not *allena*, and what does it matter if he does? But I think of him shouting *stay with me* to the mountain, the snow, the sky, and so I stay.

I'm always exactly where I'm supposed to be.

—◦—

It's no longer snowing. It's no longer gloomy either. It's dark. Night. I can't hear Acke anymore. I wonder how long he fought. How long he pretended. If he's pretending even now. Because denial has to be better than acceptance, if one side of the coin—the mirror—is death and nothing else. I shudder hard enough to again crick my neck.

When I try to get up, it feels as if I no longer exist below my waist. It takes too long to locate and change out my headlight, and the reward does not justify the effort: the thin revived glow casts only slow and frightening shadows. The drifts are high, unwieldy; the terrain is entirely changed as if I haven't made it back through the mirror at all. The couloirs are gone, their scars and fissures hidden under the weight of so much new snow.

I shine my light down on my harness. Its main carabiner is bent and twisted out of shape, probably when the avalanche wrenched me free of the line. It takes another long time to replace it with a spare; my fingers are slow, my mind slower. Finally, I move the light wider, over smooth swathes of black and white, searching for the way down. It takes the longest time of all for the truth to sink in. The fixed ropes are gone.

My panic is too slow. There's even something close to relief in it. The thin air whistles around me like I'm an obstacle, a rock in a stream. *Now* I'm fucked, there's no way I'm not. How can I ever negotiate my way out of the Death Zone alone and with no fixed lines? This is my worst Bad Thing. After years of dread, of anticipation, this, here, is how it happens. This is the *way* it happens for me.

"Sarah? Why you here?"

I swing around, slow like an astronaut; at the same time assuming the voice is inside my head. It's a not unfamiliar question.

Pasang is standing less than ten feet away, looking none the worse for wear at all. He's half-crouched, as if readying himself for a starter's gun. He doesn't look afraid *or* fucked—more startled. Because he never expected me to make it this far? I feel the pinch of familiar resentment when I should only be feeling relief. Pasang will help me. He has to.

"Jakub Hornik and Acke Holmberg are dead," I say, and my voice sounds strange, thin, like the air. It's very quiet, I realize. Nearly silent. After the storm and the avalanche, it's still enough that I wonder if I'd hear one of those blunted pins drop.

Pasang doesn't react. Chongba isn't with him, so he must have left him behind with the Slovaks, while he's come down the mountain to see how bad it is; if they can still make it down without having to bivy or call for an evac that'll probably never come. How long did I stay kneeling in the snow waiting for Acke to die? It must have been hours. Pasang's eyes scan the terrain ahead and then he looks back at the mountain behind. He never wears goggles and he never carries O. I sometimes wonder if he even needs to eat, shit, or fuck either.

He asks, "Who was higher than them?"

"Holmberg means Island Mountain. Did you know that?" I feel numb, but I no longer know which kind of numb. Something tugs at my mind, puckers my skin. Makes me remember to be afraid. I don't know what the fuck I'm doing here.

He blinks. "Sarah. Who was higher than them?"

I know why he's asking. It's because I'm the first person he's seen. And everyone else between us is gone.

"Bosse. Benoit and Savane. The Australians, I think. I don't know."

Pasang curses. This will be the end of the *8000er Experience*, I think, and I feel a guilty spark of hope that must show in my eyes because Pasang straightaway narrows his.

"Why you here?"

"What the fuck does that mean?" I look down at the snow under my boots, my crampons. Already my escape route has filled in as if it never was.

"You hate the mountains. Always." His voice is not cold, though his words are. They sound angry. "Why you come back, every time?"

I swallow because even if I understand the question, I don't understand why he'd ask it now.

"You don't belong here." His gaze grows softer. "You never belong here."

But I don't want to argue with him, because he'll never understand. He's never understood why any of us keep coming back, not really. Most of the time he manages to hide his contempt. Just about.

"You know why. I'm here for Nick."

◦►

The way is treacherous, of course. I'm clunky, *a functional climber*, Nick has always said, though I've never taken offense. It's true. But now, clambering down barely settled snow, with no protection beyond my own gear, my own judgment, I wish that I loved it, I wish that I felt it. I wish that I could reach Nick by sheer force of want, of will.

Instead my descent is anything *but* functional: I stumble and I fall and I fuck up my handholds, my footholds. My rope snags and burns; my overhangs and hitches and anchors are poor—I move too slowly because I have as much confidence in my abilities as I do in the new ground beneath me. I only have the distant lights of Camp IV and Pasang's directions to guide me, and I keep thinking of that cold, blue space and blunted pins, but I'm still doing it. I *am* doing it. And whether that's down to his help or his scorn, I suppose hardly matters.

I knew Pasang would never come with me, but when he turned back to the dark shadow of the mountain, my belly clenched all the same, and I wanted to beg him to stop. Though I didn't. His job is to look after the Slovaks. The fucking Slovaks who didn't manage to get out of their fucking sleeping bags until 2 a.m. He has to trust that I can look after myself, and that Nick can look after his group. Alone. Just as I have to trust that Pasang will be okay, even if that suffocating dread behind thick, heavy curtains suspects better.

Nick. He's all I can think about now. Not me or Pasang, Jakub, Bosse, the French Canadians, the Australians—not even Acke. Except to wonder if Nick has suffered the same terrible fate. I don't think about the others in his group either. I don't care about any of them—these idiots with too much money and too little of everything else. In that, I understand Pasang's contempt. If my reasons for being here are stupid, then theirs are moronic. Nick despairs of their inexperience: their lack of knowledge, training, equipment; their sheer bloody self-entitlement. They've paid Nick and Pasang to get them to the summit and back, and nothing less will do. They haven't paid for any kind of *Experience* at all. They've paid for a photo-op, a flag; Nick even prints them out a certificate. When Tomie Nà refused to stop after the docs at Camp II told him he could die if he climbed any higher, Nick rubbed his hands through his hair, spat into the snow, and then carried on preparing for the next section.

For all his faults—and I'm aware of them all, despite what everyone, including Pasang, believes—Nick loves these few places high above the rest of the world with a passion that could never be faked. And that's why he's here too. That's why he puts up with everything else, all the other shit that he hates. Because he has as much choice as I do.

→◇←

But it isn't Nick I find first. It's Kate. Her sobs creep up through the darkness like the wind around ice pillars; I only realize it's her when I see headlights less than fifty yards below. I don't know how long I've been descending now, or how much longer before I leave the Death Zone behind me. The lights of Camp IV look hardly closer, though the moon has moved far enough to disorientate me completely. I'm struggling to breathe, and my O is getting too low. That slow, creeping paralysis is back; a numbness inside and out that's nearly seductive. It makes me want to stop asking myself if I'm about to dive-bomb the deep end of a swimming pool. It makes me not want to care if the answer is yes.

Kate's sobs are nearly hysterical. I shout, but she doesn't hear, doesn't stop, barely draws breath. I try not to move too quickly as I edge down over still-shifting snow. The drifts are higher here, creating precarious peaks of their own, but overall the terrain is flatter, more glacial. Here is where most of the avalanche came to rest, I think. Here is where deep, dark crevasses will be hiding, waiting, beneath all that treacherous new snow. I try not to hesitate, to stop, to look for Nick, to waste precious breath of my own in more shouting. Instead, I carry on descending, descending, fucking descending, and praying a little too, for good measure. He *has* to be all right.

"We can't go! How can we fucking go?" After an avalanche, mountain air gets thicker and sounds flatter; Kate's voice is a hysterical monotone. "What about Tomie and—"

"Tomie, Jìng, and Lì are already gone, and you know it."

I allow myself the luxury of stopping, of staring at the second headlight. His voice still echoes. *Nick.*

"Jesus, how can you be so cold?"

"We're both pretty cold, Kate. And getting pretty fucking colder. It's not them you care about. It's the fucking serac between us and fucking freedom, and I can't help you with that."

By the time I reach them, I'm close to collapse. I can't feel my legs, but I know it all the same. I feel hot when I should feel cold—or nothing at all. And all I can see is Nick. He's hunkered down under a high overhang of rock, head low, gloved hands dangling between his legs. Kate sits close alongside him, and I try—and fail—not to care about that. They've been there too long, I care more about that; about the stiff, tired threat in their bodies, their voices.

"We can't free-solo around a fucking serac with fuck knows how many tons of snow weighing down on it!" Kate's digging in. Her voice is calmer, stronger. Once she makes her mind up about something, that's usually it. "We need to stay here, wait for an evac. You've phoned our position in. We can't—"

"We're still in the Death Zone. No one will be coming for us." Nick's voice is just as calm, as confident, but I know he's horrified. I know he's blaming himself. Even though it's the fault of the bloody Slovaks.

"We *can't—*"

"I *will* leave you behind, Kate," he says.

"You're a bastard."

"No," I say. "He's what'll keep you alive."

Kate gasps, looks in my direction, and her breath catches formless in the air. I wonder if she can read something in my expression that I'm usually better at hiding. I've been free-soloing since Acke, but it would be pretty petty to say so. Though I want badly to bask in Nick's uncommon approval.

Nick's head drops further between his knees, and I hear only his chattering teeth. Still none of us move. Up here, we're statues: half-frozen, half-thawed; half-numb, half-crazy. Half-alive, half-dead. It's a miracle we feel anything at all.

Nick gets back on his feet with grunted effort. He swears again; coughs. The latter rattles down inside his chest. "Let's go."

◂◦▸

The serac is a block of glacial ice as big as a three-story townhouse. Near to the start of our summit ascent, the route alongside was lit by flare lamps and set with fixed ropes. Now, its threat is magnified by darkness and formless new terrain. And all the death and weight that we've brought back down the mountain with us.

Nick wedges a metal nut into one of the rocks close to the serac's beginning. He clips a quickdraw to the wire, threading the rope through it and his own carabiner before feeding it backwards in generous loops. "We're not decking out, okay? Not fucking today."

Some color has returned to Kate's cheeks. She picks up the rope, locks into the belay. I do the same—muscle memory triggering too many other less welcome memories: me and Nick, Kate and James climbing rock faces, ice pillars, mountains. Trekking and hiking and camping all over the world. Getting shit-faced in dodgy bars and on deserted beaches. At James' funeral, Kate clung to Nick as if he was the only anchor on a Grade V vertical climb. She and I had been friends since high school, but she never again dragged me to karaoke bars or treated me to spa weekends in wanky Essex hotels, as if she'd lost me over the same sheer cliff as her husband. When I asked Nick how I could help her, he told me I'd be best leaving her alone until she came to me. And she never did.

⟶⟵

The serac radiates a different kind of cold than the mountain. It's breathless, sharp, and thin. Fragile. Silent blue dark looking up into an icy white space and sky. Endless shadow.

Nick edges along the base of the serac too slowly. The ledge is narrow—less than a foot across in some places—and the drop on the other side is big; even in the dark it has the power to squeeze my stomach, water my eyes. And it's always been Nick's cautiousness that frightens me, never his selfish recklessness. He feeds back more rope in slow turning loops, but he doesn't look around. "Don't stop," he says.

Close to the halfway point, Kate falters, one gloved hand getting caught in the gear as she tries to navigate Nick's hastily improvised line. I dilute my impatience with the memory of the couloirs, the dread and relief of *now I'm fucked, there's no way I'm not* when the avalanche stole the fixed lines. It's too easy to stop thinking past doctored routes, too easy to start shitting yourself whenever you have to unhook from their security for even a few seconds.

Kate goes on fumbling, hesitating, trying and failing to free herself, to move. Powdered snow falls through the gap between us. The serac was never stable, but now fuck knows how many tons of avalanche threaten to overload it to the point of collapse. And if that happens, it doesn't matter how careful and slow we're being; how many ropes and anchors we do or don't have.

"I'm scared," Kate whimpers, and her hands still, shoulders hunch.

Nick is far enough ahead to be nearly out of sight, so she can only be talking to me. I remember the *puja* twelve hours before we left base camp: a Lama and two skinny monks bent over a stone altar, the smell of juniper reminding me of the gins from the night before; equipment spread around us and waiting to be blessed: harnesses, crampons, ice-axes, and helmets, even our expedition flag. Pasang chanting alongside the monks, placating the spirits, making his offerings of yak milk and chocolate and rice as the Lama talked to the mountain, asked it to let us climb to its summit. Kate, hungover and dull-eyed, her smile scornful as she stifled a yawn: *Mountain says no.*

She doesn't know I hate her. She doesn't know that less than six months after James' funeral, Nick got down on his knees and told me how many times they'd fucked; that he held onto me so tightly I was nearly glad that they had. She doesn't know that he would never leave me. She doesn't know him.

"It'll be all right," I say, and her shoulders drop, she finally tugs her glove free, clips back into the line.

And at the halfway point, I start to think it might be. That maybe—just maybe—the sheer number of Bad Things that have already happened are enough. But then I feel it: the air changing just like it did before Jakub came sliding out of the gloom on the other side of that mirror—a hush, a breath too close to my ear—and I know that I'm wrong. Again.

I unclip myself from the line, and I'm no longer slow, no longer afraid. My crampons find little purchase; my left foot slips off the ledge into dark space more than once, but I keep on going, faster, faster. Until I reach Kate.

"Go!" I push her so hard she shrieks—but either she can sense the danger in my voice or in the slow deadly shifts of the wall of ice against us, because she immediately obeys, abandoning the fixed line even as Nick is screwing in another anchor up ahead.

"Go!" I scream again. "Nick! Go!"

He turns just as my headlight finds him, his face slack and pale, and then he looks up at the serac in the very moment that *it* starts to scream.

We run. And run. And the world collapses around us.

◄◦►

Kate is who I hear first. She's sobbing again, but she can't catch enough breath—the result is an oddly comforting squeak. She only stops to shout

Nick's name, and a sob comes out of me too when, finally, he answers in a hoarse shout.

I sit up, struggle to get to my knees. When I look back, the line is gone, the ledge is gone, the serac is gone. I'm finding it hard to breathe myself—I hear the thin air wheeze through my lungs—but my O is gone too.

I stand up and sway, but there's nothing to hold onto. When Nick struggles to his feet a few meters further down, his headlight glancing off Kate's helmet, her suit, I see a long streak of blood running from his temple to his jaw.

"Oh my God, Nick," she says. She sounds exhilarated and broken at the same time. "Oh my God."

He doesn't answer, just keeps staring up at all the destruction behind us, eyes still wide and wild and black.

And I stare back, but even though we're the closest we've been since the summit, I know I can't reach any closer. My dread is exhausted, heartbroken. He's safe. He's alive. But it isn't enough.

"You felt her too, right?" Kate grabs hold of his upper arms. "I know you fucking did. She was there! She was—"

"Don't touch me," he says, but he's already shrugged her off, already backed away. He keeps on looking, looking, *looking*, and something in him finally breaks as he drops to his knees, as he howls into the black, the vast ocean of white.

I look away from Nick and back at the summit. The low moon throws light and shadow against the rock, the snow, the ridges and fissures, the pillars and gullies. I think of Jakub and Acke and all the others who'll be left on this mountain, frozen in time and in place; disappeared, or dragged away from the path to become a landmark, a trig point, a cautionary tale. I think of Pasang and Chongba and the Slovaks trapped inside the Death Zone with no fixed lines, and an avalanche and collapsed serac between them and Camp IV. They may as well be on that moon.

And I think of them all sitting around that stone altar, laughing and eating. Smearing grey sampa flour on their faces; the promise that they would live to see each other become old and grey. *Mountain says no.*

Because the view from the other side of the mirror can so often look the same. Even when you know exactly what it feels like to fall, to be alone. Even when you know—as you look up out of silent blue dark into howling white light and life; as the air prickles against your skin like blunted pins—that it's already too late. Like a slow-suffocating nightmare inside thick, heavy curtains. A leaving that never feels like going anywhere at all. To be gone, but not gone.

They can't hold us both. They can't save us both.

And they didn't.

The shocking agony of plunging into that silent blue dark, Felix's weight pulling me down faster, harder, the snapped rope showering snow. To feel it coming, to *know*. A breath, barely long enough to scream, but stretching out into infinity.

Denial: a mountain climber's best and worst friend. Better to believe. Except we never do—those of us already on the other side of that coin, that mirror. Because then there really is no going back at all.

Nick still howls even as the wind picks up again and the night gets colder. But he'll come back. He'll always come back. Because this is where Nick lives. Not in our shitty Catford maisonette. Not even in base camps or trekking lodges. Only up here, in the clouds and violent snowstorms and hurricane-force winds; on the rock faces and ice fields and stony summits; in the gullies and crevasses, the ridges and jet winds and dancing tails of white snow. Up here, where people can't survive; where we start dying faster the moment we start to climb. This is Nick's home.

And mine. Because what I told Pasang will always be true. I think of Acke shouting *stay with me* to the stone, the snow, the sky. I am here because Nick needs me to be here. And so I stay. I will always walk beside him. It's the only reason I've ever climbed any mountain at all.

ABOUT THE AUTHORS

Nathan Ballingrud is the author of *North American Lake Monsters*, *The Visible Filth*, and the forthcoming *The Atlas of Hell*. Several of his stories are in development for film and TV. He has twice won the Shirley Jackson Award. He lives somewhere in the mountains of North Carolina.

◀◦▶

Laird Barron spent his early years in Alaska. He is the author of several books, including *The Beautiful Thing That Awaits Us All*, *Swift to Chase*, and *Blood Standard*. His work has also appeared in many magazines and anthologies. Barron currently resides in the Rondout Valley, writing stories about the evil that men do.

◀◦▶

Simon Bestwick is the author of four story collections, a chapbook, *Angels Of The Silences*, and five novels, most recently *Devil's Highway* and *The Feast Of All Souls*. His work has been published in *Black Static* and *Great Jones Street*, podcast on *Pseudopod* and *Tales to Terrify*, and reprinted in *The Best of the Best Horror of the Year*. His novelette, *Breakwater*, was published by Tor.com in 2018.

A new collection and a new novel, *Wolf's Hill*, are both in progress. Until recently, his hobbies included avoiding gainful employment, but this ended in failure and he now has a job again. Any and all assistance in escaping this dreadful fate would be most welcome. He lives on the Wirral with the long-suffering author Cate Gardner, and uses far too many semicolons.

◄◦►

Ramsey Campbell is Great Britain's most respected living horror writer. He has been given more awards than any other writer in the field, including the Grand Master Award of the World Horror Convention, the Lifetime Achievement Award of the Horror Writers Association, the Living Legend Award of the International Horror Guild, and the World Fantasy Lifetime Achievement Award. In 2015, he was made an Honorary Fellow of Liverpool John Moores University for outstanding services to literature. Among his novels are *The Face That Must Die, Incarnate, Midnight Sun, The Count of Eleven, Silent Children, The Darkest Part of the Woods, The Overnight, Secret Story, The Grin of the Dark, Thieving Fear, Creatures of the Pool, The Seven Days of Cain, Ghosts Know, The Kind Folk, Think Yourself Lucky,* and *Thirteen Days by Sunset Beach.*

He is presently working on a trilogy, *The Three Births of Daoloth*—the first volume, *The Searching Dead*, was published in 2016, followed by *Born to the Dark*, and *The Way of the Worm* will appear in 2018. *Needing Ghosts, The Last Revelation of Gla'aki, The Pretence,* and *The Booking* are novellas.

His collections include *Waking Nightmares, Alone with the Horrors, Ghosts and Grisly Things, Told by the Dead, Just Behind You, Holes for Faces,* and *Limericks of the Alarming and Phantasmal.* His nonfiction is collected as *Ramsey Campbell, Probably.* His novels *The Nameless* and *Pact of the Fathers* have been filmed in Spain, where a film of *The Influence* is in production. He is the President of the Society of Fantastic Films.

Ramsey Campbell lives on Merseyside with his wife Jenny. His pleasures include classical music, good food and wine, and whatever's in that pipe. His website is ramseycampbell.com.

◄◦►

Siobhan Carroll is an associate professor of English at the University of Delaware. When not plotting world domination, she studies nineteenth-century board games, polar exploration, and the history of geo-engineering. For more fiction by Siobhan Carroll, visit voncarr-siobhan-carroll.blogspot. com/p/fiction-poetry.html.

◄◦►

Dan Chaon's most recent book is *Ill Will*, a national bestseller, named one of the best books of 2017 by the *New York Times*, the *Los Angeles Times*, the *Washington Post*, the *Wall Street Journal*, and *Publishers Weekly*. Other works include the short story collection *Stay Awake* (2012), a finalist for the Story Prize; the national bestseller *Await Your Reply*, and *Among the Missing*, a finalist for the National Book Award.

Chaon's fiction has appeared in *Best American Short Stories*, *The Pushcart Prize Anthologies*, and *The O. Henry Prize Stories*.

He has been a finalist for the National Magazine Award in Fiction, the Shirley Jackson Award, and was the recipient of an Academy Award in Literature from the American Academy of Arts and Letters.

Chaon lives in Cleveland.

◄◦►

Suzy McKee Charnas has been publishing long- and short-form fantasy and SF since 1974, as well as YA fiction, nonfiction, and (so far) one play script that has had productions on both coasts. She is best known for her four-book feminist-futurist series, *The Holdfast Chronicles*, and for *The Vampire Tapestry*, a cult classic. Her work has won her a Hugo, a Nebula, a Gigamesh, and a Mythopeic award for YA fantasy.

Born in NYC, she has lived in New Mexico with her husband and various dogs and cats since 1970.

◄◦►

Stephanie Crawford works as a full-time editor in Las Vegas. When not writing about film or embellishing strange events for even stranger fictional stories, she co-hosts *The Screamcast* podcast and is currently collaborating on two scripts.

◄◦►

Brian Evenson is the author of over a dozen books of fiction, most recently the story collection *A Collapse of Horses* and the novella *The Warren*. He has been a finalist for the Shirley Jackson Award three times. His novel *Last Days* won the American Library Association's award for Best Horror Novel of 2009. His novel *The Open Curtain* was a finalist for an Edgar Award and an International Horror Guild Award. He is the recipient of three O. Henry

Prizes, as well as an NEA fellowship and a Guggenheim fellowship. He lives in Valencia, California, and works at CalArts.

—◇—

Award-winning horror author **Gemma Files** has also been a film critic, teacher, and screenwriter. She is probably best known for her Weird Western Hexslinger series: *A Book of Tongues*, *A Rope of Thorns*, and *A Tree of Bones*, and has published three collections of short fiction: *Kissing Carrion*, *The Worm in Every Heart*, and *Spectral Evidence* as well as two chapbooks of poetry.

Her book, *We Will All Go Down Together: Stories About the Five-Family Coven*, was published in 2014. Her most recent novel, *Experimental Film*, won the 2015 Shirley Jackson Award for Best Novel and the 2015 Sunburst Award for Best Novel (Adult).

Her fourth collection of stories, *Drawn Up From Deep Places*, will be out in November 2018.

—◇—

Neil Gaiman is the Newbery Medal–winning author of *The Graveyard Book* and a *New York Times* bestselling author. Several of his books, including *Coraline*, have been made into major motion pictures. *American Gods* has been made into an ongoing series for television. He is also famous for writing the *Sandman* graphic novel series and numerous other books and comics for adult, young adult, and younger readers.

He has won the Hugo, Nebula, Mythopoeic, and World Fantasy awards, among others. He is also the author of many short stories and poems.

For more information: www.neilgaiman.com/

—◇—

Stephen Gallagher is a Stoker and World Fantasy Award nominee, winner of British Fantasy and International Horror Guild Awards for his short fiction, and is the author of fifteen novels including *Valley of Lights*, *Down River*, *Rain*, and *Nightmare, With Angel*. He's the creator of Sebastian Becker, Special Investigator to the Lord Chancellor's Visitor in Lunacy, in a series of novels that includes *The Kingdom of Bones*, *The Bedlam Detective*, and *The Authentic William James*.

Adam Golaski is the author of *Color Plates* and *Worse Than Myself*. His poetry, essays, artwork, and fiction has appeared in numerous journals and anthologies, including *Bennington Review*, *Vestiges*, *The Lifted Brow*, *Always Crashing*, and *McSweeney's*. For more work, visit *Little Stories* (online).

Cody Goodfellow has written seven solo novels and three with *New York Times* bestselling author John Skipp. Two of his short fiction collections, *Silent Weapons For Quiet Wars* and *All-Monster Action*, received the Wonderland Book Award. He wrote and co-produced the short films *Stay At Home Dad* and *Clowntown: An Honest Mis-Stake*. He recently played an Amish farmer in a Days Inn commercial, and has appeared in the background on numerous TV programs, as well as videos by Anthrax and Beck. He lives in Portland, Oregon.

Glen Hirshberg's stories have earned him three International Horror Guild Awards and the Shirley Jackson Award. His collections include *The Two Sams*, *American Morons*, *The Janus Tree*, and *The Ones Who Are Waving*. He is also the author of five novels: *The Snowman's Children*, *The Book of Bunk*, and the Motherless Children trilogy (*Motherless Child*, *Good Girls*, and *Nothing to Devour*). With Peter Atkins and Dennis Etchison, he co-founded the Rolling Darkness Revue, a touring ghost story performance project. On his own, he founded the CREW program, through which he trains his most passionate students and sends them into the surrounding community to run extended creative writing camps for children with limited access to artistic instruction or formal outlets for expression. He writes and teaches in the Los Angeles area, where he lives with his family and cats.

Brian Hodge is one of those people who always has to be making something. So far, he's made thirteen novels, around 130 shorter works, and five full-length collections.

He'll have three new books out in 2018 and early 2019: *The Immaculate*

Void, a novel of cosmic horror; *A Song of Eagles*, a grimdark fantasy; and *Skidding Into Oblivion*, his next collection.

He lives in Colorado, where he also likes to make music and photographs and trains in Krav Maga and kickboxing.

Connect through his web site (brianhodge.net), Twitter (@BHodgeAuthor), or Facebook (facebook.com/brianhodgewriter).

◄◦►

Jane Jakeman is a British author who has published crime and ghost stories in *Supernatural Tales*, *Ghosts and Scholars*, and *All Hallows*, some of which were reprinted in the collection *A Bracelet of Bright Hair*. She is a regular reviewer of Islamic books for *The Art Newspaper* and has travelled widely in the Middle East. Jane lives in Oxford, UK, with her Egyptologist husband and two small black cats.

◄◦►

Carole Johnstone is a British Fantasy Award–winning Scottish writer, currently enjoying splendid isolation on the Atlantic coast of the Isle of Lewis in the Outer Hebrides. Her short fiction has been published widely and has been reprinted in Ellen Datlow's *Best Horror of the Year* and Salt Publishing's *Best British Fantasy* series.

Her debut short story collection, *The Bright Day is Done*, and her novella, *Cold Turkey*, were both shortlisted for a 2015 British Fantasy Award.

◄◦►

Stephen Graham Jones is the author of sixteen novels and six story collections. His recent novella *Mapping the Interior* won the Bram Stoker Award and the This is Horror Award. He lives and teaches in Boulder, Colorado.

◄◦►

John Langan is the author of two novels: *The Fisherman* and *House of Windows*, and three collections: *The Wide, Carnivorous Sky and Other Monstrous Geographies*, *Mr. Gaunt and Other Uneasy Encounters*, and *Sefira and Other Betrayals*.

With Paul Tremblay, he co-edited *Creatures: Thirty Years of Monsters*. One of the founders of the Shirley Jackson Awards, he serves on its Advisory

Board. Currently, he reviews horror and dark fantasy for *Locus* magazine. He lives in New York's Hudson Valley with his wife and younger son.

◄◦►

Tanith Lee passed away in 2015. By then she had written nearly one hundred books and over three hundred short stories, in addition to radio plays and TV scripts. Her genre-crossing included fantasy, SF, horror, young adult, historical, detective, and contemporary fiction, and often combinations of all of them. Her more recent publications included the *Lionwolf Trilogy*: *Cast a Bright Shadow*, *Here in Cold Hell*, and *No Flame but Mine*, and three *Piratica* novels for young adults. Her short fiction was most recently collected in *Redder Than Blood*, *The Weird Tales of Tanith Lee*, and *Tanith by Choice: The Best of Tanith Lee*.

In 2009, Lee was named Grandmaster by the World Horror Convention and given the Life Achievement Award by the World Fantasy Convention in 2013.

◄◦►

E. Michael Lewis is an aviation and ghost story enthusiast who studied creative writing at the University of Puget Sound in Tacoma. His short stories appear in *The Horror Anthology of Horror Anthologies*, *Exotic Gothic 4*, and *Savage Beasts*.

He is a lifelong native of the Pacific Northwest, the father of two sons, and the chief attendant of two cats, who are also brothers.

He can be found on Facebook and Twitter at @EMichaelLewis, and at his website emichaellewis.com.

◄◦►

Livia Llewellyn is a writer of horror, dark fantasy, and erotica, whose fiction has appeared in *Subterranean*, *Apex* magazine, *Postscripts*, *Nightmare* magazine, as well as in numerous anthologies.

Her first collection, *Engines of Desire: Tales of Love & Other Horrors*, was published in 2011, and received two Shirley Jackson Award nominations, for Best Collection and Best Novelette (for "Omphalos"). Her second collection, *Furnace*, was published in 2016. The title story "Furnace" was nominated for the 2013 Shirley Jackson Award. You can find her online at liviallewellyn.com.

◄○►

Seanan McGuire (who has written this story under the name Mira Grant) lives, works, and occasionally falls into swamps in the Pacific Northwest, where she is coming to an understanding with the local frogs. She has written a ridiculous number of novels and even more short stories. Keep up with her at seananmcguire.com. On moonlit nights, when the stars are right, you just might find her falling into a swamp near you.

◄○►

Adam L.G. Nevill was born in Birmingham, England, in 1969 and grew up in England and New Zealand. He is the author of the horror novels: *Banquet for the Damned, Apartment 16, The Ritual, Last Days, House of Small Shadows, No One Gets Out Alive, Lost Girl*, and *Under a Watchful Eye*.

His novels, *The Ritual, Last Days*, and *No One Gets Out Alive* were the winners of the August Derleth Award for Best Horror Novel. *The Ritual* and *Last Days* were also awarded Best in Category: Horror, by R.U.S.A. Several of his novels are in development for film and television, and in 2016 Imaginarium adapted *The Ritual* into a feature film.

His short fiction has been collected in *Some Will Not Sleep*, which won the British Fantasy Award: Best Collection and *Hasty for the Dark*.

Adam also offers free books to readers of horror: *Cries from the Crypt*, downloadable from his website, and *Before You Sleep* and *Before You Wake*, available from major online retailers.

He lives in Devon, England. More information about the author and his books is available at: adamlgnevill.com

◄○►

Peter Straub is the author of seventeen novels, which have been translated into more than twenty languages. They include *Ghost Story, Koko, Mr. X, In the Night Room,* and two collaborations with Stephen King, *The Talisman* and *Black House*. He has written two volumes of poetry and two collections of short fiction, and edited the Library of America's edition of H. P. Lovecraft's *Tales* and two-volume anthology, *American Fantastic Tales*. He has won the British Fantasy Award, ten Bram Stoker Awards, two International Horror Guild Awards, and four World Fantasy Awards. In 1998, he was named

Grand Master at the World Horror Convention. In 2006, he was given the HWA's Life Achievement Award. In 2008, he was given the Barnes & Noble Writers for Writers Award by Poets & Writers. At the World Fantasy Convention in 2010, he was given the WFC's Life Achievement Award.

◄◦►

Duane Swierczynski is the two-time Edgar-nominated author of ten novels including *Revolver*, *Canary*, and the Shamus Award–winning Charlie Hardie series, many of which are in development for film/TV. A native Philadelphian, he now lives in Los Angeles with his wife and children.

◄◦►

Lucy Taylor is an award-winning author of horror and dark fantasy. She has published seven novels, six collections, and over a hundred short stories. Her work has been translated into French, Spanish, Italian, Russian, German, and Chinese.

Her most recent short fiction can be found in the anthologies *The Beauty of Death: Death By Water*, *Tales of the Lake Volume 5*, *Endless Apocalypse*, *Edward Bryant's Sphere of Influence*, and *A Fist Full of Dinosaurs*. Her essay on body horror, "What's Really Under Your Skin," was recently published in *Nightmare* magazine.

A new collection, *Spree and Other Stories*, was published in February 2018.

Her science fiction/horror novelette "Sweetlings" was a finalist for the 2018 Bram Stoker Awards in the category of Long Fiction.

She lives in the high desert outside Santa Fe, New Mexico.

◄◦►

Steve Rasnic Tem is a past winner of the World Fantasy, Bram Stoker, and British Fantasy Awards. He has published over 430 short stories. Some of his best stories are collected in *Figures Unseen: Selected Stories*, published in April by Valancourt Books. *The Mask Shop of Doctor Blaack*, a middle grade novel about Halloween, will appear soon from Hex Publishers. A handbook on writing, *Yours To Tell: Dialogues on the Art & Practice of Writing*, written with his late wife Melanie, appeared from Apex Books last year. Also appearing last year was his science fiction horror novel *Ubo* (Solaris Books), a finalist for the Bram Stoker Award.

ACKNOWLEDGMENT OF COPYRIGHT

ABOUT THE EDITOR

Ellen Datlow has been editing science fiction, fantasy, and horror short fiction for almost forty years. She currently acquires short fiction for Tor. com. In addition, she has edited about ninety science fiction, fantasy, and horror anthologies, including the series *The Best Horror of the Year, Fearful Symmetries, The Doll Collection, The Monstrous, Children of Lovecraft, Black Feathers, Mad Hatters and March Hares,* and *The Devil and the Deep.*

She's won multiple World Fantasy Awards, Locus Awards, Hugo Awards, Stoker Awards, International Horror Guild Awards, Shirley Jackson Awards, and the 2012 Il Posto Nero Black Spot Award for Excellence as Best Foreign Editor. Datlow was named recipient of the 2007 Karl Edward Wagner Award, given at the British Fantasy Convention for "outstanding contribution to the genre," was honored with the Life Achievement Award given by the Horror Writers Association in acknowledgment of superior achievement over an entire career, and the Life Achievement Award by the World Fantasy Convention.

She lives in New York and co-hosts the monthly Fantastic Fiction Reading Series at KGB Bar. More information can be found at www. datlow.com, on Facebook, and on Twitter as @EllenDatlow.